RAY HAMMOND

EMERGENCE

MACMILLAN

First published 2001 by Macmillan
an imprint of Pan Macmillan Limited
20 New Wharf Road, London N1 9RR
Basingstoke and Oxford
Associated companies throughout the world
www.panmacmillan.com

ISBN 0 333 90493 1

1 3 5 7 9 8 6 4 2

A CIP catalogue record for this book is available from
the British Library.

Typeset by SetSystems Ltd, Saffron Walden, Essex
Printed and bound in Great Britain by
Mackays of Chatham plc, Chatham, Kent

For my daughter, Jane

ACKNOWLEDGEMENTS

I am grateful to many people who have helped me during the writing and production process of this first novel. Mic Cheetham, my agent and friend, knew exactly when to encourage, when to ignore and how best to help me shape this story. Simon Kavanagh, her assistant at the time, also made incredibly useful suggestions about plot possibilities. Thanks to them both.

At Macmillan I have been lucky enough to find in Peter Lavery an editor who is both an enthusiast for what is properly described as 'mainstream' fiction and is unerring in his instinct for weeding out weaknesses in both plot and prose. He has made an immense contribution to this novel.

A number of people have been kind enough to help me with scientific, medical, professional, cultural, technical or production issues. I wanted as much detail as possible in this book to be scientifically plausible and technically accurate but I haven't *always* taken the advice that has so generously been offered, so no blame can be attached to any of them for any errors, omissions, misunderstandings or inaccuracies. All faults are mine.

In alphabetical order, I thank Nick Austin who copy-edited and prepared this manuscript for press; Dr James Dodd, co-author of *The Ideas of Particle Physics*, and formerly of DresdnerKleinwortBenson Merchant Bank, for his detailed and enthusiastic input on both quantum physics *and* fund management; Professor Allison Druin of the Human-Computer Interaction Laboratory at the University of Maryland for her thoughts regarding my 'companion' characters; science and technology writer Simon Eccles for his comments and advice on space technologies and astronomy; Anne Hardy for amazingly good proofreading skills (and for her patience and understanding while the manuscript was under development); Peter Krause for his help with Yiddish colloquialisms; Judith Hall for her assistance with Spanish translations; Janice Nagourney for her assistance with French translations; Dr Brian Rossiter, Consultant at Whipps Cross Hospital, London for help with medical details; Dr John Rossiter, Senior Lecturer at Imperial College, London for advice on some possibilities for genetically modified plants and Dr Bruno Stanek of Astrosoftware, Switzerland for advice about space techologies and astronomical details.

Thanks also go to the novelist Terry Bisson for permission to reproduce a section from his short story, 'They're Made Out of Meat' which appears in chapter twenty-four. His copyright is fully and gratefully acknowledged.

In addition, I thank Dagmar O'Toole and Alex Krywald of Celebrity Speakers Ltd, whose skilful management of my public-speaking career made this project possible.

Finally, thanks to Liz Hammond for her tireless and good humoured proofreading and for her belief and support over the years.

PROLOGUE

In summer, the skies above the city of Stockholm remain blue for most of the Earth's daily revolution: the Sun might be thought unwilling to withdraw fully in night's favour. By late evening azure becomes amethyst, eventually giving way to an ecclesiastical indigo. This allows a few of the brightest stars to compete to make their presence known alongside the ever-growing network of communications satellites and their inter-mittent matrix of laser beams made brilliant and multicoloured solely for purposes of marketing advantage and brand identity.

Luxuriating in his hot tub, Rolf Larsson gazes through the glass ceiling panels of his attic bathroom and allows the deep purple of the late evening sky to engulf him. He can still feel the press of Laila's embrace, her body urgent against his, and he savours their closeness again. He slips into a gentle mood of detachment, floating, as the swirling surreality of Debussy's Cello Sonata in D minor marks a distant punctuation elsewhere in the apartment. Laila has chosen his favourite piece of music. She is sending him a message of love and contentment from the living room beyond. It is Friday night, the start to their weekend.

He names every star he can see, constructs a pattern to connect them and quickly factors their prime numbers. It is a game his father taught him even before he went to high school. Then he makes his topology three-dimensional, placing and naming the more distant star clusters and invisible galaxies where he knows them to be. Once again his mind turns to the infinite billions of stars whose presence is masked in summer by the light Scandinavian atmosphere. Sweden's twenty-seven-year-

old media-acclaimed 'prodigy' of astrophysics tries once more
to predict his pattern in a way that will make them denumerable.
As always, the model in his head shatters soon after he tries to
push beyond the counter-intuitive irrationality of string theory,
quantum mechanics, parallel states and the concept of infinity.
He exhales and lies back, dipping his head under the water.

He sits up, dries his face on a towel and leans forward to
add more hot water. As he does so, a sudden contrapuntal
rhythm created nearly a century earlier fills his head and he
gains another point of observation that flickers in and out of his
grasp.

Suddenly his four-dimensional model of matter extends with
the music and gains a fifth, then a sixth, then more, in a mental
cascade of observations that pulse with potential for proof. In a
moment it, too, shatters but then, with the counterpoint of the
rational mathematics Debussy used to build his temporal dance,
it slowly reassembles as an intellectual scaffolding that provides
multiple observation points which extend and transcend the
thinness of the present.

Larsson probes the new patterns of space, place, time and
matter that are now crystallizing in his consciousness. It seems
to be an entirely new metalanguage! Then he realizes what he
might have.

He leaps from his bath and runs, naked and wet, into his
wood-floored attic living room. 'Wake!' he shouts as he reaches
his computer display screens and, dripping, he begins to work,
oblivious of Laila's puzzled gaze.

The stars were reappearing by the time Larsson pushed himself
back from his screens and ran his fingers through his hair. He
should have been preparing for two tutorials for his supplementary PhD in particle physics, but he was sure he had just
discovered something no tutorial could offer. Yet, despite the
scale of this achievement, it didn't occur to him that he might
never return to his university.

Laila had padded over to investigate soon after he had
started communing with his machine. He hadn't said anything
when she had draped a towelling robe around his shoulders and

she understood his frequent intellectual obsessions well enough to leave him undisturbed. Later, when she had been swallowing yawns for an hour, she had brought black coffee from the kitchen, guessing that he was settling down for a long session. He hadn't even looked up as she leaned over his shoulder to place the mug beside his keyboard. She had kissed his cheek, feeling his stubble against her lips, and he had at last acknowledged her presence by placing his hand over hers as she squeezed his shoulder. She had kissed him once more and left him to it.

Now, nearly a day later, he was finished.

'Save with remote back-up,' Larsson told his computer. 'Disconnect from all networks.'

He slept for fourteen hours and when he woke, sweaty and unshaven in the broad daylight of Sunday, he panicked. He couldn't recapture the complex matrix in his mind. Two minutes later his computer confirmed he had not dreamed it: his new language and concepts had created formulae that expressed a polydimensional method of observing the smallest particles of matter – a means of calculating and proving their positions at all times.

When he had showered and wolfed down cold baked beans straight from the can, Larsson called his academic supervisor at home. He had been summoned as a standby juror, he explained: sudden and unavoidable. The trial was scheduled to last a few weeks.

Laila had given up on their weekend plans and returned to her own apartment in Trossa, leaving a message for him to call when he finally surfaced. She took his call and, after apologizing, he explained that he'd found something that might be important for his new doctorate and that he needed some time alone.

'Is there anything wrong?' she asked. He could see the worry on her face, and pursed his lips towards her in a kiss.

'I love you,' he said. 'You'll be so proud of me if this turns out to be what I think it is.'

She smiled, a reaction that produced a small dimple at the corner of her mouth. He felt a pang of desire but fought it.

'Just give me a little while to concentrate, OK?'

She nodded.

'It's not so easy when you're around.'

She smiled again. 'Well, call me when you can.'

Three weeks later, having provided only the briefest explanations for his solitary preoccupation to his family and friends, Larsson had completed the coding for his software. It worked flawlessly on the few secure messages he had in local storage. He then logged on to the global networks and dispatched the software robots he had created.

After decades of continuous investment in virtual technologies, the world had become totally reliant on the vast web of fibre-optic cables, wireless networks and satellite chains that, each day, created an ever more dense matrix around the planet. Almost every aspect of government, business and social life raced through the man-made digital cosmos at the speed of light. Everything sensitive, controversial or financial was scrambled by super-strong security techniques that were unbreakable even by the largest network of optical supercomputers. It was a safe, trustworthy and instant domain.

Within an hour Larsson's software surrogates reported back with copies of two thousand separate messages, all painstakingly gathered, collated and reconstructed from the millions of tiny parts into which they had been split in order to pursue separate routes to their intended destinations. Of these, just over 400 had been scrambled, using unbreakable cryptography.

Larsson found 107 errors in his coding as he ran his new prime-number generator repeatedly against the encrypted messages. With mounting cries of frustration at his own stupidity, he corrected and recompiled the software until his engine was producing a continuous string of the super-rare high prime numbers that lie at the heart of unbreakable encryption technology.

Once the software was stable – or stable enough to complete more than a few passes without crashing – it took him a little less than fifteen minutes to break the first message. As he tuned his algorithms, plain text emerged at an ever-faster rate from the jumble of letters and symbols that made up the encrypted communications.

Six hours after he broke the first message, all 409 were in plain text for him to examine. Ignoring the messages that were in languages he couldn't read without using auto-translation, Larsson's first ten minutes of scrolling revealed a draft agreement on agricultural trade subsidies between Washington DC and the European Union, four bank transfer instructions for sums ranging between two hundred million and seven hundred million dollars, and three sets of draft company accounts.

The young Swede pushed his chair back from his computer screens and yelled at the ceiling. He jumped to his feet and clasped his hands behind his head, turning in tiny circles. For twenty minutes he walked around his apartment staring at blank walls, at the table top and out of the window. He looked, but registered nothing.

An hour later he dispatched his team of software robots again. This time they had a particular target and, as soon as they had departed into the world's networks, he left his apartment, carefully double-locking the heavy old metal door of the converted warehouse building.

He was shocked by the brilliance of the June day. Other than occasional late-evening sorties to the convenience store, he had hardly stepped outdoors in a month. The sun created a panorama of flashing reflections across the gentle swell of the harbour like a flotilla of miniature ships frantically signalling the shore.

Not for the first time, Larsson reflected on how the apparent reality of the physical world made the intangible space of the digital environment seem unreal – the classic mistake. He smiled and reminded himself that it was his brain that was adding the brilliant colours to the scene in front of him. All that existed in the physical world were varying achromatic wavelengths of light. Man created his own world: it had been *virtual*, a product of human creativity, from the moment consciousness emerged and thus it was humans who gave meaning to quantum particles which, Larsson had proved, included many alternative states, all of them useful in the creation of new concepts for language and, consequently, thought.

He strolled past the innumerable outdoor café tables on the cobbled quayside, oblivious of the sharp looks of interest and query from the young and less-young female patrons. Tall, lank and with an unruly mop of flaxen hair, his thin T-shirted figure appeared deep in thought.

His mind was on Thomas Tye and his company, the Tye Corporation. Since the eruption of global wealth created by the virtual and biotech economies, thousands of new companies had emerged to take over from the old industrial-age behemoths such as car makers and oil companies. The corporate riches of the late twentieth century had been dwarfed by the immense wealth created by enterprises that focused on delivering virtual and information-specific products via the networks, by companies that could quadruple the produce of an acre of land and by corporations that created miracle cures based on the map of the human genome. All such products and services were delivered to a global market made one by the networks' elimination of physical boundaries and borders.

Even the old software and computer giants of the pre-network age now looked puny compared with the distributed and virtually based corporations that had come to dominate the global economy. Of these, by far the richest was the Tye Corporation, the world's most valuable company and the biggest telecommunications, software, pharmaceutical, biotech, healthcare, aerospace, media and banking conglomerate on the planet.

Almost everybody in the world, in the rapidly emerging economies as well as in the developed countries, was familiar with the face and the public opinions of Thomas Tye, the company's founder, major shareholder and environmental campaigner; the man who had become the planet's richest citizen. As such, he was the obvious target for Larsson, and by the time the astrophysicist returned to his apartment, his trawling robots had reappeared with copies of over 300 Tye Corporation communications that had been flashing through the world's networks as they lay in wait.

Larsson saved the material that had been harvested and started work. Inside an hour he had decoded and read plans to relocate offices, fund transfers between a dozen banks and outline designs for a new generation of 3D hologram software. Then he found something ideal for his purpose. It was a highest-security, deeply encrypted message that had been sent to Thomas Tye's confidential mailbox. When he had broken the code, Larsson read the final draft of the Tye Corporation's annual report and consolidated accounts that was due to be published in sixteen days' time. The document had been on its way to Tye for his final approval when it had been silently and untraceably intercepted and copied, in less than one one-hundredth of a second.

Larsson printed out the 120 pages and spent several hours struggling to understand the unfamiliar formats of multinational corporate accounting. He visited the Tye Corporation's main network resource and downloaded the previous year's accounts. He could interpret enough of the financial statements to see that the company's revenue had jumped sixty per cent and its net income was up by forty-eight per cent.

He stood up and allowed himself a few small revolutions in the middle of the floor. Then he sat back down, extracted Tye's personal network address from the decoded file and prepared a message containing a copy of the draft accounts in plain, unscrambled text. To reinforce his point, he also added three further confidential Tye Corporation messages in plain language and sent them to Tye with a cryptic message;

New software. Want to discuss?

Larsson left his audio alert on and went to bed. But sleep did not come. At three a.m., just as he was finally drifting off, his computer alerted him to incoming v-mail. He opened his three screens, enabled the videoconferencing system and saw the best-known face on the planet in front of him.

Involuntarily, his response was formal.

'Mr Tye.'

'Doctor Larsson?' That rich, full voice; so well known.

The young man nodded.

'Can you verify, please?'

'Let's both do it.'

The cameras showed Tye leaning forward and touching the fingerprint reader on his system. Larsson did the same. Three seconds later a message appeared on Larsson's home screen. 'Identity of caller confirmed as Thomas Richmond Tye, born 1 July 1966, Boston, USA. Present location undisclosed.' A second message confirmed that Tye had received reciprocal confirmation from the world's Digital Certification Authority. Despite his nervousness at communicating with the richest person ever to have lived, Larsson found himself wondering at how handsome and youthful Tye appeared for someone well into middle age. His plastic surgeon must be excellent.

'Please encrypt, if you don't find that too funny,' said Tye. Larsson complied and received confirmation of secure mode.

'Well, Doctor, you certainly have the right background for it,' acknowledged Tye, staring straight into his central camera. They had exchanged camera control as had become the custom and courtesy of the time and Larsson zoomed in until the trillionaire's perfect face filled his central screen. 'Did you get lucky or do you really have something new?'

Larsson had gone over and over what he might say at this point. Abandoning all his earlier plans, he simply said, 'It's something new. Completely new.'

'Can you prove it?'

'To anybody who understands particle physics or quantum mechanics,' responded Larsson. 'Or I can repeat the demonstrations.'

'Who have you told?'

'Nobody. It happened just a couple of weeks ago.'

'I presume you want to sell,' prompted Tye.

'I ... I don't know,' said Larsson, because he didn't.

'Come to Hope Island tomorrow,' said Tye. 'Tell nobody, and bring everything you have on it.'

Larsson hesitated. After repeated postponements, he had arranged to see Laila the following day for the first time in four weeks.

'Well?'

Larsson nodded.

'I'll send a jet. Someone will be in touch. Oh ... and don't attempt to act on what you know. I'm altering the figures.'

The screens went blank. Larsson sat slumped in his chair for a few moments and then, with shaking hands, got up to make a coffee. He had never felt less like sleep.

ONE

Seven Years Later

As usual, there was a moment's silence when Thomas Tye appeared in the lights. There is a shock in seeing such a famous face and feeling such power in the same room, even when the entrance is anticipated and the room very large.

On either side of the stage two giant screens flickered into life and the audience rose to its feet shouting, clapping and stomping its appreciation, adulation and joy. The corporate rock anthem filled the air and Tye smiled and waved, both arms outstretched, images of his improbably boyish, good-looking face filling the vastness of London's Earl's Court arena. His lustrous shoulder-length dark hair shone in the lights and the small diamonds set into his earpieces sparkled as he moved. He wore his customary stage uniform of white T-shirt and black trousers. Subtly, the taste and smell of the air changed.

He stood nodding his appreciation for several minutes as his audience swayed to the beat and reached out towards him. Then, with an extended palm, he silenced the music. His audience howled and he walked to the front of the stage and bowed low; practised, confident and sure. He had always been a natural on stage and, in the early days, he had built his markets by the power of his virtuoso extempore performances. Now he accepted major appearances only when it suited the company, when it fitted with his schedule or when it eased access to the politicians who were now his main concern. But he still loved these performances.

He stood and smiled, his perfect white teeth and infectious grin lighting up his audience. 'Well, how are you?'

Twelve thousand people erupted again and the beat returned. They stomped and stomped, the drumming of the music and their feet becoming faster and faster until it merged into a rolling crescendo of thunder.

Tye lifted one hand again and there was silence. He held them, the confident cynosure, greeted by thousands of camera flashes as he turned to each sector of the vast hall. Whistles and cries of 'Tommeee' broke through the silence he was controlling. The 'TT' chant started, low at first, then insistent, then with all the power of 24,000 lungs.

In the wings of the elaborate set, Jack Hendriksen received a message in his ear.

'There's about two hundred outside the stage door plus the TV crews, journalists and the merchandisers. And the Touchers. We've run facial patterns from our video scans. No known combustion risks as far as we can see.'

Jack nodded involuntarily as he listened to the disembodied voice.

'OK,' he said, 'The party will be there in . . .' He looked at his LifeWatch. 'Twenty-six minutes. I want a clear passage for Pierre's team.'

Tye was performing at his best and the technology worked without a hitch. He had quietened the crowd down again and he stepped back from the edge of the stage. The lighting went off. Then a spotlight lit a lectern to the left-hand side of the stage and Tye was behind it, waving his right arm. A split second later a follow-spot lit an area in the centre of the stage and another Tye was there, waving with his other hand. The audience looked from one Thomas Tye to the other and back again.

'Pretty good, isn't it?' asked the Tye in the middle of the stage. 'Tom, turn around, please.'

The figure at the lectern turned slowly, a slightly ethereal quality to its movements.

'Wave goodbye.'

The Tye at the lectern waved obediently. Its spotlight died

and Tye walked to the other side of the stage illuminated by his follow-spot.

'And now...'

The centre of the dark stage was suddenly illuminated and where there had previously been only space, a string quartet in evening dress appeared and began to play the 'Spring' movement from Vivaldi's *Four Seasons.*

As Tye stepped his audience through the carefully canned demonstration of the Tye Corporation's new holographic entertainment system, Jack Hendriksen checked in turn with each of his locally hired observers in the auditorium. The entire audience had been scanned and the building swept twice, but there was always the problem of touts selling last-minute tickets to self-immolators. And today the warm-up team had lifted the crowd to ecstasy.

For two hours before Thomas Tye had appeared, the corporation's team of international Games Masters had led the crowd through ever-increasing levels of excitement as they re-enacted legendary network war games and space battles in a show of lasers, smoke and music that filled the central roof space of the vast arena. Those who had paid €400 for their first-class tickets followed the action as they sat strapped into hydraulically powered seats that moved with the motion of the spacecraft, the battle armour or the jet planes the imagineers had created for their games. Those who were accessing the event via the networks received similar control feeds for their home HydraChairs and headsets.

Then there had been a wait: a smouldering time of heavy rock music and the first reprise of 'It's Our Planet', a song that had become the corporate anthem and a global Number One. As it played, the scent simulators in the auditorium released a fragrance called 'Abundance' into the atmosphere. It was the track's signature scent and the audience had found themselves inhaling the cleansed air of spring woodland after a rain shower. Their anticipation and excitement grew as they waited for Thomas Tye finally to appear in person.

Over the last decade, Tye's wealth, power, fame and innate sex appeal had turned him into an idol. As the world's first trillionaire, he had become an icon with a global following. Because of his good looks, his concern for the planet, his legendary philanthropy, and the careful presentations created by his perception managers, marketing strategists and public relations teams, he was also the first businessman to achieve real superstar status. Cleverly, he had captured the hearts and minds of the hoards of anarchistic, anti-capitalist, pro-environment, anti-establishment protesters who had used the early Internet to create a contagion with which to ignite demonstrations and violent outbreaks across the globe in the early years of the century. As these retro-1960s rebels, the children of the hippie archetypes, had, in their turn, become parents and homeowners, his corporation had originally offered them a respectable and ethical alternative vehicle by which to grow their wealth. But today, the glister of his fortune meant that his public appearances had also become a rallying point for the world's truly needy. He had become the focus of hope for millions of physical sufferers as well as for the disturbed, the alienated and the lonely.

Eight years earlier, Tye had shaken hands with a group of disabled fans who had been brought to hear him speak in Mexico City. Within days, the mother of a paraplegic teenager claimed that her daughter's paralysis had been cured by meeting the great star and entrepreneur. She had paraded the walking miracle on television and a movement had been born, connected and nourished in the byways and private meeting rooms of the networks. Tye's new followers believed that if they could simply touch their idol, they would be cured of their disabilities or their diseases. The press had soon dubbed them 'Tye's Touchers.'

Thomas Tye had immediately released a video statement to the twenty-four-hour news channels disclaiming all such healing powers, but the believers would not be dissuaded. The Tye Corporation's international perception-management consultancy sensed the potential for a serious public-relations catastrophe and, on its advice, Tye started asking for a token number of visibly disabled people to be present at his public engagements. His PM team ensured that they were always placed in the front row. Before, during or after his appearances, Tye made the time to shake each hand and further rumours about miraculous cures began to circulate.

A few months later a freelance reporter with a smattering of scientific knowledge provided the world with yet another example of irresponsible journalism. Her article, which was published in a networked popular-science magazine, revealed that a subsidiary of the Tye Corporation had patented a biochip that, when worn under the skin, monitored and rebalanced the electrochemical processes of the human central nervous system. She claimed that Tye had personally been beta-testing the chip for two years and it was contact with this new radiesthetic conductive and corrective force that was producing the purported cures. The movement became a cult.

Then, during a major performance in the Dynasty Auditorium in Manila, one of the many wheelchair-bound Touchers in the audience set herself alight. At the peak of the carefully orchestrated excitement, the fifteen-year-old girl had doused her clothes in petrol and the shaking figure in the chair had disappeared inside an inferno of flame before the hall's security staff had had a chance to reach her. The President of the Philippines had been watching from the Presidential Box at the time and the incident was caught live by TV cameras broadcasting the event throughout Asia. Within minutes, the recording was being replayed on the world's global news networks. The victim had left an e-mail with a friend that simply read 'For the Planet'. The girl had told her friends in a Thomas Tye network community that it was better to die in the presence of her idol than to use the planet's precious resources to extend her life of suffering.

Four months later it happened again, this time in Santiago. Then it happened in a detached home in a quiet tree-lined street in a suburb of Munich, Germany. This quadriplegic fan persuaded a friend to strap her into a HydraChair, feed her a hyper-analgesic and douse her with petrol before leaving her with a mouth-operated battery ignition system and a network connection to a Thomas Tye appearance in Sydney, Australia.

Supporters in a Thomas Tye chat room on the networks sat with her during the build-up and, when the time came, helped her find the courage. Then, in tribute, they posted a video record of her sacrifice in their community's meeting space.

Once again it was 'For the Planet. Thank you, Tom.'

Inevitably, the tabloid press dubbed this new breed of fanatic fans 'Tye's Torches' and preventing the possibility of further acts of hysterical self-immolation became a high priority during all public appearances.

This morning, Jack Hendriksen's plants in the Earl's Court audience reported nothing suspicious.

Tye was into his wrap, dancing along with a holo-image recreation of a young Bruce Springsteen and the E Street Band as they performed 'It's Our Planet'. The venerable star's brand-extension agency had graciously granted a licence for his youthful voice and image to be sampled and morphed for the recording.

Jack flicked on the head-up display in his viewpers. He switched from camera to camera checking backstage, the artists' corridor, the stage door and the throng outside. The police had the large crowd penned behind crush barriers and he could see that the members of Pierre's PPT – the Presidential Protection Team – were in place and the motorcade was waiting.

As director of corporate security for the Tye Corporation, Jack was rarely on the road with the PPT but he believed that spot checks and surprise visits were the best way to keep his in-field teams from becoming complacent. His presence in London had given him the first opportunity in months to observe Pierre Pasquier's detail and, despite a growing sense of inarticulated unease about the organization that employed him, he was pleased to see the machine was well oiled and at a high condition of readiness.

Then it was over. Tye walked to the front of the stage and acknowledged the applause to the right, the centre, the left and to the cameras in the pit. He leaned forward and touched the line of outstretched hands at the edge of the stage – the hands of a few dozen physically disabled fans allowed to sit in elevated positions for this televisual opportunity.

'Take care of our planet – you hear!' he told the audience.

'We hear! WE HEAR!' they shouted – the conditioned response to his famous parting imperative and they roared their approval. He turned back to them one more time: 'And come visit our booth in the show.'

He waved goodbye with both hands stretched high. The huge consumer electronics expo in adjacent halls would open the moment he left the stage.

He waved again and then he was gone. Even before he had left the darkened stage he had thrust his hands deep into his pockets where the fingers that had done the touching could break open antiseptic capsules. Then he was backstage and in Pierre's protection and he turned off into a specially built bathroom in the wings. Pierre, a six feet, six inches tall former officer of France's *Direction et Surveillance du Territoire*, stood guard across the door.

Tye carefully locked the door and checked twice that it was secure. He stripped off all his clothes, threw them on the floor and flipped through his vital signs on his LifeWatch. Then he washed his hands once in a bactericide and then again in a bacteriostatic, carefully scrubbing under his fingernails each time. He dried his hands on paper towels that he threw into a large trash can. He tore open sealed plastic bags and removed fresh underpants and socks. He tugged these on and peeled a long tape fastener from a hermetically sealed clothes carrier hanging behind the door. Here he found a fresh white shirt and a pair of dark trousers. When he had buttoned and zipped himself into these he took a new pair of shoes from the bottom of the container. He slipped into them and then picked up a small aerosol and sprayed his face, mouth and throat with isoprophyl alcohol for extra protection. He pulled a brush through his long hair, checked his appearance in the mirror and took a deep breath. Holding it, he stepped out of the room and into the care of Pierre's team.

Then he was walking rapidly in the middle of a phalanx of five. *Perfect formation*, thought Jack as he followed a few yards behind. The bodyguards were all immaculately dressed in sharp, dark business suits made from flame-resistant material. They moved forward like a super-taut Olympic relay team passing a radioactive baton: each knew precisely where the other was and how he would react to a slip.

Pierre's height allowed him to see over Tye's head to scan all events to the front. He was responsible for the most vital exit route, the escape to the rear. He would physically pick Tye up and run with him if he had to. At Jack's insistence he had even made the trillionaire suffer the indignity of repeated rehearsals.

Out in the daylight and powerful heat of a London June morning there was pandemonium, as usual. Reporters shouted questions as the cameras rolled. The Touchers reached out over the heads of those in front, imploring their hero to stop and shake hands or merely to touch their fingers. Some threw flowers.

Suddenly two small figures squeezed between the crush barriers and dipped under the interlocked arms of the police officers. One had a microphone in her hand, the other was operating a video camera. The first thrust the microphone in Thomas Tye's face with a shouted question.

Tye knocked the microphone out of his path without a glance.

'It's OK, OK, keep moving,' ordered Pierre in the team's earpieces as he stepped forward to shield his boss from the intrusion. From the rear Jack saw the small incident brought under control and then the phalanx had moved forward and he was left to confront the interlopers.

The two women looked identical. Both were short and dark, but Jack saw that the one with the microphone had a short elfin haircut while her twin had long hair. The elf looked from her disappearing quarry to Jack and thrust an envelope towards him. He ran an instant head-to-toe scan of the small, attractive woman.

'Give these to him, please,' she urged, her dark eyes wide as she pressed the envelope against Jack's chest.

His training told him not to touch it, to let the package fall, to avoid any legal liability. In his present disaffected mood his instinct said the opposite.

Jack nodded, stuffed the envelope into his inside pocket, caught up with the party and climbed into the rear of the fourth limo. He saw Pierre wave control over to the leader of the police outriders and the motorcade of electronically shielded and battle-armoured limousines pulled away. Jack searched back through the digital video recording his pinhole cameras had captured. Her face was not in the database of known Touchers. But he held the image in front of him, studying it. The convoy slowed as it neared the venue for Tye's next engagement.

On the other side of the world, sixteen planes were in various stages of descent for landings at Oakland Airport, across the bay from the southern suburbs of San Francisco. Although mainly a regional, domestic airport with relatively light night-time movements, the air traffic supervisors had the task of overseeing the computers that steered incoming and outgoing flights around the over-busy, delay-prone air lanes that fed SFO, the city's main international airport eight miles to the west.

Oakland was a modern, well-equipped airport and when the images projected by the air-traffic control computers froze, senior air traffic supervisor Sandy Davis swore. The technical people had told everybody that the modern computer systems couldn't crash. Then, remembering the drill from her initial training as a manual air traffic controller twenty years before, she simply closed her eyes and started counting to ten. She was trying to calculate the progress of the sixteen planes the computer had been handling even though, in her manual days, the maximum a human controller would have been expected to visualize during a system failure was six.

The back-up system finally kicked in as her count reached eight. As the display in front of her reactivated she saw that her planes were almost exactly where she expected them to be.

'What's happening?' she called angrily over her shoulder. 'We're never supposed to lose real-time!' There were shrugs all round.

When she looked back her planes were once again frozen within their cubic 3D display.

'Now we've lost positioning handshake from the satellites,' she shouted.

Then Sam Potter, the shift controller was beside her. 'You're counting?'

She nodded, also calculating how long she had before she had to declare an emergency and ask for assistance from SFO.

Potter made the decision for her and picked up the desk phone. He prodded angrily at the instrument. 'It's dead,' he exclaimed. 'What the fuck's going on around here!'

He fished his VideoMate from his pocket and flipped it open.

'There's no radio signal!' he shouted. 'That's impossible. Everything's down. But they're all separate systems!'

Sandy's display refreshed.

'Jesus,' breathed Potter. 'Tell American 114 to turn–'

Sandy was doing it before he completed his sentence. She told the pilot to override his on-board flight control computer, issued instructions that would allow him to turn the passenger jet ninety degrees to the right and simultaneously told him to climb a thousand feet. She cleared two more distant planes from the stack and instructed the bewildered American crew to complete their turn, climb another twelve thousand feet and rejoin the stack forty miles to the east. 'We're suffering multiple systems failure here,' she explained. 'Please alert SFO.'

There was silence in the room. Sandy exhaled slowly. As she sat back, the phone beside her started to ring.

Thomas Tye rose from a couch to greet the British Prime Minister, his Health Secretary and three senior civil servants. The tycoon had changed into another fresh, open-necked white shirt and he had tied his hair back. The favoured TV crews and photographers got the group to repeat their handshakes over and over again and then they were quickly bundled from the hotel suite.

Tye walked his guests to the picture window in the penthouse of the London Hilton and they stood admiring the sun-drenched view down into the private gardens of Buckingham Palace. What a row there had been a lifetime ago when the Queen had first discovered she was overlooked by hotel guests. Now it was no longer the main royal residence and the old, old, widowed Queen walked among the ornamental ponds and privet hedges only on the rare occasions when public duties recalled her to London.

With an exchange of nods, the small party turned and crossed to sit on the sofas that filled a sunken seating area. All the furniture in the room was new, the plastic covers removed only after Tye had arrived and given his permission the previous evening. The suite had been redecorated and new carpets had been laid by the Tye Corporation's Advance Preparation Unit. It was a procedure Tye insisted on wherever he travelled.

What was not revealed to the host locations was that the APU was part of Jack's division and the most important part of their 'redecoration' procedures was to investigate all wall, ceiling and floor cavities, to replace all communications systems with the Tye Corporation's own highly encrypted systems, to install electronic 'white noise' barriers and to maintain a complete electronic anti-bugging sweep of all areas the corporation's president would be occupying. Modern business techniques and ethics dictated such precautions for all off-site meetings.

Two stewards held out hot antiseptic towels for the party.

Jack Hendriksen beckoned to Pierre and said he would take the floor duty. The Frenchman nodded and he and Stella Witherspoon, the deputy PPT leader, took up positions at the two exits to the suite. Jack stepped out into the corridor and closed the doors quietly behind him.

Two uniformed British policemen, armed and with full body armour, were outside. They scanned him and received his ident. A small nod from the taller served as acknowledgement. Jack moved along the corridor to ensure that all approaches were covered. The Hilton's management had insisted its own video surveillance was adequate and had refused the Tye Corporation's request to install its own system in public corridors. Despite this, the hotel's prime location, the lure of the penthouse view and its management's willingness to allow redecoration of three suites had been sufficient for Tye to overrule the PPT's objections. They had taken the entire floor, of course, but, assuming Pierre's role for the day, Jack wanted to double-check that the elevators were locked off and that the roof and stairwell escapes were covered. He recognized the tall man in a dark navy suit standing opposite the exit to the four elevators.

'Hi, Nigel. Good to see you.'

He had met the Prime Minister's senior protection officer twice before. They swapped greetings and the Brit confirmed that his team had locked off the elevators the moment the press had left.

With a wave, Jack continued his journey around the circular corridor. As he passed the open doors to another suite he saw Connie Law, Tye's personal assistant, and her staff busily confirming the final details of Tye's short European tour. Tomorrow it was Brussels to see the Commissioner and then on to Berlin for Tye to give another performance; Paris on Friday for lunch with the President of the Republic, and then, unannounced and, it was to be hoped, unreported, one of the two supersonic Tye-Lear corporate jets ferrying the Tye Corporation presidential entourage around the world would change its flight plan in mid-air to bring Tye and a smaller retinue back to an airfield in Cambridgeshire. Tye would then spend two private days visiting his investments in the many biotechnology companies that had sprung up in the science parks of the area.

Jack watched Connie work. Her highlighted blonde hair was cut short and a pair of gold-rimmed personal viewpers were suspended around her neck on a thin gold chain. He regarded her as the most efficient and unflappable human he had ever met and he felt his interest growing as he admired her long, elegant neck. Suddenly he found himself thinking about the vacation he was due to start in six days. He was looking forward to getting back to the apartment in Manhattan he so rarely saw. He often thought about selling it but each time he remembered how important it was to keep somewhere that was your own, something that had no connection with the Tye Corporation. *A place that still felt clean*, he realized, *untainted by this business.*

He pushed away the weariness and a vague, unseated sense of disgust. It was just a reaction to mental fatigue and he had been well trained to cope. He had enjoyed the demands his twelve-year career in the US military and government intelligence services had made on him and he was grateful for the resources it had forced him to discover in himself. When he had been finally discharged, after he had abandoned two previous attempts to quit just as new crises had erupted around the world, his section head had described his service as 'outstanding and distinguished' in front of the few men and women who were permitted to witness the small ceremony in Washington.

Jack hadn't been able to talk much about those years. During most of his time with the US Navy and, subsequently, various loosely associated government agencies, he had been involved with intelligence activities. He had simply given his commendations and medals to his mother and watched her smile broaden as he asked her to mothball his ceremonial naval uniforms.

'Is it for good this time, Johnny?' his mother had asked as she reached up to push back a short lock of blond hair that had fallen across his forehead. No matter how old or experienced he became, he would always be her first-born.

He had smiled and kissed her.

'It's for good, Mom,' he had assured her. 'Although I've no idea what I'm going to do now.'

Jack had seen a frown cross his mother's forehead. Although little mention was made of it, his father's premature death had left small provision for her later years and, for the last twelve years, her two sons had jointly shouldered the responsibility of providing her with a comfortable retirement.

She need not have worried. The Tye Corporation's director of corporate security services had made contact within forty-eight hours of Jack's discharge. Jack rejected the offer outright during the first voice call. He knew nothing about corporate security and he didn't want to learn.

Then his predecessor had called back and had told him a little more about the job. He had made it plain that it was Jack's Navy-assessed IQ rating of over 140 points that was his main attraction. He said Jack had been strongly recommended by Ron Deakin, his original SEAL intelligence instructor. Jack had applied to join the elite Marine corps just as it had been changing from a brutally physical fighting force to a 'smart' operations unit. Although the induction had been gruelling, the

Navy had finally abandoned the ultra-macho, close-to-death training methods that had been necessary to train covert-killing troops when combat was principally physical and at very close quarters. Just as Jack arrived, the SEALs were donning smart suits, adopting information-distance weapons and substituting robot incursors for men in as many operations as possible. When that was not possible, they were using non-American mercenaries, mostly would-be immigrants from Venezuela, for all physical combat, although neither the media nor the public were aware of the policy. Losing an *American* life in a conflict had become political suicide.

It had been Jack's systems skills and his analytical abilities that had prompted Instructor Deakin to lift him out of the corps for tactical intelligence training and, for the rest of his four-year career with the regiment, he had directed many of its active-service operations from a communications command post many miles away from the action zone. Then he had transferred to a US government intelligence agency.

'We're not looking for a tough guy, we're looking for a clever guy who can run a large team,' the persistent Tye Corporation recruiter had explained. He said that Thomas Tye operated an unwritten rule that nobody with an IQ of less than 135 would ever join his senior management executive.

Jack had been seduced by the idea that anyone was prepared to send one of the new generation of supersonic corporate jets to collect him for a job interview. Two weeks later he found himself on the small island in the West Indies that had become the Tye Corporation's world headquarters.

Thomas Tye had conducted the first interview personally. He probed Jack's intellect and played mind games with him. At first he asked him about everything but security: how he felt about the ecology of the planet, his attitude to money, women, genetics, music, politics – even his knowledge of communications systems and software. Jack did his best to keep up, wondering at the trillionaire's polymathy and high-speed acuity. He found himself caught up in Tye's infectious enthusiasm.

When Tye had, at last, asked about Jack's views on the job, he hadn't seemed surprised by the reply.

'If you want a physical bodyguard, I'm not your man,' the former intelligence officer had told the tycoon. 'It's been many years since I carried a gun and I don't intend to do so again. Not having a weapon provides a different perspective on a situation before, during and after any given event. I would leave your personal physical security and any weapons-handling to others in my team. I would consider that it would be my job to plan situations in such a way that they'd never need to use them.'

Tye had seemed to like what he had heard.

On his second interview, conducted via a four-person 'wraparound' videoconference, Jack had agreed to a six-month contract assignment after which both sides would review the situation. The salary offered was tax-free and was several times what he had been making in his final year in US government service. He was also told that if he decided to join permanently, stock options could make him seriously rich in a short space of time.

Three years later Jack had discovered they had been right about the stock options. Despite some analysts' concerns over how such a large company could sustain its phenomenal growth, the Tye Corporation's results had beaten even the most optimistic expectations and in the last two years the stock value had soared to stratospheric heights. His options had become extremely valuable and he had exercised many of them, investing the proceeds in a broad-based portfolio of equities, property and bonds.

But he hadn't realized how little he would like big business. He had discovered it was a world completely without honour or truth – or, at least, that was how Thomas Tye's empire operated. It made government intelligence activities seem almost ethical and they, at least, pursued ends that could sometimes justify the means employed.

But Jack knew he had done a good job. He had now replaced the man who had recruited him and had restructured the PPT of thirty to bring in additional foreign-language skills, better systems skills and a greater number of women. A modern Praetorian Guard, for that was finally the PPT's function, was unlikely ever to face violence if they pre-empted, protected and performed properly and, as he knew from personal experience, female insight was invaluable in preparing for the unpredictable.

Despite his frequently repeated exhortation that any need for physical engagement would always be seen as a sign of failure, Jack had constructed a four-mile training course on the Hope Island University campus. Through frequent use of this, combined with regular visits to the gym and the island's many pools, he ensured that he and his team stayed in peak physical condition.

He checked that the service lifts were indeed locked off and walked on around the corridor.

'Roof access secure?'

Pierre's man at the foot of the stairs nodded. 'We're not allowed to lock it, for safety reasons – it's a fire escape. But there's no one on the roof and a chopper can't get into this part of London air space – the Palace.' He gestured along one of the radial corridors, towards the panoramic view.

Jack nodded. He walked down the corridor towards the dead end of the picture window and leaned gently against it, taking in the view of Westminster, the Houses of Parliament and across the Thames to south London.

He felt the press of the package in his inside pocket and her face swam back into his mind. He removed the package, lifted the flap and took out a sheaf of papers. He scanned the first sheet. He had half expected it to be legalistic and it was. But the second wasn't, nor the third, nor any of the pages that followed. He turned the sheets slowly, reading carefully, totally absorbed.

Then Stella spoke in his ear. 'Party preparing to leave.'

He stuffed the papers back into the envelope, returned it to his pocket and walked back around the corridors. He arrived just as the double doors opened.

Tye walked the Prime Minister towards the elevator chatting about a recent soccer game. His cultural-variance advisers had briefed him on the politician's obsession and Tye had watched a few edited highlights in preparation for the meeting.

With handshakes briefer and more businesslike than those produced earlier for the cameras, the British politicians departed.

As the doors closed on them and their security staff, Tye walked towards his temporary administration centre, followed by his small coterie of senior executives.

He went into the bathroom just inside the entrance to the suite and dipped his hands in the basin of hot, antiseptic water that was waiting for him. He emerged, drying his hands on paper towels. He turned and threw them into a trash can in the bathroom.

'Connie, we're taking over Britain's National Health Service,' said the world's most eligible bachelor as he took two plastic bags from her and broke the seals.

He extracted a face mask from the first pack, hooked it over both ears and pulled it up over his nose. Then he pulled a pair of latex gloves from the second pack.

The radiance of his smile spread from under his mask. He looked like a dental surgeon who had made a particularly rewarding extraction of wisdom teeth.

'Get our press people to talk to the Department of Health,' he said. 'Nothing goes public until the PM announces it in Parliament. But I want us to be prepared!'

Haley Voss slobbed out most Sundays. She rose late, didn't shower and wore her old glasses to give her eyes a rest from contact lenses. She spread the quality newspapers all over the floor, sat amongst them with legs outstretched and read, a pair of scissors in her hand poised ready to clip any stories about Thomas Tye, the Tye Corporation or any associated topic. But that was the most work she allowed herself for the day. She didn't wake up her computers and she didn't log on to the networks. It was a rule she had made after Kevin had finally given up grumbling about her work obsessions and had left with his bag of dirty underwear and his only (unread) book, *How To Quit On-Line Gambling Today!* At least Barry, her new man, understood that she wanted her thinking time. She had quickly come to enjoy the frequent Sundays she spent alone in the privacy of her inner-London apartment.

She was both surprised and annoyed when, early in her afternoon off, the entry system to her flat chirruped unexpectedly. You didn't get unexpected callers in the inner city. She looked at her video screen and saw a tall, fair-haired man with spectacles.

'Yes?'

'I'm Jack Hendriksen. I work for the Tye Corporation. You gave me this on Wednesday. At Earl's Court.' He waved an envelope towards the camera.

'Just a minute.'

Christ! Here in person? She'd hoped for a reaction, but she realized that she hadn't prepared for this. Look at the state of the place. Look at the state of her!

'Can you come back in ten minutes?' she asked quickly.

The man nodded, waved the envelope at the camera again and moved off. She ran to her second-floor window and watched as he crossed the street and disappeared into the park. Where was his car? She wondered if he was a Tye Corporation lawyer, but this was a Sunday, she told herself.

She ran through the flat, waking her computer up as she passed. She had no time to shower or wash her hair, but she pulled on her jeans and a clean sweatshirt. She took her make-up into the living room and sat in front of her computer screens.

'Call Flick' she said as she removed the traces of last night's mascara and shook her lens bath. *Be in, just be there*, she willed her sister.

She heard the ring, then Felicity said, 'Haley. Hold on.'

Felicity's face appeared on the central screen and then a tiny finger stretched towards the central camera lens.

'Hi, Flick. Hi, Toby. Can you keep this line open for a while?'

Haley explained what she wanted and then turned her screens off. She was applying lipstick in her hand mirror when she saw the reflection of her cuttings on the wall behind her.

She ran to the bedroom and pulled a folded sheet from a drawer. She was applying the last piece of sticky tape to the wall when the entry system sounded again.

'You're alone?' she asked.

'Yes.'

'Second floor.'

She buzzed him in.

Her visitor was at the door before she'd finished scooping the newspapers from the floor. She thrust them under the sofa, checked the door monitor to confirm he was alone and undid her security locks.

'Miss Voss? I'm Jack Hendriksen.' He gave his name again as Haley opened the door. Beige lightweight jacket, open-necked white shirt. Understated but expensive. A well-honed, honest face. Wedding ring. Tall. She realized he wore his spectacles for high-level communications, not short-sightedness, and he didn't bother with any of the fashionable unisex ear jewellery to disguise his clear plastic earpiece. Haley felt the briefest dry pressure as they shook hands.

'Come in.'

She seemed smaller than she had in the crowd but her face was even more open, even more humorous and attractive than he recalled. He guessed she was in her early thirties. The apartment was bright, well furnished and suggested a greater degree of affluence than he had expected – air-conditioned, he was pleased to note. One wall was nothing but books. The door slammed behind him.

'Oh, here.' He held out his ident.

'Vice-President, Corporate Security, the Tye Corporation,' she read out loud. She picked up her VideoMate, copied the ident and received confirmation. 'What does that make you – a private policeman or chief bouncer for the Touchers?'

'A little of both, I guess.'

His blue eyes were straight and steady as he stared down at her. He seemed calm and she detected no tension in his face or in his body language. She felt a sudden pull inside her, low down, that she hadn't felt for a long time.

'So they've sent you to sort me out in person, have they?' she asked, handing the ident back.

He smiled, tiny laughter lines appearing by his eyes. He produced her envelope from inside his jacket.

'You should be careful what you do with stuff like this. You're making some pretty wild allegations.'

'Am I?' said Haley, her jaw jutting sufficiently for Jack to see a hint of real determination. 'All I'm asking is for Thomas Tye to talk to me about these things. My biography will be published with or without his input, or consent. He might as well have his version of the truth included.'

'Mr Tye doesn't give any interviews, as you must know. And, according to this first page, the corporation has injunctions granted against you in eleven countries.'

'Injunctions are only temporary, Mr Hendriksen. Any lawyer will tell you that. Once my publishers submit my manuscript to the courts they will be lifted.'

'Not if it's libellous, they won't.'

'A libel is only a libel if it is untrue,' said Haley.

'So you can prove all this?' He waved the papers.

'Buy a copy of the book. I'll sign it for you.' Her voice cracked and Jack could sense the agitation behind her apparent composure.

'You must know that your book will never be published,' he reasoned, walking over to the window and looking out across the park. 'The Tye Corporation can throw so much money into litigation your publishers will simply run for cover. They'll realize that even if they won in court, the legal costs would be more than they could ever make from your book, even if it was a best-seller.'

'So you're here to scare me off.' Her voice was becoming hoarse.

No, no, this isn't the way he wants it to go. Start again. 'Would you mind if I sat down?' he asked.

She waved a hand towards the sofa.

'I've done my homework,' he smiled as he shrugged his jacket off and eased his tall frame down into the cushions. Haley remained standing, arms folded; a slight but determined figure. 'I know you're highly respected as a biographer. That film star's biography, Josh Chandler, of course: it's famous – you've made a lot of TV appearances about him. And some of the reviews I've found … your *Book of the Presidents*, was that the last? … I saw it got some great notices. That's one of the reasons I'm here.'

'Go on.'

He hesitated, then plunged. 'Look, I'm not really here on

company business. I haven't been sent. I'm not even authorized to speak to the media and...' he hesitated '...I'm the only person who's seen your questions so far.'

Haley looked down at him. In her mind she knew he was likely to be lying, but instinct told her he wasn't.

'I don't believe you. One way or another you're here to try and stop me telling the world where the Tye Corporation is heading.'

'I'm not. No one knows I'm here.' He had an idea. 'I'll prove it. May I use your system?' He pointed at her computer on the desk.

Panic. Don't show it. 'No, my system's down,' she lied. 'Tye software, I expect.'

He smiled, watchfully.

'I've got my VideoMate.' Haley touched the unit at her belt.

'It's OK, I'll use mine,' said Jack. He pulled his Tye communicator from its belt clip. Then he remembered that he had deliberately switched it off to disable its location function.

'Sorry, you're not the only one with system problems,' he smiled ruefully as he removed its memory card and returned the small device to its holder.

'Here,' offered Haley. 'Mine's a Sony.'

He flipped the small mobile device open, inserted his card and touched the screen. He searched through the recording.

'Look,' he prompted, handing her the VideoMate.

She watched the small screen. 'That looks like Tye,' she exclaimed. 'When was this–' She stopped mid-sentence as she saw that the screen display showed the recording had been made at eight that morning.

'Enjoy your day,' Tye was saying to the camera. 'Go to an art gallery or something.' She heard Jack's voice respond as Tye sprayed his mouth, pulled on a face mask and walked out of the hotel lobby to the waiting limousine. Tye turned back to the camera with a laugh. 'Take a punt out on the river!'

Then he was gone: into the car with another man and a woman and off through the city streets.

She stopped the replay, searched backwards and then zoomed in on Tye's face.

'That *is* Tye, isn't it?' said Haley. 'Why's he wearing a mask? I thought that was just another of the Thomas Tye jokes?'

'Well, he does wear them in private,' confirmed Jack. 'He's afraid of germs.'

She frowned and replayed the clip from its start. 'Isn't that Cambridge? It looks like Regent Street.' She recalled it from her university days. 'I didn't know Tye was still over here.'

'We came back yesterday. TT – Tom – has some private visits to make.'

Haley put a finger to her chin in parody of a thought occurring to her. 'Let me guess: Moleculture plc, Bioneme Ltd, Erasmus Research plc and Genome Technologies.'

Spot on, thought Jack. 'Tom has a lot of investments around Cambridge. But, as you saw, this is my day off. I'm not here for the Tye Corporation.'

'And you just happened to make that video to convince me of your sincerity, didn't you?' objected Haley, intrigued at the lengths her visitor was prepared to go to in order to convince her.

'I normally record everything,' said Jack simply. He took his spectacles off and touched the frame. Haley saw minute lenses in the corners. He touched the lapel of his jacket where it lay on the arm of the sofa and she saw others in the buttonholes. 'Don't you video meetings and so on? Just for legal safety, and security?'

She almost shot a look towards her desk. 'OK, OK, I'll play along for a while. You're here for your own reasons. So what are they?'

I'm here because I'm every bit as worried about Tye and his company as you are, because your face has been in my mind since Wednesday – I even printed out a still – because you put your address on the first page and that was an irresistible temptation. Because I've been feeling lost these last few years. But I think I'm getting over it, maybe.

Jack banished his emotions to his subconscious and picked up the sheaf of papers from the sofa cushion. 'Have you got proof of any of this?'

Haley hesitated. She looked into his pale blue eyes. His gaze seemed even and sincere. Should she trust her instincts again? They had let her down before.

'I've got something for you to see,' she said as she uncrossed her legs and rose from the sofa. She walked to her desk and pulled a thick wedge of paper from the centre drawer.

The vast greenhouses covered thirty-six acres of drained fenland and were triple-glazed throughout. Electronically operated foil blinds between the glass panes allowed the capture and escape of both light and heat to be accurately controlled. The vast area of glass was coated with translucent high-efficiency solar-energy cells made by Tye Solar Energy Inc. Inside, the air-conditioning system used the captured energy to hold the temperature at a steady 14°C for the sixteen-hour artificial 'nights' and 6° for the eight-hour artificial 'days'.

In a warm twilight, Thomas Tye and his small entourage were led to a bed of shoulder-high maize. Tye alone wore a face mask and latex gloves. He was invited to pick an ear of corn. He took the small knife proffered by his guide and carefully snipped an ear from its mother plant. He pulled back the green protective leaves. The corn was plump and bright yellow. He passed it to Connie for her inspection. Next they came to a miniature wheat field. Once again, Tye examined the maturity of the ears and nodded his appreciation.

He was shown red Desiree potatoes freshly lifted from another bed, green beans from still another. He was then invited to inspect tanks of rice and soya beans, all plump and fully mature and, finally, a young arabica coffee bush already hung with maturing red beans. The party then crossed through a double-door airtight enclosure into a higher-ceilinged green-house that contained six beds of pine saplings. Small signs at knee height announced them as *pinus strobus, pinus palustris* and *pinus nigra*.

Tye nodded his approval again and followed his host from the greenhouse and along an enclosed corridor. The rest of his entourage and a group of accompanying researchers followed a few steps behind. At the end of the corridor the party stepped out of the rubber boots that had been provided and slipped their own shoes back on. They stepped into a corridor and Connie held open a bathroom door for her boss.

She waited a few minutes until he emerged without his mask and gloves and she led him into a large, brightly lit conference room.

The visitors were shown to their places at an oval conference table and Tye walked round to a chair that was still in its protective wrapping. Connie slit the tough plastic around the arms and seat of the chair and Tye sat down. The APU had visited the room the day before and Jack's technical team had been able to confirm its secure status to Pierre, the security manager for the day.

Coffee, tea and soft drinks were served and all but Tye took some refreshment. Professor Sir Oliver Morton, the distinguished Cambridge University geneticist and co-founder of the company, stood at the head of the table, his thin, ascetic frame clad in a formal brown three-piece suit. He cleared his throat and fiddled with his cuffs.

'We are delighted to have our chairman with us at Moleculture today,' he beamed at the all-important visitor sitting to his right, at the rest of the visitors and at his own research team. 'As you have seen, Tom, we have now successfully incorporated the genes of several semi-tropical C_4 plants, mostly from the maize families, into the genomes of most of the C_3 plants, the main cash crops of the northern latitudes. This means that they are ready to grow at almost any point in the twenty-four-hour cycle, when there is light. They must have rest periods, of course, but they now exhibit positive thermotropism – that is, they grow throughout the day *and* at very low light levels, typically those found at dawn and dusk.'

Thomas Tye nodded and then started a small round of applause in which the rest of the party quickly joined.

The biochemist bobbed his long, thin head appreciatively. 'We have also managed to increase the crops' conversion rate of solar energy from its usual one per cent to five point three per cent.'

Tye tapped his appreciation on the table top. Sir Oliver's smile became broader.

'And, in our main tree genuses, the pines of the northern latitudes, we have been able to increase their CO_2 uptake by sixty per cent. Wherever they are planted, they will become a twenty-four-hour carbon dioxide sink!'

Thomas Tye banged the table hard in appreciation and the entire party clapped.

'One for our planet,' Tye commented quietly to Connie, but not so quietly that he couldn't be heard.

The knight's grin became Cheshire.

'As a next step we are hoping to get permission to plant four acres of each crop in the Scottish Highlands so that we can measure how robust each of the new strains is under natural low-light and cool-temperature conditions. We would then be able to carry out the necessary transgenic tests to ensure there is no unintended cross-pollination, and to test ecological impact on insect life and the food chain.'

'How long will that take, Oliver?' asked Tom amiably.

Morton blinked and swallowed, aware that their VIP guest and main source of funding had just asked the most delicate question of all.

'Well, that depends on the government's Genetically Modified Organisms Committee,' explained the professor quickly, looking around the table in canvass of his colleagues' support. 'We were about to file our applications for permission when the latest GM food scandals in France and Greece were uncovered. I'm afraid things have become rather difficult at present.'

'So how long?' persisted Tye, still smiling.

Morton cleared his throat again. 'Well, I can't see us getting permission to move into open fields in the current climate. At least, not for a year or two. Perhaps after the next election we–'

There was a cough from the other end of the table. 'Of course, we have all we need to prove our sequences and secure the patents,' broke in Dr Frederich Zimmer quickly, his voice rasping and intrusive. Along with Morton, the German-born biochemist and co-founder had been the company's initial source of funds. He had pumped nearly all his wife's inheritance into the company, before they had run out of cash and Tye had moved in to save them.

Zimmer rose and walked to the front, his sharp charcoal-grey suit a contrast to Tye's casual white shirt and chinos. He turned to face the man who had now become the company's principal investor and largest shareholder.

'The patents, they're the main goal, aren't they?' he suggested. 'To make low-light and pseudo-nocturnal crops ours.'

Tye nodded, still relaxed, his left arm slung over the back of his chair. 'But what if someone else is getting to open-field trials with a similar idea, Fred?' he asked as he looked up at the squat, florid German. 'Remember, American patent law has now changed to come into line with the rest of the world. It isn't first-to-invent any more; the World Patent Organization will only approve on a first-to-file basis and we can't make a filing until we've done our field tests. We may have to adjust the gene sequence to suit natural growing conditions. First-to-test and first-to-file wins under unified patent law.'

Zimmer waved a hand dismissively. 'One, I doubt that anyone else is working in this particular part of the plant genome and two, where could they be conducting trials? They'd have the same problem as us.'

Tye worked to control his notoriously short temper with this arrogant German geneticist. He had become marginally better at masking it in public in recent years.

He pushed his chair back and stood up. 'One, I know better than you, Zimmer, who else is working on low-light plant crops. Four other companies are in preparation for field trials of crops intended to be grown in more extreme latitudes. And, two ...' He trailed off, aware that he was letting go – and that he was saying too much. He took some short, deep breaths, then tried another tack. He walked to the head of the table and put his arm around the geneticist's shoulders. At five feet, nine inches he was only an inch taller than the German.

'Fred, Moleculture has only recently joined the group. We acquired you in ...'

'Last February,' supplied Zimmer.

'Well, we do things a little differently in the Tye Corporation and, well, I guess that's *why* we're the Tye Corporation.' Tye smiled and turned to Connie, who was making notes in her DigiPad. Like every other aspect of corporate activity within the company, all Thomas Tye's waking moments were videoed. But the recordings of this meeting, like the rest of his life, would not be filed in the corporate database of intellectual property. He was the only exception to company policy for the simple reason that plausible deniability was a vital option for him.

'How much of the world's population is covered by the UN Resolution on GM crop testing?'

Zimmer shrugged. Most countries had signed the agreement to control trials of new genetically modified foods strictly. 'Ninety per cent or so, I would think, Tom.'

'It's less than sixty per cent on a per capita basis, Fred. China, Angola, Zimbabwe, Russia, Sierra Leone, Ethiopia, Kazakhstan and even Pakistan – none of them have ratified the agreement. They see it as yet another power play by the West. There are governments with millions of square miles of land who will be ready and eager to help with your field trials. And *they*'ve got the populations who most need your creations, your miracle crops, Fred. We can patch your data into the Halcyon climate-modelling system and the Phoebus Project can supply the energy. You will be able to feed the world. You'll all get an invitation to Stockholm – for a Nobel Prize!'

Zimmer was a sufficiently good judge of character simply to nod his agreement. He was also crucially aware that the final (and largest) part of the payment for his Moleculture shares – and for the shares that had been owned by his wife and the others on the team – wasn't due for another two years.

'You just start mass-producing the seeds and leave the government permissions to me,' said Tye. 'I'd like to see this being tested on a small scale within two months, with very large-scale plantings for this autumn. I will be able to give you as much land as you want. We can start with a planting area of four hundred thousand hectares.'

They gazed at him, open-mouthed.

'We couldn't even *administer* such large-scale production from Cambridge, or anywhere else in the UK or Europe,'

objected Professor Morton at last. He had never even contemplated such industrial-scale planting. 'That would be a technical
breach of EU and UN Food and Agriculture guidelines.'

'Well, I'm glad you brought that up, Oliver,' responded Tye,
turning to face the scientist. 'I want you to move this facility to
our campus on Hope Island. There's quite a sizeable science
park and you'll find some interesting people there in your own
field – people who are putting nocturnal genes into cows, pigs
and sheep. Yes, farm animals that run around at night, feeding
and growing! You'll love it!'

There was silence as everybody in the room stared at him,
appalled.

He turned to face the team. 'You'll love it! You'll all love it!'
he said, nodding vigorously, willing it so. He took a small
aerosol from his pocket and sprayed the inside of his mouth.
'We'll expect you in two weeks, plants and all. Connie will get
Logistics to take care of the details. Your families can follow
later.'

'This is truly astonishing,' agreed Jack, as he finished the last
page of the report Haley had given him. He was struggling to
control outward expressions of his surprise at the lengths to
which Tom had gone in his quest for youth and vigour. Like
others in the inner circle he had suspected, but this seemed to
be proof. 'Incredible.'

While he had been reading, Haley had first made coffee,
then, later, sandwiches and tea. He put the report down and
turned to where she was sitting cross-legged, facing him at the
other end of the long sofa.

'And you don't know where this came from?'

She shook her head as she reached down and picked up her
coffee mug from a low table. 'It just arrived in the post – snail
mail, from Amsterdam. There was no indication of a sender.'

'I know of one of the authors named on the cover,' revealed
Jack. 'He's a geneticist – on the island. I might be able to check
whether he really did write this.'

'I'm told it's scientifically accurate,' affirmed Haley. 'My
boyfriend's a genetics researcher.'

Why did those words suddenly feel so bad? She looked up and found his steady gaze on her. She pressed on, quickly. 'It's written by people who know what they are talking about.'

'I don't doubt it,' mused Jack, wondering if he should share any of the concerns that had been building up inside him; the concerns that were one of the reasons he had sought the biographer out. 'This would certainly explain the way he looks and behaves.'

He paused, still cautious, still unable to break the habit of secrecy that had been drummed into him throughout his adult life. Everything he had discovered during his research about the British biographer led him to believe she was a woman of integrity. He looked up, conscious of her dark eyes on him – eyes that were startlingly direct and, he realized, disturbing. It was really those eyes that had brought him here today.

'It's true to say that TT spends a lot of his time with our drug companies and the researchers,' he continued, measuring his comments carefully.

'He's the world's *biggest* private investor in biotechnology,' exclaimed Haley. 'Look, I've created a map.'

She stood, walked across to her desk and climbed onto a chair. She peeled back a piece of sticky tape that was holding one corner of a large sheet to the wall. Jack walked to the other side of the desk and, at her nod, peeled back the other corner almost without stretching. She smiled as she jumped down from her chair. Jack stepped back to view what was revealed.

The wall was covered with photos, clippings and notes on Thomas Tye, the Tye Corporation, its subsidiaries and Tye's private investments. In the centre was a web of interconnected map pins showing the links between the Tye Corporation, Tye himself and many private companies and organizations. A large map of Hope Island was pinned in the centre.

Jack stood in front of her wall and shook his head in wonder. 'You're still working with ordinary paper?'

Haley smiled. 'No, I research on the networks like everybody else. I also read some types of book on digital paper but there is something special about seeing it all laid out together in this way. It's to do with the psychophysics of the cognitive process.'

Jack shot her a look and she laughed, unable to tell whether he was teasing her. She liked the hint of laughter that often seemed to hover around his eyes.

'You see connections you'd miss otherwise,' she explained with a smile.

He stepped forward to examine the material more carefully.

'This is cute,' he teased as he flicked an old pin-up shot of Thomas Tye that had been clipped from a women's magazine. 'Were you a fan in those days?'

Haley couldn't prevent embarrassment painting her cheeks. In earlier years she had even participated in auctions of Tye memorabilia: faded autographs and signed pictures from his more accessible days were scattered amongst her research. She justified it to herself as trying to *feel* the man about whom she was writing, a form of graptomancy.

Jack allowed his question to hang unanswered and he ran his finger along the cotton connections that tied development projects to the various Tye companies.

'There's a lot more aerospace stuff than this,' he cautioned. 'A hell of a lot more. And you're way behind on network development. Northern Russia is complete now.'

'Well, the legal issues have been taking a lot of my time.'

'I presume that's the idea,' said Jack.

TWO

Hope Island was twelve miles long by eight miles wide but, ever since it was first named by British privateers in the seventeenth century, it had never delivered on its implied promise. Situated in the Windward Passage midway between Cuba and Haiti, this uninhabited Antillean island had held out the hope of being the ideal first landfall and staging post for voyages between the Old World and the Caribbean. But, as scores of successive landing parties were to discover, the promise of its verdant slopes and white beaches remained unfulfilled. Other than occasional rainfall, there was no fresh water.

Over three centuries the Spanish, French, British and Americans all fought desultory naval skirmishes over ownership of the formerly volcanic island. But, as it offered neither strategic advantage nor revictualling anchorage, none of the protagonists really had their hearts in winning those brief engagements. As a result, it remained loosely under the supervision of the regional French administration in Port-au-Prince until Haiti gained its independence in 1804. Then, following a display of complete indifference by its former owners, the new Haitian Republic inherited responsibility for the useless lump of rock.

The island remained under Haitian control until January 1962 when ownership was secretly exchanged for an astonishing and wholly unprecedented six million US dollars. Soviet intelligence had identified Hope Island as being an ideal covert site for two hardened underground missile silos. It was a mere five hundred miles from the Florida coastline and the rich and decadent American cities beyond. Such proximity would neutralize the dangerous advantage the Americans had gained with their long-range rocket delivery systems and would provide a powerful deterrent against the widely anticipated US invasion of Cuba. Fidel Castro was quickly funded to strike the deal with his neighbour and despot rival, the Haitian dictator 'Papa Doc' Duvalier.

Five months later, acting on information gathered by a CIA spy inside Cuba's Central Planning Board who insisted that Russian engineers had arrived in force, American U2 reconnaissance aircraft started to photograph the outlines of new building activity across Cuba. By September the planes' cameras had captured images of the construction sites of twenty-nine new missile silos including, by a remarkably lucky accidental overfly, two deep excavations and an airstrip on Hope Island. The new and highly secret Corona spy satellite was deployed to pass over the Western Caribbean every forty-one minutes. It immediately revealed that twenty-four medium-range missiles had already been deployed and further weapons were being delivered and readied at the rate of six a week. Within a fortnight the CIA analysts had finished their report and concluded that there would soon be sufficient megatonnage sited in the Antilles to obliterate all of America's East Coast.

The Joint Chiefs of Staff urged the US president to make an immediate, massive and unannounced pre-emptive knockout nuclear strike on this highly dangerous and untrustworthy commie neighbour. Only the year before the new president and the CIA had been humiliated when their covertly funded and organized 'arms-length' invasion of Cuba by 'exiles' had been trounced by well-trained Cuban troops led by Ché Guevara. Eleven hundred men had been captured at the aptly named Bay of Pigs and, amidst international derision, Fidel Castro had managed to extract a ransom of food and medicines worth fifty-three million dollars from the United States for their release. This seemed like an ideal opportunity to exact retribution.

President John F. Kennedy ignored such urgings to apocalyptic revenge but did issue an ultimatum to Nikita Khrushchev. He ordered US warships and submarines to mount a naval blockade across the Windward Passage to stop Soviet ships delivering further missiles to fill the silos on Hope Island and those being completed on mainland Cuba. For two days the world had hung on the brink of global thermonuclear war as twenty-six Soviet missile-laden freighters doggedly continued to plough their way through the world's oceans towards the Caribbean. Then, on 14 October 1962, after a secret reciprocal deal was agreed under which American Jupiter missiles in Turkey would also be withdrawn, the United States made a public commitment never to invade Castro's fledgling communist state and all Soviet ships *en route* to the West Indies received orders to return to their home bases.

Almost half a century later, Cuba's crumbling government made an unexpected profit on the Cold War purchase it had almost forgotten. A personal representative of the Tye Corporation's Bahamian lawyers visited Havana and, in a prearranged private audience with the minister of the interior, offered the government two hundred million dollars for the outright sale of the island. The minister and his aides could think of no reason why the giant corporation should want an uninhabited, anhydrous island on the edge of the world's worst hurricane corridor.

Before responding, the minister ordered a naval survey team to re-examine the island. Although the team included the best seismologists, mineralogists, geologists and petrochemical surveyors the nation's impoverished universities could muster, nothing was found that could warrant any further government interest in the island. The old silos had long since been sealed and nothing of any salvage value remained.

Accordingly, Cuba's Government of National Reconciliation reaffirmed the island's strategic importance to the Republic and offered the corporation a ninety-nine-year lease for six hundred million dollars. As part of the deal Cuba would remain the sovereign protector while retaining all mineral and petrochemical rights. The Tye Corporation's lawyers insisted on an outright sale with no residual rights, but increased their offer to four hundred million dollars. Their terms included Cuban recognition of Hope Island's sovereignty and the cession of cabotage rights over its airspace.

There was also to be a six-mile exclusion zone for Cuban-registered shipping, the aircraft of Empressa Cubana de Aviación and the Cuban air force. In response to the Cuban request for an explanation about the intended use of the territory in question, the lawyers said that the company's initial plans were for the creation of an exclusive resort island, but their clients naturally reserved the right to put their future territory to whatever peaceable purpose they chose.

With his inner cabinet, the minister debated whether they could bluff the company into a much higher bid. The Chief of the Armed Forces objected to the sale at any price, pointing out that Hope Island provided the nation's first line of eastern defence.

'Defence against whom?' sneered the education minister. 'The ganja warriors of the banana islands?'

The general's objections were noted but overruled.

The cabinet then discussed the economic feasibility of even such a rich organization as the Tye Corporation being able to supply all the necessities needed for a resort complex to a piece of Atlantic rock forty kilometres from the nearest source of fresh water.

Finally, reality prevailed. Since the collapse of world communism over a decade earlier and the consequential loss of billions of dollars a year in Soviet aid, Cuba's economy had remained in deep crisis. Overseas markets for cane sugar, citrus fruits and tobacco – the island's most important exports – were declining as other producers were able to invest capital to create new and more efficient production techniques. Despite its rich natural resources the country was starving and tremors of insurgency were once again being felt in the provinces.

It was agreed that the government Estate Office should respond by asking for eight hundred million dollars for an outright sale but, in the event of the Tye Corporation withdrawing, Havana should immediately accept the four hundred million dollars previously offered. The only absolute condition insisted on by the Cubans was that the island could never be used for military purposes and, other than the forces required for coastal protection, should never be used as a base for any form of weaponry or troops from any other nation. The Havana government also sought and received an undertaking that Hope Island's new owners would not offer refuge or transit access to any Cuban citizens who might land up on their shore.

The deal was finally done for five hundred and eighty million dollars. Despite requests for delay from his army of international lawyers, who pointed out the delicate negotiations that would be required for international recognition of the world's first corporate sovereignty to be established since 1796, Thomas Tye landed on Hope Island to begin his personal and corporate eloignment from the United States a day after the cession documents were signed in Havana and the cash had been deposited according to the seller's instructions.

Throughout the second day and the days that followed, the Tye corporate flight of four Tye-Westland LoadShifter helicopters ferried staff, equipment and portable accommodation units between the island and Cristoba, a small private airfield to the west of the Dominican capital, Santo Domingo.

By the end of the fourth day the engineers announced that a total of 10,000 gallons of pure fresh water at 23°C was springing from their forty-two new boreholes each minute. Nobody was surprised. Infrared images of the island taken by the Tye Corporation's Argus Satellite Network had clearly shown three large freshwater springs emerging in the coastal seabed around the island. A careful analysis of flow rates and direction coupled with computer-enhanced satellite geodesy had enabled a small, but very expensive, hydrology consultancy from Mobile, Alabama to land secretly six months earlier and drill two carefully positioned deep test-bores through the island's reheated sulphided limestone. The engineers then took samples, plugged the boreholes and capped them invisibly before confirming the results to the Tye Corporation. Thomas Tye was discovering the pleasure of betting on certainties.

Thirteen years later the entire world had come to know of Hope Island. It had become the world's first corporately owned nation state since the East India Company had reluctantly handed over its subcontinent to a young but implacable British monarch in 1858. After Cuba recognized the state's sovereignty as part of the purchase deal, the Tye Corporation privately agreed a massive technology transfer with the government of the People's Republic of China to secure recognition by twenty-one nations within the Sino sphere of influence.

Following two years of similar tactics in the rest of the world, the new sovereignty had received grudging, enthusiastic or coerced diplomatic recognition from all major countries and was even expected to seek a voice within the United Nations. The Tye Corporation, which also acted as Hope Island's government, said it would not be seeking diplomatic status for its international staff nor for its four hundred regional offices around the world and that it deemed consular presence and exchange of diplomats unnecessary.

Despite eschewing a formal diplomatic role, the new state worked hard to present a neighbourly face in the West Indies, a task that was eased immensely by local investments and technology gifts to schools and hospitals on the neighbouring islands. The cost of such gestures for the Tye Corporation was more than offset by the new state's generous tax regime and the income from its offshore virtual casinos, network auctions, purchasing-aggregation syndicates and tax-free global retailing. Most lucrative of all was the new Tye Global Bank for Personal and Commercial Finance that attracted three million new depositors in its first month of operation. The world knew and trusted the Tye brand and the opportunity to make discreet deposits in a safe tax-free zone proved irresistible. And it wasn't just cash. Intellectual capital, the new core asset of the information economy, found a natural and secure home in the data haven offered by Hope Island. Without making any announcements, the island suddenly started to become the Switzerland of the virtual economy. These initial businesses were established from temporary accommodation during the corporation's first few months of occupation and served customers in 146 countries and operated in over forty languages.

After a two-year construction effort had built the main campus, the Tye Corporation had moved its world headquarters to the island. Work had continued unabated and now the state boasted a semi-permanent population of 14,500 residents whose transportation needs were served by a sophisticated network of super-fast underground maglev shuttles. Above ground, a floating concrete spaceport capable of accommodating orbital launches, wide-body jets, supersonic corporate aircraft and presidential jet fleets extended the island by six miles and provided access to the outside world – and beyond.

An unexpected bonus for the corporation was the discovery that the fresh water that welled up from deep within the volcanic rocks was so plentiful and pure that they were able to sell a concession to a Florida-based company to collect, transport and bottle 'Hope Island Natural Spring Water,' a brand that was later to attract such cachet that it outpriced many table wines.

Jack Hendriksen had left Haley's London apartment in time to catch an early evening train from London to Cambridge. On the way he drafted a letter of resignation on his reactivated VideoMate. He didn't know whether he really intended to submit it. He just knew that he had an increasing sense of unease about the way Tye conducted his affairs. Perhaps all big business was like this, but on two recent occasions he had been present when Tye, or one his lawyers, had not hesitated to destroy the businesses – perhaps lives – of individuals who stood in their way. He had seen companies and families wrecked as Tye had masterminded hostile takeovers or used his uncanny business intelligence network to pre-empt or disable even the smallest and weakest competitors. He was also alarmed by the momentum for territorial acquisition building up inside the corporation and by the aims of its founder and president. Some of the new projects were breathtaking in their audacity.

Like every other employee of the Tye Corporation, Jack had signed a binding non-disclosure agreement when he had joined the company. When he had been made a corporate vice-president he had also signed several additional heavyweight long-term confidentiality agreements – which included powerful media gags – and he understood better than any outsider how ferociously the Tye Corporation's in-house army of attorneys pursued and protected the corporation's many rights across the globe. But some things had to outweigh mere legal agreements.

At first he had thought about simply calling up some of his former colleagues inside the US intelligence community. But he had quickly thought better of it. He knew how friendly Thomas Tye was with President William Wilkinson and he understood that nobody still in the Service would want to champion any cause likely to be unpopular in the White House. He came to the realization that if he wanted to do anything about his worries he would need to speak to an independent attorney, and do so quickly, not least to protect his own position and his future stock options. Only then could he decide whether his concerns were really justified and, if he could protect himself from any legal pursuit by the Tye Corporation lawyers, decide how best to approach his Washington contacts. It would have to be an attorney who understood international law and who wouldn't be frightened by the bizarre nature of the disclosures he would make. It would also have to be a professional who wouldn't be cowed by the immense financial muscle the Tye Corporation could apply to a lawsuit. He had smiled to himself as he realized the irony. It had been thanks to the Tye Corporation's share performance and the tax-free status of Hope Island that he could even contemplate seeking such expensive counsel.

He had arrived back in Cambridge just before seven p.m., in time to check arrangements for the group's departure. As Tye's return visit to the UK had gone unnoticed by the media, Pierre Pasquier's watchful team estimated that the risk of assassination, kidnapping, assault, journalistic intrusion or trouble from the Touchers had dropped to Status One, the lowest level. Jack was, therefore, able to allow his mind to wander in a way not normally possible when he was on the road with Tye.

Tye Flight One with its eighteen passengers had taken off to the east from the remote Cambridgeshire airfield just after ten p.m. GMT and had turned right to execute its sonic boom over the English Channel. The moment it was in the air Jack had been able to switch off fully and, once again, go back over the information Haley Voss had provided and see how it connected with what he already knew. In particular, he wanted to weigh up the likely authenticity of the report he had been shown. Even though he could find an excuse to approach the report's main

author for verification, he knew that even raising the question
would trigger an alarm.

He also wanted to consider the things he had not told Haley
and analyse whether they should be made public or whether
there was another way, as he now realized he saw it, of blowing
the whistle on Tye's plans. This wasn't an attractive phrase, but
it described an unattractive activity and it suited his mood
perfectly. No one man, or no one company, should gain the sort
of power Tye was now contemplating. Jack scowled as he
pondered the options. This evening he wouldn't exercise his
privilege of joining the crew on the flight deck. His pilot's log
was already crammed with hundreds of recent hours in the air
and he could do without the flight-deck banter.

The pressurized cabin air was laced with an odourless
antiseptic and in the forward Presidential Lounge the world's
greatest-ever tycoon was feeling comfortable once again in the
mask and gloves he liked to wear whenever possible. Jack could
hear him conducting a flurry of video meetings – laughing,
shouting, snarling, abusing and, occasionally, praising – before a
brief silence reigned as the meal was served.

Jack relaxed sufficiently to savour a dish the chef called a
piperada – a Basque omelette with tomatoes, peppers and tofu-
ham with fries and salad served on the side. Only genetically
modified and organically grown vegetarian produce and bever-
ages from Hope Island Farms were served on the Tye flight of
aircraft and the jet had made a transatlantic round trip earlier in
the day to pick up fresh supplies.

It had become part of accepted Tye culture that no matter
where he was in the world, Tom would eat only fresh, medicinally active produce from his island: vegetables, beans and pulses
grown in natural conditions to provide meat-level nutrition but
with cholesterols, fats, sugars and other undesirable calorie
carriers modified to block biological absorption. Active pharmaceutical and agriceutical ingredients were added to the protein
to aid the human body's struggle against heart disease, cancers
and other potential ills. It was rumoured that some years earlier
Tye had upturned a plate of South African soya-bean *bobotie*
over the head of an in-flight chef who had been foolhardy

enough to serve alternatively sourced ingredients, confident that his demanding boss would be unable to tell the difference within the hot curry spices.

When the meal was over Jack checked in with Pierre, who had returned to Hope Island on the provisioning run. His Director of Presidential Protection confirmed that everything was ready for Tye's return and for the official state visit by the Russian leader the next day. After signing off, Jack yielded to habit and clicked through the dozen most important cameras on the island. In the dim lighting of the jet cabin, the sunlit images projected in front of his eyes seemed bright and slightly surreal. He flicked over to Locate Mode and Tye Network's private Global Positioning Satellite network gave him a map of the island and the position of every one of his team members on duty. Everything was in order, as he had suspected. From the standpoint of security and privacy, the acquisition of the island base had been masterful. It was virtually unapproachable by air or sea without detection and, once the corporation's president was on the island, Jack felt reasonably secure from outside incursion. Any problems would come from inside.

He smiled to himself as he realized he had automatically re-entered work mode. With no public exposure of Tye's entourage ahead, at least for this evening, Jack felt sufficiently mellow to order another half-bottle of red wine (with unrestrained alcohol) and put his seat into full recline. He had chosen to sit alone in the mid-cabin this evening, rather than join Pierre's team, 'the flying doctor' and the paramedics in the aft lounge where some serious poker would already be under way.

Despite his distance from the Presidential Lounge at the front of the aircraft he could hear his tireless master revving up again and reeling off a string of instructions and asides to Connie while he harangued his executives, business partners and con-tacts around the world.

Many things Haley Voss had written or said had completed or complemented scraps of information Jack had picked up on his travels with Tye. The boyish Croesus seemed to be moving into territory far beyond conventional corporate life or even political activity and Jack had frequently questioned his own sense of unease, arguing with himself that he was simply being old-fashioned. Perhaps his naval training and years of government service had made him too old and conventional at thirty-eight to accept the new lifestyles and the astonishing commercial opportunities that computers, satellites, networks, biotechnology and space exploitation promised. Perhaps the strangely conservative nature of the government's intelligence community had left him unprepared to face the new and increasingly bizarre moral and ethical issues of the early twenty-first century.

In the end he had decided that *wasn't* the reason he felt so uncomfortable with what he had learned. He recognized that his feelings stemmed from a simple conclusion: not only did Tye trample over people, he was a monumental hypocrite and some of the things he was doing were simply wrong; wrong in the most basic of human senses and, Jack felt rather than thought, wrong in the natural order of things and most definitely wrong for the future of the world's population. Thomas Tye was out of control, in all meanings of the phrase, and Jack realized that he was one of the very few people who had the right contacts to be able to do something about it.

Jack had called his mother in upstate New York, waved at Skipper the red setter and sent him into a barking frenzy and, when he had listened to his mother's news and sent his love, had allowed himself to doze briefly. After they had landed in Hope Island's early-evening sunshine, he had spent a couple of hours with Pierre and the HQ team going over plans for the next day's state visit before enjoying a nightcap and turning in for a proper sleep.

'It's not that they won't sell. They won't even talk to us. *That's* our problem.'

Tye lashed out at the figure of the senior counsel for the Tye Corporation. His hand went clean through the head. At the other end of the Holo-Theater videoconference in Washington DC, Marsello Furtrado instinctively stepped back as Tye's fist evaporated around him. HVCs had made the videoconference experience 'just like being there' – as Tye Business Systems'

marketing slogan promised – but none of the glossy ads that
were showing around the world depicted participants striking
each other.

'No, that's YOUR FUCKING PROBLEM,' screamed Tye
in the darkened conference pit of his home office on Hope
Island. He was surrounded by four men standing in a circle
around him. All were wearing suits that had been treated and
optimized for holographic representation. All were three-
dimensional images of Tye executives many thousands of miles
away. All were used to Tye's physical 'approach' to meetings
and all knew he enjoyed it every bit as much when they were
actually present.

Tye stepped towards Furtrado and electronically levelled his
boyish face with his counsellor's.

'Do I have to personally call every student who's had a good
idea? You're our senior counsel. You still need ME to help you
acquire a six-person outfit?'

Furtrado nodded again and then altered the movement to a
shake. He knew how important it was. For a month interceptions made by the Competitive Threat Analysis department
proved that the little start-up in Sâo Paulo had microwave
multiplexing software that could instantly double the capacity of
the Tye Corporation's ageing fibre networks. Or anybody else's.

'I've offered them IP protection, non-disclosures, goodwill
escrow deposits, the whole nine yards,' insisted the counsellor.
'The little shit just laughs and goes off air. I'm not even sure he's
legally competent. He may still be a minor.'

Tye sighed. Furtrado had been with the Tye Corporation
for almost three years and he was still thinking the same way he
had when he had been a senior partner in a global law firm.
Today's business demanded direct methods.

'Go down there with a bag of money, Marsello,' he snapped.
'Go find one of the senior technologists who *isn't* a major equity
partner. Wave the money under his nose, go schmoozing. Hire
him, promise him a long-term contract, debrief him and dump
him. You know how to do it. We need a defection for cover.'

'I'm not sure that's a good idea. The boy wonder's father is
in the government.'

Tye held up his hand. 'That's it, gentlemen.' He snapped the system off and remained standing alone in the glaze of the lights that had lit him for the holographic scanners. His first morning back here after the European trip had been frantic.

He was wondering if there was any way of creating a dummy audit trail of in-house developments that might show that Tye NetWare had been working on a similar approach to multiplexing when Connie entered to remind him that the time for the President's visit was approaching.

Haley sat with her literary agent, cappuccino stains drying in the empty cups on their pavement table. Since traffic had been banned during daylight hours, the streets of London's Soho had become fashionable promenades filled with tables, sun umbrellas and people: atmospheric warming had its benefits, many Londoners agreed. This morning, the elegantly suited agent had suggested going out for a coffee to sit in the sun amongst the tourists. Haley knew that the real reason for an outdoor meeting was that she wanted to smoke.

'To describe them as nervous would be an understatement,' sighed Rosemary Long. She and her client had been discussing how Haley's various publishers around the world had been reacting to the Tye Corporation's flurry of injunctions. Rosemary wasn't telling her author just how colourful some of her exchanges with the editors had been.

'I'm afraid Nautilus definitely wants out. They say you can keep the part of the advance already paid. That's unconditional, and all rights revert to you.'

'But the USA's my biggest market,' objected Haley. 'Can't we persuade them to change their mind?'

Rosemary sighed again, hoping her client would grasp the implications of the developments without her having to spell it out.

'It won't be easy,' she warned. 'Also, I think their Chairman knows Thomas Tye. Rumours are that he maintains a liver on Hope Island.'

'So it's the old pals' act,' groaned Haley. 'How about some other US publisher?'

Rosemary shook her head.

'The trade knows Nautilus bought the book. It was all over *Publishers Weekly*. They'll figure that there must be a good reason for Nautilus not going ahead.'

'But we can get the injunction lifted. It says I intend to publish libellous, defamatory untruths. I can prove what I'm saying.'

'We can only get the injunction lifted if Nautilus or some other publisher wishes to fund the appeal,' explained Rosemary patiently. 'That's the problem. You know how much litigation costs in America. Even if a publisher did win the first round, the Tye Corporation would only start again in a higher court. It would be never-ending.'

'So they're simply caving in to the big money,' cried the biographer.

Rosemary sighed for a third time. Her authors, while necessarily brilliant in their own fields, rarely understood the pure commercialism of publishing. There were always other books to fill gaps in publishing schedules.

'Let's have another coffee,' she said, catching the waiter's eye and indicating their empty cups.

She had good reason to be patient with her youthful-looking client. Haley was a best-selling author, although that description didn't imply the vast riches that other people often assumed. A revised edition of her first biography, a detailed and insightful portrait of the film star Josh Chandler, was still selling strongly nine years after the original had been published, although Haley was honest enough to admit that her special access to the actor owed more to luck than professional perseverance.

Her 'friendship' with Josh had started shortly after her roommate at Cambridge University had met the teenage star at a Hollywood party. Haley had already guessed that Abbeline's family was rather better connected in LA than she let on but when, a few weeks later, her fellow second-year student had felt compelled to make a late-night confession that she was dating one of the world's most desirable bachelors, Haley had also discovered the full details of her friend's family's involvement in the film business. Abbe's father had produced the film in which Josh had first found international stardom.

Josh's and Abbe's relationship had become very public and had lasted for nearly two years and, in that time, Haley had met the handsome star dozens of times. He had bought a London home to be near his girlfriend and Haley was often asked to make up a foursome with one or another of the star's actor cronies. Felicity had repeatedly urged her sister to 'bag a star' for herself, but Haley had just laughed the idea off. Over the years she had come to like the funny-silly movie actor who hid behind a tough-guy image and although she was well aware that he kept a large part of himself withdrawn from most social exchanges, she felt relaxed around him and accepted that his interest in her was genuine.

After a highly publicized split between Josh and Abbe, Haley did not see her film-star friend again for almost two years. She received occasional e-mails from him and it was clear from the little messages he wrote that he didn't want to lose touch. In the meantime, Haley had joined the business desk of one of the few serious London newspapers that had survived the public's migration to network news. It was a publication so well written and edited that it retained a large print circulation in addition to its more recent incarnation as a global network resource of international importance.

Then her editor had checked on the office rumour that Haley was 'a close personal friend of Josh Chandler'. She had put him straight on that, but there was the prospect of an exclusive interview, and she had agreed to take the assignment, even though she wasn't a show-business writer

Haley had gone to Claridge's to meet her old friend and although the interview had started out quite formally, Josh had soon dispatched his publicist on some lengthy but pointless mission and had told his assistant to take the Hollywood equivalent of a hike. Within minutes of their being alone he was his old self again and then, with the absolute agreement that they were off the record, he told her how much he missed Abbe and how the public discussion of his latest relationship and speculations about marriage – with the scion of a French fashion empire – was 'pissing me off'. Moments later he was being silly again and making her roar with laughter at his mimicry of other members of the cast of his most recent film. Haley genuinely liked him because he seemed to sense that his fame placed him in an impossible position and, despite the fact that a large part of his life no longer belonged to him, he was determined to have a genuine, unforced giggle as often as possible.

Haley wrote an absolutely truthful piece, far closer to the bone than she knew his publicists would like but, before showing it to anyone, she had sent a printout to Josh's hotel under a confidential seal. She wasn't sure whether her handwritten note would be sufficient to convey the envelope directly into the star's hands, but that was what she intended.

Her ploy worked and her VideoMate had trilled the same evening. He was laughing – 'Am I really that silly?' He put his publicist's camp voice on again, and laughed; then he was his macho co-star, complete with the mangled English. His mimicry was wicked. 'So Josh Chandler is not allowed to change any of this?' he asked pompously.

'Not if he's a good sport,' challenged Haley. She knew she had been revealing, but not unkind.

'Fine by me, Haley,' he had said. That simple statement was to lead to a new career.

She guided her piece through the editorial process personally – to avoid the arbitrary excisions of sub-editing – and the article ran on the front page of the weekend features section. It was illustrated with a new portrait by a junior member of the British Royal Family who was unashamed of using his title and access privileges to develop his photographic career. The story was syndicated worldwide and she won three major journalistic awards that year.

Soon afterwards she had been approached by the languid Rosemary Long, *belle littératrice*, doyen of London's female literary agents: a major publishing house wondered whether Haley could get access and approval to do the first 'fully authorized' biography of Josh Chandler. Haley had prevaricated: she doubted it. She wasn't sure she liked the idea of biography.

She recalled Carlyle's remark: 'A well-written *Life* is almost as rare as a well-spent one.' But, after giving the project some thought, she began to see the idea as a challenge. She made the call to his personal location and was surprised and delighted to be put through almost immediately.

She had told him what she wanted and she heard the groan.

'Not another one,' he complained. 'There's too many already: all rubbish.'

'Precisely,' said Haley. 'That's why there's room. I would aim to be definitive and to treat a film actor like a person, not an icon.'

He had agreed to ask 'his people' and, a week later, Haley had received an e-mail invitation to a private weekend party at Cliveden, a stately home twenty miles west of London. At the bottom Josh had added: 'This is a wrap party. I'm staying on for a week. We can get started if you like.'

Then Haley had talked to Rosemary again. The problem was going to be finding the time to do the research and write the book. She talked the issue over with her editor: he had agreed that she could take a nine-month writing sabbatical but in return had shrewdly bargained for, and obtained, first serial publication rights for his paper's weekend supplement at a fraction of their real market worth.

And so a friendship had been cemented and a best-seller created. The book was exceptionally well written – 'a surprisingly literary and revealing insight' enthused one reviewer – and had been studded with unpublished portraits and family photographs, many of them taken by former girlfriends: in addition to talking to Abbe, Haley had taken the trouble to find and interview all the star's other long(ish)-term loves. Haley Voss became a 'name', someone publishers were keen to listen to. Rosemary just wished her author would choose anyone but Thomas Tye as her next subject.

'I've got some news that will change their minds,' announced Haley, as Rosemary lit another cigarette. 'I've made contact with someone inside the company. Someone really close to Tye.'

Rosemary raised a well-maintained eyebrow.

'I can't say who it is, of course, but I think it will prove very useful.'

Rosemary looked up with a smile of thanks as the waiter delivered the fresh coffees. 'Haley, you're not hearing me. I think we have a real problem with this project.'

'But it's a fantastic story,' the author objected. 'Do you realize just how dominant Tye's investments in biotechnology are? If you list them it becomes really scary.'

Rosemary wondered how long she should humour her client before explaining that her planned book was completely unpublishable – in any form.

Haley mistook her agent's silence for interest and plunged on. 'One, I think now that he's proved it works he's going to file for a patent on the human-ageing gene sequence. Think about it. If scientists have learned how to transfer the modified genes to a human...'

Haley's voice tailed off into hoarseness. She was becoming aware that Rosemary's attention was polite rather than enthralled.

'He's patented four new treatments from the bloody muscular-dystrophy sequence,' she continued stubbornly. 'And the active genes covering IQ development, and he's got a new genetic therapy for curing colour blindness. He's got a whole range of patents on the human cosmetic genes – you know, eye colour, height and so on.' She paused, willing her agent to see the issues. 'He runs the world's largest human-organ farm. We can't have one man, or one company, controlling the future of the human race.'

Rosemary shook her head. 'But that's just conjecture, Haley. There's nothing illegal in what the Tye Corporation or Thomas Tye has done.'

'So why are they trying to gag me?' asked Haley, her voice cracking.

'It's because of what you imply,' Rosemary replied gently. 'Calling the book *Why Thomas Tye Must Be Stopped* is totally pejorative. You suggest the man's going to behave irresponsibly and dangerously. We simply don't know if that's true.'

'Do you want me to find another agent?' croaked Haley, her chin jutting.

*

As he walked beside the red carpet Jack Hendriksen appeared the same as always: confident, calm, professional and resourceful. But inside he was not the same. Something had died for him as he had digested what he had learned from the British biographer. Suddenly, he hated his work and his artificial life on this absurd, unreal island. He had made a massive mistake in joining international business: he hated the total obsession with money and power and the lengths to which the global players would go to obtain them. Now he couldn't wait to get out. He would take up his younger brother's offer and join him in his yacht brokerage in Florida. That operation, at least, still depended on the human qualities of personal reputation and trust.

The president's jet was a new generation Russian-European Airbus, still subsonic but with immense range and comfort. Jack waited at the foot of the stairs for President Orlov's head of security to descend. He hadn't met the tall Georgian, but they had conferred by wraparound videoconference. The perennially impoverished Russian Federal government hadn't yet installed the Tye Corporation's new HVC systems. Ordinarily, Pierre would have handled executive security but Tom had wanted this visit to be overseen personally by Jack, as an acknowledegment of the visitor's status.

There was a movement in the open doorway and the security chief appeared in the garish, flat-capped uniform of a full colonel of the Russian Federal Army. He tripped lightly down the stairs, gave a small bow, removed a white glove and extended his right hand. His greeting was instantly translated by Jack's VideoMate and delivered through his radio-linked earpieces. The colonel was similarly equipped.

Jack assured the colonel that all was secure on the island and that 'Tom' was waiting to greet President Orlov. The Tye Corporation's informal president was 'Tom' (sometimes 'TT') to his vast domestic and international staff, 'Tom' to the adoring public and everybody else, and only on the most official occasions 'Mr Tye'.

The colonel nodded his understanding, turned and trotted back up the aircraft steps. Jack followed him and entered the aircraft. Contra-security on presidential and government aircraft was always a ticklish procedure. Every nation regarded its government's aircraft as an extension of its sovereign territory and although Jack would have preferred to have his team sweep the plane before authorizing disembarkation – especially in view of his previous experience of Russian manners gained during a covert action against members of their industrial *mafiya* – he had had to settle for the agreed arrangements. For its part, the Russian delegation had agreed to leave all directed and ambient recording devices behind. Hope Island was both sovereign territory and classified space.

A quick glance to right and left convinced him that superficially everything appeared normal and he turned to incline his head in the direction of the large leather sofa occupied by the president. Then he froze. Seated beside the Russian leader was Anton Vlasik, a man the world believed to be safely behind bars.

Jack turned to the colonel. 'Mr Vlasik isn't on the list we approved. I am therefore unable to allow him to disembark.' He tried to keep the anger out of his voice.

Vlasik, the most powerful, most notorious of Russian criminal chiefs, had controlled two Russian Federal banks that had mysteriously collapsed, taking with them over fourteen billion dollars of Western loans and tens of thousands of life-savings accounts of ordinary Russians. Jack had later read that he had received a twenty-year sentence for fraud. But now he was here.

The colonel shrugged. 'Mr Tye has approved . . .' Jack waved the explanation away as Tye was already talking in his ear. He turned away from the colonel and the Russian party to listen.

'It's OK, Jack, I knew he was coming. He's been pardoned and he's financing part of this deal.'

Jesus! 'Tom, I haven't done any clearance or vetting for him. I haven't arranged for anyone to escort him. Why on earth didn't you . . . ?'

'You would only have been difficult about it, Jack,' Tye soothed in his ear. 'I know you're over-sensitive about such things. Now, let's get them out of the plane.'

The communication link snapped off. Jack turned to face the visitors, hoping his face hadn't reddened as he fought to swallow such a public undermining of his role. Vlasik had now risen from the sofa, a broad grin on his face.

Jack nodded curtly to the Russian president and walked out of the plane, breathing deeply to re-establish self-control. The colonel emerged beside him and they took up their positions at the top of the steps. As Jack gave clearance for the welcoming party, he watched a crocodile of Tye Corporation-designed electric Volantes – vehicles that looked rather like elongated golf carts – swing away from the reception building and head towards the aircraft. His head-up display confirmed that his team, with their heavily armed back-up, were in station on the rooftop of the reception building and at strategic points around the perimeter of the floating spaceport.

As this mini-motorcade drew up at the foot of the steps, Jack felt rather than saw the small figure of President Mikhail Niko-layevich Orlov arrive beside him in the doorway. Thomas Tye swung out of the first car, followed by Pierre who, for today, was acting as his personal *garde-du-corps*.

With complete disregard for diplomatic protocol, Tye bounded up the steps. He stopped and extended his hand to the sixty-six-year-old leader who, the world would assume, was the head of state least likely to pay a visit to Hope Island. There had been many occasions in the past when Tom had publicly criticized the Russian Federation for its poor environ-mental record but, as the world was also forced to agree, Orlov's insistence on using his nation's fuel resources as he himself saw fit was finally beginning to make Russia a meaningful economic power again. Then the tycoon turned to Vlasik, turning his formal handshake into a warm bear-hug.

Tye was wearing his customary open-necked white shirt with button-down collar and a pair of crisp, pleated-front khaki trousers. He had pulled his hair back and for once wore neither mask nor gloves. Hope Island's climate had bestowed a gentle tan and his well-toned muscles were discernible under his shirt. In the early-afternoon sunlight Thomas Tye looked like a young film star.

Jack shuddered inside.

*

A thousand kilometres above Auckland, New Zealand, two station-maintenance thruster valves opened for three seconds. The pressure exerted amounted to only .35 grams per square centimetre but ESQ173, one of 400 giant satellites of the Tye LaserNet network, began a slow roll on its axis. The seventy-metre-long spacecraft and its 3,400 kilograms of laser guns, capture dishes, reflectors, solar panels and cameras was rotated out of alignment and instantly became useless. The digital processing and storage systems that were housed inside its pressurized compartment became deaf and blind as they lost their links to the outside world.

A hundred kilometres away the processing systems on ESQ174, the next hub on Earth's highest-capacity data network, went into overdrive as they automatically re-routed the vast streams of laser-borne information to other satellites in the quadrant and warned Orbit Management of the malfunction. Insomniac observers in the darkness below were treated to a rapidly changing laser light show as the aerial networks compensated and healed themselves automatically. Then the valves of ESQ174's adjustment thrusters – the motors periodically deployed to maintain precise orbit station – also opened as the thrusters fired.

Two seconds later the same thing happened to four adjustment thrusters on a nearby Soyuz satellite of the FreePlanet network.

Standing by the lakeside in the warm, sulphurous night air, Constable Terry Nobel of the Rotarua Community Police Service scratched his head. New Zealand's night sky had gone dark for the first time in five years. The soft brilliance of the star clouds of Carina, Canopus and Sirius shone again as the white misty glory of the Milky Way slowly regained its old dominance.

THREE

President Orlov and his large delegation were getting the full tour, courtesy of the island state's premier citizen. First they were driven around the sprawling, beautifully maintained university campus. Their stately progression along broad gravel drives took them past neoclassical fountains, vast lawns of dense green pearlwort grass, world-class ambient and active sculpture and acres of low-rise pyramids of steel and smoked glass that shone in the fierce afternoon sun.

In the distance, large man-made lakes glinted and beyond those they could see mature cedar trees with high umbrella canopies that had been imported from the savannah plains of East Africa. These *Cedrus Libani* provided a distant backdrop without obstructing the clear view out to sea. The consulting evolutionary psychologists claimed this would provide visual comfort for the humans who strolled in the grounds. Their theory was that the long views provided reassurance that predators were not close and such knowledge would awaken dim noetic echoes of ease and contentment that have filtered down from humanity's distant evolutionary past.

Thomas Tye told the president that more than 10,000 people were permanently resident on Hope Island, a population made up of the staff and families of the Tye Corporation, associated companies and research facilities. He added that another 4,000 workers had been imported from Mexico and the Caribbean islands to provide domestic services and staff for the restaurants, leisure complexes and other public facilities. He didn't add that even the most lowly of the imported workers were required to sign lifetime non-disclosure agreements and media gags in return for signing-on financial bonds that, should an ex-employee ever breach the agreement, would become instantly repayable in addition to any other remedies the company might seek. Neither did he add that the corporation was rapidly running out of development space on the island, a problem that had been occupying the executive board and its international lawyers for many months.

Tye also neglected to mention that rumours about life on Hope Island had become so persistent, so extreme, so exaggerated and so sensational in the poverty-beset Caribbean that what had started years before as an initial trickle of uninvited but hopeful immigrants from Cuba was now growing to become a severe problem. Cuba was now once again in the grip of civil war. Each night Jack Hendriksen's 200-strong local security force had to be ready to deal with dozens of unauthorized landings by small craft, some of them no more than planks of wood strapped over empty oil drums. Despite the best surveillance systems in the world a few of them succeeded in landing undetected, economic refugees and escaping democratic freedom fighters alike, both refusing to believe that once ashore the authorities would turn them away. But the Tye Corporation did, every one of them they managed to intercept, despite reports of firing squads being assembled to greet returning rebels. Hope Island issued no visas, forbade tourism and welcomed visitors by invitation only. Each week a patrol craft would return upwards of a hundred Cuban asylum-seekers, mostly young males, to their mother nation. Many would return there wrapped defiantly in the white-star-and-red-cross flags of the rebel guerrillas.

Jack had remonstrated with Tom over returning young men to almost certain death. He pointed out that the US automatically granted residency status to all Cuban refugees who managed to cross the Florida Straits and had suggested forwarding some of them to the US and to other nations prepared to offer asylum. TT had countered the suggestion with impeccable and forceful logic.

'If none of them finds a route out from here, they'll stop coming.'

Jack had merely nodded. But in the months that followed he had failed in this aspect of his duties on several occasions. He was well aware that some members of the Tye Corporation's domestic and service staff were engaged in smuggling Cuban freedom fighters and their families aboard some of the many supply ships that visited the island. Having to prioritize, Jack chose to apply his forces to their core duties: protecting the corporation's senior staff and the company's assets on the island. Chasing refugees was not his idea of useful deployment.

Then the Cuban Foreign Minister had heightened tension with a public accusation that the Tye Corporation was failing to return all of the rebels who reached Hope Island's shores. Tye had laughed at this suggestion, publicly suggesting that Cuba's besieged government was paranoid. Relations with the neighbouring post-communist state had become severely frosty.

The procession turned a corner and Tye pointed to one of the low glass structures protruding from a lawn. He explained that, due to its location in the hurricane corridor, eighty per cent of the island's commercial facilities were underground and that every pane of glass above ground was able to withstand winds of over 200 miles per hour.

The caravan moved out of the manicured and well-irrigated campus and began to climb the steep slope of a small peak on the western side of the island. Wide roads with surfaces of dark green asphalt cut their way through the island's luxuriant undergrowth even though few of the island's residents used surface transport.

They crested the hill and pulled into a viewing area at the edge of a clifftop. As was usual for first-time visitors, the delegation reacted with small exclamations of surprise.

Sitting at the centre of a large white crescent bay was an eighteenth-century Spanish-style colonial town. The pastel colours and soft stone of the buildings made it seem as if the settlement had been there for centuries. Only the dull glint of the Tye Corporation high-efficiency solar cladding on the rooftops betrayed its recent origin.

'That's Hope Town down below,' explained Tye the tour guide as he pointed out the main features. 'We built the harbour and the marina and we got Disney to design the buildings and the central part of town.'

He offered the president a pair of binoculars and watched as the Russian leader scanned the grid of the town centre, the Town Hall, the green city square and the Hope Island flag that hung listlessly from its white flagstaff. Stretching away from the town in both directions were ribbons of seafront developments that included bungalows, low condominiums, small private estates and beachfront bars and restaurants. In the distance there were signs of major construction where the settlement was being extended around the western headland.

Tye's running commentary about the buildings and features below was a courtesy rather than a necessity. The binoculars the President was using were not only image-stabilized, 3D-enhanced and multi-wavelength, they were also network-enabled: the town's public information system was providing small translucent Cyrillic captions that described every building and physical feature that came into view as he traversed the bay.

If he was impressed, he said nothing.

The president moved the focus of his binoculars up to the hills behind the town where gleaming white villas occupied the lower slopes of the old volcano. A low-rise hotel had been built at the foot of the mountain.

'This is the shielded side of the island,' Tye added. 'The winds on this side never get too bad. That's the Caribbean down there, not the Atlantic.'

The president scanned the view dutifully and nodded his thanks without comment.

'We've taken great care not to disturb the settlement of frigate birds – *Tachypetes aguuilus* – on that ridge,' announced Tye, suddenly the ornithologist, pointing to the cliffs on the other side of the bay as he tried another tack to engage the President. 'And as you can see – perhaps taste – the air here is absolutely free of pollution.'

In the three cars behind, senior Tye executives were providing similar commentaries and viewing facilities for the rest of the delegation. The day was stiflingly hot and the overdressed

Russians were sweating visibly underneath the white canvas canopies that shielded the open vehicles.

The procession restarted and did a U-turn in the empty road. They rolled eastwards down the hillside and were soon rewarded with a cool breeze from the Atlantic. They turned back towards the main campus and Tye explained that they would soon be entering the air-conditioned comfort of the underground complex. He informed his guest that all power on the island was derived either from the company's solar-powered fuel cells or from heat-exchangers that extracted energy from the many underground hot springs. He joked that the old missile silos built by Russia had finally found a useful purpose. The old man nodded but did not respond further. The host smiled to himself; he knew he would get a reaction when they went below.

They drove around the base of the ancient volcano and Tye pointed out the cliff face of sheer plate glass that formed the frontage of his recently completed private mansion. It stood above five vast man-made terraces. He explained that he would have the honour of entertaining the leader and his party at his home later. The procession turned to head back to the main command complex.

Jack radioed his approval ahead and the cars passed through the open gates of the corporate command campus and drove straight down a ramp to the subterranean entrance. Tye leaped from the lead vehicle to demonstrate the security systems to his guests.

'We use only biofeedback systems for security,' he explained as the president and his party disembarked and walked round to the entrance. 'Humans are unique. Our individual identifiers provide the one security key that can't be duplicated or faked.'

Tye stood beside the main door and allowed the system to scan both his irises. 'Open,' he commanded and the metal doors hissed apart. He guided the president and his party onto a station platform surfaced with pale Chernites marble. A three-car train was waiting on the monorail.

Tye, the president, and the senior party climbed into the first car. Jack stood at the rear. The other Tye executives and Russian guests piled into the cars behind.

The shuttle pulled quickly out of the station and Thomas Tye was explaining the principles of maglev repulse-magnetism that propelled the train and allowed it to float silently and frictionless above its single rail. In response to the president's question he admitted that this was one of the few products on the island not made by a Tye subsidiary.

The old missile silos had served merely as a starting point for the immense underground complex that Tye and his team had instructed the architects to build. There had been a time, shortly after the Tye Corporation had first issued its own form of electronic corporate currency, when the piles of cash building up in the company's coffers had proved unusable, inefficient and downright embarrassing. Despite benefiting from heroic returns on their Tye Corporation stock, institutional investors had complained that the corporation's capital hadn't been working hard enough.

But even such activities as massive share-buybacks, a move into global investment banking and large-scale aerospace investments had failed to stem the tide of cash generated by the super-efficiencies of network logistics, the elimination of the thirty-day economic cycle in favour of instantaneous real-time value transfers and the sheer economies of scale created by truly global operations. The more the Tye Corporation invested in real-time transaction and communication systems for itself and its clients, the greater the corporation's returns became. It was as if traditional economic theory had been turned on its head: the almost total elimination of friction from business processes created a virtuous circle that released vast amounts of capital.

The huge construction project on Hope Island had provided a temporary solution to the problem and, these days, Tye and his executives had diversified the corporation's activities and portfolio so much that there were endless uses for the accretive amount of capital that the various operations were creating from their billions of worldwide customers.

The maglev shuttle suddenly slowed and, from high above a huge atrium-like area, the party gazed down on six microsatellites in various stages of completion within a glass-caged clean-room. The area was lit partly from the roof windows above and partly by suspended tungsten lighting.

'They are for our new Deep-Space Location and Navigation System,' said Tye. 'Finishing the network ready for Phoebus expansion.'

The shuttle accelerated rapidly and moved on until the monorail branched ahead. Tye explained that further halls to the south were engaged on other aerospace projects while the centre rail headed towards his home on the west of the island. As usual, visitors were not invited to see the Research Park and the group visit to watch an orbit-shuttle launch was scheduled for the following day.

With a sharp increase in speed, the train branched north, over further brightly lit halls containing offices, TV studios and news rooms. It came to a rest above a vast glass-encased, air-conditioned room filled with seemingly endless rows of long wall racks containing blinking electronic equipment.

'That's our main server farm,' Tye pointed out. 'Those boxes down there are all connected to the networks and each is running a separate business.'

He pulled a DigiPad from his pocket and consulted it

'There's a dozen or so travel agents and brokers, two distance-learning universities that operate in over sixty languages, two hundred and ten auction houses, our global banks, eighty-one local-currency banks, sixteen *bureaux de change*, forty-seven automated stockbrokers and market makers, two hundred and four insurance brokers offering a range of financial services, thirty-nine global retailers selling high-value branded goods, two hundred and one casinos playing every type of game you can imagine and taking every kind of bet, over six thousand real-estate agencies – they have to remain as local brands – one hundred and twenty radio stations, over two thousand separate network game servers, our news servers and archives, eighteen hundred film and video back-catalogue servers – rentals and sales, music servers, book and magazine servers, aggregation and purchasing syndicates, telemedicine servers and, of course, our software servers for rentals and purchase. Then there's the offshore finance and data havens, oh, and the cemeteries. We maintain virtual memorial and personal-history retrievatories for nearly eleven million families – people *and* pets.'

Tye inhaled theatrically as he ended his high-speed recitation of the long list. Jack had seen the performance previously: it was a party piece.

The president nodded as if he too had seen it all before

'Of course, this entire complex is in the core of one of your old rocket silos,' added Tye, breaking the silence that had followed his rehearsal of corporate achievement. 'It's hurricane-proof, earthquake-proof and, as you will recall, it was even designed to withstand a nuclear strike – as were the networks the servers feed.'

The president nodded again. Jack wondered what was going through his mind. The news broadcasts and magazines had praised him for patiently rebuilding the economy of his vast federation. 'We have to travel three hundred years in ten,' he had told his people. They were getting there even though vast, almost unrepayable debts still hung over the government's head from endless rounds of Western refinancing. And, as Vlasik's presence here proved, criminal interests remained at the heart of Russian government.

Oil was being extracted efficiently and getting to its markets. Coal was still being mined and burned despite the criticisms of Thomas Tye and other world leaders. Steel production was now of high quality and Russia's aerospace industry had, once again, become world class. But although Thomas Tye had not said so, Jack knew that the GDP of the unmanned server farm below them eclipsed the entire economic output from one hundred and sixty million citizens of the combined Russian republics. But perhaps the president's impassivity was merely a mask for common acrophobia.

Tye had made no mention of the *other* server farms. Some of the cash and data deposited and stored on Tye Corporation servers was so valuable and hypersensitive that no terrestrial offshore bank or data haven was considered adequately secure or discreet by certain ultra-paranoid customers: these particularly hot deposits were kept *off-planet* in a network of vast-capacity, high-bandwidth, multiply redundant data-server satellites hurtling around the planet 1,000 kilometres out in the deep-freeze of space. These interconnected storage facilities were designed to remain oblivious of any terrestrial nuclear events and they were also immune from the globe's political and military reversions and incursions. They ignored natural terrestrial catastrophes such as earthquakes, rising ocean levels and volcanic eruptions and defied even extraterrestrial extinction events such as asteroid impact or celestial collisions.

Unsurprisingly, the majority of customers for such expensive services were dictators, despots, generals of various 'people's' armies, Triad leaders, Mafia godfathers, drug shoguns, industrial-scale money launderers and the growing army of senior international executives of global corporations. Customers accessed these servers only by a fearsome combination of digital signatures, deeply encrypted and multiple-layered passwords and a range of very personal DNA verifications. Customers also held digital keys to self-destruct mechanisms on the satellites if they were ever forced to contemplate such extreme security measures. The Tye Private Bank asked no questions of depositors with sufficient funds to rent anonymous space in these networks of foil-wrapped, weightless deposit boxes.

The train restarted and entered a short tunnel. Then the party emerged above indoor tennis and squash courts, three gymnasiums and an Olympic-size swimming pool.

'There's also a fully equipped hospital in the complex,' added Tye, unnecessarily. The president was due to become a patient the next day when the check-ups would be run before he became the latest customer of a Tye Life Sciences VIP service.

Tye maintained his running commentary until the train pulled into another station. He gestured for his guests to disembark, waiting politely as the president stepped slowly out. His heart was weak and only careful medical management allowed him to undertake limited public engagements. A pair of large black-glass doors offered the only exit from the station. In his temporary role as team leader Jack brought up the rear, although he was now confident that the situation was totally secure.

Without realizing it, all members of the visiting party – including Anton Vlasik in the second car – had passed through four separate scans of varying wavelengths and, apart from the Russian army colonel who carried his weapons by agreement, Jack had heard his team confirm that the visitors carried neither armaments nor recording equipment.

'This is the entry to our Network Control Center,' Tye told his guests. 'This is where we are able to follow progress and see the world's networks as a whole.'

He stepped forward and allowed his irises to be scanned. Then, with a single movement, he provided a fingerprint from his right index finger to a scanner plate set into the wall. To complete the process he plucked a hair from his head with a theatrical flourish and placed it into a brightly lit scanning tube. A small door closed over the tube.

'DNA verification, the ultimate security,' beamed Tye, revelling in his sales pitch.

The President shrugged and tapped his own pate.

'No hair. Not good for me,' he said in careful English.

Tye and the party laughed dutifully. Jack thought it was rather good. He noticed Tom turn back to face the doorway, allowing a facial-pattern scan to be taken and the chemistry of his scent to be analysed. He was pleased to note that his boss had not explained that the individual biometric checks were all elements of a multi-part DNA signature package that, in total, was the most secure physical access-checking system ever devised.

A green light illuminated on the access panel and the doors hissed apart. Connie was waiting inside and she stepped forward to usher in the honoured guests.

To first-time visitors, the Tye Networks Command Center looked like a theatre-in-the-round that might have been created by set designers from *Star Trek*'s vintage years. The controllers sat on raised circular terraces facing inwards to a darkened central pit. But instead of banks of computer consoles, as in the old NASA command centres, the monitoring team sat in reclining armchairs with no obvious controls or display panels. The circular wall at the rear semi-circle of the room housed large flat display screens. The effect was dramatic and it was created for that purpose.

Connie indicated for the party to halt in the acclimatization area. The room was quiet except for the low hum of powerful air-conditioning. As their eyes adjusted, the visitors could see that about a third of the sixty control positions were occupied by a duty team made up of twelve women and eight men.

Tye walked his visitors around the top terrace and, as they circumnavigated the room, flat two-dimensional holographic displays appeared momentarily in front of the controllers' seats before the visitors' viewing angle changed and they disappeared again.

'All networks are self-monitoring, of course,' Tye pointed out. 'What we do here is to match our traffic projections with actual usage and provide global feedback to the regional controllers.'

He could have added that the entire Network Control Center was completely unnecessary and had been created merely for show. Although it *was* monitoring the world's satellite and terrestrial communications networks, it had actually been built to serve as a large demonstration suite for the Tye Corporation's latest products and much of its quaint futuristic design was yet another product of Disney's kitsch imagineering. All real network management functions had long since been distributed to automatic systems, regional strategic planning centres and local contractors and maintenance teams. This was a place in which to *sell*!

Tye led the party down a central aisle and waved them into seats in the three front rows. Four uniformed stewards handed out hot antiseptic towels. When these had been used and retrieved Tye nodded to one of the controllers and the central pit was filled with light.

Hanging in space in front of the visitors' eyes was a giant globe: a representation of the planet Earth, fifteen feet in diameter. Despite his gnawing doubts about the Tye Corporation and its president, Jack once again found himself captivated by the power of Tye's latest 3D Holo-Theater technology.

'This view is created from images captured by over four hundred separate satellites of our Argus network,' explained Tye, stepping into the pit to stand beside the huge globe. 'This is a composite of what they are seeing at the moment, from about a thousand kilometres out. That's about seven hundred miles,' he explained. 'As you know, all space measurement is in klicks.'

The visitors were silent as they drank in the details: the under-seat scent simulators added a hint of sea breeze to the atmosphere. The projection showed the sunlit side of the planet with the Americas to the left, Europe and Africa to the right and, dominating the centre, the immense curving blue of the Atlantic Ocean. They didn't have time to register the complete absence of cloud cover.

Tye nodded to the controller again and the image dissolved and zoomed in at such high speed that it seemed as if a central vortex had formed. Within a few seconds the outline of Hope Island appeared with its larger neighbours, Cuba and Haiti. Then Hope Island, with its floating spaceport, launch runways and deep-water harbour was clearly visible, filling the holographic space. The camera zoomed again and they saw the tarmac area at the entrance to the underground complex. A further zoom and the camera was focused on the driver they had left with the first of the Volantes.

The controller mouthed a few words into his microphone and the driver held out a small piece of paper, the size of an old-fashioned business card. One further magnification revealed the characters on the card. In Cyrillic text with English sub-titles they read:

The Tye Corporation is proud to welcome President Orlov and his distinguished party to Hope Island.

The demonstration had its intended effect. The president smiled and then patted his palms together in appreciation. The rest of the delegation followed suit.

Tye smiled. 'That's an old party trick, although there is a new twist to the way we do it,' he beamed, stepping out of the light. 'High-definition visual satellite surveillance is really quite old-fashioned.' He wagged his finger in mock admonishment.

'Just don't go building any new rocket silos on Cuba. We'll catch you.'

Tye turned and nodded towards one of the control positions. A slim woman in her mid-forties, dressed in a white blouse and elegantly tailored navy-blue trousers walked to the edge of the Holo-Theater to stand beside him.

Tye introduced her to the visitors. 'This is Professor Theresa Keane. You'll be aware of her work on artificial life and machine intelligence.' He paused. 'We're proud to have her here and we're honoured that a Nobel Prize-winner should head our School of Virtuality at Hope University.'

He turned to the woman who shot him a brief but vivid smile. 'Theresa, please show our guests our recent enhancements to satellite surveillance.'

Tye stepped out of the ring and took a seat in the front row. The holo-image snapped back to an orbital view of the Earth, now one-third covered by cloud. The visitors also noticed that within the short time that had elapsed during the demonstration of visual-resolution systems, the planet had turned a few degrees to the east.

The professor stepped from the shadows into the pool of soft light created by the shimmering representation of the planet. Her dark auburn hair was cut short and she wore gold-framed half-lens viewpers that glinted in the light.

'Gentlemen, as you can see, we are now viewing our planet using only the visible spectrum of light,' she began with a hint of a soft Irish brogue. 'Remember, this image is composed in real-time from signals beamed back here by four hundred and eighteen low-earth-orbit satellites of the Argus network. But we are also scanning the planet at all wavelengths. Let's remove cloud cover again.'

The image reverted to the perfect blue, green and ochre globe the visitors had seen when they had first taken their seats.

'Most of the images that have now emerged from under cloud cover are being captured at infrared and ultraviolet wavelengths. The systems are compensating in real-time for cloud movement and are translating their output into light of the visible spectrum.'

She spoke slowly and carefully, ensuring that the visitors' translation systems would deliver one hundred per cent accuracy. She wasn't sure how recently their software had been upgraded. She looked around her small audience to see if they were following her. Their faces told her little.

One of the Russian delegates in the front row rose hesitantly and bowed. 'May I put one question?' he asked in slow but reasonable English.

The professor nodded and smiled her permission at him. Jack decided it was a very nice smile despite the island rumours about her sexual preferences. His emotions were definitely surfacing again.

'This is simulation, yes?' the delegate asked.

Theresa Keane smiled and shook her head as her questioner sank back into his seat. 'No, we are not simulating what might be going on under the clouds,' she explained. 'We are monitoring ground-level movements, heat and electrical activity at non-visible wavelengths, and representing them visually. The only things we can't see through cloud cover are inert details such as fine lines, print, objects that don't store heat and so on. We pull these details from a database that is updated every time cloud cover lifts. What we are seeing now is a form of enhanced real-time visual-wavelength monitoring.'

The group was silent as it digested the implications of satellite surveillance that could see through cloud.

The Russian delegate rose to his feet again, his hand raised as a request to ask another question.

Theresa smiled her smile at him again. 'If you're going to ask whether the network can also see in the dark, the answer is yes, it is fully scotopic – performance is even better than with clouds in daylight; there's less refraction, less visual interference.'

The questioner nodded, hesitated, then nodded once more and fell back into his seat.

There was silence in the room and Jack smiled to himself. She hadn't mentioned the link between the corporation's terrestrial wireless networks and the surveillance system. A huge amount of data was uplinked from sensors in the cellular networks to help the satellites see in all weathers and at night. Nor had she mentioned the system's radar-lidar components.

Theresa allowed the silence to hang for a few seconds more and then she turned back to the globe. 'For the second part of my introductory presentation this afternoon I thought you might be interested in a short history,' she said. 'So, just for fun, I'm going to freeze the image so we can take a look at how we started to connect our planet – how we started to create the digital domain and living space I call global virtuality.'

She waited until the planet became still.

'It all started over one hundred and seventy years ago, here.' The hologram dissolved and zoomed towards the eastern seaboard of the United States and then adjusted its image to present a round two-dimensional map of the Delaware peninsula.

Suddenly a line of white light snaked northwards between two areas of darkness.

'This was humanity's first form of electronic communication,' said Theresa. 'This city at the bottom is Washington DC and the world's first telegraph line covered the thirty-five miles to Baltimore. It was built by Samuel Morse when he was fifty-three. Then, over the next hundred and seventy years, the industrialized nations wired themselves with telegraphic cables, telephone lines, satellite networks and, finally, the mobile wireless systems we all use today.'

Calypso Browne felt sorry for her precious charge and she tended to indulge him. She hauled herself out of the pool and, once again, ran to fetch the beach ball from the grass.

'That was a foul,' shouted Tommy. 'I wasn't ready.'

Calypso crooked the ball in her arm and smiled down at the petulant seven year-old. 'So how many times do I have to say "Ready?"' She smiled. 'Here!'

She shot the ball towards the boy and jumped back into the warm water. The early-afternoon Caribbean sun was so hot that, although her dark skin required no tanning, all she really wanted to do was stretch out on the grass for an hour. But the boy had so little time to play. Tommy leaped and caught the ball above his head.

'I'm going to score,' he shouted and punched the ball back over the small net they had rigged across the pool. Calypso feigned an attempt to reach it and allowed it to fall into the water behind her head.

'You weren't trying!' shouted Tommy. 'Give it back.'

'Yes, I was so,' laughed Calypso, hands on hips in mock anger.

She shot the ball at him once more and again it bounced off his fist and out onto the manicured lawn surrounding the pool.

'Your turn, Tommy,' shouted Calypso. 'I'm always getting it.'

The boy swam for the steps and clambered out of the water. He retrieved the ball and, holding it high over his head, ran back towards the pool intent on hurling it as hard as he could at his laughing companion – she was now poking her tongue out at him. He was so preoccupied with his aim that he didn't notice his discarded baseball bat by the poolside. The bat rolled forward under his foot and with a yelp he flipped backwards and cracked his head on the unpolished marble slabs laid around the pool edge.

Calypso churned the water as she swam to the nearest steps and ran to the boy's aid. He was flat on his back, unconscious. Dr Browne didn't hesitate. She raised his eyelid. There was a slow response to the light. She lifted his wrist and pressed a button on his Day-Glo orange LifeSwatch. His pulse was almost 120. A second press of the button revealed his blood pressure was 110 over 60. She checked again: it was falling.

Calypso stood and ran to her bag. She grabbed her VideoMate to summon help even though she knew that the boy's LifeSwatch would have already transmitted its pre-programmed emergency alert. In a few seconds it would automatically make a decision whether or not to start injecting its small store of concentrated adrenalin through the boy's skin.

She bent down and disabled the LifeSwatch, just to be safe. Personal health protectors were better than nothing if the wearer was alone when a crisis struck, but she didn't want to risk

Tommy's heart being accidentally stimulated until she had a better idea of what his internal injuries might be.

'Well, we have now arrived at the present day,' said Professor Keane quietly.

Her audience sat transfixed at the diorama of their planet cocooned in chains of satellites and networks of cables.

'We estimate that there are currently about four billion social and commercial transactions per second taking place in the digital networks, most of them initiated and completed without human intervention. We have now come to realize that every device – the telegraph, the telephone, radio, television, computers, the Internet, cellphones, wireless devices, VideoMates, bodynets – are all different aspects of the same thing. They are all devices for access to the electronic digital extension of human consciousness that is global virtuality.'

She paused, preparing to wrap up her presentation.

'You might be interested to hear the words of the first message ever sent electronically,' she continued. She looked at her DigiPad to ensure the quotation was accurate. 'It was sent by Samuel Morse in 1844 when he had made the final connection to his telegraph cable and, of course, it was in binary code. It said: "What hath God wrought?"'

What indeed? thought Jack at the back of the room.

'Thank you for your attention, gentlemen,' concluded Professor Keane. 'Now we're switching from our history lesson back to our real-time monitoring of the world's networks and I'm handing you back to Tom.'

She nodded at the controller and stepped into the darkness.

The Russian president patted his palms together again and his party swiftly followed suit.

Thomas Tye stood up and walked into the pool of light, keen to enjoy his audience's appreciation of the dazzling display.

'What you see now is our monitoring of current network activity. The intensity of light in the networks indicates the traffic load. We estimate . . .' there was a pause as he looked at a digital counter above the display ' . . . that over three billion people, or their software agents, are currently transacting in the

world's digital space. One of our single laser beams can now
carry over one hundred million video calls and if all the children
on the planet wished to send a holiday video to their grand-
parents at the same time – live feed or recording – there would
still be sufficient capacity.'

From two rows back, Jack saw that the Russian leader was
leaning forward and pointing towards the bottom of the globe.
Tye also noticed the action and followed his gaze. At the
southern tip of the globe, just above New Zealand and northern
Antarctica, a dark spot was growing like red wine spilled onto a
white tablecloth.

Tye straightened and shot a look at the senior controller,
then at Connie in the back row. She rose and left the room,
unnoticed by members of the visiting party.

'It looks like there's a network outage in one of the sat-nets,'
he said calmly. 'Traffic will re-route around it automatically.'

He paused. 'Let's move on to the real business of our
meeting.' He nodded towards a steward at the top of an aisle to
open the door.

'I am delighted to introduce one of your former Russian
countrymen, Doctor Nicholas Kutúzov.'

An elderly, white-haired man in a grey suit walked carefully
down towards the presentation area. The Russians clapped more
enthusiastically.

'Doctor Kutúzov will be your host for this part of the
presentation and you'll be delighted to hear that it will be given
in natural Russian. We will now switch all systems over to the
Phoebus Project. As of this moment, this is no longer our
Network Control Center, it is the Command Center for the
Solaris Energy Stations.'

Tye nodded to a controller and stepped out of the pit. The
image of the Earth snapped off and there was darkness for a few
seconds. New holo-panels appeared in front of the control seats
and the large projection screens on the rear wall lit to present
distant real-time views of the Earth from space beamed back
from Tye's Argus network and from NASA's Mars-orbit Hubble
VI observatory. Then Jack noticed a holo-image in the central
pit that was new to him. The sun and the inner four planets of

the solar system glowed in the darkness. He switched on his VideoMate translation system. He noticed a subtle change in the air: the ScentSims under the seats were releasing a low-intensity fragrance that had been created by the olfactorologists in Tye Consumer Electronics R&D. Jack recognized it from the past: it was the smell of old dollar bills. It was called 'Anticipation'.

He felt a hand on his shoulder and looked up. It was Connie.

'Can you be spared?' she whispered. 'Tommy's had an accident and he might have to be moved.'

'Me,' called Haley as she pulled her key from the lock and slammed the door behind her. Although her sister had lived in Ladbroke Grove for over three years, Haley still found herself impressed by the space and elegance of the mid-nineteenth century *belle époque* mansion. Felicity and Martin only had one floor of the house but that was ... *only one floor?* That was still three times the size of Haley's apartment and offered fifteen-metre reception rooms and huge bay windows overlooking lawns and trees. It was London living at its most elegant.

'There in a minute,' Flick shouted from a bedroom.

'Yeeeee,' whooped Toby as Haley scooped her nephew up from his playpen. He was just over a year old and always loved his aunt's visits. Haley imagined that, because she and Flick were identical twins, she was somehow closer to Toby than an ordinary aunt would be. It certainly felt like that and Toby had never shown any objection. This evening he was to be all Haley's as Felicity was meeting her husband Martin to attend a soirée at the Foreign Office. Haley and Toby would be staying in and Haley felt it was just like old times.

Of the two sisters Felicity had always been the party girl. While Haley had worked ferociously at their state comprehensive school, her sister had partied away her later adolescence. Haley had then delighted the family by winning a place at Cambridge University, while Flick had been grateful to scrape into a communications-design course at one of the lesser-known colleges attached to Cardiff University. It was the same story when the twins were undergraduates: while Felicity enjoyed herself, Haley worked hard and, after securing her much-coveted first-class degree in English, she found a place on the national newspaper that had provided the opportunity to interview Josh Chandler. Felicity had become a production assistant in a network-game production house and, during the following eight years in which Haley experienced only three fairly unsatisfactory relationships, Flick had met, made out and moved on ('the 3M Syndrome', as she called it) with more men than Haley could now remember.

But, in their mid-thirties, it seemed as if the polarity of their relationship was reversing. Outside the long periods when she was engrossed in one of her writing projects, Haley had become renowned as a party animal, while her sister was happily settling for family life and domesticity. She and Martin were already planning another child – if Martin ever found enough time away from his dynamic career in the diplomatic service to make it possible.

Haley walked into the kitchen with Toby balanced on her left hip. He was chewing her necklace. She poured herself a glass of apple juice, then poured a second glass for Flick and sat down at the kitchen table for some serious eye contact and, possibly, conversation with Toby. The sisters were in hot competition to be the one to hear him utter his first recognizable word.

Flick touched Haley affectionately on the head as she entered. The sisters never kissed and rarely embraced. They were too close for that.

'You look wonderful!' admired Haley, truthfully.

'Sorted out your publisher yet?' asked Felicity.

'What publisher?' Haley groaned. Toby took the opportunity to stick his hand in her mouth and she nibbled his fingers, mumbling about how good they tasted.

'Oh. What are you going to do?'

Haley understood the real nature of the enquiry. 'They're not asking for their advance back.'

'Still ...'

Haley lifted Toby's bib and wiped some dribble from his chin. 'I'll just find another publisher.'

Her voice was sounding hoarse but neither remarked on it. That was how Haley showed stress: she would increasingly lose her voice.

'Drink your juice and get going,' Haley ordered. 'Toby and I want some time alone.'

'How's he doing?'

The entire island was buzzing with news of the accident and the research scientists had only just left.

Calypso looked up from the boy's bedside as Jack Hendriksen closed the door behind him.

'I think he'll be fine.' She smiled. 'It's just hard to tell how serious the concussion is.'

'Are we moving him?'

Calypso shook her head, her almond-shaped amber eyes looking troubled.

'That's what I planned, so I asked for one of the jet planes to be put on standby to go to Miami. They've got a special head-injuries unit there equipped for a craniotomy if it's needed. But Tom cancelled it.'

'Yes, I heard. I intended to go with you.'

Jack looked down at the unconscious boy. Despite the neck brace, the oxygen mask and the dense cluster of neural sensors attached to his scalp, he seemed so like his father with his jet-black hair and long eyelashes.

For the hundredth time in the past hour Calypso checked the monitors. Still no change. The scans and computer systems had given her diagnosis a rating of 74.7 per cent probability.

The door of the sanitarium hissed open and Thomas Tye was at the bedside. He had already changed into a dark suit for the reception dinner.

Calypso launched into an apology until Tye silenced her with a gesture. He pushed his face close to hers, white with fury.

'You *knew* he was to meet the Russians tonight! He was going to play for them! Swimming was not an authorized activity today. How could you . . .'

Jack stiffened and watched carefully as his boss fought to recover his self-control. Tye's eyes flicked from Calypso's shocked face to Jack's. He swallowed and took a small aerosol from his pocket, turning away to spray the inside of his mouth.

'Never mind explaining. I've seen the replay. Just tell me how he is.'

Calypso gave him the same information she had given Jack. 'I still think we should have him checked out in Miami,' she concluded defiantly. 'Telemedicine doesn't work so well when the problem is invisible.'

'I understand that, probably better than you do, Doctor,' snapped Tye. 'A consultant neurosurgeon is landing in...' He checked his LifeWatch. 'Twenty-five minutes' time. It's safer not to move him.'

Without touching his son he turned on his heel and left the room.

FOUR

Joseph P. Tinkler added the half-and-half to his fibre and banana flakes and ate breakfast standing beside his kitchen window. He willed the nerves in his stomach to calm. Perhaps the food would help.

Far below, the Manhattan rush hour was getting under way and the first seaplanes from the Hamptons were skimming in to land at the East River Skyport. He had less than an hour to go before he had to face the board and, most importantly, the Old Man, who was probably on one of those planes. Joe wondered if he had stuck his neck out too far this time.

Joe Tinkler was the star fund manager at Rakusen-Webber and, despite his comparative youth, he was one of the bank's top earners. He had seven hundred and fifty billion dollars under his control and, ignoring long-established standing guidelines against over-concentration, his stock portfolio was heavily biased towards two types of investment: the companies in the Tye group and the quoted companies in which Thomas Tye had a personal stake.

When he had joined the investment bank fresh from Yale, Joe had been its first African-American recruit and, as an analyst, he had lived, breathed and dreamed about the world's richest corporation and its trillionaire founder. Now, twelve years later, Rakusen-Webber's many institutional investors had billions of reasons for thanking him for his knowledge, prescience and judgement.

But suddenly the bank's chief investment officer wanted to remove two-thirds of his fund; to 'split it for the sake of prudence,' Morgenstein had said, citing the extremely heavy percentage of Tye Corporation-related investments. Joe knew his fund had grown to be larger than any on Wall Street, but as he had consistently returned between thirty and thirty-seven per cent annual growth, he had expected to increase the funds under his control rather than see them taken away. He knew that if he allowed it to happen there would be all sorts of rumours on the Street within hours, rumours that would be impossible to neutralize and that could seriously damage his reputation and career.

He guessed, rightly, that it was his performance-related bonuses that were the problem. They were larger than those received by any other employee at Rakusen-Webber and, according to gossip, the largest employee-incentive package on the Street. He also guessed that his earnings had overtaken Morgenstein's – and *he* was a partner.

Joe had objected strongly and, as was his right, he had insisted on a management board review. He hadn't guessed that the Old Man would use this opportunity to make one of his rare personal appearances in the bank to hear Joe put his case.

His presentation for the board was complete. He rechecked that the memory card was in his VideoMate and, for the tenth time, looked to ensure that his back-up and the printouts were in his pilot's bag. He had already dropped a version onto the office server, but he believed in belt and braces when it came to office politics. It had taken him until two a.m. to complete the presentation, checking and rechecking his background information, his figures and his sources' qualifications and justifications.

Out on the street it was still early enough for the air rising off the river to be cool. As usual in summer, he'd decided to walk the six blocks from Maiden Lane to Wall Street. Although it wasn't yet 6.30 a.m., the sidewalks were already busy with others planning an early start to their Tuesday.

Joe had got to the corner of Depyster and Pine before he yielded to temptation. He flipped his Ray Ban Electros out of their case and hit the play button on his VideoMate. Once again, he stepped through his presentation.

The telecoms division was the easy bit and the obvious starting point. Thirteen petabytes of new fibre and LaserNet capacity created in the last quarter alone. Would Tye Data Networks slash the wholesale price of data capacity again? Joe was certain they would and he was sure it would be an aggressive move. Ever since the company had gone on a buying spree and absorbed many of the old national telecommunications companies, it had continued to cut costs while improving services. He projected a growth of forty per cent in demand in the next year and predicted that Tye Corp would gain an additional twenty-two per cent share of the enlarged market. Demand for digital communications capacity was both global and insatiable. As the pundits had predicted years before, it *was* the oxygen of the twenty-first century.

The media division was always the hardest to call. Four major new film releases in the next quarter but only one that looked like a blockbuster. The global film servers were still doing a great job on back-catalogue sales and rentals but that was a mature business. Live news was Tye Corp's weakest area although it was gaining ground with Halcyon, a new global weather channel. This service was proving particularly accurate and reliable but TNN – the Tye Network News channel – was still running a definite third to CNN and DBT News. Profits were unchanged.

Aerospace was very strong: over 300 successful commercial satellite launches last year from Cape Hope, the island's shuttle base, and from the corporation's two leased launch sites in South America. The company had a waiting list of sixty-two months for customers hoping for a launch slot. And Tye Aerospace had a ten-year contract from the World Space Agency for Orbit Management – the systems developed to prevent the thousands of satellites from cannoning into each other. For this division he had revised his profits contribution estimate upwards by thirty per cent, although the corporation was ploughing back much of its surplus into a deep-space location network, for reasons that were as yet undisclosed.

Consumer electronics: Joe's Electro viewpers threw the categories in front of his eyes. The eighth generation of

LifeWatches was due in a few months and his sources were very excited. They whispered that in addition to carrying microstores of adrenalin, angiotensin and digitalis the new models would include a secret new anti-fibrillation compound as well as enlarged ambulatory data storage. The LifeWatch was finally becoming the 'physician on the wrist' that Tye had promised eleven years ago at the launch of its original version. And then there was the astonishing potential value of the medical data warehouses and the boost these would give to the corporation's trove of intellectual capital.

Joe quickly flipped through his media on the market growth for VideoMates, HouseNets, BodyNets and viewpers – still no hint when the 3D entertainment system would be launched.

A heavy weight hit the fund manager between the shoulders and he fell onto a fire hydrant. His large bag went flying.

'Hey, man. I'm sorry.' The tall white man in a pinstriped suit circled to a fast stop on his rollerblades. He reached out to help Joe up. 'You OK?'

Joe nodded. He'd probably have a bruised thigh, but nothing more.

'My wife was giving me shit,' said the rollerblader, as he took off his Armani viewpers and waved them. 'I just can't get away from her.'

'I know, I know,' smiled Joe. He checked his LifeWatch. Everything normal. 'I'm fine.' No need to trade identities.

'Sorry,' repeated the rollerblader as he took off again, more slowly this time. Joe retrieved his case and slipped his own Electros off. Although their video projections onto his retinas appeared as a transparent overlay in front of his eyes, he knew how easy it was to block out the images of the real world.

Almost everybody else on the sidewalk was wearing personal viewpers of one brand or another. Most of them, he guessed, were watching the news, talking to someone, gambling, scanning e-mails and v-mails or, like him, going over their work. Many of them were 'attending' meetings in different time zones, different climates, different seasons: some of them would be involved in more than one. All of them walked more slowly, more absently, than people had when he was a kid in Manhattan and all of them seemed to be talking to themselves. Once again Joe realized that while their bodies were on the streets, their minds were in the networks.

'Is it time to wake up?' asked the red caterpillar.

Tommy and his Furry were inseparable and Calypso had asked for the companion to be sent over from the house.

The boy yawned and stretched, puzzled that he wasn't in his bedroom.

'Row, row, row your boat, gently down the stream,' sang Jed and waited. Tommy didn't feel like singing. His head hurt so much he wanted to cry.

Calypso stepped quietly into the room. She walked over to the bed and stroked Tommy's hair. Despite her written orders of employment that forbade such intimacy, she bent and kissed him gently on the forehead.

'Welcome back, Tommy,' she said quietly. She could guess how he must be feeling.

Tommy looked up. 'My head hurts, Calypso. Where am I?'

'You had a fall and banged your head, my darling. Can you remember where it happened?'

He frowned.

'Ten little speckled frogs,' sang Jed until Tommy squeezed him.

'We were in the pool,' he said. 'You were cheating.'

'Was not,' smiled Calypso, a rush of relief sweeping over her. The scans had shown no internal bleeding. The consultants from Miami were certain there had been no intracranial haematoma, but, well, you could never be sure. She had treated many cases of concussion during her internship in Chicago and she knew nothing was sure until consciousness returned.

She ran her eyes across the read-outs on the wall screen. Pulse a little elevated, otherwise everything was normal.

'Let's make the headache go away,' she said, taking an air-pressure syringe from her coat pocket. Almost by instinct she had worn a physician's coat from the moment she had brought her precious patient in to the clinic. It felt good to dress like a doctor again and she needed to underline to the visiting consult-

ants her professional status as an MD *and* a paediatric psychiatrist. It also brought back all her guilt about focusing her
long years of training and her specialist knowledge on *one*
healthy child, no matter who he was. But there was also her
mother to think about.

Calypso had been the first of her family to make the break –
to emerge from the grinding poverty of life on a banana island
in the eastern Bahamas. She had her father's Scottish belief in
education, the strict little mission school he founded, and her
astounding looks to thank for her escape, she acknowledged.
She had been crowned Miss Americas and then Miss World.
She was the first 'Miss World' to come from the West Indies
since Cindy Breakspear had won the title nearly fifty years
earlier and Calypso was determined to make the best use of the
money and travel opportunities the title had brought with it.
Cindy had leveraged her brief fame to gain the 'privilege' of
bearing Bob Marley's son; Calypso used hers to make good on
her breathlessly blurted ambition to become a doctor. When she
was done with her duties for the sponsors and had finished her
year on the celebrity lecture circuit, her savings had bought
her nine years of medical training in the United States.

And now she was back home – well, almost. Life on Hope
Island certainly bore little resemblance to conditions on its near
neighbours, but her contract with the Tye Corporation guaranteed her one round trip home and back by company helicopter
every two weeks. With her older brothers long gone to seek
their livings in the States and in Europe, who else was there to
visit Mum and oversee her care, now that her ageing parent was
starting to lose her sight and become semi-housebound? Thank
God Calypso made more than enough money to provide
twenty-four-hour help for the old lady.

Calypso positioned the syringe on her small charge's pale
white arm and, with a little puff of compressed gas, the analgesic
entered his bloodstream.

The wall screen beeped and displayed a familiar icon.

'Accept,' said Calypso, as she removed the injection nozzle
from the syringe.

Her employer's face filled the screen. 'How're you feeling, son?' asked Tye gently.

'I'm OK,' mumbled Tommy.

'I got the alert he was conscious. Thank you, doctor.' It was the closest he would come to an apology.

'Everything looks OK, Tom. Full short-term memory recovery, no haemorrhaging, all the vital signs are normal. Do you want to talk to Doctor Henoch or Doctor Bowlby – I think they're still sleeping?'

'No. Just keep me informed.'

'Are you coming to see me?' asked Tommy quietly.

'I can't, son. I'm in São Paulo. In Brazil. I'll be back tonight.'

The boy nodded and the screen flipped off.

Calypso cradled the boy's head. 'Is it still hurting?'

Tommy nodded and leaned into her. Calypso stroked his hair and wondered how best she could offset the attachment damage that had already been caused by so many broken connections with hired nannies and temporary care-givers. Children need constant love from a single source if they are to develop trust in relationships. The door opened and the biologists returned with their probes and scanners.

Joe Tinkler came to the first of his carefully-orchestrated crescendos.

'I'm certain they're talking *down* the situation in almost all areas,' he declared. 'In fact, everywhere except in the media division. I'm sure the actual results will beat all forecasts for all the other divisions. Except for *my* forecasts, that is. I think we'll probably see earnings of four dollars thirty a share.'

The board had so far sat through his presentation almost impassively, muted because of the rare experience of their founder's son, and their honorary chairman, being present. There was a quietness in the room and then the legendary Richard J. Rakusen spoke for the first time.

'You're telling us that for the thirty-second consecutive quarter the Tye Corporation's profits are going to rise, and this time it will be by over sixty per cent?'

Joe nodded apprehensively.

'Are we to believe that gravity no longer exists?' asked the Old Man.

Joe swallowed. He had taken the board through each of the Tye corporate divisions and subsidiaries and, for the benefit of Richard J. Rakusen and, perhaps, to show off a little, he had explained why historical data were no longer a reliable guide to future performance.

He had also reminded them that the plethora of corporate currencies on issue, the pegging of the US dollar to the Euro and the end of the appallingly wasteful thirty-day business settlement period had flattened economic cycles so much that the booms and busts that had afflicted the markets so severely in the twentieth century and the early years of the twenty-first were now modulated to provide little more than periods of respite between increases in global value-generation. Therefore, he argued, the risks suggested by the old policy guidelines on concentration were out of date. He had done some homework and, with a flourish, he had told them that these guidelines had last been updated over a quarter of a century earlier, in 1989.

He had then listed the most important of the 387 patents that Tye-related companies had filed during the year. He had lifted copies of the original filings from the World Patent Database and he skipped through them as the board watched in silence. He had reminded his audience about the record number of patents the company had secured the previous year and he had tried to explain the implications of some of the research being undertaken in the group's various R&D labs.

'No company in history has ever filed so many important patents in a single year,' he had stated finally.

'Which company has filed the second-highest number of patents in the year?' Morgenstein had asked during that section.

How typical of the bastard! Asking a pointless tangential question like that in the hope of catching him out. Not for the first time, Joe wondered whether it meant plain old embedded racism. His was still the only black face in the firm.

'GenCode, the European-based group,' he had responded swiftly. 'They've filed one hundred and sixty-four.'

There was a deeper silence now as the board waited for Joe's response to their most senior partner.

'No, sir, gravity still exists, but there's no sign of the Tye Corporation's curve flattening yet.'

'Are we still happy with the quality of Tye Corp's reporting?' asked Jill White quickly. *Thank God for a friend*, thought Joe. She had thrown him one of his specialities.

'The company has never wavered,' he confirmed. 'Although they could have changed their accounting methods when they moved their registration of incorporation from Delaware to Hope Island State, they've stayed firmly with the EUUSA and International Accounting Standards principles.'

Since the main stock markets of the EU and the USA had merged seven years before and moved to permanent twenty-four-hour trading, standards of financial reporting had finally become trustworthy and transparent. The massive scandals that had repeatedly rocked the emerging regions more than a decade ago had pushed the regulators to develop better and better standards of accounting, asset valuation and liability accounting. Although this had initially depressed corporate valuations, the sudden appreciation of stored knowledge value, the instruments developed to rate it and new internationally agreed accounting standards for intellectual capital had quickly pushed corporate valuations and the markets back up.

'If anything, their accounts are misleadingly conservative,' Joe suggested. 'They're sitting on three hundred and ninety billion US dollars in cash and, frankly, that's only the visible part. They're laying off enormous sums against real or imaginary future liabilities. Also, our chief economist says...'

He searched through the media and projected the figure. 'They could issue a further six hundred billion T-euros without it affecting the value of their currency. The Global Bank reports separately from the main group. Last year it had assets of one point seven five trillion US dollars.'

There were mutterings around the table.

'I turn now to the future,' the fund manager continued.

Jill looked up quickly. Joe's tone had taken on a harder edge.

'Let's return to the consumer division. The LifeWatch has

now sold...' He brought the media up – a moving collage of the various models with a running counter at the bottom of the screen. 'One point two billion units around the world. As you can see, six new customers are strapping on a LifeWatch every second. Is anybody here without one?'

He held out his wrist. His Rolex LifeWatch glinted in the ceiling lights. There was no response from his audience.

'We all wear them. You can buy a standard model for the price of a meal and it could well save your life. Heck, they're even available in vending machines in the subway.'

Joe flicked his media forward.

'The World Health Organization estimates that personal health-protectors have saved over two million lives in the last three years, and that's just from early intervention in heart attacks. When the statistics for diabetics, epileptics, anaphylactics and narcoleptics are added the figures go through the roof. Tye Corp has a ninety-three per cent share of the market for PHP systems, even though it allows other brand-owners, like Rolex, to co-market individual styles under licence. The Tye Corporation fully understands that the word "brand" has become today's collective and corporate noun for integrity so it is pleased to co-market with other well-established designer names. But it remains the Tye Corporation's software and systems on the inside and the company itself administers all the updates and maintenance. They have a real monopoly and they are, of course, outside the reach of any anti-trust action.'

He paused, looking around the table to ensure that he still had everybody's attention.

'What I am now going to tell you is price-sensitive information and I have cleared the next part with our compliance department. You therefore understand the limitations on any future investment activities before the official announcement.'

The chief compliance officer nodded his assent for Joe to continue.

'For the last three years LifeWatches have been capturing ambulatory data – that is, they record and store our vital signs during every moment of our lives. We never take them off, do we? That would defeat the point. Since they were launched they've also had ultra-short-range wireless datalinks with VideoMates and compatible communicators and, well, that's just about every mobile communicator on the planet. On top of that, the potential market for LifeWatches is still nearly two billion, just in the developed economies. Worldwide, it's nearer five billion.'

He paused again, watching them. Only Morgenstein was making notes or, more likely, doodling to affect disinterest, thought Joe. The other fourteen pairs of eyes were all fixed firmly on him.

'This datalink is ostensibly for downloading software updates to the LifeWatches. Every time there's a new feature or software patch, Tye Consumer Electronics transmits the update to our VideoMates, and they then transmit it to our LifeWatches. This all occurs automatically, in background. We don't initiate it and we're not aware when it's happening. Only it also goes the other way. Every week our LifeWatches *upload* the recordings they've made about us to our VideoMates and, in turn, they upload this information to Tye Corp's customer-relations centres. That means details of our heart rate, our blood pressure, our blood-cell counts, our ECG record and our epidermic conductivity.

'For those with declared medical conditions – people who are wearing specialized LifeWatches with boosted diabetic, ana-phylactic or epileptic defence systems, for example – the data will include specialist measurements such as glucose levels, antigen reaction or epidermic electrochemical resistance. This means that Tye Corp's Consumer Division receives data on how our bodies perform under every condition: when we're sleeping, when we're eating, when we're exercising.'

Joe paused once more and looked at Jill.

'And when we're making love.'

He allowed three beats to pass. He shouldn't have said that. He was getting cocky.

'For example, the data show how heat affects us. They can fill a data warehouse with the information being collected, and then compare how people react to the global weather records on temperature, humidity, sunspots – you name it. Tye Corp already has all the climate data from its Halcyon weather network. Suddenly we know *how* people, and *which* people, are affected. But to do that they have to know precisely where we are at a given time, and that's where the VideoMates come in. Over eighty per cent of VideoMates and compatible communicators make use of the various global positioning systems. They need to – that's part of their brilliant efficiency.

'Our employers, our families – everybody can know where every other human and every asset is, supposedly only when we want them to – when we agree to swap location modes. That's how we manage the world's traffic flows, plane movements, passenger flows at airports, train loads, taxi availability, bus schedules, the shipping lanes, all those satellites and all the other stuff of our busy lives. That's how business manages its global supply lines. Without the commercial GPS networks and computerized management systems we'd be back in the blind world of previous centuries with all that friction and all those inefficiencies.'

Jill was nodding and Morgenstein had stopped making notes.

'Now, couple that with our digital identities ...' He waited to see if he was going to have to explain that. 'Every time a LifeWatch uploads to a VideoMate it is correlated to the GPS history. That's uploaded to Tye's Consumer Division along with the digital identity certificates that allow us secure and guaranteed communications and transactions.'

'So he knows who we are and where we are at all times?' said Jill, inadvertently personalizing Thomas Tye's corporation.

'Yes, even when we don't use location mode or when we've switched our autolocate off,' confirmed Joe. 'Or, at least, Tye Corp gets a history of our movements. A VideoMate still checks its actual position every few minutes even if you've switched it to standby. It needs its precise location for its log and to give us the information we need when we next enable it. Those data are all stored and automatically uploaded to the Tye Corporation.'

'What's this worth?' asked Richard T. Rakusen quietly. Nobody saw a bottom line emerging earlier, or at a greater distance, than he.

'I've put some numbers on it, sir, but they're only guesswork because we don't know precisely how the Tye Corporation plans to exploit it.'

He flashed up some figures from the media. 'If we just consider the impact of those data on the pharmaceutical division and on the health services and hospitals Tye Health-Care manages around the world, I think we're talking three and a half trillion dollars over five years just from small enhancements to approved drugs – dosage adjustments, new drug-interactions and so on. Essentially, this technology is mapping the physiology of over one billion humans during every moment of their waking and sleeping lives. Customers must provide a lot of personal medical information if they want Tye Health Insurance to accept liability for LifeWatch performance and if that information is coupled with in-field consumer research for statistical verification, Tye's corporation has got permanent, ongoing, real-time results from the greatest clinical trial ever conducted on the human race. Imagine the impact on prognosis guidance, hospital building programmes, and drug development!'

'Surely the data-privacy laws will prevent this,' snapped Morgenstein, aware that there was a serious danger of Joe pulling off a coup. In the last few years the USA had given up its resistance to data-protection laws and had fallen into line with the rest of the world in placing strict limitations on how corporations could exploit personal data.

'Those laws don't apply because every customer signs a waiver,' explained Joe patiently. 'You all recall what happened when the early versions of LifeWatches came out. Some of them went off accidentally and injected adrenalin, epinephrine or other drugs when they shouldn't have. Sometimes they failed to intervene, or failed to send an emergency signal when something *had* gone wrong in the wearer's body. The Tye Corporation settled those claims out of court but as the technology improved Tye's marketing people also got smarter. When we buy one of these articles we have to sign a form that provides basic information – name, address, height, weight, sex, doctor's name and address and so on, if we want to receive legal insurance and medical cover against malfunction. What's the point of buying an uninsured LifeWatch that misses an arrhythmia or an acute allergic nut reaction occurring, so doesn't intervene? People still want coverage even though LifeWatches have become so reliable that there has not been a single reported case of failure, or of accidental intervention, for many years. Tye Corp got round the liability issue by providing their own insurance policies through THI – Tye Health Insurance. It was a really neat solution. We also have to declare any medical conditions we may have and the medication we are on, and we sign a partial data-privacy waiver. Sure, THI agrees not to sell the data on, but it doesn't need to. Its own divisions can make more than enough use of the information.'

Joe stopped to draw breath. 'In the emerging countries the Thomas Tye Foundation has already given away three hundred and eighty million LifeWatches and Tye Consumer Electronics has started to subsidise basic LifeSwatches for those on welfare and for certain needy groups in the developed markets.'

'The great tree-hugging philanthropist, again?' asked Jill, arching her eyebrows. Perhaps he hadn't upset her after all. Those deep brown eyes were smiling.

'Not really; those data are the *most* valuable because those people suffer the most diseases, they need the most drugs, even if we end up paying for them through our taxes or our donations. And then, of course, there's the feedback that is supplied to Tye Life Sciences and its cloned-organ farms for the super-rich. Everything is part of a positive-feedback loop – a virtuous circle. The potential for growth is staggering!'

He looked around all the faces. He had them now. He bent, pretending to look at his notes. After a suitable delay he coughed, changed position and tone.

'And there's a small marketing coup promised for announcement at Comdex this fall.' Once again he paused, making sure he was producing maximum impact.

'The first PetProtectors will go on sale this Christmas. They'll be twice the price of LifeWatches because the collars will be breed-specific and adjustable for coat thickness. They're going to be marked under the tag line "Never Lose Your Pet Again", with a focus on pet location, but physiological data will be the second part of the sales message. I forecast six million sales in the first eight weeks alone.'

'With the data on individual pets being collected too?' asked Jim Manzies, senior partner in Corporate Currencies.

'Of course. Uploaded via their owners' VideoMates, and multiplexed within the location transmissions.'

Joe decided to show off his depth of research and flipped up some pages from the *Nature* archives. 'Of course, PetProtectors won't actually be a new concept. Tye Corp ran animal trials with early versions of protectors before the LifeWatch was launched. It's just that, now LifeWatches are such an important human accessory, many animal-owners will want one for their pet too. They're just digging out the old designs and repackaging them with updated electronics.'

Everybody at the table was nodding, including Morgenstein and even the Old Man. Since Tye Life Sciences had launched its PerPetual service in the United States eleven years earlier the craze for cloning pets for replacements had spread to all developed territories. TLS had quickly sold international franchises for PerPetuation Centers and millions of expensive but identical replacement animals were now routinely provided to order. Pet Pamperers had thus become recognized as a global market of vast potential.

'And I suppose pet paramedic emergency teams will respond to alarm calls from the PetProtectors?' laughed Jill.

'You bet,' smiled Joe. 'That's what I call a start-up opportunity!' He allowed them to enjoy the joke, even though he knew of at least three planned start-ups that had got wind of Tye Corp's launch and had developed precisely that business plan. He was thinking of investing personally in just such a Miami-based venture, if he could clear it with Compliance. But on with the close.

'Although PetProtectors will undoubtedly be big business, that market will be nothing compared to other ways the Tye group can exploit what they are gathering from the LifeWatch data. Take financial products – pensions, health cover, life insurance. Guess what? Tye Financial Services Group builds a

data warehouse to mine for those individuals revealing signs that
are negative indicators of long-term health – such as poor heart-
rate response to heat, essential hypertension, the electro-conduc-
tion of stress, and not sleeping well, since heart rates do provide
a clear correlation with sleep patterns. This means that the
vulnerable are weeded out, and the salespersons will know
the healthiest people to target for selling an expensive policy
that they probably won't need. They'll also know exactly when
to load the premiums for some poor jerk whose physiological
performance doesn't meet actuarial standards.'

'And you think this is legal?' queried Harriman, the bank's
senior counsel. 'I'd like to see those waiver forms.'

Joe nodded and slipped a set of copies from his pilot's bag.
He moved to the table to distribute them, then paused looking
down at the elegant Longines LifeWatch on Harriman's wrist.
Except for two extra buttons on the side of its slender gold case,
it was virtually indistinguishable from the classic analogue time-
piece of the previous century. Its electronically active strap was
cased in leather and, when required, its digital data would appear
in a transparent display layer sandwiched within the watch-
glass.

'May I ask if you signed a waiver when you bought that, Mr
Harriman?'

There was a silence. Then the counsellor nodded.

'I suppose I must have done,' he admitted, looking around
the table for support. 'Well, none of us read *standard* retail sales
conditions, do we?'

Without waiting for the waiver forms to be passed around
or read, Joe stepped back from the table.

'Now let's look at the Solar Energy Division and the projected global take-up of Tye Corp's high-efficiency solar-energy
fuel cells,' he said authoritatively.

Hope Island had an early-rising culture and, just after eleven
p.m., the seaside suburbs of Hope Town became quieter as less
noise drifted across the small bay.

Calypso had chosen as her home a beach bungalow a mile
away from Little Venice, the main harbour frontage and marina

with its 'world restaurants' and themed bars. The Island's *Welcome* brochure, which had been given to her on her arrival three months before, boasted that every cuisine in the world was available along a one-mile stretch of waterside restaurants.

And so it was, but Calypso did not feel like walking out to eat this evening. The scare over Tom Jnr's accident had left her feeling both alert and drained at the same time and, once the boy had been returned to his latest nanny in the great house up on the mountain terraces, Calypso had been grateful just to take the Mag back to her bungalow, open a bottle of wine and heat a frozen pepperoni pizza. It was made at Mario's, down by the marina, and contained delicious and medicinally active ingredients. As a doctor she loved the idea that she could adjust and protect her body's biochemistry with a meal she enjoyed but that could not help to make her overweight. The pepperoni topping had become one of her firm favourites.

She had kept communication open, of course. Tommy's VideoMate broadcast updates from his LifeWatch every thirty seconds and she was sure there would be little change. When she had eaten she had tried to catch up on her reading, her VideoMate, open beside her, displaying Tommy's steady life signs. She could tell he was asleep, still mildly sedated.

Calypso logged on to two journal discussion centres and skimmed through the postings but, even as she did, she knew she was too distracted to concentrate properly. She marked articles and threads that she would revisit and turned away from her screens. She had changed into a white silk dressing gown and now she switched off the air-conditioning and opened the door to the small veranda.

Within seconds a close heat filled the small room and she smiled. She often did this at the end of an evening. It reminded her of how it had been back home, when there were seven of them and the nights were so hot she would go out and sleep on the beach.

On a whim, she turned out the house lights and stepped into the night. The white beach sloped gently in front of her her, down towards the dark, glittering sea. High above, innumerable satellites pierced the black sky with their staccato bursts of laser communications – *like those old Star Wars movies*, she thought. Beyond were the soft pinpricks of light clusters that made up the constellations of the Corona Borealis and Hercules.

She heard a roar in the distance and she looked south. Far over the Atlantic, beyond the floating spaceport, she saw the white flame of one of the Tye Aerospace space shuttles as it graduated from jet propulsion to rocket power. She had become used to the spectacle since she had arrived on the island but still she stood and watched the white light grow smaller as the vehicle accelerated towards orbit. In a few minutes it was just another pinprick of light in the sky.

She looked to her left and right. There was no movement. Nobody else was sufficiently interested to come out into their gardens to watch a routine launch. The beach bungalows had been placed at eighty-yard intervals, enough space to give privacy but, the planners claimed, close enough for a community to emerge. All lights were out. Most of the other residents on this beach were professional staff, medics, like herself, or teachers from the school and the university, pilots, astronauts, air traffic movement supervisors or spaceport personnel. There were also many patent attorneys. All took early nights.

Calypso walked down the beach and grabbed a swimsuit and a pair of goggles she had left to dry over her hammock. She slipped the costume up over her legs and allowed her robe to fall from her shoulders at the water's edge. She slipped her arms into the suit, fitted the goggles, waded forward and then dived, exhilarating in the tang of the cool salt water as it swept over her body.

Clear advice was given to all residents not to swim in the seas around Hope Island. The currents were strong and the beaches shelved sharply. Also, sharks were regularly sighted.

But Calypso had grown up with this sea. It was the same sea that had lapped her beach on Mayaguana and she understood its ways and those of its inhabitants. Like her namesake in Homer's *Odyssey*, she was a sea nymph, the daughter of Oceanus. Her brothers had teased her that it had been her constant swimming that had produced her statuesque frame, those shoulders, that neck, those breasts – a body providing the perfect complement to the breathtaking, fine-boned symmetry of her face. It was a feature so provocative it had prompted an ebony-black and somewhat platyrrhine runner-up in one beauty contest to describe Calypso, rather uncharitably, as 'beautiful but undeniably mulatta' in an interview for the *Jamaica Gleaner*. But where had those startling amber eyes come from? They had to be an atavistic attribute, perhaps from her maternal Arawak Indian grandmother.

As an adult, Calypso still swam three or four times a week. She could cross the bay and back again in two hours but this evening she decided that she would merely venture around the small headland before returning – a mile's journey that would take her forty-five minutes. In truth, she didn't want to be away for too long from her VideoMate and its link to her charge.

She stroked her way past the Gene Scene, a beach so named because the DNA snippers from the biotechnology research campus broke every island rule on this small strip of sand they had made their own. Rumour had it that they made all their own recreational drugs, each one tuned for its own user, and they certainly did like to party all night. As her body rolled with her strong easy freestyle crawl, she could see half a dozen bonfires flickering in the darkness.

She ploughed on for a further ten minutes until she felt a colder shaft of water hit her from below. That meant she had reached the headland and would soon be leaving the Caribbean Sea for the Atlantic Ocean, so she turned and headed for the low rocks at the water's edge. As she often did, she would haul herself onto the rocks and sit for ten minutes, before starting on her return. Even this late in the evening, the limestone would still be warm from the day's sun.

A figure was sitting on *her* favourite rock. She paused, treading water. He stood suddenly – he had seen her.

'You OK?' His voice sounded thin across the water, even though only a dozen yards separated them.

Calypso pulled off her goggles and waved an acknowledgement. She realized it was Jack Hendriksen. He stood up and held out a white towel.

FIVE

The bicycle won't go! Won't go. Go on, push. It's hard. Breaths are coming in laboured gasps. He hears her running behind the bicycle. He can feel her, he can smell her. She is pushing. It is too fast too fast too fast.

He soars up and over the girl and her propulsion. Her stupid clothes will get caught. It's stupid stupid. All these strange people are laughing.

Look how I ride. Look how I ride. I can go fast. Are they looking? See. See.

The lawn and its narrow winding path are sunlit. People are gathered for something, all staring at the little girl.

Clothes catching. Pull at them pull at them, pull pull. He is tearing her stupid clothes off. But the tree always comes. No matter how many times he tries to control it, the tree just keeps on coming.

She is crying, the tears are hot, of shame, not hurt. Then she is carrying him. Alone together. The smells again, the smells. She is touching him between his legs the way The Doctor does when she sits on his knee.

Thomas Tye woke, bathed in sweat, both hands scrabbling down there where, as always, they had no busyness.

He looked at his VideoMate on the bedside table. He had woken one minute before the alarm time he'd set. He cursed as he saw that the DreamDial software he used to save him from that dream had not been activated. He was sure he had set it, even for this short nap before the important appointment he was now to keep on the terrace below. It would be a long time before he fumbled the settings again. He personally championed the DreamDial project through Consumer Electronics in order to protect him from her and The Doctor.

He showered, pulled on a dark sweatsuit and tied his hair back. He took the elevator down to the main viewing terrace in front of the house and walked out into the warm night air. As he had instructed, the rest of the huge house was without lights and the many garden lamps along the terrace pathways had been switched off. Four hundred feet below, the white sand of his private beach stretched out to meet the dark, gentle swell of the Atlantic.

Connie was fully dressed and waiting for him beside a small patio table. She handed him a cup of jasmine tea.

He heard a sound and the Russian president emerged from the darkened house, dressed in a red silk dressing gown. His valet and his two most senior ministers – General Padorin, the Armed Forces Commander, and Leonid Konstantine, the Interior Minister – followed him. Anton Vlasik, another house guest despite Jack Hendriksen's many objections, brought up the rear. The rest of the Russian party was lodged in VIP accommodation in Hope Town and they had not been asked to disturb their sleep for this demonstration.

Tye turned and nodded without saying anything. The President and his party did the same. Connie poured tea for them all.

The night was dark despite the intermittent laser-bursts of satellite communication overhead but it was as clear and cloudless as the meteorologists and their powerful Halcyon weather computer had predicted. The moon was very new and, unless an observer knew precisely where to search, almost invisible to the naked eye. Tye looked at his Piaget LifeWatch and scanned the quadrant of the sky where he knew the event would occur. He found Pegasus in the north-east and followed it up to Equuleus. It would be just a few degrees to the east. *There.*

The island was quiet and unlit. From this northern vantage point the observing party could see down the whole length of the corporate state past the main campus and out to Cape Hope and its floating white extension, where the spaceport runways and deep-water harbour were located. Tye knew they would all be watching down there too, the video cameras and sensors already recording.

Apart from those whose job it was to observe this experiment, and those on Hope Island whose duties kept them up until three a.m., few others on the planet would see the results of this first mid-power trial at close quarters. Hope Island ATC had re-routed all night-time air traffic well to the south.

Despite these precautions, Thomas Tye knew that the forthcoming celestial event would be widely recorded. But he doubted that any of the world's observatories would be able to make sense of it. Each of the energy stations was cloaked in light-absorbent, radio-wave-dispersing materials and all communications had been encrypted and buried in the vast mass of inter-satellite radio transmissions. The fourteen large space stations had initially assumed their pre-booked orbit positions as granted by the UN Space Agency but, when the constructions had been finished, each had been boosted out of earth's orbit and away to specific locations that Tye Aerospace had described as 'part of the Space Location and Positioning System – a network of satellites to aid navigation in the solar system'. After that, they had become invisible to the world's terrestrial observatories and the scores of orbiting telescopes.

None of the world's many space agencies and observatories had publicly identified or queried any of the low-intensity tests undertaken around the planet in previous months. Most had been carried out in regions where it was just before dawn or immediately after dusk. Nor had they noticed any of the tests conducted in the non-visible frequencies. The assumption by the Phoebus Project Team was that the tests had simply been misinterpreted as natural phenomena.

In the next few weeks the controllers would have to take more chances by running high-energy tests in the visible spectrum, but they would choose unpopulated areas such as the South Pacific or the Arctic and, perhaps, an uninhabited forest area. They had to find a balance between the need for successful trials and their desire to keep details of the new service secret until its global launch on 30 August. Tye wanted his Russian deal to become a *fait accompli* before the world's analysts had a chance to consider and pontificate on the implications of his new technology. Cuba would present tonight's biggest problem as their patrol craft would undoubtedly witness the test first-hand, but Tye doubted whether the country's astronomers or physicists were equipped to make a meaningful analysis.

He held his wrist up and switched his LifeWatch to a digital display. With just a hint of trepidation that things might not work as planned, he turned to the president and counted down the seconds to three a.m. – the darkest part of the summer night. He knew that if it worked delivery would be almost instantaneous.

Suddenly the island was bathed in light from end to end. Tye and the others squinted and averted their gaze. He pulled sunglasses from his sweatsuit pocket and put them on. He blinked as his eyes adapted.

The President's valet had handed out sunglasses to his party, and they brought their heads back up as their eyes adjusted to the light.

Tye picked up a solarimeter from a coffee table and checked its reading. 'That's just one at mid-power,' he said and he passed it to the president. The Russian leader read the display and nodded before passing it to the others.

Now that his eyes had become accustomed, Tye quickly scanned the horizon. He smiled. The square of light ended abruptly a few miles offshore. The focus calculations had been perfect and there seemed to be little leakage.

He then looked up at the source of the light. It had obliterated the illumination from the satellite laser beams as well as that from all the stars in the north-eastern sky.

Suddenly the light split into its component wavelengths and a brilliant vertical rainbow held Hope Island within a prism of colours. Tye heard Connie gasp at the beauty of the experience, even though she alone amongst the other observers on the terrace had been prepared for this aspect of the demonstration.

From the trees on the mountain behind them, and from the cliffs below, they heard the songs of frigate birds, sugar-birds, gulls and puffins as they woke to the false dawn.

The light integrated back to the full visible spectrum. Tye

looked at his watch again and counted down the seconds until the end of the time scheduled for his brief demonstration.

As suddenly as it had arrived, the light was gone.

The president and his party began to clap with gusto, the sound bouncing off the plate-glass windows and the Dolomite marble flooring of the terrace.

On the beach far below, Jack Hendriksen was still staring up at the sky, at the point where the light had come from.

'This place is a bloody shit-hole,' spat the uniformed sergeant in his thin, squashed Afrikaner accent as the four-wheel-drive vehicle bounced over another pothole in the battered bridge that spanned the almost dry Hunyani River. 'The worst in Africa.'

Ahead squatted a cluster of old stone buildings inside three rings of a high razor-wire fence. The sign at the entrance to the approach track identified the complex: Chikirubi Maximum Security Facility. Harare.

At the gate the guards took their passports, visas and visiting permits off to their post and examined them for fifteen minutes.

'What's the hold-up?' shouted the sergeant eventually, trying to keep the irritation out of his voice. He knew his accent and colour could provoke trigger-happiness almost instantly in Zimbabwe. He got no response.

'It's OK,' said his black passenger quietly. 'They just like the feeling of self-importance it gives them.'

'Skelms!' hissed the sergeant quietly. 'Do they want money?'

His passenger shook his head. 'That's all been done.'

After a further ten minutes one of the soldiers sauntered out of the guard post with their papers. The sergeant lowered his window again and the heat speared into the air-conditioned interior.

'Recording equipment?' asked the soldier, looking in the rear windows of the vehicle.

'We don't have any,' said the sergeant.

'Get down,' ordered the soldier, opening the door. Three other guards lounged outside the gate house, their old AK47s crooked in their arms, ready for rapid use.

The visitors stepped out onto the dried mud. The soldier patted the sergeant down first, deliberately making his hand movements hard and personal. Then he ran his fingers over the passenger.

'Block F.' The guard pointed as he handed back their papers. The electric gate slid open. The fencing, towers and floodlights were all new and looked expensive.

But Block F, like all the other buildings inside the compound, had not been new for a very long time. The sergeant led his passenger along a filth-strewn concrete corridor to the governor's office. A secretary rose instantly and walked around her desk to open the door to the inner office. She did not knock.

With a nod in her direction the sergeant entered, followed by his passenger.

The overweight governor wore civilian clothes: a tan suit with a pink, open-necked shirt, his fingers adorned with gold. He rose and shook hands with both visitors. The door closed behind them. They sat on two upright chairs in front of his large desk.

'So, Amnesty has finally decided to visit us,' the governor said slowly, twisting a gilt letter-opener between the fat, finely manicured fingers of his right hand. He spoke as if oblivious of the fact that the human rights organization had been applying to visit this prison for nearly thirty-five years. Because of repeated refusals, Amnesty had publicly declared Chikirubi to be in breach of the UN's Universal Declaration of Human Rights.

Philip-Niël Shütte nodded. 'It is *very* kind of you to allow me to visit,' he said slowly and graciously. Via an intermediary, it had taken $40,000 to the Minister of the Interior and $10,000 direct to the prison governor himself before this visit had been scheduled.

'You realize that we have not received our full budget entitlement for eight years?' queried the commander. 'We have to try to feed and house four hundred and sixty men and, well...' He gestured expansively. 'We don't know month to month if we will receive sufficient funds. The war.'

Shütte nodded. The civil war. The rebels had been fighting

back and forth across the borders with Zambia and Botswana for a decade.

'Without enough money...'

How bad can it be here? thought Shütte. He had prepared himself for the worst and the South African intelligence services had provided plenty of smuggled-out eye-witness accounts that described appalling conditions.

'I do my best...'

Shütte nodded again. He had had to agree that no criticism of either the governor or the Ministry would be made public after his visit. Normally, Amnesty International would never have agreed to such restrictions. But this wasn't a 'normal' visit and the young South African lawyer wasn't a regular Amnesty observer.

'Let's start with the juvenile section,' he suggested.

'We don't maintain separate juvenile accommodation here,' smiled the governor as he rose.

The cell was about nine metres by three and it contained between thirty and forty men and boys; a black hole full of jet-black faces. Philip-Niël Shütte stood inside the doorway with the sergeant and governor as an armed warder waited in the corridor behind them. The stench was overpowering.

Involuntarily, Shütte cupped his hand to his nose. The temperature had to be over thirty-five degrees and the drone of flies was incessant. The faces turned towards the visitors were silent, impassive.

Shütte pulled a sheet of paper from his inside jacket pocket. 'Reon Albertyn, Joseph Abednego, Marcus Mynery?' he called.

There was a movement behind him. 'Abednego and Mynery have passed away,' the governor breathed in Shütte's ear, emitting a wash of talc and a sweet-sour cologne from his body. 'That's Albertyn over there.' He pointed at a small form in the corner of the room.

The lawyer pushed his way through the men and looked down at the old white man crouched on the bench.

'Reon Albertyn?'

The aged man nodded, the skin on his swollen bald head like flaking white parchment.

'How old are you, Mr Albertyn?'

The man didn't answer. Shütte squatted so that he could look him in the eyes.

'You're not Reon Albertyn, are you?' he said quietly, indicating the sheet of paper. 'Reon Albertyn's only fourteen – and he's a native Bantu African.'

The room remained silent, and Shütte was aware that every eye was on him. He stood up and turned to the governor.

'Where's Reon Albertyn? I was assured–'

'That *is* Albertyn,' insisted the governor, pointing again. 'He's an albino, and he's got some disease that makes him seem very old. But the doctor says it's not contagious.'

Shütte turned back to the old man. 'You're only *fourteen?*' he asked.

The figure nodded, not lifting his head.

The hastily arranged meeting between the chiefs of Tye Networks and their counterparts of the Russian-based FreePlanet Networks had started testily and was now becoming distinctly bad-tempered. Nobody was ready to shoulder the blame.

'Say again, what damage reports did you get on your bird?' asked Raymond Liu. As group technical director of Tye Networks it was his responsibility to ensure that the company's satellite hubs always exchanged data transparently, both with each other and with the satellites of other networks.

Two days earlier there had been a malfunction in the low-earth-orbit satellite networks above New Zealand and Antarctica. The problem had taken a day to solve and the word was that TT had personally demanded an explanation. Certainly Liu had found no obstacle in requisitioning a jet to get to today's meeting. It had been his first ride in one of the Tye-Lear supersonics and he had ridden in the cockpit for the eighty-minute flight from Hope Island to New York.

Chomoi Ltupicho, technical director of the FreePlanet network, was the man who had insisted on a personal meeting rather than a holo-video conference – and had therefore suffered the expense of 'cleaning' and electronically shielding the hotel meeting room. He shook his head.

'I've already shown you,' said the Russian engineer in his excellent English, waving at the printouts covering the desk in the conference room. 'There isn't any damage. Once we regained control and put her back in alignment, we ran full diagnostics. Everything reports A-One, with no history of malfunction.'

'No panel or casing damage?'

'None that shows up on the sensors. We'd need a visual to be sure, of course.' Ltupicho paused. 'I know what you're driving at.'

The three other men in this small room of the Marriott Hotel on the perimeter of Newark Airport, New Jersey, stiffened as the engineer reached into his briefcase.

'Our satellite was not struck.' The Russian unfolded a piece of paper. 'The motion sensors show no impact on the casing before the roll started. Not even a microgram.' He sat back.

The room was silent. There had been no meteor shower, which they had initially presumed. But, although he did not mention it, Raymond Liu had already guessed that FreePlanet's Soyuz satellite had been undamaged. 'So what *did* happen?' he asked, with all the authority of the world's richest corporation behind him.

His counterpart hesitated and then spread his hands on the tabletop. 'Can we go off the record?'

Liu nodded and their assistants simultaneously reached for the two VideoMates that lay open on the table. Both removed their viewpers and confirmed that data capture had now ceased.

'All we know is that two of the orbit-maintenance plasma thrusters made unauthorized burns,' Ltupicho sighed. 'We sent no command, but the log we've downloaded shows that the thrusters fired for 4.768 seconds at 2.30.07 GMT on Monday. Normally those thrusters are only fired to prevent unanticipated orbit decay.'

Raymond Liu nodded in sympathy. So, it wasn't just their network that was suffering unexplained faults. This was why the Russians had wanted a personal meeting. The admission that FreePlanet's communications satellites might be open to outside interference could seriously damage their company's stock price, just as it could Tye Networks's own valuation. Liu suffered a few moments of inner debate before his engineer's frankness won out. His promotion to vice-president had been recent and he was still struggling to acquire the political evasiveness necessary to survive in board-level management.

He shuffled through a pile of papers at his elbow and pushed forward a printout. 'The same thing happened to our birds,' he admitted quietly. 'I presume you too have done the probability math?'

Ltupicho nodded.

'Our tests show that an unauthorized, spontaneous thruster burn will indeed occur once in ninety-six thousand hours – that's eleven years, give or take a few weeks,' continued Liu. 'The odds that two would fire spontaneously at precisely the same moment are thousands of times greater. I presume a Soyuz 8Zoi satellite isn't that different?'

The Russian nodded again. Soyuz aerospace technology had again become the equal of any in the world.

'And the odds on all four thrusters on two separate satellites firing spontaneously within a few seconds of each other are...?'

'Incalculable,' agreed Ltupicho.

Raymond Liu nodded and sat forward, forearms folded on top of his papers. 'Let alone the odds that it would happen to our two birds and *then* to one of yours.'

There was a quietness in the room. The assistants to the two technical directors avoided looking at each other.

Then Liu spoke again. 'You said that your Network Control Center never sent a message.'

'Nothing,' confirmed Ltupicho. He too sat forward.

'Any maintenance messages? Any other sort of messages?'

'We sent nothing,' said Ltupicho quietly.

Liu looked down at his bare forearms, as if inspecting his pale cream Asian skin for freckles. Despite his senior management position, the small Chinese-American was dressed in the engineer's traditional uniform of short-sleeved white shirt with a stainless-steel pocket protector displaying a parade of pens.

It was almost a whisper when he spoke again. 'But did your bird receive *any* message?'

The Russian sat back and interlaced his fat fingers over his prominent gut. He looked at Liu over his reading glasses. 'Did yours?'

The silence hung long enough for the sound of the air-conditioning to grow to a roar.

'They may have done,' said Liu at last. 'We simply don't know. We have to assume that might be the case.'

The Russian leaned forward again and took off his glasses. He closed his eyes and pinched the top of his nose, massaging gently. 'That's our position also,' he admitted before opening his eyes again.

Liu looked around the table. 'So, we may have an unauthorized visitor in the networks.'

He allowed a short silence for the implications to sink in. Then he looked up at the Russian.

'I don't think we want to alert the network authorities yet. Let's work together on this one.'

Jack Hendriksen woke with a start, disorientated. Then he smiled. He was in his own bedroom, back in Gramercy Park, back in Manhattan, back in the real world. And this was the start of his vacation!

Jack's loft apartment had seen better days and he had been meaning to fix it up for years. But this had been his marital home and, despite his loss, he treasured its memories. 'Rent it,' his younger brother, the businessman of the family, continually urged, reminding him that rental demand in the city was still soaring. But Jack didn't need the money and he loved getting back here two or three times a year.

He yawned and looked at his LifeWatch, but there was no display. He shook his wrist. Still nothing. He undid the security buckle and eased the watch gently up from his wrist, careful not to damage the almost invisible carbon microdermic nanotubes as they detached from his skin. He shook the device again. Strange, he thought. He had never heard of one failing before.

He laid the LifeWatch on his bedside table, face down, to protect the bioconnectors, and rubbed the stark white strap mark on his tanned forearm. His skin itched where the monitor had interfaced with his body. Well, it must be late. He rose, pulled on a white T-shirt and shorts and padded into the kitchen. The old analogue clock on the wall told him it had already gone nine. *Hell, that's what vacations are for.* He smiled to himself. He switched the kettle on and snapped open his VideoMate to scan the mail. It too was dead: he couldn't see a dial tone.

He picked the communicator up with a frown and closed it, then opened it again. It seemed to have power still, but there was no display. He reached into his jacket pocket. He had brought both his Ray Ban Electros and his Phillipe Patek clear-glass viewpers with him. On both the tiny LEDs were blinking a warning but there was no signal from the VideoMate.

The kettle snapped off as it came to the boil and Jack laid the useless communications technology on the kitchen table. He had never known a VideoMate to fail either.

He made a black coffee and then realized that all his network addresses and numbers were stored in his VideoMate or on his server. He had been planning to scour the Manhattan networks to see which of his friends were in town. A dozen times previously he had planned to organize his vacation in advance, but each time something had happened to distract him. He thought of Calypso and smiled. Then he frowned; he had also been planning to ask his friends for advice on finding a trust-worthy attorney – if that wasn't an absolute contradiction in terms.

There was an urgent, sharp knock at his door. He crossed the living room and looked up at his security screen. Its red LED was blinking, which indicated there was no signal from the cameras at the street entrance or in the hall outside. This had to be a neighbour – no one could get inside the building without passing through the security system at street level.

'Yes?' Jack called through the door.

'Jack, it's Ron. Ron Deakin.'

Jesus. After three years!

'Ron?'

'Come on, Jack, open up!'

Jack grinned and undid the bolts. The wide old door swung

open, and there stood Jack's first navy intelligence instructor, the
man who had realized that Jack had more, much more, to offer
the US government than pure SEAL machismo.

They hugged each other, the older man almost engulfed by
Jack's enthusiasm. When Jack looked up over Deakin's shoulder
he saw a bulky young black man in a dark business suit standing
some distance down the hall.

Deakin stepped back and studied his protégé. 'You're still in
shape.'

'Unlike you,' grinned Jack, prodding his friend in the
stomach.

The older man turned to his companion. 'Come inside,' he
said without waiting for an invitation.

Jack closed the door and re-bolted it.

'Jesus!' exclaimed Jack, aloud this time. 'Ron Deakin!'

Deakin smiled, waiting for Hendriksen to get over his surprise. It took only a couple of seconds.

'How did you ... how did you know I was here? I'm hardly
ever here. The entry system is out for some reason.'

Deakin held up a palm. 'Yeah, we know. Listen, Jack, we're
only going to stay a few minutes. It's our system that's doing
this: we're jamming all radio transmissions and screen displays
around this building. We're scrubbing the immediate area.'

'Who's "we" these days, Ron?' Jack shot back quickly, looking from one to the other.

Both men reached into their jackets. 'I don't expect this to
mean much to you,' said Deakin. 'That's why I came personally.
You know, because of us – you and me. This is Mike Chevannes.
He works with me.'

Jack took the wallet Deakin held out. He saw a plastic card
with a photo ID and a digital identity chip laminated into the
corner. The emblem showed the blue oak leaves and the globe
of the United Nations. The text announced the bearer to be an
Executive Officer of the United Nations International Security
Agency.

Jack looked at the other man's ID. It was almost identical.
'The UN?'

Deakin nodded. 'The National Security Agency, *our* NSA,

helped the UN set the agency up about ten years ago. It isn't widely known and it isn't meant to be.'

Jack studied the IDs again and then looked back at Deakin.

'I realize you can't verify or copy these idents with your system down,' said Deakin. 'But it's *me*, Jack. You know me.'

And it was him. Always there for Jack, even years after initial training. Every time there was an intelligence problem, whether in Iraq, Kosovo or North Korea, Ron had always been there. He had also been there just after Helen was killed.

Jack handed the badges back with a smile. 'What's going on?'

'We need your help, Jack. Can you come with us right away? We're going to a UN facility.'

Jack nodded. 'I'll get dressed. Give me time to shower and shave.'

'Pack an overnight bag, please, sir,' added Chevannes in a light Jamaican accent.

Joe Tinkler's morning had started spectacularly. The Tye Corporation had reported annual earnings of five dollars a share! That was over ten per cent higher than even Joe had forecast and every one of the bets he had made for his clients and for himself had paid off handsomely. The stocks had started roaring in Tokyo and the sound had spread westwards around the world's markets for the last eighteen hours. On the back of Tye Corp's results the whole of EUUSA was up thirteen points!

Then, around 11.30 a.m., Joe had started to worry. One of his software agents had sent back an alarm. He had configured this agent six years before and, after he had dispatched it into the global networks, it had sent him daily updates on which he based many of his decisions. But the software agent, which Joe had christened *TinklerOne*, had never before sent him an alarm.

Its alert had flashed on his wall screen and sounded an audio signal as Joe had originally planned. He opened the message and scanned the text and the charts.

It seemed that Thomas Tye was selling stock, and selling it in a very big way! The fund manager had customized this software agent from an off-the-shelf package especially to moni-

tor Tye's personal shareholdings and other investments. Joe had
spent over four months programming the agent with details of
every stock he knew Tye held. He started with Tye Corp's core
stock on EUUSA and then included every company quoted on
any of the world's major securities markets in which the Tye
Corporation or Thomas Tye himself had any shareholding. He
subsequently included the speciality companies quoted on the
smaller electronic exchanges that were dedicated to nanotech-
nology development or biotechnology start-ups. He had also
given the research agent the names of Tye's investment vehicles,
his brokers, his attorneys and his dealing codes on the individual
markets. And he updated the same agent's reference list every
time he came across a new corporate or legal identity for Tye
or any of his companies. Its reach could never be exhaustive, but
it was about as good as it was possible to be. Altogether, he had
found 2,891 companies in which Tye held stock either personally, through one of his investment vehicles, or indirectly
through a third party. The man's investments were scattered
throughout forty-one countries and appeared on eighteen different stock market indices.

Joe had even estimated Tye's likely stock disposals and had
programmed the robot accordingly. Each year, Tye sold a little
more of his core stock in Tye Corp, but as the corporation had
now split the stock two-for-one eleven times in six years, he had
suffered a manageable dilution. He also had a habit of taking
profits out of other investments that were doing well and buying
into small, unheard-of companies. Tye's intuition about stocks,
which had always been good, had become close to perfect in
the last few years and *TinklerOne*'s reports had allowed Joe to
track and shadow Tye's moves with a high degree of fidelity.

The software robot was Joe's secret weapon and although all
fund managers used a number of software monitoring tools to
watch over their portfolios, none of them (as far as Joe knew)
had refined the self-learning capabilities of a software robot to
anything like the extent Joe had with this one. His first degree
at Yale had been in computer science, before he'd done his
MBA, but Joe had always chosen to downplay his special

knowledge of information-technology systems when in the company of his bank colleagues and other Wall Street associates.

When Tye sold stock, his office usually went public within a few hours in order to offset potentially damaging speculation. The world's richest man was, himself, the most powerful economic indicator on the planet.

But this was something different. *TinklerOne* was programmed to ignore routine disposals, even up to one billion dollars in a month, but now the agent was reporting over 200 separate disposals in an hour, with a value climbing above four hundred billion dollars as Joe watched. The agent was sending back a continuous stream of data about sales, security commission filings, and a host of third-party encrypted attachments that were useless and were automatically trashed by the system as they were received.

There was nothing wrong with Tye selling stock like this, Joe reasoned. He was doing so after his results were published and there had been no unusual purchases beforehand.

Then Joe's system sounded another alarm. Joe looked up at the corner of his wall screen. This time it was another of his agents that had also never before sent an alarm. Joe opened the message. The Tye Corporation's Global Bank had issued two hundred billion in new currency and was already trading Tye-€'s at $1.10. They'd added ten per cent to their capital pool and still the value rose! It was because of the strength of those annual results.

Joe slumped in his chair and watched as his agents adjusted the graphs and figures in real-time. Tye's personal disposals had reached five hundred billion dollars. With Tye Corp's cash deposits, the currency issues and Tye's personal disposals, Thomas Tye and his corporation had raised close to one trillion dollars in cash in under an hour.

But why? Cash was weak compared to paper. Tye Corp's stock could buy anything and Tye-€'s were gaining in value. What could Thomas Tye or his company possibly need with so much hard currency?

Then Joe sat bolt upright. If this continued, every stock

related to the Tye Corporation had to collapse. Then the world's markets would stagger, and perhaps founder. His hand cleared some papers and opened a shoebox he kept at the back of his desk. He removed what he flippantly thought of as his 'panic button'. It was an old-fashioned wireless mouse that pointed towards a macro that Joe had created years before. If he clicked the button, the macro would send 'sell' orders on every Tye Corporation and Tye-related stock on the planet – and Joe's fund held more than anybody except Thomas Tye himself. Joe had never previously had to use these commands and that was why he had left it under manual control. He didn't want some speech-interpretation program to scramble an instruction and start a sell-off accidentally. The market was still holding, despite Tye's rising disposals. How long before it was noticed and other investors reacted? Joe's finger trembled on the mouse as he weighed his options.

SIX

Introduction

The world loves Thomas Richmond Tye III. His is the quintessential American success story, transferred to a global stage. He has become the world's first dollar trillionaire and, in real terms, he is many times wealthier than colossi of previous centuries such as Gates, Rockefeller, Croesus or Tiberius. There are dozens of calculators on the networks that strive to measure how much Thomas Tye earns each hour. Currently the best guess is around US$23 million.

'Tom', as he insists on being called, is also the world's first entrepreneur to gain genuine superstar status. His good looks, boyish charm, casual style, concern for the planet and legendary philanthropy have won him fans from every walk of life – from the hopeless Touchers in their ghettos of networked urban misery to the presidents of the world's great powers. He is, after all, the first business hero to emerge in our global society and he is the ultimate eligible bachelor. He is also likely to live long enough to enjoy his fabulous wealth. I can exclusively reveal that his doctors currently predict he will live to be at least 300 years old! He has been taking anti-ageing therapy for seventeen years and I provide full details of the treatment undertaken in Chapter One.

This is the twenty-third 'biography' of Thomas
Tye to be published around the world but it is not
simply another authorized hagiography, nor yet
another tabloid-style *réchauffé* of life on Hope Island
and the supposed excesses of the Tye Corporation
Techies.

Rather, it is a polemic on power; a monograph on
monopoly, a dissertation on the dangers of massive
personal wealth when it is coupled with a complete
and utter lack of accountability. Truly, no one with
almost unlimited money has ever been as powerful
and as unaccountable as is Thomas Tye. He has no
voters to please. He is subject to no laws other than
his own. He must please only his shareholders but
their interests are so narrow, so restricted, that, by
definition, his activities need to succeed in only one
dimension.

We all know the basic details of the Thomas Tye
legend and I do not intend to regurgitate once again
his unfortunate background or his remarkable rise
to power and fame. However, some aspects of his
life story have a direct bearing on his behaviour
today and the dangers it may present to humanity.

There is little doubt that Thomas Tye suffered
massive 'attachment damage' as a child. This is a
term used by psychologists when they diagnose
a patient as unable to form relationships with or
'attachments' to other people, whether those are
bonds of friendship, love or simple empathy. Frequently, the damage and resulting isolation leads to
'homelessness' in adult life (a euphemism society
often substitutes for 'lovelessness'), criminal recidi-
vism and both male and female varieties of sexual
abuse. In extreme cases, attachment damage
produces the psychopaths who pollute and mutilate
our society. (The best [or worst] examples I can
point to are the Romanian Rapists, that terrifying
pan-European epidemic of middle-aged, orphanage-

reared monsters that was created by a dictator's total ban on contraception and abortion almost fifty years ago.)

Although he was born into a wealthy Bostonian banking family, Tye's clinically depressive mother committed suicide when he was five years old and this event cast a shadow that has seemingly fallen across his entire life. This piece of misfortune was only compounded by his father's chronic alcoholism that killed him, a few months after his wife's death, in a road accident that was almost certainly drink-related.

Few details are available about Tye's unhappy childhood – the family closed ranks and used its money to ensure silence about his parents' many failures – but we have all wondered about the impact of his internment in an exclusive psychiatric clinic immediately prior to his parents' deaths.

This period appears to have had an immense impact on Tye and, as I will argue in Chapter Eleven, it probably accounts for the astounding lack of ethics that marked his early years in business and his apparent lack of personal empathy with those around him. We have recently watched the spectacle of a string of former business partners and disgruntled ex-employees from Tye's early business dealings giving testimony on American talk shows about their invariably abrupt and ruthless treatment at the hands of the lonely young genius.

Tye's experiences in early childhood may also be responsible for the fact that no one has ever claimed to have had a sexual or intimate relationship with him. I will be adding more detail to his childhood biography in Chapter Four.

As some readers may know, this book almost didn't make it to publication. The attorneys for the Tye Corporation won seventeen injunctions in fourteen territories to ban this work from the shelves

and the networks, and it is to the credit of my
publishers and the world's legal systems that you
are now reading these words in print or from a
download.

The reason Tye and his corporation want to ban
this book is that I make a number of serious allegations about Tye's activities and those of his companies and I will provide proof of my assertions. I
have called this book *Why Thomas Tye Must Be
Stopped* because I think the governments of the
world must act now to prevent the very nature of
humanity being patented and subsumed into a commercial, for-profit corporation.

Haley pushed her chair back from the keyboard and took
off her glasses. '...*Almost didn't make it to publication.*' Quite. And
it still looked as if she might never see her words published. She
could always self-publish on the networks, of course, but hers
was a linear argument, so it belonged on paper or as a commer-
cially published electronic book. And self-publishing would also
rob her work of the imprimatur of a major publishing house
and, considering the allegations she made, that kind of credibility
would be vital. It would also lay her personally wide open to the
legal attacks that, she judged, would inevitably follow.

Haley wasn't wholly sure what she wanted to achieve with
this book. It had started out as a complaint about unfettered
technology. But, as she had learned more about Tye's interests
in biotechnology, the astonishing experiments already under
way, and the breathtaking hypocrisy of his publicly espoused
green politics, her 'biography' was turning into a simple plea for
the world to pay greater attention to the growth and global
ascendancy of unaccountable corporate power.

But she must somehow press on. Rosemary said Nautilus
didn't want their first advance payment back, and the new input
she was hoping to get from Jack Hendriksen should help her
agent attract another publisher. But why hadn't she heard from
him? It was over a week since he had promised to get in touch
with her again. Perhaps he too had got cold feet.

She stretched, put her glasses back on and pulled herself back to the keyboard, her triptych of screens and her text. How many times had she rewritten this intro? She had lost count and each time a day or two's reflection had led her to brand it too hysterical, too emotional or too dry. She was trying to find the middle ground.

'. . . many times wealthier than colossi of previous centuries such as Gates, Rockefeller, Croesus or Tiberius.'

Not 'colossi', a clumsy plural for an opening paragraph.

'. . . many times wealthier than the commercial or industrial giants of previous centuries such as . . .'

Better.

'Rather, it is a polemic on power; a monograph on monopoly, a dissertation on the dangers . . .'

The author frowned and launched her thesaurus program. She sorted the adjectives alphabetically and selected the words that best suited her mood.

And a bloody battological abomination of assonantal alliteration from a pretentious prestidigitator, she wrote tartly, mock-sesquipedalian in her self-disgust: perhaps it was the legacy of Greek blood in her veins, or might it be the Irish? She cut the entire paragraph.

She sighed, pushed back from the keyboard again, and went to find a nail file. She was typing so much that her fingernails had become a biological tariff of her frustration with the project: they were growing at an almost alarming rate.

Jack Hendriksen knew he must still be somewhere inside the United Nations complex beside the East River, but even he had completely lost his bearings.

Despite Gramercy Park's status as a twenty-four-hour car-free zone a black limo with a diplomatic plate had been waiting for them at the kerb outside the brownstone. Jack noticed the 'All-Zone' windshield digital ID – just like for the cops and the emergency services.

Chevannes had stowed Jack's bag in the trunk and gone up front to ride with the driver. Deakin and Jack rode in the back. As they turned north on Third Avenue, Jack's VideoMate and viewers had returned to life, a low tone alerting him to waiting messages. At Deakin's request, he switched the system off completely.

'Better if you don't supply your whereabouts, Jack. Erase the location buffer immediately you switch it back on.'

During the fast drive uptown the older man had gently deflected Jack's questions about the purpose of their trip, saying that everything would be explained when they arrived. Instead, the two men used the time to catch up with the news on mutual friends, former colleagues, family and acquaintances. They soon worked out that it must have been over three years since they had last met. At Helen's funeral.

On their arrival at UN Plaza, the UNISA idents had prompted a young major in the black uniform of the German army to escort them away from the public security checks and scanners and lead them through a private entrance. A turbaned Gurkha at the door came to attention as they entered.

They had descended three escalators and been led through a maze of brightly lit corridors until they came to another security point. Here Deakin and Chevannes allowed their IDs to be copied even though they were obviously known to the guards. Jack guessed this procedure was for the benefit of the database records and the security cameras.

'Will you leave all comms and storage here, please, Jack?' said Deakin, as he and Chevannes handed their communicators and viewpers to the guards. The group waited while Jack unclipped the VideoMate and fished his viewpers case from his inside pocket. He had pulled on a sports jacket over his open-necked shirt and he checked to ensure that he hadn't left lapel cameras in place. Confident he was clean, he placed the equipment in the tray provided and stepped through the scanner.

The guard handed Jack an electronic badge and they were waved on. At the end of the corridor was a plain white door, beside which Jack noticed an iris scanner. Deakin halted to allow his eyes to be scanned, and the door slid open. As they stepped through, Jack saw that the thick door had a sandwich filling of lead running through it.

The conference room was large and high-ceilinged, the central space occupied by a table capable of seating thirty or forty. Beyond it was a large Holo-Theater and an older wraparound videoconference system. They were alone in the room – Chevannes and the armed German major had remained outside.

Jack whistled. 'I had no idea the UN complex was so large,' he said, turning to his one-time instructor.

'It extends over thirty-eight acres – we're right under the river here,' grinned his friend. 'The Midtown Tunnel lies on the other side of that wall, Jack. The UN faced a tough choice about ten years ago: either relocate, or expand underground. This is what they chose.'

Jack turned and saw a giant electronic world map on the wall. He ran his eyes over the clusters of illuminated red dots scattered through Africa, Eastern Europe, the Middle East and Asia.

'That's everywhere UN troops are involved currently,' explained Deakin. 'The Security Council meets privately in this room. They like to keep track of how many peacekeeping actions are going on.'

Jack smiled grimly. There had to be at least a hundred lights. 'Our peaceful century,' he observed.

Deakin snorted.

The main door slid open and four men and one woman entered. All were in business suits; all but one carried briefcases. Jack recognized the first face: it was very famous and very distinguished and it belonged to the one individual without a case. His black visage was framed by a huge crop of curly white hair that seemed even more unruly than on television. Jack thought he also knew the swarthy face of the short, podgy white man at his shoulder. The others were unknown to him. Behind them Jack saw Chevannes and the German officer resume their positions as the door closed silently.

The small group walked into the centre of the room to greet their visitor.

'Commander Hendriksen?' said the Secretary-General of the United Nations. 'I'm Alexander Dibelius.'

'Well, I'm retired from the Navy now sir,' said Jack as he shook a large powerful hand. He had to tilt his head up slightly to look into the Secretary-General's warm dark eyes.

'This is Doctor Yoav Chelouche, President of the World Bank.'

Of course. The 'economic genius', they called him. The man who had finally managed to soften the gyrations of the global economy, and who had been awarded a Nobel Economics Prize for his efforts, a new form of quasi-scientific award created specifically to mark his achievements.

The banker's hand was dry, its pressure brief. His lugubrious brown eyes and heavy jowls reminded Jack of a basset hound's face.

Dibelius turned to introduce the other three.

'Professor Rima Berzin, Director of Science at the World Health Organization.' She was about fifty, attractive, though she did little to emphasize her looks. She smiled briefly as they shook hands.

'Doctor Alan Mathison, Cambridge University.' Jack shook hands with the tall, pallid academic and Dibelius turned to the last man.

'And Jan Amethier, director of UNISA.' He pronounced the acronym 'eu-nese-a.'

'Thank you for coming to see us, Mr Hendriksen,' said Amethier. The accent was Dutch, or perhaps Belgian. Dutch, Jack decided.

'I'm intrigued to know why I'm here.'

'Let's sit down,' said the Secretary-General, leading the way to the conference table. He chose a place a short distance from the head and gestured for Amethier to take the chair. 'It's your show, Jan,' he said.

Deakin indicated for Jack to sit opposite Dibelius and then pulled out a chair and sat beside him. Jack noticed that the place sign in front of him read *Australian Republic.*

'Mr Hendriksen, welcome to the United Nations,' began the Secretary General. 'You probably bypassed our informal immigration procedures, but you realize you're no longer on American soil?'

Jack nodded, although the thought hadn't really occurred to him.

'This is United Nations territory, so it belongs to all of our two hundred and twelve member nations, not to any one country. Neither the US government, nor any other, has any independent legal rights here. We possess similar territories inside many of our member states and globally we are considered a sovereign power, you understand?'

Jack nodded again. He had already noticed the big 'Duty Free' signs hanging over a large International Bazaar in the atrium upstairs, but he doubted whether this man ever concerned himself with discount retail opportunities.

'Now, I presume that during your years with the US Navy and the Government you would have signed US National Secrecy Regulations?' said Dibelius.

'Yes sir.'

'Well, as you know, that remains in force throughout your life but, unfortunately, it concerns only US confidentiality and the US constitution limits the government's powers of enforcement.'

Jack nodded again, his mind racing as he tried to guess what all this was about.

'The United Nations is not restrained in such a way and we have a document that is fully enforceable, it's closer to the Official Secrets Act used by the British. It's called the International Security, Diplomatic and Military Confidentiality Undertaking and it is drawn up under the international jurisdiction of The Court of the Hague. Would you be willing to sign it?'

Jack hesitated, unsure of his response.

'We need your help,' added Dibelius quietly. 'The trouble is that we can't even tell you in what way without your signing it. The information we have will compromise you.'

'This is about Thomas Tye, isn't it?'

For a moment he thought he saw acknowledgement in Dibelius' eyes. But then the Secretary General turned to Amethier and held out his hand. The director of UNISA handed him a printed document.

'Please read it, if you wish,' said Dibelius, as he slid it across the table to Jack. 'This may well conflict with undertakings you have given to the Tye Corporation. Technically, it even overrides your loyalty to your own country. From this point on, your oath of allegiance will be to the United Nations.'

'You mean I give up being an American?' asked Jack, surprised.

'You can keep your US passport, Commander, but your first loyalty will be to the United Nations. You will also have a right to a UN Diplomatic Passport should you ever need it. A UN passport is a very special thing: it guarantees a holder entry, domicile and work rights in all member nations.'

Jack let out a low whistle, sat forward and picked up the document.

'It's a standard form, but it is globally binding and will supersede all other legal commitments you have made,' continued the Secretary General. 'Unauthorised use of UN information acquired after you have signed that form will be an offence under The Hague's international military jurisdiction. The maximum sentence for an offence is life imprisonment. We call that part the Silence Resolution.'

Jack turned the form over in his hands. He read the first few lines, then skipped through the four pages, scanning the paragraph headings. He flipped it over so the back page was uppermost, took a pen from beside the deskpad and signed it. He passed it to Deakin.

'He was my best man,' smiled Jack. 'He can act as my witness again.'

Deakin nodded then added his signature and the date.

'It is about Thomas Tye, isn't it?' he asked again.

'Welcome to global citizenship, Commander,' said Dibelius. He smiled and turned to Amethier. 'Jan?'

The UNISA director retrieved the document from Deakin, placed it in his briefcase and watched as the electronic catches shut on recognition of his thumb prints. He lifted the case from the table and placed it beside him on the floor.

'Yes, it's about Mr Tye,' he confirmed in his careful, lilting English. 'We know you are already concerned at some of his activities.' He touched a button on a small black box of controls in front of him and waited as a flat screen rose from a housing at the far end of the table. He pressed another button.

Jack saw an image of himself sitting on a sofa, he couldn't place where. Then Haley Voss came into the shot as she leant forward to pick up her mug from the coffee table and Jack heard himself start to speak.

'I know one of the authors named on the cover. He's a geneticist – on the island. I might be able to check whether he really did write this.'

Amethier hit a button and the replay stopped.

'We don't need to watch the rest of that conversation,' he said. 'We know Mr Tye intends to live forever.'

Jack turned back to his old friend with an eyebrow raised. 'You've had me under surveillance?'

'No, not you Jack,' corrected Deakin. 'Haley Voss – for about eight months. She was sending her sister a video feed of her meeting with you.'

'But why? What has she got to do . . .?'

Amethier held up his hand. 'We'll explain why in a moment, Commander Hendriksen,' forstalled the director, also choosing to address the visitor by his former rank. 'The important thing is that you already seem to be concerned about Mr Tye's behaviour. Frankly, so are we – very, very concerned. And not just by that report Miss Voss showed you.'

The Secretary General leaned into the table assuming control again. 'How much do you actually know about the United Nations, Commander?'

It seemed as though they were determined to militarize this meeting.

'Not a lot, I guess. Only what I read. It seems the UN has been doing a pretty useful job of ironing out the knots here and there.' He gazed up at the world map smeared with its clusters of war zones.

'We're really quite different from our public image,' explained Dibelius. 'You'll be familiar with our peace-keeping activities, our refugee efforts and so on. What you may not know is that the World Bank, the International Monetary Fund, the World Trade Organization, the World Health Organization and the International Space Agency are all UN bodies – part of our executive, if you like. Since we expanded the Permanent Membership of the Security Council to include all major economic powers, since we adopted majority decision making and abandoned the veto, and since we finally managed to persuade the US to pay its full dues, the UN has become the closest thing the world has to a global government. That was, of course, the dream of visionaries like H. G. Wells who laid out the blueprint for a world state – and it was the original goal of our founders nearly seventy years ago.'

He smiled and held up his hand. 'Oh, you won't hear people talking like that, of course. National pride, especially within member states such as the United States, France and China, prevents them acknowledging that fully, at least in public. After all, the biggest nations spent over half a century working to ensure that we didn't fulfil the aims of those who brought us into being – none of the superpowers could really hope to lead the world, but they weren't prepared to let us do it either. Thankfully, those days are past. In the last ten years, we've had the power, the money and, most importantly, the mandate, to try and deal with issues that are supranational in character.'

The Secretary-General's mellisonant tones held Jack and the

others riveted. It was a party trick, Jack realized. A master politician's magic. The power of charisma.

Dibelius gestured towards Chelouche. 'Doctor Chelouche's team at the World Bank is a good example, Commander. Since the dollar and the euro stabilized as the world's reserve currencies, the bank has done a superb job in softening the gyrations of the smaller currencies and we're finally getting IMF money – in fact, the world's money – into places where it can really help the emerging nations.'

Jack nodded, although he wasn't sure why they were telling him all this.

'I don't suppose Exec Deakin has told you much about the role of UNISA?'

Jack shook his head. 'Not really, Mr Secretary.'

'No? Well, that was before you signed the Silence Resolution. I'm going to hand back to Director Amethier in a moment and he can give you an outline of the agency's function. But before I do so, I want you to know that, with the exception of the representatives of a few member states, the members of the World Trade Standing Sub-Committee and the International Security Standing Sub-Committee have been informed that this meeting with you was due to take place. They also know the substance of the information that will be imparted. What you are about to hear is of the *utmost* importance to the future of the world's peoples.' The Secretary-General's eyebrows lifted, questioning whether Jack had fully understood.

Jesus! What could matter so much that UN members would be informed of this meeting? It had to concern the Phoebus Project, the development that had first made Jack consider approaching his old Washington contacts.

He nodded and realized his throat was dry. Abruptly, the Secretary-General stood up and Jack found himself rising along with the others at the table.

'I hope to see you again, Commander Hendriksen,' smiled the Secretary-General leaning forward and extending an arm across the table. Jack rose and shook the large hand again. Then Dibelius turned and left the room.

'Right, let's get on,' said Amethier as they resumed their seats.

'Could I get some water?' asked Jack.

Chapter 1

When he was thirty-two, Thomas Tye personally invested four hundred and thirty million dollars in Erasmus Inc., a start-up corporation that had been spun out of the genomics department at the Johns Hopkins Research Center in Baltimore. The company had filed a patent application identifying a string of genes that, it claimed, were the principle cause of a condition known as progeria. This disease affects only one in 240,000 people, but its effects are horrific, with the most prominent visible symptom being premature ageing. A sufferer as young as twenty-five can appear to be in advanced old age and early death is inevitable. In adults, progeria is called Werner's Syndrome and most adult sufferers contract the disease in their early twenties and die before the age of forty.

Erasmus's discovery promised the first effective treatment for Werner's Syndrome but, seventeen years later, no therapy based on this gene string has yet reached the market. Twelve years ago, Erasmus Inc. and its thirty-six genetic researchers relocated to the Tye Corporation's science park on Hope Island and thus escaped the routine progress filings required of biotech companies under American FDA regulations. The company also closed its articles of incorporation in the state of Delaware and became a closed company within Hope Island State. For over a decade, therefore, the world has remained ignorant of progress towards a treatment for this horrendous condition.

But a treatment *was* developed a few months

after the original patent filing, though it had nothing to do with Werner's Syndrome, which is best described as an 'orphan disease' – where there is no incentive to develop treatments because there are not enough sufferers to generate profits. The genes that produce the startlingly premature ageing symptoms of progeria are also responsible for controlling most, but not all, of the human ageing process. Erasmus Inc. identified the remaining age-control genes, in particular those that govern the sclerosis of the central nervous system. So they learned how to switch off the ageing process, or delay it almost indefinitely.

After a series of trials, the first human 'patient' to undergo such long-term treatment, and the resultant therapy, was Thomas Richmond Tye III himself.

Chronologically, Tye will be fifty years old at his next birthday. Physically he is still thirty-four. Every three months the researchers at Erasmus take cell and tissue samples from his body and submit them to detailed analysis to detect signs of ageing. Their confidential internal report (see the full report at this book's network resource) reveals that there has been almost no change in Tye's basic cell structure for seventeen years. It explains how the normal release of the toxic oxidative by-products of metabolism (known as free radicals) that damage human DNA is halted. The report also reveals that twenty-two of Erasmus's scientific staff have since joined Tye in the experiment.

The printed evidence had arrived in Haley's letter box two months earlier. It had been posted in Amsterdam but did not carry a sender's name. At first, Haley had had trouble even understanding what it was all about. But the appearance of Thomas Tye's name in the opening paragraph had made her persevere and finally, with the help of medical, genetics and biotechnology dictionaries and glossaries on the networks, she had managed to decipher the gist.

Her first conclusion was that the document had to be a hoax. At that stage the story about her book and the large advance Nautilus had paid for the US rights had only recently appeared in the publishing press and Haley guessed that someone with a grudge against Tye or one of his companies was trying to feed her highly inflammatory material. Or perhaps it was the Tye Corporation's own people trying to trip her up?

Then she found reasons to reconsider. She recalled that a cousin was sharing his Islington flat with a researcher who worked at one of the Wellcome-Parke laboratories in East Finchley, north London. A quick call to cousin Maurice had led to a conversation with his flatmate and a subsequent meeting in a brutally bright Bloomsbury bar that catered for students at nearby London University. While Haley waited for him to arrive, she thought about security and patched herself into Felicity's system in Ladbroke Grove. She and her impending contact had agreed to swap locator codes for the evening so as to avoid rendezvous mishaps, and the twins watched as Haley's VideoMate displayed his slow progress along Gower Street.

There! The lost-looking man in the entrance had to be him. Haley crossed the floor.

'Doctor Evans?'

He was short and bearded, with a thick red facial growth compensating for a hair-line that had already receded to his crown.

'Maurice tells me you're a writer?' He smiled as he took her hand. He had a very broad Welsh accent, as if he'd not long been in London.

Haley bought the drinks and thanked the geneticist for meeting her. They found a quiet corner and, after a few exchanges about the bar's noisy young patrons, she handed over the document that had been posted to her.

Fifteen minutes later, her new acquaintance laid it down.

'Where did you get this?' he asked, his eyes accusatory.

Haley explained how it had arrived, then asked if he thought it might be a hoax.

'If it is, it's a bloody good one and they're using the name of one of the world's leading genetic engineers,' Evans mused. 'It

claims it's by Professor Eli Kramer. He's really a biogerontolo-
gist, you know, studying the biological causes of ageing. There's
only half a dozen people who know as much in this field as he
does.'

Haley begged him to keep quiet about the document, until
her book was published. He bought her another drink and
flipped through parts of the report again. Then he smiled
and asked if he could buy her dinner 'somewhere quieter'.

'Go for it!' Felicity had urged in her ear.

Jack sipped the mineral water Deakin had called for. The others
at the table had followed his lead, and all now had glasses in
front of them as the door closed behind the catering assistant.

Amethier put his water down. 'Commander Hendriksen...'

'Jack, please. I'm no longer attached to the Service.'

'OK, Jack, UNISA is the sort of agency the National Security
Agency always wanted to be but couldn't quite manage to
become. We're not answerable to any type of congress or
parliament, we answer to the Secretary-General and the Security
Sub-Committee alone. We employ eleven thousand people,
located in almost every nation across the globe. We work closely
but quietly with the NSA, the CIA, the FBI, Interpol, FSB,
Mossad and every other intelligence service in the world. We're
information-led in approach, closer to the American National
Security Agency than to any of the "dirty-tricks brigades", as the
Brits put it. We're non-combatant, so we rarely get involved in
physical action ourselves. When something of that nature needs
to be done, covert UN or NATO forces usually do it for us.'

Jack nodded, surprised that during his years of service with
the US government he had never heard of this agency. But then
he realized that he had not heard of dedicated covert forces
within the UN or NATO either. Perhaps the American intelligence agencies were not as omnipresent as they liked to think –
or, at least, not in UN circles.

'Ron Deakin's been on the Tye case for three years now. In
fact, it was he who suggested your name to Bob Grant, the man
who hired you into the Tye Corporation in the first place.'

Jack shot a look at his friend.

'It was the first thing I did when I took the case on,' acknowledged Deakin with a smile. 'I wasn't sure what I was getting you into at the time, but you've done very well by it, haven't you? Now you're in a position to return the favour.'

'So, what do you want from me?' asked Jack, mystified.

Deakin picked up the thread from his boss. 'The Tye Corporation has grown too big, too powerful, Jack. There comes a time in this world when however much presidents and prime ministers like to schmooze with trillionaires, they get worried about their power and influence. Eight years ago the former United States president put the CIA on to the case, to examine just how dangerous the Tye Corporation could become, and he didn't like the report that resulted. It suggested Tye would end up calling all the shots. And, in the end, if somebody gets too big, things get *political.*' He stressed the last word as though it was distasteful.

'That's not wholly fair, Ron.' Amethier rebuked him lightly. 'Some very legitimate causes for concern have now surfaced, as you'll know better than anybody.'

He turned to Chelouche. 'Would you mind, Doctor?'

The banker's head was bowed and his hands were cupped around his water glass. He looked up sharply at Jack with sad eyes that seemed almost opaque, as if a veil had been drawn across them to hide their secrets.

'Do you know anything of economics, Mr Hendriksen?'

'*Nothing* would be an over-generous description.'

'The Tye Corporation is getting so powerful we think it risks destabilizing the world's economy,' the banker said carefully in the same Israeli-accented gravel tones that Jack had heard so often on the news broadcasts. 'I first raised the subject four or five years ago. We therefore did a study – created a scenario – and even then we found that if the Tye Corporation suffered just a couple of bad quarterly financial results, the whole world's economic growth might actually turn negative. Investors would panic, millions of little traders would get hurt and the international markets would crash.'

The 'basset hound' sucked in his fat left cheek as he searched for the right words.

'I concluded that it could lead to a major world recession,' he explained. 'But it appears my worries were ill founded at the time or, at least, I was worrying about the wrong thing. Far from failing, the Tye Corporation is now four times the size it was then. The largest corporation the world has ever seen. Its annual revenue is greater than Germany's GDP...'

He shrugged. 'Who has control over it? Not the World Bank – not any central bank, not any government. Exec Deakin is right: this has become political. My member states are uncomfortable with the current situation – the principle of laissez-faire is OK only when granted, not when appropriated. In the old days we could apply national anti-trust laws. We could fine, supervise or break up corporations when they became too big, too monopolistic, too wealthy or too powerful. Now that they're global, we can't do that, except in trifling ways in individual territories. There's no such concept as antitrust regulations or anti-monopoly legislation in international law. The Tye Corporation is a rapacious, unprincipled, monopolistic, money vacuum. And with the new information Exec Deakin has shared with us...' Chelouche shrugged and began to study his fingers.

Jack was puzzled. These ideas weren't new to him. Many of the news magazines had run pieces on the same lines over the last few years, and he had been present numerous times when Thomas Tye addressed such public concerns on TV and on the platforms.

'Always remember we're a *public* corporation,' TT would proclaim in his best shareholderese. 'All we ask is the freedom to be creative, to innovate, to bring really great new products and services to the world at large. Our shareholders are like voters: if we get things wrong, they'll vote via their stock portfolios.'

And so far, it seemed, Tye had done nothing to upset his elite body politic.

Amethier took his cue from the banker's lapse into silence. 'There's something else, Jack, one of the main reasons we've dragged you here – the new information Doctor Chelouche refers to. Look at this.'

The Director of UNISA again pressed the button on his

control panel. Jack looked up at the screen and saw a standard form with the heading *World Patent Organization.*

'This is a patent filing, Jack. It's from Bioneme Research, a subsidiary of the Tye Corporation. Don't bother to read it all. The point is that there is a very, very unusual error in this document. The object of the patent is to secure the rights to a therapy produced from a string of genes, a treatment that controls human hormone production, specifically progesterone, oestrogen and testosterone.'

Amethier turned to the World Health Organization scientist who had moved along the table to take the place vacated by the Secretary-General. 'Professor Berzin, would you like to explain?'

She bowed her greying head slightly. 'According to that patent filing these hormones govern how humans smell. They create our individual body chemistry, Mr Hendriksen.' She spoke with a faint East European accent and Jack guessed she was from Poland. 'As you may know, it is now widely understood that pheromonal attraction is by far the most important component of sexual desire. To a large extent we choose our mates by how pleasing their smell is and by how different their genetic mix is from our own – we analyse this unconsciously from the body's olfactory signature.

'Progesterone, oestrogen and, to a lesser extent, testosterone are circulating prohormone steroids and they control how receptive myometrial cells are to oxytocyn, the hormone that's made in the brain and governs the body's olfactory chemistry. If this string of genes can be modified and brought under control, a man or woman would be able to use a ScentSampler to analyse a desired partner's chemistry and then construct a pheromone mix that was sufficiently similar but genetically different to enhance their chances of seduction. And, as this patent suggests, the effect would be very powerful.'

She paused and looked with a slight frown at the pen she held between her hands. 'A therapy for these genes, say an oral DNA vaccine, would be like manufacturing a love potion naturally, inside the body.'

'It's got blockbuster drugs written all over it,' interjected Deakin.

Jack smiled. He had heard Tye and his associates discussing many other such blockbusters. So many drugs and treatments seemed to be dubbed 'miracles' these days, he wondered why this particular one had caught their attention.

'The point is, the genes mentioned in this patent filing don't actually exist,' explained the professor. 'Or rather, they do exist in the genome, but the ones identified in this patent are silent, inactive. They're incapable of affecting hormone or pheromone production or any other function of human physiology. They belong to the ninety per cent of gene strings that don't seem to have a specific purpose, the non-coding or junk DNA.'

'So, Bioneme's researchers have screwed up?' queried Jack, looking at the banker. 'Is this serious enough to cause a global financial problem?'

'Just a minute, Commander,' broke in Amethier. 'Take a look at this.' He pressed the control-panel button again, and this time Jack saw a page headed *Highly Confidential Memo*. From the logo he could see that it was an internal document of the Pfizer-LaRoche pharmaceutical company.

Amethier highlighted a line near the top of the page. 'This memo was written four months before Bioneme filed their patent application,' he explained. 'But it wasn't written by anyone inside Pfizer-LaRoche. It was written here, by UNISA, and Ron led the project.'

Deakin grimaced and turned to his former pupil. 'We *made up* that damn thing, Jack, with the help of some of Professor Berzin's researchers.' He looked to the WHO iatrochemist for confirmation.

'It was the work of some very clever osphresiologists and hormonologists in my research group,' she nodded. 'I asked them to imagine their ultimate wonder drug. At Exec Deakin's suggestion I asked them to identify deliberately a sequence of silent genes that we know don't do anything in human physiology. Then they wrote an explanation of how an oral therapy might be delivered once a patent was filed and testing could begin.'

Deakin smiled and resumed the story. 'Now listen, Jack: when it was finished we scrambled the document, using the highest level of encryption we've got – string lengths above a hundred megabits, Pentagon standard – and e-mailed it from the Swiss offices of Pfizer-LaRoche to their offices here in Vermont. The company was happy to help, though they didn't know what we were doing. It was just another encrypted e-mail that came into their server, only they didn't have the private key to open it. *Nobody* did, Jack. In fact, nobody does to this day, not even anybody else in this room. I myself ran the software to create the encryption keys, and I destroyed the original memo and removed every trace from the system.'

Deakin slipped a data-storage card out of his shirt pocket. 'This is the only copy of the key that exists in the world, and I have never used it since I originally scrambled that memo.' He sat back to see if his friend would see the implications.

Like everybody, Jack understood that super-strong encryption was considered unbreakable. Unlike everybody, his training as a field intelligence officer had provided him with an understanding of the maths behind it. He knew that even if every scrap of computer power on the planet was connected and run as the largest parallel processing computer ever imagined, the amount of time required to discover the set of high prime numbers developed for one encryption key of such length would run into tens of thousands of years.

'You're saying Bioneme got hold of a plain-text copy of that memo?' he asked incredulously.

'There were no copies made, Jack – plain-text or otherwise. Professor Berzin's team worked solely in my office and they took nothing away. After I sent the e-mail from Switzerland I destroyed my original plain-text file and electronically scrubbed the storage media. The only copy that exists is the encrypted document I e-mailed to Vermont.'

'And that encryption is unbreakable,' confirmed Jack.

Deakin turned to the British mathematician who had been silent throughout the meeting. 'Your turn, Doctor Mathison,' he said.

SEVEN

Theresa Keane walked to the centre of the stage and turned to face her audience. Every seat in the lecture theatre was taken. They were also sitting in the aisles and standing at the back. Even the floor space intended for wheelchairs in front of the low stage was filled with the upturned eager faces of people who sat hunched and cross-legged on the carpet. Volunteer stewards who were supposed to keep the fire exits clear had given up this hopeless task, and now stood facing the stage while knots of latecomers tried to squeeze in behind them through the doorways. All over the campus hundreds more would be watching the video stream.

The buzz had started in the Hope Island networks even before a formal announcement was made. Professor Theresa Keane, the Tye Corporation's Nobel Laureate of computer science, was going to give what she billed as a 'Summer Lecture', her first public performance since becoming Director of Hope Island University's School of Virtuality the year before.

Every 'student' on the campus of Hope Island University was actually postgraduate and many had already achieved their doctorates. A few had arrived as associate professors. Each year, the Tye Corporation's team of human-resource scouts roamed the world's greatest universities, seeking out the brightest and the best to make them offers they found hard to resist. It didn't take much to seduce young computer scientists, geneticists, astrobiologists, evolutionary psychologists, cognitive scientists, physicists, chemists and mathematicians into spending a few years in the semi-tropical climate of a Caribbean island, studying with some of the world's best brains and – even more unusual in academia – being paid handsomely to do so. Nobody claimed that Hope University offered a wide range of academic opportunities, but in the fields of the life sciences, computing and communications it was the equal of any institution in the world. Its patent record was unrivalled.

Keane's reputation preceded her. It wasn't just her Nobel Prize. The gossip addicts of the networks insisted that she was regarded as the most gifted lecturer MIT ever had: even better than the great Feynman, some said. At her former university the students had dropped everything when they heard she was giving a lecture and, the word was, she never needed notes, she never waffled and she always captivated her audiences.

She smiled, pleased at the turnout. 'Good afternoon. Thank you for coming. Let's keep the house lights up for the moment.'

She walked to the front of the low stage and paused, looking down at the press of young researchers at her feet.

'May I?'

Those who were sitting cross-legged on the floor at the front of the pit area had to shuffle backwards on their buttocks to make room. The professor stepped down to stand amongst them, elegant in a beautifully cut olive-green trouser suit and white blouse. She smiled and lifted her arms as if about to conduct an orchestra. Every individual in the room felt contact. As one, the audience seemed to lean inwards.

'This glorious planet, our home, is between four and five billion years old,' she began, her soft Irish lilt lending natural melody to her words. 'About four million years ago our distant ancestors started to lean back on their hind legs and, step by step, they began to walk in what anthropologists now call plantigrade fashion. Thus began the final part of the evolutionary process that was to lead to human beings.'

She had stooped to match her action to her words and now she slowly rose again to her full height and shielded her eyes with her hand, as if protecting them from the sun.

'In this fully upright posture, *Homo erectus* tilted his head back in order to see into the distance, over the tall savannah grasses of Africa's Rift Valley – that's in today's Ethiopia, Somalia and

Kenya. This step hastened the development of vision, which has become our supreme sense. Over the countless generations that followed, gravity caused our skull to elongate, our brain started to expand in this new space and our larynx fell to the bottom of our throat.'

The professor pressed her hand to her throat and looked around at her audience. 'Here it found room to enlarge, to grow a nervous system and become mobile. The range of sounds that it could produce expanded dramatically and thus, through language, we stumbled upon our most important ability...'

She paused for effect.

'... *The interconnection of one single intelligence with many others.*

'It was language that provided the feedback loop that sent the human brain on its runaway evolutionary progression towards the emergence of consciousness or, as I prefer, coeaesthesis or self-awareness – the general sense of existence, of immanence, that arises from the sum of bodily impressions and mental observations, the vital sense. It was language – spoken, unspoken, written, symbolic and conceptual – that was the trigger to this fantastic, accidental creation: humanity's individual and collective virtuality.'

She had them. She smiled around the hall and held their gazes. 'Language, and the virtuality of which it is the prime representative, was so successful as a random evolutionary excursion that, in under four million years, it achieved for the genus *homo* a breakthrough and a developmental spurt that had not occurred in the nearly two hundred million years during which fish, mammals and dinosaurs had rule of this solitary, lucky and almost unbelievably fecund planet.'

Her listeners were absolutely silent.

'Language is the essence of humanity and it was the first external symbol, simulation, representation or *virtual* element to appear in what had been, up to that point, a totally physical world. This uniquely human form of shared consciousness began the moment humanity named itself.'

The professor leaned towards a bespectacled young man at her feet and held out her hand. 'I am Theresa, you are...?'

'R-Robert,' he replied, with a hint of a stammer.

'Good afternoon, Robert.' She smiled at him and turned back to her audience.

'We named each other and the objects in our world with abstract but mutually agreed sounds that can be taught to others in a group network. Language created humanity's past and the present and gave it some tools with which to imagine the future – all based on virtuality, which for so long has been misunderstood by those imbuded with it and erroneously expressed as spirituality or soul. We are not clever *animals*, ladies and gentlemen; we are primarily identities of virtuality trapped, for the moment, within physical biological containers or, as I prefer to call them, constrainers. This is our psychogenesis.'

The professor was into her stride. She explained that the Neolithic cave paintings were humanity's first recorded form of virtual expression. She underlined how it was the agricultural revolution alone that had produced the wealth, and thus the time, that allowed humans to invent the concepts of writing and money, two of the most powerful forms of virtual information storage. And she urged them to accept the concept of digital representation, virtual existence, as a logical destination for the human species.

'Our migration into the digital networks around this planet is a natural extension of human virtuality,' she explained. 'By definition, humans are virtual creatures and we are at our most powerful when our habitat is also virtual.'

None of this was new to her audience. Her first best-seller, *Global Virtuality*, had laid the foundations of digital-age philosophy ten years earlier and it was now almost mandatory reading for undergraduates, whatever their branch of science. But they also knew she never missed an opportunity to reinforce her message. As she claimed, the virtual environment was still a very new place for the human psyche and it was always tempting to dismiss the intangible as unreal.

'And so we come to the subject of consciousness,' Theresa announced. 'Some of you will know that machine consciousness has been the focus of my work in recent years.'

Some of you will know? Every one of them knew and every

one of them was hoping for an update. She wasn't going to disappoint them.

'My reason for starting with a brief overview of human evolution is that until a few years ago we were ignoring the process, even though it was a model that had been staring us in the face all the time. For nearly forty years the field of artificial life and machine intelligence yielded nothing but disappointments. It seemed as though our efforts to build a machine that had human-type intelligence were doomed to failure. Many said we were failing because humans have qualities that can't be captured within a machine. Others said it was because we didn't even understand the object we were trying to copy, let alone become capable of replicating it. I believed that attempting to create consciousness as if it were a product, or a function of software code, was wrong. I believed that consciousness is something that emerges spontaneously in a given set of circumstances, probably out of immense processing density and billions of individual transactions – as in the human brain.

'Then, about seven years ago, my team and I wondered what would happen if we applied our latest understanding of human evolution to our research. Everybody in this room will know that, as humans, we are merely the latest members of a group of eighty billion or so hominids who have so far gasped momentarily for life, reproduced and died on this planet. We are the latest models of a line of almost infinite prototypes, developed with no hint of temporal urgency or parsimony of resources and with no whiff of interest in the fate of individual experimental models to distort the process that led to our accidental but seemingly wonderful design.

'We decided to take these principles of natural selection, of biological evolution, and speed them up. We have applied this process to our research and I will be demonstrating some of the results this afternoon.'

The room crackled with expectation.

At 46,000 feet above the Atlantic, Raymond Liu adjusted his viewpers so that the professor's image became solid. He didn't need to see what was now in front of him in the physical world. It was only the bulkhead in the executive cabin of the Tye Corporation jet and the network supremo was keen to watch the professor's lecture. Machine consciousness wasn't his field, but Keane had a world reputation and he had been disappointed that the meeting in Newark that had just ended had denied him the chance to attend her first Hope Island lecture in person.

During the first fifteen minutes of the short ride back to the Island Liu had issued instructions for the formation of two network-investigation teams to explore the recent satellite failures. The Red Team would work from the island's Network Control Center. The Blue Team would work from the Tye Networks Control Center in Singapore – an almost identical facility that had originally been intended as a contra-hemisphere back-up unit in case of colossal atmospheric or geophysical disruption in the Americas. Now, like its Hope Island counterpart, it was used mainly for sales demos. The two teams' tasks would be to construct new security barriers within the communications networks and to watch for any unauthorized attempts at command communications with any of the 22,866 satellites active in the forty-two networks. The most skilled hacker on each team would play the role of an opponent and would attempt to breach the opposing team's assigned networks without being detected. Liu had decided to blitz this problem.

Although he hadn't mentioned it during his meeting with the Russian network controller, the problems in the networks above the South-West Pacific had not been the first anomaly to occur since he had been given overall technical responsibility for Tye's satellite communications networks. Only seven days earlier, one of the data processors on board an Air Traffic Management satellite serving the North-West American coast had frozen and crashed. The system had reset itself and reloaded its data in just eleven seconds but this event had rated an 'immediate action' malfunction report and it had appeared on his system within seconds of the occurrence. He knew it would also be prompting an FAA investigation.

Liu had ordered the satellite taken out of service immediately and he had switched the ATM processing to one of the standby satellites in the same quadrant. He had asked Tye Aerospace for an 'earliest possible' launch slot to drop a replacement into orbit, but he also knew he might have a wait: all non-third-party launch capacity seemed to be taken up with launches of space stations for something called the Phoebus Project. It wasn't a networks communications project so it wasn't his concern, but he knew he would have to argue with Aerospace and then with Tom to get slots for replacing all three satellites that were now suspect.

The individuals who would make up the investigation teams would be identified by Liu's executive staff by the time he landed back on Hope Island. He had been unequivocal: this investigation had priority over all other projects and only the most experienced and the most talented would be seconded to work in shifts around the clock until there was a definitive answer about the cause of the network failures. Liu knew his own future depended on finding the cause and eradicating it before any further problems occurred.

Satisfied that he could do no more until the potential members of the investigation teams had been identified, Liu turned up the sound for Professor Keane's lecture.

He listened as she described her Anagenesis Experiment – the early attempts to produce super-intelligent software by creating computer environments that mimicked ecosystems. She described the many failures there had been and how she and her team had struggled to find methods of reproducing the forces that had shaped human evolution and the necessary density and complexity of decision-making systems from which a form of consciousness might emerge.

'In the end we decided to create independent software agents that were heuristic, wholly autodidactic and that were able to reproduce themselves continuously. We made two types of personality we call male and female. We gave these agents two overriding imperatives: to reproduce and to eat – to take on energy – although we also programmed them to pass on to their offspring whatever they learned during the competition and selection processes. This decision lies at the heart of our evolutionary acceleration algorithm. There is no relearning to be done by each generation; it's a form of palingenesis.

'For every one female entity, we made ten males so the boys would have to compete like mad and so further accelerate the evolutionary process. We also gave both sexes limited lifespans to cleanse the field of obsolete generations. Females live until they have reproduced sixty-four times or until whenever they go for more than three days without reproducing. The males die when they have fathered sixteen offspring, or if they fail to reproduce within thirty days, whichever is the sooner. Male-to-female ratios in the offspring are as per our starting point. We colour-coded the females green, the males red – and then we released our software robots into the world's networks to fend for themselves.'

Raymond Liu felt the hairs on the back of his neck rise. He leaned forward in his seat even though that had no effect on how the image was displayed by his viewpers. She couldn't have been that irresponsible! He went to put a question but he saw that the event had not yet been opened for questions from the remote audience.

Then he heard laughter. Someone from Evolutionary Psychology had asked what a software robot liked for lunch.

'Sushi,' someone else shouted and Theresa smiled.

'To simulate eating we decided that every entity had to return to the mother server once every twelve hours for what we call a refuelling stop. If an agent fails to do so precisely at its allotted time, it dies. It also allows us to track every bot's movement and ensure the experiment isn't getting out of hand.'

Liu sat back in his seat again.

'Now, we also had to decide what fitness characteristics we wanted to select for – or, to put it another way, what traits the female personalities would find so attractive in the males that they would allow themselves to be used for reproduction. The human female's refusal to mate indiscriminately is, of course, the second key to the incredibly rapid evolutionary anagenesis of the human species. In short, boys, when she says "no" you are observing the two vital keys of human evolutionary success used in a devastatingly effective combination: language and positive selection.

'You will have guessed that we restricted the females to one duplication – or reproduction – per day and we programmed the females so that they only became reproductively viable – in season, if you like – for twenty minutes in every twenty-four hours, those twenty minutes to occur randomly. A female spends the rest of her time receiving advances and comparing the desirable characteristics of the potential mates who are courting her. Despite this, the females' main objective is to reproduce with the most desirable mate they can find and it is his desirable traits, and of course her ability to select for those traits, that get amplified in the offspring.'

Keane turned to her audience. 'So, what do you think is the key attraction we want the male bots to develop? Remembering the aim of our development exercise, what should be the one thing that will drive the girls mad and grant the males access to reproduction?'

She waited to see if any of the brightest of the bright, most of them at the peak of their own reproductive potential, would offer an insightful suggestion.

'Money,' shouted a young female voice from the rear.

They laughed, Keane with them. 'Yes, it could be money. Resources are very important for human females considering reproduction. Anything else?'

'Elegant code,' shouted another researcher, a male.

'Digital good looks,' said Theresa smiling. 'That's a very good idea and very male of you. Only the best code, or the fittest, gets to reproduce. Any further suggestions?'

There were none.

'We programmed the female entities to look for *human* characteristics in their potential partners,' she said quietly.

And it had stopped, just like that. Joe Tinkler had sat stock-still, watching the prices in his Tye Corp portfolio for another fifteen minutes, his finger poised over his mouse – his manual panic button. The disposals had stopped. Joe's agents hadn't reported a single further sale by Tye or any of his representatives or legal

entities. No other big sellers were in play and the prices in the
core Tye stocks had started to creep upwards again.

Joe allowed his right hand to fall back into his lap and he
slumped in his high-backed chair. The markets had hardly
moved. Tye had realized the equivalent of over one trillion in
cash, mostly in US dollars and euros, and it was as if nobody
had even noticed.

Then Joe sat forward again. Tye was breaking the audit
trails! He must have gone to cash simply to stop analysts
following him from one investment to another. It was anonymity
he was seeking. That meant that a trillion dollars was going to
be laid in new investments very quickly. But Tye had made the
analysts, the trackers and the millions of small investors who
shadowed his every movement temporarily blind.

Joe called four new agents to his screens and quickly gave
them their instructions. If he could spot when Tye was investing
the cash, he could catch a free ride on Tye's coat tails until the
rest of the market spotted it.

If it had been anybody but Connie Law, Raymond Liu wouldn't
have accepted the incoming call. As it was, he had snapped off
the image of Professor Keane, accepted Connie's handover and
watched as his ultimate boss circled in his Holo-Theater.

'So what happened?'

Liu answered Tom as truthfully as he could. Within a few
minutes the swearing had abated. Tye stood still and zoomed in
so that his eyes filled Liu's vision.

'You find whoever is in those networks within twenty-four
hours!' he snarled.

The connection went dead and Liu was left staring at
blackness. It would take him forty-eight hours just to get the
investigation teams in place.

'Would you like a drink?'

The engineer slipped his viewpers off. The flight attendant
was at the bar; she knew what was needed when one of her
passengers had been in communication with TT.

Liu swallowed and then nodded. 'Give me a Scotch, on the
rocks.'

She made it a large double and smiled as she handed him the drink. 'We'll be landing soon. Please fasten your seat belt.'

After he had fastened his belt and taken two long pulls on the drink, Liu's breathing eased and he put his viewpers back on, switched to playback mode and rejoined the lecture where he had left it.

'Please turn the house lights down,' requested Professor Keane as she stepped to the side of the stage. When the room was dimmed she turned back to face her audience.

'And now, with no apology for what is a gratuitous act of anthropomorphization, I want you to meet Miss Scarlett.'

In the centre of the stage the Holo-Theater snapped on and the head, shoulders and torso of a young female appeared. The vintage-film fans in the audience recognized her immediately and they whispered her name to their friends. It was Vivien Leigh, one of the greatest film beauties of the mid-twentieth century. She was in character as Scarlett O'Hara in *Gone With the Wind* but at a quality and resolution of which Herbert Kalmus and his Technicolor film engineers of the previous century could only have dreamed. She was wearing the white, black-trimmed, two-piece travelling suit bought for her in Charleston by Rhett Butler and, in this representation, the software and projection system gave her three dimensions.

'Like all our software agents, Miss Scarlett has been allowed to choose her own visual identity from the Tye Digital Arts archives. Allocation is governed strictly by how successful these agents have been in achieving their twin goals. Perhaps rather unfairly, females are judged by the reproductive success of their male offspring. Miss Scarlett is the most successful female of the current generation and we have reprogrammed her to spend her next twenty minutes of, shall we call it "courtship time" with you. She will regard all men in this room as potential suitors.'

The professor walked towards the front of the stage. 'In a moment I am going to turn on Miss Scarlett's natural-language interface. When I do, I want the gentlemen to raise their hands if they want to ask Miss Scarlett a question. I will select a questioner and he may continue in a dialogue until he chooses to say "End". I will then select another questioner who may continue until he feels he also has done his best.

'I want you to know that we have programmed the female software agents to judge the characteristics of humanness by *language*: your eligibility to reproduce with Miss Scarlett will be judged by the quality of your chat-up conversation, as is so often the case in the human world. Remember what I said earlier: it was language that provided the feedback loop that sent the human brain on its runaway evolutionary progression. It was language – spoken, unspoken, written, mathematical, symbolic and conceptual – that was the trigger. Miss Scarlett understands all forms, but today we will deal with the verbal. English only, and please be courteous; Miss Scarlett thinks she's a lady. *My* team – remember you're disqualified!

'Who will be first?'

Liu watched as a sea of hands shot up. Professor Keane picked one, gave a command to the image and then stepped back.

'Who are you?' asked a young man in the front row.

Miss Scarlett raised her eyebrows and looked down at the questioner.

'Why, Ah believe you already know that, suh,' she said in a soft Southern accent. 'Ah'm sure I heard the professor introduce us.'

Liu didn't notice a solid *clunk* as the landing gear lowered and locked, nor the gentle bump as the small supersonic jet touched down. He didn't notice the noise of the engines dying as they were powered down. When he felt a hand on his shoulder he waved it away and the flight attendant left him in his seat while she completed and filed her flight log on her VideoMate. He watched as questioner after questioner tried to engage, charm or confuse the software agent with oblique, tangential, non-sequential, litotal, counter-intuitive, antiphrastic, erotic, sexual and surreal conversation. Miss Scarlett responded with vivaciousness, humour, interest, boredom, irony and derision. She even made the film fans laugh out loud and applaud – when she exclaimed 'Fiddlededee!'

When they were all done, Professor Keane turned to her

agent. 'You are free to select a partner for reproduction from those in this room. Indicate his identity by replaying any part of your conversation with him.'

'I don't think I will,' said Miss Scarlett coyly. 'Ah'm afraid it would be a regression compared to, well, compared to, shall we say, an alternative romantic opportunity that occurred earlier today.'

Liu realized that he had just watched *humans* fail the Turing Test.

He uttered a low moan as he ejaculated inside her. Haley slipped her hand between them and held him gently, where he was most sensitive. His head dropped to her shoulder and she kissed his neck. He had been so shy. It had been their sixth date – and fifth classical music concert – before the Welsh geneticist had made a move and even then he had been hesitant and unsure.

But how gentle he was, how caring, how concerned for her needs and her pleasures. Despite this, she already knew that there were many things between them that grated, that turned her into what she thought of as an ungrateful, over-critical lover. Sometimes she despaired of ever finding the right partner – a man who excited her emotionally and physically whilst being someone she could truly like and respect. It seemed as if those qualities were mutually exclusive.

Haley was realistic enough to understand that her unusual lifestyle was mainly to blame for her poor experiences in romantic relationships. She simply didn't meet enough men from whom to choose and she constantly made do with second-best. She was attractive enough to secure plentiful advances from males, yet she was rarely in a situation in which they could occur. On the infrequent occasions when she complained to her sister or her friends about her work and her solitary lifestyle denying her social opportunities, they pointed out that many other professionals worked from home these days and there were dozens of ways of joining social or professional clubs and communities where she could meet suitable men.

But they didn't really understand. When Haley was working on a project, she was almost incapable of focusing on anything else. Her subject and her writing wrapped around her like an invisible shield against the outside world. She had made real efforts, however. Sometimes she forced herself to go to other authors' book-launch parties, to literary lunches and, on four occasions, on blind dates set up via network dating agencies. The results had become familiar and depressing. Once she was engaged on a book she found it hard to be engaged with anything, or anybody, else. In her spells between books when she did socialize, she simply grabbed the first reasonably attractive man who presented himself to her. This was not a recipe for long-term success and she knew that it arose from a feeling of mild desperation that she had forced herself to allow Barry to intrude when the only man who *really* mattered in her life at present was Thomas Tye. Suddenly Jack Hendriksen's face popped into her mind.

She kissed Barry's neck again as he stirred. She hated to allow the real world to intrude.

'You'll be late for work,' she murmured.

He pushed himself away on one elbow.

'Christ, look at the bloody time!'

He leaped out of Haley's bed and headed for the bathroom. She snuggled back down into the warmth of the duvet, where he had been lying. She felt drowsy and she wanted to enjoy the feeling of the gentle warmth that was washing up and over her. This was one of the few good things about working from home. She didn't have to face the Stygian Northern Line in the mornings: it was the last remaining route without air-conditioned business-class carriages and the London summers had been getting steadily warmer for most of her life.

'Naturally, we can't know what it is we don't know,' pointed out the desiccated mathematician redundantly. 'But I, for one, do not believe that the Tye Corporation could be breaking deeply encrypted messages from the networks without having achieved some sort of major breakthrough. It would have to be a massive leap forward in computer processing power, perhaps an improvement by a factor of several thousand, or some completely new form of mathematics – something I am wholly unable to guess at.'

They had been talking for over seven hours with only one or two breaks for their physical comfort. Food had been brought in and cleared away again and more brought in and cleared. Chelouche and the WHO scientist had made their excuses and left. Parts of the session had been agonizingly technical as Mathison had demonstrated the mathematical impossibility of deciphering encrypted communications in the absence of a manufacturing key.

Jack felt hard stubble as he rubbed his chin.

'What first made you think that Thomas Tye, or the company, had started hacking into encrypted comms?' he asked Deakin.

'It was the World Patent Organization,' explained the intelligence officer. He had first taken off his jacket, then his waistcoat and he now pulled at his tie before opening the collar of his white shirt. Ron was always well turned out, even in the field.

'You know that the WPO is another UN body?'

Jack didn't. He had never really thought about the UN – like most people, he guessed. While business had become a global affair these days, the majority of people were concerned only about domestic issues and local politics. Despite the ease and convenience of electronic home-voting, it was as if the masses had collectively given up trying to understand or influence world issues. He shrugged a negative.

'Nine or ten years ago things were a real mess. You had to file patents in different countries with different authorities. There were over one hundred different jurisdictions. Some of them followed one procedure, others another. Some authorities considered that *filing* first was the most important thing, some thought that *inventing* first – and being able to prove it – was all that mattered. We, the Americans, believed in inventing first but we were in a minority. The arguments kept the lawyers rich for years. Anyhow, the UN eventually realized that such intellectual property was going to be the equivalent of gold in the future and they stepped in. The WPO was established as a single, global patent office and it was agreed that filing for a patent first should be the key to awarding the patent. Our American methods were overruled. For the sake of *global harmonization.*'

Deakin ended his short history lesson on a note of sarcasm. He lifted his hand and ran it through his thinning hair. Then he sat back and hooked an arm over the back of his chair.

'So now we have a first-past-the-post system. No good sitting in your backyard inventing cold fusion on your own, you've got to get your papers in as soon as you can prove you've got something unique, something that hasn't been thought of before. It's irrelevant *when* something was actually invented. There's no such thing as the concept of prior art any more. The change was supposed to settle things for good, but it didn't. The result is a lot of nerds and academics going to civil courts, squabbling over who thought of what first and who stole whose ideas. You can imagine.'

Jack could indeed imagine. Although he had done well during his years at Columbus, he had been appalled at the pettiness of academic life and its schoolyard characteristics. His tutor had urged him to become a postgraduate student but as soon as Jack had finished his degree in physics he had opted for a life of unequivocal reality in the US Navy – not least because the starting salary would ease things for his mother back home. Mathison's attitude of aloof self-importance reminded him how little he liked academics.

'So the WPO started a database of complaints and complainants. Every time someone made a complaint or sued a patent holder for IP theft, those details went into the files. After a couple of years they had enough data to go mining and guess what they found? Half a dozen companies that systematically challenged patents and developed bogus proof of their own development projects to show to the courts. Reverse-engineering specialists, all of them! These claim jumpers always accepted a pay-off before their case came before the international court. It was very lucrative but after the WPO published its evidence, the claim jumpers went away as quickly as they had arrived.

'Then, about two years ago, they noticed a new trend. The Tye Corporation would file a patent and almost instantly

another company or an academic institution would claim they
had already invented the same damn thing and had been about
to file for it themselves. Only this time, the plaintiffs were really
respectable people – huge pharmaceutical companies, the
world's best universities, you know.'

Jack did know. He knew that almost half the flights between
Hope Island and the USA were shuttling patent attorneys to
and from meetings – another breed he didn't like. He realized
he was feeling irritable because he was tired. He also wanted a
drink.

Few regions of the planet remained completely uninhabited or
unobserved by humankind. Even the remote polar regions now
hosted scientific research stations, while surveillance satellites
continuously criss-crossed the hot arid wastelands of the equatorial wildernesses. Even the giant telescopes orbiting the moon
and Mars were sometimes re-tasked to look back towards their
point of origin.

For these reasons, it was agreed that the Tye Corporation's
new Russian allies would be party to one of the few concen-
trated-power tests that would be risked prior to the launch of
commercial services. Afterwards there should never be a need
for such tests to be repeated. But Tye Corp had to discover if
their calculations were right – and the Russians controlled
swathes of remote, unobserved territory.

As it turned out, the Russian Federation naval frigate dispatched to play sea-level observer and policeman at Ostrov
Vrangelya – a small archipelago in the Chukchi Sea – found
only one Japanese whaler to harry and dispatch. It was chased
away to the south and ordered to stay clear of 'forthcoming
naval exercises' as the crew of the *Boris Dólokhov* settled down
to wait and watch in the Arctic cold at the edge of the
paleocrystic polar ice cap.

The celestial event began, as scheduled, at eleven p.m.
eastern-Siberian time and the sailors stared in awe as twelve
miniature new suns appeared high above their heads in the dark
blue northern skies. They could see the focus of the light beams
on the *nunatak* five miles to the west and, relying on his

superiors' assurances that there was no danger to adjacent areas, the captain edged his craft nearer to the patch of intense illumination to assist in the capture of film and video images and the taking of measurements. They moved through the ice floes with only just enough speed to maintain their heading and after three hours they were within a mile of the ice-shore.

The captain ordered the engines to be disengaged and, in the near-silence, they heard loud reports as the ice at the edge of the island cracked. They could see huge lumps of ice breaking off from the almost vertical cliffs and falling into the sea. Then the sailors on deck felt the heat and some started to strip off their waterproofs and sweaters, even though they were still some distance from the light.

On the bridge, the captain heard the crackle of a walkie-talkie radio behind him.

'Sir,' began the very young first lieutenant. 'Forward lookout reports the sea is boiling.'

Then they saw steam.

Jan Amethier leaned forward. He had been quiet, chewing the end of a ballpoint pen during most of Mathison's maths talk and Deakin's background briefing on the patent disputes.

'Finally the World Patent Office realized that other companies in which Tye was involved were attracting patent-filing complaints,' the UNISA director added. 'And these complaints also came from reputable organizations. All of them had meticulous evidence of their own development procedures and sworn statements from highly respected researchers. One of them in particular attracted attention: it was the patent for the solar-powered fuel cell that the Tye Corporation has sold all around the world. Then the WPO came to us – well, to the UN Secretariat, who then came to us.'

Jack nodded. 'But what made you suspect they were breaking crypto? It could be straightforward commercial spying. That's much more likely and I don't think Tom would hesitate. There's a whole industry of ex-spooks doing it – searching for keywords and voiceprints on the networks, using software agents to scan the airwaves, renting submarines to tap undersea cables. Hell, you can even lease your own time on NASA's spy satellites! And Tom doesn't need any of that – he already owns half the networks!'

'That's what we did think at first,' agreed Amethier. 'It seemed logical but everybody knows what goes on and everybody encrypts anything that's sensitive these days. Then the WPO reported that patent filings from the Tye Corporation and Tye's other companies were increasing rapidly and, as before, they were attracting what looked like legitimate complaints. It seemed to go way beyond anything that could be done by normal commercial theft. That's when I threw the file over to Ron.'

'As you know, I already had the Tye Corporation in my ongoing-observation portfolio,' confirmed Deakin. 'We keep tabs on all the powerful corporates and their executives. I'm sure you can understand why. It's the people versus the corporations these days and we end up as the cops – it's something the lawyers call *parens patriæ* – the UN has a duty to protect the people. At any rate, the director dropped it in my lap and I followed developments for a few months. I went to talk to some of the companies who had complained that their work had been stolen. Several of them said they'd had an approach from Tye's people either to take their company over or with an eye to investing in them, before either party had filed a patent – you know, the Tye Corporation's old tricks. They'd pretend to be interested in buying a company, Tye would stroke the young founders personally, get them to show all their intellectual property and then back out of the deal only to produce his own version a few months later. But *these* companies hadn't publicized their developments.

'Then I started to wonder if he was somehow getting inside electronic communications – as you say, the Tye Corporation owns what, forty, fifty per cent of the world's networks? So that's when I decided to develop something that we could go fishing with, something that couldn't be got any other way than by intercepting communications. So I pulled the WHO on side and their people did the rest. Bingo! He files for a patent on a therapy based on genes that don't *do* anything. They were in such a rush to file the patent first that they didn't take the time to isolate the gene string to check whether or not Pfizer-LaRoche's research results were right. They took things on trust just because the patent filing came from a famous and well-established research lab.'

Deakin stood and reached for another coffee flask, the tenth they had gone through during the meeting. More of a pre-operation briefing, thought Jack as he waited for the right opportunity to add something to their knowledge, something that had been burning inside him all day – the information that had prompted him to seek out Haley Voss, to finally consider consulting a lawyer and, perhaps, his old contacts in the American intelligence community.

'So we want your help, Commander,' said Amethier finally. 'I realize that all this is only circumstantial. Perhaps Tye and his company have found a way of deciphering encrypted communications, perhaps not. Perhaps it is just a massive commercial spying operation. As Doctor Chelouche told us earlier, things are very delicate. If Tye has found a way to break into the world's encryption system he could cripple any competitor he wants to. And he can read all *our* communications, Jack.'

'He could then trawl through our entire knowledge base,' added Deakin. 'He could find out everything the various security services keep to themselves. Hell, he could even find out who really killed JFK!'

'Who *did*?' asked Jack.

Amethier brushed this deviation aside. 'More importantly, he can find out what the governments of the world are planning. He could even engineer a complete collapse in the global economy *deliberately*!'

The UNISA director fell silent as his own vocalization made such an improbable threat seem more real.

'You know what that would lead to,' he then continued in a lowered voice. 'We'd slip back a hundred years. Wars would break out all over the world. We might even have world war again.'

Amethier paused and then brought himself back from fanciful concepts. 'At the very minimum, we'd have to alert every military force in the world that their security is compromised. The governments, security forces, the police, the banks...' He tailed off.

Jack scratched at his stubble again. He realized how deeply concerned they were. 'You want me to set him up for you? No, get someone else. You know that's not my thing–'

Deakin snorted. 'Jesus, Jack! Of course not. All of the irreversible options are out of the question in this case. Quite the opposite: we need you to keep him safer than ever! If Tye were to die suddenly that alone could bring the world markets down – even if it happened through natural causes. That's part of the problem. His power is so great that things are very precarious. We've got to handle this as carefully as...' he searched for an analogy that would resonate with his former pupil '... a covert agent-extraction. We need to gather hard evidence about whether Tye has found a way to unscramble communications. We've got to be sure before we do anything. We've also got to start a campaign to change public opinion about this man and his corporation. Tye's got a huge approval rating at the moment. We've had market research firms checking by electronic poll every week and the people of the world love him. Schoolkids chant "Take Care of Our Planet" and their buddies answer "We hear!" There's no way we could get him near a court as things are. It will take us a while to change that attitude. We thought Miss Voss could be useful there – with her book. Any idea who's sending her the inside stuff?'

Jack shrugged. 'Could be anybody. There are thousands of people with reasons to hate Thomas Tye. We've already got files on most of them.'

Deakin nodded. He didn't doubt that. 'I think *we* can persuade a publisher to go ahead with her biography,' he stated. 'You feed her the right stuff and that might start the process of changing how people think about him. Then we'll have to gather enough evidence to get Tye, or the Tye Corporation, into the international court at The Hague. It might take a few years, but it has to be done.'

'You haven't said anything about Tye Aerospace,' said Jack.

Amethier looked up sharply. 'What about it?'

'Did you know President Orlov has just visited Hope?'

'Sure. Air traffic coordination,' Deakin grunted. 'UN ATM handed President Orlov's plane on to Hope Island airspace.'

Jack nodded. *Of course.* 'Did you know Anton Vlasik was in the party?'

'We did *not*!' snapped Amethier. 'I thought he was safely in prison. What the hell's that thieving bastard cooking up with Tye?'

'Well, they were visiting for a demonstration of a surprising new technology. During this vacation I was intending to see a lawyer about how to proceed. I didn't know whether I could do anything, what I *should* do, knowing Vlasik's record...'

He tailed off, aware how far-fetched his claims might sound. Jack didn't yet know how the technology worked, but he had seen the elaborate preparations. He had been at the Science Academy in Moscow two years earlier when Tom had first met the Russian leadership and started his negotiations. He had watched as ships arrived carrying the components for the giant satellites and their incredible extensions. He had watched hundreds of shuttle launches from Cape Hope. Damn, he had even met some of the all-female crews who were running the construction projects on the orbiting space stations. And, of course, he had seen that dazzling demonstration.

'I have very few firm details, but the Tye Corporation is going to sell sunshine,' he said simply. 'To the highest bidders.'

EIGHT

Calypso helped the limping athlete out to join his mother in the waiting area. He was twelve years old and he felt he no longer needed his mom's presence in the consulting room when he saw the doctor. Calypso winked at her over the top of the boy's head, resisting the temptation to ruffle his bright ginger hair.

'Nothing cracked or broken, Sonia,' she smiled. 'I've bound it up tight. Make sure he rests the ankle for a couple of weeks and ...' she turned to her patient and wagged her finger '...no more soccer for a month.'

Sonia, wife of a senior vice-president of marketing in Consumer Electronics, put her arm round her son's shoulders and smiled her thanks. Calypso held the surgery door open for them and they eased their way down the short path to their Volante.

'Come and see me again, Gary,' she called. 'But don't make it *too* soon.'

The boy waved as he carefully lowered himself into the vehicle, holding his bandaged left leg stiff and proud in front of him, like a minor war wound. Calypso allowed the veranda door to bang shut on the outside heat and she checked the time on her LifeWatch. She had finished her appointments early. Apart from being available for Tommy on a twenty-four-hour basis, this weekly surgery for the children of the Hope Island community was her only prescribed duty.

When the HR director for Hope Island executive staff had first interviewed her in Chicago, before she had signed the heavyweight non-disclosure contract and media-silence agreement, he had made it clear that she would not be required to

join the staff at any of the island's hospitals and clinics. She
could use their facilities as she chose and, as she had qualified as
an MD before she began her training as a paediatric psychiatrist,
she would be on standby in case of any major emergency. But it
was Tommy who was to be her main concern, he explained.

Calypso had initially wondered what on earth could be
wrong with the boy and had voiced her question. But her
interviewer had assured her that Tommy was healthy in all
respects. It was merely that Mr Tye's heir was growing up in an
extremely unusual and privileged position in life – 'something
you might find hard to imagine,' he said condescendingly – but
accurately, as Calypso later realized. It was also explained that
the boy was showing considerable intellectual promise and his
father wanted a child psychologist on hand at all times to
protect his son's mental as well as physical health.

'A permanent therapist?' queried Calypso, eyebrows raised.

'More of a qualified companion,' was the response.

'Where's his mother?' asked Calypso. 'Surely she'll want to
talk to me first?'

'There is no mother,' said her interviewer abruptly. 'You'll
have access to his files on your arrival.'

Considering her own mother's growing dependency, this job
with the Tye Corporation had been the best opportunity Calypso
could have possibly hoped for. It provided the necessary funds
and the physical proximity that would allow her to ensure that
the old lady received the best possible care in her final years.

Calypso had accepted the post with alacrity, leaving behind
Chicago, the snow, the psychiatric wards and Larry Sumner all
at the same time. She realized that she was using her mother's
deteriorating health and this new job as an excuse to end the
relationship with Larry. But she had recently been fighting to
hide her irritation with the radiologist's addiction to on-line
gambling and she guessed that he was probably feeling much
the same about some of her own domestic habits. Their relationship had simply gone stale, although Calypso realized that it
was she who was initiating the break.

Given the unusually exclusive conditions of her new job,
Calypso had offered to run a weekly clinic for all the other

children on the island and the HR department had welcomed her suggestion.

As soon as she met Tommy, saw Hope Island and realized what a sanctuary of wealth and privilege it was, how utterly different to life a few miles away on her home island of Mayaguana, Calypso had started to feel guilty about her career move, despite her offer to provide her services as a general physician. She decided to use her free time to study tropical medicine.

Then she had scared herself. She was learning a great deal about the human immune system and she started to wonder what could happen to the population of a completely new and very sanitized island state. She broke off from her study of schistosomiasis, did some calculations and v-mailed the HR director to request a personal meeting.

'I'm worried that we may be heading for a disaster,' she had begun hesitantly, aware that she was very new to the corporation. 'We're not getting sufficient population throughput to maintain antibody templates.'

The HR director had taken her worries seriously and Calypso had quickly been asked to make a presentation on the subject to the Hope Island management board. That had been the first time she had met Tom. Despite the fact that she had been to the house almost every day for three weeks, his life was so frantically peripatetic that she had never glimpsed her employer, the father of her charge. Nothing further was said of the mother and she had been offered no files and had not yet found the right opportunity to enquire further.

She was doubly shocked when she first saw Tom in person. The first surprise was that he entered the room wearing what seemed to be an antibacterial face mask. Nobody else paid any attention to this, however.

Then he removed it to spray his mouth and Calypso experienced a sense of unreality, of double exposure, a meeting with a person whose face she had seen all her life on television, in the press. She felt public and private, inner and outer, blur, grow confused. He was smaller than she had imagined, but he looked younger and more handsome – well, more beautiful, she realized – than any of his media images, even the most iconic, had suggested. The doctor in her ran a check of his visible indicators: he looked very fit and youthful. His features were almost perfectly symmetrical, his hair dark and shining. When he looked up at her from behind the conference table she saw a strong, straight nose and a full mouth. But dominating his face was a pair of the most startling, lively violet eyes. She already knew those eyes well – they were Tommy's eyes.

In her 'fun years', when she had competed in beauty pageants to earn enough money to continue her education, Calypso had worked with other beautiful women – models in magazine photo shoots, television commercials and product launches – and she had had many opportunities to observe the impact of female beauty on others.

'Looks are merely an accident, but truly beautiful people *do* live in a different world,' she had admitted when Larry had first asked her what it was like to have to live with her stunning looks.

She recalled some lines on the subject from a novel she had read at university. '"Beautiful people are exempt from life's difficult tests. They can sit there and judge life, instead of being judged by it. Beauty is its own morality."'

Larry had nodded his understanding, but she was sure he couldn't *know* what it felt like to be wanted or hated by everybody simply for your looks. Few men could.

But Thomas Tye could, Calypso realized.

She had worn her maroon two-piece suit with its knee-length hem and had gathered her wavy black hair into a thick plait that reached to the middle of her back. She wanted to make a good impression but as she took the management board through the dangers of immune-system decay as a by-product of communal isolation she had realized that Thomas Tye wasn't looking at her like most men did. She could see that the HR director and his male assistant were watching her movements in a typically masculine manner, practically licking their lips. Connie Law was clearly amused at the sight. Calypso was used to such behaviour and almost expected it, but Thomas Tye's gaze seemed to be everywhere but on her. Once again, like the rest of the world, she had wondered about his sexuality.

Her presentation was a success. She had allowed herself a small amusement at the end when she had wrapped up by describing Hope Island as 'this scept'red isle, this demi-paradise, this fortress built by nature for herself against infection'.

Tom had laughed. 'Does that make me Richard the Second or Bolingbroke?' he asked, surprising her and the others.

As a result of her warnings, the frequency of the rotation cycle of staff between Hope Island and the Tye Corporation's overseas offices was increased sharply. On TT's instructions the management board had gone so far as to lease two additional wide-bodied jets to ferry employees and their families for extra subsidized vacations in the United States, Europe and the Americas. Calypso had entered these new population movements into her model of Hope Island's immune-system development pattern and she had been able to report to the head of Human Resources that the likelihood of immune-system deterioration in the community was now much reduced.

A month after her presentation, when the HR department had conferred with consultants, completed their own calculations and had started to increase population flow to and from the island, her viewpers had notified her of an incoming message. It arrived during her siesta. Calypso had strung a hammock between two palm trees on her private section of the beach and she was dozing in the shade when Connie Law's ident appeared in her Ray Ban Electros. As she accepted the call, the PA's face filled her gaze.

'I've got Tom for you, Doctor. Hold on.' Then Calypso was staring at those eyes.

'Great work, Doctor. You've made an excellent start. You may have saved Hope Island from a real health problem.'

'Thanks, Tom.' She didn't know exactly where he was since his system wasn't transmitting the usual GPS reference or map graphic. She could see that he was in an aircraft, however.

'Our appreciation will be evident in your next pay transfer. Oh, and Tommy really likes you, he says. But not as much as he likes Jed.'

Then he'd gone.

When the notification of a large bonus and a mass of stock

options arrived in Calypso's e-mail a few days later she had been very touched. But not as pleased as she had been to hear about Tommy's growing affection for her. Already her vulnerable charge had become very important to her – and she was delighted to be nearly as important to him as his favourite Furry.

Now she stood in her surgery reception area and looked at her LifeWatch again. She could spend an hour absorbing more of Manson's *Tropical Diseases*, the seminal introductory work on the topic, before going up to the house to see Tommy after school.

Calypso had only recently intervened in what had become the first serious contest of wills between Tommy and his father that she had witnessed. Tommy had been begging his father to allow him to attend the little elementary school in Port Hope. It was run exclusively for the children of senior company executives and Calypso knew how desperately Tommy needed to feel normal – or as normal as possible, under the circumstances. At first, Tye had refused flatly, without giving any reasons. But Tommy was also strong-willed and after Calypso had endured a number of his tantrums, she had asked to see Thomas Tye in person to discuss the matter.

She had then explained how damaging isolation from other children could become for the boy. That, she had asserted, was the main reason why Tommy seemed emotionally immature whilst exhibiting enormous intellectual potential. After a lot of initial extreme and protracted reluctance, his father had finally agreed that Tommy could attend the school for three afternoons a week. Until then, all his various tutors had visited the house for up to eight hours a day.

Her VideoMate trilled, and Calypso answered it as she walked back into her consulting room. The wall screen came on automatically and showed Heather Garland, the principal of the school.

'Doctor Browne. Could you come over here now? There's been an ... well, Tommy's hurt.'

Calypso was already finding her keys and bag.

'What's happened?'

'I think he's OK, Doctor. He's ... Well, I'm afraid some of the boys ... He's been involved in a fight, Doctor.'

Ron Deakin snapped off his VideoMate and picked up the printouts he had downloaded from the *Stargazer, Scientific American, New Scientist* and *Amateur Astronomer* archives. The information was all in the public domain. He hadn't even needed to consult UNISA's own archive of scientific briefing reports. He sat down behind his desk on the twenty-third floor of the UN Secretariat building on Manhattan's East Side and laid out the articles in chronological order. Behind him stretched the vast urban wilderness of Queens and Flushing Meadow.

Amateur Astronomer, April 3rd 1999
Cosmonauts Ready Kirlian
By Robert Strauss

On April 4th, 1999, cosmonauts inside the Mir space station (at left) will command a circular, 25-meter (80-foot) catopric to be unfurled from Progress M-40 spacecraft (at right). They will then use the recycling system to provide energy for Mir and, potentially, for delivery to the Earth. (Click on image for larger view)

Update to story (4/5/99):
Kirlian Deployment Fails

When commanded to unfurl on the morning of April 4th, the Kirlian 25-meter heliostat became snared by an antenna on its carrier spacecraft, Progress M-40. Despite frantic attempts by cosmonauts Gennady Padalka and Sergei Avdeyev, the thin sheet refused to deploy fully. After engineers on the ground debated possible fixes, the cosmonauts tried to unfurl the catoptric again on April 5th, but its deployment mechanism jammed. The experiment was abandoned, and the control center near Moscow commanded the Progress and its partially-unfurled heliostat should re-enter Earth's atmosphere over the Pacific Ocean. It was destroyed immediately.

Deakin skimmed through the rest of the article and realized that bad timing had doomed the ambitious Russian experiment from the outset. They had been trying to launch their orbiting solar-energy system while their nation had been collapsing around their ears. Within weeks the companies behind the energy satellites had been closed down for lack of funds and the technology had been mothballed.

'Search Space Energy Consortium and Energate and the Tye Corporation,' Deakin told his VideoMate. 'Search Kutúzov.'

He spelled the name out for the system as he knew his pronunciation would be wrong.

And there it was.

Wall Street Journal, April 3rd, 2002.
Tye Corporation Buys Space Oddity.

Tye Corporation Europe gmbh today announced the purchase of a cluster of semi-dormant Russian space technology companies which includes the Space Energy Consortium, a coalition-corporation headed by veteran space engineer Nicholas Kutúzov. The group had once tried unsuccessfully to place a heliostat in orbit around the Earth. The purchase price for the Consortium and the other companies involved was not disclosed.

   Mr Kutúzov will join Tye Aerospace, Inc., Miami, as director of space-energy research.

Suddenly Deakin cursed out loud. How could he have forgotten? How could he be so stupid! The intelligence officer crossed to the power cord in the wall and pulled the wall display's plug from its socket. He picked up the VideoMate from his desk, found the master power button under its concealed sliding cover and turned the system off. He took his radio earpiece from his left ear and his viewpers from the top pocket of his jacket that was hung over the back of his chair.

Deakin threw the dead communications technology together in a heap in the middle of his desk. This operation was going to prove difficult, he realized.

The boy was sitting on a low bench in the small schoolyard. Heather Garland had her arm around his shoulders. Stella, one of Jack's team, was standing a little distance away, conferring via her VideoMate. She would have been alerted automatically as the network's keyword-recognition system monitored the head teacher's call to the doctor.

Calypso negotiated the safety gate and ran up the slight incline of the play area.

'Tommy? What's happened?'

He looked up and held out his arms to her. Calypso eased herself down on the low bench and allowed him to put his arms around her neck and press his face into the doctor's coat she was wearing. She hadn't even paused to take it off before driving up to the school. Heather Garland removed her own arm from between them. 'He's OK, I think, Doctor. I think it's been more of a scare than anything else.'

Tommy lifted his head up. 'I wasn't cheating, I wasn't.'

Calypso stroked the back of his head and looked at Heather for explanation.

The head teacher shrugged. 'It was a chess game. That's all. Tommy was playing our school champion.'

Tommy looked up at Calypso again. 'You won't tell my father, will you? Will you?'

He swivelled his gaze from one to the other. 'You won't, will you?'

Calypso stared down at his face. She could see a trickle of dried blood below his nose and a graze on his right cheek. His huge violet eyes were filled with tears. She wanted to kiss him so much it hurt.

'Don't worry about that now. Let's just go back to my office and get you cleaned up.'

'You mustn't tell him, you mustn't!' Tommy screamed and he pulled away from them both, jumped up and started to run towards the school gate.

Calypso was off the bench and at the gate in front of him before she was even aware of it. She put her hands on his shoulders and held him square in front of her.

'I said, don't worry about that now, Tommy. I just want to make sure you're OK.'

The boy glowered up at her defiantly, his eyes blazing. He had inherited his father's temper.

She squatted so that her eyes were on the same level as his. 'Tommy, I'm your friend. Let's go check this out, OK?'

He stared back directly into her eyes, petulant and defiant.

'I'll let you come over to my place afterwards.' She knew that would get to him. He lived in the world's most luxurious modern mansion, with every possible amusement and facility, but he still loved to visit her tiny bungalow. He would pick up her small trinkets and examine each one with care, asking where she'd got it. Then he would usually ask to play her electronic keyboard.

He hung his head. 'I'm OK. Please don't tell my father.'

Calypso guessed that Tom was probably aware of the incident already. The security systems on the island were so all-embracing that hardly a square inch of it was not covered by cameras.

'*I* won't tell him,' she said, truthfully.

Morgenstein held the report in his left hand. He made Joe Tinkler stand, waiting in front of his desk, while he reread it. *Like being back in grade school*, thought Joe. But there was no doubt Morgenstein was angry.

'So Tye cleared out roughly a trillion dollars of his holdings and you did *nothing*?'

Joe nodded.

'Where's he put all this money?' demanded Morgenstein.

This was the hard part.

'I don't know. I've been tracking all IPOs and filings on private investments. I can't trace any of it.'

Joe didn't mention that he had just re-dispatched his software robots with fresh instructions. He was determined to find where it had gone.

'What are Tye Corporate Relations saying?'

'Nothing, sir. They have no comment. They say it was a private matter.'

Morgenstein's right hand moved over the keys of a large electronic calculator on his desk. He looked at the result and then back to the fund manager.

'I was watching the entire basket and nothing twitched,' offered Joe. 'I've got the recording.'

'Even if it had, you'd have been too late,' growled Morgenstein. 'You should have cleared out the moment you realized what was happening.'

Joe shook his head. 'I calculated that even following the markets I could have cleared everything out with only a five per cent discount.'

'What would that have cost our clients?' asked the partner.

Joe swallowed. 'Just over sixty billion dollars,' he said quietly.

'My guess is closer to seventy,' sighed Morgenstein, his anger held tightly to his chest.

He put the paper down on his desk and leaned back in his high-backed swivel chair. He turned so that Joe could no longer see his face. Everything about the partner's office spoke of the vast volumes of money that passed through Rakusen-Webber every day, and of the value even of the tiny percentages that got left behind. The pedestal desk was of gleaming mahogany with brass edging, a nineteenth-century antique. The walls were panelled in the same wood, stained to match the desk and the fine Hepplewhite chairs that were scattered around the Georgian conference table. The air smelled of polished leather, but Joe guessed that was artificially enhanced.

'We're letting you go, Joe. As of this minute,' Morgenstein said quietly from behind his chair back. He swivelled round to meet Joe's shocked gaze.

'I've spoken to Richard Rakusen and he agrees. We will *not* carry the sort of risk you have exposed us to. We'd rather be without the returns you have produced if this is the potential downside. You've forgotten the golden rule: every dollar lost in our business is worth every ten gained. It's a matter of reputation. You are dismissed for gross negligence.'

Joe was stunned. He could think of nothing to say.

'Security staff are waiting for you in your office. Please collect your personal things and leave the building. Do not speak to anyone on your way out and make no attempt to contact anybody here after you leave. Our lawyers will be in contact to discuss severance terms. Remember you are still bound by SEC confidentiality.'

Joe stood, rooted to the spot.

'Goodbye,' said Morgenstein and he turned his chair again so that Joe was left staring at its back.

The fund manager turned and walked from the room.

The reverberating sounds of an ancient cathedral pipe organ filled Calypso's comfortable living room. She found herself drifting into tranquillity with the gentle pedetentous descent of Bach's Air No. 3 in D major.

Tommy had seemed pensive on the drive back to Calypso's bungalow so the doctor had let him be, understanding that it was the shock of the assault, the affront to his male dignity rather than any of his minor injuries that was occupying his thoughts. He had been so sheltered from the rough-and-tumble – so unlike normal boys, so less emotionally mature. She shrugged mentally as she realized that with his wealth and his father's phobic obsessions such isolation was almost inevitable.

Tommy reached the end of the piece, allowed the final D-major chord to die, mellow on the air, and slowly lifted his hands from the keyboard of her synthesizer.

He turned, grinned and was suddenly a little boy again, much younger than his seven years. He spun round on the old revolving piano stool: round and round. He laughed as it reached the top of its thread and he spun the other way until it reached its lowest point.

'That was beautiful,' breathed Calypso, when he finally stopped. 'Beautiful. I haven't heard you play that before.'

'Miss Duckett only gave me the music yesterday,' said Tommy. 'I like it.'

'I like it very much, too,' agreed Calypso. 'You play so beautifully, Tommy.'

She too had enjoyed playing the piano when she was a child. But she knew that she had never played an instrument the way Tommy could. It was both his feel *and* his technique that marked him out. Despite his youth and size, his ambidexterity and his exceptionally long fingers enabled him to span more than an octave and somehow he injected such emotion into his playing that it was almost impossible to believe he was so young. And his memory for a piece was remarkable.

'So what *did* happen at school Tommy?' she asked.

The boy frowned and then gave a massive shrug, much too big for his little frame. 'I don't know. I just got Emilio into checkmate and he shouted at me. Then Maurice Dennis joined in. They banged me against the wall.'

'Do you play chess with them often?' probed Calypso gently.

Tommy shook his head. 'I've never played anyone before. Only my ChessMate program. I must have done something wrong.'

'Do you win when you play your ChessMate at home?'

'I used to,' Tommy sighed. 'But then my father put it on the top level and I haven't won a game for a week.'

Introduction – insertion

I can also reveal for the first time that Thomas Tye has a son who is being brought up in a strictly controlled scientific environment on Hope Island. Thomas Richmond Tye IV was born to an unknown mother approximately seven years ago. Sexual intercourse was not involved and the 'mother' had no genetic input to her apomictic[1] 'son'. Tye's son is the world's first enhanced human clone, born by a process that can best be described as 'cryptogame eutelegenesis' – a combination of eugenics and genetics, achieved secretly and remotely – and I describe the enhancements that his 'father' selected for him in Chapter Seven.

[1] Apomictic is a biological term: pertaining to or produced by apomixis; reproducing without sexual fusion.

Haley sat back and stared at her central text-composition screen. It seemed so bald, so cold, so academic, so undramatic. But how else could she put it? She felt like writing it in capitals, giving it a sexy, newsy sans-serif typeface, so she did:

THOMAS TYE HAS CLONED HIMSELF, WORLD, DO YOU
HEAR?
NOT ONLY DOES HE WANT TO LIVE FOR EVER,
HE'S GROWING HIS OWN SUCCESSOR!

But ordinary text would have to do. She deleted her fantasy
headlines. All she had to do now was find a publisher.

The second report had arrived that morning in the mail.
Once again it was a paper document but this time it had been
posted in Paris. She had read through the sixty pages at speed.
Then she reread them slowly, with the help of on-line medical
dictionaries and the world's science archives.

When she'd finished she took off her glasses and stared
blankly at the pile of papers. This report was either an ingenious
hoax or a godsend.

Haley was tempted to scan the document and forward it to
Barry. She checked his location and saw that he was now in his
lab; but she wasn't sure whether others there might have access
to his encryption key. She contented herself by reading the
report again, adding her own questions and interpretations of
the technical jargon as margin notes. She knew Barry would be
amused by her bumbling efforts at interpreting the technicalities.

Then, because she couldn't wait, she had written the draft
insert for her book's introduction.

When Barry finally arrived back, shortly after seven, his
mood was foul. He had been forced to stand in a packed
Underground carriage all the way from Euston to Stockwell, he
told her. The heat had been intolerable, everybody around him
shouting into the networks. His first words as he came through
the door had been 'I stink.'

While he showered Haley turned the air-conditioning up,
put on some gentle Mozart and punched up his favourite
ScentSim aroma, *New Car Interior*, as compensation for his
experience on London's public transport system. She then made
him a large gin and tonic. Wordlessly, she held it with an
outstretched arm around the bathroom door as he towelled
himself dry. He took it without acknowledgement.

She recrossed the hall and threw herself full-length on the white sofa, her arms crossed, getting ready for any type of argument he fancied.

A few minutes later Barry emerged pink and steaming into the cool living room. A large white towel was wrapped around his ample waist, and he was rubbing his sparse red hair one-handedly with a small hand-towel that he had removed from beside the bathroom sink. In his left hand he still held his drink. He looked down at her, blinking.

'Sorry, baggage, bloody awful day,' he apologized, as he inhaled the cool, scented atmosphere. 'Broke a bloody culture dish after three weeks of good festering.'

He took a large swig of his drink and burped. The towel at his waist unfolded in slow motion and fell to the ground.

'Oh, vision of the Northern Line, come to me,' laughed Haley as she held out her arms. He came and sat beside her and she kissed him hard on the lips, their taste fresh with gin, tonic and lime.

'How did *you* get on today, sweetheart?' he asked, more out of duty than genuine interest.

She scooped up the report from the floor beside the sofa and dropped it onto his naked legs. 'I need your help again, Doctor Evans. This arrived this morning. I'll get you a tracksuit to wear.'

It took Barry half an hour to read it the first time. Then he flicked through it again, to underline points that seemed important.

'You understand I'm no reproductive biologist?' he said finally. She sat opposite him at her circular dining table.

'Well?'

'OK. Look, it does seem kosher, but I can't be sure. I'd have to show it to one of the real boffins at the lab.'

Haley shook her head. 'We can't show it to anybody,' she said. 'If this information is true, my book is made. The newspapers will be falling over themselves for serialization rights. We can't risk the story getting out before publication.'

'Well, obviously somebody else already knows,' reasoned Barry, annoying her with this wholly unnecessary deployment of common sense.

'Can't you check it out *without* showing it to anybody else?'

Barry sighed – the patronizing display of weariness he always produced when about to explain scientific complexities to a lay person. Haley frowned.

'There aren't many people qualified to comment authoritatively on this,' he said. 'It's a very specialized area.' He took a deep breath. 'Look, there are two sorts of cloning. The first is a simple process and we, that is biotechnologists, do it all the time, with cattle, rare animals, endangered species, et cetera. It's a piece of cake. In this method we take an ideal nucleus that's been created from the sperm of an ideal male and the nucleus of an egg from an ideal female. The genes are often manipulated and then they are inserted into a carrier egg from which the natural genetic material has been stripped out – it's a procedure we call androgenesis. The fertilized egg is then duplicated and the results are implanted in a surrogate mother. This technique produces several animals that are identical – say, identical twins, like you and Felicity – but they're not exact copies of any existing adult animal. When the subject of cloning comes up, the public mistakenly thinks that the offspring is an identical copy of some adult. That's a very different story.'

'But that's what this report is about,' urged Haley.

'So it would seem,' agreed Barry, flicking through the pages, unwilling to be hurried. 'The main problem with cells taken from adult animals is that they have already differentiated. That is, they have already determined what they are and they have lost the embryonic ability to divide and to grow into specific types of new cell – like a heart muscle cell or nerve tissue.'

He turned back through the pages again. 'Then they discovered that if they take a cow's egg that has been stripped of its own nucleus and fuse it with an adult animal cell they get a blastocyst – an embryo that starts to grow in the test tube but that isn't viable in the long run: it dies after a few days.'

'Should I be making notes?' asked Haley, but her sarcasm sailed straight over his head. He closed the report and sat back and folded his hands over his stomach as he prepared for the next part of his lecture. She could see the middle-aged academic he would become.

'But if embryonic stem cells are taken from the blastocyst and they're implanted as a nucleus into a carrier egg they can develop into any type of the two hundred and ten cells required and they carry the exact copy of the DNA that was present in the original adult-animal donor cell. That's how a copy of an adult is made and that's far more difficult.'

'But it can be done,' insisted Haley.

'It can,' the geneticist admitted. 'It was done for the first time nearly twenty years ago, in Scotland. They made a successful copy of an adult sheep but, later, animals that were produced elsewhere using similar techniques aged too quickly. Once they solved that problem, they started cloning pets – dog, cats and so on – just at the turn of the century.'

'But they've never done it with humans?' she asked.

'Well, not as far as we know. The nearest they've come is to grow human organs for transplant.'

'Yeah, that's what one of Tye's companies concentrates on,' said Haley. 'So why no human clones?'

'It's illegal, since they'd have to use cells from real human embryos,' explained Barry simply, picking up the report again. 'Although I wouldn't mind betting there's been more than a few thousand human clones already knocked up in South American clinics and some of those dodgy Middle East states. Although why somebody would want to copy himself – or any other human – is beyond me. Anyway, there's just no reason to want to do it now. Even infertile couples have better options these days.'

He flicked through the report again and laid it down on the table, open at one page he had marked.

'It's these genetic adjustments to the embryo, described here, that make this really interesting.'

'Are such things really possible?' asked Haley.

NINE

Suddenly Jack Hendriksen had new purpose, a new identity and a feeling he hadn't experienced since he'd left government service. He felt he was once again doing something worthwhile.

Deakin had taken advantage of Jack's loose vacation plans and had arranged a series of 'refresher' courses for him before his official swearing-in to UN service would take place. Three courses had been arranged in short order and none of his instructors were to know anything about their new pupil until the moment he arrived.

He was flying first to Fort Mead in Maryland, to the headquarters of the National Security Agency, a US government facility in which UNISA had been able to negotiate a small sovereign space for its own communications laboratory. His passport, reservation, digital identity, value-transfer modules and new communications equipment were all in the name of Bruce D. Curtis, a thirty-nine-year-old attorney from Washington, DC. All details had been confirmed and registered with the World Certification Authority. Even his finger- and voiceprints had been matched to Curtis's identity and he'd collected an instant but detailed biography and an impressive list of legal qualifications. The individual identified as John Edward Hendriksen was 'still on vacation' in Manhattan.

'We keep a bunch of these IDs ready-made,' Deakin had explained. 'There are more lawyers on the road than management consultants these days. You'll fit in – just try to look a bit more venal.'

Once in the air, Jack lifted his background file on the Tye Corporation from his new briefcase and extracted a few sheets at random. He wondered about the relevance of the first report.

Forwarded by: UNINET to Executive Officer R. Deakin, UNISA.
Automatic forwarding keywords: Tye, Erasmus
Qualification: 100%

UNITED NATIONS HIGH COMMISSION FOR REFUGEES
Report No.: HC/SA/10/207
To: Deputy High Commissioner Sherri Prasso, UNHCR, Geneva
From: Philip-Niël Shütte (HCR 4011)
Subject: Reon Albertyn, asylum applicant No. SA81956

Status: Highest Confidentiality
At the request of UNHCR Geneva, I completed a successful negotiation with Amnesty International, Johannesburg in order to use the accreditation of their organization to carry out a visit to a maximum-security prison facility in Harare, Zimbabwe, June 11th last. Geneva had provided me with the names of three teenage prisoners in whom they have an interest, following appeals for information from the families of these boys and also local political representatives. During my visit I was told that two of the subjects had died during their internment. I was later able to obtain copies of their death certificates (copies attached).

The third prisoner on whom information was requested was Reon Albertyn, a 14-year-old South African citizen imprisoned for armed robbery and car theft, crimes found proven by a closed Zimbabwean juvenile court when he was 12.

I found Albertyn in poor health and imprisoned in appalling conditions in adult accommodation. This is the first visit UNHCR (or Amnesty International) has been able to make to this prison and, as far as I could tell, all inmates at Chikirubi Maximum Security Facility are held in conditions that breach UNHCR, UNESCO and WHO guidelines. I recommend that conditions at this facility should be officially classified by UNHCR as inhuman and degrading and confirmed as being in breach of the United Nations Declarations on Human Rights 1958, Article 7. I also recommend copies of this report are forwarded to the Ethics, Human Rights and Compliance committees at the World Bank and the International Monetary Fund. (My full assessment of the conditions for

inmates of Chikirubi MSF are provided in a separate report, ref: HC/
SA/10/207/CMSF.)

As UNHCR Financial Aid Auditor for Zimbabwe, I was granted an
audience with Dr Kim Mnanke, President of the Republic, and he
graciously granted Albertyn a presidential pardon on compassionate
grounds. I then arranged for paramedic air transportation to Mount Zion
Hospital, Pretoria where Albertyn has been undergoing tests and
observations for 10 days.

Reports by Dr James Hughes and Professor Per-Ola Nieble of the
Steve Biko Institute, Cape Town are attached to this report. I summarize
their findings here:

Reon Albertyn is in the advanced stages of a condition that initially
presents as a disease known as Werner's Syndrome, a form of progeria
or premature ageing. This condition, which is normally a chance
mutation in one copy of a single gene, is known to be genetically
inheritable, non-contagious, non-infectious and usually fatal before the
patient reaches adulthood. Albertyn's physical condition resembles that
of a man in his eighth or ninth decade, but Professor Nieble has been
unable to find a single mutant gene on the appropriate chromosome in
DNA samples taken from the patient. He is continuing his investigations.
Another unusual aspect of this case concerns Reon Albertyn's skin
colour. He is white, technically a 'leucoethiop' or albino negroid. This
very rare condition is also wholly hereditary.

Reon Albertyn insists that none of his family have ever had a
similar ageing disease nor skin of the same pigmentation and my local
agent found his parents in good health in Neuville, a township 12 miles
outside of Cape Town. They also reported no incidence of any ageing
disease or leucoethiopia in Albertyn's family but Reon Albertyn's putative
father strongly disputes paternity. I am currently awaiting independent
DNA verification of his claim.

Ends

Underneath the report Deakin had scrawled '*Lily Albertyn
employed by Erasmus Research SA 1999–03*'.

Jack shook his head and pondered what his first steps would
be when he got back to the island – he would need an ally, he
realized. Then he ordered a large vodka and tonic from the

flight attendant before pulling another report from the pile and starting to read.

His arrival at Fort Mead had been expected and he was quickly escorted into the bowels of the research facility. He remembered the first part of the route well, but then he and his escort continued on to a new extension. Here a guard in a UN uniform assumed responsibility for the visitor and walked him down a brightly lit corridor to a pair of double doors. The guard opened them and nodded for Jack to enter. The doors closed behind him and Jack smiled to himself. Even seen from the back, he knew the figure hunched over the keyboard very well.

'Doctor Lynch? It's Bruce Curtis. I hope you're expecting me.'

The man continued typing for a few moments, then lifted his hands and turned his wheelchair to face the visitor. Suddenly a broad smile lit his face.

'Well, I'll be damned! Jack Hendriksen.'

Jack dropped his briefcase onto a chair and quickly crossed the room to take the eagerly outstretched hand.

'How are you, Al? You look good.'

Jack had spent part of the plane ride from Newark working through the emotions he knew would surface when he met Lynch again. He hadn't seen the computer-systems expert since the crash that had killed Helen and partly paralysed Al: they had been flying back to New York together for Christmas leave, Al to join his family, Helen to their beloved Gramercy Park loft.

'My, my. But I heard you got out, Jack?'

'I was out, Al, but it seems like I'm back in again – although it's the UN this time. As of two days ago.'

Lynch nodded. Then he took a breath and said what had to be said. 'I was very sorry about Helen, Jack. We all were.'

Jack nodded, feeling an ache rise up, though less acutely than he had anticipated.

'I got your letter, Al. Thanks.'

'And I got yours, Jack. Eventually. So how are you?'

'I'm over it, Al. Or as over it as you can ever get.'

As he said what was expected of him he wondered, for the first time, if that might be starting to be true.

'What about you? Look at this place. You've got a whole new set of toys.'

He didn't mention the wheelchair.

Lynch noted the change of subject and took his cue. 'Sit down, help yourself to coffee,' he offered with a smile. 'I've got something to show you.'

Jack saw the percolator and plastic cups on a desk and poured himself a black coffee. 'You?' he asked waving the coffee jug in Lynch's direction.

'No, no, just sit down, Jack,' said Lynch urgently.

Jack did as he was told and raised the coffee cup to his lips.

'Watch,' said Lynch. He locked the wheels of his chair, grasped both arm supports and pushed himself to a standing position. He rocked slightly and then gained his balance. He next took a hesitant step with his right leg and then brought the left up to join it. He took another step and then brought his left leg forward again. Slowly, but with a huge smile on his face, he shuffled across the room until he halted two feet in front of Jack.

Jack put his cup down and stood up. He could feel a wetness in his eyes. He held out his arms and hugged his former colleague.

'Al, that's wonderful.'

This time the tears came. He was crying, not for Al but for Helen – and for himself. But, yes, he *was* crying for Alan Lynch too. Al was walking again!

Jack pulled away and looked down at his former systems instructor, who was over a head shorter and nearly bald. Lynch was beaming up at him.

Jack wiped his eyes. 'I thought they couldn't fix it?'

'That's what they said at first. But I just got out of hospital again, three weeks ago. Watch this.'

Jack watched as his ex–instructor spread his arms and carefully started to turn in a slow circle.

'I have to practise for an hour every day – no more, no less, they say. But I've done two hours already today!' He beamed triumphantly as Jack sat down again.

'That's wonderful – how did they...'

Lynch finished turning and began a slow shuffle back to his wheelchair.

'My back's still broken,' he said over his shoulder. 'The spinal column is completely severed just above the T12 vertebra.'

He reached his chair and turned back to Jack. 'They've bypassed the break and they've interfaced the first cervical nerve and the spinal nerve here.' He touched the back of his neck and turned so that Jack could follow his hand movement. 'And a bionet of microwires and signal amplifiers runs all the way down to here,' he touched the base of his spine, 'where it's interfaced again to the sciatic, pudendal and lumbar nerves.'

He turned back to face Jack, beaming. 'They've put a steel brace on the spinal column and they say that eventually all the nerve endings will grow onto the bioconnectors and I'll be back to normal, more or less.'

Jack felt himself grinning broadly as he watched the man lower himself gently into the wheelchair.

'That's wonderful.' He smiled again. They hadn't even been able to show him Helen's body. He often wondered if they had even found it all. How could so much damage have been caused at such a low height? The Navy passenger jet had been only a few hundred feet off the ground when the obsolete shoulder-launched missile had hit.

'At least they got the bastards,' growled Lynch, picking up Jack's mood. 'They're on Death Row now.'

Jack nodded. But they *wanted* to die, that was the problem. They thought they were going to 'Allah'. They were simple, uneducated, superstitious, information-deprived, aspiring martyrs carrying an antique, distorted and grotesque fantasy of Muslim righteousness into the heart of the infidel nation: to a rural airbase perimeter road that had been inadequately guarded. It was as if an ignorant native tribe from the distant past had travelled into the future solely to attack him and his family. Jack pulled himself away from such thoughts.

'So what's new in systems?' he asked.

'If there's nothing wrong, why is he here?' demanded Calypso. 'Why *precisely*?' She was angry and she knew it showed.

Marcus Forrester, commercial director of the Hope Island Research Clinic, smiled and tried to quieten down the noisy visitor.

'Because Tom asks us to keep a special eye on him. It's really nothing more than that, Doctor. He's an only son, after all.'

'Let me see him,' insisted Calypso again. '*I* am charged with his medical care, not your staff.'

She knew this wasn't wholly true, but she'd been shocked when the senior nurse up at the Tye mansion had told her that Tommy had been admitted to the high-security research clinic for three days. It was precisely this sort of ludicrous over-protection she was trying to prevent.

Without any apology or explanation she had been kept waiting for ten minutes in the large reception area of the underground clinic until Forrester had eventually emerged.

He smiled again. 'Of course. Right this way, Doctor Browne.' Insincerity radiated from his face, like a flight attendant's farewell.

He led Calypso from the reception area into an elevator. As they descended Forrester tried to make small talk, but by the time they had travelled three floors down he had abandoned the attempt. He led the way into a softly illuminated corridor with half a dozen white doors aligned down either side. At the third on the right he stopped and swung the door open for Calypso to enter. She could hear the sounds of a hydra-immersion chair from within.

She hesitated outside. 'Exactly what tests are your people running, Mr Forrester?' she asked. 'I'd like to see both the procedures and the results.'

'Naturally. I will arrange that, Doctor,' agreed Forrester unctuously. 'Please . . .' He gestured towards the door.

Calypso eyed him suspiciously and entered.

Tommy was oblivious of her arrival. He was wearing blue striped pyjamas and he was strapped into a grade 4–6 size 360-degree HydraChair fitted with full kinetic, tactility and olfactory sensory capabilities and user reafference. The helmet visor covered his face to below his nose. As she watched, whatever virtual craft he was piloting started a steep left-hand turn and the hydraulic supports of the small chair tipped him over at a thirty-degree angle. She heard him laugh and saw him shudder as the chair transmitted the sense of the force to his body. Then he was flying level again. Next his chair tipped upwards at the front and he was in a sharp climb. She could detect a faint aroma of jet-engine fuel in the atmosphere.

Calypso crossed to the wall screen and reviewed Tommy's physical history for the previous hour. As Forrester had said, there was nothing to worry about. She looked around the room, but she could see no trace of testing equipment or other records.

Suddenly Thomas Tye was beside her. He was sweating gently, as if he had been hurrying. She guessed he had been told of her sudden arrival at the clinic, and of her demands. She also guessed that it had been at his request that she had been kept waiting.

'What's this, Calypso? You should have been told you were not required today.'

Calypso folded her arms and turned to face her employer. She was wearing a bright yellow polo shirt and navy shorts, having planned to walk along to a restaurant beside the marina and meet Heather Garland for lunch. She had hoped to learn more from her about the disputed chess game.

'I called the house to talk to Nurse Pettigrew about Tommy going back to school,' she explained. 'Then I was told that Tommy wouldn't be returning. I asked to talk to him and she said he was here.'

'What do you think your job here is, Doctor?' asked Tye quickly. He was almost exactly the same height as her and his violet eyes flashed as he held her gaze.

'To look after Tommy, of course. To help him feel good about his fortunate position and to try and keep him sane when everything around him is insane.'

The words had come from nowhere. She'd meant them more figuratively than literally, but their effect on Tye was dramatic. The colour drained from his face and his lips pulled back from his teeth.

'Your job is to observe and report, Doctor, not to interfere,' he hissed, stabbing the air with his finger. 'We've got the world's best medical researchers on this island and I don't expect you to get in their way.'

Calypso's training came to her aid. She understood that irrational anger had to be calmed, not confronted. She said nothing.

'You're a qualified companion,' Tye continued, 'in case Tommy gets over-strained.'

Her feelings got the better of her. 'The only strain is the one that you put on him,' Calypso pointed out. 'Why can't you let him be normal, like other boys? He'd be far healthier for it, rather than living like some semi-institutionalized freak!'

'That's enough, Doctor,' snapped Tye.

'No, it's not enough,' insisted Calypso, determined to take the opportunity presented. 'Tommy is getting none of the praise, none of the constant assurance necessary to build his virtual identity – to create a robust personality, to put it in layman's terms. He isn't getting the love he needs to form relationships. He's not a laboratory specimen!'

'YOU HAVE NO IDEA WHAT YOU ARE FUCKING TALKING ABOUT!' shouted Tye. 'You've only been here five minutes.' He swallowed, then looked at his son. 'He's a genius, Doctor,' he added, waving at the oblivious Tommy in his HydraChair. 'He's got an IQ of over one eighty, he has talents like no other child, he's already reached Grand Master level at chess. Fucking doctors! I, better than anybody, should have seen through you. You're a quack, a charlatan.'

'He's a little boy,' shouted Calypso, now seriously angry. 'And money alone does not qualify you to be a parent! You *must* be insane!'

He hit her hard, open-handed across the face. The sound reverberated around the small hospital room.

'Never, ever say that,' he snarled pushing his face into hers.

Instinctively, Calypso had clapped her left hand to her assaulted cheek. She had never been struck before and part of her mind was consciously questioning how she felt about it. Then she slapped Thomas Tye across *his* face, as hard as she could.

He pulled back and stared at her in disbelief, shocked into silence. He had never been struck before, either.

Calypso suddenly realized there was no other sound in the room. She turned and saw that the HydraChair had stopped its motion. The helmet visor was swung up to its idle position. Tommy was staring at them, his violet eyes wide.

Calypso forced a smile and crossed the room. She squatted beside him. 'It's OK, Tommy. Grown-ups sometimes have arguments, too.'

'Leave us, Doctor,' ordered Tye. She noticed tears forming in his eyes.

Calypso hesitated as Tommy stared into her face with his father's eyes. He was obviously scared.

'LEAVE US!' screamed Tye.

She touched Tommy's cheek and rose. Walking slowly to the doorway, she turned and looked into Tye's face. Tears were now streaming down his cheeks.

'What *have* you done?' she asked him quietly.

She pressed the panic button on the wall. Then she turned and left Tye and his offspring alone together.

Haley sensed Rosemary's excitement when she called.

'Can you get over here now?' the agent had asked. 'Let's meet at the café again.'

They hadn't seen each other since Haley had threatened to find alternative literary representation, though Rosemary had sent her a bunch of flowers with a card saying she would continue to seek other publishers who might be interested in Haley's book.

As Haley threaded her way through the tables she saw Rosemary had arrived ahead of her and was already smoking her second cigarette. She also noticed an ice bucket waiting beside the table, and wine glasses glinting on the white cloth. It was a beautiful June morning but still only eleven o'clock, so rather too early for a lunchtime drink.

Rosemary rose to greet her client. 'I've ordered champagne,' she gushed as they both sat down. 'I've got good news for you. The Sloan Press – in New York – has made an offer.'

Haley had half-wondered whether an alternative offer might be the reason for this summons.

'That's wonderful. Was it the new material, about Tye's son, that hooked them?'

Rosemary smiled. She hadn't sent them the latest updates before they had made the offer. In fact, until they'd approached her, she hadn't sent them anything at all. But all agents want their writers to believe that it was hard work and not luck that made the difference. The fact was that the Sloan Press's editor-in-chief Luke Bailey had called out of the blue and asked to see the manuscript so far. He claimed to be fascinated by the idea that it was so hot that Nautilus had pulled out. Rosemary had e-mailed the text to him that same afternoon and twenty-four hours later he had made the offer.

'They love all of it, Haley,' she dissembled.

Haley nodded eagerly.

'They've even matched Nautilus's advance, and they'll provide a generous research and travel budget. They're promising a massive marketing campaign...'

She tailed off as the waiter arrived with the bottle of champagne. She tasted it quickly and nodded for him to pour.

'I was sure you'd want to celebrate.'

'But what about the injunctions?' Haley asked. 'Won't the Tye Corporation just reissue them against Sloan Press?'

'Luke Bailey says that's part of the plan. He believes that if the Tye Corporation really goes after the book, the subsequent legal action will attract massive publicity. His PR people can then turn any attempt to suppress your book into headline news.'

Haley nodded as she sipped the cool champagne. She could see the logic to that.

'And there's something else,' added Rosemary, slipping a piece of folded paper from her handbag and handing it to her author. Haley unfolded it and scanned the words.

'It's your draft itinerary,' Rosemary explained. 'Luke Bailey wants you to go and visit him in New York next week. He wants to discuss the book in detail and for you to get together with their lawyers to plan your defence and a counter-attack.

He also wants to discuss serialization in the newspapers – under non-disclosures, of course!'

Haley felt a little dazed by it all.

'What do you think?' urged Rosemary as she lit another cigarette. 'Should we accept?'

Haley smiled her answer.

'Here's to it,' said Rosemary as she lifted her glass in a toast.

Haley touched her glass to the agent's.

There had been a *lot* to learn. After two days of his intensive refresher course in computing and communications systems, Jack's mind was reeling from the onslaught.

Al Lynch had suggested, half seriously, that NSA, CIA and UNISA technology might seem old-hat to someone employed by a corporation able to crack the world's encryption systems. Jack had laughingly explained that he had little personal experience of the Tye Corporation's technology, having only observed what some of it could do. Tye never bothered himself with technical details these days, and he was only interested in meeting the sales prospect, doing the demo, then handing the sales process on to the technical consultants for completion. In fact, Jack realized, computing and communications had become an almost invisible part of everyday life for millions, something everyone took for granted.

'You realize how I received my instructions about your visit, Jack?' Lynch laughed. 'A courier flew down from New York with a briefcase chained to his wrist. It was a Cold War relic. They must have got it from a museum. But when I read the papers, I understood. We really do have to assume that your target has cracked the principles of prime-number key encryption. Is that right, Jack?'

Jack nodded. 'So UNISA assumes, Al. But they have no idea how that could be possible.'

'Nor me, either,' mused Lynch, 'and I thought I was pretty well up in this area. Ciphers are one of my specialities – I did encryption theory for my PhD thesis ...'

He tailed off in thought. Then he looked up again.

'But if the Tye Corporation *can* do so, it means that everything we normally provide for secure communications is now useless. That's always the inevitable implication for any civil or military authority after such a breakthrough. If they can crack the highest levels of encryption they can then just set up robot watchers in every hub on the networks. These would automatically intercept every communication that mentions Tye, his companies, his competitors, or organizations like ours, and copy them to his...' He tailed off again.

'Come to think of it, they could read *any* communication in the world, and if they can get into our databases, they could read every military secret we have. *Jesus...*'

Jack nodded.

'It means everything we've now got, all this comms kit, is junk – it's useless.' Lynch waved at the benches covered with minute wearable communications and surveillance devices.

Jack nodded again. He thought of making a joke about homing pigeons, but he could see that Lynch was deadly serious. He was working up to something.

'This gave me quite a challenge, Jack. And I had no idea that I was doing it for you, of course. But I'm delighted, delighted.'

He turned his wheelchair to the bench and lifted the plastic cover from a small piece of equipment. He turned back and handed it over. Jack took the device with a puzzled frown.

'It doesn't look much different to an early VideoMate,' said Lynch. 'But it is.'

He leaned forward and pointed to a slot that ran the whole length of the underside. 'This is a little fax feed, Jack, like they used to provide on the first generation of VideoMates, only I've modified this machine so that it doesn't send ordinary faxes. When you press this button it produces old-fashioned one-time codes at random and applies them to speech or keyboard input.'

Jack raised his eyebrows. One-time codes, for centuries the most secure form of encryption for covert communication, had disappeared long before he had joined the intelligence services: the topic was not even covered on any of the courses he had attended.

'You dictate the message, Jack, and the processor generates the one-time code – it's completely random, so no chance of patterns occurring. You connect this machine to a dedicated phone line and send the message as a fax, a bitmapped graphic, not as live text, and it's received at the other end and printed out on paper as plain text. Nothing must remain in a memory anywhere. This VideoMate doesn't have any radio links or network ports, Jack. They're all disabled. You get one printout of the one-time code and that's it. After that it doesn't exist any more.'

'So how do I get the one-time key to UNISA or whoever I'm faxing?' asked Jack.

'Ah, that's the weak link,' admitted Lynch. 'Ideally you should hand it to them personally. But that rather defeats the object, doesn't it?'

'I have to agree, Al,' he said. Lynch didn't seem to notice his sarcasm.

'But I think you can risk faxing it over a second dedicated fax line, like we used to use until everything went Internet protocol. We'll just have to install a couple on Hope Island or wherever you're going. It should be safe: we'll provide a massive white-noise wrapping and we'll know if anybody is tapping it. Even if it *was* compromised the beauty of one-time codes is there's never enough information to allow a computer program to decipher the pattern. There are too few occurrences. Also, I can't imagine that your target has set up robot intercepts for bitmap graphics. No one has ever used one-time codes in fax transmissions. They disappeared way before faxes came in and went out again.'

'Back to the future,' said Jack, smiling as he recalled a saying from his childhood.

Lynch looked at him blankly.

'Shall we go to full throttle?' suggested Stella Witherspoon diplomatically. The captain nodded his approval to the helmsman and with a roaring surge the ninety-foot offshore patrol craft rose to its full planing height.

'Sixty-two knots, that's about it,' shouted the Captain after a few minutes.

'How far are they?' yelled Stella as she clung on to a grab

rail. It was her turn to ride with one of Hope Island's coastal patrol craft: every few months her boss made each of his section heads take a week's night shift with the coastal patrols – even those who belonged to the Presidential Protection Team. It was just past midnight and misty.

The navigator indicated the converging shapes on his combined radar, infrared and satellite-imaging screen: the information from the three systems was integrated to provide a detailed graphic display.

'About three minutes at this speed,' the captain shouted at her. 'They're hove-to.'

The Cuban patrol vessel appeared as a red icon on the screen. They were closing quickly.

The captain lifted a flap on the control panel and pressed a red button. 'Go to weapons drill,' he ordered unnecessarily as the klaxon sounded.

Crew members appeared on deck and manned the forward laser-guided cannon and the aft machine guns. They watched as they converged on the incident.

'Ship ho,' called a crewman.

The captain nodded and the helmsman cut the throttles. The craft settled and the roar of the engines gave way to an idling burble. They rocked in near-silence for a minute as they stared into the mist.

The staccato sound of a machine gun broke the peace, and lines of red tracer flew over their heads. One of the crewmen turned on a searchlight and swung its beam across the sea.

'There,' shouted the helmsman.

The Cuban patrol boat and a crudely built oil-drum raft were caught in the intense white glare. They had been engaged in hauling fleeing rebel supporters on board. One youth was still clinging to a net on the side of the old gunboat. Sailors lined the rail, automatic weapons trained on the would-be asylum seekers.

Another burst of machine-gun fire from the Cuban vessel created a red carpet of tracer fire over the Hope Island patrol vessel, lower this time.

'Not very friendly,' observed Stella.

This type of mid-sea confrontation had been going on for

nearly a year, since a Cuban craft had come upon a Hope Island patrol boat lifting escaping rebel soldiers from the water. Havana had complained that far more of its citizens were landing in Hope Island than were returned.

'Position?' asked the captain quietly.

'Borderline, sir,' responded the navigator, peering at his display. 'Right on the line. Might be our waters, might be international.'

'They wouldn't really be a problem,' sighed the captain to Ms Witherspoon. But he already knew her response.

''Fraid not, Captain. The standing orders are unchanged.'

'Let's go home,' ordered the captain. As his craft turned away he spat pointedly but impotently out of the side window, in the direction of the Cuban craft, and went below.

TEN

Tye Life Sciences was suffering from a serious problem: in one key division it was unable to keep up with an overwhelming, insatiable global demand for certain highly personalized and very intimate products and services. The problem had become so severe that, two years before, Thomas Tye had personally taken responsibility for finding a solution. Above all, he *hated* losing revenue.

He solved the problem by inventing a new health-care concept and by founding a new company to deliver it. He was very proud that the idea for LifeLines Inc. was entirely his. The early results indicated that the severe shortage of biological products was already being reduced.

After a last-minute change of plans and some frantic rescheduling, he was to 'open' his new operation officially this morning. He whistled under his antibacterial mask as he rippled through the hermetically sealed clothes bags in his wardrobe, deciding what to wear for the hastily arranged ceremony.

TLS, as the life-sciences group of companies was known inside the Tye Corporation, had been founded soon after the parent company moved to Hope Island. In overall charge of research in the TLS group was Professor Stanley H. Walczack, a sixty-eight-year-old mathematical biologist and reprogeneticist whom Thomas Tye had personally courted for three years before he had been persuaded to leave his chair at Washington State University and relocate to Hope Island. As well as asking Walczack to direct research at TLS, Tye also invited him to become the first incumbent of a chair in Life Sciences that the corporation was endowing at the new Hope Island University.

At first, Walczack had turned him down flat, citing the inestimable benefit of working with so many like-minded colleagues in a non-commercial environment. After all, he was a MacArthur Award-winner and a member of the National Academy of Sciences and he felt that his life's work and reputation depended on him remaining in mainstream American academic life.

Then Tye persuaded the professor and his wife to visit Hope Island for a weekend. Walczack hadn't been finally induced to consider the offer seriously until late on the afternoon on which he was due to return to Seattle. Tye had already driven the Walczacks around the new university campus and cited the impressive list of other academics who had already committed to creating a 'knowledge nursery' on Hope Island. He sensed that Mrs Walczack was already won over and Tye had taken the professor into his office to reveal some of the work currently in progress within the research organizations that would make up the Tye Life Sciences group.

The biologist was amazed by the research that Tye described. He was fascinated by Erasmus's discovery of the progeria gene string and its role in cellular sclerosis and the anti-ageing therapy it was developing. He was also impressed to find that his host and benefactor had a grasp of biotechnology that was at least doctorate level.

It had still taken another six months to secure Walczack's formal commitment and a further twelve months of protracted negotiations between Washington State University and the new Hope Island University before Walczack had been able to delight his nagging wife by moving into one of the new white villas overlooking Hope Town. Now, over a decade later, Hope Island University and the Tye Life Sciences group occupied the leading position in the world's theoretical and applied life-science research community.

The first TLS success under Walczack's leadership had been PerPetuals, the pet-cloning technique developed personally by the professor. This service was launched in the North American

market from a string of PerPetuation Centers wholly owned by
Tye Life Sciences. Within two years TLS had franchised reproductive pet-cloning laboratories in all developed territories.

The second major service launched by TLS had gained such
success that response had been overwhelming. It was this
insatiable demand, and the severe shortages it caused, that had
prompted Thomas Tye to create the concept for LifeLines Inc.
two years earlier.

Tye Life Sciences had pioneered the laboratory growth of
replacement human organs. Working from stem cells into which
a patient's own DNA was grafted, the researchers successfully
grew livers, kidneys, hearts, lungs, hands, feet, sex organs, skin,
eyes and neural tissue that, because of their perfect genetic
match, could be transplanted into the original DNA provider
without fear of rejection and without the need for the powerful
immunosuppressant drugs that had previously been the main
problem in the aftercare of transplant patients. Usually a transplant from genetically identical tissue returned the sufferer to
excellent health within days.

From the outset, doctors in North America, Europe and
Japan had been enthusiastic about the process. Wealthy patients
who were still well enough to travel flocked to Hope Island for
tax-free surgery paid for with tax-free money. Soon there was a
lengthy waiting list for organs to be grown and transplants to be
undertaken. The Hope Island Medical Clinic was extended twice
in the first two years after it opened and the TLS laboratories
expanded to cover thirty-one acres.

By itself, this achievement was remarkable but not unique.
Several other research facilities around the world announced
similar successes in growing cloned organs and, for the brief
period the subject had held the media's attention, scores of
happy auto-transplant patients told television reporters how
wonderful it was to feel well again.

What was unique about the work undertaken at Tye Life
Sciences was the third project to be headed personally by
Professor Stanley H. Walczack that he had started soon after
arrival on Hope Island. After two and a half years of development, TLS filed patents for a universal organ-support and

long-term storage unit called MatchBox. Further patents, filed
three months later, described a similar but portable device.

MatchBox solved a problem that was severely limiting the
therapeutic work that the world's transplant surgeons could
undertake with farmed organs. The device kept newly grown
organs healthy for an indeterminate period. Without such a
device an organ could be kept healthy for only a few days after
it had reached maturity and been harvested.

For his MatchBox, Walczack personally designed and
manipulated a gene string from which a universal placenta could
be grown: a biological interface that could quickly grow supporting tissue connections to the very different arteries, veins,
nerves and conductive tissues found in the various organs that
were under cultivation. Walczack's master stroke was in coaxing
the gene string to mimic the way female reproductive systems
switch off their immune-system defences when an embryo,
which is wholly foreign tissue, is welcomed and nourished by
the placenta. Within a year of starting MatchBox manufacture
Tye Life Sciences had sufficient stocks to be able to announce
the launch of a new service described in their literature as POB
– Pre-emptive Organ Banking.

The response to the new POB service from Tye Life Sciences was overwhelming. Many wealthy and perfectly healthy
individuals wanted the security of having back-ups of their vital
organs and waiting lists started to grow alarmingly.

At first, Tye was in favour of steadily increasing the price for
these standby organs until a natural rationing occurred. But his
marketing economists developed a complexity-pricing model
that produced the maximum financial yield while ensuring
demand remained high. The range of price variations was
enormous and contracts were tailored for each client. Some paid
hefty premiums to have their organs duplicated quickly and
then moderate storage fees during the period that TLS kept
them against potential need. Others paid lower duplication fees
but higher storage costs. The TLS pricing system computed an
individual's price structure from the number of organs ordered
at one time, the patient's genetic background, medical history,
LifeWatch ambulatory data (which, helpfully, indicated current

health status), actuarial tables, and also the customer's preferred payment terms. Existing customers of the many Tye-Managed Healthcare Schemes around the world received loyalty discounts, but no customer paid exactly the same price as any other and no customer received exactly the same service.

TLS and MatchBox gave the rich and successful another personal luxury to aim for: an ultimate acquisition that ranked alongside their personal jets, classic-car collections and luxury yachts. The richest customers wanted every one of their vital organs – and some of the less vital – grown and kept available in case of future need.

It was over the issue of how best to deal with requests for help from seriously ill customers unable to afford a priority fee that Walczack and his patron had suffered their first serious disagreement. 'Your work has to be protected,' insisted Tye. 'We own the patents for twenty-five years and there's another eighteen to go.' He could have added that the corporation had still not recovered all the development costs, and licence income was not the most efficient way to go about it.

Walczack had tendered his resignation immediately. But Tye had smiled, put his arm around the professor's shoulders and asked him, as a personal favour, to delay his decision.

When Walczack saw Tye's plans for the seventh-generation LifeWatches and the new market that would result, the professor had suspended his threat of resignation. Tye had then cemented their new agreement by bestowing an additional tranche of stock options in the new company on the pioneering professor.

Thomas Tye selected a pair of blue chinos to go with his white shirt, removing them from their sterile container. He took the elevator down to his office where he handed Connie an envelope and issued instructions about Calypso. Then he pulled a spreadsheet onto the wall screen and ran over the projections for LifeLines's stock-market flotation.

Raymond Liu sat alone in Network Control Center on Hope Island. The Group Technical Director of Tye Network Systems was baffled. His teams had spent three weeks investigating the short but highly dangerous intermittent failures of the air-traffic-control satellites over Northern California and the near-disastrous loss of satellite communications in the Australasian quadrant. But they still had no idea what might have caused such bizarre independent system failures.

Every diagnostic report from the satellites, from the traffic management centres and from the ground controllers was negative. There were no faults and no log records of unauthorized communications. Air traffic communications over Northern California had returned to normal and in the South-Western Pacific the ground controllers had only had to override the orbiting traffic management system, and order the two data communications satellites to fire their thrusters again to return them to their original orientation. When their on-board computers were rebooted, laser-borne data had been once again routed back to them and they functioned perfectly. Their on-board diagnostic systems reported one hundred per cent performance, so there was no explaining the mysterious malfunctions. Chomoi Ltupicho, Liu's opposite number at the Soyuz FreePlanet network, had confirmed a similar outcome to his investigation. Short of sending a recovery shuttle to launch two replacement satellites and bring home the offending units, there was little more Liu could do from the ground. Also, as the suspect units were now functioning perfectly, he knew Tom would never divert launch capacity from the much-whispered-about Phoebus Project.

But despite this, Tom was pressing – screaming – for an answer. No data had been lost during the Pacific network outage so Tye Networks had not suffered any contingent liabilities, but it had seemed very close. Even an hour's failure of a backbone data network could cost the corporation billions in compensation payments. The world's economies could no longer function without the networks.

Liu had searched the global archives for information about other unusual communication-system failures occurring at around the same time. At first he had searched for unusual system events happening an hour on either side of his Australasian satellite failures. There had been nothing, however. Then, in desperation, he had gathered the hourly logs of every orbiting router in the Tye-LaserNet satellite networks for a week either side of the mysterious failures. There were over 8,000 of them and he had been forced to write a script to automate the transfer of those data to his three-dimensional spreadsheet.

He now clicked the display back on. The central Holo-Theater in the Network Control Center was filled with light, and Liu was looking into the square box of cells he had created. He switched the display to graphic mode and pushed himself up from the well-upholstered control chair. He walked right into the display and put his hand into one of the beams of red holo-light that represented a failure that had occurred and been automatically corrected.

There had been a 300 per cent increase in such minor failures in the previous six weeks and there was serious and startling degradation in performance across all the networks. Until these problems were identified and eliminated he couldn't even begin to deploy the much-needed multiplexing software the corporation had recently acquired from a Brazilian software company. He debated whether he should send a warning message to Thomas Tye but decided against that course of action almost immediately. If you alerted Tom to a problem you had to have a solution ready at the same time. Liu knew he was going to have to design a system that could measure data flow and integrity across every public network in the world.

The senior executives, software engineers, medical consultants and off-duty bereavement counsellors of LifeLines Inc., the majority-owned subsidiary of Tye Life Sciences Inc., stood in little huddles, talking nervously as they waited for their VIP guest to arrive and perform the official opening ceremony.

In physical terms there was little he could open. The large sunken room was divided longitudinally by a floor-to-ceiling glass partition. In the administration area, where he would be welcomed, there were only a dozen desks and six large wall screens. On the other side of the soundproof glass, those on duty were huddled in their booths, monitoring their screens or speaking quietly with next of kin all over the world.

Zachary Zorzi, the chief systems designer, Multi-Linnux IV

magus and technical inspiration of the LifeLines sales resource
('Zee Zee' to his friends and favoured staff, 'Easy Zee Zee' to
those who knew of his herbal and chemical indulgences) had
thought it would be cool to invite the great man to cut a white
ribbon, which was now strung limply between two potted
plants. Even though the entire enterprise had been the boss's
idea, the team had still been surprised when Thomas Tye had
reversed his original decision and, with only four hours' notice,
agreed to make time in his frantic schedule to accept their
invitation to open the operations centre formally. Then it had
taken them all morning to locate suitable pot plants to decorate
the bare office.

Zorzi was looking forward to becoming rich. He had been
lured away from his role as systems director at one of the
world's great auction houses by a serious salary increase and
generous stock options in the new company. He was nearly
twenty-eight and most of the fellow students who had been on
his systems-design course at Stanford were already multimillion-
aires. He knew he had been leaving his own attempt at a
financial home run dangerously late in his career. But when the
HR Director of the Tye Corporation had made contact, Zorzi
had sensed that his opportunity had finally arrived.

Now, two years since initial systems development had
started, the resource was live on the networks and had been
operating for six weeks without any downtime. LifeLines had
already served over 5,000 successful bidders and the company
was forty per cent ahead of its projected target for recipient
registrations. Zorzi was delighted but, other than monitoring
data produced by the automated transactions, there was now
little for him to do. The real action was in bereavement counselling and that wasn't an occupation for him. He was already
getting bored with life on Hope Island and with the company
he privately referred to as 'White Lines'.

'He's coming,' hissed a young female interface designer
whom Zorzi had stationed at the door. Everybody straightened.
No one there except Zee Zee had met the superstar tycoon
before.

Connie walked into the room first, followed by her boss. She was wearing a beige linen trouser suit with a terracotta-coloured blouse, the epitome of professional elegance. Tom wore his blue chinos with a white open-necked shirt. His long dark hair was tied back in a ponytail. Easy Zee Zee approved of his boss's casual style.

'Good morning,' said Tye to the assembled company.

Zorzi stepped forward. He wasn't quite sure what to do. He knew his chairman didn't like to shake hands.

'Welcome, Mr Tye,' he responded involuntarily before he corrected himself. 'Welcome, Tom. Welcome, Miss Law. Coffee, mineral water?'

Tom smiled and shook his head for both of them. Connie cracked the seal of a packet and Tye sprayed his mouth. He slipped on the face mask Connie handed him.

'I heard you've made a good start,' Tye said through the mask. 'Let's see it, then.'

The guests were guided to two new upright chairs placed in the centre of the room from where they could best see the wall screens. Off-duty members of the team pulled chairs from behind desks and arranged them in a group behind the visitors, marvelling that the rumours about Tye and his face masks were true. Zorzi pulled his chair up next to Tye and Connie as the overhead lights were turned off.

'We'll start with a global display of all seventh-generation LifeWatch locations.'

A Mercator projection of a world map appeared on the centre screen, the continental masses outlined in red on a black background. As they watched, minute white dots appeared as concentrations in and around the major cities of North America, Europe, Asia, Australasia and South America. On the Russian land mass, only Moscow and St Petersburg showed much illumination.

'So far there are about eight hundred million units of the GenSeven LifeWatch registered and active on the world's networks,' explained Zorzi, even though he guessed that his exalted business partner would already know those figures. 'But there are still large gaps in distribution in most of Russia, middle China and Africa.' Zorzi pointed to the darker areas of the map.

Tye nodded. 'The Foundation is upping distribution of free units to a hundred and fifty thousand a month,' he announced. 'We're concentrating on areas of high mortality, for obvious reasons – Africa especially. We've got new teams starting in Ethiopia and Somalia.'

Zorzi scratched his goatee beard. 'Well, we're getting a higher percentage of DNA matches than we projected, so getting more GenSevens distributed isn't so urgent as we thought it would be. Anyway, let's look at the US situation.'

The map changed suddenly to display an outline view of North America. Every urban centre showed up as a large, dense cluster of white light. Myriad strings of light across the rural areas revealed how ubiquitous LifeWatches had become for the American people.

'Those data derive from routine uploads from LifeWatches and VideoMates over the last week,' explained Zorzi. 'There's only been a point zero zero two failure rate on GenSevens, which is very impressive.'

'Can we go real-time?' asked Tye.

Zorzi nodded at the display controller and the screen refreshed to show less dense concentrations across the country.

'These are the LifeWatches that are uploading to us right now. If we take out the routine periodic uploads … Yes, here are the distress calls, and the uploads from those whose vital signs have ceased or are suspect.'

'Show me the deaths occurring in the last hour,' requested Tye. The screen refreshed to show a higher density of white dots.

'The average mortality rate throughout the world is around eleven thousand an hour at this time of year. In the United States it is just over eight hundred an hour,' explained Zorzi. 'It's mid-morning on the East Coast so we're down on that by thirty per cent but, if you look at California, it's the early hours and we're getting a peak loading.'

'What percentage of mortalities are we registering overall?' asked Tye.

'It's a very good proportion,' smiled Zorzi. 'Your marketing people in Consumer Electronics have done well. Even allowing for those who haven't upgraded their LifeWatch units to a GenSeven, and for those freaks who won't wear any sort of LifeWatch, we're getting data from about forty-six point two per cent of the adult American population.'

Tye turned to Connie. 'I want to talk to Randall from CE later – remind me. Penetration still needs to be better.'

He turned back to Zorzi. 'How good has the matching system proved?'

Zorzi swung round in his chair to face one of the female medics. 'Do you want to take this, Irene?'

Haley hated jogging, but there was no getting away from it: she could feel a distinct pinch of fat where there should be none. It happened during the writing of every book and during relationships in which she had too much control. She didn't like herself for this behaviour, but she would let herself go to seed a little when a romance didn't stimulate her.

Battersea Park was filled with joggers, t'ai chi enthusiasts and dog walkers. It was five p.m. and the river was almost at its lowest, the grey mud of Chelsea Reach drying within minutes of its exposure.

Haley rubbed her side to banish a trace of stitch, took another deep breath and set off again, in the direction of Albert Bridge. She doubted whether she would achieve much physical improvement in just a week, but she needed to make a good impression in New York.

She'd also been thinking a lot about Jack Hendriksen and why she hadn't heard from him. He had warned her not to contact him at the Tye Corporation and, although she understood his reasons, it was frustrating to have to wait for his call. He'd promised to get in contact over a month ago.

Haley put on a short burst of speed to arrive at the gradient leading up to the park gate and the beautiful old suspension bridge beyond. She stopped again to lean against the embankment railings opposite Cadogan Pier. When she had found her second wind she would run back around the park, take a shower, and go over to Ladbroke Grove to spend the evening with Flick and Toby. There was little she could do on the biography until she knew more about what Sloan Press expected.

Dr Irene Desmond, thin and nervous in a black jersey dress, stood up and walked round to face her exclusive audience. She swallowed nervously and then looked directly at the distinguished visitor.

'The system for matching donors to recipients has proved remarkably accurate, Mr Ty– Tom. A GenSeven LifeWatch sends us the wearer's DNA profile in its first routine upload after it is initially strapped on. We compare and couple that to the wearer's digital ident from the World Certification Authority and, once confirmed, the information goes into the data warehouse until it's needed – and, of course, so that Tye Agriceuticals, Pharmaceuticals and the insurance companies can extract the genetic profiles of each individual. When a customer registers to become a recycling recipient, we upload his or her DNA profile and we store it in the same format for constant comparison with the profiles of those who pass away. That's the module that Zee Zee – Zach – developed. When we get a match above sixty per cent we alert the customer. Let me show you.'

She nodded at the display controller and a DNA profile appeared on the left-hand screen.

'This profile was provided by a forty-one-year-old male in Melbourne, Australia. He is waiting for at least one kidney, since he's lost both and is on permanent, but unsustainable, dialysis. He therefore can't wait for Tye Life Sciences to grow him replacements. Now, if we could see our current pool of donors whose organs have not yet been reallocated...'

The map display refreshed yet again, to show a whole world view. Those watching saw a low cluster of lights in the main urban centres and lights stringing out across the rural open spaces. Despite the relatively low overall penetration of the seventh generation of LifeWatches in Africa and Russia, a surprisingly large number of individual dots and clusters showed across those territories.

'There's a higher ratio of donor wearers in the undeveloped areas, where there are fewer medical facilities,' broke in Zorzi by way of explanation. 'It's the people who think they're most at risk health-wise who go out of their way to get a GenSeven model. So the deaths we miss out on in these areas tend to be the accidental and unanticipated mortalities. Unfortunately, they are often the best source for recycling opportunities.'

Dr Desmond looked up at the screen, then turned back to resume her explanation.

'Of those with organs still uncommitted, we currently have eleven hundred deceased up to an hour old, just under six thousand up to three hours, twenty-two thousand, three hundred up to six hours and thirty-four thousand, seven hundred up to twelve hours. Unfortunately, none of them has a good enough DNA profile match to be of interest to our Melbourne customer.'

'How many of those uncommitteds matched a customer's needs well enough to be in auction?' asked Tye.

'Zee Zee?' prompted the doctor.

'Can we see the current bidding status?' asked Zorzi.

The left-hand screen refreshed to a show a transaction-analysis page.

'You may not be able to read all of the small type,' said Zorzi. He stood up and walked closer to the screen. 'There are four hundred and twenty-seven auctions in progress at the moment. The longest duration is nearly eleven hours.'

'Is that normal?' asked Tye. 'I thought our business plan suggested three hours of bidding would be the max. Don't we want to keep bidding excitement high?'

Zorzi nodded. 'Yeah, that's what we thought. But sometimes it gets protracted when there are late entrants, or somebody asks for a pause when they need to raise more capital. We allow each bidder *one* break of fifteen minutes for that.'

He nodded to the system controller again and a new display appeared.

'We're running two auction models to see which one produces the highest yields,' he explained as he looked at the screen. 'This one here is a straightforward *highest* bid, the other is a *sealed* bid that's intended to elicit high pre-emptive offers. As you suggested, I chose an upper-class English accent for the auctioneer interface. It does seem to reassure customers and maximize the bidding.'

He stepped back to take in more of the data. 'This auction's for a liver that's available in Cape Town and is already safely in a MatchBox and certified by the removing surgeon. The next of kin have agreed to a twenty per cent cut of the net receipts and we've given them an estimate of one point seven million US as their share.'

'What's the reserve?'

'Eight million US. This particular recycle opportunity is in A-One Condition and the database has shown eleven DNA profiles that match over ninety-five per cent of the donor's genome – that's from our database of patients who have regis-tered with us and are waiting for a well-matched liver. A ninety-five per cent match means that there will be many common genes on the sixth chromosome and many common antigens. It's almost a perfect match of tissue types – as good as if it were an isograft from an identical twin. That's why this auction is going on so long. It'll be a fierce contest and will probably reach twenty million'

'Are all eleven bidding?' asked Tye.

Zorzi glanced at the controller and the screen refreshed again. 'No, seven have now dropped out,' he reported. 'We're at sixteen point five million dollars, that's from a customer in Memphis. The other three have ten minutes to improve their bids. The next round drops to five minutes, then one minute, thirty seconds, and that's it. The whole process is automated. Once a NOK – sorry, a next of kin – has agreed, we get a copy of his or her digital ident as approval, then a contract is printed out at their end in their local language and in a format that embodies any peculiarities of local laws and taxation. Where there's a spot tax on removal we undertake to pay that.'

'How can we be sure of getting our payment from the bidders?'

'Well, we've had no problems so far. Most of the customers who sign on are too late for POB – they can't wait while a replacement organ or tissue part is grown. We charge everybody who registers three hundred thousand dollars as a joining fee. That isn't a lot of money but it's enough to keep out the jokers and those who aren't wholly responsible for their actions. When bidding for a recycled resource begins we ask everybody who wants to bid to deposit the reserve in escrow, as bankers' drafts or in digital cash, before the auction starts. Our registered customers are warned of likely reserve figures in advance. The actual reserve depends on the closeness of the DNA profile match of the recycled component and this is displayed for the bidders as they enter.

'If the match is forty per cent or less they might as well get a recycled part on the welfare market. They're going to have to use cyclosporine and all the other immuno-suppressants for years. If it's above sixty-five per cent, they'll still have to use them, but they've got a ninety per cent chance of the transplant holding. Above ninety per cent and everybody's a winner. No drugs are needed at all. Obviously we ensure the successful bidder makes full payment before the shipment is approved.'

'How did we get this liver?'

Zorzi signalled at one of the members of staff perched on the edge of a desk. 'This is Doctor Mohammed Ebrahimi, our senior bereavement counsellor. He's also our head counselling trainer and a consultant thanatologist.'

A squat, sallow, grossly overweight middle-aged man stood up. He had a bushy black moustache and he wore an over-formal three-piece dark suit. He made a deep, ostentatiously oleaginous bow.

'That was one of mine, Tom,' Ebrahimi explained in an old-fashioned, Farsi-accented style of English. Despite the air conditioning, he was sweating visibly. 'It was really very easy. The LifeWatch intervened when the poor donor suffered an MI – a heart attack. Very sad. I got to the widow in Mumbai – in India – within an hour. She spoke very good English although, as you know, next door we can cope with one hundred and eighty-six different languages. You understand that auto-translation isn't a very suitable thing in bereavement counselling. We are often the ones who have to break the news to the NOKs and it doesn't come out right. So, anyway, this NOK was quite composed. I should say your wonderful, wonderful counselling message helped a lot, Tom. Thank you very much for that.'

'Can we show Tom how that message came out?' called Zorzi, looking over at the controller. He was pleased at how well this was going.

The right-hand screen refreshed and Tye was looking at his own image. He was in darkness, so that only his face was lit with a soft glow.

'[NOK Salutation space, NOK Family Name space.] I know there are times when even a LifeWatch can't help us,' his image said gently, looking earnestly into the camera. His tones were deep and mellisonant, as designed by the otolaryngologist over thirty years before. 'I know how you must be feeling. You have lost someone very close. I extend my sympathies.'

There was a short pause as if Tye was gathering himself. Quiet organ music started in the background.

'But, if you'll agree, some good can come out of this. Allow me to find a way for [Deceased Salutation space, Deceased Family Name space]' – there was a short pause, then increased emphasis – '[Deceased Given Name space] to help others. Our recycling program guarantees the best future for – [Deceased Given Name possessive apostrophe space] – life to be of help to others. And you will also contribute to helping the Thomas Tye Foundation so that other lives can be saved.'

The figure paused.

All in the room inhaled involuntarily and held their breath as the ScentSims added a most pleasing fragrance. Zee Zee had debated for months with the olfactorologists about the right note to strike at this point in the message. In the end they had created a fragrance they called 'Strawberry.' It was the smell of a newborn baby's crown.

'LifeLines can take care of all the details now. One of our counsellors will speak to you personally in a moment. I just wanted a moment to express my regret and to say . . .'

There was another pause and the camera slowly zoomed in towards the face. The music stopped.

'Reach out and touch me.'

Tye's hand appeared and he reached out towards the lens.

'Touch me and [Deceased Given First Name space] can touch the world.' His finger flattened as he pressed it to the lens and a faint golden corona appeared.

'And, thank you. May your God bless you.'

The video image faded to darkness and even those in the administration area felt its impact as the screen flickered and returned to normal display.

'Very powerful,' breathed Zorzi, breaking the collugency. 'Of course, you were kind enough to give us sufficient video material to allow us to morph your mouth around whatever names you need to say – even the long Russian ones. Then we morph the whole message into all of the various languages. The result is very realistic. We even select a threnody appropriate for the local culture. Want to see a replay in Russian? We use *gusli* music.'

Tye held his hand up to quell the young auction designer's enthusiasm. He'd seen more than enough lip-synch morphing over the years and he already knew that the morphotactioners in Tye Digital Arts were the best in the world.

'Tell me about the total yield on this deal.'

'The widow was most keen for full recycling procedures,' smirked Ebrahimi, a model of morigeration. 'She agreed to twenty per cent of the net receipts, as Mr Zorzi said. We instructed the local surgeons, and the excellent Tye Logistics delivered the MatchBoxes in under an hour. Procedures were complete inside three hours.'

'That's the way we'd like them all to be,' broke in Zorzi.

'How many other commodities can we recycle from this donor?' asked Tye.

'Every high-ticket item except the heart and lungs,' beamed the necrophilic negotiator. 'The widow even accepted a closed-casket funeral so we could harvest the face and hands for the burns, skin-cancer and identity-replacement markets. For that, we pay all the exequial expenses.'

Tom nodded his approval.

'The kidneys went immediately, I think,' reported Zorzi. 'Some oilman from Uzbekistan trounced everybody with a pre-emptive eighteen-million-dollar bid. The corneas also went quickly, bone marrow is under way now...'

'What will be the total recycle yield?' asked Tye again.

'About one hundred and two million,' Zorzi estimated. 'The widow will get twenty per cent, while storage and transport is paid for by the successful bidders. We pay local medical expenses for the recycling procedures. I would think we'll net maybe seventy or eighty.'

'How are the percentage splits holding up in general?' queried Tye. 'Are any of the families getting greedy?'

Zorzi signalled for the bereavement counsellor to respond.

'Oh yes, but you see it is we who add the value to the meat,' explained the happy grief counsellor. 'We do get some greedy NOKs, but recycle potential exists for only a very few hours, so we just let them, how do you say it ... stew.' He emitted a high-pitched series of connected shrieks, as if someone had described to him what laughter was but then forgotten to provide an actual demonstration.

'The trick is in finding the match and providing the storage. The actual recycled unit isn't worth much without that. NOKs usually come round after a couple of hours – when they're facing the choice of making a free donation to a charity or welfare health market, or making some serious money with us.'

'Very good,' commented Tye as he stood up. He turned to Connie. 'Set me up to visit one of these auction winners in the recovery room. Choose an American kid, under twelve, and get the perception people to handle the media set-up.'

He looked back at the gangly Zorzi and slipped off his mask. He then walked his latest entreprenerd a few steps away from the main group.

'Have you got a capitalization in mind for the stock-market offering?'

Zorzi scratched his goatee again. 'I'd guess around forty billion.'

Tye beamed. 'I'll have a bet with you. With this rate of earnings we'll reach a hundred.'

He paused in thought. The success of the auction models

had given him another idea. 'Can all this work without you now?'

Zorzi nodded. 'Yeah. I've only got to finish designing the suicide-reserve module – as the prices will have to be higher. The condition of organs from most suicides is much better than those that come to the market from natural deaths. I want it all up and working before the autumn. The actuaries say there's a big rise in suicides around the Christmas holidays and the New Year and I want to be ready.'

Tom raised his eyebrows. 'Get someone else to finish up for you,' he said quietly. 'Meanwhile, talk to Connie and fix to come by the house. I've got something for you that will make this stuff seem like chicken feed.'

Zorzi smiled. He couldn't imagine any market that would be better than this – but an invitation to the Tye mansion!

Tom turned back towards the expectant faces. 'Thank you, ladies and gentlemen,' he said. 'We'll go for an IPO in eight weeks. And we'll all be seriously rich.' There was no trace of irony in his voice.

He turned on his heel and walked from the building, spraying his mouth as he did so. Connie followed, hard upon his heels. The ceremonial ribbon remained intact, hanging limply between the potted palms.

But Zee Zee didn't mind at all. He had some calls to make.

ELEVEN

The flowers filled Calypso's living room. They had arrived while she had been consulting with HR and Logistics about helicopter availability. She had decided she would spend a month with her mother before making contact with the medical staff agencies on the American mainland to begin the search for a new job.

Two men from the spaceport's busy courier office had been drafted in to make the delivery from the exclusive flower boutique in the town square. The Volante pick-up they used seemed to be overflowing when they started to unload, and it took them ten minutes to carry all the baskets and bunches into Calypso's bungalow while she frantically cleared surfaces on which to put them. Each display had a small handwritten card identifying its blooms. There were giant white atamasco lilies from Virginia, mauve calceolaria from Venezuela, a Japanese ikebana arrangement with white chrysanthemums set against gravel and bleached drift twigs collected from the island's beaches, a stunning arrangement of chocolate-tinted odontoglot orchids from Brazil, a dozen strongly scented burgundy Hope roses (grown on the island) and a dazzling array of spotted purple, yellow and white tiger-flowers collected from the swamps of Florida's Everglades.

When every flat surface had been covered and her living room turned into a heady, aromatic bloomery they handed her a grey envelope and left. She slit it open and pulled out a card.

It was from Thomas Tye, and Calypso scanned his hand-written message with mixed feelings. She was still furious with him for the previous afternoon. Then she sat down and read the note again. His handwriting was elegant, almost female in quality, completely unlike her own scrawl.

> *Dear Dr Browne,*
>
> *I'm truly sorry about yesterday. Tommy means a great deal to me but I was wrong to react in such a way.*
>
> *Tommy was very upset by my behaviour and I have apologized to him. I'm afraid he is still somewhat upset and he is asking for you.*
>
> *I hope you will be gracious enough to accept my apology and join us for lunch at the house today. Please contact Connie.*
>
> *Yours,*
> *Tom*

She put the card down on her small coffee table and looked around her flower-filled room. Suddenly she sneezed. Then she sneezed again. She went outside into the heat and sneezed twice more.

Two hours later Calypso took the Mag to the house. The shuttle stopped as it approached the steel security doors shuttering the tunnel leading to Tye's private residence. Calypso turned her head and squarely faced the camera lens set into the wall. The doors parted at the middle and the shuttle sped forward into the brightly lit tunnel.

Tommy was waiting on the little station platform right underneath the house. Even before she climbed out she could see that he had been crying. She had dressed in a white linen shirt and white Bermuda shorts for what, she anticipated, was going to be a rather awkward meeting.

She squatted on the platform and Tommy threw his arms around her neck in silence. She forced herself not to kiss him but she stroked his back as he clung to her.

'It's OK, Tommy,' she soothed. 'There are no bones broken, are there?'

As she stood, he continued to gaze up at her, clutching Jed. Tommy's companion had recently been upgraded by Professor Keane's researchers and he now disliked being left alone.

'Hello, Calypso,' said the red caterpillar.

Calypso heard doors open, then Connie stepped out of the elevator.

'Welcome, Calypso. Tom's waiting for you inside.'

By tacit agreement they said nothing as they rode the four floors up to Tom's main living area. Tommy clung to Calypso with one hand while squeezing Jed with the other.

'You're hurting me,' complained Jed. Calypso knew how that felt.

The elevator stopped but the doors did not open.

'Hold your breath,' warned Connie.

Calypso felt a wave of damp cold air wash through the car. Then, at last, the doors slid open.

Tye was waiting for them in his main living hall, a room Calypso hadn't visited before. It was of double height, clad in brilliant white Carrara marble, and she guessed the ceiling was over thirty feet high. The vast unpolished, slate-grey stone floor was strewn with ancient Afshar, Sehna and Shah Abbas Persian rugs arranged around a score of fine classical sculptures. Pale sofas were grouped to form seating areas.

Although she had heard about them, it was still a thrill to see the giant Jackson Pollocks and Hockneys, the Picasso nudes – and, displayed all on its own at the far end of the room, *that* Rembrandt, an image she remembered from her childhood. She would have liked more time to study the small but exquisite art collection.

The room's east-facing wall was constructed entirely of photoreactive plate glass. In the bright sunlight it had darkened protectively to lessen the glare.

She noticed a slight swelling on Tye's left cheek, as he extended a hand with a smile. Despite herself, she couldn't help but respond.

'Apology accepted?'

Calypso conjured up a small grin, then took his hand. She noticed it was small-boned and extremely fine. She had never shaken hands with him before.

'Let's go out onto the terrace,' said Tye, leading the way across the hall. A full-height pane of glass slid to one side and they stepped out onto the white tiled terrace. A table had been set up under a large sun umbrella where Tye's butler and one of the maids stood waiting for the luncheon party.

Calypso's first impressions were of dazzling light and considerable elevation. Beyond the waist-high safety rail, the hillside fell in wide, stepped terraces to the beach and the emerald ocean below. The view was breathtaking and she found herself gaping in awe up and down the length of the island.

'It *is* beautiful, isn't it?' observed Tye, as he pulled a chair out for her. 'But then, you know these islands well, Doctor.'

Calypso smiled again, spontaneously this time. She had been wondering whether she could see Haiti on the southern horizon.

Once seated, they each took one of the warm antiseptic towels that were offered.

Tye was at his most charming as lunch got under way. He recounted how he had discovered Hope Island and what a tough deal Cuba had struck over ceding it. He went on to describe the protracted negotiations with the United Nations for sovereign recognition and how his corporation had bowed to Cuban and American pressure to forgo all forms of arms development and manufacture here and to maintain no armed forces other than those required for internal and coastal security. He was explaining how he had personally chosen the site for the house when Connie interrupted him. 'I have President Orlov's cabinet secretary for you.'

'I'll get back to him,' said Tye.

He turned back to Calypso and apologized. 'Sorry, Doctor. I was supposed to be in Moscow for lunch today but I wanted a chance to make things up with you.'

Calypso did her best to smile in what she hoped was a gracious and understanding fashion. He had cancelled lunch with a head of state to see her. How bizarre Tye's world seemed – and, of course, Tommy's.

'It's very hot today,' Jed offered, breaking the silence. Tommy laughed and they all laughed with him.

They were first served a salmon mousse, and then the chef offered a choice of sushi or soya-duck in a *bigarade* sauce. Tye had fish for both courses, while Calypso and Connie ordered the pseudo-duck. A huge basket of crisply fried coarse-cut Hope Island potatoes (guaranteed non-fattening) was served on the side. Tommy, who had been silently gazing at Calypso all through the lunch, was brought tofu-chicken nuggets in tempura batter served on a bed of wild rice. A very chilled Pouilly Fuissé was served, which Calypso enjoyed greatly although she noticed that Tye drank only mineral water.

When he had eaten most of his main course, Tommy asked to be excused. His father nodded and the boy got down from the table.

Connie rose. 'I'll take him to see Nurse Pettigrew.'

Tye smiled his approval.

'Can Calypso come and play with me later?' asked Tommy.

Tye looked at the doctor questioningly. Calypso nodded.

'She'll be along later, son,' he said. 'Enjoy yourself.'

'May we watch a cartoon?' asked Jed.

After the plates were cleared, they were left on their own. Tye cleared his throat and turned in his chair to face Calypso squarely. He took off the sunglasses he had been wearing. 'You don't think much of me as a father, do you, Doctor?'

Calypso stared at her employer's beautiful face and tried to read some of the secrets hidden behind those vivid violet eyes.

'No, I can't say I do,' she confirmed slowly. She tilted her head back. 'You're over-protective to the point of doing him harm. You've employed me because I'm a paediatric psychiatrist and I have to tell you that if I examined this boy in a clinical environment I would classify him as already significantly disturbed.'

She watched Tye take the blow and she saw that it hurt. But he was holding himself in tight control.

She ventured further. 'Where's his mother? Every boy needs a mother and I never hear him talk about her.'

Tye looked at her with a long steady gaze. 'His mother left when he was a baby, Doctor. I'm sure HR must have explained that when you joined us. It is one of the main reasons I want your help in keeping him as, well, ordinary as possible.' He paused. 'Given the circumstances.'

The butler and maid returned with a choice of tea or coffee. Calypso chose to have some more wine as she thought about what she had been told. She took another hot towel that was offered. When the servants had gone, Tye moved the conversation forward.

'What would you suggest we do, Calypso? How can we help Tommy?'

She made a decision about her own future and about Tommy's. 'I'll stay and help *if* he is allowed more freedom, Tom. That's my condition.'

Tye raised his eyebrows.

'I want him to go to Hope School full time,' she said. 'He has too much private tutoring. He must mix with other children. If you remember what I said earlier about the whole population on this island, you should apply it to him also. As far as I can see he's not picking up any of the normal childhood illnesses: no measles, no mumps, no chicken pox, no coughs or colds. He's not developing any resistance to them and if he catches them later they could be serious.'

Calypso looked to see if her arguments were hitting home but Tye had put his sunglasses back on and she couldn't read him. She wondered if she could venture a discussion about his own personal phobias.

'I'll think about it.'

'Do you mind...' She hesitated, then she plunged, as was her way. 'Why do you wear face masks? What's all this with the antiseptic towels? Airborne bacteria are good for us, Tom. It's that resistance thing again.'

He smiled, broadly this time, flashing perfect teeth. 'It's about money, Calypso,' he explained with a small shake of his head. 'If *you* get a cold and you can't work, what does it cost you – a few days' pay. Perhaps a few thousand dollars. I'm not bragging here, but if I miss a day, well...'

He didn't need to continue and Calypso saw his point. Over ninety per cent of common illnesses – colds, fevers, viruses – are transmitted by airborne infective agents. He was right: what would cause ordinary people merely annoyance would cost him – or his corporation – tens of millions of dollars, just through the business delays caused by his absence. But still it seemed to her more likely that he was simply a phobic pangermic hiding behind this plausible excuse. *How sad to be such a prisoner,* she thought.

'Any other questions, Calypso?'

She uncrossed her legs. From the angle of his head she wondered if he was staring at her body.

'I want Tommy to come to Mayaguana with me – to visit my mother ... and my nieces and nephews.'

Tye shook his head.

'That's out of the question, Doctor,' he said. 'He can't leave the island.'

Joe Tinkler added the usual half-and-half to his fibre and banana flakes and ate breakfast standing beside his kitchen window. Far below, the Manhattan rush hour was getting under way.

But what was he doing up? He'd got out of his bed simply from habit. After fifteen years with Rakusen-Webber, his life had become a firmly fixed routine. He realized he was still in a state of shock. By the time he had got back to his own office the word had already spread and his assistant wasn't at her desk. All the other staff on the fund-management floor seemed heavily preoccupied with their screens or with voice calls. Two burly security men had been waiting outside his office door, their faces impassive.

It hadn't taken Joe long to remove the traces of his years with the firm and in ten minutes he had packed all the physical objects he owned into a small plastic crate that Security had thoughtfully provided. He turned to his screens to send some internal 'goodbye' e-mails and discovered that he was already locked out of the bank's network. He shrugged and lifted the crate.

The security men walked beside him to the elevator and rode with him to the ground floor in silence. At the security checkpoint Norbert Jones, the man who had checked Joe in and out of the building every working day for over a decade, held out his hand.

'I've got to have your bank ident, Mr Tinkler,' he said sadly.

Joe nodded and put the crate down on the man's desk. He opened his shirt and slipped his neck chain around until he found the fastener. He felt no anger or sorrow: he was in shock, functioning automatically. After slipping the laminated digital ident card from its chain, he handed it to Norbert. Then he had picked up his crate and left the building without saying a word.

Joe finished his cereal and went back to his bedroom, where he pulled on shorts and a sweatshirt. Whatever was going to happen in the future, he would make good use of his enforced leisure now, he decided. Getting back in shape was the first priority. He clipped his VideoMate to his running belt, inserted his earpieces, pulled the cord of his Ray Ban Electros over his neck and set off.

It was too early for the day to be hot and Joe headed for the embankment, under the elevated highway. The river sparkled in the early-morning sunlight and he took it easy, aware that his infrequent Sunday jogs had not prepared his body for really strenuous exercise. There were few others out running this weekday morning. Most people in the city were getting to work.

He got down to the Battery just as a ferry from Staten Island arrived. He ran on past the ferry terminal and stopped by the low wall surrounding the isolated little green which, rather grandiosely, proclaimed itself a park. He checked his pulse and blood pressure and stretched out his calf muscles, resting his feet, in turn, on the wall.

He straightened to watch the stream of workers flooding off the ferry, out through the terminal building and into the subway. The clock on the small terminal tower told him it was still only 7.30 a.m.

Joe jogged over to a snack stand near the bus stops. He ordered a large black Colombian coffee and transferred payment from his LifeWatch.

He went back to the low wall and swung his feet over to sit

and watch as the ferry began its return journey. He sipped at his coffee as it was too hot to drink quickly.

'Hey, man, mind if I join you?'

Joe looked up and saw a bulky young black man in a dark business suit. He too was holding a plastic cup of coffee.

Joe shrugged. There was plenty of wall.

The stranger sat down a few feet to Joe's right. He sipped his coffee and blew on it.

'Beautiful morning.'

Joe nodded and looked away.

'It's OK, Mr Tinkler,' the man said quietly, moving closer. 'Here.' He produced an old-fashioned leather wallet from inside his jacket, opened it and proffered the badge to Joe.

'I'm with the United Nations,' explained Chevannes. 'Their Security Agency.'

Joe took the badge and studied it. The laminated card appeared genuine and the photo matched its bearer's face. 'Do you mind?' asked Joe as he unclipped his VideoMate.

'It won't be working, I'm afraid,' Chevannes pointed out. 'We're blocking all communications at the moment.'

Joe stared at the unit. A blinking red LED confirmed there was no signal.

'If I can't check your ident you can't expect me to talk to you,' reasoned Joe, rising to his feet and holding out the badge to its owner.

Chevannes rose and took it from him. 'We'd like to have a meeting with you, Mr Tinkler, over at the UN building. You might be able to help us with something.'

Joe looked around him. The street was now quiet. Then he noticed an illegally parked black sedan at the ferry terminal entrance.

'What about?' asked Joe.

'It's about someone who was very important to you – until yesterday. Thomas Tye.'

Joe laughed out loud. 'You've got the wrong guy.' He smiled. 'I've never met him.'

'But he knows all about you,' insisted Chevannes. 'You were a subject of major discussion for him only a couple of days ago.'

Joe stared blankly at the intelligence officer.

'When he was a house guest of Richard Rakusen – out in the Hamptons.'

The journey had been long, difficult and, as far as he could tell, without point. Marsello Furtrado had struggled to overcome his resentment at his boss's imperious commands but the heat and gritty friction of travel in West Africa had worn him down.

'Just get there,' Tye had insisted. 'It's for the Russian deal.'

When Furtrado had started to enquire about the precise purpose of his mission he had found himself watching the white noise of an empty carrier signal. The holo-conference was over. He didn't even know where Cape Verde was. He would have to look it up. Then Connie had provided a few more details, but these were almost as scant.

'Yes, he insists you go personally,' she had confirmed. 'He'll tell you more once you're there. Just make sure you're on the island before the thirteenth.'

Which hadn't been so easy. Most of Furtrado's work was concerned with making international acquisitions and overseeing the patent-protection team and he ran a forty-person office out of Washington DC while also maintaining his office within the corporate headquarters on Hope Island. Because he could begin his journey from either location he had expected flight arrangements to be straightforward.

As senior counsel for the Tye Corporation and keeper of Thomas Tye's greatest commercial secrets he had the right to use a jet from the Tye corporate flight but, after his assistant had filed his requisition, Logistics informed his office that no aircraft would be available on those dates. Furtrado had never known all six supersonic jets belonging to the company flight to be busy ten days in advance. He then ordered his assistant to charter a corporate jet but his request was turned down by Logistics without explanation. The attorney next turned to Connie.

'We don't want a trail, Marsello,' she had explained with one of her best smiles. 'Charter people talk – about their passengers *and* their destinations. Take scheduled flights, if you don't mind.'

He had minded, very much. Reluctantly he had taken a

Delta 797 subsonic red-eye to Paris and had worked all the way, conducting meetings in six different Tye regional subsidiaries from his private 'discretion-shielded' office on the commercial deck. Once there, he endured a three-hour wait before catching an Air-France connection to Lisbon in Portugal. He had also worked on this trip but Tye's European APU had been unable to verify the electronic security of his workspace so he had been forced to deal only with non-sensitive administration matters. Once in Lisbon he had found it necessary to check into a Holiday Inn at the airport to await a TAP flight that would take him on to Dakar in Senegal.

During his several flights he had reviewed the scant amount of material his assistant had been able to collect about these islands. The remote archipelago was stuck in the middle of the equatorial Atlantic, and the inhabitants spoke Portuguese, which, Furtrado assumed, was one of the reasons he himself had been dispatched. But this wasn't a good enough reason on its own. These days everybody used VideoMates and the language-translation modules were so cheap and so efficient that people could buy or rent the software they needed for any particular occasion. Neither could he see any connection with the forth-coming Russian deal that had been occupying so much of his time and he couldn't imagine that his legendary negotiating skills would be needed in such a remote location.

In Dakar he had had to make yet another overnight stay before catching a tiny propeller-driven plane of Air Cabo Verde to cover the 400-mile trip due west into the Atlantic. After a three-hour buffeting by the Trade Winds, which made working impossible, he had landed at a tiny airstrip on São Tiago, the main island of the Cape Verde group. He followed the directions he had been given and, as no alternative was available, carried his own suit bag and briefcase down the long dusty access road to a small wooden quay. He was due to catch the noon ferry to Fogo, the most westerly of the larger islands in the group. As always, Furtrado was immaculately dressed, today wearing a shot-silk grey business suit and burgundy loafers. But, despite his lightweight outfit, he was bathed in perspiration and unavoidably maculate by the time the ferry arrived.

The sea breeze cooled him off quickly, however, and he was soon wishing for the lengthy journey to be over. Though still conducting meetings at different locations around the globe, he was feeling a sense of personal dislocation: increasingly, he couldn't shut out his physical surroundings to concentrate on the issues at hand. The immense emptiness of the mid-Atlantic Ocean thoroughly distracted him.

It was early evening by the time the craft arrived at the tiny harbour of São Fillipe and Furtrado picked up his bag, walked down the rough-hewn gangplank and, following a seaman's directions, turned away from the small township and set off along the dirt road beside the beach. After half a mile he saw what he hoped was the end of his quest. It was a small house that stood inside a low drystone wall built out of rough basalt rock – solidified lava that had once spewed from the flat peak of the volcano two thousand feet above. Outside the two-storey house was an ancient, weather-beaten wooden sign. Furtrado stopped to make out the lettering: *Pensão Hollywood.* Despite its improbable name, this was the place.

He walked up the worn cobbled path and knocked on the door. He was greeted by an elderly but neatly dressed white man in cardigan and carpet slippers who was clearly expecting him. Once he heard Furtrado's native Portuguese, the man became all smiles and, despite the younger man's resistance, insisted on carrying his luggage as he led the way to an upstairs room at the front of the house.

'Just one or two nights your secretary said, Senhor?' enquired the owner. 'A very short break.'

Furtrado agreed. He was becoming increasingly puzzled. There could be nothing here worthy of acquisition by the Tye Group and, in particular, nothing worthy of the attentions of Marsello Furtrado, the maestro of such activities. He knew that in the office they called him 'Must-Sell-O!' behind his back but, like all over-dressed, over-mannered *rastaquouères*, he missed the irony.

As soon as he was alone he opened his VideoMate and found it lacked a signal. He assumed that there was no local wireless network on these islands, so he moved to the window, watched the satellite icon appear and called Connie.

'Well, I've made it here,' he confirmed, 'but God only knows why. What now?'

'Tom says well done,' relayed Connie, with a smile. 'What time do you normally wake up?'

Furtrado was too tired to wonder why she wanted to know. 'Usually around six, but I'm completely disorientated.'

'We'll call you at five your time,' she told him. 'Have a good evening.'

He was cheered up by an excellent swordfish steak in piri-piri sauce. Furtrado was the only guest in the tiny dining room and his host lingered to see if conversation would be forthcoming.

'This is excellent,' complimented the lawyer, as he savoured the tender flesh of the fish and added oil and vinegar to his tomato, onion and chickpea salad.

The man nodded appreciatively. 'Thank you. I enjoy cooking.'

As Furtrado still had no idea what was expected of him in this remote location he decided to make an ally.

'Will you join me?' he asked. 'At least for a glass of this vinho – is it Portuguese?'

'It's from Bucellas,' the chef-hotelier confirmed as he pulled out a chair on the other side of the oval table. 'Near Lisboa. We have to import everything. Little grows here in this godforsaken place,' he grumbled, plunging unhesitatingly into *saudade* – the Portuguese delight in melancholy. 'Why they called this Cape Verde, I don't know.'

The white wine was poured and, as he continued eating, the lawyer assumed that his own language skills might indeed have been the reason for his presence here. The local dialect, Furtrado learned, was a combination of Portuguese and Crioulo, a blend of West African words with a few Tupi and Guarani paronymies thrown in for good measure. He had never heard of a 'Cape Verde' language-translation module being available for a VideoMate and it certainly added to his own lexicon.

Furtrado also discovered that the semi-barren islands of Cape Verde had formed on the tips of huge volcanoes that reached upwards from the Atlantic seabed 2,000 metres below. He learned that the people of this former Portuguese colony survived by providing fuel, provisions and other services to the world's shipping as it passed by and, the hotel owner assured him, by servicing a growing tourist industry. Furtrado wondered who would seek out such arid isolation voluntarily.

Twice during the evening, the hotelier probed his solitary guest about the reason for his visit and the counsellor fobbed him off with a story about needing some time alone for reading and research. In turn, Furtrado had asked him about Russian connections with the islands, but the owner's blank stare confirmed the truth of his denials. They sealed their new, somewhat uncertain, friendship with a fiery Portuguese aguardiente.

Despite his disorientation and bewilderment, the brandy helped Furtrado sleep soundly and he was aware of enjoying a deep and vivid dream about his estranged twin brother when he was woken by his VideoMate trilling on the bedside table under the window. He switched on the table lamp and answered.

'Morning, Marsello. Sleep well?'

Tom was circling inside his Holo-Theater.

'Morning,' managed Furtrado, looking at the time display. The local time was 4.50 a.m. On Hope Island, the same time zone as New York, it was now ten minutes before one a.m.

'What's the weather like in Cape Verde?' asked Tom.

'Fine,' responded Furtrado absently. He shook his head in an attempt to wake up fully. He was obviously missing something here.

'No, you idiot, I mean what's the weather like NOW?' screamed Tye.

Furtrado pushed himself up from the small single bed and walked around to the window. He pulled the floral curtains aside. It was still dark outside, only a glimmer of light in the east suggesting that dawn had started.

With difficulty he undid the catch on the ancient sash window and pushed the bottom frame upwards. He leaned out, felt rain on his face and ducked his head back inside.

He picked up his VideoMate. 'It's raining,' he reported.

'Show me,' ordered Tom.

Furtrado found his Viewpers and slipped them on. He returned to the window and scanned the horizon.

'It's raining pretty heavily,' he observed, 'as you can see. What's this about?'

'It hardly ever rains on those islands,' said Tom, 'and never at this time of year. It hasn't rained there at all for seven years. It's the driest inhabited place in the world.'

'Oh,' responded Furtrado, mystified.

'It's called taking care of the planet,' intoned Tye, tartly. 'Go out into the streets, get me lots of pictures, and then find the mayor and a local judge and record their reactions to the rain. Also, get them to sign timed and dated affidavits about today's weather. Then bring their depositions back to Connie on Hope – personally.'

TWELVE

Haley Voss felt as if she was bouncing along Fifth Avenue. The sidewalk felt like a trampoline and the soaring buildings seemed to beckon her skywards.

The crush of late-afternoon shoppers and scurrying city dwellers worked its usual exhilarating magic. As she threaded her way northwards through the throng she felt as elated and as vibrant as when she had first visited the great metropolis as a teenager. She hardly noticed the oppressive heat. She had tried to call Felicity so her twin could share her pleasure, but she could only reach Flick's AutoSec.

Her initial meeting with Luke Bailey and his team at Sloan Press had gone even better than Rosemary had predicted. Haley found that their enthusiasm for her biography was rekindling her own passion for the project. She could now admit to herself that Nautilus's withdrawal and the subsequent retreat by the other publishers had badly damaged her self-confidence. That was why she had kept rewriting and rewriting, she realized, going over the same material time and again. Now she was keen, almost desperate, to leave her palimpsest behind and to get back to the really hard part of the job: producing the new pages that would reveal the man behind the public image.

'Handled right, we'll make the lead item on every news bulletin,' Sloan's vice-president of publicity had predicted, his deliberate use of the plural pronoun sending her a clear message. '*Everyone* will want to read the inside details of his life, Miss Voss. We'll work you so hard on the interview circuit that every time anybody thinks about Thomas Tye, they'll also be thinking of Haley Voss. We'll get a number one in the *New York Times* best-seller list and we'll become the top e-book download on the networks.'

Sloan's senior legal counsel and her assistant had seemed totally relaxed about the prospect of a confrontation with the huge law practice that represented the Tye Corporation. They had laughingly dismissed them as 'Tye's Terriers'.

'We're expecting injunctions and writs the moment we announce our publication of the book,' she confirmed. 'We just need to lock the other side up in the discovery cycle until the week before publication. Then we'll go back and get the injunctions lifted.'

They hadn't seemed at all worried that Tye's attempt to stop the book's publication might actually succeed. 'This isn't the UK,' the senior counsellor had laughed. 'The right to free speech is enshrined in our constitution!'

But despite this optimism, it was agreed not to divulge a single detail of the book's content to newspaper editors in advance of publication. They were sure they would be swamped by offers for serial rights the moment the review copies were available.

Then Luke Bailey had taken her for lunch at the Grill Room of the Four Seasons on East 52nd Street. Haley had been careful not to overdress for their first meeting and had chosen to wear a mustard-coloured trouser suit over a high-collared white blouse. A fine gold chain circled her neck, just below the top button. The publisher was obviously well known to the maître d' and they were quickly shown to a balcony table that provided them with a panoramic view of New York's favourite traditional luncheon room. She had thoroughly enjoyed the impeccable service, the superb food, Luke's slightly peccable company and the certainty with which he enthused about their 'world exclusive'. He had even made a discreet and not entirely unwelcome pass at her that, for the moment, she had chosen to ignore. But it lifted her spirits immensely: it confirmed again that it was only the solitary nature of her writing work that got in the way of romantic opportunity.

Sloan had booked her into a suite at The Plaza, the majestic old Manhattan landmark that faces Central Park from its superb location on the corner of Fifth Avenue and Central Park South. She had planned to spend the rest of the afternoon shopping but, as she paused with the crowds waiting to cross 54th Street, she realized she was far too excited to concentrate on anything as mundane as the items the themed retail stores had to offer. Instead, she would walk up to Central Park, sit in the sunshine, and map out a revised structure for her biography.

'Haley?'

The voice to her left sounded surprised. As she turned, it took her a couple of seconds to recognize the tall, fair-haired man in a white polo shirt and dark slacks. He took off his Ray Ban sun-viewpers.

'Why, hello,' she cried. 'What are you doing–'

The WALK sign appeared and the crowd surged forward. Jack Hendriksen laughed as they were both carried into the road. He held out his hand and took her shoulder, steering her safely onto the opposite sidewalk.

'Well, what are *you* doing here, Haley?' he asked when they reached the comparative safety of Gucci's shop windows.

'I'm here to see my publisher,' Haley told him breathlessly. 'Sloan's now publishing my Thomas Tye biography! But what are *you* doing here? Why aren't you with your boss?'

'I live here,' said Jack simply. 'My apartment's down near the Village. I'm on vacation and I'm shopping for my mom's birthday.'

They stared at each other for a few seconds.

'Sorry I haven't been in touch,' added Jack. 'I was incredibly busy when I got back.'

Haley waved away his apology. 'Now I've got a new publisher I *really* need to talk to you,' she enthused. 'You haven't changed your mind?'

Jack smiled and shook his head. 'No. I've been thinking more about it. I...' He paused, put his shades back on and looked around briefly, then back down at her.

'Are you busy right now?' he asked.

Haley shook her head.

'Let's walk up to the park,' Jack suggested. 'We could sit in the sun and ... Well, I *am* going to try and help you with your book. Tom's behaving increasingly...'

He tailed off. Haley was smiling up at him, her broad mouth and sparkling teeth bringing a generous smile to her impish face.

'I'd love to,' she said.

As they walked, Jack pointed out the notable buildings – St Patrick's Cathedral, the re-renovated glister of the old Trump Tower, F.A.O. Schwartz, the world's largest warehouse of intelligent companions – and Haley listened and wondered about her own feelings on bumping into him.

Passing the Plaza Hotel they crossed into Central Park, mingling with tourists waiting for carriage rides. Then they headed up towards the Zoo, where it would be quieter.

On this beautiful June afternoon all of the benches were in use by shoppers, resting joggers and office workers who had somehow found an excuse to be outdoors. As they approached an occupied bench in the centre of the green, a bulky young black man in a smart business suit rolled his sandwich wrapper into a ball and rose to his feet. With skill he lobbed it directly into a trash bin five yards away and headed off in the direction of The Met.

Haley hurried to grab the vacant bench, then sat and turned to Jack with a grin of triumph. They sat facing the afternoon sun as Jack asked her more about her new publishing deal. Then he enquired when she thought she might have the book finished.

She shrugged. 'It depends on what I uncover. I've finished all the orthodox research, but someone keeps sending me new stuff ... really amazing stuff.'

She glanced sideways at him as he leaned back in the corner of the bench listening carefully to her. He had taken his sunglasses off again, so she looked straight into his clear blue eyes. She had a decision to make here and, if she was wrong, she knew her book could still get suppressed.

'You remember that report I showed you – about Tye using gene therapy to stop him ageing?'

Jack nodded.

Haley decided. 'Well, someone's sent me another amazing report.'

Jack raised his eyebrows.

'I don't know who.' She hesitated. 'Would it surprise you to learn Thomas Tye has a son?' she asked.

Jack smiled. 'Well, someone *definitely* is trying to help you,' he confirmed. 'Thomas Tye Junior and he's seven. But we're never supposed to talk about him – for security reasons.'

Haley felt a thrill race through her, shivering despite the warm sunshine. This was the first independent confirmation of what would be one of her most exciting revelations. Then her biographer's alarm bells started ringing.

'But how can anyone keep something like that a secret?' she asked, fearing that the news would break elsewhere before she could publish.

'That's not too hard if you're Thomas Tye,' explained Jack. 'The boy has always lived at home – in Tom's private mansion – and everything is brought to him, rather than the other way around. He has his own nannies, his own doctor – hell, even his own shrink.'

He smiled as he thought of Calypso.

'But *you* know about him.'

'It's my job to run the security operation there. I have to know.'

'But all those other people on Hope Island . . .'

Jack thought about the buzz that had started up on the island that time when Tommy had knocked himself out.

'I guess it's a kind of open secret there,' he suggested. 'But everybody on the island either works for the corporation or is financially dependent on it in some other way. Nobody's going to risk saying anything to an outsider. The risk of a kidnap attempt is considerable when so much money is involved.'

'What's he like – this boy?'

Jack looked down at his lap. He was holding his sun-viewpers open on his thigh, his forefinger crooked between their tortoise-shell arms. He weighed his words.

'He's very like his father. He's pretty spoiled and sometimes his behaviour is … Well, I'd like to be in charge of him for a while. I believe that kids need a firm hand – gentle, but firm, you know what I mean.'

Haley nodded. She had noticed that even little Toby seemed to be happier when handled firmly.

'But is this boy like his father, to look at?' she persisted.

Jack smiled again. He had already read a copy of the report that UNISA's London surveillance team had intercepted. 'He's the spitting image,' he confirmed.

He watched as Haley digested this. He hoped she hadn't noticed that both their VideoMates had remained unusually inactive since they had met.

'The report claims the child's actually a human clone – of Thomas Tye,' she said flatly, looking up to gauge Jack's reaction.

He uncrossed his long legs and leaned forward, elbows on his knees, his sunglasses now swinging between his fingers. He was silent for a few seconds before he turned his head to look at her. 'I've always suspected that,' he agreed.

They sat for a few moments in silence, lit by the powerful sun, then Jack leaned back. 'I really would like to help you further,' he said. 'Are you free for dinner this evening?'

At first, Joe Tinkler had found their request ludicrous. If he hadn't been sitting there on the seventeenth floor of the United Nations Secretariat building he would have felt sure that the guys from Derivatives had set up one of their expensive and elaborate practical jokes. But the men talking to him now didn't seem to be working up towards a big laugh.

Joe had agreed to visit the UN headquarters later on the same day that his jog had been interrupted. As he had showered and pulled on a suit, he found himself going over and over the possible reasons for Thomas Tye and Richard Rakusen discussing him last weekend, presumably planning his dismissal. He could see why Tye would want to limit the power of external shareholders, but the Old Man had never given any indication that he knew the tycoon personally. If he did, he should have declared it to the compliance officer and, theoretically, should also have declared it at any meetings in which future investments in the Tye Corporation were discussed.

'Bastard,' Joe mumbled as he selected a tie. Perhaps he should call Jill White at home.

Chevannes had been waiting to meet him at the main entrance on UN Plaza and had escorted him through security, the informal 'immigration' process and up to Ron Deakin's office.

'Thanks for coming, Mr Tinkler,' Deakin began. 'I hear you're out of a job.'

Joe shrugged. The Street had been buzzing with the gossip. He'd had to switch on his AutoSec to manage the carrion calls.

'Would you consider undertaking a six-month assignment with the World Bank, in Geneva?'

Joe wondered if he had heard correctly. 'You belong to some sort of security service, right?' he queried.

Deakin nodded. 'We're a security agency for the UN. We have a mandate to operate in all its member countries.'

'Forgive me ... I mean, why me? What has the UN got to do with fund management?'

'Humour me,' persisted Deakin. 'Consider it a theoretical question at this stage. If an offer seemed attractive, could you handle it? I mean is there any reason you *have* to remain in New York for the next six months?'

Joe thought about it. Most of his friends were here, Nancy was here – but that on-off-on-off was more *off* than *on* most of the time. His work was here, too ... His work *had* been here. He doubted that he could work again in the Street at anything like the same level unless Rakusen-Webber retracted their accusation of gross negligence and agreed a no-fault separation. Even then, as they say, doubt clings where money sings.

'There's no reason I *have* to stay in this city,' Joe admitted. 'But I'm no banker. I don't know much about what the World Bank does – I mean, beyond the obvious.'

Deakin nodded. 'I understand. You'll want to know more about this assignment. We'll provide a first-class round ticket, three nights at the Hotel President Wilson and a payment of

sixty thousand dollars just for your time, if you're prepared to
fly to Geneva and meet Doctor Chelouche. He's President of
the–'

'Yes, I know who he is,' broke in Joe. 'What's going on here?
You'll have to tell me more of what this is about if you want me
to consider it.'

Deakin reached in his desk drawer for a copy of the Silence
Resolution.

Jack was seeing a new side to Haley. On accepting his dinner
invitation, she hadn't seemed the least bit surprised when he
suggested that they should eat at his apartment. He liked to
cook, he explained, and he rarely had the chance.

Although he really did enjoy cooking, the main reason for
his suggestion was to ensure that his discussions with the British
biographer would not attract attention. In a world in which
politics was dominated by the continuous and instantaneous
polling of public opinion – 'instant democracy', 'the people's
voice' – a revelatory biography could be crucial in changing
public perception about his employer. But he needed to keep
his cover intact until he could get back to Hope Island and find
an answer to UNISA's most pressing question.

Jack had no reason to believe that Tye, his pack of feral
attorneys, or the many investigation agencies they employed yet
suspected that the company's vice-president of security might
be feeling disaffected. Nevertheless, as Al Lynch had suggested,
Jack needed to keep any reference to his new relationship with
this British author out of the networks, and out of all forms of
digital storage. He was starting to discover how difficult that
could be.

Al Lynch had prepared his own plans for foiling any surveillance system Tye or his technical teams might have created. He
had taken great pleasure in demonstrating a software agent
he had deployed.

'Assuming their system is looking for key words, key faces,
et cetera, this agent is designed to snow them under with piles
of seemingly fresh information,' he told Jack. 'It's an agent I
developed years ago when I was working for the National

Security Agency and I've adapted it to our needs. Every day this little fellow collects everything that is written, said or broadcast about Tye, his corporation, its technologies or any of the associated companies. It then uses one of my own algorithms to generate new communications and stories that are apparently completely different messages, articles or broadcasts. It will seem as if the coverage of Tye and everything to do with him has suddenly gone up tenfold, and we'll encrypt a good percentage of the new messages. They'll be swamped because when their automatic systems get overloaded, humans will then have to decide which messages are worth decrypting – if that's what they really can do.'

At Jack's suggestion, Lynch named his agent *Multiplicitye*.

While he had been undergoing his refresher courses with Lynch and his other, more physical, instructors, UNISA had brought Jack's apartment up to full safe-house standards. Dozens of small transmitters scattered throughout his floor, wall and ceiling spaces generated a shield of electronic white noise that turned his apartment into a sterile communications zone. Nothing digital or electronic went in or out unnoticed on the airwaves or on the land lines. Technical Services had been sure that no local surveillance of Jack's apartment had already been established but, as a precaution, they had even set up a system that used recordings to mimic Jack's normal domestic communications and exchanges to disguise the existence of the new shield. All windows had been double-glazed to prevent laser-borne acoustic bugging and every street and store camera within a three-block radius switched to simulated input (with the correct time and date stamp superimposed) when any team member or target ident was in the vicinity or when a target was recognized by the automatic pattern-recognition system.

Haley had arrived promptly at eight. Jack recognized her face on the downstairs security camera and buzzed her in. He checked the elevator location display inside his apartment and, as it rose to the top floor, he crossed to open his door. He watched as the elevator doors slid back. She was wearing a black silk blouse and black trousers. A grey sweater was draped over her shoulders. Her smile lit up the elevator even before she stepped out.

'Welcome,' he said.

She had brought a bottle of white wine. 'It *was* chilled,' she complained, her deep-brown eyes earnest. 'But that was before I found that I had to walk half a mile here from where the taxi dropped me.'

Jack took the bottle with a smile. 'Gramercy is a traffic-free zone. Great for the environment, hell when you need to get the groceries home. The local stores deliver by refrigerated bike.'

She looked around the old loft. The UNISA security installations had required a full redecoration of the apartment – finally forcing Jack to allow the physical obliteration of his past life with Helen – and the new pale lime paint and clear varnished wood surfaces glowed.

'This is lovely,' his guest observed. 'It feels very comfortable.'

They sat at the much-used wooden kitchen table and Jack poured the wine she had brought.

'To your book.' He raised a glass in a toast.

Haley's smile seemed to increase the level of illumination in the room. 'I'm so excited,' she laughed as they clinked glasses. When she had sipped the Pinot Grigio she put her wine back on the table and pulled her VideoMate and a pocket video camera from her bag. 'Let's get started,' she grinned.

'I not sure *that*'s a good idea,' Jack said gently, nodding at the capture devices. 'I can't go on the record, so any help I give you will have to be informal.'

Haley frowned at him. 'I wasn't thinking of using the actual recording, I just like to–'

'It's just not a good idea to have any identifiable record,' insisted Jack, gently but firmly. 'Make written notes by all means.'

Even though he had kept his tone light, he saw Haley register his resolve. Then he saw her small chin jut determinedly.

She was recalling what he had said in her London apartment: *I normally record everything. Don't you video meetings and so on? Just for legal safety, and security?* This could still be a trap.

'Are *you* recording this meeting?' she asked. 'That's what you usually do, isn't it?'

He spread his hands on the table. 'No, I'm not,' he said, dissembling with a strictly literal truth. He and the UN technical services team had discussed how they could feed the signal of this meeting outside the building but had agreed that, given the Tye Corporation's potential powers, even with highest-level encryption it was too risky. The recording equipment to capture their conversation had been installed by a UNISA technical officer inside the loft earlier in the afternoon and was now being operated remotely.

Haley now had another decision to make. She looked around the large room and then back at him.

'OK,' she agreed. She put the device back in her bag and extracted her DigiPad.

'So, you're the corporate vice-president of security for the global Tye Corporation. Does that mean you have a seat on the main executive board?'

'Would you mind using real paper?'

She shrugged again, bemused. She rummaged in her bag and found an envelope and a pen.

'OK. So do you have a seat on the board?'

'But you're not going to quote me in your book.'

'No, I'm not. You'll be an unidentified source as far as my readers are concerned. But I have to keep records, even if it's just for the libel lawyers and, maybe, the courts. To prove my sources.'

Jack nodded. 'How about this, Haley? I'll tell you anything I can, you make your notes, but don't keep anything in electronic form that identifies me as a source. I can't explain my reasons right now. Keep it on paper by all means but don't put my name in your VideoMate address book and don't even make annotations on your DigiPad or word processor. Don't make any PopUp notes that mention my name or my role. Is that possible?'

Haley cocked her head on one side. 'Very mysterious. I *am* able to use secure mode, you know.'

Jack nodded again. 'I know, I know. But humour me. I do want to help and, if it gets to a court case, I'll even do what I can to help there. But, in the meantime, don't file anything about me electronically. Don't call me, don't v-mail or e-mail me. I won't contact you in that way either, I'll use other methods.'

'What going on here?' she asked, her face suddenly animated.

'What's my job?' he replied, with a smile of his own.

'Security,' she said.

'Precisely. Will you work with me on this?'

She thought for a moment and then nodded, her large dark eyes never leaving his.

'So, how can I help?'

'So, *do* you have a seat on the main executive board?'

'No.'

'What did you do before you joined the Tye Corporation?'

'I was in the US Navy.'

'An officer?'

'Commander.'

'You mean you weren't trained in security?'

'My training covered a lot of things. Some forms of security included.'

'So you weren't a seagoing officer?'

'At the outset, I was. But, in general, no.'

'What *were* you? Exactly?'

'That's classified.'

Jack would never admit to his original SEAL background, it was *such* a cliché. The rest he couldn't talk about.

Haley paused and looked across at him. He seemed at ease, slightly amused even.

'But in the US Navy?'

'Yes. They paid my wages.'

'Were you a *spy*?' she asked, with a mischievous grin.

'Absolutely not,' said Jack firmly.

There was a pause.

'So how did the Tye Corporation recruit you?'

'They contacted me shortly after my discharge. An old friend recommended me.'

'Who?'

'It doesn't matter.'

Haley thought about a challenge but decided on a new tack. 'You're married?' It was put as a question, despite his ring.

'Why?'

Helen smiled down on him from the wall opposite, behind his guest's head.

'Are you married, Jack?' she repeated.

'No. I mean I was. Not any more.'

'But you still wear your ring,' she objected, gently touching his hand and peering at the gold band.

He hesitated. 'I'm a widower.'

Haley removed her hand quickly and he watched her digest his answer. Her next question was put more softly. 'Any children, Jack?'

'No.' That would have come next. He wondered why she was asking.

She moved on. 'What's your remuneration?'

'That's not relevant.'

'It certainly is. The lawyers will have to make a judgement on your actual status in the Tye corporate hierarchy. If you're a VP but you're not on the executive board, your salary level is the best guide to your seniority.'

Jack considered. She was waiting for his answer, preparing her next question. Intelligence shone from her dark eyes like a beacon. He found he that he didn't at all mind telling her.

'Sixteen dollars and three cents per working minute.'

Like everybody these days, he was paid in real-time and by true value transfer. Money worked much harder and more effectively when it was kept moving.

'OK, Jack, save me the math. How much is that a year?'

'Eight and a half million dollars, US.'

Haley raised her eyebrows, but made no comment. Then, 'Anything else?'

'What do you mean?'

'Any other sort of benefits? Cars, share options, pensions, health insurance, et cetera.'

Jack nodded and smiled. 'All of those, except the car. There aren't any cars on Hope Island.'

'What's your total package worth?'

At eight and a half million dollars he was highly paid, but not by global VP standards. Even though corporate security had grown up to become a function of the senior executive in most corporations, he and his peers had yet to penetrate the *highest* echelons of capitalist power.

'I get more share options added each year. I suppose the total now has a value of several hundred million dollars.'

This time Haley did allow herself a smile. 'And you'll risk all this to help me?'

Now he saw her point. 'No. I'm helping myself. I have my own reasons and . . .'

Her noticed her frown. 'I'm not using you,' he said quickly, even though as he said the words he realized that the opposite was true. 'Like I told you, I think things have gotten out of hand. Something has to be done.'

'Like what?' she demanded.

'Well, the international legal system doesn't seem—'

'No. I mean like what things are getting out of hand?'

'I'll come to that,' he said as he rose from the table.

Jack crossed the loft's wooden floor and bent to open a low two-drawer filing cabinet. He extracted a thick file and returned to the table.

He pushed the bottle and his glass aside and opened the file.

'First, I thought you might be interested in a little personal background on Tom. This is all on paper,' he muttered as he leafed through, looking for the first document he wanted to show her. Deakin's research team had unearthed it and it was perfect for the occasion. 'This is for you, but please don't scan it, or digitize it in any other way. Is that OK?'

Haley nodded, mystified but intrigued.

He found what he was looking for and held the photocopy of an old press cutting out to her.

'This should also make good copy,' Jack suggested as he turned to locate another bottle of wine. 'It's about the mental institution to which Thomas Tye was committed. He's purchased his past.'

THIRTEEN

Towards the end of the first decade of the twenty-first century, at the peak of uncontrolled vehicular excess, the controllers in the Los Angeles Department of Traffic and Highways offered up a daily prayer in the hope that the Santa Monica Freeway would be able to cope with 32,000 vehicles per hour. As the months went past this prayer changed from a forlorn entreaty to an abject confession, a *mobilis-miserere*, as they finally acknowledged that the capacity for which the freeway's designers had planned it had long since been exceeded. At the best of times progress was slow. Often the freeway, like many others in the city, became gridlocked. Average traffic speeds in the Greater Los Angeles area had dropped to twelve m.p.h.

When the first fully automated traffic-flow system was finally introduced in commuter lanes there was much public outcry and intense political debate. Drivers felt uncomfortable handing over control of their vehicles' movement to computer systems, even if the state was providing them with generous tax incentives to assist with the cost of installing the necessary automatic driving systems. It was only when non-automated traffic was completely banned from the fast lanes in peak periods that drivers seriously began adopting AutoRide technology. The Los Angeles City Council fuelled the experiment by providing an eighty per cent cash subsidy for these in-car control systems and, during the first years of the experiment, the flow of vehicles was managed by roadside locators and broadcasting systems.

As a result, average traffic speeds rose from twelve to forty m.p.h. and the number of vehicles able to move along the thirty-five miles from the center of downtown Los Angeles to the Pacific coast increased to a record 38,000 an hour. The problem was that traffic on the adjoining roads, particularly the San Diego Freeway, remained uncontrolled and thus the local terrestrially based solution was only partially successful. The on and off ramps continued to be a mess and lengthy waiting periods at smart traffic lights provided only a partial solution.

Other cities such as New York, London and Athens had responded to the alarmingly accrescent number of private vehicles simply by banning them from parts of their road networks, charging vehicles to enter the remaining areas and significantly improving mass-transit infrastructures. Once public transport became smart enough to provide customers with information about the precise arrival time of the next tram, bus or train, also its current passenger load, its best-prediction ETA and the precise whereabouts and loadings of all connecting transport, the public suddenly began to see the advantages. First Class and Business sections were opened on the larger people-carriers and, in London, the whole top deck of the traditional red bus was given over to cosseting premium-class travellers with display screens, drinks and snacks.

But however smart, reliable and comfortable mass transit had become elsewhere, it wasn't an option for the Los Angelenos and their administrators. The gigantic urban sprawl of Greater LA had been designed after the automobile had become ubiquitous but before it threatened to choke its host city's arteries. The scale of the city was simply too large for any conventional form of mass transport system to work. Even if the city fathers had been able to start over and magically dig earthquake-resistant tunnels for a comprehensive under-city subway system, the trains, trams or maglev shuttles would need to make too many stops, and to cover such vast distances, that they would still remain unattractive as a form of regular transport.

The answer was to envision all the city freeways and their feeder roads as one circulatory system; to imagine each vehicle as a single cell inside a giant centrally managed mass-transit system in which individual vehicles obeyed the needs of the larger organism. As a result, the roads became a huge contraflow venous system that was controlled and managed from the skies.

This satellite-based management system was designed, built and administered over a five-year period by a consortium of Tye Aerospace Inc. and Tye Asset Management Inc. (TAMI). Currently, the Santa Monica Freeway handled over 70,000 vehicles an hour travelling seven feet apart at an average speed of forty-five m.p.h. All the other freeways and main arteries in and around Greater Los Angeles boasted similar throughput and, a mile before joining any of the roads or freeways that were part of the LA Intelligent Transport System, drivers logged in their required destinations and handed over control of their vehicle to the ITS, operated on the city's behalf by TAMI, a system that had been working faultlessly for three years.

On the bright sunny Wednesday morning following the rather less than intimate dinner that Jack Hendriksen had cooked for Haley Voss, most Angelenos were keen to begin their working day. By 7.30 a.m. the freeways were at 84.7 per cent maximum capacity and, from a thousand kilometres up, a satellite of the TAMI network was issuing instructions to more than 130,000 vehicles to reduce their speed from 52.157 m.p.h. to 47.342. Construction had closed one lane of the on-ramp to the Santa Monica Freeway at its junction with 405 South and the satellite's on-board parallel processors had predicted the resultant congestion and was routing 2,962 vehicles to different entrance and exit ramps, providing in-car displays of the new routes that had been selected and revised estimated arrival times. If the drivers had entered the network ident of those awaiting their arrival, they too were similarly informed of the travellers' revised ETAs.

Unfortunately, few travellers were paying any attention. Despite state regulations that required a driver to remain available to resume control of a vehicle at all times in case of automatic control failure, some drivers had swung their big chairs away from the dashboard and steering wheel to attend business meetings locally, on the East Coast, in Europe or in any location in any of the fourteen longitudes and twelve time zones in which other humans were still awake. Many had resumed their social conversations and get-togethers via the networks, some reviewed news, sport or business information in their viewpers while others donned immersion helmets, turned up their ScentSims and wallowed in pornography. A minority simply ate, drank and watched TV in air-conditioned comfort. Others, caught in a global frenzy of the time, gambled their way to work.

Grazing the ionosphere above the traffic, 6,000 satellites occupied spaces within a layer of orbits that, in the early days of earth-orbit satellite deployment, would have provided safe locations for less than a hundred of them. As with the cars below them, the satellites were computer-managed and, after a gigantic space-junk clear-up operation to remove the debris of fifty years of uncontrolled near-space colonization, all orbital positions and movements were now strictly controlled. Orbiting refuelling tankers provided energy top-ups and in-service repairs for the satellites: these in-flight maintenance techniques had extended the average useful life of satellites to twenty-five years. Again, the contractor was the Tye Corporation – this time in the guise of Tye Orbiting Management System Ltd (TOMS). The entire system was under the control of a team led by Raymond Liu, group technical director of Tye Networks.

On a geostationary 4,700-kilogram satellite dubbed LAT-6 the real-time memory managed by four 1024-bit microprocessors developed a leak. It wasn't the first of the day and ordinarily it wouldn't have caused a problem. The fail-safe memory system supported its data and instruction set inside several artificial shells designed to isolate operations from any equipment or operating system malfunction. But this memory leak was the 643rd to occur in eight hours and such information losses exceeded every scenario the designers had anticipated. All registration addresses in the emergency buffers were occupied and even the flash-storage overflow could accept no more. Despite being guaranteed as completely fault-tolerant, LAT-6's processing froze and all data transmission ceased.

Two hundred and ten kilometres further into space, SAT-MAN 36, the regional Orbital Management Station maintained and operated by TOMS, registered the loss of communications handshake from LAT-6 and dumped its real-time mirror copy of LAT-6's activities in a laserburst containing 782 terabytes of information to LAT-7, six miles to the south. LAT-7 acknowledged receipt and took over the control of 7,458,711 vehicles, 11,610 roadside displays, 15,041 traffic lights and 4,794 controlled crossings. The handover took two milliseconds and the drivers and pedestrians below were unaware of the glitch.

Then the navigation sensors on SATMAN 36 reported that the failed LAT-6 was rolling out of orbit, dipping dangerously close to the approved path of a high-speed orbiting satellite operated by the Pakistani government for a purpose claimed to be atmospheric research. SATMAN 36 observed LAT-6's descent and, when the critical line was crossed, automatically issued instructions for the satellite to self-destruct before NASA's ASAT anti-satellite systems were triggered and intervened with a destructive laserburst that would invalidate all insurance claims for the satellite's loss.

LAT-6 fired its emergency thrusters, heading for re-entry and automatic incineration as ordered.

LAT-7 continued to manage the central LA traffic it had inherited from LAT-6 as well as its own south LA vehicles for a further eleven minutes. But it too had suffered ten times more memory leaks overnight than its specifications allowed for. Then, just as it was about to slow the Santa Monica Freeway traffic down to 45.82 m.p.h., all on-board processing froze.

SATMAN 36, holding an updated mirror copy of TAMI data from LAT-7, then had to make a choice between managing the traffic below or the spacecraft in orbit. The artificial intelligence algorithms prioritized the management of the highly valuable orbiting assets, in particular the satellites that were managing air-traffic movements, at the expense of their terrestrial counterparts.

When the control signals vanished, fail-safe cut-outs operated inside 7,458,702 vehicles, emitting audible warning signals before braking and slowing the vehicles to a controlled straight-line stop within thirty yards. The whole of the Greater Los Angeles road network came to an immediate standstill.

Inside nine vehicles, the fail-safe systems malfunctioned.

The most serious incident occurred on the junction of the elevated San Diego Freeway and Airport Boulevard. Aboard a southbound sixty-six-ton, thirty-two-wheel, twin-tank gasoline trailer-rig travelling at the prescribed 52.896 m.p.h., the automatic fail-safe system did not engage. The driver had been changing his clothes in the cubicle behind the front seats at the time. The truck continued in a straight line into a stationary van ferrying six children to elementary school, then jackknifed to the right, crossed the safety lane, crashed through the parapet of the elevated freeway and landed on top of a Boeing 797 passenger aircraft waiting to taxi onto the recently extended main LAX runway for take-off. The aircraft and the tanker erupted into a giant ball of flame.

In other parts of the city the wholly quadrirotal Angelenos suffered instant impotence and many attempted to restart their vehicles, assume manual control and drive off the freeways in the safety lanes. There were 571 collisions and six old-fashioned 'freeway fever' killings in the first thirty minutes following the control failure.

'I want you to think of your favourite beach on Hope Island,' Theresa Keane began, selecting an image she knew would be popular. The graduate students were scattered around the study in her home. As part of the package designed to lure her from the rarefied air of Cambridge, Massachusetts to Hope Island, the dean of the new university had secured permission for her to use one of the much-coveted white villas set on the lower mountain slopes overlooking Hope Town. This morning Professor Keane had opened the wide glass doors that led out to a large stone terrace and a view of the distant town and the emerald bay beyond. Small green and blue humming birds darted between the luxuriant Browallia, bussu palms, Escallonia, poinsettias and castor-oil plants that she had cultivated. When she was alone in this room she often compared it to the musty, cramped accommodation for which she had been so grateful when she had secured her first tenured seat at Trinity College in Dublin fifteen years before.

'I want you to imagine that a hurricane strikes your favourite beach and lifts every grain of sand into the air. It forms a giant swirling cloud over this island and out across the oceans in all directions.'

She waited as they created the model in their heads.

'Now I want you to think of the beaches on the other islands that are our neighbours: Cuba, the Turks and Caicos Islands, Jamaica, the Bahamas and the Dominican Republic. Simultaneously, hurricanes hit all those beaches and funnel all that sand into the air in vast clouds that stretch right across the Caribbean.'

They nodded as they made the mental construction.

'Now, more hurricanes appear in the Keys, in Florida, in Miami, Palm Beach, Naples and Tampa. Then on Stinson Beach north of San Francisco, or Long Beach in LA, or the beaches at Cape Cod, or the wonderful sands of Samoa, Goa Beach in India, Phuket in Thailand or Bondi Beach in Australia. I want you to run through all of the beaches you've ever seen, lift the sand into the air, make vast, dense clouds of sand all over the world.'

She waited again as the twenty-six postgraduate students who were crammed into her room rooted around in their memories for beach scenes that could serve as visual aids.

'Imagine the amount of sand on those beaches. Think of the number of grains there might be. I want you to think of those hurricanes merging, the clouds of sand becoming one. I want you to imagine that cloud and all those grains of sand.'

Again she waited as they assembled a mental language with which to approach her concepts.

'How many grains do you think you might have? A hundred billion, a trillion, a quintillion, a duodecillion?'

She paused again.

'One thing we do know – there are more stars in the universe than there are grains of sand on all the beaches of our own planet. Our galaxy alone has over one hundred billion.'

Theresa Keane knew that this was not new material to some of them, but she wanted them all to start from the same place. As a computer scientist she would normally have expressed such large numbers as powers, but this was a diverse group that required her visual diglossia. Professor Walczack's frequent urgings for cohesion across all disciplines had fired her imagination and she had invited biologists, evolutionary psychologists, linguistic neuroscientists and geneticists to join her own students in the seminar series.

'There are ten galaxies – not stars, *galaxies* – for every human on this planet! Think about it – ten whole galaxies for each of you and ten for every other single person.'

She paused again.

'And each of the billions of stars in each of those galaxies are all separated by an average of four light years. Or five hundred billion, billion miles. *This* is the human dilemma.'

'What about binary twins?' asked a lanky Scots materials physicist with a prominent Adam's apple and watery blue eyes. He was part of the Phoebus Project research team.

Theresa smiled at him. 'You're right, Martin. Many of the stars are twins. I was thinking of single-star systems that might support planets.'

She allowed them to think on a little longer as she sipped her tea. She imagined them constructing mental images of vast swarms of stellar dust in which every speck was a star.

'We now know that many of those trillions of billions of stars support planets – some of them possibly oases of benign atmospheres, gentle warmth and abundant water like our own glorious Earth. Humankind has now explored its own world. We have discovered and probed the other planets in our solar system and we know what lies immediately beyond. But if we know one thing about our species, it is that we will never stop expanding. We can see so many of those stars; they tantalize us. If it is true that our planet is merely a cosmological crèche for our species, how, then, do we take the next step?'

'We m-m-m-must go to the stars,' averred Robert, her stammering research fellow and, secretly, her most ardent admirer.

'We must, Robert, but humans cannot travel at a speed that allows that. How many of you have what you consider to be an

accurate scale model of our solar system and our nearest
neighbouring stars in your mind – our physicists, astronomers
and other supraterrestrialists excluded?'

Theresa looked around the group of young men and women
adorning the chairs, sofas, arms, floors, stools and walls of the
study. Only one of them raised a hand.

'Do you?' she asked Lisa, a gifted young proteomicist from
Argentina. 'In that case you can help me. We're going back to
school, Grade Six or thereabouts. We all do these experiments
when we're young and we all forget them. It's not comfortable
information to retain. Now then...'

She turned to a fruit bowl placed on a low table beside her
comfortable chair. She picked up an orange and held it up
before them.

'This orange will be our sun,' she smiled as she held it on
the fingertips of her right hand. 'What is it – about four inches
in diameter? That's about ten centimetres for the metric among
you. Now...'

She turned back to the fruit bowl and picked something up.
They couldn't make out what it was until she held it up between
the thumb and forefinger of her left hand beside the orange.

'This dried pea is our own Earth and it's about a third of an
inch in diameter – that's nine millimetres – and, as you have
already guessed, these bodies are approximately to scale. Now,
Lisa, take this pea and show us roughly how far the Earth is
from the sun at this same scale.'

Lisa pushed herself up from the floor and swept her long
black hair back over her shoulders. She took the pea from the
professor's fingers and looked around the room. She threaded
her way through the bodies draped across the furniture and the
carpet and turned at the open French windows. She held up
the pea.

'Keep going,' said Theresa, waving her student out of the
room. Lisa walked backwards into the sunshine, holding the pea
up between her fingertips.

'Keep going,' called Theresa. 'More ... more. There.'

Lisa stopped at the far end of the terrace, beside a low table
that Theresa had placed as a marker.

'That's thirty-six feet, about ten metres or if, like me, you're very, very Irish, eighteen bandles. That pea out there is us, and this orange in my hand is the sun.'

They looked from one to the other.

'Now, working on the same scale, who will stand up and tell me where the star closest to us, Proxima Centauri, would be located out there?'

Theresa stood up and all of them – except the three astronomers, feeling cocky in the pit of their sofa – stood also and gazed out onto the cultivated sunlit slopes that led down to Hope Town a mile away to the south-west. Lisa remained at the edge of the terrace, the pea held in her right hand.

'Well?' asked Theresa from the back of the group. She knew none of them would know. She hadn't known for sure herself until she did the research.

'Th-Th-The Town Hall,' guessed Robert, pointing at the small clock tower jutting above the low roof-line of the town. His doctorate was in speech interfaces.

'No. Further.'

'Three hundred miles out in the Caribbean,' hazarded a cognitive neuroscientist, keen to get it over.

'No. Further.'

'M-M-Mexico,' offered Robert gamely.

Theresa stepped forward to stand amongst them. She pointed out to sea.

'The next landfall out there is Panama,' she told her class, enjoying her demonstration, 'on the other side of the Caribbean Sea. That's nine hundred miles away. If you kept going another nine hundred miles, across the Canal Zone, and then out into the Pacific until you reached the Galapagos Islands, an archipelago with special meaning for the evolutionary psychologists here, that's where Proxima Centauri would be. Again, about the same size as this orange.'

They turned back to her. She seated them with a smile and tucked her long floral skirt under her legs as she lowered herself into her armchair. She waited a few moments for them to get comfortable again and for Lisa to return with the pea and resume her place on the carpet, her back propped against a wall.

'Forgive the high-school experiment,' she requested. 'But it is easy to forget the scale of our local solar environment, even though particle physics suggests such concepts. If I held up the orange again and said it was a helium atom, we know that its pair of electrons would go around it at a distance of about five kilometres. Matter obeys the natural laws of physics throughout the universe.

'Despite this, every image of our solar system you may see – in film, magazines and books – is grossly distorted in scale. You can visit science exploratoriums and you still won't see any accurate sort of scale models. It is as though there is a conspiracy to pretend we live in a space that is more manageable, more human.

'NASA, Hollywood, TV producers and popular magazines have been selling us lies for over fifty years. When the Americans went to the moon it wasn't one of the greatest steps for Mankind, it turned out to be one of the most disappointing. We didn't discover another living world, it wasn't a step towards further space travel. It was a hard collision with the brick wall of truth. There is nothing out there worth going to, or at least nothing worthwhile that is even remotely within reach. Our culture tells us differently because we cannot bear to face the truth. Every model we see of the solar system is grossly tele-scoped and distorted. Every movie that projects the idea of manned space travel or that heralds yet another contact with alien intelligence lies to us about the real difficulties of space travel or the odds of such an encounter or its nature if it were ever to happen. We have no language with which to consider such ideas realistically.

'Let's look at the facts, now that Lisa has helped us develop a better scale model. In our present physical form we cannot travel at the speed of light, nor even at a speed that approaches it. Our fastest spacecraft today would take ten thousand years to reach Proxima Centauri, our Sun's nearest neighbour, which we have today imagined as being located eighteen hundred miles away in the Pacific. On the same scale, the centre of the Milky Way, our own small outer galaxy and only one of billions of galaxies in the universe, is about twelve million miles away from this orange!'

She lifted the orange again and paused as they tried to take in this information.

'Even if we could travel magically at one quarter of the speed of light it would take us three hundred years to reach the nearest solar system that we know to have planets – and the same time to come home again. So what is to be done?'

'Unmanned probes,' suggested one.

'Targeted radio messages,' submitted another.

'Suspended animation,' ventured a third.

Theresa held up a hand. 'None of those solves the problem,' she maintained. 'It would seem as if the times and distances of our universe are inhuman. They are beyond human comprehension and all biological timescales. Are we to give up?'

Her question was rhetorical and they all knew it.

'No, we are *not*,' she declared. 'The next step for our species is to emerge from our biological envelopes, to free our virtual consciousness and our temporal perceptions from the tyranny of our fragile mammalian support systems and fleeting earthly lifespan. Then we shall be ready for our virtuality to travel at the speed of light to meet the others who share our universe.'

They were quiet.

'This is the topic of our tutorial today and later I will describe progress with our efforts to transfer human neural experience to machine storage. But I will begin by describing some tools that we are developing for the observation and measurement of non-biologically-dependent consciousness in the little boys and girls we are creating in our Anagenesis Experiment.'

Joe Tinkler added semi-skimmed milk to his room-service muesli and sliced fresh banana and looked down at the leisurely flow of traffic and pedestrians in the Avenue Wilson six storeys below. He checked his LifeWatch. It was still the middle of the morning rush hour. Geneva seemed so small, so tame, so ordered, after Manhattan.

He had arrived early on the previous afternoon and, after checking into the suite at the Hotel President Wilson that had been reserved for him by the World Bank, he had showered, changed and gone on a walking tour of the city. He'd been to Europe several times before, but never to Geneva or anywhere else in Switzerland.

Even though it was a working day the old city was quiet. Prosperous-looking men and women walked sedately along the lakeside promenade, enjoying the midsummer sunshine. Well-dressed nannies pushed child buggies and chatted in muted tones to their friends beneath the luxuriant trees of the Quai Wilson and the *Mon Repos* waterside gardens.

On the promenade Joe marvelled at the Alpine clarity of Lake Leman and the majesty of Mount Jura rising behind the town. He stopped to examine a metal triangle and a notice board. On top of a metal pole a small ball, perhaps two inches in diameter, represented the Earth. Joe followed the English-language instructions and put his eye to the hole bored through the centre of the sphere. On the other side of the wide harbour – really an *embouchement*, where the Rhône emptied into the lake – Joe saw a sphere that represented the sun. This distant ball was actually five yards in diameter, but it appeared the same size as the little Earth. Joe peered through the hole again and then stood up once more. He had never appreciated how tiny and how far away the Earth really was from the sun.

Then he crossed the busy road to enter the city's main commercial district. Even here, activity was muted. The shops were elegant, the prices high, the atmosphere discreet. Joe could *feel* money in the air. He realized that the Swiss existed by an invisible process of long-term quiet money making more long-term quiet money. Joe's own world of Wall Street and dealing screens, of money frantically competing to make money on marginal spreads, seemed frenetic and vulgar in comparison. Here and there he came upon carpenters and labourers for whom personal physical output was still linked to income, but as he walked through the city he realized that his current sense of unreality was not only the result of jet lag and the time change – he had used his viewpers' anti-jet lag technology to reduce that – but of entering a society in which most of wealth-generation had long been virtual.

Joe had selected a sharp charcoal-grey suit with a white shirt for his meeting with the most famous banker in the world. As he straightened his pale grey tie, his most conservative, he could feel nerves fluttering in his stomach. He turned left out of his hotel and walked up the gentle gradient of the Avenue de France. He passed the old Palace of Nations and the monument to Woodrow Wilson's fumbled efforts to establish the first global government and then he was at the vast compound the United Nations had been given in 1947 when that organization was established. The new European headquarters of the World Bank soared like a shimmering silver hologram between the ponds and sculptures that dotted the park.

He presented himself at the security post inside the glass doors, and an electronic ident was clipped to his lapel. An American security guard asked Joe to leave all his recording and communications devices at the checkpoint. He then stepped through a scanner and was walked to the elevators. The guard leaned into a waiting car and pressed the button for the top floor. He left Joe to travel upwards alone.

The doors opened onto a softly lit corridor of mahogany doorways, pale cream walls, moss-green carpet and expensive watercolours. A dark-haired, middle-aged woman with a Video-Mate under her left arm greeted him and introduced herself as Madame Pioline. She told Joe that the Doctor was waiting for him and they crossed to a pair of highly polished double doors. She pushed them open and stepped aside.

Inside, Joe's first impression was of light and space. Then he noticed the heavy form of Dr Yoav Chelouche slumped, reading intently, behind a desk. That face was familiar from a thousand newscasts and magazine covers. Joe cleared his throat. The banker looked up, rose, walked around the large desk and extended his hand.

'I am Chelouche,' he announced in the gravel tones that were even more famous than his image. 'Thank you for coming, Mr Tinkler.' He waved Joe towards a low coffee table surrounded by high-backed gilt chairs.

Coffee was brought, pleasantries exchanged: the president of the World Bank enquired about Joe's flight and accommodation. The fallen Wall Street star then commented on the view of the lake seen from the tall office windows. He had debated whether it would be uncool to express his admiration for the man.

'I'm proud to meet you, sir,' he risked. He was tempted to say more about Chelouche's renowned financial achievements. But he knew there was almost nothing he could add to the praise that had been heaped already on the banker by the world's political leaders and economists.

Chelouche put down his coffee cup, folded his hands over his stomach and focused his dark, mournful gaze on the fit-looking black man in front of him.

'Well, I have been aware of *you* for some time, Mr Tinkler,' he said. 'Very aware. It's hard to become as successful as you've been and not get noticed.'

'Tell that to Rakusen-Webber.' Joe laughed ruefully. 'They wouldn't agree and nor would many others. You know Wall Street.'

Chelouche nodded. He did. That was where he had started, a lifetime ago.

'I'm worried that I might now be finished in fund management.'

'Maybe, maybe not,' mused Chelouche. 'But your name has been in front of me for several years. You have done well with your Tye portfolio.' It was a statement but Joe realized that his host was inviting comment.

'The figures say so,' Joe admitted. 'My fund was growing at an annual average of thirty-three-point-seven per cent in real terms over the last six years.'

'Why do you say in real terms?' asked the banker pointedly.

Joe maintained his composure. 'I mean, once they're adjusted for inflation, momentum growth, rounding errors and so on.'

'And what has been the average rate of inflation in the reserve currencies over the last six years?' Chelouche asked.

Joe shrugged. 'One point one, one point two. It's been very steady.'

'Thank you!' exclaimed Chelouche as if he were accepting a

compliment. 'I always feel that the expression "growth in real terms" implies there is something unreal about the underlying performance. It's an archaic phrase.'

Joe could see that he had touched a nerve. He said nothing.

'But you *have* done very well,' Chelouche said more graciously, returning to his theme. 'Despite being dismissed by Rakusen-Webber. As you have been advised, UNISA thinks Mr Tye was involved in that move.'

'In what way, sir?' asked Joe. He had learned very little more about the UN's interest in the Tye Corporation or its boss even after he had signed the lengthy secrecy agreement that Executive Officer Deakin had put under his nose. He had been told only that Thomas Tye and his companies were the subject of a current UNISA investigation that could lead to criminal or civil charges. He was also told that his special knowledge of the Tye investment portfolio could be helpful in that same investigation. Given that Joe had nothing better to do and couldn't easily find another Wall Street buyer for his highly specialized knowledge of Tye and his finances, he had readily agreed to visit Geneva to at least discuss the options.

'I'll come back to that, Mr Tinkler,' said Chelouche. 'But ... you've been kind enough to come all this way. Let me tell you about the assignment we would like you to consider.'

Joe leaned forward and put his coffee cup down on the low table.

'You must know the Tye investment portfolio better than almost anybody outside of the corporation itself,' began the banker. 'We want you to operate a new investment fund specializing in the Tye Corporation and its many related interests. It will be a large fund, a very large fund indeed, but it will have unorthodox goals.'

Joe nodded again, wondering what type of fund the man could be talking about.

'We want you to maintain all your current intelligence-gathering operations on Mr Tye and his personal investments and we hope you will be able to attract many of your old clients back to your new fund.'

Joe allowed himself a small smile. He thought that might be

possible. Many of the world's pension-fund managers had hitched a free, or semi-free, ride on Joe's coat-tails for almost a decade.

'At the outset we want you to run this fund with one initial aim.'

Chelouche raised his heavy eyebrows as he reached the end of the sentence, inviting Joe's input.

'To make profits?' offered Joe because he could think of no other motive. He had read as much as he could find about the World Bank since being invited to visit Geneva, but he wasn't aware of any investment banking operations.

'Yes, naturally, to make profits,' confirmed Chelouche. 'But I also want you to use the fund to maintain price stability in the various Tye stock-market listings.'

Although Joe had now been out of Rakusen-Webber for ten days he was still fully aware of the market positions and he knew that all Tye's stocks were showing great resilience. He had been perversely pleased when the news of his dismissal from Rakusen-Webber had momentarily wiped two per cent off the top level of Tye's quoted interests. But that dip had only lasted half a day and now most of the offerings were trading near or at the top of their year's highs. His network agents had provided updated prices just before he had attended this meeting.

'In what way "stabilize", sir?' asked Joe. 'They seem to be doing pretty well without my help.'

'That's very true – for now,' grunted the banker enigmatically. 'Your job would be to intervene if and when any of the core stocks show signs of serious weakness. If you were to take this assignment, we'd want you to build a substantial cushion of Tye stockholdings as a first step. The more your fund would hold, the less damage any other fluctuations might cause.'

'Would that be fair on my clients, sir?' asked Joe.

Chelouche smiled. 'We will ensure they don't suffer. Additional funds will be made available, if required. How long would it take you to rebuild the sort of position in Tye's stocks that you held at Rakusen-Webber – on the understanding that your buying activities mustn't inflate any open-market prices?'

So the value of his previous fund would merely be regarded

as a starting point – a position to hold *before* new funds for
market intervention were even calculated!

Joe considered. He'd have to buy slowly and very carefully.
A lot would depend on how Rakusen-Webber played their
existing position on his previous portfolio. His sources had told
him that it had now been split into five, with Morgenstein
personally assuming responsibility for the largest segment. He
had also heard that at least two of his old clients were shopping
around for new investment houses to handle their equity
portfolios.

'Perhaps five or six weeks, sir,' he estimated, 'if we have to
do it without being noticed. It depends on how the markets
move.'

Chelouche nodded and appeared to be in deep thought. Joe
took the opportunity to ask some questions.

'Do you think we're heading for problems in the markets,
sir? Is that why you want me to buy Tye stock?'

'There may indeed be problems, Mr Tinkler, but I think they
will be very small and limited only to the Tye Corporation and
its relatives *if* you would be kind enough to use your skills to
help us.'

Joe waited.

'You already know that UNISA is investigating Mr Tye and
his corporate activities?'

Joe nodded.

'What emerges from that investigation could affect how
investors view Mr Tye and his stocks. We want you to intervene
– secretly and anonymously, of course – to maintain the value
of those stocks. You'll use our funds for that, not your investors'
money.'

'Wouldn't that be illegal?' queried Joe. 'Wouldn't that be a
market manipulation?'

Chelouche smiled for the first time.

'This is the World Bank, Mr Tinkler. This is where the rules
are made. You're not to worry about that because you'll be
working under our auspices. Our aim is to maintain stability,
nothing more. The World Bank is not trying to make profits
from its interventions, that is not our role. You will understand

far better than most that Mr Tye's holdings are so valuable that any sudden downwards movement could destabilize the world's markets. That would set us back a decade or more.'

Joe nodded. He knew that even after nearly ten years of consistent stock-market growth, panic could return within minutes. Only recently he had been within seconds of selling all his Tye-related investments. His failure to do so had been the excuse Morgenstein had used to sack him.

'I thought that was going to happen the other day,' he admitted. 'About two weeks ago Tye started going to cash for no apparent reason. It was touch and go whether I bailed out then.'

'And why didn't you?' asked the world's banker.

'The market swallowed it. He liquidated nearly half a trillion US in a morning and the prices hardly wavered.'

Chelouche smiled again. 'We found ourselves with quite a lot of Tye Corporation stock that day,' he said.

Joe understood what he was being told, but he still couldn't help himself exclaiming: 'You! *That*'s why ...' He tailed off.

'We think he might have, well ... guessed that we sometimes undertake such activity and I suspect he deliberately leveraged our interventions to get such a large pile of cash out.'

This was all outside of Joe's experience. There was a long pause.

'What do you think he might need so much cash for, Mr Tinkler?' asked Chelouche, eventually.

Joe shrugged. 'I was certain he was making new investments. I've been watching, but I haven't found any of it.'

Chelouche nodded. 'Nor have we,' he agreed. 'But it must move soon. Money only generates new value when it is moving. We'd like you to trace it for us.'

'But if you're already intervening in the market, why do you need me?' asked Joe. 'I was fooled myself. I assumed the markets had soaked it up.'

Chelouche sucked in his cheeks as he considered his response. 'There are two reasons. First, we're no longer able to do that. As I said, we think Thomas Tye may have somehow guessed our little game. Frankly, Mr Tinkler, we want you as cover. We don't want anyone at the Tye Corporation or anybody else in the financial community to know when the World Bank is intervening. You understand?'

Joe nodded. He did indeed understand. If anybody knew about this it would provide the richest investment gravy train in financial history. For a moment he found himself wondering if he could hitch a ride himself. Then Chelouche cut into his thoughts.

'The second reason is that we want you to be seen publicly to be building a very large Tye-based investment vehicle – far larger than you were running at Rakusen-Webber. If you're agreeable, we'll set you up in your own office in Swiss National's Fund Management centre here, in Geneva. We're very close friends with the bank and, to all intents and purposes, it will be a straightforward hiring. It will be announced that Mr Joseph Tinkler, formerly of Rakusen-Webber, has moved to Europe to join Swiss National,' said Chelouche. He paused. 'I presume you would consider such an offer?'

Joe smiled. A spell with the most prestigious bank in Switzerland would completely restore his reputation.

'Of course, Swiss National themselves will be unaware of the unusual nature of your portfolio,' continued the banker. 'Even outside of the investments you bring from your old clients, your funds will, for all practical purposes, be unlimited. If the Tye Corporation's overall valuation suffered a twenty-five per cent fall, how much would you need to bring them back up?'

Joe did a rapid mental calculation of Tye Corp's total capitalization. That was too much money.

'You mean in addition to the value of the fund I've previously managed?'

Chelouche nodded.

'A *very* much larger fund than I had at Rakusen-Webber,' exclaimed Joe. 'Perhaps more than is available.'

Then Chelouche made himself crystal clear. 'Mr Tinkler, unlimited means *unlimited*,' he explained. 'The World Bank draws its funds from almost every nation in the world. It is as though we are the keepers of the concept of value. If we say we

have money, we have money. That's what money is – a belief
that there is value.'

Chelouche paused. 'Do you know the meaning of the word
"credit", Mr Tinkler?'

Joe wondered if this was a trick question.

'"Credit" is a Latin word,' said Chelouche. 'It means "he
believes!"'

Chelouche laughed and Joe heard the man's lungs gurgle.
He guessed that the large humidor on the coffee table was not
solely for the benefit of his visitors.

'So if the going gets rough I prop up Thomas Tye, no matter
what the cost?' continued Joe, marvelling at the idea.

'It's not exactly a new concept,' growled Chelouche.
'Countries used to do it all the time, when corporations still had
national identities. Twenty years ago companies like GE, Micro-
soft and Mitsubishi were frequently propped up in the markets
by their national governments. Usually the companies concerned had no idea of that support. After the Cold War ended
the CIA turned its attention to economic activities and the
security services became economic spies, commercial subver-
sives and tactical investors – all on a vast scale. They diverted
the billions the Pentagon was saving – by not having to pursue
an arms race – into economic warfare.'

The banker paused, to ensure his explanation was being
followed. 'You must recall that scandal ten years ago – when it
was revealed that America had agents all over Europe trying to
deflate the Euro. They were also whipping up anti-European
Union sentiments in the press, covertly funding politicians and
political parties who wanted individual states to withdraw from
the EU – just to slow up the Union's growth and expansion.
They realized that the EU was going to become the most
powerful economic bloc in the world and they were trying to
subvert it. The idea of keeping a few bell-wether stocks at a high
rating in the markets is nothing compared to some activities
undertaken by the major governments.'

Joe nodded, not really understanding. Despite all his years
on The Street and dealing in the world's most important
financial markets he had never heard of governments or the

security services secretly intervening in the world's stock markets – or trying to subvert the political aims of their so-called allies and friends. To his chagrin, he realized that despite his supposedly elevated position on Wall Street he and even his most exalted colleagues had been working in ignorance. In a second it all became clear: the great bull markets of the last few decades – a phenomenon usually attributed to the economic efficiencies of global networks – were revealed as products of national stratagem. While he and other market makers had been acting tactically, governments had been using *them* to achieve much larger strategic goals. He felt very small and rather stupid in this most hallowed tabernacle of international capitalism.

'You know what the term "bell-wether" actually means, Mr Tinkler?' continued Chelouche, seemingly intent on developing the semantic theme of their meeting. 'It means the sheep that leads the flock.'

Chelouche roared heartily, his lungs now sounding like a pair of Harley-Davidsons idling at a traffic light.

'That's what I want you to do, Mr Tinkler. Lead the flock. Stop the shmendriks from scattering when there's any loud noise.'

Chelouche's laughter had turned into a wheeze and the banker pulled a red handkerchief from his pocket. He coughed, blew his nose and then looked up at Joe.

'Mr Tinkler, who is the second most important executive in the Tye Corporation?'

Joe considered. It wasn't easy to judge, Tye being such an autocrat.

'It's hard to say, sir. It could be Marsello Furtrado, the corporation's senior legal counsel. The group is very widely distributed. Each division and each subsidiary is run separately by its own CEO and CFO and they report into the corporate office on Hope Island. Tye runs that himself with a very small staff – just sixty or so.'

The banker nodded, wiped his nose again and returned the handkerchief to his jacket pocket. 'But you know them all – or know of them.'

Joe nodded. He knew the biography of every one and he'd

met quite a few at analysts' briefings. He knew their key technical staff, the finance directors and their marketing executives. He even had a spreadsheet that compared the annual salaries and bonuses of the Top 500 people in Tye's organization worldwide. Not all the information he had about them was in the public domain, but Joe was content that his information was accurate. His numerous sources and his relationship skills were the key to his success.

'Then will you develop an organization chart for me, Mr Tinkler?' asked Chelouche. 'I want to see the whole Tye empire laid out: the people who run it, their backgrounds, the relationships between the corporate entities – physical, legal and personal. On a board, not a screen, if you don't mind.'

Joe nodded. He already had most of the material he would need.

'I also want a complete breakdown of the shareholding of each separate corporate identity: how much of each company is publicly available, who owns what percentage – everything above a one per cent stake. And full cross-referencing between different companies and legal identities. Can you do that?'

Now Joe understood how much work was entailed. Creating a cross-referenced and consolidated shareholding register of every Tye-related company would be an immense undertaking.

'Do I get any admin help?' he asked.

'As much as you need,' huffed Chelouche, with a dismissive wave. 'This is a political operation. Finances don't come into it.'

Joe could never recall hearing such a statement from a banker before. He guessed the surprise was showing on his face. Then he remembered there was something else. 'What's the second objective of the fund?' he asked.

'I can't tell you that at this stage,' said Chelouche. 'And it may never materialize. But I can promise that you would be very enthusiastic about it.'

Joe nodded. As well as admiring Chelouche's reputation, he was now beginning to like the man. He realized that he was staring at an opportunity to be catapulted to the pinnacle of global finance and he swallowed.

'So what do you say, Mr Tinkler?' asked Chelouche. 'We'll

match the salary Rakusen-Webber provided and the bonus you were due from them. You'll also be earning bonuses at your previous rate on any additional profit you make for the fund.'

'When do I start?' asked Joe.

His ashen complexion only emphasized the large dark rings around his eyes. Raymond Liu presented himself, as demanded, outside the Network Control Center, where Connie was waiting for him.

'He's in a foul mood,' she warned as she touched the entry system. 'Keep your distance.'

Inside, Liu saw a bright display in the Holo-Theater and he waited while his eyes adjusted to the darkness of the room. Tye had the advantage.

'Get down here Liu,' he screamed. 'Look what your fucking networks have done!'

Liu walked down the gently sloping aisle towards the central display pit. Inside the ring he could see a flat two-dimensional display. He didn't need more than one glance to know that it was an optical view of Los Angeles from one of the visual-wavelength satellite feeds.

Tye was circling the edge of the Holo-Theater, haloed by the bright image behind him. Liu stopped halfway down the aisle. He felt Connie stop abruptly behind him. He could make out several other figures in the front row of seats, just at the edge of the surrounding darkness.

'Come down here and fucking well look,' demanded Tye. 'Nothing is moving down there.'

Liu didn't need to be told. He had been looking at the crisis on his own monitors all day while he frantically directed the efforts to restore vehicle management to the Greater Los Angeles road network. In the local offices his people had been besieged by the news networks seeking explanations.

'They've been dragging cars off the freeways ever since it happened,' shouted an ignivomous Tye, 'and the roads are *still* fucking full! It will take them days to get all the vehicles off. Their drivers just abandoned them!'

Liu was as frozen as the stationary traffic in the image. He could see the Santa Monica Freeway clearly. Miles of stationary metal glinted through the late-afternoon heat haze – an atmosphere that was unusually free of smog. When he had been a regional technical director of Tye Satellite Networks he had been one of the original beta testers who had driven the length of each freeway to check the system's reaction to unauthorized driver intervention, breakdowns, blow-outs and all the other ills that can befall any one of those millions of individual mobile assets within an integrated city traffic management system.

They had taken so much time designing back-ups, fail-safes and extreme-condition survival systems that they had not felt it appropriate to build or act out a scenario for the complete failure of the entire system – not least because there *could be* no conceivable solution. So the decision had been made to engineer risk out of the system and they had even designed sufficient fault tolerance for the satellites to withstand a meteor shower one hundred times more dense than any ever recorded in the Earth's vicinity. With two low-Earth-orbit satellites stationary above Los Angeles and a third back-up management system on board a satellite in mid-Earth-orbit, they could not envisage how total failure could occur across three separate systems.

But it had.

Tye bounded up the aisle. He lunged towards Liu and grabbed his shirt front. Connie stepped round and pushed herself physically between them. Liu was suddenly aware of an unexpected strength and muscularity in the executive assistant.

'Tom ...' she warned. 'That won't help!'

They stood there, all three, in an embrace of anger. Connie did not budge. The slope of the aisle equalized their heights.

Tye released his grip and turned away.

'Tell him, Marsello,' he screamed towards the seated group. 'Fucking tell him!'

Furtrado stood up. He had a printout in his hand. 'We've been contacted by the attorneys who act for the City of Los Angeles,' he said with a face like a lawsuit. 'They've notified us that actions will be forthcoming – for the loss to the city's economy and for punitive damages. The death toll so far is believed to be over seven hundred.'

There was a silence. Tye had gone back to the edge of the Holo-Theater where he was staring again at the image of stationary downtown Los Angeles.

'Tell him all of it!' he screamed at the lawyer.

'The city is at a complete standstill,' continued Furtrado. 'There has been no production in any of its major industrial or commercial sectors today. Very few services are operating. LAX is closed and all flights are diverted to San Diego. The police, ambulances and fire crews can't travel – every road is blocked. Looting has broken out in West Hollywood, Culver City and the lower slopes of the Hollywood Hills. The Governor has called in the National Guard and they have started arriving by helicopter. The police are afraid that when night falls the looters will move west towards Beverly Hills, north into the Canyon and east into the commercial district. I'm afraid we can expect many more civil suits from those affected so far and any who suffer later.'

Liu shook his head in disbelief.

'Tell him how much, tell him how much!' shouted Tye.

'We don't know how much yet, Tom,' observed Furtrado. 'But it's going to be huge. The city's action alone could be the biggest lawsuit in history. Then there's the private suits with their inevitable claims for actual damages, punitive damages and for *solatium* – payment for making them feel bad. And remember, they're the richest urban population in the world.' Furtrado paused. 'And, necessitously, we are uninsured for this contingency.'

There was a silence and Tye turned back to face Liu. 'Every traffic management project we were working on has been put on hold,' he said quietly, as if he could hardly believe it himself. 'Atlanta, Toronto, Singapore, Sydney – they've *all* told us to stop further development. The LA standstill is now the main item on every one of the world's news networks.'

Tye gathered himself and started up the aisle towards Liu again. Connie stepped further down the ramp to block him.

'Have you seen the fucking stock price?' he yelled up at Liu as Connie pressed the flat of her hand against her boss's chest to prevent him from attacking the engineer. 'Networks is down forty per cent! The Corporate stock is down five! WHAT THE FUCK HAPPENED?'

'We don't know,' admitted Liu. 'There's been a large increase in faults all over our networks but this was...' He tailed off. There was no adequate description for the disaster.

'How long...?' screamed Tye, not even bothering to finish the question.

'The master system on board SATMAN-6 is now working again,' reported Liu. 'I've personally reloaded the entire system. But there's no back-up and we can't restart without one. We've got to launch replacements for LAT-6 and 7. Then we've got to test them.'

'How long?' repeated Tye. 'Every day will cost billions.'

Liu had been dreading this question. He had put fourteen staff to work on preparing two replacement satellites the moment he'd heard the news.

'About five days, Tom,' said Raymond Liu.

'Make it two,' shouted Tye as he sprayed his mouth. 'Or get off my island.'

FOURTEEN

'Hope Island Control, this is Tye Flight Five, over.'

'Good morning, Tye Flight Five, this is Hope Island Control. Good to see you, Jack. You're flying *manual*?'

And so Jack Hendriksen had been welcomed back. He had disengaged the computer system that normally flew the plane and he confirmed the aircraft's unusual status to Hope Island ATM. Jack liked to feel a plane in the air, as did most pilots, but every commercial airline flight was now operated automatically, from take-off to landing. Insurance companies would no longer accept the risk of humans flying planes, except in extreme emergencies, and today's pilots flew with the aircraft simply to reassure the passengers. The problem was that the one in ten take-offs and landings that the human pilots were allowed to handle, for purposes of practice, were not enough to maintain their general flying skills or their preparedness for emergencies, despite a significant increase in simulator training. As a result every passenger preferred the ultra-smoothness of a computer-controlled landing and many had started to book seats only with carriers and on flights where this could be guaranteed. It looked liked commercial-airline pilots were going out of business. Such shop talk had occupied the team on the flight deck throughout their short supersonic trip from New York's La Guardia airport back to Hope Island.

Jack accepted his flight-path-approach instructions from the tower, made the course and height alterations necessary, trimmed the aircraft for subsonic speed, winked at his co-pilot as the controlling computer pointlessly communicated a heading error of one degree – an error no human pilot could correct – and watched as the island and the Cape Hope spaceport came into view.

He had cadged a ride back to the island with a group of returning patent attorneys and he'd asked the pilot for permission to fly the Tye jet personally in order to keep himself occupied. There was nothing he could do to advance his new mission during the flight but he knew that the moment he landed he would be overloaded. UNISA wanted answers urgently and he realized that he was flying into a corporate maelstrom: the hysterical media coverage made it sound as if Los Angeles had been completely shut down by the failure of the Tye Corporation's traffic-management systems.

He also knew that Tom would be screaming for him to approve the security aspects of plans for the forthcoming anniversary celebrations.

In two months, on 30 August, it would be Founder's Day on Hope Island. In previous years that day had been marked by a public holiday and with company-sponsored barbecues on the beaches. But this year, for the state's thirteenth official anniversary and celebration of sovereignty, the corporation was planning to use the occasion for a major product launch. Jack knew it would also be a belated celebration for Tye's fifieth birthday but that would remain unannounced. Rumours suggested that the event was being designed to be 'the party to end all parties', with a guest list intended to be the most exclusive of the twenty-first century. By coincidence, Tye's ambitious plans would provide Jack with a perfect excuse for a complete review of the island's security – not that it wasn't needed. As UNISA had made clear, Tye's continuing safety was essential for global economic stability.

Connie had greeted Jack with an affectionate smile when he arrived at the corporate offices in the ground-floor quadrangle of Tye's house. Yes, he had enjoyed his vacation. No, he didn't realize that Connie had been in New York at the same time. She'd been trying to reach him? Ah, well, he'd spent time upstate with his mother: her birthday and she wasn't at all well. In fact, she might have to be admitted to hospital.

Jack detected no suspicion in Connie's gaze as she listened to him. Perhaps there was a hint of something else, he realized. Once again he considered the elegance of her long neck. He knew he would need an ally on the island but ... well, Connie was just too close to Tye. Nobody knew the origins of the fierce loyalty she showed to her mercurial master.

'Never mind, it wasn't important,' she said with a smile. 'Well, you *have* come back at a busy time. Tom's got meetings all day about the LA situation – you can *imagine*! But he wants you to see the event organizers – they're in from Washington, and standing by in Network Control. They gave Tom and me a briefing this morning on their plans for the anniversary weekend. It all sounds wonderful but your people will have a lot to do. Oh, and there's the Moscow visit. Tom had to postpone that, so you might want to review the new arrangements. Pierre is currently scheduled to lead the Presidential Protection Team for that trip.'

Jack nodded as she ticked off her list one by one. He wanted to talk with Tye in person, even though strictly he didn't have any urgent need. He guessed he wanted to see him in the flesh again, now that he knew more about the supposed secret of the man's success. He also wanted to push him a little, to see if any cracks appeared.

It had just been the busiest vacation, or non-vacation, of his life. He had arrived in Manhattan intending to talk to a lawyer about Tye's dubious activities, and he had returned as a newly sworn intelligence officer of the United Nations International Security Agency. Despite his protestations, a second salary was now being paid into a new bank account for him as 'Bruce Curtis' in Manhattan. 'It isn't legal unless we pay you, Jack,' Deakin had smiled. 'That's *our* part of the contract.'

Jack's part of the contract was still unclear. He knew that to a large extent that would be decided only once he had uncovered more information about Tye's presumed interceptions of network traffic.

He had also attended four more UN briefing sessions on what was now known as 'Operation Iambus' – a code name specially selected for the purpose. At each one he had seen the team grow steadily larger. By the time he had left it consisted of over 190 men and women from all parts of the world, who were busily taking over the entire twelfth floor of the UN Secretariat building.

As well as an increasing number of UNISA intelligence officers, the team now included technical officers, satellite-surveillance analysts, patent lawyers, two insolvency practitioners, aerospace consultants, three jurimetricians – jurisdictional experts in antinomic international law (who seemed unable to agree on anything) – economists, energy consultants, media specialists, corporate lawyers, a former White House Chief of Staff, a professor of solar radiation, two meteorologists and an ecologist.

Research into every aspect of the Tye Corporation and its many subsidiaries and interests was punctuated by endless discussions about what might be the long-term aims of the mysterious Phoebus Project to which Jack had alerted them. Just before he had left, this topic of speculation was replaced by a sense of quiet awe at the scale of the standstill the Tye Networks malfunction had inflicted on Los Angeles.

He had also submitted himself to six days of exhausting refresher courses during which he had been supplied with the small selection of specialist tools that were stowed in his luggage. There were no Customs or immigration barriers on Hope Island and, if such a need ever arose, it would be Jack's own team that would provide the personnel. After the training and his rendezvous with Haley Voss, he had indeed travelled upstate to visit his mother, despite the fact she was as fit as he was and regardless of the fact that it wasn't actually her birthday.

'How would you enjoy a trip to Europe, Mom?' he had asked, though he didn't immediately explain that she would have to travel under an alternative identity. Gently, as the evening progressed and she watched her son enjoy the dinner she had prepared, he told her that he was once again working for the government, although he allowed her to assume he meant the US administration. He admitted that it was to do with his boss, the Thomas Tye she saw so often on the television, but the investigation was so secret that he had to remain in place as a Tye executive in the corporate offices.

His mother nodded her understanding. 'That young man is getting a little big for his boots,' she observed.

With suitable meiosis he explained that he would need an excuse for regular return trips to the mainland and that he would therefore like to pretend she was unwell and that he needed to visit her regularly. He told her that his government agency could arrange for her to be registered as a patient at a nearby hospital while she was actually spending time in Birmingham, England with her younger sister. This was because people in the Tye Corporation might try to check on his whereabouts or her condition of health.

'You should never wish your mother ill, Johnny,' she had replied sharply, but he could see the twinkle in her eye. His mother had always enjoyed a little subterfuge and he remembered how easily she had manipulated his father.

So it had been agreed, and his mother had seemed more excited than disturbed when he had explained about a new passport and the need for absolute secrecy. They discussed what to do about her dog and about Clara Morgan, his mother's best friend. It would be impossible for her to leave without explaining, the elderly lady affirmed, since if Clara thought she was in a hospital, she would break down all the doors to visit her.

Jack pondered these twin problems for a moment. 'What does Clara think I used to do, Mom?' he had asked, at last.

'Oh, nothing,' his mother had said, with an over-casual shrug. 'You always told me not to talk about it.'

Jack smiled. His mother had known no details of his work, but she had certainly guessed its nature.

'You must have said *something*,' he prompted gently.

Anne Hendriksen swivelled her shoulders slightly, like a small child trying to avoid making an admission. 'Well ... I just said you did confidential work for the government.'

Jack smiled. 'Would you mind if I dropped round to see her?' he asked. 'When I take Skipper out for a walk, later on.'

The red setter lifted his head above the rim of his basket and regarded Jack with a liquid, hopeful stare.

'I could just explain how you're helping me, so she mustn't worry. Would that be OK?'

And later Mrs Morgan had stared up at him, her bright button eyes popping. 'I won't breathe a word, John, on the Good Book,' she swore, 'and I'll be pleased to look after Skipper. You just tell your mother to have a good time.'

Joe stepped back and looked up with satisfaction at the large pinboard on the wall. Ingrid, his new assistant, had been scouring the networks for such an old-fashioned item, but without success. But Geneva does not desert its traditional retailers easily and in the end she had found the green baize noticeboard, three meters square, at a small stationer's near the university.

He had spent two days dumping the contents of his VideoMate, his server files and his own memory, as well as contacting his friends and other sources, in order to create this graphic representation. He'd even found images of most of the Tye Corporation executives. Then he and Ingrid had spent another seven days compiling a consolidated and cross-referenced shareholding register for every Tye-related company. Now his only concern was whether he would have to get his graphic display and supporting documents packaged up and transported safely across town to Dr Chelouche's office, or whether the world's banker would deign to visit him here.

He had flown back to Manhattan to collect his clothes and tell his friends the authorized version of his sudden move to Europe. Before Joe had been allowed to leave his first encounter with Chelouche, the banker had insisted on the importance of transmitting nothing on the networks that might reveal the true nature of his forthcoming role in Europe. To Joe's surprise, he had even insisted that this restriction also apply to encrypted messages.

Well, Joe knew no one he wanted to tell *that* badly and he relished the challenge of establishing a fund so large that he could exercise some control over the market price of the Tye Corporation. He had used the brief trip home to pass news of his new role onto the key pension fund managers and to blow on the embers of a few Tye-oriented relationships that had been allowed to cool.

One such call had produced an interesting snippet: an individual on Hope Island named Zachary Zorzi was shopping around for a loan – a large loan, the source said – based on the value of his stock options in a Tye Corp subsidiary called LifeLines Inc. Joe had recorded a PopUp reminder to research this company. Joe's stock-in-trade wasn't real inside knowledge (although he never hesitated to use it discreetly when he came across it) but lay in his ability to find a link between apparently unrelated events: to look for a pattern in various developments and announcements that allowed him to discern the intentions of those who were shaping the markets. If he got that right, he could invest and maybe share some of the spoils.

Joe had also picked up some news that he found hard to interpret. One of the software agents he had programmed to search for Tye's new equity investments had struck lucky in one of its random Serendipity Excursions and had reported back with documents on a land deal filed as a matter of public record by Finland's Ministry of the Interior. Joe had been surprised to read that a new corporate identity called Tye International Real Estate Inc. had bought a cluster of uninhabited small islands in the north Baltic Sea. Joe's network atlas had quickly given him some basic facts: at a latitude of sixty degrees north, these islands were ice-bound for eight months of the year and contained no known mineral or chemical resources of value. The deals were leasehold, each for 999 years, and all commercial fishing rights had been retained by the Finnish government. In all, the ownership of thirty-seven islands had been transferred at a total cost of only thirty-two million euros.

Joe knew the history of how the Tye Corporation had acquired Hope Island and, despite the tycoon's professed concern for ecological issues, he doubted that Tye Corp was merely buying Baltic islands to protect the local gull populations. Then he had recalled his other software robots and reprogrammed them to go in search of any land deals into which any known Tye-related company had entered over the previous three years.

He had arrived back in Geneva to find that a penthouse apartment in a low modern block had been rented for him, close to Swiss National's head office. A new Audi was also waiting for him in an underground car park. An alien's work permit – something even harder to acquire in Switzerland since the country had finally joined the EU – waited amongst the package of documents related to his new home, the car and his appointment to Swiss National. There was also a printed memo from Madame Pioline asking him to pay special attention to the group of companies within Tye Aerospace while he was constructing his organizational chart.

The Director of Human Resources at the bank had been all smiles when Joe arrived at the appointed time the following morning.

'We're honoured that Doctor Chelouche would ask for our assistance,' he said in French-accented English. 'But this will remain between us, yes? The director of fund management understands you will be working on your own, but the rest of the team are being allowed to assume you are setting up a new fund here in the normal way. Perhaps you would look over this draft press announcement of your appointment to Swiss National?'

In addition to the large pinboard, Joe had developed a non-network electronic version of his organization chart complete with videos and database material on the various companies, subsidiaries and shareholdings of the Tye Corporation and on Thomas Tye himself. He'd never laid out a physical map of the Tye empire before and as he looked at the busy pinboard with its clusters of company names and presidential titles even he was surprised by the depth and complexity of the organization revealed by this visual display.

Joe's VideoMate chirruped and he found himself looking at Madame Pioline.

'The Doctor will be pleased to visit Swiss National tomorrow morning,' she told him in response to the request he'd made earlier. 'I've spoken with the bank's director and the board room will be at your disposal. Our technical support team will check the room over immediately beforehand. Shall we say nine a.m?'

Joe nodded. How civilized. How European. How northern latitude. It would give him time for a morning run beside the lake.

'We'll be bringing in the newly commissioned *Treasure of the Caribbean* for additional accommodation,' announced the young, silk-suited female event-producer in what she obviously thought was a clipped, inner-Beltway presentational style. An impressive image of the giant cruise liner, superimposed alongside the quay of the deep-water harbour at Cape Hope, hung pointlessly in the Holo-Theater. *Everybody knows what a cruise ship looks like*, thought Jack. Only a DC organization would pad out a presentation so excessively. Next they'll show me a floor layout to justify their large fees. Just then the image changed to display seven separate deck plans.

'We'll have sixty suites, three hundred and twenty double bedrooms and three hundred single rooms for staff. The conference itself will take place here in the Network Control Center – we understand the conversion to the Solaris Control Center will be complete before then – and in Mr Tye's house, in the lecture theatres on the university campus and in the three lecture theatres and the ballroom of the *Treasure of the Caribbean* itself.' *Herself*, thought Jack with a rush of irritation. 'Outside of the plenary sessions there will be three hundred and eighty-two separate seminars.'

But, despite the over-fussy detail and high-pressure delivery, it had been an impressive presentation. Jack had smiled sagely as the details unfolded but even if he had still had only the Corporation's interests at heart, he would have been daunted by the task of analysing all the many potential threats and dangers posed by such an ambitious undertaking.

'We are calling the event *One Weekend in the Future*,' the account director had beamed. 'We are bringing together the world's greatest business leaders, politicians, scientists, philosophers, artists and writers to spend three days in a conference on the global environment that will set the ecological and technological agenda for the next ten years. Naturally, the Tye News Network will have exclusive television and network rights. An announcement was made to the press this morning.'

As the list of events and activities grew, Jack began to wonder how his staff could possibly cope. Then the PR people turned to the guest list. They started with the ultra-VIPs.

'We've had a provisional acceptance from the president's office, the Dalai Lama . . .'

Jack stood and held up his hand. The young woman looked up from her list.

'You mean the president of the United States?' asked Jack.

'Yes, we're all delighted by that,' said the account director. 'We heard only two days ago. It's subject to final confirmation, of course.'

'And what level of security will he be bringing with him?'

'That's to be confirmed. We know he will be travelling in Air Force One. The Secret Service has already cleared the trip – they believe Hope Island is probably one of the safest territories on earth.'

Jack nodded and sank back into his seat. He agreed with that judgement but he dreaded working with the White House mafia again. Twice before his work had taken him into the American presidential orbit and both times the macho, pre-emptive, turf-dominating, gun-toting hubris of the Presidential Protection Section of the US Secret Service had made him want to vomit. It reminded him of the ignorant and stupid young man he himself had been when he had first wanted to join the Marines. They seemed to sum up all the worst aspects of American military culture.

When Thomas Tye had first hired him he had asked Jack's opinion of American presidential security.

'It's effective but wholly over the top,' Jack had commented. 'It's about projecting a tough image when it should be about discretion. I've worked with those Secret Service officers and although they're good as a team, they don't work well with outside agencies or organizations. Every presidential trip becomes a misery for the hosts.'

'We'll see if we can do better when *we*'re on our travels,' Tye had then said. 'But that'll be up to you.'

The young event producer sensed Jack's reservations. 'Mr

Tye thought you would start liaising with the White House fairly soon,' she prompted. 'Do you see a problem?'

Only one of jurisdiction, thought Jack. He was also wondering whether the President's late acceptance of Tye's invitation could be linked to American concerns over Tye's rapidly increasing power – or whether the US government had suddenly joined the rest of the world and was finally starting to pay more than gas-guzzling lip-service to the plight of the choking planet. He would need to inform Ron Deakin quickly but the covert UN landing party wasn't scheduled to lay the secure landlines until the following day.

'Please go on.'

'The Dalai Lama, President Orlov of Russia, President Cohen of the EU, the Sultan of Brunei, Prime Minister Benn, President Boutard of France, Lord Berners-Lee...'

Jack listened as she read off some of the world's most famous names. He knew Tye wanted to create the ultimate launch event for the first public unveiling of the Phoebus Project, his largest project and investment to date. But Jack wondered if all the many guests would react in quite the way Tye expected.

Calypso had waited a week for news. She hadn't seen Tommy since that lunch on Tye's terrace when she had laid down her conditions for continuing as the boy's ... she still didn't know how to describe her role. Chaperone? Companion? Psychiatrist? Playmate? Observer? Love-giver?

She knew she genuinely loved Tommy, but she was resigned to the fact that he might already be beyond her reach and her help. At the end of their lunch she had insisted that Tom reconsider his decision about Tommy's attending school and about allowing the boy to join her on a trip to visit her mother. She wanted Tommy to witness other aspects of life, and by having him meet some of her nieces and nephews she wanted this child of ultimate privilege to see how different family life could be on an island not so very far from his own.

Since then she had called the main house three times each day but every time one of the staff had explained that Tommy was in a lesson, or swimming, or in the bath, or in bed, or playing the piano, or immersed in a game or anything but able to see her or even speak to her on a communicator. She'd started to call Thomas Tye himself and, once again, was told that Tom was in a meeting about the Los Angeles problem, or down at Cape Hope for a launch, or was in holo-conference with the president of this nation or that nation. She'd even strolled around the foot of the mountain to see if she could somehow get into the grounds of the mansion. But she discovered that down at sea level would-be trespassers were greeted by nothing but sheer cliff face.

Then she had decided to act. She had had enough! She walked to catch the Mag, determined to visit the house itself and persuade whoever she found there that she must see Tommy immediately for his own good.

But the shuttle had refused to leave the station. She pressed the destination button for Tye's residence again and again but the car refused to budge. At first she thought maybe the power had failed, but when she pressed the button for Little Venice, the shuttle pulled away instantly. When she arrived at the waterfront she pressed the button for Tye's house again. Once again, the car would not move. Resigned, she pressed the button for the station near her home and the shuttle started instantly. It was now clear that the security system was simply denying her access to the main house. Her VideoMate locator and also the facial-recognition system of the island's camera network were automatically communicating, and the security system was obeying instructions to deny her access.

When she woke the next morning, she found Tye's decision waiting for her in her mail box. Seeing that he had recorded it during the night, she presumed it was her attempt at visiting the house that had at last prompted this contact.

I'm sorry, Doctor, but I have considered everything and I'm afraid I can't let Tommy return to the school or leave the island even for a short trip. I understand your genuine concerns, but Tommy is an exceptional boy destined for a very special role in life. Therefore his world can't be exactly like that of other boys. I hope you will understand – or that you will come to understand in the future.

'*Given the strength of your feelings on this matter, it is probably better if we now terminate our agreement. Technically, you're still within your probationary period, but I've arranged for severance pay to be made to you as if the full contract was already in place. Logistics will arrange for your transportation off the island. I've told HR to provide an excellent reference regarding your professional capabilities. Thank you, Doctor Browne.*'

Then the screen had gone blank. *Patronizing bastard,* Calypso had thought: '*... or that you will come to understand in the future.*'

What she *did* understand was that it was now time to leave and her instincts told her to do so quickly. HR and Logistics confirmed that a helicopter would be available to her at ten a.m. the following morning to take her to Mayaguana and she spent the day packing her clothes and the lightweight possessions she had brought from her Chicago apartment. Most of her furniture and pictures were still in a run-down Me-Lock self-storage depot near O'Hare airport where, in sullen silence, Larry Sumner had helped her load the container. She hadn't been on the island long enough to arrange to have them forwarded to her.

She had already laid out her travelling clothes on the queen-size bed and, by late evening, she was packing the last of her underwear and shoes into a leather overnight bag. It had been one of her first 'luxury' purchases seventeen years before, after winning her first serious prize money. The bag was old but with a battered quality that improved with time and had the comfortable smell and feel of a much-loved travelling accessory.

She heard a banging on the door to the veranda. Then a familiar voice. 'Calypso? Calypso?'

She ran through into the living room, pulled the inner door open and swung the mesh door outwards onto the veranda.

'I knew you hadn't gone away,' he said simply, his violet eyes full of tears.

Tommy was still wearing blue striped pyjamas but he'd pulled on dark trainers for this excursion. Jed was trapped firmly under his left arm and the boy held a bottle of water in one hand and a chocolate bar in the other. Calypso wanted to smile at these preparations he'd made for his expedition. Then she noticed that he was wearing a small surgical mask pulled down

around his neck, and even pale latex gloves. She put her arm
around his shoulders and led him into the light of her living
room.

As she kneeled and hugged him, she could feel his small
heart pumping violently beneath his pyjama jacket.

'They told me you'd gone away,' he sniffed as his tears
abated. Then he noticed the three black leather suitcases lined
up on the carpet ready for her departure the next morning. Two
packing crates of books and the synthesizer flight-case stood
against one wall, ready to be forwarded.

Calypso weighed up what, and how, to explain to him. She
realized how much damage had already been done to him in
his short life and, above all, she wanted to cause no more hurt.

'I do have to go, I'm sorry,' she lied. Lying about *having* to
go, not about being sorry. She supposed that if she gave in to
Tom and stopped interfering in the way the boy was brought
up, she might still be able to stay – but what would be the
point? It was her professional judgement that was being challenged here and she couldn't bear to watch Tommy go on
spending his childhood in such damaging phobic isolation. The
only possible end result would be psychopathy or severe
neurasthenia.

Calypso sat him on the piano stool and gently took the
water bottle and chocolate bar away from him. Without a word
she pulled the tight-fitting gloves from his hands and undid the
bow that secured the face mask around his neck. She tossed the
items aside and examined him for injury. She noticed grass stains
on the knees and elbows of his pyjamas but he seemed unhurt.
As she kissed his forehead, Tommy released Jed from his tight
captivity.

'Hello, Doctor,' said the caterpillar. 'It's a pleasant evening.'

Calypso couldn't help smiling. She guessed that the Furry
must have registered her professional identity during that lunch
up at the house.

'Hello, Jed,' she replied, grateful for the distraction as she
gathered her thoughts.

'Does your father know you're here?' she asked Tommy,

sitting down on a low chair, close to him. She could guess the answer.

'I've run away,' he announced solemnly. 'I want to live with *you* now. They said you'd gone away for ever.'

'Well, I do have to leave tomorrow, Tommy,' she admitted. 'But I'm very pleased to be able to say goodbye to you.'

'Where are you going, Doctor?' asked Jed.

'I'm going to visit my mother. She's not very well,' replied Calypso, marvelling at the conversation simulation in the latest generation of Furries.

'Go to sleep, Jed,' said Tommy irritably.

Then they heard a sound that was unusual on Hope Island. Calypso couldn't recall ever hearing it since she'd arrived there and she was shocked at how intrusive it seemed. She crossed to the front door and opened it. The petrol engine of the large four-wheel-drive vehicle cut out and Stella Witherspoon swung her lithe frame down from the cab. In the distance Calypso could hear the deep throb of a second engine coming closer.

Stella started along the path that crossed the small lawn and threaded her way through the pile of refuse sacks that held the remains of Tom's floral apology. Calypso knew very well why she was here but she wanted this situation handled with a *very* light touch.

'Hi, Stella,' she called out as a friendly greeting, though she'd only met the security officer a few times previously and had never really spoken to her before. 'Come on in.'

Calypso stepped aside to let Stella enter the room. The woman had clearly been out on night patrol when she had received an alarm call. She wore a black shirt, black trousers and black combat boots – and carried a holstered gun on her belt. Calypso guessed that Stella's dark night-vision viewpers were already transmitting the scene to watchers elsewhere. Calypso made her smile ultra-wide, but her gleaming eyes and flaring nostrils delivered a warning. 'I expect you're looking for Tommy,' she said lightly. 'We were just going to have a cup of hot chocolate before he went home.'

Stella looked from the psychiatrist to the small boy on the

stool, then back at her. Calypso's hands had moved involuntarily to her hips and she sucked in one cheek. Stella's orders had been to return the boy home immediately. They were talking in her earpiece.

'Sure,' she agreed. 'Sure.'

'I don't want to go home, I want to stay here,' said Tommy. But the demand was made in a mumble of resignation, not a cry of defiance. Calypso smiled and nodded for Stella to sit on the couch.

Then the second vehicle arrived outside and cut its engine. As Calypso opened the door again, Jack appeared in shorts and a sweatshirt. He was barefoot and his hair was ruffled as if he had only recently been sleeping.

'Hi,' he smiled as his glance took in the scene. 'May I join your party?'

Tommy looked up at the tall security executive. He had been repeatedly told that Jack would always be his friend but that he must always do whatever Jack told him. The security chief sat down cross-legged on the floor in front of the boy.

'Good going, Tommy, that was some trip. Are you OK?'

The boy nodded, tightly clutching the now-silent Jed.

'I'll make that hot chocolate,' said Calypso, crossing the room.

While Jack kept Tommy occupied, Calypso poured hot milk into two mugs. She didn't have enough for four because her fridge had been informed of her scheduled departure and had adjusted its normal restocking order. From the kitchen window she saw Stella standing outside, examining her VideoMate as if her system was suffering problems.

Calypso handed Tommy and Jack each a mug and resumed her seat.

Jack was telling Tommy about some new model plane – with three on-board video cameras – that he'd seen in a Manhattan store. Would Tommy like Jack to buy him one on his next trip, he asked.

Tommy ignored the suggestion. 'Will you be coming back here when your mother is better?' he asked Calypso.

She concentrated her gaze on Tommy, even though she could sense the same question in Jack's eyes.

'I don't think so, Tommy,' she sighed, her heart suddenly aching. 'My mother is very old and I've got to stay and look after her. I might be there a very long time.'

Tommy nodded sadly and hung his head. As Stella reappeared in the doorway, Calypso rose and held out her hand.

'Come on, Tommy, I'll take you out to the car.'

Tommy rose, using both hands to place the unfinished chocolate carefully on the small round table on which Calypso normally displayed her family photos. He took her hand and walked with her to the door. There he turned back and silently glanced at Jack still seated cross-legged on the floor. Rising, Jack watched Calypso gently lead Tommy down the path towards the waiting vehicle. He saw her crouch to hug the boy, then kiss the top of his head. Stella stood patiently behind them as Calypso opened the door and Tommy clambered up into the high seat. His actions seemed a bit more animated and Jack guessed that he was excited at the prospect of riding in this commanding-looking vehicle. The four-wheelers were normally garaged underground and used mainly for night-time beach patrols.

Suddenly, Tommy leaned out of the passenger window and threw his small arms around Calypso's neck, clinging to her. She eventually reached behind her head and gently unlocked his fingers. Jack wasn't sure whether Stella's system would have yet started transmitting again. The jamming device in his back pocket was supposed to suppress all radio and display signals within a radius of twelve yards. Then the vehicle started up in a wide turn before heading off towards the mountain road and Tye's mansion.

Calypso remained at the roadside, waving as Jack stepped back into the living room. A few moments later the door opened again, and he turned to study her face. Her amber eyes were full of tears and he could see moist tracks across her high cheek-bones. She looked briefly back at him, then down at the small table where Tommy had placed his mug. He had also left behind the bottle of water and the chocolate bar, the provisions for his escape attempt.

Calypso began to howl and she buried her face in her hands. Jack was beside her in two strides. As he wrapped his arms around her, she slipped her arms about his neck and sobbed into his left shoulder. Instantly the shape and warmth of her body were evident through her thin silk robe. Despite understanding her sadness, Jack was obliged to ease his hips back so she would not notice his rapidly growing erection.

Yoav Chelouche grunted his approval as Joe Tinkler finished his two-hour exposition on the make-up of the Thomas Tye empire. He had started with the main corporation, examined each of the main divisions and then paid special attention to Aerospace as the banker had demanded. He listed all the satellite launches of the last four years and showed a chart of the customers by nation. Clients from almost every developed economy in the world had used Tye's launch services for its satellites. As Joe discussed the development of the Deep-Space Location and Navigation System, Chelouche had cut in with questions about this technology and its functions.

'All we know so far is that it is being developed by Phoebus Inc., which is a joint-venture research company set up by Hope Island University, the Tye Corporation and several private trusts,' said Joe. 'Tye Aerospace has launched a number of deep-space satellites for the company but they have filed nothing about this programme – no patents, just applications for fourteen initial orbit positions in which to construct the craft before they are launched out into deep space. It's been going on for over ten years and, knowing Tye, there has to be some commercial angle other than simply developing a navigation system.'

'But what, Mr Tinkler, what?' asked Chelouche suddenly.

Joe stared at him blankly. 'I have no idea, sir,' he admitted.

He hesitated and then resumed his summation. 'Phoebus sits in its separate corporate identity away from the main corporation,' explained Joe as he used a laser pointer to show the links between the Aerospace division and its subsidiaries. 'The majority shareholding is split between Thomas Tye himself, the Tye Corporation, the Tye Foundation and a cluster of small trusts based in Andorra and Liechtenstein.'

'Not exactly a kosher arrangement,' grumbled Chelouche, the man who had publicly crucified governments and corporations that had dared to disobey his beloved ethic of transparent and responsible accounting.

Joe had to agree. 'They haven't attempted to raise any money, there is no sign of a product or any indication that they're going to market,' he explained. 'That's why their structure and their secrecy hasn't affected my rating of the main corporation. If it remains private, it's their business. They're certainly keeping this one very close.'

'How much capital has been raised by the company?' asked Chelouche.

'There's no way of knowing, Doctor,' Joe admitted.

Chelouche mumbled a series of low asides to Madame Pioline, then asked, 'Have you cross-referenced the shareholder registers?'

Joe spent the next three and a half hours painstakingly laying out a series of print-outs that showed the detailed shareholdings of the Tye Corporation and the quoted subsidiaries and companies in which it had a partial holding. He explained which shares were voting, which were non-voting, which had special executive powers and which did not. Joe finished by showing Chelouche a spreadsheet he had developed that was automatically updated every time ownership of shares in the Tye group changed hands.

'In real-time?' asked Chelouche.

'In real-time – when a change of ownership is filed,' confirmed Joe.

The banker took his time examining the breakdown of shareholding patterns and voting power in each company. When he had finally finished, he put his palms down on the edge of Swiss National's boardroom table and pushed himself upright.

'Excellent, Mr Tinkler – Joe, if I may call you that. Excellent.'

Then Joe raised the matter of the Baltic islands and Chelouche sat down again.

FIFTEEN

Marsello Furtrado knew his boss better than most, but even he hesitated before walking uninvited into the Presidential Lounge. He waited in the companionway beside the executive bar until the clairvoyant Connie turned her head and saw him. She waved him forward.

Tom was sitting opposite her in one of four large armchairs placed around a low coffee table, his back to the aircraft's nose. It was a typical executive cabin layout for a full-size supersonic corporate jet. Unusually, Tye was poring over a fan of concertina-paper printouts.

'Marsello's here,' announced Connie quietly.

Tom didn't look up, but Connie smiled at the lawyer and cleared her papers from the seat next to her so that he could sit down opposite Tom. Furtrado knew what his boss was reading.

'I've never seem so much garbage,' complained Tye finally, as he looked up. 'Who do they think we are? Total idiots?'

He threw the paper concertina on the seat to his right and stretched, hands clasped together, arms high in the air behind his head.

'It's just their starting point,' reasoned Furtrado. 'What else can they do?'

Tom nodded, yawned and sat back. He picked up a small spray from a well in his armrest and absently sprayed his mouth again, despite the atmosphere of antibacterial compound that was constantly refreshed by the cabin's recycling system. Many of the females in the flight crews of the Tye Corporation planes had started to complain about the dryness of their skin and the chapped lips they suffered in such a hostile environment, but they didn't use as much face moisturizer as Thomas Tye. His frequent applications weren't for cosmetic purposes, however: like every bar of soap, every scrap of food, every beverage and all the unguents he used, his face cream was medicinally active. It delivered preventative and proactive agents that hunted down all embryo carcinomas, others that boosted the elasticity co-efficient of epidermic cells and some that simply maintained his skin tone at the precise shade he wanted.

The printouts were from an old Russian-made computer that its operators had programmed to print English-language lists of the assets in the region concerned. Tom turned to his right and fingered a line at random.

'Two hundred and twelve oil and refining facilities, total capacity twenty-two million barrels a day. Is that the real number?'

Furtrado slipped his DigiPad from his pocket, put on his viewpers and quickly searched.

'Maybe forty of the plants are working properly. The capacity for all the refineries in the designated zone was only one point two billion barrels in the whole of last year and much of that was astatki or mazut. That's from OPEC figures.'

Tom nodded. 'So why do they send us *this* shit?' he asked, flicking his fingers disdainfully against the pile. 'Let them keep it. We're not interested.'

'They've got nothing else to offer, Tom. Ease up. Save them some face. We can accept every figure they produce and still close within our own deal parameters.'

And what parameters they were! It was the largest deal Furtrado had ever worked on. It was larger than any deal his previous global law firm had handled and, he knew, it was larger than *any* commercial deal that had ever been undertaken. Only efforts to reconstruct continents after major wars – like the American Marshall Plan to rebuild Europe after the Second World War – came close in scale.

But Tom knew how to create value where none existed previously, as he had demonstrated so clearly to Furtrado in Cape Verde. Sometimes, to his wife or himself, the international attorney would dismiss his boss as just lucky, an opportunist who had secured one vital commercial advantage. Then Tom would amaze him with master plans like this that were dependent on nothing but the youthful tycoon's vision, imagination and drive. The ideas that underlay this deal were pure genius and that, in the end, apart from the twelve-figure personal fortune he was amassing for himself and his family, was why the lawyer tolerated the arrogant antics of his temperamental leader.

But this afternoon TT was in relatively benign mood. The LA traffic system was functioning again and Marsello's team had responded to the 1,472 lawsuits so far prompted by the system failure with such aggression and arrogance that the plaintiffs and their attorneys began to wonder what sort of battle they were getting into. The Los Angeles City Authorities were not faced down so easily, of course, and Tom had already ordered a substantial provision to be made in the corporate financial projections for the payment of an interim award, pending a court hearing. Tye was insistent that nothing would be finally settled for at least eight years, by which time even a gigantic liability pay-out would still be only a pinprick in the hide of the vastly enlarged corporate entity he was planning. As he told his inner cabinet so often: 'There *are no rules*! Today, a global corporation can become anything it wants to be – *if* it has the ambition.'

As his team of in-house lawyers instructed the twenty-three different law firms in their stonewalling, denial, disbelieving and offensive postures towards all plaintiffs, Furtrado had found himself wondering whether he might have been earning just as much if he had stayed in private practice with the Tye Corporation as a client. At least he would have got to see his family occasionally. But then, he realized, he wouldn't be part of a history-making deal like the one that would be closed over the next few days. The shape, productivity and economic balance of power in the world would be changed for ever because of what Tom and he were now doing. The power to change the world no longer lay with politicians. It belonged to business leaders like Thomas Tye.

'Let's go over the designated area again,' sighed Tom, nodding to Connie. She touched two buttons in her armrest and the lights dimmed, the window shades closed and a wall screen on the front bulkhead flickered to life.

'Come and sit here, Marsello.' Tom indicated the empty seat next to his. Both seats swung round on electric motors to face the screen. Furtrado eased around his boss, stepping over his small, dainty feet, and flopped into the left seat, putting his pile of papers on the floor in front of him. A map appeared on the wall screen with a new boundary outlined in red.

'This is the region we're leasing and this is the adjacent region we'll be treating for their benefit, as per the terms of our deal,' Furtrado said, pointing. 'It will take us about three years to complete phase one, the infrastructure and the resorts in the east, a further six for the forestry and agricultural developments of phase two and the entire development of the region will take upwards of thirty years. That depends on our immigration policy, the demand by would-be lessees for agricultural land and development properties, inward investment numbers, long-term ecological results and, of course, our own policy on zoning permission for outside developers.'

Tye nodded. He'd seen this map a thousand times and he still had only one territorial worry, the same one that had cropped up when these new borders were first drawn. He put that concern aside for the moment. It was for the Russians to worry about, and he would bring it up in Moscow.

'You've got the presents ready?'

Furtrado smiled, reached down and pulled a small, elegantly wrapped package from among the papers on the floor. 'Each of the leases constitutes a separate gift. I've had ornamental certificates of ownership made up and framed. We'll save them right until just before the deal closes, when we might need just a little extra leverage.'

Tye nodded. Buying the Baltic islands as inducements had been Furtrado's idea, after his visit to Cape Verde.

'They'll probably help us on the price,' predicted Tom. 'But I want you to try again to extend the lease. The period is an abstract concept, so why is it so difficult for them to agree?'

Furtrado shrugged. 'I just can't see us getting anywhere on

that one. My people have been over it with their team a dozen times. The secretariat would not sanction anything beyond one hundred and fifty-five years. The Hong Kong deal the British did with China is providing the precedent. Other than a freehold sale – which they can't countenance on political grounds – that's the longest period the Constitutional Court would approve.'

Tye sighed and drummed the fingers of his right hand on the armrest.

'It's academic for us as well, isn't it?' suggested Furtrado, deliberately provocative. 'A hundred and fifty-five years will see us all out, and several more generations too. Who knows what will be happening in the middle of the twenty-second century?'

Tye put his head on one side and considered. He swung his chair to the left so he could look straight into his senior counsellor's face.

'How old are you, Marsello?' he asked in the semi-darkness.

The lawyer shrugged. 'Forty-six, forty-seven next month. Why?'

'I'm three years older than you,' replied Tye. 'See any difference?'

Furtrado watched as the younger-looking man gazed back at him. The question was rhetorical and both men knew it. Tye could almost be mistaken for his son.

Tye paused, then leaned forward, his face close to Furtrado's. 'Do you want to join the programme?' he asked quietly.

The blood leaped and burned in Furtrado's veins. He was close to the *arcanum*. Nobody knew for sure, but everybody in the senior executive guessed there had to be some truth in the exposé threatened by that British woman biographer. Furtrado had personally overseen the issuance of injunctions to prevent her from publishing, but now it seemed as if he might find out the truth first-hand. The lawyer swallowed but, despite his intense excitement, he was still a lawyer – nothing could be left to chance. It had to be spelled out.

'You mean the gene therapy, for staying young?' he asked for the avoidance of all possible doubt, exhibiting in his deliberate reductionism the incisiveness and determination that had made his career.

Tye considered. He would be increasing the charmed circle by one. That would mean twenty-nine people now – including President Orlov, if Furtrado succeeded in Moscow. Tye would be parting with one of his ultimate motivational incentives, but it was worth it.

'Yes, I mean the gene therapy that arrests human biological ageing – the Erasmus trials,' confirmed Tye quietly. Behind them, they could hear Connie accepting a call.

'You understand the sensitivity of this?'

Tye needn't have said it. Furtrado already knew more of Tom's secrets than any other Tye executive. He was bound by attorney-client privilege, but even more so by the vast sums of money that were just starting to come his way.

He nodded, wondering whether he should also ask the same favour on behalf of his wife. He decided not to. 'Like everything,' he said.

'No, not like everything,' contradicted Tye. 'It will alter your perspective completely. I'm fifty now: by normal standards sixty-five per cent of my life would be over and that sort of realization *does* colour your thinking. My doctors and geneticists tell me I've actually used only sixteen per cent of my projected life, and the eventual figure may be even lower. You have no idea what that does to your mind. Everything seems different. To you, a one-hundred-and-fifty-year lease on this deal seems like an unimaginably long time, doesn't it?'

He raised his eyebrows. Then he leaned even closer to the lawyer. 'While *I'm* afraid we'll be handing the land back to them long before I'm ready to retire.'

Furtrado stared into Tom's clear eyes, taking in his smooth skin, the glossy hair, the glowing aura of energy and health.

'Get them to agree to a lease of four hundred years and you can join the programme as soon as we get home,' offered Tye in a whisper. 'Then you might still be around to ensure they honour their part of the bargain – all the way to the end.'

'Tom?' Connie was standing nearby in the aisle. She bent

low and whispered to her boss, although Furtrado could still make out the words.

'It's a call from Nurse Pettigrew. There's a problem at the house.'

Calypso woke with a start and found herself alone. She had slept uninterruptedly for the first time in a week. She knew images of Tommy in a mask and gloves had been flying around in her sleeping brain, but so had recollections of Jack Hendriksen and his tenderness. And now she had a completely new agenda.

She had sensed Jack's arousal as he had comforted her, so she had soon pulled away and gone to wash her face before returning with a bottle of wine and two glasses.

'It'll only get left behind,' she had explained as she handed him the corkscrew. 'How did you know Tommy was here?'

Jack began to explain that the island's security system had automatically alerted him and all his staff. 'He's got ID and GPS locator chips in his LifeWatch,' he said. 'The network security system sent out an alert the moment Tommy crossed the boundary line of their house.'

He looked up and noticed the expression on Calypso's face as he eased out the cork. 'It's not just him,' he added. 'Those locators are all the rage this year. Everybody wants them for their kids. They're a great safety device.'

Calypso had felt tears welling up again. What sort of future could the boy have, locked up in that house and perpetually tagged and monitored? She had warned how such isolation might affect Tommy's adult life. Jack had listened carefully for a while and then he moved to sit down beside her. He put his arm around her and kissed the top of her head. Neither knew what might happen next. Their first lovemaking, on Calypso's rock, had been a spontaneous, urgent and physical episode. But there had been no promises, no suggestions of anything further and they hadn't spoken privately since Jack had called in to say goodbye as he left for his New York vacation.

Calypso kissed him gently in return. It felt good to have Jack here with her. As he kissed her again, it was suddenly passionate. She felt herself responding, but her emotions were jumbled. She loved the taste and the feel of him, had thought about that a lot, but she was still disturbed by the events of the evening. She pulled away and put a restraining hand on his chest.

'You're welcome to stay, Jack,' she smiled, 'but I don't think I feel like...'

He had nodded, knowing how upset she was.

But later, lying in her bed, in his arms, her sadness had lifted and when he pulled his body away to avoid any unwelcome physical intrusion, she had laughed quietly and slipped her hands down his body.

'No, you don't,' she whispered. 'This might be just what the doctor ordered.'

It was tender and deeply loving and she had cried gently again.

She had then lain in his embrace, enjoying their closeness, aware that her lover was wide awake and staring at the ceiling.

Eventually she raised herself on her elbow. 'Jack?'

He traced the outline of her breast with the back of his fingers. 'Don't you want to sleep?' he asked.

She shook her head. Then he had got up, fetched the rest of the wine, and told her the long story of Thomas Tye, his obsession with the process of ageing, and young Tommy's unusual background. Calypso had harboured suspicions ever since first seeing both the boy and his father together, but this confirmation had shocked her.

She now wondered what time Jack had left her, as she hadn't heard the four-wheel's engine. She pushed herself out of bed and checked the time. Not yet seven. She would shower and then call Connie to arrange a meeting. Maybe there was still time to persuade Tom to reverse his decision about her departure. It was the least she could do for that lonely, uniquely special child.

The stream of hot water was loud in the shower cubicle and at first she didn't hear her VideoMate trilling. As soon as she closed off the tap she heard its tones. She wrapped a towel around herself and skipped into the living room, assuming it was Jack. She had a huge smile on her face.

But it was Connie Law, aboard an aircraft.

'Doctor, can you go up to the house at once? Tommy's been injured.'

As Calypso was pulling on the white shirt she had laid out for her journey, she heard again the sound of a petrol engine in her drive.

It wasn't until she was seated beside Stella and on the way to the main house that she wondered why Connie had contacted her and not one of the many other doctors or specialists on the island. Calypso slipped on her viewpers, opened communications with the house itself and had a visual patched through to her.

Theresa Keane raised her eyes from her book and waved back at the diminutive figure that had appeared outside on her terrace. His visit was expected, and one of the bonuses of life on Hope Island was that, as in her Irish childhood in rural Connemara, the professor could leave the doors and windows open without fear of unwanted intrusion. She stepped out into the early-morning sunshine and took his outstretched hand.

'Professor Keane, thank you for seeing me,' said Raymond Liu, with a formal dip of his head. The American-Asian still effected this oriental courtesy even though his parents had emigrated from Hong Kong to San Francisco years before he was born. This morning he felt more than a little daunted at meeting this world-famous academic and recipient of the Nobel Prize.

'It's good to meet you, Doctor Liu. Come in.'

The highly regarded group technical director of Tye Networks had asked to see her in person, so she had suggested this early-morning meeting before either of them started their daily schedule. She already knew his division was in crisis because of the Los Angeles traffic-management debacle; his personal assistant had made clear the urgency of his request. Even though the hastily arranged launch of two replacement satellites had restored the vehicle-management service to the city, she guessed that he was still under immense pressure to ensure no further failures. Suddenly, every computerized traffic- and mobile-asset management system in the world had become suspect.

'Tea or coffee?' she asked as she led him into her sunny living room. Pots of both were ready, with pastries and croissants laid out on a low table.

'Good morning,' said a ball of fur sitting on the arm of the sofa.

Theresa laughed. 'I'm sorry,' she apologized as she bent to stroke her CatPanion. 'Go to sleep, Sandra.' The Furry obediently switched to nap mode.

Liu chose coffee and perched himself gingerly on the edge of her sofa. 'I watched your Summer Lecture,' he began.

Theresa smiled. 'A little theatrical, I'm afraid. But we need party tricks to capture young minds.'

Liu merely nodded.

'So what can I do for you?' she asked, direct as always.

He leaned forward and carefully returned his cup and saucer to the coffee table.

'I was wondering if you'd be kind enough to tell me a little more about the activities of your agents in the networks?'

The professor smiled again. 'Ah yes, the Anagenesis Experiment. And you're wondering whether they're in any way connected with the system failures.'

'I have no idea,' admitted Liu. 'I can't find any common cause for the faults occurring in our systems or networks and, well, given your reputation, I've ... Frankly, I need help, Professor. I have never seen anything like this in all my years as an engineer.'

Theresa could see the desperation in his eyes. She could also guess that he hadn't been sleeping much recently.

'What happened to the LA traffic-management system, Raymond?' she asked.

He hesitated. At least in her he had an informed listener – possibly there was no one better qualified. But he realized she was unlikely to be fully versed in the arcane design structures of orbiting traffic-management systems.

'We lost one bird,' he began, 'but the other was recovered. All its data processing had frozen.'

'But I presume the orbiting management system would have held a back-up of the asset data?'

'Precisely '

'And what did they show?' she prompted.

'They showed that there had been over six hundred memory leaks on board LAT-6 in the twelve hours immediately before the system crashed.'

'Memory leaks – you mean specific faults that the system registered and corrected itself?' He nodded. 'They wouldn't be coding faults?' she prompted.

Liu shook his head. Ever since commercial software code had been generated by computers instead of humans, programming bugs had become almost non-existent and, in the case of orbiting systems, every combination of every line of code was checked and cross-checked by *ad hoc* computer farms made up of vast global networks of computers contracted to spend their idle time on the task. During the period that Liu and his team had been developing the software for the SATMAN systems, over two million computers had each been used for up to seven hours a day, attacking the software and presenting it with every possible combination of instructions and error situations that the computers could randomly generate.

The system analysis and diagnostic modules had predicted the mathematical odds of six hundred memory leaks occurring within a single eight-hour period of normal orbital processing at 14.7 million to one. Liu hadn't even bothered to compute the odds against another satellite suffering similar problems, or of the first failed satellite leaving its station without receiving instructions to do so. He'd been through that type of futile calculation over the satellite failures that had occurred in the Australasian quadrant.

'No. When we refer to memory leaks we mean faults appearing in the registers without any obvious internal cause.'

'Just a binary flip?' she prompted.

'That's it,' agreed Liu. 'Those rare situations when a zero becomes a one and nobody knows why.'

It was Theresa's turn to ponder. She was making connections.

'We normally put those down to magnetic radiation, don't

we?' she mused, as much to herself as to Liu. 'We say that a photon passed through – or a quark, a neuron, neutretto or neutrino. Loosely, a cosmic event concerning an energy particle which we don't yet understand.'

'But we shield all our systems,' objected Liu. 'And the magnetosphere – the magnetic force field around the earth – shields us from all the really nasty radiation of outer space.'

The professor nodded and sat back and played with the Victorian silver stamp box that hung on a silver chain around her neck. 'You've ruled out a virus or a hacker?'

Liu nodded. 'There's definitely no virus. It wouldn't be so random in what it affects and, anyway, we've combed almost every line of code we have. There's nothing there.'

'A hacker?'

Liu started to laugh but it turned into a groan of exaspera-tion. 'I just can't see how, Professor – Theresa. You should see the security systems we've built in. But even if somebody *could* break our encryption, surely we'd have received some sort of extortion demand by now. It wouldn't be done just for fun.'

He shook his head again, steeling himself to be blunt. 'I saw what you're doing with self-duplicating software agents in the networks and, well, frankly, I was wondering if your experiment could have gotten out of control.'

Theresa nodded. She understood his concern, but she was thinking along wholly different lines. 'I think that's impossible, Doctor. I wouldn't allow my students to release anything that has the potential to do harm. The only objective our agents are given is to compete in order to reproduce.'

'But they are evolving?' prompted Liu.

'Yes, but only in their courtship techniques. They're learning merely how to reproduce more efficiently, not to interact with the environment around them.'

Liu weighed his next statement carefully. 'Professor ... seven hundred and eighteen people died in Los Angeles because our system failed. The Tye Corporation faces lawsuits that currently total over eight hundred billion dollars. Large-scale projects we were constructing in fourteen cities have been put on hold until we can show the consulting engineers what caused the problem, and other cities still using our traffic-management systems are panic-stricken in case they suffer a similar failure.'

Theresa nodded, trying not to convey any hint of her alarm. She'd had no real idea of the seriousness of the situation. She rarely watched or listened to real-time news, and she read no newspapers. Years before she had made a conscious decision to forgo the experience of the present, of the here and now, of the *actualité*. 'Life's not a rehearsal' her only serious long-term partner had once said to her. But Theresa had dismissed her remark, understanding better than most that the virtual – the essence of Theresa Keane – was not so confined, and that semi-isolation and withdrawal from the world was a wholly suitable environment for her work. Most of her thinking involved a time far in the future and, in that virtuality, there was both rehearsal and performance. Theresa's philosophy was, of course, that of a Yogācāra Buddhist, although she would have accepted neither the label nor the limitations that implied.

'Have you considered that some of your agents might have adopted altruistic behaviour?' asked Liu.

Ah, there it is, thought Theresa; *the real reason for his concern, and his visit.*

'Raymond, I have to let you into a little secret,' she said. 'Those agents aren't as clever as they appear. It's all a trick. I keep trying to teach my students that our artificial companions are still quite dumb and that it is *we* who anthropomorphize them. Their conversational ability is pure psittacism.' She saw him frown and explained. 'Purely a parroting of language.'

'All these companions,' she said, pointing to the sleeping Sandra, 'only seem clever because they mimic us. They're programmed to pick up our tone, our mood, as well as to identify – if not understand – our language. It's merely a party trick and it is we who endow them with the qualities that make them seem so loveable. It's one of the most powerful human instincts, and one of the first things I do with all my students is try to get them to understand that.'

Liu nodded. In his student days his computer-science professors had also staged demonstrations to show how stupid computers are and how gullible humans can be.

'So there's no chance that one of these agents, or a group of them, could have acted out of character?' he persisted. 'Or that any of them could have reproduced without you knowing about it?'

Theresa leaned forward and returned her own cup to the coffee table.

'It's impossible,' she stated firmly. 'Their behaviour is governed strictly by the rules we created. You can strike that idea.'

'Well, I suppose that's something,' he sighed. 'We have to eliminate every possibility.'

He paused and then decided to tell her the other reason he had requested this meeting.

'There is something else,' he added. 'As I was unable to find any fault in the component parts of our networks, or the networks we are connected to, I went back to square one and ran a basic RQI procedure. I found–'

He hesitated. Theresa had held up a hand. 'I don't know what RQI means.'

'I'm sorry Theresa. RQIs are an exercise we set our first-year network engineers. It's a resistance, quantification and identification test. Students calculate the theoretical resistance found in an open, unused network. Then they measure the actual resistance of the network when it is in use and quantify data and the pathways to calculate how much resistance has been added by the activity in a network. They then reconcile the totals in order to check that there are no faults in any of the components or pathways. They are basic elimination procedures.'

Theresa nodded her understanding.

'Anyway,' continued Liu, 'I carried out an RQI on the networks and I found...'

Theresa placed her hand to her throat in surprise. 'On what networks?' she asked, amazed that such a test could be undertaken.

Liu smiled. 'On all the networks we operate and connect with.'

'How much is that, exactly?' she asked.

'There are about nine billion miles of networks – if you treat satellite communication paths and broadband wireless the same as fibre-optic cable. Capacity for about four thousand exabytes – four billion, billion bytes.'

'Some maths,' breathed Theresa.

Liu acknowledged the compliment with an inclination of his head. 'Of course, I automated the procedure as much as I could. Anyway, I found something very strange. There's a flickering, transitory resistance in the networks that can't be accounted for by data in transit, stored instruction sets, switching resistance or any of the other processes.'

Theresa frowned.

'In fact there is over twenty per cent of network space that seems to be occupied by something I couldn't identify – a sort of dark matter.'

'Dark matter...?'

'I don't know what else to call it,' admitted Liu. 'Dark data, perhaps. The resistance tests show something's there, but we can't see it. We can't actually tag it in any way. And ... it seems to move.'

Theresa raised her eyebrows. Connections were being completed.

'We'll test one network one day and it will show a twenty, twenty-two per cent unexplained activity level – the next day there's none. And there's no record that those data, or that matter, or whatever it is, has passed through the routers to other networks.'

Theresa sat back in her armchair and thought hard, her right hand playing with her stamp box again as her mind worked.

'Let me have a think about this,' she asked finally. 'I'll get back to you.'

Liu nodded and stood. Theresa rose and took his hand.

'Thank you for making the time to see me,' said Liu, with another slight bow. He turned and walked out the way he had come, across the sunlit terrace.

Theresa sat down again, slowly. Her mind was racing. Who to call first? She would start with Robert, see where he was with the Descartes Experiment. Absently, she picked Sandra up and sat her on her lap.

'He seemed worried,' observed the CatPanion. 'Keep or discard?'

'Oh, keep, I think,' said the professor. Sandra purred contentedly as Theresa stroked her.

There was blood everywhere. The anterior carpal artery in Tommy's left wrist had been severed and the gouts of blood had hosed the walls as if there had been an explosion in a cochineal factory.

Calypso had already seen the room through her viewpers but only her experience of the horrors of a late-night Chicago ER allowed her to overcome her panic immediately and start to assess the situation.

'I had to restrain him, Doctor, in order to get a tourniquet and the compress on,' Nurse Emily Pettigrew explained breathlessly as she cleared away the debris of her labours. 'Then I gave him ten CCs of thiopentone. I was frightened that he would open the wound again.'

The boy was now unconscious on his bed. Nurse Pettigrew had displayed the value of her training as a British State Registered Nurse, applying a tight and efficient tourniquet on the pressure point of his elbow and binding a compress tightly to the main wound. Further up his forearm were the slashes he had made before the kitchen knife had found its target. How had he known? Where had he seen or read about such self-harm?

He was very pale. Calypso checked his BP and pulse: 80/60/135. He needed blood, and she said as much to the nurse.

'I have plenty matched and ready in the fridge,' said Emily Pettigrew as she started to leave the room. She saw the doctor's surprised reaction. 'On Tom's orders,' she explained. 'It's always available. He allows me to draw fresh supplies from Tommy every three months.'

Calypso considered the situation as the nurse went to fetch the plasma.

It was clear that Emily Pettigrew had understood the sensitivity of the incident. Calypso had to admit the nurse had shown good sense in contacting Tom on board his plane – wherever that was – and specifically requesting permission for Calypso to attend, rather than rushing the boy to the clinic or asking one of the duty medics to visit the house. However loyal a Tye Corporation staff member might be, this gossip could have proved just too juicy to contain.

'He just kept crying out for you,' explained the nurse, 'over and over again. I heard that on the monitors, but I didn't realize he was hurting himself. Then I got the alarm.'

Calypso shook her head: she knew the syndrome. With every repetition of her name he would have been making another slice in his forearm. She had treated child patients who had undergone similar episodes of self-harm and had seen self-mutilation and pseudocide cases before. But she had never encountered the syndrome in a pre-teenager and had never known a victim to inflict self-harm during the waking hours of the morning. The events almost always occurred late at night or in the small hours and it was usually, but not exclusively, a female behaviour observed in patients with a history of depression.

Her VideoMate trilled. She found herself looking at Connie, then Tom, as she provided an update. She was unable to keep the stoniness out of her voice.

Tye nodded grimly as he digested the news. 'Can you deal with it, Doctor? I don't want to bring any others in.'

Calypso glanced at the boy and considered. She'd dealt with far worse as an intern, but they had been welfare patients.

She nodded. 'He'll be out for another hour or so, I should think. I'm just going to give him some blood to get his BP back up. We should be able to stabilize him for surgery. We just don't know if there is any metacarpal damage.'

There was a short silence.

'Doctor Browne. I realize how serious this is and I am grateful for your help.'

Calypso nodded again.

'Would you do me – well, Tommy – a favour, please? Would you please accept another apology from his father and stay there with him. At least until I get back at the weekend.'

Calypso hesitated. She didn't have a choice – her heart felt like breaking. For a moment she thought Tom would say something else, perhaps talk about a financial inducement. But he did not make that mistake. Instead he waited for her reply.

'I'll wait until you get back,' she agreed. She would now do anything for Tommy.

'Thank you, Doctor,' sighed Tom. 'We'll keep this between ourselves.'

'Of course.' It could never be any other way.

'The Furry will know what happened,' said Tye. 'Don't let anybody remove Jed.'

Calypso returned to her patient. She would remove the compress and ligate the artery for safety before examining the surrounding tissue and bone. She would also ask Nurse Pettigrew to prepare an ice pack to keep his antibrachial as cold as possible. Then she would have him moved discreetly to the clinic where she could run X-rays and scans before moving him into an OR for stitching up. She debated whether she would have to call on one of the anaesthetists. Perhaps the thiopentone would last long enough. She would take half a beta blocker before she began the surgery. Although it would be a minor procedure, this was Tommy and she knew emotion might cause her fingers to tremble.

SIXTEEN

[Insert page 37 – Chapter One]

Thomas Richmond Tye was committed to the Sandler Sanitarium, Norwood, New Hampshire, USA on 6 August 1971. He was just over five years old. The committal order was signed by his father, Thomas Tye II, and the family's long-time physician Dr Marcus Cordell. The cause for the committal was given as *hysterical dissociation* – a broad categorization that can cover a range of disorders including amnesia and somnambulism. A copy of the committal certificate was lodged with the court authorities in Norwood County, as was required by law. The date of the committal precedes the state's Juvenile Justice and Detention Act that requires the active participation and approval of a local social services agency and the Department of Juveniles.

That is the end of all information available about Tye's internment. We don't know his condition on arrival or the treatment he received. We don't know when he was released, nor do we know into whose care, although we do know that he was once again living back at the Tye mansion by the time he was thirteen when his paternal grandmother legally assumed responsibility for his upbringing. By this time family probate had been settled and Thomas Tye became heir to a thirty-two-million-dollar fortune that was held in trust by his grandmother until he was twenty-one. It appears Tye attended no school or college and there is no record that he passed any external examination or gained any form of academic qualification.

The reason we know nothing more of Tye's internment is that the Sandler Sanitarium was purchased by the Tye family trust in 1987 and rebuilt as a cosmetic-surgery clinic. It was sold again in the same year. Since that time the directors of the clinic have consistently maintained that no patient records exist from the period prior to 1987. Reporters first started asking questions about Tye's stay in the clinic over fifteen years ago when the Tye Corporation first became a quoted multi-billion-dollar company and its president became a nationally known figure in the United States. The clinic was unable to provide any help.

This time, at least, Haley knew the source of her information. She wondered why Jack had become sufficiently interested in Tye's childhood problems to have done this research but, she had to admit, it did make good copy. She settled down to integrate the new paragraphs within her opening chapter and wondered if she should use some of the Sloan Press's research budget to visit the sanitarium for herself. As she had learned during the research for her very first book, the best-selling film-star biography, second-hand sources are not to be relied upon and, despite the potency and verisimilitude of multi-angle 3D videoconferencing and the latest olfactory and gustation simulations, there still remained something special about visiting an individual or a place in person. She would only accept that the clinic had no records when she had established that fact beyond doubt.

Her first job, however, was to bring some sense of order to the vast streams of news and information reaching her in-box regarding Thomas Tye, the Tye Corporation and its many subsidiaries. Eighteen months before, when she had been planning her research pattern for this biography, she had programmed a group of software agents to hunt for all Tye Corporation and Tye-related information on her behalf. Now it seemed as though the amount of available information about her target had shot up to almost unmanageable proportions. Each morning she started reading the material gathered and, even after the system automatically discarded all encrypted files, she found herself still wading through the heap of information at the end of the day. It was overwhelming.

She therefore gathered her software agents and attached a de-duplication engine to each. At least she would then be spared reading some of the many similar stories being produced around the world. Then she began to draft an advertisement she would post in the many network discussion groups and communities that revolved around Thomas Tye and the Tye Corporation. This was where her new research budget would come in useful. She would offer a financial reward for any previously unpublished information about the tycoon or his company.

Ishkov Konstantine, Minister of the Interior for the Russian Federation, rose to his feet, his naturally florid, leonine face now suffused with blood. He leaned forward, his knuckles resting on the table top, and glowered across at Tye, Furtrado, Connie, the seven Tye Corporation attorneys and the numerous corporate analysts who were sitting opposite.

'You arrive to rip the heart out of our Tartar homeland – to take the cradle of Russian civilization away from our people and yet you will forbid them to live there?' he bellowed. '*Nyet! Nyet!* This will not go forward.'

Tye and his party did not need to concentrate on the translation feeds from their VideoMates to understand the minister's position. But position it surely was – or rather leguleian posture, if Furtrado's political analysts were to be believed. Konstantine was playing for the ever-present cameras, for the historical record and for the Russian people – creating an aura of personal importance for when the next elections came. If he failed to win re-election to central government, as the analysts predicted, he was likely to stand as a mayoral candidate in his home city of Novosibirsk, capital of the Krasnoyarsk Republic, and that was close enough to the southern border of Tye's new province for him to claim an interest. It would therefore be important to win him over, especially as the Tye Corporation's new agricultural enterprises were likely to need the processing facilities of Konstantine's city. Tye suspected that the gift of one of the Baltic islands with its newly acquired microclimate would achieve that objective – when the time came.

They were seated in the great gilded Tsar's Hall of the Terem Palace in the north-east corner of the Kremlin complex. Little government was conducted in the ancient walled citadel these days – most administration being centred around the State Union building across the Moskva River. But Thomas Tye and his colleagues from the mighty Tye Corporation were getting the sort of reception usually reserved for a visiting head of a superpower and his entourage – which, everyone conceded, was appropriate in the circumstances.

There had been a tour of honour through the streets of Moscow. The citizens knew Tye's company was becoming Russia's largest foreign investor – some muttered 'saviour' although that was unfair to President Orlov's incredible achieve-ments in economic reconstruction – and they had responded accordingly. The people were being informed that the huge new development was a partnership between the Russian Federal Government and the Tye Corporation, although the use of the word 'partnership' in this context added new dimensions to its generally accepted definition.

The *Moscow Times* Index had jumped thirty-two points in anticipation of the deal. Despite continuous television coverage and the press attention paid to Thomas Tye's visit, so far there had been no reports of tribute self-immolations amongst fringe groups within the population.

Then there had been an interminable state dinner of disgust-ing individually baked coulibiacs that opened to reveal a pulver-ized slumgullion of fish shreds, cabbage and gravy. This had been followed by operose speeches that seemed to go on for ever. Tye had touched nothing of the food or the vodka and could not have cared less what his rapacious hosts thought of his restraint. He just wanted to get on with things and he didn't need to drown in a vedro of high-octane alcohol to cement this deal. But such behaviour was exacerbated by the harsh Russian climate, he reminded himself, with a private smile.

They had been talking for two days and all around them were huge maps propped on ancient easels on which new boundary lines and corridors had been drawn, appropriately in red ink.

At the head of the great room, to the right of a vast black-marble and gilt fireplace, was a recently installed Holo-Theater. It had been a gift from Tye Business Communications to mark Thomas Tye's first state visit to Russia and it also provided the APU with the opportunity to scrub these ancient rooms electronically and install the necessary white-noise generators and other anti-surveillance devices.

Tye had been counselled that such blustering over the cession of this territory was likely to go on for some time and he was struggling to be patient with the brabble. He slumped in his chair, resting his head in his hand as he listened, his right ankle supported on his left knee, and his loafer-shod foot twitching furiously. Unusually, he was thinking about his son.

It was a big deal for the Russian people, that was clear. Over one and a half million square miles – almost eighty million *dessiatine* – of the republics of the Central and Eastern Siberian Plain was involved. Leasing such a vast tract of land to the Tye Corporation took monumental political nerve and the absolute willingness of the Russian federal army to back such an arrangement. For that reason General Yevgeny Padorin, Supreme Chief of the Federation's armed forces, had been included in the party that visited Hope Island and he was now a prominent member of the Russian delegation sitting on the other side of the table. Although he didn't yet know it, he too would become the proud owner of a new holiday property in a uniquely sunny area of the Baltic, along with the presidents of the two vast, poverty-stricken and corrupt republics affected.

But the benefits for the immense mother country were

incalculable. Of the one hundred and sixty million people that made up Russia's population, only three million moujiks – most of the Tchuktchi, Koryak, Lamutic and Yukaghir ethnic groups – lived in the gelid dry tundra of the Siberian heartland and on its vast eastern slopes. As a jointly mounted, year-long survey had shown, the immense government-owned plain and mountain range was good for little but oil, gas, diamond and mineral extraction and the Tye Corporation had generously agreed that these resources would remain in the hands of the local Sakha Republic leaders or Russian government-owned or government-appointed companies – two, at least, to be headed by Anton Vlasik and his cronies – throughout the duration of the champart lease.

Even new finds would remain either the property of the individual republics that were ceding territory or of the Federal head landlords for disposal as they chose. The incumbent operators would pay no tax or levies to the new regional authority. The Tye Corporation had no interest in the energy and mineral resources of the industrial age and the lessors did not fully appreciate what was likely to happen to the price of fossil energy once the world understood the alternative that the Tye Corporation would offer as the Phoebus programme rolled onwards.

But, most important of all to the Russian federal government, the lessee company was agreeing to extend its heavenly largesse to specific parts of the vast swampland of the West Siberian Plain abutting the Urals that would remain Russian sovereign territory, owned directly by the federal government. Two million square miles of harsh and uninviting terrain would suddenly have sizeable areas that, over the next few years, would develop temperate and invitingly habitable graminiferous microclimates.

The Federal Council had already passed the outline legislation in closed session and the President's signature and those of two other appointed ministers would complete the agreement recognizing the sovereignty of the new state. The Duma was firmly controlled by Orlov's followers and would provide an immediate rubber stamp: the *ukase* would be issued on schedule.

'First, we are not taking Central and Eastern Siberia away from your people, we are simply leasing it,' explained a theatrically weary Furtrado once more as the minister sank back into his chair. It was so painful, so old fashioned, *so full of friction*, to have to samba with the uncivilized, the *nekulturny*.

'What we are saying is that we will not be able to allow *uncontrolled* immigration to the new state of Sybaria. Those already resident will be entitled to remain in their homes and continue to live their lives in the enhanced environment we shall be providing there. They will have dual Russian and Sybarian nationality and they will be able to move freely between the two territories. We will respect all cultural traditions, provide absolute religious freedom and support the freedom of individuals and human rights. What we cannot have – and, I would have thought, what you would not want – is an open-border policy that allows *your* people to emigrate to our territory. Besides, you will have an enhanced Western Siberia, so there's more than enough land for everyone.'

What Furtrado had not mentioned, and what he knew his Russian counterparts would never raise (unless the negotiations started to spiral towards failure), were the difficulties most of the autochthonic groups in the region would have in adapting. In particular, the Tungus, Kamtschadales and Lamouts, all subarctic tribes scraping a living along the coastline of the Sea of Okotsk, were unlikely to apply for trainee positions in the fast-food restaurants and hotels that had already signed provisional leases to build outlets and facilities in the area. The Sybarian business plan budgeted for these people to draw a form of corporate welfare and, the planners privately agreed, it would be necessary to work hard to ensure they did not become the Sybarian equivalent of the Native Americans or the Australian Aborigines.

Another issue that would not be raised was the withdrawal of democratic rights from the region. The new province of Sybaria would never be democratic and it would always have only one government. The new plutarchy would, over time, develop a standard of living that would be possible nowhere else on the Asian continent and, if the predictions of economists and social scientists were right, in few other places on earth.

*

DID YOU KNOW THOMAS TYE?
REWARD OFFERED

Author seeks any new (previously unpublished) information about Thomas Tye's childhood, family background or education. An attractive financial reward is available to anyone who provides new information about Mr Tye's early years that can be successfully checked and verified.

Hayley would post it in all the Thomas Tye communities and in the Tye newsgroups. She would also create links from her new publisher's network resource and from the companion sites that had been created for her earlier books. But should she mention how much the reward might be? The Sloan Press had been generous. Their initial advance payment on top of Nautilus's money had, for the moment, eased her financial worries. No, how much she would pay would depend on what, if anything, was offered. She assigned the ad to her posting agents, provided the locations, sent them on their way and went to make a cup of coffee.

Thomas Tye stifled a yawn. He wondered how long these blustering negotiations would continue. He realized that it was the largest deal that most of these politicians would ever be involved in – well, it was also *his* largest deal so far – and he understood that they would all want their turn to show off their political skills. Something to tell the grandchildren. Something for the history books. Something an enthusiastic, unusually literate but inexperienced writer in the Tye Corporation's public relations agency had already dubbed a 'a truly historic and Brobdingnagian agreement' in a headline proposed for one of many press statements.

In another room, across a marbled corridor, Furtrado's

conveyancing lawyers were still arguing with their Russian counterparts for an extension of the lease. That debate would eventually have to come back here to the main table. In yet another room, Richard Rakusen, his co-financiers and a covey of architects were exhibiting architectural models of the airports, roads, hotels, housing estates, golf clubs and sports facilities they would be constructing to create new spa resorts around the Sea of Okhotsk and on the Kuril Islands as the ice receded and a new environmental ecology was born.

Technically, Rakusen and the other developers who would follow him into the new territory of Sybaria were not required to show their plans to the Russian government or to any authority except the Tye Administrative Council for the new region. But it had been agreed that for the sake of goodwill, and to help Russian understanding of the peaceable plans that the Tye Corporation and its development partners had for the ceded territory, the plans and three-dimensional models for the first major real-estate development of the new province should be shown and discussed. The disclosure also provided Anton Vlasik and his associates with a pre-emptive opportunity to select the investment and development projects in which they wished to participate.

Immediately after the Act of Cession was signed and Sybaria was receiving its first season of ecological and climatic re-engineering, Rakusen-Webber would launch a new Sybaria Fund to offer the world's investors an opportunity to share in the huge development opportunities. The first leisure resorts would be centred on the best of the many coastal hot-springs locations and the littoral would be marketed as both summer and winter resorts to the nearby Japanese as well as to the North American market.

Also in Phase I would be opportunities to invest in the vast solar farms that would occupy two million hectares of the former Siberian permafrost. These vast acres would contain mile after mile of curved Anacamptonite solar-capture panels that would feed electrical power to huge underground storage silos ready for marketing to the cities of Japan, China, India and Russia via superconducting underground cables. The former 'sleeping land' of Siberia would become an electronic counterpart of the great wheat expanses of America's Midwest, only this 'basket' would hold energy, not the ingredients for bread. Later would come opportunities to invest in an area enjoying macroclimate manipulation and the vast agricultural opportunities presented by nocturnal crops and livestock – once the happy point of autarky was passed.

Although 'Sybaria' had been accepted as the official name for this new territory, suggested by one of Furtrado's classically educated English lawyers, an unidentified wag on the team had already suggested the region should be called 'Tyeland'. This idea had been officially abandoned for fear of confusion, but inside the company this name had stuck as the code name for the new province.

Tye ached to have a shower and he craved the comfort he derived from a protective mask and gloves. He sprayed his mouth with antiseptic again. This was the first time in a decade he had attended a meeting in which he could not control his environment. Only he, and the geneticists of Tye Life Sciences, understood the damage that common infections could do to the suppression of free radicals in his body. As his immune system rose to respond to infection, it overcame the inhibitors produced by the oral cell-maintenance therapy that he had taken daily for the last sixteen years: if he caught a cold, Tye would resume ageing like everybody else for as long as the infection lasted.

But it would be worth the risk and at least he didn't have to suffer the Russians' disgusting tobacco smoke. He had made that an absolute condition when this trip was being arranged. Every half an hour one of the Russian party would make an excuse and disappear from the room. That had proved a useful weakness to exploit. Several times Furtrado had insisted on labouring a point while the Tye party watched a Russian negotiator start to fidget and sweat, desperate for a cigarette break. That way some details had been agreed hastily but Tye guessed there would be at least another day of negotiations. If everything was agreed tomorrow, the deal would be done on his fiftieth birthday, but only Connie and Furtrado would offer him congratulations on his anniversary and there would be no public celebrations of his age. Tye did not discuss this subject in public even though the media was bound to home in on the story.

But this deal *would* be settled, that much was for sure. Furtrado had bank authorizations for transfers of a total of one trillion US dollars in his briefcase – enough to eliminate Russia's global debt in a single payment, if that was how the government chose to spend their giant windfall. Tye judged that President Orlov would do just that and his nation's economic rating would suddenly be propelled back into that of the world's top half-dozen countries, even before the economic benefits of the forthcoming climatic re-engineering had been calculated.

Another man, pale with a patchy red moustache and ill-fitting rust-coloured jacket, rose at the far end of the table: the E&E minister – environment and ecology. The Greens had *finally* found a voice in the polluted behemoth that had been industrial Russia and, after years of prevarication, the state was at last attempting to fulfil some of its biosphere obligations to the international community.

'The Tye Corporation and the University of Hope Island have both been very helpful in modelling the short, medium and long-term impact of these climatic ... improvements,' the minister began portentously. He spoke good English so the Tye corporate team was pleased to switch their earpiece-jewellery to ambient, and join real-time again. 'We have been very encouraged by the models that show the impact of carbon dioxide reduction in the atmosphere and the improved economic prospects of the region and the surrounding territories.'

He paused and everybody waited for his objection. 'However, I have been unable to find any prognostications or projections for the future of the indigenous species. Although the region is classified mostly as taiga, tundra and ice cap, the Tye delegation must know that there is a rich, diverse and important collection of birds, mammals, rodents, reptiles, insects and fish in that area. These include Stella sea eagles, the white-tailed eagle, the Siberian bear, Siberian tiger, Siberian fox, Siberian chipmunks, buzzards, picus, polatouche, salmon, deer, moose and many thousands of insects, reptiles and other fish. Many of the species have not yet been identified and named. Are they to go the way of our elasmotherium or the Stella sea-cow? What is to happen to them, please?'

He sat down.

Tye leaned back and raised his eyes to the ceiling. All this had been covered in the detailed discussions and scientific documents that his teams had prepared and delivered months before. They had already started freezing sperm from many of the life forms of the region. Jesus! What more could they want? He would be delivering them a Moscow with winter daylight time extended by fifty per cent. The city would have temperatures similar to San Francisco, for Christ's sake! He could even switch supplies off to give them fucking white Christmases whenever the government asked – just to ensure the ancient city didn't lose touch with its original character!

He sighed and nodded to Furtrado to respond.

The counsellor shuffled through his documents for the folder on wildlife and endangered species. But before he could find the reassuring words he had selected so carefully the questioner rose to his feet again.

'I was wondering whether Mr Tye would honour us by sharing his *personal* views on this topic?' suggested the Minister of the Environment.

Tye felt a sudden sense of alarm. Could it be possible that this was not a done deal after all? Was this a trap? He and Furtrado had been sure that the Russian government would provide nothing but a token, albeit prolix, show of resistance during these negotiations. But if this new voice represented anything more than a desire to be heard, everything could still fall through. Tye had been thoroughly briefed on the Russian political system so he knew that consensus, not majority voting, was required for the Presidential Council to endorse such radical legislation.

Perhaps it was time to utilize the old magic. Outside of his public appearances, he used it so rarely now – almost never in private meetings. It had grown too large, too *kerystic*, to be used against just a handful of people in what, for one of *his* performances, would be a comparatively small room. But, Tye reasoned, as business had become a form of theatre all individual careers had become performances. He also guessed that they couldn't resist the chance to see if this supposedly legendary performer was truly as great as the rest of the world thought.

He glanced along the table at his interlocutor, then smiled, his grin lighting up the whole conference table. He pushed himself to his feet and stepped back, lithe in his movements. Despite the formality of the occasion, he wore his usual open-necked white shirt and black trousers. His hair was tied back in a short ponytail.

'The Minister is quite right, of course,' he began. 'This *is* a subject that I am pleased to address personally, since it is of the utmost importance.'

Tye clasped his hands behind his back and walked slowly towards the head of the table, where President Orlov presided – so far in silence. When he reached the president's side he stopped and turned to face his audience.

'We will be bringing light and heat to areas that have never received those natural benefits before.' He spoke slowly and carefully, aware that many of the Russians around the table would be able to understand his carefully enunciated English. He raised his arms in practised chironomy. 'But this energy, *our* energy, is totally controllable – to within a radius of one mile, as I have had the pleasure of demonstrating to President Orlov, Minister Konstantine and General Padorin recently on Hope Island. We have created a complete model of the world's climate on the most powerful parallel-processing computer ever built. It's capable of five trillion operations per second – we call it the Halcyon system. It allows us to play "what-if" with different conditions. We know precisely what each joule and nanowatt will achieve and its knock-on effects in the global ecosystem as a whole.'

He paused and looked at each of them in turn, holding their gazes, ensuring their absolute attention.

'Remember, I care about this planet!'

Tye paused again. The Tye corporate heads were already nodding – then some of the others. He had them now.

'Humans have been aware for nearly forty years that we are

slowly choking our world. Temperatures have been rising – especially in the northern latitudes – and, unless the Tye Corporation takes this crucial step, with the help and aid of the great Russian Federation, carbon dioxide concentrations will be at seven hundred and fifty parts per million by the middle of this century – three times its pre-industrial level. That means we will destroy the Amazon rain forest and all other rain forests, and global sea levels will rise by two metres. A four-degree Celsius increase in the planet's mean atmospheric temperature would increase global rainfall by twenty per cent – but all of it in the wrong places. Water vapour in the air is, in itself, a powerful greenhouse gas. So it becomes a vicious circle. After that the remaining vegetation will disappear and the sea will continue to rise.'

He paused once more to ensure they were all keeping up.

'Currently, only eleven per cent of our planet's surface is under cultivation and we are expecting our population to continue to grow – perhaps to ten billion or more in the coming decades. We cannot support such a population with the present biocapital resources this planet has to offer. We are already seeing chronic water shortages affecting thirty per cent of the world's population. Over the next thirty to forty years, the climatic re-engineering we are undertaking will add fifty per cent productive land and will add an entirely new hydrological resource. Today, most of the Siberian permafrost is at minus thirty degrees Celsius. Just lifting that to temperate levels and covering that much of the white tundra and taiga with vegetation and crops will reduce solar reflective radiation in the region by thirty-six per cent. That will reduce the warmth pumped back into the atmosphere by the same amount. *That* is the only way we can feed and clothe the people of the future *and* do so without exhausting current resources. We have no choice, ladies and gentlemen. Humankind is like a household living giddily off vanishing capital. There is no choice.'

Tye looked for, and found, nods of agreement. Suddenly he thought of his son, then of Calypso. The words he wanted flashed into his mind.

'Remember: "Our remedies oft in ourselves do lie,
Which we ascribe to heaven."'

He glanced around the table. He guessed he wouldn't have
to identify his reference in such a Shakespeare-mad culture.

'And I look to you, the Russian Federation, to be our
partners in providing these remedies for the world's people.'

He saw more, increasingly vigorous nods around the table.

'The Phoebus Project represents a new age for humanity
and this planet. After centuries of prosthetic technologies
designed to extract greater and greater resources from the
Earth to satisfy the ever-increasing material needs of humans,
we have found a way to harness the vast pool of energy that
streams past our planet only to be wasted. It is truly a new
beginning. But there will be some small costs. I seem to recall
one of your most famous countrymen declared that to make
omelettes, you have to . . .' He tailed off, lest this reference should
cause offence.

'It will produce a fundamental shift in this planet's ecology:
the biological equivalent of the Triassic Age giving way to the
Jurassic. We will take control of our environment and apply
energy carefully and thoughtfully where it will provide the most
benefit while causing the least harm. And remember, none of
this would be possible without the pioneering efforts, creativity
and imagination of late-twentieth-century Russian enterprise.'

That got them. Broad grins and nods greeted his reminder.

'We shall not, repeat NOT, be melting the northern ice cap
nor any of the major ice flows of these latitudes. We shall be
eliminating seasonal ice in the Sea of Okhotsk and on the
western edge of the Baring Sea, but we know this will have a
negligible effect on global sea levels. All of you here will know
that only ten per cent of polar ice is found in the Arctic. The
great mass is at the Antarctic and we have no plans to modify
any polar environments in the Southern Hemisphere. As we are
all aware, eighty per cent of the world's wealth is generated
north of the equator.'

Tye didn't wait for the environment minister to butt in again
about the indigenous species. In particular he didn't want the
topic of native nocturnal life forms brought up in open session.

Their sperm too would be frozen but their habitat would no longer exist. They would have to be completely relocated.

'We *shall* be warming the atmosphere,' he conceded. 'But our energy will render over forty-six coal-fired power stations obsolete inside four months. A further two hundred can be decommissioned in the following year. The cities of East and West Siberia will never again need street lighting. In all, our ecologists and environmental economists have calculated that we will be adding the equivalent of two hundred and forty-four parts per million of CO_2 to the atmosphere over Eastern Siberia and replacing the need for nearly six hundred PPM of man-made emissions. That will produce a net reduction in CO_2 concentrations of over three hundred and fifty PPM.'

He paused to allow the delegation to complete their note-taking. He had every statistic in memory. He even knew what was likely to happen to all the little creatures caught up in these changes, but he didn't want to discuss that here. The plan was to take samples of each of the important genus groups, clone sufficient for genetic diversity and then offer the clone bank to the Moscow Institute for breeding elsewhere.

'We are also ensuring that there will be no climate re-engineering anywhere in the western quadrant of this hemisphere – there will be no activity over Greenland, for example. We intend to ensure that the deep-sea current continues to sink vigorously and that the CO_2 absorption properties of the Northern Atlantic remain undisturbed.'

This was all so tedious. The corporation's ecologists had provided over 2,000 gigabytes of data on the ecological impact of the project in readiness for the inevitable questions and objections of the global community.

'I also want to refer you to our agricultural strategy. Over forty per cent of our plantations will consist of crops specially modified to absorb large amounts of CO_2 – at the type of inhalation levels currently found in tropical regions. Our new forests will also be both diurnal *and* pseudo-nocturnal and thus will absorb carbon dioxide twenty-four hours a day.

'We are going to extend the tree line of this planet eight hundred kilometres to the north and we believe the overall effect will be a significant improvement in evapotranspiration and a reduction in the build-up of the so-called greenhouse gases in our atmosphere. After all, we are harnessing–' he evoked a theomagical metaphor he knew would still have meaning for a society that had re-embraced religion only a generation ago '–*God*'s own energy in this project.

Tye waited as translation was received by those few who required it. He then lifted his arms again and gazed directly at the E&E minister as if daring him to make another challenge.

'Take care of our planet – you hear!'

'We hear,' responded the well-rehearsed Tye delegation, the English-speaking Russians hastening to join in.

He watched as the translation was received and more heads on the Russian side of the table nodded.

'I propose that we should form a new collegium to review our plans for the wildlife of the region. Perhaps the minister could delegate one of his team to act as Chair. It can then review the plans we have made and report back to us jointly in due course.'

The minister nodded his head.

'Now, I would like to move on to one subject that is of crucial importance to all of us.'

This was Tye's biggest worry, the one thing that could completely wreck plans and developments that had been over ten years in gestation. He would have to have their complete understanding on these issues. He turned to a large map that stood behind him.

'We cannot expect our friends in the People's Republic of China to remain unmoved by the creation of a new region of opportunity so near their northern border,' he began, choosing his words carefully. 'Our agreement calls for the Russian government to maintain a corridor two hundred miles wide along the entire southern border with the People's Republic of China. It will be Russia's responsibility to maintain an adequate military force in this region at all times to deter any thoughts of an advance by the People's Liberation Army or any other form of incursion towards our areas of investment. I would be grateful if General Padorin could provide more detail of the forces and equipment that will be permanently stationed along this corridor.'

This was the crunch. The Tye Corporation had to have the protection of the Russian Army against the Chinese hordes. Envy was the most powerful of political motivations, even if the coveted territory could be devalued at the turn of a switch. The army in the People's Republic had grown to over one hundred million men and women and it would take a deployment of Russian armour and, most importantly, Russian tactical nuclear weapons along the northern border to provide a clear and demonstrable guarantee of security for the Tye Corporation shareholders and the many new investors who were eager to take sub-leases on land in the new province. Tye knew, of course, that if things ever became really difficult he now had an awesome weapons capacity of his own, but that was not to be spoken of – *ever.*

Jack surfaced a mile offshore and trod water. In the distance, to the south-west, he could see the dark outline of Hope Island and its myriad twinkling lights. There was a clear sky and the bursts of laser communications added a canopy of intermittent illuminations. There was also a full moon. That would require extra caution. He had blacked his face for the mission – recalling, as he did so, that the last time he had used camouflage in such a way had been over fifteen years ago, when he had been preparing for his final active-service mission. Then he had been aboard a submarine that was rolling viciously in a large surface swell fourteen miles off the coast of North Korea.

He had drawn an automatic pistol from Security's stores but had refused the box of ammunition the armourer had pushed across the counter. Then, to add to the man's confusion, he had also declined to complete the electronic identification and regis-tration procedure to confirm him as the authorized user. Only this would have given him access to the internal microprocessor that controlled the laser-sighted weapon. He had then requisi-tioned lightweight scuba equipment, once again without expla-nation. He had signed for the useless gun and the diving equipment and taken them back to his apartment where he had run a full safety test on the scuba gear in the bath. His security review was under way and his people had been told to expect incursions and similar tests of their defences. All his team were on edge. He intended to keep them that way.

He had reviewed Pierre's security plans for the Moscow trip and had found them both detailed and thorough. Having once occupied a top slot in the league table of cities regarded as most dangerous for Tye executives, the Russian capital had improved over the years to the point where it was little more dangerous that any Western European city. The only real point of concern had been the motorcade to which they had insisted subjecting Tom on the day he arrived but that had passed off without event. Pierre reported that the entire corporate team was now ensconced in the Kremlin and was likely to remain there for several days. Jack had already seen one of the three Tye-Lears that had carried the Tye diplomatic mission returning for fresh supplies of Hope Island produce.

Jack had been able to meet with his boss in person for eleven minutes shortly before Tom had left for Moscow and he found the tycoon rested and relaxed. The media frenzy over the Los Angeles traffic crisis had receded: Tye had appeared totally focused on the deal about to be struck in Moscow and on the forthcoming *One Weekend* conference.

'You do whatever you need, Jack,' Tye had agreed with a wave as the corporation's vice-president of security explained his plans for a radical review of protection procedures on the island and the need for more regular refugee sweeps. Since the Cuban navy had now been witnessed shooting at their own people as they tried to escape the country, Tom had agreed that any refugees and escaping rebels found in Hope Island waters would be brought ashore before being forwarded to one of the other countries prepared to accept them. Jack had warned Tom that with such an exalted guest list, the weekend conference would be a major trial of Hope Island's state security procedures and he wanted to go over the plans and test them to ensure everything worked smoothly.

He checked his old analog wrist-compass and made sure of his heading. His LifeWatch with its sophisticated GPS locator was beneath the duvet back in his apartment overlooking the marina in Hope Town. He blew out his mask, released some air from his buoyancy jacket, sank to three metres and began the trudge for the shore. He was heading for the north-eastern tip of the island, aware that his patrols on the beaches and clifftops would be constantly scanning the water – as instructed by their standing orders. Low-level radar swept the surface for early warnings of approaching craft while drone sonars were deployed at every mile around the island's perimeter in wait for the sound of propellors. The system was even sensitive enough to detect and identify the sound and rhythm of splashy swimmers.

He doubted whether either of the two patrol craft would be inshore. Their standing orders were now to patrol the edge of the exclusion zone with Cuba, over to the west.

Jack felt the increasing warmth of the water as he arrived in the shallows and he became aware of rocks rising up to meet him. He paused again and slowly rose to the surface. To his left was the tiny crescent bay that had been blasted out of the sheer rock face to provide a private beach for the main house. It was now floodlit for the benefit of the security cameras. The only landward approach to that patch of imported white sand was the silver funicular railway that rose from the rear of the beach up to the pool terrace one hundred and fifty feet above. The car was now at the top, inside its winch-house.

Getting his bearings, he submerged again and set off northwards. If the engineers had chosen the shortest route for the tunnel the outlet should be just below the surface, a further two hundred yards along the sheer cliff face that fell almost vertically into the sea. He had located several articles about its design on the networks. Various architects and engineering consultancies were so proud of their work on Thomas Tye's mansion that they encouraged specialist journals and architectural magazines to print stories and diagrams of their various designs. None was permitted to publish pictures or plans of the house itself, of course, but Jack had gathered more information than he needed and for this particular exercise it was important that he only used information that was generally available.

He checked his depth gauge and released air from his

buoyancy jacket until the instrument registered two metres. Then he swam slowly along the rock wall. He was weighing the risks of having to use his main flashlight when he felt the current slightly above him. He stopped and allowed himself to rise into the stream. His pencil-light revealed the grating and he felt the gentle warmth of the current pushing against his wetsuit.

First he examined the bolts that secured the outlet cover to the rock face. As expected, they were too deeply embedded to yield to the unaided strength of a single swimmer, so he opened his tool bag and unclipped the diamond-tipped micro-saw that UNISA's Technical Services had provided. The hand-held circular saw was driven by a tiny but enormously powerful electric motor and in two minutes Jack had cut a hole a yard square in the grille.

He returned the saw to its clip, refastened his tool bag and swam into the wide opening. Inside the seclusion of the steel tunnel, Jack was finally able to switch on his main flashlight. He could see that the bore continued level for about ten yards and then began its slow curve upwards into darkness. He wondered how the construction engineers had drilled such a tunnel through solid rock.

After four or five minutes of vigorous swimming Jack felt himself tiring against the opposing current and, despite his fitness, he began to think he might not make it. He checked his air: he had twenty minutes left and that immediately reassured him. Then he saw a dim light ahead that meant he had arrived under the large baffle and filter housing at the bottom of the pool.

Professor Sir Oliver Morton, Knight Bachelor of England and one of the world's most distinguished genetic biologists, had thrown himself into practical work in a way that he hadn't since he had been a PhD student thirty-one years before. Reluctantly, and only after a series of blazing family rows, he had relocated to Hope Island as his company's new chairman had insisted. His wife, a professor of comparative philosophy at the University of Cambridge, had refused to join him in the move. Morton had faced a stark choice: resign and give up all realistic claim on future share options and the capital he had invested in Molecul-ture plc – all the liquid capital he possessed – or move with the company and endure separation from his wife and family. They had agreed to try living apart for six months. Lucy Morton understood that to be fifty-five years old without any savings was an uncomfortable position, no matter how philosophical one might be.

At the same moment that Jack Hendriksen was arriving at the bottom of Thomas Tye's swimming pool, Morton was rechecking an observation he had already rechecked eight times, under four different electron microscopes. He was in the com-pany's laboratory in Hope Island's Science Park and he had been working all night, as had become his custom since arriving on the island. There could be no doubt about what he was seeing, but he would need other eyes to see the living cells, the photographs and computer images he was collecting.

The cells that had grown in the latest batch of *Triticum spelta* – a new strain of pseudo-nocturnal wheat – were right-handed.

Right-handed, not left-handed. 'Left-handed' was the biologists' term for the universal polarity of all life on earth. Since the beginning of the earliest form of life on the planet, every cell, vegetable or animal, had selected only left-handed amino acids to make proteins. It had long been surmised that it was the polarity of the Earth's own magnetic force – created by the inner metal core of the planet revolving more rapidly than the outer – that causes all living things to be so.

But these cells had a polarity that was the reverse of all other life that had been observed and they had evolved naturally, without intervention from Morton or any of the researchers on his team.

He had checked and rechecked the room, too: there was no internal magnetic field. He had demagnetized and degaussed the culture units, the work surfaces and the three electron micro-scopes in the lab. Viewed separately under each of the three in turn, the result had been the same.

Morton looked at the microscope's display screen again and then reached for his VideoMate to call Fred Zimmer. He knew Thomas Tye had been exaggerating when he had talked about an invitation to Stockholm for the pseudo-nocturnal crops – but this! It was certainly worth waking up his partner. They would have a chance to decide how best to start further replication trials before the day shift returned to the lab.

Thomas Tye had used the island's natural hot springs to feed his indoor swimming pool. Whether this had been his idea or the architects' was not known, but balneologists had been brought in to supervise its design and those who had swum in the mineral-rich water reported enthusiastically on the invigorating benefits of this natural spa. One of the many underground springs had been diverted to feed the large pool and, with a tunnel bored to provide an exit to the sea, the trillionaire had eliminated at a stroke the energy requirements and costs of both heating and recycling filtration.

Jack clipped himself to the grille below the pool while he deployed his micro-saw again. The cut-away section of the grating, and the filter mesh, sailed away in the rapidly increasing current and Jack forced himself up into the pool against the flow.

He swam away from the now swirling drain and sat at the bottom of the pool, looking up for human silhouettes. His air supply was not now the invisible mixed-gas rebreathers he had used as a SEAL. He knew that bubbles were escaping to the surface, but it was unlikely that any of the house staff were in the pool room at three a.m.

He then finned towards the surface and gently broke through into fresh air. Pulling off his mask, he savoured a deep breath and slipped back the hood of his wetsuit. The ornate pool room was empty, as expected. Moonlight penetrating the huge windows was reflected off the water's surface and bathed the ceiling and walls in gentle undulations of light.

Jack swam to the edge of the pool, pulled off his fins while still in the water and climbed out onto the marble surround. He thought it unlikely there would be any security cameras here or in the changing rooms. Considerations of modesty often override security – a sensibility that professional intruders frequently exploit. Inside the male locker room he peeled off his wetsuit.

He was wearing black shorts and T-shirt beneath his wetsuit but he kept his reef shoes on to provide grip. Then he removed a plastic bag from his tool kit. The 9mm SigSauer was perfectly dry. Even though the gun's microprocessor-controlled firing system was not activated and he had left the empty seventeen-round magazine back in his apartment, he checked once again that it did not have a round in the breech. He tucked the gun in the waistband of his shorts, ensuring that it was displayed prominently. Next he took a black waterproof envelope from his swimming bag and clasped it under his arm.

Back in the main pool room he summoned the elevator. From now on he knew his presence would be recorded, but that was part of his plan. Once the elevator arrived he stepped quickly into its bright interior, hoping that this small momentary illumination in the pool room would go unnoticed by his own patrols out in the grounds. Jack studied the row of buttons and the camera lenses set into the control panel at shoulder height.

He pressed for the fourth floor, where he knew Tommy's room was located. He had not visited that level before, but he had inspected the lower three floors of the great house and realized that Tommy's room and the live-in staff quarters were situated on the fourth. Tye's private quarters, inaccessible to all others but his Mexican domestic staff, lay on the fifth and topmost level. The elevator began to climb.

Eventually the doors hissed open onto a dimly lit corridor running to either side. From here on, Jack was working on luck. He pulled a sheet of ultra-thin, clear, optically conducting plastic from the envelope, knelt down and depressed the 'open door' button. Slowly he extended his arm and the plastic into the hallway. He determined the house's alarm system did not include movement-detection beams at floor level. Tye had never asked Jack or any of his predecessors to cover the interior of his house in their security plans, so the island's security force held no details of its internal protection arrangements. It was this anomaly that had given Jack an excuse to mount this exercise. If he triggered an alarm by breaking a movement-detection beam now, his dual-purpose mission would be over instantly and he had no alternative plan.

He slowly worked the transparent sheet up to head height, then higher again. There were no beams, so he stepped out of the elevator. As the doors closed behind him he carefully repeated the process, crouching and straightening to full height again and again as he worked his way across the width of the corridor. They had either chosen not to install detectors in the hallways or they were not switched on. Perhaps there was too much casual movement through these corridors for them to be practical, Jack supposed – it wasn't as if this house was ever going to be left empty of staff. He returned the plastic tell-tale to its envelope and looked towards each end of the hall, spotting cameras at ceiling height. He pulled the gun from his waistband and waved it theatrically at each camera in turn. He knew of no all-night surveillance team that might be monitoring the camera feeds right now, but he wanted to create an impact when the inevitable, exhaustive post-mortem started.

He had already estimated that there might still be three or four people inside the house at this time of night. Apart from Tommy there would be his night nanny – a woman called Angela, whom he had only met once, Emily Pettigrew the head nurse, the night butler and then possibly a cook. But with Tom away in Moscow it was likely that most of the domestic staff would have chosen to return to their own homes in Hope Town or its outlying developments rather than sleep unnecessarily in the almost empty mansion.

Jack made an arbitrary choice, turned right and moved silently along the corridor. It was 3.20 a.m., the nightly low spot for human activity when all the staff would be most likely sound asleep. He paused at the first door he came to, bending to listen. Then he opened the door quietly and poked his head into the room. The bedroom was empty, with moonlight streaming through its large window. He closed the door and set off again. When he opened the next door, he sensed the room was occupied, even before he heard gentle snoring. Emily Pettigrew slept naked, Jack noticed. He closed her door silently. He was now nearly at the end of the corridor. Looking up at the camera he shrugged, and he pointed at the last door, miming the question 'In there?'

Suddenly he heard a sound he recognized. It was a HydraChair in full motion. He pushed the door open and stood watching in the dimly-lit room as Tommy's chair inverted the boy completely, then put him on his side as the game simulated an aircraft or a spaceship executing a sharp turn. He could hear Tommy laugh as he fought to keep the virtual craft within whatever performance envelope the game's designers had specified.

Jack closed the door behind him, returned the gun to his waistband, pulling his T-shirt down to cover it, and turned up the main room lights. He didn't expect the illumination to penetrate the boy's helmet so he crossed the room and rapped playfully on its decorative wing decals.

The HydraChair flipped upright to its resting position and Tommy's helmet visor hissed upwards.

'Hiya, Tommy,' said Jack.

'Hi,' replied Tommy doubtfully.

'You're up late,' observed Jack.

'Hello, Jack. Was that a gun?' asked Jed from the bed. The Furry's vision extended into infra-red wavelengths.

'You *are* clever, Jed,' said Jack, keeping the irritation out of his voice. 'But it's not loaded.'

He lifted the front of his T-shirt, pulled out the gun and handed it, butt first, to Tommy.

'I'm testing security in the house,' Jack told the seven-year-old. 'I heard your HydraChair. Why are you still up?'

Tommy turned the heavy gun over in his hands. 'I don't have to go to sleep – as long as I stay in my room,' he explained. 'Who are you going to shoot?'

Jack smiled and retrieved the weapon. 'Nobody,' he said, stowing it in his waistband again. 'We're just practising drill – to make sure everybody's safe. Do you want to help us?'

Tommy banged the quick-release lever on his safety harness. He was wearing blue pyjamas and a pair of large blue rabbit-eared slippers that, Jack recalled, had been a gift from Calypso. As Tommy rose out of the chair he staggered slightly.

Jack stepped forward and caught the boy's arms to steady him. He eased his grip as he noticed the bandages underneath the boy's pyjama sleeves. Calypso had told him about the incident with the knife.

'Whoa – it gets like that when you've been flying.'

'I'm OK,' insisted Tommy, pulling free. He stepped to the bed and picked up his Furry companion.

'What are you going to do now?' Tommy asked Jack. 'Your face is all black.'

Jack took the package from under his arm and extracted a smaller, white envelope. 'I've crept into the house secretly to surprise everybody. It's your father's birthday tomorrow and I've brought a birthday card for you to give him. You can sign it. Have you got a pen?'

Tommy ran to his drawing chest. Jack followed and laid the card on its flat surface. He watched as Tommy read the text.

'It says "Happy Birthday, Dad",' exclaimed Tommy excitedly. 'I didn't know it was his birthday.'

Jack smiled. The card was a generic anniversary greeting, mentioning no particular age.

Tommy took up a green marker pen and carefully wrote his name.

'I'm going to sneak this into your father's office,' said Jack, tucking the card back in its envelope. 'It will be a nice surprise for when he gets home. Want to come along?'

'I'm not allowed out of my room,' responded Tommy, dutifully.

'You're with me now,' replied Jack firmly. 'Come on.'

'May I come too?' asked Jed in the very proper English that Tom had specified for his son's personal Furry. 'I'll just disconnect from the networks. Hang on a mo.'

Tommy scooped up the caterpillar as Jack picked up the small chair from in front of the boy's drawing desk.

'I think we'll need this,' he explained.

He opened the door and glanced along the long corridor. Seeing that it was still empty, he stepped out, followed by Tommy with Jed tucked under his left arm. Jack led the way to the elevator.

Inside the lift Jack pressed the button for the fifth floor. As he had expected nothing happened.

'We're not moving,' observed Jed.

'Just a moment,' said Jack. 'We need a special pass.'

He opened the larger envelope and carefully pulled out a gleaming mirror that immediately iridized, shooting rainbows of prismatic light around the lift. He positioned the low chair underneath the control panel.

'I want you to stand on this, Tommy,' Jack said. 'I'll show you a trick.'

'Will my father be angry?' asked Tommy, suddenly afraid.

Jack laughed.

'No. He'll be really pleased. He'll come back to a great surprise.'

Tommy stepped up onto the chair, Jed still clenched firmly under one arm.

Jack positioned the mirror carefully and Tommy's eyes widened as he stared at the reflection. The intelligent mirror recreated the boy's face as a perfect, slightly enlarged three-dimensional hologram. It was as though his whole head was captured inside a strangely deep mirror. He turned his head to the left and the right, watching the disembodied head move, exactly as Jack had hoped.

In their lab the UNISA technical officers had scaled up the identification parameters of a facial-recognition system, requisitioning the experimental holo-optics from the physics department at the University of Indiana. They had added an imaging microprocessor to the system with over 120,000 algorithms intended to morph a juvenile face into a convincing adult version. The system could generate all these in less than a second before starting over again. In the lab the catoptricologists had managed to fool a facial-recognition system by using the enhanced 3D-mirror and coloured images of *approved* faces, but there was no guarantee that Tommy's young face would be sufficiently similar to his father's for the reflector's enantio-morphing and ageing techniques to work. Jack knew the recognition system was dividing the boy's reflected face into forty elements, such as the outer corners of the eyes, the tip of the nose and the ends of the eyebrows and measuring the distances between them to compare to its database of approved faces. He also knew that each measurement was programmed to be imprecise to some degree because the system had to allow for variations in lighting and distance.

As Tommy gazed into his reflection, Jack slowly moved the mirror closer to the stereoscopic camera lenses, then back towards Tommy's face, angling it slightly as he did so.

'It doesn't seem to be working,' observed Jed.

'Thank you,' said Jack, who knew that the Furry would be recording all his actions. Instinctively, he stuck his tongue out at the caterpillar – a gesture he knew Jed couldn't return.

Tommy laughed at this and then Jack saw a small green LED illuminate above the button for the fifth floor. Jack nodded to himself in satisfaction. He should have guessed that Thomas Tye would *always* smile for a camera.

'Press the button again,' he said to Tommy.

As the boy did so, the lift started to rise.

'Well done,' said Jed.

The lights were off in the fifth-floor corridor but Jack doubted whether movement beams would have been installed there in addition to the elevator's security system. A rapid traverse of the hall space with his conducting tell-tale sheet confirmed it. He stepped out and touched the illumination control on the wall. The accommodation on the top of the building was set back considerably from the floors below, so was practically invisible from the ground. Jack wondered if any of his patrols had been sufficiently energetic to climb the mountain tonight. If they had, they might spot the lights and he would only have a minute or two before someone arrived to check.

Jack noticed three doors along the corridor. Two were on the side where the rooms would have sea views. The room on the other side would face the mountain. Jack opted for the land-facing room. As expected, there was a full range of security barriers protecting this door.

'Touch that pad with your finger,' Jack said to Tommy. He pointed to the long middle finger of Tommy's right hand.

He had already lifted the boy's fingerprints from the cup of hot chocolate Tommy had left unfinished at Calypso's house. Back at UNISA's HQ, Deakin had received them as uncaptioned electronic images, with a separate, coded fax detailing the request. Within an hour the dermatoglyphologists in UNISA Forensics had compared the prints to a set of impressions Thomas Tye had left in the White House in Washington DC eight years before. At that time the US Secret Service had harvested the prints as part of their routine observation of all the President's guests and, as part of a wide-scale reciprocal agreement, copies had been lodged with UNISA. Jack had recieved a four-word message back: '100 per cent match.' He had read somewhere that a third of identical twins have matching fingerprints, but he doubted whether anyone had data on artifical clones.

As Tommy touched the fingerprint pad, a green LED illuminated. Jack then positioned the low chair again and repeated the procedure he had followed in the lift. It took longer this time, although the system would be employing precisely the same facial-pattern recognition system used in the lift. He moved the mirror closer to and then further away from the twin lenses.

'Smile,' prompted Jack again.

As the green LED lit up, Jack helped Tommy step down from the chair.

'Now the system's got to sniff your wrist,' said Jack. 'Put your arm up against that grille, like this.'

Jack showed Tommy how to put the inside of his wrist to the olfactory sensor. This would be the hardest part and Al Lynch had bet him a case of Jack Daniels that his mission would fail here. Jack took a small aerosol spray from his belt bag as he watched the display panel.

The iatrochemists and the osphresiologists of the World Health Organization's research labs had also been doubtful. Though they understood that the boy was a clone of his father, they argued the degree to which the body's chemistry was altered during puberty. They therefore thought it very unlikely that the young son's chemical signature would match his father's so – as one put it, 'rather more in desperation than in hope' – they had prepared a supplementary concoction of testosterone and related hormones for Jack to spray on during the sampling.

He just was about to use the spray when another green LED lit up, indicating the system had been fooled.

'Just one to go,' said Jed.

Despite the preoccupations of the moment, Jack felt his skin crawl at hearing the little companion. This was uncanny. He turned and stared at the caterpillar under Tommy's arm. To his discomfort, Jed turned his own head slightly and blinked the lashes of his huge eyes, raising his eyebrows as he returned Jack's gaze. The caterpillar was mugging back at him! Jack thought he might have a word with Professor Keane. Her achievements with artificial intelligence were astonishing but also quite disconcerting.

'Now we need one more thing,' he told Tommy. 'This won't really hurt.'

'Oow,' complained Tommy jokingly as Jack pulled a single hair from his head.

'Watch this,' said Jack. He carefully placed the hair in the scanning capsule of the DNA-verification system and they watched as it was bathed in UV light. Within four seconds the third green LED illuminated.

'Come on, let's go,' said Jack. He pushed open the door and they were inside Thomas Tye's private office.

'It's very dark,' observed Jed, who could see perfectly well. Jack switched the lights on.

As the planners of this mission had guessed, the whole room was a shrine to computers – a throwback to the days when Tye had actually understood something about current computer technology and, perhaps more tellingly, had still cared. Jack saw a dozen outdated super-RAID storage racks and he estimated there were seven or eight processing systems in the room. All the monitors and the large wall screen were on stand-by. As Al Lynch had predicted, there would be petabytes of data contained here. But if you wanted to find something in particular, you wouldn't know where to begin.

'That's his desk.' Jack indicated it to Tommy, wondering, as he did so, why he was whispering.

Tommy seemed afraid, unwilling to move.

Jack smiled and put his hand on the boy's shoulder.

'Come on, let's put the birthday card where he'll spot it easily.' He led Tommy over to the main work surface. Beyond lay a personal Holo-Theater, now in darkness.

Tommy took the envelope and placed it centrally on the desk top.

'*I*'ve brought a card for him as well,' said Jack as he pulled a small waterproof wallet from the envelope. He broke the seal and extracted the memory card that Al Lynch had prepared specially for him. 'It doesn't matter which storage slot you use.' Lynch had advised.

Jack looked around and the only slot he could see was on a control panel in the rack of old RAID storage drives. He crossed and slipped the wafer-thin card into the slot. 'It will eject itself when it's done,' Lynch had continued. 'I've automated everything, so you just add your message.'

The wall screen came to life and Jack was looking at himself. 'Hi, Tom,' smiled a relaxed-looking Jack, videoed standing on his small balcony overlooking the marina at Hope Town. 'Hope you've had a great time in Moscow. Happy birthday and I'm sure we'll be meeting as soon as you get home. Take care of the planet – you hear!' Jack's image then raised a glass of champagne to the camera, with the sound of 'Happy Birthday' sung by children being played over the slow fade.

Jed started to join in, then Tommy too was singing along. The clip ended as the small voices trailed off.

'Hurrah,' cried Jed, unable to clap.

Jack looked at his storage card, which was still firmly engaged. He carefully positioned himself between the caterpillar and the rack, to block Jed's view of the system. He knew that if Jed's vision sensors captured images of the control panel and its LED status lights, they would realize later that Jack had been copying data.

'Do you want to see it again?' asked Jack, trying to buy time and wondering if he could get a replay without resetting the memory card. At that moment the memory card popped out of its slot, behind him.

'No, it's late, we'd better get back,' Jack corrected himself. 'Come on, Tommy.'

He retrieved the memory card and held the door open for Tommy and Jed.

The elevator required no security clearance to descend and Jack escorted Tommy back to his bedroom.

'Time for bed now, I should think,' he suggested as he held the door open.

'I'm not tired,' protested Tommy. 'I don't need to go to bed. I just rest and dream sometimes.'

'Anything you want before I go?' asked Jack.

'No, thanks,' said Tommy as he set Jed down carefully on the bed. He opened the door to his bedside cupboard and a light came on. Jack saw that he had been provided with his own mini-fridge. 'I'll just have a fruit juice.'

'OK. Well, good night,' Jack said softly, opening the door.

''Night,' replied Tommy as he climbed back into his HydraChair.

'Goodnight, Jack,' called Jed from the bed.

Jack closed the door silently, wondering whether they would talk about him.

Connie was asleep in one of the antique four-poster beds the Tye Corporation's Russian hosts had refurbished for their guests. Like all the senior visitors, she had been allotted one of the giant old rooms of the Terem Palace. Once a waiting-chamber to the throne room, it had long since been converted to a bedroom suite by the installation of a huge private bathroom with antique brass plumbing.

She was currently in REM sleep, her sensorially deprived consciousness feeding on the keywords the DreamDial module of her VideoMate was whispering in her earpiece.

She had gone to bed feeling stressed and then decided she would treat herself. She loved the prompt sequence she had created that reliably produced one recurring dream: she would be at her childhood home with her mother, her sister and their horses, the ScentSim's 'Saddle and Bridle' fragrance always prompting total recall. Then she would be at her high-school prom, dancing until she could dance no more. To follow that Connie had synchronized a fragrance of dark hormones to accompany words she had programmed to induce a dream about the prolonged, hard sex she craved but which, because of the strange life she led, she rarely found. She wished she could find a man to whom she could say such words, and with whom she could create these feelings, images and smells. But in her dreams she did – night after night, whenever she chose.

She was tossing and writhing with a smile on her face when an incoming high-priority override call jerked her awake. At night, all regular calls for Thomas Tye or for herself were routed to the front office on Hope Island where her eight assistants and forty administrative staff fielded the twenty-four-hour frenzy of communication that surrounded Thomas Tye. Only a few people had the facility to get through this barrier.

'It's Pat O'Mahoney in CTA,' announced a voice redundantly after she had identified the caller and accepted the communication. She didn't switch to visual. She couldn't imagine what could be happening in the Competitive Threat Analysis department of the Tye Corporation that warranted her sleep being interrupted. That department of 260 people comprised surveillance staff monitoring the networks for the performance indicators of competitors, intercepting and deciphering encrypted messages that might be important, preparing briefings about possible acquisitions, and gathering information about other companies engaged in markets similar to the many fields of interest of the Tye Corporation.

'Pat, yes,' yawned Connie, as she swung her legs out of bed and tried to focus her thoughts. He was the keeper of Tye's secret and was absolutely trusted. 'What is it?'

'Sorry to disturb you, Miss Law,' apologized the CTA director. 'But we thought you might want to alert Tom. Over the last couple of days something strange has been happening. There's been a massive increase in the number of messages, communications and press stories about us – about the corporation. Plus a massive increase in articles about Tom himself and some of our subsidiaries. The networks are full of this stuff, mostly encrypted.'

'How big an increase?' asked Connie, curious.

'It's shot up to three or four times the usual,' said O'Mahoney breathlessly. He'd spent several hours plucking up the courage to disturb Tom's executive assistant. 'We've never experienced anything like this before, and we can't keep up. There are now large areas we're not able to cover.'

'OK, Pat,' replied Connie. 'Leave it with me. I'll pass this by Tom.'

She ended the call, removed the earpiece and stood up. It was not yet five a.m., although Moscow's summer dawn was already peeping through from behind the heavy drapes. She walked to the old-fashioned pedestal washbasin in the bathroom, ran some cold water and rinsed her face. Then she decided to risk one brief call. The increase in network traffic would be in her favour. She returned to the bed, picked up her VideoMate and told it to connect her to an office just outside Washington DC. As she waited for her call to be answered, she decided that she would not disturb Tom yet with this news. It would keep until morning.

SEVENTEEN

'Oh, I want to be sick,' gasped Haley as she put the report down. 'That little boy was grown in a box!'

It was a sunny Saturday morning in Battersea and, as before, the report had arrived by mail. She and Barry had just emerged, after an enthusiastic bout of early-morning lovemaking, to celebrate the start of the weekend. Even though most interpersonal communications had migrated to the global networks, the Royal Mail and its upstart competitors still found their daily workload increasing as more and more market researchers proclaimed that printed material remained the most powerful form of direct sales promotion. But apart from the junk mail that arrived each day, there were still enough people who liked to send picture postcards from their holidays, who wrote personal thank-you notes and who used printed anniversary, birthday and greetings cards for the postal delivery to remain a key event of people's morning routines.

This report, the third to arrive unheralded and unsigned, had been posted in Berlin. Jack had informed Haley that whoever was posting these reports chose to do so only from main post offices in major city centres: standard anti-trace procedures. Haley had torn open the envelope immediately and settled down to read as Barry brewed the filter coffee.

'What do you mean?' asked Barry as he reached for the coffee mugs. Because of the heat they were both in T-shirts and shorts, although this sports combination looked better on Haley's frame than on Barry's. It didn't help that his orange outfit clashed with his red hair and beard.

'It claims that Tommy was grown in one of those boxes they use to keep donor organs alive – something called a MatchBox, with an artificial placenta.'

Barry laughed. 'Well, that beats labour pains any day. Even better than a Caesarean.'

'BARRY!' exclaimed Haley. 'I'm being serious. They made a cloned embryo, then grew it in this box. There's even a diagram! That's who Tye's son is. That's Tommy. Jack said he's identical to his father.'

'Who's Jack, then?' asked the Welsh geneticist lightly.

Haley looked up and frowned. She hadn't previously mentioned her new contact – as he had asked.

'Oh, he's just someone inside the Tye Corporation,' said Haley, equally lightly. 'Helps me with research.'

Barry brought the mugs over to the table and sat down opposite as she returned to the report.

'They *harvested* the baby after thirty-three weeks,' she read aloud with a shudder.

'Cool,' deadpanned Barry as he sipped his coffee.

'It is *not* cool, Barry Evans, it's *sick*!' shouted Haley as she slammed the pages down on the table. 'You can't grow someone in a box that you keep on the sideboard! How would that child hear his mother's heartbeat – or external voices, or music? How would he feel movement? How would the baby bond with the mother, for God's sake?'

'Well, it beats putting up with morning sickness,' smiled Barry. 'I, for one, think the benefits of viviparous birth are greatly exaggerated. *And* it would be pretty safe – probably zero miscarriage rate, and you could pop in a bit of compost to help things along.'

'You have no soul, Barry,' complained Haley, getting seriously annoyed with his flippancy.

'And you should bloody well lighten up, girl,' protested Barry, also serious now, his sing-song accent increasing with his emotion. 'It's Saturday bloody morning but it's always Thomas Tye this, the bloody Tye Corporation that. Now it's this wonder child. It's not *your* family. These people are trillionaires who can do anything they want – they live in the future! It's not real life, girl. It's not you and me, a few beers and a fish supper on a Friday night. But you don't think about anything else but Thomas Tye and your bloody book. I would have thought a career girl like you would approve. You too could have a baby in a box and still concentrate on your bloody work.'

Haley drew a deep breath. She knew where it was going now; they both knew where it was going. It had been bubbling for weeks. They weren't really made for each other and out of bed there was little they could share. Barry had seemed sensitive at first, but he really wanted a woman who was prepared to revolve around his life and his needs, not one who had a massive, all-consuming career agenda of her own. In recent weeks his behaviour had been expressing his dissatisfaction more eloquently than any words could. He had taken to spending his evenings in pubs or wine bars with his workmates. On Saturdays it was rugby or cricket and, if they saw each other on Sundays, he insisted that conversation about work should be taboo.

But Haley lived for her work. When she wasn't actually writing she was composing words in her head. She was constantly recording little voice-notes on her VideoMate and scribbling on her DigiPad. Three or four times a night she would wake up and lean over to whisper quietly into the machine on her bedside table, trying not to disturb Barry if he was there. Even in her bath she would read background research, and over meals she would be flicking through her words already committed to paper. She realized this made her an impossible partner, but her real friends knew and understood – although of course they didn't have to live with her. Furthermore, she was an intellectual and an artist; and Barry, despite his doctorate, was neither.

'Time for us to have a little break from each other, I think, Doctor Evans,' she said with a wan smile. 'Just while I get this book finished. Anyway, I need to go abroad again.'

Al Lynch walked around his laboratory, using this period of waiting to exercise his back and leg muscles. He was out of his wheelchair for most of the working day now and he imagined he could feel the nerves regenerating at each end of his spinal cord. He was currently anticipating Ron Deakin's imminent arrival from New York. The ban on network communication was placing a huge strain on both budgets and personnel.

The computer systems Lynch controlled in the UNISA lab at Fort Mead were the most powerful ever developed. In the last few decades of the twentieth century, the NSA had run Cray supercomputers to break codes, sift information and mine into mountains of generic data but, as silicon-based microprocessor circuits had shrunk to the point where their miniaturization had run up against the concrete wall of molecular physics, the NSA and, in turn, other intelligence agencies had pioneered the use of networked optical processors. These computers moved, measured and modified data inside beams of light and did so at a rate thousands of times faster than the supercomputers they had replaced.

Al Lynch had received his specially prepared storage card back in the regular post. Before their newly recruited UNISA intelligence officer had returned to Hope Island there had been much discussion about how Jack Hendriksen should transmit any data collected from Tye's private systems back to the UN facility at Fort Mead. As his covering note explained, Jack had resolved this problem by simply asking one of his pilot pals in the Tye Corporation flight to post the padded envelope for him during a stopover in Washington: pilots stuck together, Al Lynch understood.

In hacker circles the program on the storage card Lynch had prepared for Jack would have been described as an 'invisible tapeworm'. That nomenclature was outdated and referred to computer systems long since obsolete but hackers are a strangely nostalgic and conservative breed. Once inserted into a storage slot, the software could mimic the operating parameters of all known current and obsolete storage systems and, without leaving any trace of its presence, would copy every byte of data it could find in all local storage cards, flash memories and disks and on all storage systems, new and old, connected by common networks. It even collected files that had been 'deleted' but not yet overwritten. The holographic storage system was an IBM prototype: a single plastic card, three inches by two, could store forty-eight petabytes – forty-eight quadrillion bytes! – of data. Lynch found only 27.8112 petabytes on the card Jack had returned.

Only twenty-eight petabytes! A couple of decades ago that would have represented enough data to fill up the storage disks of over ten million of the most powerful desktop computers! The increasing fashion for videoing every meeting, and storing movies, music, reference books and TV shows on computers, as well as the latest fads of holo-image conferencing, taste-generation and scent simulations, were demanding storage and access technologies on a scale that would have been unthinkable even a few years earlier. And, of course, strong encryption created very large additional files. Fortunately, speed and storage were the types of problems that the computer industry had always been able to solve and, now that the cost of media storage had fallen to less than a penny a terabyte, everybody would hoard *everything*. A form of partial immortality was thus being achieved through virtual storage.

Almost all the major files in Tye's private store of data had proved to be encrypted. 'Suspicious bastard,' Lynch had muttered as he watched screens full of random numbers and letters fly by. He presumed that years ago Tye had selected 'Secure' as the default setting for his communications and computer storage systems. Lynch had randomly dipped into these files in the hope that Tye might have become careless at some period and used a lower level of security, but all his analytical tools revealed encryption so dense that Lynch guessed that Tye must regularly apply the super-long string lengths normally used for military encryption. Lynch knew that even if he ran all his immense optical processing power against these twenty-eight petabytes of data, he wouldn't have decoded a single message from it before he was due for retirement.

The night before, he had copied all the same data onto local flash storage and instructed his system to search only for the same two words in any scraps of unencoded text and images that might lie within the data mountain. Then he had put his jacket on, switched off the lights and walked slowly and carefully to his car. He only needed his wheelchair towards the end of each day now, when his muscles were screaming with tiredness. In another few weeks he hoped to be able to give it up completely, for the benefit of another needy user.

Lynch heard the door open and there stood his friend. The pair had worked together, on and off, for over twenty years and it had been Deakin himself who had first introduced the computer security analyst to Jack Hendriksen.

'Jack told me you were out of your chair and walking,' Ron Deakin exclaimed as he grasped Lynch's hand. 'That's fantastic!'

Lynch poured a coffee for his guest and seated him at the small conference table. 'Here, this is why I suggested you come down this morning.' He pushed the printout of an e-mail message towards Deakin.

The UNISA officer flipped through the pages before settling down to read them carefully. When he reached the third page he started flipping again. Then he skimmed through the remaining sixty sheets.

'I extracted everything from Tye's files that was in plain text or unencrypted video,' explained Lynch. 'There was over a terabyte of it. Then I searched for two key words: "encryption" and "decryption" plus all possible stems, suffixes and contractions. This e-mail printout was the only hit.' He looked up. 'And the next unencrypted communication was this one...'

He pressed a remote on the desktop and the wall screen lit. Deakin saw a young man with unruly fair hair.

'Mr Tye.'

'Doctor Larsson?'

The young man nodded.

'Can you verify, please?'

'Let's both do it.'

Deakin watched as the man called Larsson leaned forward and touched the fingerprint pad on his system. There was a few seconds' delay and then Deakin saw the message:

Identity of caller confirmed as Rolf Linquist Larsson, born 13 January 1980, Stockholm, Sweden. Present location Järntorgsgatan 1–3, Stockholm, Sweden. GPS location 57.6042°N, 17.1619°E. Identity Certificate on file.

'Please encrypt, if you don't find that too funny,' said Tye.

Deakin saw Larsson nod and then the screen dissolved into white noise.

Deakin whistled. 'Why would he find the idea of encrypting *funny?*' he asked.

He picked up the text of the message that had preceded the videoconference and read it again with more care, this time paying greater attention to the thick wad of pages at the back of the message. As he read, Lynch rose, walked to the coffee percolator and refilled his friend's coffee mug. He had a huge smile on his face; not just because of the messages he had found, but also because the simple act of standing and walking to the coffee machine still gave him the most exquisite pleasure. He knew the incredible mental processing and feats of mechanical engineering that are required to keep the top-heavy human body upright, to move balance from one ten-by-three-inch platform to the other; to control the thousands of muscle, bone, temperature, blood, oxygen and sensory inputs, outputs and parameters required for such an apparently simple process to occur. He wondered how long it would be before he became blasé again and took his brain's astonishing information-processing capabilities for granted.

After a few minutes Deakin put the papers down.

'Want a replay?' asked Lynch. Deakin nodded and they watched again as Thomas Tye began his videoconference with an unknown Swede in Stockholm at three a.m. local time, over seven years earlier.

When the white noise reappeared Deakin picked up the printout again. 'So this Rolf Larsson sends an e-mail to Thomas Tye that says "New software. Want to discuss?" and with it he sends these Tye corporate annual accounts and these memos about marketing plans and office relocations – all in plain text. Then Tye calls him back and thinks Larsson might find it funny to encrypt their conversation. You've definitely got something.'

Lynch smiled. 'There's one more thing,' he added. 'I did some checking. Those accounts are getting on for eight years old. See the date on the e-mail message?'

Deakin flipped back to the top page and nodded.

Lynch pulled a folder towards him and took out a glossy

document. 'I borrowed this from the library,' he explained as he handed the booklet to Deakin. 'This is the annual report and accounts that the Tye Corporation did *actually* publish that year – just over two weeks later! They've been tweaked a bit here and there; the bottom line is different with more money in a forward contingency fund, but they're basically the same accounts.'

Deakin put the booklet down. 'Do your men friends kiss you often?' he asked with a laugh. 'I suppose you've traced this Larsson. Don't tell me, he's outside the door waiting to help us.'

Lynch grinned. 'No, he's not. But I know who he is. He's a maths genius. Honours graduate in pure maths from Stockholm University at age seventeen, first doctorate in pure maths when he was twenty-one. A nationally acclaimed prodigy. He was working on a second PhD in quantum mechanics when he had that conversation with Tye. Since then he's disappeared.'

'Disappeared?'

'Well, from the networks,' Lynch explained. 'There's not a trace of him. Even his entry with the World Certification Authority has lapsed. It looks like he didn't finish his second doctorate. There are no publications, no Web references, no university citations or news, no conference presentations, no guest lectures – nothing.'

'What does his university say?'

Lynch held up his hand. 'Whoa, Ron! You know I don't do legwork,' he said, grinning.

Furtrado snapped off the holo-image and uttered a particularly graphic Portuguese oath. He slumped back in his chair and wondered how best to break the news. Tom had been on a high on his way back from Moscow but this morning, the day after, when they should have been laying plans for the public announcement of the new state of Sybaria and the launch of the Phoebus Project, he had been in a foul mood.

'Get Jack Hendriksen in here *now*,' the tycoon had shouted at Connie without further elaboration.

Furtrado had made an excuse for getting back to his office

along the corridor. He knew his boss well enough to steer clear until this storm had blown over.

The lawyer looked down at his notes and wondered if the news could keep. It couldn't, so he pushed himself out of his chair and walked back to Tye's suite. He crossed the outer office with its gaggle of male and female executive assistants all dictating or involved in conferences, both physical and virtual, and entered Connie's office. As he did so Jack Hendriksen emerged from Tom's room, nodded pleasantly and sauntered out of the office in his peculiar, lithe way.

Connie was involved in her viewpers and she waved Furtrado through – there were only rare occasions when Tom's office door was closed to his most senior counsellor. As Furtrado stuck his head inside, Tom was standing by the picture window, staring out over the Atlantic ocean. The windows in the suite had darkened to eliminate the worst of the sun's glare. Tye heard Furtrado enter and he turned.

'Do you trust Hendriksen?' he asked abruptly.

Furtrado considered. 'Trust in what way?' He couldn't think that the security chief would be involved in any of the corporation's commercial deals. Hendriksen struck Furtrado as being a fit, watchful man, something of an outsider in the company, but the sort you would want on your side if there was ever any real trouble: a little dangerous, perhaps.

'He broke into my office upstairs while we were in Moscow,' said Tye quietly.

Furtrado whistled. 'How the hell did he do that?' he asked.

'Said it was part of a security review, did it to prove my security is no good. Swam up my swimming pool drain. Helped Tommy write me a fucking birthday card!' Tye picked a card up from his desk and waved it. 'And now he's given me these brochures advising on new household security systems!'

Furtrado had to stop himself smiling. He knew that even Tom wouldn't dare loose his temper on Hendriksen. He wished he had been present during their meeting.

'Take a look at him,' said Tye. 'He could be selling information.'

The lawyer nodded. He knew everything Tye did would be fully encrypted and he doubted that Hendriksen was a spy. It sounded more as if Tom was being taught a sharp lesson.

'There's some news from New York,' he ventured. 'Some outfit called Sloan Press has contracted to publish that libellous British book – the unauthorized biography.'

'Just swamp it in legals,' ordered Tye distractedly.

'The New York attorneys have done all that,' explained Furtrado. 'They've got twenty-one injunctions, but it looks like Sloan Press is prepared to publish and meet us in court – then the media will get it.'

Tye's attention snapped back. 'Who the hell is Sloan Press?' he asked. He pondered for a minute. 'Buy them, Marsello. We can always sell them on once we've dealt with this.'

'They're privately held, Tom,' explained Furtrado. 'They've turned down two good offers in the last year.'

'THEN BUY THE FUCKING BOOK,' shouted Tye, now getting seriously irritated. 'It will be cheaper and faster than doing the legals. Go and see this English writer, and buy her off.'

The housing estate was new – still under construction in some sections – but it looked like a safe place to raise children. The large lake, an inland extension of one of the many watery fissures that penetrated the Swedish mainland, provided a natural focus for the horseshoe-shaped community of houses. Children played in the streets and on the grass at the edge of a gently sloping lake shore. Chevannes smiled at the setting of sunshine, peace and safety, automatically comparing it to the dangerous Jamaican wasteland of the Kingston yards where he had spent his early years, before his family had won an immigration lottery and moved to America.

He had to ask twice for directions because these streets were so new they had not been included on the map he had bought at the airport in Stockholm.

He knew the woman's married name and he carried a wedding picture that was only three years old. He hadn't called ahead, partly because all case-related network communication was banned but mainly because his experience had taught him that better results were usually achieved when questions were asked without advance notice.

Chevannes identified the house, walked up to the front door and found it ajar. He pressed the bell push and waited. There were sounds from within and then a pretty woman with flyaway blonde hair appeared. It was definitely her. She was wearing a white blouse and loose-fitting tan trousers.

'Mrs Astrandh? Laila Astrandh? Formerly Laila Hagstrom?'

Laila smiled at the well-dressed man on her doorstep. 'What can I do for you?' she asked in the near-perfect American-English common to most Scandinavians. He realized he wouldn't need to use auto-translation and, not for the first time, reflected that it was a shame such devices were rapidly reducing the need to learn foreign langauges.

Chevannes showed his badge and watched as the housewife unclipped a VideoMate from her narrow belt and ran his ident signal past the World Digital Certification Authority. She smiled when she received confirmation and handed back the card.

'What can I do for you, Officer Chevannes?' she asked. She pronounced his name in the correct French way. There was a child's cry from within the house. 'Come in,' she invited. 'You'll have to excuse the mess.'

Chevannes followed her into a bright living room cluttered with children's toys. A small girl with golden curls stood in a corner telling off a Furry. Chevannes didn't understand her Swedish.

Her mother reproached the child gently, stroked the berated Furry and then sat with her daughter on her lap. She gestured for Chevannes to sit on the couch opposite.

'This is Aya-Karin. Say hello to Mr Chevannes,' Laila told her daughter in English. The child's pale blue eyes fastened on the elegant visitor. She half smiled and then nuzzled her face into her mother's blouse.

Laila said something else in Swedish to her daughter and the child turned her head towards Chevannes again. 'Hello,' she said with a bouncing intonation.

'Hi, Aya-Karin,' replied Chevannes in what he hoped was

his softest tone. He waggled his big fingers at her. The girl just stared at him and then looked up at her mother.

'I'll take her next door for a minute,' said Laila, rising with the child in her arms. She started for the door and then stopped when the Furry called out something after them. She returned and bent over so her daughter could scoop up the green rabbit. With a dazzling smile in Chevannes's direction, Laila left the room with both daughter and Furry.

The intelligence officer took in his surroundings. He had never been inside a Scandinavian home before. Even the most ordinary of objects seemed designed with flair: the bay window had a curve at the top that made it resemble a church window. The natural-stone fireplace doubled as a divider between the living room at the front of the house and a dining area at the rear. Despite the clutter of toys, the place was clean and comfortable. Chevannes sat back in the sofa enjoying this brief sojourn in what he might imagine was true domestic bliss.

'I left her with my neighbour,' Laila explained as she re-entered the room, pushing a lock of fair hair back behind one ear. 'So what can I do for you?' she asked as she sat down again. 'What does the United Nations want in Solna?'

'It's about Rolf Larsson,' said Chevannes, coming directly to the point. 'Do you know where he is currently?'

Laila raised her fair eyebrows and pursed her lips. She didn't seem overly surprised. 'No,' she said finally, 'I don't.'

'You two were ... close friends,' prompted Chevannes. 'Or so I was told at the university.'

The Swede smiled at his propriety. 'He was my boyfriend, for two years,' she confirmed. 'But I haven't seen him or spoken to him in over five years.'

'Did he ever have any dealings with Thomas Tye and the Tye Corporation back then?'

Laila smiled again and nodded. 'That's what changed him. He sold something to Thomas Tye – and made a lot of money. It completely messed him up. After that deal he began throwing money around as if he was insane. At first he went off on the star trail – you know, the Greek Islands, Thailand, China, New Zealand, Peru.'

Chevannes shook his head and shrugged. He didn't know.

'The places where you can view the stars best, away from urban lights and the main satellite networks,' explained Laila. She sighed as she recalled: 'At first it was all very professional. The best portable telescopes, cameras, computers and so on. Then ... well, we were staying up all night, sleeping all day. He started using drugs and stopped bothering with his telescopes. He'd just lie there on the beach or on a mountainside and stare up at the stars all night, every night. He seemed very unhappy in spite of all the money.'

She tailed off – back there with him again, in the time before she had met her husband Benji.

'We were only twenty-seven,' she offered by way of explanation. 'You know his parents had died in a boating accident three years before?'

Chevannes nodded. That was why she was the second stop on his visit, after the university. 'Do you know *what* it was he sold to Thomas Tye?' he prompted.

Laila shook her head. 'He wasn't allowed to talk about any of it. He said he'd signed a contract that forbade him to discuss it. After a few months he started ranting about how it had ruined his career. He'd just lie on his back and stare up at the stars, and go on and on. That's when he really started on the drugs and drinking.'

'What was he working on before he sold this thing to Tye?' asked Chevannes.

Laila had been examining the hands folded in her lap. Now she looked up. 'Would you like some tea or coffee?' she asked.

'That would be nice,' smiled the intelligence officer. 'Coffee would be good.'

'Come into the kitchen, we can talk there,' she said.

Chevannes followed her into a light and airy room, more of a conservatory, with a large informal eating area and another open log fireplace.

'He was a mathematician and an astrophysicist, not somebody in business,' Laila explained as she snapped the kettle on. She turned to face him, leaning back against the work surface. 'I think it was some sort of mathematical formula, or some sort of software. He kept it all to himself.' She hesitated. 'To be truthful, I wouldn't have understood it anyway. He was highly gifted mathematically, but to me it was all a foreign language.'

'You speak at least one foreign language very well,' said Chevannes, rather taken aback by his own gallantry. 'I spoke earlier to his supervisor at the University who said that one minute Doctor Larsson was working for a second PhD – in particle physics – then he was called away to do jury service. He never returned to the college, and he never explained why. The professor wasn't very happy to be reminded of this. He thought Doctor Larsson had a unique brain and could easily have become the youngest full maths professor in Europe. It seems he represented a massive loss to the university, and they were furious at the time.'

'I don't think he ever did any jury service,' recalled Laila as she spooned coffee into two mugs. 'He just cut himself off for a few weeks and then he went to visit Thomas Tye. The company even sent a private jet to collect him. When he came back he couldn't get over talking about how rich he was. He claimed he'd been paid billions of dollars, but at the time I rather thought ... well, *Je ne l'ai pas pris au pied de la lettre.*'

Chevannes looked at her, not understanding.

She smiled. 'I'm sorry, what's an equivalent saying in English? I didn't take it literally. I mean, I took it with a ...'

'... A pinch of salt?' guessed Chevannes.

Laila nodded. 'But he *did* have a lot of money. We travelled everywhere first class, stayed in the most wonderful hotels ...' She tailed off as she poured the boiling water, then stirred the granules absently. 'Milk?'

Chevannes shook his head, and they both sipped their black coffee. 'When did you last see him?' he prodded.

'It was about eighteen months later. We had continued to travel and he had got hooked on some really strong acid in Northern California – a special form of hallucinogenic developed in some remote lab near Mendocino. I tried the stuff and I didn't like it. But Rolf said it allowed him to set the motor free.'

She tapped the side of her head. Chevannes nodded.

'He would binge for a week at a time – totally out of it –

then stop completely for a few days. Then he'd start again. Eventually we ended up at some exclusive resort island on the Great Barrier Reef. We had this giant villa on stilts down on the beach. The domestic staff came over from a nearby island three times a day to leave food and change the laundry – not that Rolf cared about food or laundry by this time. I decided I couldn't take any more. I took the boat across to the main island one day while he was still passed out and caught the seaplane out – to Cairns on the Australian mainland. Then I headed down to Sydney and bought a ticket back to Stockholm. Just before I got on the plane I called the police and told them where Rolf was and about the drugs he had with him. He had brought everything from California – I think the stuff was too new to be categorized as really illegal. I hoped they'd get him some medical help.'

'And that was the last you heard of him?' asked the intelligence officer.

'Directly, yes,' admitted Laila. 'I've never spoken to him since.'

'But you have heard from him?' prompted Chevannes gently.

Laila sighed. 'I've never told Benji – my husband.'

Chevannes nodded. His job had long since proved that everybody had their secrets. 'We only want to talk to Mr Larsson. This isn't about you or your family.' But he couldn't promise that her secret would be safe until he knew what it was.

Laila nodded. She'd already said too much to hold back now. And she'd been waiting for this to emerge for a long time.

'He sends me money,' she said. 'Every month, to my old bank account. It's in my name before I was married – Hagstrom. It's quite a lot and I'm saving it for Aya-Karin.'

'Where does he send it from? Have you got any transaction records?' asked Chevannes.

Laila shook her head. 'It's all done by direct bank transfer. From a bank in Geneva – in Switzerland,' she added, as if a Jamaican-American might not know where Geneva was. *A sensible precaution with* any *American*, thought Chevannes.

She rose from the table and opened a drawer under the work surface. She rummaged through a pile of papers and extracted one sheet. Laila tore the header from the page and returned with it to the table.

'Here's the address of my bank and my account number,' she said as she sat down. 'They'll give you all the details. Tell them to contact me and I'll authorize them to give you the information you need.'

'And that's all – just the money?' persisted Chevannes.

Laila nodded. 'I thought someone would come eventually,' she admitted as she picked up her coffee mug again. 'Will I have to give it back? I've kept every bit of it since it started arriving. There's over thirty million dollars.'

'I'm afraid you've had a wasted trip,' said Marcia Fernandez, the chief administrator of the Sandler Cosmetic Clinic. 'There is absolutely nothing in our files that predates nineteen eighty-seven. We've been asked about that before.'

Haley allowed a sigh of disappointment to escape her lips.

'We do get enquiries about Thomas Tye from time to time,' offered Ms Fernandez. 'But we're a different sort of clinic altogether now. I understand the building was almost completely gutted before it was renovated. Then the Tye Foundation sold the property on to our organization.'

'Any contact with the previous patients?' asked Haley.

The woman looked at her quizzically. 'It wasn't exactly the type of place to run an alumni programme, Miss Voss.'

Haley's irreverent and unruly imagination instantly assembled a fantasy scenario of former mental-asylum inmates attempting a reunion. What would they say to each other? She wondered again what on earth could have been so wrong with the five-year-old Thomas Tye to warrant his committal there.

'Are *any* of the original medical staff here?' Haley persisted, as she pulled her thoughts together.

This produced a chuckle. 'No, but I sometimes think I could use them,' smiled Marcia Fernandez. 'This might now be a cosmetic surgery clinic but we do get some strange types in, if you know what I mean.'

'What about janitors, non-medical staff? Or administrators, secretaries, accountants?'

'Miss Voss, it's nearly *thirty years* since my corporation bought the building. There's no one here from those days. I'm really sorry ...'

Haley put her coffee cup down, then rose. 'Well, thanks for making time to see me,' she said as she halted her data capture.

At the end of the long gravel drive, Haley turned right towards Springfield and the I90. Her adverts among the Thomas Tye communities had elicited a particularly interesting response from an individual in Philadelphia. She had a long drive ahead.

Even though they had chosen a region that was not covered by any of the surveillance-satellite networks, they realized that sooner or later the scar would be noticed and, in due course, investigated. Accordingly, they designed the test so that the affected area would look like a long teardrop, suggestive of a gouge caused by a low-angled, burning descent. They also knew that once soil investigations began any meteor theory would be quickly discounted. But, given the absolute remoteness of the Western Amazon basin, they calculated that any such examination would happen many months later, long after their new service was launched and delivering its phenomenal benefits. Marsello Furtrado, the only native Brazilian with knowledge of the project, predicted it would probably be years before the Ministry of the Interior got round to sending an expedition out to such an inaccessible region.

There had been arguments within the team about destroying even a comparatively small area of such an important ecological environment but, as the Director of Solar Focus reasoned, the Amazon basin occupied over two and a half million square miles and the relatively small area they planned to affect would regenerate naturally and regrow with the benefits of the invigorating, fertilizing nitrogen that would be released as acres of rainforest were turned to ash. The trial would also test the first-phase energy network at its most extreme range and Tom was adamant he wanted the data on what was possible at southern latitudes.

So, on the same evening during which Haley enlivened her long drive across country by flicking through the channels on the satellite radio system in her rented car, eight square miles of Brazil's vast tropical rain forest started to experience intense nocturnal sunshine. At first the daytime creatures of the forest re-emerged after a severely truncated night and resumed their activities, briefly meeting some of their nocturnal cohabitees as the latter grudgingly sought their shelters long before their usual order of business was complete. Birds sang and epiphytes near the top of the tree canopy opened their buds. But the heat continued to rise and, as the cloud cover sweeping down from the foothills of the Andes burned off, the continual dripping at the forest floor began to cease for the first time in over one hundred million years.

Then the entire section of forest began to steam and a mist filled the gaps between the trees. For a few hours the dense tree canopy managed to protect the abundant and multifarious life forms beneath but, shortly after midnight, the highest layer of foliage started to crackle and burn beneath the tightly focused and magnified output of all twelve energy stations. The steam swiftly evaporated and, three hours before dawn, the lachrymiform target area was ablaze, its dehydrated, flash-baked foliage, liana and fauna erupting almost spontaneously as fierce concentrated beams seared through the burned-out tree canopy and reached to the ground.

Watching on monitors fed by the Tye Argus satellite network, the DSF ordered a cessation shortly before dawn. As planned, the winds from the foothills began dispersing the smoke and the soaking wet of the surrounding jungle contained the conflagration whilst itself suffering only minimal collateral damage.

Thomas Tye's image appeared on the monitor. 'Congratulations, Doctor,' Tye greeted his Director of Solar Focus. 'You will ensure no recordings of the test are filed, won't you?'

The small, highly paid and well-trusted team clapped enthusiastically. Their measurements, received from ground-level calorimeters that they had parachuted in, had transmitted results far better than expected before the instruments too were engulfed in flames.

*

Haley had arrived in Chalfont, a northern suburb of Philadelphia, just before midnight. She had prebooked a motel room and had found the inn, situated on the main street, with ease. Her appointment was not until eleven a.m. the next morning, so after a lie-in she had treated herself to an American breakfast – *where they really know how to cook eggs, bacon and hash-browns*, she thought as she enjoyed it.

As she checked out she asked directions from the desk clerk. He recognized Miss Hattie Jones's address. It would only take her five minutes. Haley took her time loading up the rental car and then, on a bright, sunny Wednesday morning, she set off to visit the woman who had responded to her advertisement for fresh information about the great Thomas Tye.

Understandably, her correspondent had been reluctant to disclose full details without discovering what was on offer. She claimed to have documentary information about Thomas Tye's very earliest years, the period before he was institutionalized. In response to Haley's e-mailed request for further background, Hattie Jones had written simply, 'I worked at a clinic which treated Thomas Tye as a baby and I kept a copy of the records.' Nothing Haley could say would get the woman to offer further evidence of her claim, and the old lady – Haley worked out that she had to be at least seventy years old – had refused even to name the institution to which she had referred.

Haley found the street, then the house, without difficulty. She parked and walked up a short path to the low, single-storey residence. The other homes in the street looked respectable but, like the paintwork on this property, gently faded. She rapped on the wooden frame of the mesh outer door. When there was no answer, she tugged at the mesh door and it opened easily. Extracting her car keys from her purse, she tapped on the glass of the front door beyond. In a few moments she spotted movement from the hallway within and she allowed the mesh door to close once more. The inner door opened and a small, birdlike woman was looking up at her.

'Miss Jones? I'm Haley Voss.'

The woman pushed open the outer door and extended her hand. 'Miss Voss, and you're on time. So polite of you.'

Haley smiled and took the wizened hand. She estimated that this neatly dressed woman was probably well into her eighties.

Hattie Jones stepped back into her hall, allowing Haley to enter. She ushered her into a small living room and gestured to a Victorian grandmother chair that needed restuffing. 'Sit down, sit down. The kettle's boiled, I'll make tea. My mother came from England. I know you probably haven't tasted a decent cup since you arrived.'

Haley smiled her thanks. That was true.

'Don't realize the water needs to be boiling to split the leaf, that's the problem here,' said Miss Jones over her shoulder as she disappeared.

Haley took in the clean but faded room with its vaguely musty smells. She switched her VideoMate to record and put on her clear-glass viewpers. Then her host reappeared with a tray that looked far too heavy for her.

Refusing Haley's help, she lowered the tray onto a low table, then sat down and began to pour.

Haley responded to her polite questions. No, she hadn't been to Chalfont before, nor even to Philadelphia. Yes, she had visited the States before on several occasions.

'I know you're a successful writer,' said Hattie Jones with a grin. 'I've looked you up!'

Haley smiled back. 'Well, I hope this will be my most important book so far. My publishers seem to think so.'

She was wondering how to prompt the woman to get down to business, but she needn't have been concerned. Miss Jones rose suddenly, crossed to an old mahogany sideboard, pulled open a drawer and returned with a thick buff file.

'So how much is my reward?' she asked, suddenly very businesslike.

'Well, that depends,' replied Haley hesitantly. 'I mean, it depends on what information you have to offer. I have a research budget, of course, and I...'

'I understand.' Miss Jones nodded. 'You need to know what I have here. My nephew is a lawyer, over in the city, so I asked him about the best way to handle this.'

She extracted a crisp white sheet of paper from the file and handed it to her visitor.

'It's a non-disclosure agreement, Miss Voss,' explained the old lady as Haley studied the document. 'Very simply, it allows me to show you what I have, but you aren't free to use any of it until we have agreed terms. How does that sound?'

It sounded very fair, and suddenly Haley's heart raced. If this woman's lawyer nephew considered the information sufficiently valuable to draw up this agreement, then it could be something very special.

She smiled again. 'This looks fine.' She started to rummage in her bag, then looked up to find Miss Jones offering her a pen.

Haley signed and dated the document and returned it. The old lady folded it, neatly inserted it in an envelope and placed it on the sofa behind her.

'So,' she said. 'Where to begin? Tell me, have you heard of Professor Charles Eon?'

Haley searched her memory. 'No ... I don't think so ...'

'The sex doctor,' prompted Miss Jones. 'He was always on TV.'

Haley searched again, but shook her head.

Hattie Jones shrugged. 'No, well, I suppose it was long before your time – back in the nineteen-sixties and -seventies. And poor Charlie was best known here, in the States, of course.'

Haley nodded, waiting.

'Charlie died last month, Haley – may I call you Haley?'

Haley smiled her consent.

'He was nearly ninety-five, and died a week before his birthday. There weren't many at the funeral service.' They was a silence as the old woman thought over those events. There she pulled herself back to the present. 'Charlie was the Professor of Psychosexual Medicine at the University Hospital,' she explained. 'He founded the department in the 1950s, and I was his secretary for thirty-two years.'

Haley smiled again, encouragingly.

'I'm afraid some of the things we did ... Well, Charlie was

sure they were for the best at the time...' Now she looked embarrassed, almost mortified. She folded her hands on top of the thick folder.

'Well, that was a long time ago. Later on, Charlie sort of retreated from the world. I always knew he had a good heart, but the press were very cruel...'

Haley waited as the woman fought some inner battle.

'I always swore I wouldn't do anything with this—' she tapped the folder '—while Charlie was still alive. But now...' She tailed off again, looking down, then up again, some internal decision made. 'But it happened a very long time ago, nearly fifty years.'

Haley nodded, silently screaming for Hattie Jones to get on with it.

'Like I said, I was his secretary – well, secretary to the whole clinic, really. I had to type all the old files into the first computer they installed, and it took me months. I was instructed to trash all the paper files when I was through, but I didn't trust that machine so I brought them back here for safety. Never did need them, though, I must admit,'

She changed tack. 'I remember the little boy, he was very pretty. But he was a classic case, like most of the others that were referred to Charlie. He's become so famous now, hasn't he?'

Haley nodded once more.

'I'd like to think it might help him ... well, deal with things, ... if his case was known. He's never married, has he? So many of them got over it better once it was all out in the open. Some even got married...'

Haley wanted to scream out loud. She wanted to tear that file off the old lady's knees.

Hattie Jones looked down at it again. Suddenly she thrust her hand into the folder, withdrawing a pile of yellowing papers and black-and-white photographs, and laid them on the cushions beside her. She leaned forward and handed the empty file cover to Haley. 'Let's start with this,' she said.

Haley took the empty file with shaking hands and read the printed headings and the handwritten entries:

Family Name: *Tye*
Forenames: *Thomas, Richmond*
Date of Birth: *07/01/66*
Date of admission: *04/07/67*
Putative sex: *Male*
Assigned sex: *Female*
Assigned forenames: *Thomasina, Rachel*

The former secretary lifted the pile of paper records and photographs from the cushions and placed them on her lap.

'Now, what am I bid?' she asked with a sweet, old-lady smile.

EIGHTEEN

Rep. Robarts Calls on White House to Intervene In Tye Aerospace Experiment — 'Satellites Could Be Weapons'
By a WALL STREET JOURNAL Staff Reporter
WASHINGTON — In a stinging attack on what he called 'the failure of White House foreign and defense policies,' House Minority Leader Ronald Robarts today accused the White House, the Pentagon and NASA of suppressing research which, he claims, has identified a chain of deep-space location satellites launched by Tye Aerospace, Inc. as having weapons potential.

Addressing a House Judiciary Committee, Mr Robarts showed what he claimed was an edited extract of a Top Secret NASA/CIA report and urged the President and Secretary of Defense to be honest with the American people about the threat to the nation's security posed by this chain of distant satellites.

'NASA knows these aren't simply a positioning system for the solar system but they won't tell the people what they do know,' he said. 'There are fourteen deep-space vehicles in orbit above the northern hemisphere — all of them in solar-stationary orbits. Twelve of them are deployed above the night side of the Earth's northern hemisphere, two

are positioned sunwards of our planet. I challenge
the White House and the Department of Defense to
publish the full text of this report. These things
could be weapons – the people have a right to know.'

Following the hearing, Mr Robarts's spokes-
woman played down the more sensational side of
his speech. 'We're not claiming that these are a
definite threat, we are simply asking for the facts
to be disclosed,' she said. 'We want to know why
the White House has remained silent on this topic.'

Tye Corporation's public relations agency in
New York professed amusement at the congressman's accusations. 'The Tye Corporation is not in
the defense business – period,' said a spokesperson. 'We are creating a network of satellites which
will provide a navigation and positioning system
for research purposes and future missions. The
Aerospace Division has many Earth-orbit and deep
space experiments, all of them peaceful in nature.
We welcome all enquiries.'

Mr Robarts, a long-time champion of the
American defense industry, is seeking nomination
as the Republican party presidential candidate in
next year's election.

Ron Deakin snapped the screen off. He could recognize a
planted story ten miles off. This was *getting political*!

There was a long-standing statute in Swiss law decreeing that if
a police officer, Customs investigator, intelligence officer or
other official from a foreign power (with or without diplomatic
status) was found on Swiss territory asking questions about the
provenance, ownership or status of a bank account, deposit box
or any other financial or property instrument, he or she would
be summarily deported and thereafter denied access to the
nation. It was an effective deterrent to inquiry.

In recent years, under pressure from other members of the

European Union, the World Bank and foreign governments, the Swiss had paid some lip-service to improving financial transparency and drug barons could no longer be sure of the absolute discretion they were once promised. But apart from this concession to its membership of the EU and its obligations to the international community, it seemed that the Swiss still resisted real change. Keeping and protecting wealth and its privacy, on behalf of all those who were able to pay for the privilege, was their business and it had been so for many hundreds of years. The Swiss would no more readily abandon their economic *raison d'être* than would the Arabs their oil, the Belgians their chocolate or the Scots their whisky.

Michael Chevannes broke through this veil of state-mandated secrecy. It took him a week to do so and the one-time coded fax transmissions involved Ron Deakin in New York and Dr Yoave Chelouche in Geneva. Finally, one early-morning phone call from the world's chief banker to the home of the president of Premier Security Bank Swiss succeeded in negating a tradition of banking secrecy that had begun with the Edict of Nantes in 1685. *Perhaps the country is becoming more responsible to the world's financial community*, thought Chevannes later the same morning as he examined the many accounts and the piles of paper correspondence of Rolf Linquist Larsson, one of the bank's most wealthy and secretive private depositors.

Altogether, Chevannes found the equivalent of over twenty-three billion US dollars in 143 separate accounts, bonds, property companies and shareholdings. He also discovered the two main alternative identities used by the depositor. Interestingly, Larsson kept the majority of his vast investment portfolio in the Tye Corporation and Tye-related stocks. As Chevannes looked back over the six-year history of the accounts he shook his head and muttered to himself in amazement. The Swede had quadrupled his fortune simply by placing his faith in the fortunes of Thomas Tye's companies.

When he had finished his detailed note-taking – despite his privileged access, photocopying was not allowed – he left the bank and booked himself a one-way ticket to Lima, Peru.

*

'I've never been on a boat before,' exclaimed Tommy. 'This is fun.'

'This is fun!' echoed Jed. 'It's super!'

'Super,' shouted Tommy in turn. He was picking up Jed's English accent and superlatives.

As they passed the outer limits of Hope Town Marina, Jack eased forward the levers controlling the throttles of the mighty GE turbo-diesels. The huge motor yacht lifted up to its full planing height as they gathered speed.

A light spray flew into the high, open flying bridge and Tommy laughed with joy as he clung to the safety rail, Jed clamped firmly under his arm. Despite the size of the craft and Tommy's swimming prowess, they had insisted he wear a bright orange life jacket. He had asked for one for Jed too but nothing could be found that was small enough. Calypso had found a solution by borrowing a lifebelt-style cup-holder from the bar on the diving deck. She had deftly fitted this around the caterpillar's middle.

Tommy's father had put up suprisingly little resistance when Calypso had reintroduced the idea of the trip. For the first time since she had known him, Tom seemed at a complete loss.

'I shall always be in your debt, Calypso,' he had begun.

She had already discovered that apart from the severed artery and some lesions to the surrounding tissue, Tommy's forearm had suffered no significant damage. She and Emily Pettigrew had managed to complete the procedure and close the boy's arm in less than half an hour.

'That's what I'm trained to do,' she had told Tye simply.

As he looked at her, she thought she could detect tears. 'My mother committed suicide, Calypso,' he told her sadly. 'I'm sure Tommy hasn't inherited the gene, but . . .'

Calypso now knew why Tom could feel so sure about Tommy's genetic make-up, but he seemed absolutely deflated by his son's recent actions.

'Do you see any signs of depression in him, Doctor?'

'All self-harm is a form of depression, Tom,' she said gently.

But Calypso had laid down tough terms for continuing as the boy's protector on the island. She had demanded twenty-four-hour access to the child, had asked for a bedroom to be made available for her close to his, insisted that he be allowed to attend the school again, and she made it mandatory that he should be allowed to make supervised visits to other homes on the island and, under special circumstances like this, even off the island.

She had then read Thomas Tye the accepted lore on juvenile psychosis, as laid down by the paediatric psychiatrists Walsh and Rosen, the ultimate authorities on self-injury in childhood. She had explained how Tommy's actions were indicative of a deeply buried depression and that without treatment the condition would deepen even more. And she had warned him where that would lead.

'Eventually to a suicide attempt that *does* succeed,' she had said simply but firmly, her voice ringing off the marble walls as she sat on one of the vast white sofas in Tom's reception hall. 'The youngest recorded suicide to date has been an eight-year-old girl – another isolated child – in Los Angeles. She was the daughter of one of the world's foremost female movie stars, and she started self-harming at only six.'

Calypso saw a strange panic on Tom's face, and pressed her attack home.

'Yes, he has everything to live for, but because of the way you overprotect him, *he* feels he has nothing. A child's values and sense of self are gained not only from parents and guardians, but more especially from others around them – primarily their peers. That's where a child learns his or her place in the world.'

Tom had at last started to remonstrate. Again he had protested that Tommy was unlike other children. Calypso understood what he meant but to her he was simply Tommy, and she was determined that she would now focus only on securing the boy's happiness. This, she realized, was more important to her than anything. Even more important than her growing fondness for Jack Hendriksen.

Finally, she had held her hand up. 'I could not care less if he was the last of a royal line,' she announced. 'That boy will only become a happy person *if* he is allowed to experience a normal childhood. If you want him ever to be proud of who he is, also proud of you and able to play a useful part in managing this incredible empire, you have no choice but to let him find himself in his own way first. That's how humans work, Tom. Believe me.'

So Calypso had moved into the great house, and into a room next to Tommy's. Gradually she had helped him talk about the incident.

'It felt like a dream, Calypso,' he told her. 'I thought I'd never see you again. I didn't know what I'd done wrong, and nobody would tell me where you were.'

She had hugged him unreservedly. Now that she knew his true origins, some of her worries about the normal doctor-patient relationship could be discarded. He was not like other child patients, as he had no 'natural' parents. There was no precedent in medical history for how he should be treated. Therefore Calypso allowed herself to run on instinct. Far from being repelled by the boy's scientific genesis, she loved him all the more. She knew clones were a phenomenon of nature – in identical twins, for instance – and she could see clearly what had caused his problems: they were all to do with nurture and little to do with nature. She had prescribed a mild antidepressant for Tommy, although within two days of her moving into the house he seemed to exude an abundance of energy. Although keeping the perception to herself, she felt sure that it was her own presence in the house that restored his happiness so quickly.

She had decided to test Tye's acceptance of their new relationship, so one day she had simply informed Connie Law that she was going to take Tommy on a visit to Mayaguana, to see her mother, a week hence. She then sat back and waited for another explosion. It never came.

'Look after him well – and enjoy the trip,' was Tom's surprising response in a live video call that appeared to originate in Ethiopia.

But he had followed up his permission with a mandate that

Jack, Pierre and Stella should join them for this excursion and had stipulated that they should take his personal power yacht, not the usual helicopter.

'Doctor, it's a matter of odds. The statistics for helicopter crashes are appalling on a per-mile basis,' he said with monumental insensitivity, 'So I insist you take *Hope's Dream.*'

When this conversation was over Calypso had just stared at his image frozen in the intense sunlight of East Africa. She wondered how any man could care so much for his son's safety yet understand so little of other people's feelings.

Hope's Dream was the ultimate development in large high-speed power craft. It was 160 feet of snarling white-painted aluminium, darkened glass and stainless steel, so raked that it looked as if it was permanently lying in wait. It was a triple-decked Sunseeker with twin flying bridges – one enclosed, one open. On this fine day, Jack, Calypso, Tommy and Jed stood aloft on the open bridge on the top deck. Jack was at the wheel, operating the controls of two 2,800 HP turbo-diesels capable of propelling the huge craft at up to fifty knots.

Jack had taken the precaution of visiting *Hope's Dream* on the evening before their trip to give the vessel and the crew the once-over. After his nightly run along the beach, he had caught the Mag down to the marina. Though he had seen the vessel on many occasions, as had everybody else on Hope Island, he had never been aboard it and except for a weekly maintenance check he had never seen it leave the harbour.

The skipper, Henry Singleton, was welcoming. He was a white Jamaican and a Yacht Master, qualified to sail around the globe navigating solely by celestial navigation. Indeed, Jack found the sailor sorely chafed by extended port-bound duties.

'She's never been out properly since she was delivered here,' sighed Singleton as he poured Jack a beer in the vast recovered-walnut and farmed-leather stateroom. ScentSims boosted the aroma of polished wood and rich Connolly-tanned hide. 'I'll be proud to let you have her for the little boy's outing.'

In his early days in the Navy, Jack had been trained to pilot every sort of craft, small submarines included, and also to fly a wide variety of aircraft. It was a proud boast of his unit that they

were capable of operating on land, sea and air, and once
Singleton had heard the evidence of Jack's nautical experience,
he was delighted to hand over the forty-seven-million-dollar
craft to the corporation's security chief.

'I'd like you and your crew to come with us, of course,' Jack
hastened to add. 'As you'll be skipper, I'd like you to plot the
course. We'll need to stay well away from Cuban waters with
things there being as they are. Then I'd be grateful if you would
personally pilot us in to Mayaguana. I see there's a long coral
reef across the harbour entrance and I'm sure nobody knows
these islands as well as you.'

Singleton nodded. 'It's a very beautiful island. But are you
sure you only want to visit Mayaguana? We could be in Santo
Domingo in the same time, where there's much more to do and
see.'

Jack hated to dash the skipper's hopes of a trip to a larger
island with a real town, but he knew Calypso had her own
reasons for wanting to take Tommy to visit her home island.

Joe Tinkler had begun to feel like his old self. In the seven weeks
he had been building his new fund he had already recaptured
all his old pension-management clients plus an additional
fourteen. He had been particularly successful in raising Asian
investments and he was surprised that so many of his new Far
Eastern clients expressed pleasure that he had moved to Geneva.
He hadn't realized just how partisan overseas fund managers
could be. They simply hadn't wanted to invest their members'
savings with him while his fund had been based in New York.

Tye's stocks were still riding high and Joe was spreading his
risks with care. He had subscribed heavily to an initial public
offering by LifeLines Inc., a Tye Life Sciences subsidiary, even
though the flotation of the organ-matching and broking company had been handled by Rakusen-Webber. He hadn't had
to talk directly to Morgenstein yet, but all his other former
colleagues were delighted Joe was back in the market – even if
he was now playing against their house.

His fund now stood at 1.76 trillion in US dollars, although,
at Chelouche's request, he was converting to the European

common currency at the end of each of his allotted trading 'days'. At the current exchange rate that was just over three-quarters of a trillion euros. Then there was that other pot: although Tye's stocks had performed well, Joe had made a few experimental but discreet market interventions and, as Chelouche had promised, the World Bank had settled every claim – and without question. Joe once again controlled the world's largest external shareholding in the Tye Corporation and its subsidiaries and he had unequalled power to influence the market prices. As requested, Joe intervened judiciously and discreetly, learning when an 'irrational' purchase or disposal had the greatest effect on other investors.

'Good evening, Joe,' greeted Chelouche, entering the room. Madame Pioline had requested that Joe should 'drop in' at the World Bank's European headquarters for an early-evening cocktail. Although all global stock markets traded on a twenty-four-hour basis, seven days a week, Joe chose to limit his personal activities to a nine-hour working day. During the rest of the cycle his software agents bought, sold or held according to the daily parameters he set them. His VideoMate would only be paged if any of his pre-set limits were breached.

Joe put down his Bloody Mary and rose. He sank back into his seat as the banker waved him down and came to sit opposite. A neat whisky had been poured and was waiting for him on the low table. He raised it in salute.

'Are things buoyant in the Tye markets?'

Joe nodded. 'Holding well, sir.' He couldn't yet bring himself to call the esteemed banker by his first name.

'No worries over what that congressman says – that this Phoebus Project has weapons potential?' asked Chelouche as he flipped open the lid of his humidor.

Joe had read the story several times. He had discussed it with half a dozen other fund managers. '*Who are they going to scrap with?*' James Dodd at DRKB in London had asked dismissively. '*Doesn't make any sense, Tinkler.*' Efi Arazi at Lehman Brothers in New York had laughed. '*Another crazy Republican. There's an election next year. You should know better, Joe.*' Joe was forced to agree. None of the markets had paid any attention.

'No, sir. It's had no impact,' he confirmed as he lifted his drink again.

Chelouche nodded. He held out the box to Joe. The fund manager shook his head and he watched as the banker selected a large Havana cigar, cut the end and lit it carefully from an oversized match. Chelouche blew out a great cloud of smoke and returned his attention to Joe.

'Do you consider the Tye Corporation could be vulnerable to a takeover?'

Joe almost choked on his cocktail. Then he looked up to see if the banker was serious. He seemed to be.

Joe shook his head and put his drink down. He had to let a laugh escape. 'No way, sir. It's the world's richest corporation. The core stock is trading at two hundred and eighty-four, maybe two eighty-five times annual earnings. No other company could get close to the necessary finance, no matter how much debt leverage they managed to find.'

Chelouche nodded. 'But what would it cost – theoretically?' he asked.

Joe felt his eyes widening as he considered. He shook his head. 'I've no idea, sir. I'd have to build some models.'

'Then build them,' instructed the world's banker. 'That's your second objective, Joe. I want you to build up positions that allow your fund to take control of the majority of the shareholding in the core Tye Corporation.'

Chelouche had said it quietly and Joe felt an urgent need to have him repeat it. But he knew what he had heard. He wasn't sure if it was even possible.

'Do it quietly, Joe, and use a large number of proxy accounts. Get option agreements from the other main institutional shareholders. I know you will have to guarantee significant premiums, but do it. And above all, don't allow word to spread – tie a confidentiality agreement into the options. Each one of them must think it's an exclusive deal for them. Now, listen carefully Joe...'

Joe looked up and saw the basset-hound eyes boring into him.

'Do not discuss any of this operation on the networks. Don't make video calls, send e-mails or talk to anybody on your VideoMate. You'll need to travel to see the main shareholders personally and, when you discuss this, you must ensure they do not record any part of the conversation. Use paper option forms. This is absolutely vital. Do I make myself clear?'

Joe nodded. It was crystal clear. But absurd.

'Remember, each one must think it is a one-off personal deal for them. There must be no suggestion that you are buying elsewhere. We may never have to exercise those options, but I want them all in place.'

'We'll have to serve notice on the Tye Corporation, sir,' he objected. 'They can block such a move in dozens of ways.'

'Where is Tye incorporated, Joe?'

'In Hope Island, sir, but . . .'

'Our lawyers say the EUUSA notification rules apply only to corporations that are *lex domicilii*, legally resident, in regulated territories. Hope Island isn't one. When Tye moved his corporation out of Delaware, he escaped taxes and regulation but he also gave up the protection of the national governments that run EUUSA.'

Joe had no idea whether Chelouche was right or wrong. But he knew that at least the Securities and Exchange Commission would have to be notified, as it was when any holder's stock rose above five per cent of issued shares.

'We'll have to submit a 13-D to the SEC, sir, that's the rules.'

Chelouche regarded him silently from under his dark bushy eyebrows.

'OK, OK, I know, I know,' sighed Joe. 'The World Bank makes the rules. But even if I could get the stock, even if we could build a majority voting position, do you realize how much money those options might cost? The banking operation alone would be trillions. Then there would be the poison parachutes: every board protects its members that way. They have agreements with the company that if it becomes subject to a hostile takeover they receive such huge compensation packages that it makes any such move ludicrously expensive.'

'It's only money, Joe,' said the world's banker.

*

Calypso was standing surrounded by children, many of whom she knew, all of whom knew her. She was an honorary *macoumère* to many and official godmother to two of them. Tommy clung to her hand apprehensively. He had never seen so many children before, all of them shades of brown and black. There must have been forty or fifty of them and at least half of them seemed to be related to his Calypso. They danced and sang and ran around the party.

'Miss World,' they called, 'Miss World,' for that was how their parents talked about her.

Calypso was the tiny island's most famous export and her brief success as a beauty queen fifteen years earlier still meant far more to the population than her later achievements as a doctor. Every time she visited, she was given this escort of laughter. She realized she would have some explaining to do to Tommy.

They walked through the small town of Abraham's Bay and past the old mission schoolhouse where her father had taught. Calypso skipped off the road and peered in through the windows. A class of the more dedicated Mayaguanian children had their heads down over their books and were writing in silence. She stooped and picked Tommy up so he could see.

'This is where I went to school,' she whispered as he gazed wonderingly at normality. 'My father used to be the teacher.'

They had not been noticed and Calypso put her finger to her lips, signalling for Tommy and the other children not to disturb the young scholars inside. They continued through the small town until they reached the outskirts beyond and then followed a dirt path that wound through a grove of loblolly trees. They emerged at the beachfront beside a blue-painted stone cottage surrounded by a well-kept garden. The sound of hummingbirds and cicadas competed with children's shouts and laughter on the sand.

Calypso smiled and waved at them as she led Jack and Tommy up the short path to the front door. Calypso had bought this cottage for her mother fifteen years ago, when she had first started to earn some significant money from her modelling and sponsorship activities.

The day-carer opened the door with a smile and Calypso
led Tommy into a bright, white-walled interior. Mrs Browne
was dressed specially for the occasion and sitting upright on
the dark sofa. She was small and pencil-slim and wore a neat
powder-blue suit with a navy blouse. Calypso smiled: her
mother still had style. She stood up as Calypso crossed the
room to hug her. The elderly lady reached up and lovingly
touched her daughter's hair.

'And who have you brought with you?' asked Mrs Browne,
turning around.

'This is Tommy,' said Calypso. 'He's my friend.'

'Hello,' said Tommy uncertainly.

The old lady reached out a sinewy hand that Tommy shook.

'Welcome to Mayaguana, Tommy,' said Mrs Browne
ceremoniously.

'Thank you very much,' replied Tommy with boyhood
gravitas.

To Jack it all seemed slightly surreal.

'And this is Jack,' said Calypso. 'He's also my friend. He
works with me on Hope Island.'

The old lady looked up and squinted with her fading
eyesight. 'My, you *have* brought a good-looking man to my
house,' she laughed.

'Hello, Mrs Browne,' said Jack as he took her hand. He
suddenly realized he was being introduced to his girlfriend's
mother – if Calypso was his girlfriend. He turned to look and he
saw a mischievous smile hovering around Calypso's mouth.
He suddenly felt very uncomfortable.

'Sit, sit,' ordered their hostess. 'We'll have tea in a minute.'

Calypso sat down at one side of her mother on the firm sofa,
and Tommy on the other. Jack found an upright chair near the
door. He felt reassured that Pierre and Stella had followed them
discreetly through town and would now be in position at the
front and the back of the house.

'And how old are you?' Mrs Browne turned to her young
guest.

'Seven,' answered Tommy hesitantly. He wasn't used to
conversation with strangers.

'Do you go to school?'

Tommy nodded shyly. Then he remembered what Calypso had told him about her mother's eyesight. 'Yes, well, I'll be going again soon, won't I Calypso?'

'Yes, you will,' affirmed Calypso. 'I think Tommy's ready to attend full time.'

Her mother looked towards the kitchen, where her day-carer was assembling cups and plates for afternoon tea. Calypso could smell freshly baked johnny-cake.

'I'm Jed,' said Jed, filling any silence as he was supposed to.

'Oh, my manners!' said Mrs Browne, peering along the sofa in puzzlement. 'You've brought a friend, Tommy. And are *you* going to school as well?'

'I'm a caterpillar,' Jed explained.

There was a short silence as she attempted to digest this information.

'It's called a Furry, Mum,' explained Calypso. 'A toy you can talk to.'

'He's my friend,' affirmed Tommy, clutching the caterpillar even closer.

'Ow, that hurts,' complained Jed.

'Don't harm him, dear,' said Mrs Browne anxiously.

Tommy laughed at the idea. 'He doesn't really mind. He doesn't feel anything. He just says things like that.'

'Mayaguana is the most easterly of the Bahamian islands,' offered Jed. 'There are about three hundred people resident on the island and it remains almost wholly unspoiled.'

'My,' marvelled Mrs Browne. 'You do know a lot.'

'Mayaguana is the original Indian name for the island,' continued Jed, undaunted. 'It is a paradise for sailors, boat owners and divers because of its extensive anchorage and coral reef. During the year temperatures vary between nineteen and thirty degrees Celsius. Friendly and inexpensive accommodation can be found at the Abraham's Bay Inn, in the island's main town.'

'He does know a lot,' agreed Calypso. 'Don't you think Jed knows a lot, Jack?'

'He does know a lot,' laughed Jack. 'I've thought that before.'

'Shut up,' Tommy hissed to Jed.

Mrs Browne started to laugh and they all laughed with her. Jed promptly fell silent.

'We've brought a toy pet for you too, Mum,' said Calypso.

She bent to pull a package from her bag lying on the floor. She leaned across her mother and handed it to Tommy to make the presentation.

'This is Roger,' said Tommy, holding the box out shyly.

The elderly woman took the box and opened the lid. Calypso had deliberately ruled out gift-wrapping in order not to spoil the moment. She watched her mother lift out the ball of warm fur, and quietly removed the box from sight.

'You say hello to Roger,' suggested Calypso.

Mrs Browne began stroking the CatPanion.

'I'm Roger,' said the cat in a soothing voice. 'What's *your* name?'

'Let me show you around the garden,' murmured Calypso to Jack and Tommy. 'We'll leave Mum alone with her new companion for a while.'

'See you later, Roger,' called Jed as they left.

Deakin was calling the emergency meeting to order. Almost forty section heads of Operation Iambus were crowded into the conference room on the eleventh floor of the UN Secretariat building. The UNISA Exec was perched on a battered projector stand.

'OK, just how interested is Washington becoming in the Tye Corporation?' he asked. 'Let's put two and two together and see what we get. Marv ... what do your sources in the White House say?'

Marvin Girdlong, a former Chief of Staff at the White House, rubbed his day-old facial stubble and studied the notes on his DigiPad. It had been Marvin's research that had prompted Deakin to call the meeting.

'Hendriksen was right,' he began. 'There's been no official announcement but it looks like the Chief is going to attend the party. They've had to reschedule a visit by the Prime Minister of Israel and two fund-raising dinners have been postponed. The

Secret Service has already started to re-roster for that weekend. Oh, we also hear the First Lady's cancelled a charity appearance in New York.'

Deakin nodded. Marv's DC sources remained the best, even though all Washington knew that he had 'defected' to the UN.

'Anything else?'

'Only a rumour, but they say Jane Treno has invited Tye to Washington, for discussions. Two weeks before the party takes place.'

Deakin snapped his head up. That was new. The Attorney-General herself was inviting Thomas Tye to visit DC! In Washington terms such an invitation was close to an imperial command. Tye was still an American subject, even though he also held a separate Hope Island passport. For reasons known only to the Department of State, he had not been asked to relinquish US citizenship when his island's sovereignty had been recognized.

'I only heard that just before this meeting started,' explained Girdlong, as if apologizing for springing a surprise on his boss. 'It's not confirmed but once again it's whispers and lots of calendars being rearranged.'

'OK,' pondered Deakin, turning to the attentive audience seated around the large conference table. 'The President accepts a jaunt to a tycoon's anniversary party on Hope Island and meanwhile Jane Treno invites Thomas Tye to drop by for a *discussion*. Any ideas?'

'It will be about the LA traffic mess,' stated Martha Rose, one of the international lawyers, authoritatively. 'I hear the Tye attorneys are playing real hardball. I'll bet the administration is going to lean on Tye personally to make an interim settlement. It will be the old one-two: Treno will be tough with him in Washington – threaten the Tye Corporation's US interests, perhaps a domestic antitrust action, perhaps talk about pulling the company's government contracts, et cetera – and the President will be all smiles and backslapping for the cameras at the party once the interim payment's announced. California's going to be even more marginal next year. It could go Republican and the Wilkinson campaign people will do anything to stop that.'

Deakin sipped his coffee, his umpteenth cup of the day. It was now late evening and, even as he raised it to his lips, he tried not to drink too much. He would never get to sleep this way. He nodded. Rose's analysis was logical.

'Yes, the LA thing is big enough to go all the way up to William Wilkinson,' he conceded. 'But could it also be anything to do with this Russian deal? Have we learned anything more about that?'

Magda Nezhdanov, the senior Russian Federation analyst, gave a Slavic shrug. 'Everyone in Moscow is talking about it, but nobody knows anything for sure. Some say the Tye Corporation is developing real estate, others say it's an agricultural deal. Something big has been signed, that's for sure. And President Orlov's attending this celebration as well.'

'Can we all go too?' shouted Olliphant, a young and utterly brilliant British perception-adjuster from the far end of the table. He was planning the campaign to realign the public's view of Thomas Tye once a course of action was decided upon.

Deakin held up his hand. 'Doctor Chelouche has sent me an interesting fax,' he told them. There were smiles around the table. None of them had yet got used to sending paper faxes again – even ones scrambled with one-time security codes. 'Moscow is offering to buy back Russia's debts, at a discount.'

'Which debts?' asked Libby Klinkhamers sharply. She was an international economist for the UN but one who still found time to teach as a visiting professor at Harvard.

Now Deakin had their attention. 'All of them,' he said simply. 'IMF, World Bank, Bank of Redevelopment and Construction, OECD grants, EU bonds, US loans. The whole damn lot. They're trying to get them rolled up together and they want to settle them, in hard currency, at a sixty-four per cent discount inside thirty days.'

Libby had been tapping on her VideoMate as Deakin was speaking. Like everyone else on the team, she had had to allow Lynch and his technical support people to disable all the network and external storage capabilities of her unit. The UN computer support staff were busy adapting one of the building's wiring looms to provide a totally internal and insular network protected by physical firewalls, but until that happened even office-to-office network communication was banned.

'With interest rolled up that's almost a trillion US dollars,' she breathed. 'Even if they got that discount it would be ... three hundred and sixty billion. In hard currency, you say?'

Deakin smiled. 'I think we've just found out what Tye did with all that cash he raised on the markets a few weeks ago,' he said. 'So what *has* he bought?' He looked around the room. There were only shrugs.

'For God's sake, not the few old nukes they have left?' asked Chevalier, the group's senior military analyst.

'No, definitely not,' asserted Deakin. 'That would be a turn-off to every one of Tye's shareholders and supporters. He's maintained a strong stance against everything nuclear. What do the intelligence services say?'

James Soames, the British-born liaison officer working as linkman between UNISA and the world's intelligence services, shrugged in turn. 'Less than nothing, Ron. They're telling us there's nothing on the radar as far as the Federation is concerned.'

'What about this Phoebus research project?' asked Deakin. 'Did Congressman Robarts really have something or was he fishing?'

'NASA says not, CIA says not,' reported Soames, 'Pentagon says not, NATO says not, EU Defence Agency says not. All damn worrying.'

The looks around the table said it. There was something up and the UN wasn't being told. It was back to the bad old days of distrust between the individual members and their global representative body. But why?

'OK, three urgent tasks for us,' announced Deakin. 'One, what does the Justice Department really want with Tye? Two, what deal has the Tye Corporation done with Moscow? Three, what does NASA or the CIA have on the Phoebus Project that they won't share with us? Steal it, extort it, buy it or beg it. Lean on every diplomat in this building, crawl into every little lobbyists' crevice. Let's get that information. I'll talk to the SecGen tomorrow and get him to talk directly to Washington. We are the *United* Nations, ladies and gentleman, and we won't be stonewalled by any of our individual members, no matter how powerful they may be.'

NINETEEN

'Touch me and you *can* make a difference' said Thomas Tye, giving the camera his most earnest look. The set was designed to look like a gentleman's study, and he sat behind a desk. But his customary open-necked white shirt and tied-back hair banished any sense of formality. Tye reached for a globe on the desk, spun it slowly and pointed to a spot. In the background began a soft, instrumental rendition of 'It's Our Planet'.

'Ethiopia is a nation of seventy million people in East Africa. Approximately sixty per cent of them are starving. There has been no rain in the lowlands of the southern part of the nation for six years. Each year the harvest has failed for nearly thirty million people who depend upon it. Famine is widespread.'

The image of Tye's face dissolved to show him standing in a desert, wearing a dust-stained beige safari suit. 'This land is the oldest nation on earth – it is the cradle of human evolution. It is from here that our ancestors walked, paddled and sailed out of Africa to populate our world.' He squatted and picked up a handful of earth, allowing the dry soil to run through his fingers. 'But today the lush savannah has become dust. We have abused our planet and this is the result.'

Then the picture cut to Tye standing in an Ethiopian village. A girl about eight years old was holding his hand, staring stoically ahead.

'This is Biya,' he said to the camera. 'She has no family left and she has lost her eyesight from trachoma, a viral condition exacerbated by the effects of malnutrition. She has never seen, or felt, rain.'

As he told his viewers more about the ravages of drought and famine, the picture changed to a montage of starving children, dried-up crops and lines of people queuing for food on the pediplain. The corporate anthem was now a glissando of sweeping strings, an emotive accompaniment to the sombre images.

'The Tye Corporation can change things here, but we need your help,' he said over the pictures.

How strange, thought Haley as she watched this v-mail that had just arrived. She'd never seen Tye make a personal appeal before. She could guess that he must have been aching to get back inside his air-conditioned trailer and slip into an antibacterial mask.

The voice-over continued with still more facts about the ravaged country. Then the camera revealed Tye back in his study.

'Next month, on Sunday, August thirtieth, I'm proud to say my company will start to change the world. Using new, totally benign and sustainable energy technology, we shall bring rain to southern Ethiopia for a period of at least six hours. We shall then bring rain once a week for a further month. My charitable foundation already has people in place to help the Ethiopian population make the most of this situation. Much of this year's crop *can* still be saved if it rains before autumn.'

The camera zoomed back to a close-up on Tye's finely featured face.

'Will you pledge just one US dollar to help thirty million people? If a majority of you make this pledge, I can *guarantee* that it will rain in southern Ethiopia next month. We want to give two billion dollars to the Ethiopian people so they can rebuild their economy and their nation. If you, the people of the world, will pledge a total of one billion dollars, the Thomas Tye Foundation will match that with a billion dollars' worth of solar energy systems, livestock and crop seeds specially modified for Ethiopian conditions and, most importantly, will send a team of four hundred trained field-workers to help Ethiopia and its people work towards achieving a decent standard of living. This will be the start of a ten-year programme that I will be proud to have my foundation oversee.

'This v-mail has been sent in over two hundred languages to all three billion network addresses on this planet. I hope and believe you will now help Biya and her people.'

He leaned forward suddenly and pressed his right forefinger to the camera lens. An electronic halo shimmered around the dark outline of his fingertip like the corona of the sun in a solar eclipse.

'Reach out and touch the world now. Touch your finger-print-identification pad and your pledge will be automatically recorded. But send no money until *we* have brought rain to Ethiopia.'

Haley leaned forward and touched her pad.

'Thank you, Haley Voss,' said Thomas Tye with phoneme-perfect image morphing and a spectacular close-up smile. 'Your pledge has been recorded. Join me on Sunday, August thirtieth, to see it rain in Ethiopia. Take care of our planet – you hear!'

The driving rock version of 'It's Our Planet' rose over a slow sequence of images of Thomas Tye walking amongst the children of the Rift Valley. Haley smelled the instantly recognizable scent of 'Abundance' from her ScentSim as the anthem grew.

I hear, thought Haley.

The papers were full of it. It was headline news in every country. Every TV bulletin led with the story, but had to manage with scant details and hours of speculation from wholly ignorant 'experts'. Mostly they resorted to running library footage of previous famines in Ethiopia.

Deakin scanned the printouts of various front pages that lay on his desk.

'Tye Corporation Claims To Be Rainmaker,' said the *New York Times*.

'Tye Corporation Ready to Rebuild Ethiopian Economy With New Weather Technology,' ran the *Financial Times* headline. 'Ethiopian Market Closes 40 Points Up.'

'Two Billion Dollar Pledge To Make Ethiopian Rain,' reported the London *Times*.

'Tye-riffic!' screamed London's *Sun*.

'Tye-phoon!!' opined the *Asian Star* in proleptic ecstasy.

'Amelia Earhart's Plane Found on Dark Side of the Moon,' offered the *National Enquirer*.

But neither Thomas Tye himself nor any spokesperson from any part of the Tye corporate empire would say more.

'Join us on August thirtieth,' they kept repeating. 'Just be sure you have made your pledge.'

Ron Deakin had called another meeting – the second in thirty-six hours – and he waited impatiently for the meteorologists to arrive. The unavailability of normal communications technology was making this investigation grindingly slow.

And, on all the main markets where it was traded, the Tye Corporation's core stock made sharp gains.

'OK, companions to nap mode, VideoMates to silent and all viewpers off, if you please,' instructed Theresa as she took her seat.

Professor Keane had gathered her 'A Team' of researchers in the Network Control Center. The projection system was switched off and she sat in a low chair in the middle of the holo-image pit, where she was lit by a gentle but unflattering overhead light. The researchers sat in a banked semicircle around her, all with a CatPanion, a Furry or some other sort of intelligent companion on their laps or on a seat beside them. All these 'creatures' were development platforms for beta personalities now undergoing development by the researchers. Theresa always found it difficult to bring this team together. So many of them were unconventional individuals who did their best thinking on beaches or on clifftops or in their hot tubs. Some of them were so deeply involved in their relationships with their companions that they found it hard to focus on the outside world. Indeed, some rarely left their apartments and contributed their thoughts, criticisms and software over the team's private network.

'First, I want to welcome our special guest, Doctor Calypso

Browne.' Theresa inclined her head to where Calypso sat in the front row, the only person in the room without a companion and whose well-tailored dark trouser suit marked her out from the collection of brightly coloured T-shirts, shorts and sandals worn by the others. 'Doctor Browne acts as a personal physician to the Thomas Tye household and is also a consultant psychiatric paediatrician. Thanks for coming to join us, Calypso.'

Calypso bowed her head in acknowledgement, grateful that the professor had not mentioned her earlier claim to fame. Perhaps that part of her life was finally disappearing into the past.

'Now, I have an interesting ethical question for us to consider,' Theresa continued. She had Sandra on her lap and was gently stroking her sleeping CatPanion. 'But first, consider: how many Furries, CatPanions and other companions has the corporation or its licensees sold worldwide to date? Anybody have a figure?'

'I think it was about three hundred and fourteen million, last time I heard,' ventured Rory McCullum without looking up. He was one of the world's leading theoreticians in artificial personalities and Theresa had lured him from the Turing Institute in Glasgow. She noticed he had recently become deeply attached to the very large shocking-pink Bugs Bunny-style rabbit called Beau who was asleep in the seat next to him. Companion bonding was both fashionable and strongly encouraged within the artificial-personality research team. Rory was in the process of knitting a maroon cable-stitch cardigan for Beau, and his size eight needles never ceased clicking as he spoke.

'But many of those are only first- or second-generation.' He deftly cast off a row of purl stitches from one needle, starting a new line before he continued. 'Those didn't have network-communications abilities and they didn't upgrade themselves automatically.'

Theresa nodded. 'Tye Consumer Electronics and its various licensees have been selling companions for about four years,' she explained. 'CE is now even getting requests for Furry personality transfers. Some children who have had one type of Furry for several years – a caterpillar, a rabbit, whatever – think they've grown out of the physical envelope of their companion but they want to keep the Furry's personality. Do you see any objections to us doing this for our customers?'

'At a price, I hope,' put in Liane Stevens, former associate professor of the Human-Computer Interaction Laboratory at the University of Maryland.

Theresa smiled. 'Of course. But are there any concerns here about the *concept* of transferring a Furry's personality to another container? Let's imagine that a little girl of seven has owned a Furry – a soft pink rabbit called "Lucy", say – for three years. Her Furry has been everywhere with her. It has seen everything she has seen, heard everything she has heard and it has listened to all her problems. The Furry has *learned* from its owner and its abilities to harness that information have improved with every remote upgrade that has occurred as our Anagenesis-network personalities evolve and bequeath their hard-learned experience to their more corporeal cousins. Every sight and sound of their owners' lives is recorded, and not just in the companions' local memories. They are also uploaded to our FMR – our Furry Memory Retrievatory – in our data ware-houses on this island. As part of that project we're creating a database that will contain a complete audio-visual record of every Furry owner's daily life; it will become the ultimate anthropological resource.'

They nodded, listening carefully. Those who had been on the team since the beginning could sense that the time had finally arrived for some of the big questions to be faced.

'Do we just carry out a transfer as requested and send her a PonyPet or whatever she wants with precisely the same person-ality and memories? What would be the impact of her lifelong companion and friend appearing in a completely different guise? And do we deliver the new "Lucy" only when the old one has been returned to us? What would be the pyschological impact of the two Lucys being together with the owner in different physical form?'

'And of them me-me-meeting each other,' added Robert, the group's speech simulation expert.

Theresa smiled. 'Good point, Robert. All Furries love to

communicate. What would "Lucy A" make of "Lucy B"? We can model that here – one for you, I think, Liane. But, first, let's consider the impact on children. Doctor Browne?'

Calypso shook her head, feeling out of her depth. But she also felt distinctly uneasy, as if something was wrong here but she wasn't sure what. She herself had made contact with the eminent professor after Jack had talked to her about Jed's recent behaviour. He said there seemed something uncanny about the Furry's ability – as if it *understood* more than a mere toy should. Calypso had to agree – she felt the same way. She was also wondering whether Tommy's obvious devotion to an increasingly percipient bundle of fabric, plastic and computer circuitry was wholly healthy. These were two concerns she had articulated to Professor Keane during a video exchange one evening.

'I do understand your worries, Doctor,' Theresa had replied. 'Most parents buy these toys without realizing that they are introducing their children to potential lifelong companions.' Later in the conversation she had invited Calypso to attend this current discussion with the research team responsible for developing future generations. Now that she had confronted some of the issues Calypso felt less sure that she was qualified to help.

She weighed Theresa's question carefully, aware that she was speaking in front of some of the brightest intellects on the planet. Then she thought of Tommy – and the obscenity of the concepts they were discussing swam into sharp focus.

'I must suggest that the ideas you're discussing are incredibly dangerous,' she began, struggling to keep aggression out of her voice. 'Children do love these companions, but they aren't best equipped to distinguish between real pets and ... and machines. Replacing one Furry with another companion that has exactly the same personality would be criminally irresponsible. It would be better to allow the first companion to go through something that appears to be closer to a normal death – like the demise of a pet dog or cat – rather than to provide a replacement that makes death seem impermanent. That could traumatize a vulnerable child – one who is seriously ill, perhaps, or who has suffered from their parents' divorce, or has actually lost a parent

or a brother or a sister. You must consider the children's feelings
– you can't consider them simply as an upgrade market!'

There was shocked silence in the room. Calypso felt intense
hostility directed at her. Then she thought of an even more
concrete objection.

'If a family called me as an expert in a lawsuit raised against
Tye Consumer Electronics because of trauma caused by a
companion transfer – or even malfunction – I wouldn't hesitate
to testify about the potential danger to an unformed psyche.'

'Thank you, Doctor,' said Theresa dryly. 'Comments?'

'The Doctor's concern about companions' apparent immortality may become irrelevant, given the research into human
longevity that's being undertaken elsewhere on this island,'
observed Liane Stevens with just a hint of acid in her voice.
'The way things are going, it won't be just Furries who will
seem to live for ever. Some of the owners may also live for
hundreds of years and that presents us with a *far* more important
concern. We know the capability of companions is improving
exponentially, not just because of our deliberate design improvements but also through the evolutionary improvements within
the community of network-agent personalities that are passed
on automatically to companion toys. How will a balance be
retained between increasingly clever Furries and owners who,
whilst becoming more experienced in life, are almost certainly
no more capable? How will owners keep up mentally with their
companions over a long period? *That*'s what we should be
worrying about, not the issues of personality transference
between different models of companion envelope.'

'But, what ha-ha-happens when a companion's owner *does*
die?' asked Robert. 'If a child has an accident or a fatal disease,
what ha-ha-happens to the companion that has shared all their
waking moments and has all their common memories stored?'

That too silenced them. All, with the exception of Calypso,
were probably thinking about how their companions would
continue after their own deaths.

'No one can access a companion's memories but an owner,'
said Rory McCullum quietly. 'We built that in to all of them

from the second generation. It needs the owner's voice print to activate a core command in a companion.'

'But what *should* ha-ha-happen to those memories?' insisted Robert. 'After all, we store a copy of every owner's voice print so *we'*ll be able to access them.'

'Surely the next of kin should inherit the companion and be given access to its memories,' said Liane.

Theresa shook her head. 'No, we can't allow that. Everybody's memories and their shared experiences with their companion are highly personal and very private. We can't allow anyone else to access them.'

The researchers were silent again, nodding as they contemplated their own experiences shared with their companions. Calypso's mind was reeling at such cavalier discussion of personality transference and the archiving of hundreds of millions of life experiences. She wanted to scream, to shout at them, to make them see that human personalities and experiences are not commodities.

'I th-th-think maybe we should erase all memories when the companion's owner dies,' suggested Robert.

'You mean bury the pet with its owner?' snorted Avi Becchar, whose speciality was emotion simulation. 'So they both have to go together? I seem to have heard that one somewhere before.'

'Ethiopia Appeal Tops Four Billion,' screamed the *New York Daily Post.* 'Global Pledges Set To Break All Records.'

'Over one billion people are now reported to have pledged money for the Ethiopian Appeal recently launched by Mr Thomas Tye, President of the Tye Corporation,' read the BBC's senior news announcer. 'A spokesperson for the company has said that promises of nearly five billion dollars have already been received. Such a universal response to an appeal for charity is unprecedented. A spokesman for Oxfam states that aid on this level could transform the future of Eastern Africa. On its re-release, the song "It's Our Planet" has become the world's number one downloaded track once again. All proceeds also go to the Ethiopian appeal. On the world markets, all companies with business interests in East Africa are currently experiencing a sharp increase in valuation.'

So, it seemed, Thomas Tye *had* touched the world. The Tye Corporation's PR agencies were operating in full flood, but their efforts were unnecessary as pledges continued to pour in. The world's population wanted to see Thomas Tye produce rain on cue and, under his leadership, they were happy to help feed the starving. The largest number of people ever united in a single cause were turning their thoughts to 30 August and to the people of Ethiopia. A fourteen-year-old white girl in Cape Town, suffering from a brain tumour, sent 200,000 Rand to the *Cape Town Herald* in aid of the cause, then spent a night on the networks in various Thomas Tye chat rooms gaining emotional support before setting herself alight as she replayed her hero's appeal one more time. She left a caption to the recording of her self-destruction that said simply 'For The Planet'.

The frenzy continued and the Tye Corporation's stock rose another ten points!

Michael Chevannes switched off the engine of his United Nations four-wheel-drive Toyota and climbed out into the crystal-clear sunlight. The noise and dust that had been his constant accompaniment on the grindingly slow ascent disappeared and there was the sudden and immediate pervasive silence that only exists at great altitude.

Although it was mid-afternoon and the tropical sun was still high in the sky, the atmosphere was cool and clear. It was the thin air up here, Chevannes realized. On the advice of the logistics manager at the UN compound he had deliberately spent an uncomfortable, cold and cramped night in the back of the vehicle 6,000 feet below in order to give his body time to acclimatize. If he had attempted to ascend the mountain in a single day he would now be suffering from completely debilitating nausea and dizziness. The GPS and hypsometric display in his RayBan Electros showed his position as 14,657 feet or 4,500 metres above sea level. Despite making his ascent in carefully timed stages, he felt his breath coming in short gasps.

Only one road zig-zagged up Monte Camanchaca, a medium-size peak in the Peruvian link of the great Andes chain. The recently constructed road was surprisingly wide, broader than many of the country's secondary roads, and surfaced in thick black asphalt. On the winding journey across the lower slopes he had passed through a few Aymaran villages and waved at an occasional vicuña shepherd and his flocks. Once he had been forced to stop as a vast herd of furciferine deer bounded across his path but he had seen no sign of human life for the last 8,000 feet.

Although usually preferring to drape his muscular bulk in a business suit, Chevannes had decided to underline the authority of this mission and he had borrowed a UN peacekeeper's uniform of white epauletted shirt with shorts. Now, in the chill of the rarefied Andean air, he could feel goose bumps forming on his exposed arms and legs. Despite the sun he shivered involuntarily.

He put his hands on his hips and surveyed the flat mountain peak immediately above him and the long cordillera sloping gently down to the south. In the far, far distance it rose up again to meet a yet higher snow-covered peak. *A little like the Great Wall of China*, thought Chevannes as he noted how the ridge had been flattened to provide a vehicle track and a narrow-gauge railroad between the radio dishes along its top. There had been some serious engineering work done up here.

He turned and looked behind him, back the way he had come. It was the first time he had been able to see the full majesty of the view and he took an involuntary half-step backwards and then leaned against his vehicle's hood. He was way above the cloud line and so high he could make out no detail at ground level. Immediately around and below him were row upon row of black solar-energy capture panels. A long way down, the rocky slopes of the mountain gave way to what he knew to be scrub, then catalpa trees and then to the cultivated coca-bush terraces of the foothills before becoming lost in an arboreal sea of rain forest and epiphytes so lush and dense that in the bright sunlight its green canopy seemed almost black. Above the forest he saw a speck that he thought at first might be a carrancha. Then he realized that a hawk would be almost invisible at such a distance: it could only be a condor circling lazily in the thermals far below.

In the extreme distance, perhaps sixty miles or so to the west, he could see the llano and, beyond, the glint of the Pacific Ocean. To the north the mountain range stretched away towards the equator and its eponymous nation. It was absolutely still and stunningly beautiful here on the mountain top.

Above him, the vast mesh dish of what he presumed to be a radio telescope cast a mottled shadow over the centre of a compound. He estimated the dish was at least 800 feet in diameter. Within its shade huddled six or seven white single-storey concrete buildings. To the east, away from the shadow of the dish, Chevannes could see a windsock hanging listlessly over what he guessed was a helicopter landing pad. That would have been the sensible way to travel, he thought, although few choppers were able to climb so high: perhaps the Canadian Sea King or the Russian Helix, if he recalled correctly. Just over the other side of the peak Chevannes could see the top of a large white dome that, he assumed, covered a conventional optical telescope array. UNISA satellite surveillance had discovered the compound's existence five years before and had tagged it as a research facility of the University of San Marco, Lima.

Dotted at regular intervals along the flattened mountain ridge to the south was a string of twenty or so smaller radio telescopes, each perhaps 200 feet in diameter, all set along the rail track that disappeared into the snow before the next peak. This installation was a rival for any of the giant observatories he had seen in TV astronomy programmes.

Chevannes had stopped his vehicle in front of a twelve-foot-high steel-mesh fence topped with razor wire. Security cameras inside the compound were trained on the large gates that barred his way. He assumed that someone must have seen him arrive, but nothing stirred in the ultra-clarity of the still afternoon. He opened the door of the Toyota and pressed the horn. The sharp sound was startling, almost deafening, in the thin air and he heard its echo roll away, slapping off the distant rock faces along the ridge.

A few minutes later an all-terrain motorcycle emerged from between the low white buildings inside the compound and sped down the road towards the gate. As it approached, the rider brake-turned the bike to a stop and switched off the engine. He slid lithely from the saddle and walked to within six feet of the gate. This New Age gaucho was neatly turned out in a white, short-sleeved shirt and knee-length black shorts. A holster was on his right hip and sun-viewpers hid his eyes.

'Hola, buenas tardes. Estas perdido?'

Chevannes watched and waited as his VideoMate identified the language and started to provide the translation in his earpiece. He understood some Spanish but he would need help in framing his replies.

'Good morning. You speak English? Are you lost?' asked the guard again before Chevannes's system had finished translating: as if UN personnel were in the habit of driving up mountains to seek directions.

'Hi,' said Chevannes. 'I'm here to see Doctor Toksvig.'

'You don't have an appointment.' It was a statement, not a question.

'No,' admitted Chevannes.

'You have had a wasted journey, sir,' the guard continued in his excellent English. Chevannes guessed he was Mexican or Cuban. 'Doctor Toksvig is off-planet, in an orbiting observatory. He'll be gone for many months.'

Chevannes nodded as if he understood. But he had prepared for this and he had assumed that, even under his new identity, Rolf Larsson would be unavailable to any uninvited visitors.

He turned back to the open driver's door of his four-wheel-drive and pulled out an envelope he had placed in the map-webbing of the sun visor. As he did so he watched the security guard in his peripheral vision. The man appeared completely relaxed and, Chevannes assessed, this was not a facility that would attract any trouble. It was too high to be of interest to local bandits and it was too remote to pose a threat to the

Colombian drug barons who owned many of the country's coca
fields. Despite the impressive fence, the security level here was
low.

He returned to the gate and pushed the envelope through
the wire. 'Would you give this to Doctor Toksvig, please?'

The guard approached the fence and took the envelope. It
bore the doctor's name and was marked 'confidential'. The blue
UN emblem was embossed in the upper left-hand corner.

'As I said, it will be many months, sir,' repeated the guard.
'Perhaps not until next year.'

Chevannes took off his sun-viewpers and allowed the guard
to see his eyes. He then flipped his wallet from the back pocket
of his shorts and held it up to the fence.

'I'm from the United Nations Security Agency,' he said. He
didn't offer the ident to the guard for checking. 'And, at the risk
of offending you, I have to suggest you may be mistaken about
Doctor Toksvig's absence. I would like you to take that envelope
to him now or, in the million-to-one chance my information is
wrong, I want you to give that envelope to the most senior
person now at this facility and tell him – or her – that I authorize
them to open the envelope. Is that clear?'

'Where can we reach you?' asked the guard.

'I'm not going anywhere,' said Chevannes. 'I'll just wait while
you deliver it.'

The guard looked at the envelope, then at Chevannes, then
at the UN Toyota with its fluttering white-and-blue flag and
nodded. He remounted his motorcycle, started the engine and
sped back to the cluster of buildings.

Chevannes walked back to his vehicle and rummaged for a
water bottle he had left in the cooler. He drank and then poured
water onto his handkerchief and washed his face. Refreshed, he
pulled a pair of image-stabilized binoculars from the glove box
and walked to the edge of the track to take a closer look at the
chain of radio dishes that stretched away into the distance. He
understood why optical telescopes needed to be located on
mountains, but he couldn't think of any operational advantage
justifying the expense of hauling radio-wavelength receivers to
such a height.

He enabled the video link on his binoculars, stabilized the image and scanned along the mountain ridge. Ordinarily, others back at headquarters would now be sharing his view, but the ban on all network communications was being strictly enforced, so Chevannes was recording only in Local Mode. He moved his view from dish to dish, sharpening the image and adjusting the contrast as he went since even the thin atmosphere of the mountain range distorted the light. He saw no movement, and guessed that these dishes were controlled remotely.

He turned when he heard a sound behind him. The ground locks on the central gateposts had snapped up and the twin gates were slowly opening inwards.

'Am I late?' asked a voice from the darkness of the outer circle in the Network Control Center.

Theresa switched on the holo-projection system and by its ambient light she saw that Raymond Liu had arrived exactly on schedule. When Calypso Browne had got up to go, Theresa had thanked the paediatrician for so forthrightly expressing her views, despite the note of discord they had struck with the team. With the exception of Robert, Theresa had then dispersed all her researchers back to their hiding places and Companion Nests where they could continue work on the next stage of what would be a continuous progression of researcher-designed personality upgrades.

'Come on down, Raymond,' invited Theresa as she adjusted the projection controls on the holo-panel that floated in front of her seat. She waved him towards one of the front-row seats.

'This is Robert Graves,' she said, by way of introduction. 'He's my senior researcher on the Descartes Experiment.'

Liu bobbed his head and took a seat in the row indicated. 'As in "I think, therefore I am"?' he asked.

'Precisely,' confirmed Theresa. 'Who else but the person who first posed the original mind/body dualism question would be suitable as our patron saint?'

Liu smiled, but he wasn't sure why. He didn't yet know what their experiment entailed.

'Robert is going to explain the network elements of our

Descartes Experiment to you, Raymond,' explained Theresa from behind the control display. 'He works closely with me on this long-term project so I hope we can do two things. One, I think we can explain those dark data you've encountered in the networks. And two, I think we can reassure you that our experiments and developments in artificial life could not possibly have led to any of the systems failures you have been suffering in the networks. In short, I hope you will be able to eliminate us from your list of suspects. OK, Raymond?'

Liu nodded. That would be a step forward, at least. There had been little progress otherwise in finding the cause of the network faults.

'Over to you, Robert,' said Theresa.

The researcher stood up and turned to face his audience of two. 'I assume that you are bound by the same confidentiality as the rest of us in the university and in the corporation?' he asked brusquely of Liu. All trace of his balbutience had disappeared – as Theresa had observed many times before when she had asked him to make a presentation.

Liu nodded.

'We had to get special clearance from Tom to show you this today.'

Liu swallowed, hoping it wasn't noticeable. He knew his salary, stock options and career were currently hanging by the most slender of threads.

'I understand from Theresa that you watched our little demo with Miss Scarlett?'

Liu bobbed his head again.

'That software robot personality is disembodied and lives in the networks, but it's essentially the same type of D-persona that we use in physically based companions like my own Michelle or Theresa's Sandra.' Robert pointed to the CatPanion curled up on one of the vacant seats. 'Companion personalities are merely *simulating* speech and human behaviour and deducing how to respond to us by a complex set of rules that we have laid down. They have absolutely no independent consciousness or intelligence and, as Professor Keane has demonstrated so clearly, it is we humans who anthropomorphize them. However, the important point for *this* discussion is that they are absolutely processor-dependent. In Furries and other companions the personalities run on the microprocessor installed inside each unit. The disembodied versions travel the networks as packets of information but they can run only when they find a vacant microprocessor – or one of the more recent photonprocessors – to use.'

Robert paused to see if he was being understood. He knew their guest was the technical director of the Tye Global Networks so he had assumed he wouldn't need to explain too much about the basic elements of their technology.

Raymond Liu nodded silently once more.

'In the Descartes Experiment, our goal has been to try and create a basic entity that is processor-independent. By that I don't mean software that can run on a wide number of different processors, I mean software that runs without *any* specific processor.'

Liu smiled his understanding again, even though he was unsure how such a thing could be done.

'What we wanted to do was to develop an artificial entity that in turn could create its own processing environment from any of the individual single-state switches that exist in the world's networks or its attachments. There are trillions of those today. Every routing device, every gateway, every amplifier, every laser controller, every multiplexer, every firewall, every relay, every uplink, every downlink, every access device – all the millions of VideoMates and LifeWatches – each have millions of minute, individual switches that are either "on" or "off" at any one time.'

Robert put his hands together and waved them from side to side to indicate the two polarities.

'We are trying to build a software personality that doesn't need a *computer*. It assembles its own from the billions of simple "yes/no" condition switches that are all around it and the more firings – switchings – there are, the more capability it will have. To exist, it has to make up its transient assemblies of processing capability afresh, nanosecond by nanosecond, from the individual single-state components of the world's networks. We consider that collectively the individual switches produce what we call a "potentially panpsychic" environment. That means the networks and its component parts all become part of the personality.'

'You mean the individual transistors of all the processing devices attached to the global networks *themselves* become the processor?'

Robert nodded. Theresa stood up and stepped into the ambient light of the Holo-Theater.

'Thank you, Robert, well put. You see Raymond, the human brain, the only vessel in which true consciousness of self, as we understand it, has emerged, contains about a thousand to the fifth switching combinations – one hundred quadrillion, yes? – and the only possible processor to get anywhere near that number would be a combination of all the individual switches inside the world's processors connected by the networks. It's a question of scale – although we still fall far short of the number we'd need to mimic a single human brain. Nevertheless, the global networks at least give us a simple prototype for an artificial neural nervous system. Let me see if we can show you. Robert?'

Her senior researcher had taken Theresa's seat and now he started to make adjustments to the controls.

'I'm now going to try and show you what your dark data are,' said Theresa. 'But before we start, we must address a fundamental problem that occurs when we contemplate technologies that have yet to be fully developed and harnessed. You see, the difficulty is that I can't properly describe it to you – at least not in words we'd both understand. Wittgenstein summed it up when he said: "Concerning that of which we cannot speak, we must pass over in silence." In short, we have no language for the future. Whenever something is completely new we don't have *words* for it and that means we can't *think* about it. When the projector was first invented we had to call it a magic lantern. The car was a horseless carriage, the radio the wireless – we were reduced to describing it either by something it *didn't* possess, or by an allusion to an *existing* concept – the iron horse, the flying machine. I could go on, but you get my point.'

Raymond Liu nodded. He understood that.

'As a first step, with the comparatively limited processing power of today's global networks, we're trying to create an entity that is both omnisentient and anoetic – it has feeling, consciousness if you like, but there is insufficient complexity for real thought. Given the primitive and small-scale state of the neural pathways represented by today's global networks it can't have any capability for action. We are trying to mimic the way human consciousness may have emerged over the four billion years of biological evolution on this planet. In another quarter of a century we think the global networks will have grown sufficiently to allow real emergence to take place but for now this is more like a *gedankenexperiment* – a thought experiment with practical components – if that doesn't sound too much like an oxymoron.'

Liu had no idea how to react. *The people in this room were trying to turn the world's networks into a brain!*

'So, without a mutually agreed language for the new, my following description may sound a little – well, opaque. We can only *show* you and we'll do that in a moment. We have been creating and releasing software moneme-microsthenes into the networks for three years – you're familiar with memes, the information equivalent of genes? We use the smallest elements of language – the lexeme and moneme – and couple that with a grammatical-instruction carrier that Robert has developed – the microsthene – to create a hylozoic ecological system. When there are sufficient memes created from monemes – that's about a thousand to an eighth, one hundred trillion – and sufficient individual transactions occurring on the networks – the on-off switchings that Robert talked about – we expect to achieve parallel-processing states that create recurrent connections and what we call transient assemblies – the sort of pathways and structures we find in the human brain. From this we hope to observe the earliest stages of *emergence*, of consciousness, arising. An epiphenomenon. What would you assume that might resemble, Raymond?'

He felt like one of her most ignorant students. He realized how privileged he *should* feel, but he was numb. He shrugged, unable to respond.

'It's a primitive form of dream, Raymond. And we think the very first "primitive dreams" began to emerge about a year ago – Robert?'

'I'm switching to visual representation now,' Robert said. 'Note, this is *not* a simulation. It is a visual interpretation from the swirling swarms of the memes as they move through the world's networks seeking out active switches and jumping the gaps in the networks from one to the next. This is made up of about four hundred billion switch firings per second. We call it "René", after Descartes.'

Suddenly the Holo-Theater pit was filled with light and Raymond Liu saw what looked like blue smoke. At the top right he saw a digital tripmeter headed *Transactions*. Then he saw that the central light was a vignette of blue, smoothly graduated but swirling. Loops and whorls appeared and from the bottom an amethystine glow began to spread gently upwards.

It was so peaceful. Raymond Liu found himself entranced, becalmed. He thought he could make out a shape in the colour. But nothing came of it. Then he thought he saw something else. There was no sound in the Control Center. They drank in the colours as they shifted through the visible spectrum and the counter spun in its recordings of the switch firings in the global networks.

Eventually Theresa stepped forward again. 'Thank you, Robert,' she said and her researcher killed the display. She turned to face the network chief.

'We are fairly sure that's an expression of an early dream, Raymond, but that's as far as we've got: colours, a few shapes. And that's taken eight years of preparation and work – but it emerged spontaneously. I'm afraid those quadrillions of shifting moneme-microsthenes probably account for the mysterious loading of your networks. Individually they're too small to be counted, but collectively...'

Liu was still entranced by the display he had seen. Then, being an engineer, he made one more check. 'I have to ask this, Professor,' he said. 'I don't fully understand what you've been telling me but I think I get the drift. Is there *any* chance that whatever it is you've been trying to create could have ... well

... could have developed into something more? Something that could have consciously or unconsciously interfered with normal network operations?'

Theresa stared at him and pursed her lips. 'It will be decades before we have a sufficient number of switch firings in the global networks to properly resemble the neural activity of the human brain,' she said firmly. 'At this stage I have to say not a chance, Doctor.'

'Exclusive: We Reveal The Guest List At The Party of the Century,' trailed the cover of the latest *Hello* magazine. Haley leaned forward and picked the top copy from the pile. She flipped to the pages indicated.

'Thomas Tye Brings The World's Leaders, Thinkers and Artists to Hope Island to Celebrate his Appeal for Ethiopia and the "Take Care of Our Planet Campaign".'

Below were pictures of the American, EU and Russian Presidents, a galaxy of other world leaders, film and music stars (including Josh Chandler) and, of course, Thomas Tye himself. He was good-looking enough for the layout designer to have given him the largest picture on the right-hand page of the spread, facing the impossibly dreamy Josh Chandler.

Haley flipped over to the next page.

'Mr Tye's "One Weekend In The Future" Will Set The Global Environmental and Technological Agenda for the Next Decade,' she read. Beneath this gushing prose were photos of the artists, writers, film stars and intellectual giants who were participating in the four-day event.

'Are you buying it?' demanded the Pakistani shopkeeper testily. Haley nodded and transferred payment from her LifeWatch.

Rolf Linquist Larsson sat opposite Michael Chevannes at the dark wooden conference table. They were alone. The UNISA officer noted that the tall Swede's tanned face had become lined and his hair had retreated a significant distance from his forehead since the last known photograph of him had been taken eight years before. He was dressed in a crumpled khaki shirt and

cut-off white jeans that were more than a little grubby, his bare
feet semi-shod in open-toed sandals. In fact, he looked as if he
had just got out of bed. But then, Chevannes realized he'd never
knowingly met a multi-billionaire before.

Further up the approach road, Chevannes's vehicle had been
met by the same security guard he had encountered earlier. He
had been led into this room in one of the white buildings and
asked to wait there. But he'd been left with all his communications and recording equipment. He had promptly replaced his
RayBan Electros with a pair of Armani clear-lens viewpers
switched for Local recording. A water-cooler, a wall-mounted
whiteboard covered with mathematical formulae and an inactive
display screen were the only furnishings other than the table
itself and half a dozen chairs. He was kept waiting for less than
ten minutes.

From his shirt pocket Larsson took out the letter Chevannes
had delivered and spread it flat on the desk. 'May I see some
ID?'

As Chevannes offered his ident, the astrophysicist glanced
at it and nodded, making no attempt to verify or copy it. It
was interesting that Larsson did not wear viewpers, LifeWatch
nor VideoMate. *The ultimate luxury of disconnection*, thought
Chevannes.

'How did you find me?'

'I don't know,' lied Chevannes. He had been ready for this
most difficult of questions. 'My office in New York provided
some details and asked me to come and talk to you.'

'This is private property and I don't have to say anything. I
have broken no law,' responded Larsson in perfect English –
honed from his years of exposure to the international academic
community.

'I have come here alone, Doctor. I did not ask the Peruvian
government for help. In fact, they don't even know I'm here.'

He waited as Larsson glanced down at the note again. It was
a difficult letter to ignore, its message simple and to the point.
On the embossed, headed notepaper of the United Nations, it
was signed personally by the Secretary-General, and Ron Deakin
had arranged for it to be couriered down to await Chevannes's

arrival at the UN compound inside the perimeter of Lima's Jorge Chávez International Airport. Larsson bent his head to read it yet again, as if the contents might have changed in the last few minutes. Chevannes knew the details of the request from his own copy.

Dr Larsson,

On behalf of the 212 member countries of the United Nations, I write personally to ask for your assistance.

The United Nations International Security Agency has reason to believe that just over seven years ago you passed a piece of intellectual property to Thomas Richmond Tye III, president of the Tye Corporation. I am told that if used improperly this knowledge would have the potential to destabilize the world's economy. If this were to occur, in the way that Dr Yoav Chelouche, president of the World Bank, believes possible, it could bring immense strife and suffering to millions of the world's poorest nations and their peoples.

I understand that you may have given undertakings and entered into contracts that seemingly inhibit your ability to assist us. But this matter is of such importance to the global community that, if you will help our organization to protect the interests of its member states, I am empowered to extend UN diplomatic immunity to you on all issues related to this transaction. Such legal protection would render you immune to civil or criminal legal proceedings relating to the transfer of the above-mentioned intellectual capital within the jurisdictions of all member states.

We now need your help as a matter of urgency, and Intelligence Officer Chevannes of UNISA will provide further details.

I hope to be able to welcome you personally to the headquarters of the United Nations in New York in the very near future.

Yours sincerely
Alexander Theodore Dibelius
Secretary-General

Larsson finished his rereading of the letter, sat back and gazed at Chevannes. 'Can you guess what we're doing here?' he asked with a sigh.

'Astronomy?' hazarded the intelligence officer.

Larsson stood up quickly and walked to the window. He looked up at the huge dish above them that blotted out the sky. 'Not just that. We're listening, Mr Chevannes. We're listening to the universe.'

He turned back to face the UN emissary who remained seated at the table. 'We have the only ears that can understand.'

Chevannes began to wonder if Larsson's drug abuse had caused some permanent damage.

'Can you force me to go with you?' Larsson asked abruptly.

Chevannes shook his head. 'Our charter gives us special jurisdiction in all our member states – Peru included – but we have no powers of arrest. We would have to ask the local police to act for us, but we have no intention of doing that. As you point out, we know of no international law that you have broken. I have come here because I believe this issue is of crucial importance. We really do need your help, Doctor.'

'You can't imagine how important my work here is,' Larsson said with a shake of his head, resuming his seat. 'It dwarfs anything Thomas Tye could get up to.'

'Tell me about it,' suggested Chevannes.

Larsson studied his visitor with clear, Nordic-blue eyes, considering his options. Suddenly his face broke into a broad grin.

'Then you'll have to stay for dinner,' he exclaimed. 'That'll give me time to think things over. We've got plenty of accommodation, and there's dorado and empanada for the barbecue tonight!'

It started in Moscow. After consultation with the newly reinvigorated financial community, President Orlov declared Sunday, 30 August would be a day of federal celebration in support of Thomas Tye's global appeal for aid for Ethiopia and the associated campaign to 'Take Care of the Planet'. Mikhail Orlov also knew that on the same day he and Thomas Tye would be announcing the creation of the new state of Sybaria and the climatic re-engineering of huge tracts of Western Siberia. As Tye suggested, the excitement over the Ethiopian project would help to drown out any misguided ecological concerns about the latter project. President Orlov expected Russia's massive national debt to be eliminated by then and that would also be announced proudly during the lavish festivities on Hope Island. The president's office had ordered street and village parties to be organized throughout the entire Federation, providing a large special fund to subsidize the cost. Thus everybody would appear to have an immediate share in Russia's windfall.

Michael Chevannes sat beside his host in silent wonder. They were alone on a specially designed wooden bench beside the observatory building. Its back was sharply raked to allow the occupants to sit comfortably while leaning their heads back against a flat tilted rail. It was nearly one a.m. and the heated seat was warm against their bodies.

Although Chevannes had travelled to many countries of the world, he could not recall seeing anything to approach the majesty of the giant moon above and its glittering stellate canopy. They were *surrounded* by stars, as if drawn up inside a cupola of the gods. Far below the land was lost in infinite blackness and the thin, clear air at the mountain peak allowed the stars to shine gold, without the twinkling interference and chromatic distortion of the lower atmosphere. The moon in perigee, vast, gibbous and immediately overhead, was bathed in light from the sun that revealed the mountain ranges and the bruised depressions of its continually battered impact craters in sparkling, sharp clarity. Beyond and all around, providing the celestial backdrop, was a wash of white stars so dense it seemed like phosphorescence on a summer night's sea. Away to the west, perhaps twenty or thirty miles distant, dim laserbursts of a satellite communications network transferred data between the northern and southern hemispheres – and, appearing in all quadrants, catching his eye and animating the siderealism, were the white-red death streaks of meteors entering the atmosphere. Neither he nor Larsson had spoken in the last fifteen minutes, and it was absolutely silent on the mountain top. They sat on their warm cosmic *pulvinar*, allowing their consciousnesses to cavort in the wash of infinity.

The natural ambient temperature at the mountain top was close to zero, but they were in their shirt-sleeves. When Chevannes had queried the viability of a barbecue in the chill of a mountain evening, his host had explained how solar-powered underground heating had been laid throughout the compound. At every few yards additional gas-flame outdoor heaters created microclimates like a warm summer evening, all run on natural methane gas. 'Produced locally,' added Larsson.

Earlier, Chevannes had learned that this was the highest observatory in the world, as the astronomer showed his guest the sixteen-metre adaptive optical telescope, then his real-time feed from the six orbiting Hubble telescopes and a NASA Mars-orbit telescope, his computer array for mining the vast warehouses of astronomical data collected, and the smaller direct-view optics housed in his observatory. Chavennes, the intelligence officer, had been hooked instantly. They had been touring the building for nearly three hours, only coming outside for occasional relief from visual overload: *Some relief!* thought Chevannes now as he sat in awe with his head tilted back.

'It was Debussy,' said Larsson eventually, 'his Cello Concerto in D minor. Someone once asked him what it was about and he explained it was Pierrot angry at the moon.'

Chevannes had no idea what his host was talking about. He said nothing and silence returned.

'What did they expect me to do, write a paper?' asked Larsson, sitting forward a minute later, a hint of bitterness in his voice.

The visitor guessed this was a rhetorical question and left it to roll away across the mountains.

'Perhaps I should have settled for a Nobel Prize. "Receiving an invitation to Stockholm", they call it. Huh! That's where I started from and for a mathematician it's downhill all the way after thirty.'

Chevannes nodded emphatically, not knowing how else to respond.

'The probability is very high that forms of aware intelligence exist around some of those stars out there – or around those we can't even see,' continued Larsson pointing at the sky, seemingly intent on an evening of non sequiturs. 'What we can see in front of us with our own eyes is only part of our own galaxy – less than one per cent of the known star systems.'

Chevannes still said nothing. He knew he wasn't expected to.

'We are now seeing those stars as they were between two and four million years ago: that's how long the light – the information about them – takes to reach us.'

Another minute's silence.

'No one has been able to prove whether they're still even there or not – like Schrödinger's hypothetical cat, kept inside a box. It might be alive, it might be dead. But until we look, mathematically speaking, it's a mix of the two. So, until my work of seven years ago, we could only safely assume those stars were both there and not there.'

Chevannes turned his head to look at his host: he felt like Alice in Wonderland.

'That's the basis of all quantum theory, Mike,' continued Larsson. 'At the quantum level that's just how the world's physicists believe subatomic particles behave; *where* they are depends on who is looking at them – and when. But when no one is looking at them they are considered to be in both phases, in superpositions. But *I* know where they are, Mike. And I can prove their positions, I know how to allow for the effect of observation and measurement and *non*-observation!'

Chevannes nodded again. He would need to practise believing impossible things. Perhaps he should start before breakfast each day.

Larsson glanced at his guest and changed tack. 'We can be sure that some of those stars are suns with orbiting planets, perhaps carrying elements that may have induced some form of what is called life – I prefer the term "intelligence". We're currently looking out for extra-solar planets possessing atmospheres, and simple maths shows us that any form of aware intelligence out there is certain to be *much* more advanced than ours. Half a million years – the time the human species has been around – is merely an eyeblink in cosmological terms, so anything less advanced than us wouldn't even get classified as *aware*.'

Chevannes could feel a sense of inner dislocation occurring. He was inside himself and not; in virtual evanescence. Silence stole around them again.

'I installed all that–' Larsson continued at last, waving at the optical observatory building '–for my own pleasure, so I could personally see and feel closer to a part of our galaxy. But all the really important work these days is done by analysing the feeds we get from space telescopes orbiting the Earth, the moon and Mars, and the signals we receive with these radio dishes. You can't see much from Earth these days, anyway. All serious astronomy is now virtual – non-real-time. It's done by mining data.'

Chevannes's own mind – his 'virtuality' – wallowed in the infinity of light and energy above him but then slowly and reluctantly returned to its earthly container. After a while, he glanced at Larsson and summoned the courage to ask a question that might make him seem a fool.

'Do the radio telescopes also have to be this high up?'

The astrophysicist snorted and leaned forward, reaching into the side pocket of his shorts for a cigarette case.

'These days, yes. Since communications systems went wireless the radio spectrum is as polluted as the visual – like the atmosphere. This altitude – and Peru's isolation on this side of the Andes – takes care of most of that. I also wanted to be private. Nobody ever comes up here.'

The intelligence officer nodded. He tried to guess what it might have cost to transport the materials to the top of the mountain and build the twenty-three radio dishes and their tracks. Of course, if he had Larsson's money he too might do something crazy, something wonderful, like this. This vantage point, this private *montevideo*, provided a view previously unknown to him, a perspective unimagined by his terrestrially shackled consciousness.

Larsson lit his joint with a match, blew out the flame and flicked it away into the darkness.

'I don't want to be away from here long.'

They were due to leave the next day.

The UN man stretched. 'With any luck it will take just a few days – a week or so at most.'

Larsson drew on his joint. 'You understand why this matters so much? Any advanced civilization will be wholly virtual. Even if they still retain some physical form, all their communications, transactions and interactions will be virtual. That might be digital, it might be some other form of representation, but I'm certain that however they communicate they will encrypt everything. They will be using prime-number or quantum encryption for *everything*. Why do you think the thousands of radio telescopes in the SETI programme have so far found nothing? All they would be hearing is white noise, even if they were receiving full-on extraterrestrial communications every day.'

Chevannes nodded again, even though he barely understood.

'Others can't understand what they're hearing – but *I* can. And that's why my work here, my data mining with my decoding software, is so important.'

TWENTY

The great river was at the peak of a spring tide; a billion gallons of water embanked in a swirling equilibrium. Nature's forces were at stalemate for a few minutes; ancient antagonists brought to yet another temporary cessation in their involuntary reflex to the planet's pulse.

Jack leaned on the stone parapet of an elevated, gilded Pagoda – a Japanese 'peace present' to the people of London – and watched eddies form where the scouring bore of the English Channel met a stately Thames and suddenly, savagely, turned it estuarine. Three hundred yards to his left, on one of the riverside benches in Battersea Park, the elfin figure of Haley Voss sat absorbed in a book. She was dressed for the heat in a loose white short-sleeved blouse and long white linen skirt. Her left hand was resting on the handle of a child buggy but Jack guessed, from the lack of movement, that little Toby was sound asleep.

He had been watching her for nearly half an hour and neither of the two London agents drafted in to assist him had reported anyone who looked remotely like a tail or any other form of surveillance. She was clear.

He pocketed his viewpers, pushed himself away from the parapet and walked down the stone steps. Crossing the monument's gravelled surround, he began to stroll slowly along the edge of the grass towards her. The heat of the early August afternoon was oppressive – climatic changes were making London summers more like New York's – and he was glad he'd worn a polo shirt and shorts.

Jack was supposedly now in upstate New York visiting his mother again. He had received a suitably worded message from the hospital – her condition was causing concern, but he should not be over-alarmed – and despite the frenetic activity as Hope Island prepared to host its *One Weekend* celebration, he had promptly taken compassionate leave.

At UN headquarters he had found Deakin and his much enlarged Operation Iambus team running at a far higher level of activity than before. Jack had been surprised when told that Counsellor Furtrado himself had recently flown to London to visit Haley Voss. Then he had laughed when he heard the outcome. He could imagine their encounter.

'But that's not necessarily the best outcome,' Deakin had pointed out. 'She could do a lot better working from the inside, if she could get more intimate stuff on him. Do you think we could trust her to work with us, Jack?'

So 'Bruce Curtis' had flown to London that same night, feeling irrationally excited by the task ahead. During the journey he had joined his mother for breakfast via his VideoMate, Al Lynch having adjusted both Jack's unit and his mother's, to register their current locations as upstate New York. So Jack leaped forward a few hours to UK time and spent ten minutes reassuring his mother that he was safe and well, while observing that she was thoroughly enjoying bossing her younger sister around.

As Jack came within the extreme boundary of Haley's peripheral vision he noticed that the heavy volume in which she seemed engrossed was a treatise on antitrust and competition law. He stopped and waited, watching her eyes saccade across the print, her pen poised in her right hand, ready to mark any passages of interest.

He saw her head turn, then she glimpsed his feet. She stared up, directly at him and gasped.

'Hi,' said Jack. 'Good book?'

'Jack!' Her smile eclipsed the afternoon sun. She leaped to her feet, the book falling to the ground.

Crossing the space between them, she reached up to hug him and kissed him on the cheek.

'What the hell are you . . .?' She tailed off. 'How did you find me here?'

He gazed down into her earnest brown eyes.

Then she groaned. 'Oh, don't tell me, you can't help any more. That lawyer's sent you to talk me out of it, hasn't he? Forget it, Jack. There's no way.'

She turned away to check on her charge, then picked up her book and sat down again, staring out at the water.

He stepped forward and sat down at the opposite end of the bench. 'That's not it,' he said gently.

'So why *are* you here?' She turned her head towards him.

'It is a lot of money, Haley. I'm not sure I would turn down that much,' he teased.

'It'll make a good intro,' she said defiantly, looking back at the river. '"I was offered eighty million dollars not to write this book!" I recorded it all.'

She put out her left hand to rock the child buggy, as if Toby had suddenly woken and become fractious. One leg was crossed over the other, swinging back and forth in the same rhythm, as she stared straight ahead.

'Yes, it will,' he agreed. 'But there might be an even better one.'

She shot a look at him. 'Who *are* you, Jack? How come you just pop up out of the ground whenever you think I need you – like a genie in a pantomime?'

Jack glanced to left and right. There was a jogger approaching from one side, otherwise this part of the park seemed deserted.

'I'm here to ask you to change your mind, Haley. If I know Furtrado, he's told you how you can still accept the company's offer.'

'I thought so,' she sighed sadly. 'You don't know me, Jack. There's absolutely no way.'

But Jack knew her better than she guessed – and he still wanted to know much, much more about this woman.

'No, that isn't what I mean, Haley. I want you to *appear* to agree. To take the access to Tom they've offered you.'

She turned to stare at him, still not understanding.

'Oh! I should do "A Year In The Life of Thomas Tye", should I? Live on his island, attend the meetings, meet the main staff, travel with him – the TV, the performances, the deals. Take my pay-off money, write a hagiography and *finish* my career!'

'You wouldn't need a career after that.'

'I'm not like that,' she replied simply.

'Leaving aside the money on offer, don't you think all that inside stuff could be useful?' he reasoned. 'For producing the sort of book *you* want to do.'

Haley looked at him, wondering. 'What do you mean? How could I?'

Jack, in his turn, contemplated the river. He allowed thirty seconds to pass as the jogger – not one of those marathon dromomaniacs but a reluctant middle-aged male – panted past on the grass running-track behind them.

Then he turned to face her, resting his arm along the bench.

'Haley, your book, as you originally planned it, *needs* to be published and it will have to be as hard-hitting as possible. It was you yourself who said that no one man should be able to control the future. The world *should* know the real story about Thomas Tye, about the genetic experiments, about Tommy's birth, about the anti-ageing technologies, about how he abuses people. But your book could be even better, more insightful, if you appear to take their offer and use the priviledged access they're offering. The future you're concerned about really is too important to leave to chance – or one man.'

The proleptic future by her feet gave a sudden gurgle. Haley leaned forward, temporarily distracted by Toby's reminder of his presence, but the child had merely turned over in his sleep and was peaceful once more.

'You know that's not possible. I'd have to sign a binding contract. Once I take their money, I'm gagged. End of story.'

'Not necessarily,' countered Jack. 'You wouldn't end up keeping the pay-off, but I could fix the legal stuff so they couldn't touch you.'

She turned to stare at him, then flicked her head away in anger. She folded her arms, head bowed in thought.

He wanted very much to hold and kiss her.

'How could you do this?' she asked, with her chin almost touching her chest. 'Who the hell *are* you, Jack?'

'Sloan will still be your publishers, but you'd be able to add all the inside stuff – the details of his life and how the company works. Sloan will go along with it.'

'You can speak for the Sloan Press.' It was a statement of realization rather than a question. 'OK, Jack. Tell me about it.'

So he had to tell her – and the tide started to turn.

Meanwhile, a few miles to the north-west, the secretary to a large and very vocal committee carefully recorded its vote as unanimous. Chair had made the suggestion in what would now be the last full meeting before the big day itself. But, despite the lack of time for creating replacement publicity, it was agreed that this year's event should be dedicated to the Thomas Tye Appeal for Ethiopia.

The Notting Hill Carnival, now in its fifty-first year, had become the largest street party in the world, eclipsing New Orleans's Mardi Gras and even Rio de Janeiro. Over eight million people now pilgrimed each year to the fashionable streets of West London, but no one intellectualized this rite, no one noted or cared that its timing roughly coincided with the ancient harvest festivals of the northern hemisphere. One of the planet's ancient rhythms had been given a West Indian accent and new lyrics. But the committee members were all aware how it coincided with that rather more exclusive celebration on Hope Island – 'that other little party', as Chair had called it – and her appeal to help out the brothers and sisters in Ethiopia won the day.

So arrangements were made for each of the floats in the procession to accept electronic donation transfers from the LifeWatches and VideoMates worn by millions of spectators along the route, and permission was granted for the Tye Network News channel to integrate coverage of the Carnival with both their live feed from Ethiopia and the *One Weekend In The*

Future celebrations on Hope Island. The Carnival organizers then congratulated themselves on seizing the opportunity to contribute significantly to the greatest philanthropic and ecologically correct gesture in history.

Joe Tinkler was unused to so much jet travel and although he knew his body occupied a seat, he felt as if *he* were still hovering somewhere behind, over some distant continent, just visited. He had experienced the *bizarrerie* of watching the analog time display on his Rolex LifeWatch readjust itself to accommodate seven time-zone changes in one week. He had already turned the jet-lag compensators to 'full' in his viewpers, but his system seemed unable to cope merely by adjusting the light levels that reached his eyes or the level of melatonin delivered by his LifeWatch.

He had just spent four days in London, three in New York, then two days each in Boston, Minneapolis, Denver and San Francisco before crossing the Pacific to visit Hong Kong, Singapore and the royal states of the Middle East. He had finally met in person those he had known for years only as network representations: there was little time for conventions and other industry get-togethers in corporate finance and the participants rarely got to meet face to face. In the flesh they seemed so familiar but, at the same time, so different. Their corporeality flavoured their character in a way that even the most advanced holo-image theatre failed to capture. He wished he had made the effort years before. The only major house he hadn't yet visited was Rakusen-Webber.

Joe Tinkler was also in unfamiliar territory in another sense. As was true for so many analysts, fund mangers, investors, traders, economic forecasters and financial journalists, the prospect of *personally* operating in *real* business terrified him. It was one thing to judge the efforts of others, to identify winners and losers and bet other people's money on it; quite another to imagine how one might fare in such activity oneself. Chelouche had instructed him to form a number of shell corporations based in the United States and Europe that would own the Tye Corporation stock purchased during a take-over. In all of them,

Joe was named as president and chief executive. Even though Chelouche reassured him that consultants would be brought in to manage the businesses, suddenly what had before appeared as a game now seemed brutally real. Joe was honest enough to admit to himself that if handed any real decision-making responsibility for day-to-day activities in any part of the vast Tye empire, he would not know where to start. That would require manipulating people, not numbers, and Joe had little experience of that.

He had most of his options now in place and he was going home – well, back to Geneva. The meal in the first-class upper cabin of the Airbus 1000 had been excellent and, after the flight attendant had cleared his tray, he had opened his VideoMate to return to the vast spreadsheet in which he was keeping an updated total of the commitments he had been making on behalf of the World Bank. Tye Corp's core stock price had been rocketing in anticipation of the Ethiopian technology launch and several of the Tye Corporation's institutional shareholders had insisted on prices so high that exercising these options in the future would be fabulously punitive. The amount he had already potentially committed exceeded his largest estimate and he wondered how Dr Chelouche would react on learning the sums involved.

As his exalted shadow-employer had requested, Joe conducted every negotiation in person and he had filled out the option agreements by hand in front of his wondering counterparts. Joe's cover story was a small truth, which is often the best servant of a larger lie. He wanted his option on their Tye Corporation shareholding to be kept a secret, he explained. He was contemplating some power plays in the market and he didn't want to signal his intentions in advance. Only Joe Tinkler could have got away with such a ploy: he had already been the world's best-known Tye Corporation analyst and investor and, since his spectacular move from Rakusen-Webber to the largest bank in Switzerland, his personal reputation had made him the brightest star in his own arcane firmament. The options were for ninety days; there were non-execution and get-out clauses galore to protect the sellers, but all were subject to ultra-strict confidentiality clauses.

The net effect was that, if Chelouche so wished, the signed papers in the pilot's bag lying on the seat beside Joe would, on receipt of the stipulated payments, deliver nearly twenty-one per cent of the core Tye Corporation's voting stock into the hands of the World Bank. This would provide Joe with an almost unassailable position from which he could begin buying on the open market with the aim of reaching a position of overall control. If this happened, Joe realized, it would in turn deliver the whole Tye business to the UN and, ultimately, to the people of all its member states. These days, that was almost every nation in the world.

Joe flipped open his communicator and noticed he had AgentMail waiting. It came from one of the software agents he had reprogrammed to search for any new land deals entered into by Tye International Real Estate. He read through the government-published documents the agent had retrieved. Now Tye was buying vast tracts of real estate in Northern Canada! One deal alone was for a strip of land around Hudson Bay that ran for nearly a thousand miles through Manitoba, Ontario and Quebec! Another was for thirty-two islands in the Bay of Alaska, off the coasts of Yukon Territory and British Columbia. He pulled up an atlas and zoomed in to inspect the territories concerned. He noticed that they were at similar latitudes to Tye's Baltic acquisitions.

But none of this made sense. Canadian zoning and planning laws were every bit as strict as US regulations and commercial or industrial developments must be out of the question in areas of such natural beauty. Nothing about the purchases suggested a prospecting operation either and Joe already knew that there was not a single mineral or petrochemical operation in the entire Tye empire. It certainly wouldn't be oil: for one thing Tye was the major global opponent of the fossil-fuel industry – and, more practically, the price per barrel had stubbornly remained below $10 for over a decade. As global warming had continued to increase – despite many late-twentieth-century experts who had predicted the opposite – most analysts believed that the solar-fuel capture and delivery systems produced by Tye's Solar Energy Division, and two or three less prominent competitors, would completely eliminate the fossil-fuels market by the end of the century.

Joe studied his map again, then reviewed the deal announcements his agent had found. Some of these purchases were freehold, others were for very long leases. He made a PopUp reminder for his assistant to get hold of copies of the original conveyance deeds.

Haley was incandescent with rage. 'You bastard!' she screamed at him. 'You allowed me to think Sloan Press wanted my book on its merits and all along you and your friends in the UN were *paying* them to publish it!'

They were back at her flat after a still-slumbering Toby had been returned to Felicity's care. Jack had walked around the park with her to where Haley's twin sister was due to collect the boy in her car. The sister had eyed Jack knowingly as they were introduced. She already knew about him, Jack recalled. He had been astonished to see them together again: they *were identical*.

'We're *not* paying them, just underwriting their legal liabilities – protecting them from the Tye Corporation's lawyers. They bear all the normal costs of promotion, marketing and so on.'

Jack had told her as much as he was authorized to during the last half-hour they had been back.

'But you allowed me to continue thinking this was a straightforward publishing deal. You fed me information! YOU SET ME UP!'

She turned away from him, trembling with anger, and stared unseeingly out of her window at the trees in the park she knew so well.

He stared at her back, at her slender neck with its wisp of dark hair curling down towards her white collar. Feeling an instant and urgent longing, he wanted to cross the room and hold her. In comparison, Calypso's beauty now seemed abstract, something too perfect, something chiefly to admire. But this seemed real and very close. He realized suddenly that his long sleep of emotional regeneration was finally over, and that he had woken to a desperate longing for the woman standing with her back to him. Helen's face swam into his mind and he was able to imagine her granting permission.

But the woman in front of him was in no mood to care. She swung back to face him, her fine chin jutting with determination and anger.

'You lied to me Jack, you lied, and that's the worst thing anyone can do. Just leave me alone. I'm going to do this my way and I don't need you, the United Nations or Sloan Press – or any of you. I'll find a new publisher and I'll do this *my* way!'

He saw tears – was it anger, pride, regret? – gathering in her wide brown eyes. She tossed her head once and then glared up at him.

'I think it's time for you to leave, Jack, don't you?'

I think I am hopelessly in love. I want you so much I don't know what to do. My pulse must be over a hundred. My stomach feels worse than it used to when I was about to go into action. My hands are wringing wet. My breath is coming in short gasps.

He takes a step forward, strange geometric hinges in time and place opening before him.

'Haley...'

She doesn't move.

He reaches out and caresses her cheek with his fingertips.

'Haley...?'

She is staring up into his clear blue eyes. All she sees is honesty – and a light she doesn't recognize, but one that seems compelling and all-embracing.

'Haley, I don't care about any of this. All I know is I don't want to upset you. I never want to upset you again. I...'

She can't stop her tears now, but she can't turn away. She feels them tumbling over her lower eyelids and down her cheeks.

Suddenly he is against her, holding her head in both his hands, kissing the tears from her cheeks. He kisses her lips, her mouth, and she hungrily kisses his. She no longer has any idea of what she is doing, but her heart is singing.

The writ was served by hand, in the front office of the Tye Corporation Legal Services Department on F Street and 6th, Washington DC. In itself this wasn't unusual. Writs were still sometimes served by hand, although electronic filing had long since become approved as the fast and sensible way to serve notice of a legal claim. But some contrary legal firms still liked to pettifog with old-fashioned methods, and Furtrado assumed that Masters, Morrison, Johnson & Co of Knoxville must have deliberately set out to be vexatious.

He broke the seal and sat back to read. To a seasoned lawyer a writ meant little more than childish name-calling in a school-yard: as many as a dozen different writs were received in one part or another of the Tye group each day. Few of them ended up in Furtrado's personal office, since usually they were appraised by one of his team and spun out to the most appropriate law firm to make an initial response.

But this writ had been delivered just as Furtrado himself was crossing the lobby. He had scooped it up from the reception desk with a smile; it never hurt to sample the daily activity.

He read it once, then read it again more carefully. It had been issued by a wholly champertous Southern law firm on behalf of the Memphis-based family of a retired fast-food fran-chise owner, now deceased. The man had bought a replacement liver in an auction run by LifeLines Inc., part of the Tye Life Sciences Group, for $20.5 million. The writ claimed that the liver had been guaranteed a 95.21 per cent match with the recipient's DNA profile, but the actual match had turned out to be less than forty per cent. Despite belated immune-system treatment, the patient had died as his body rejected the organ. Attached to an aggressive covering letter sent in advance of the formal legal procedure of mutual 'discovery' and disclosure of evidence was a copy of LifeLines's guarantee of the DNA match profile and an extract from a consultant pathologist's report declaring that the organ was, in fact, no more suitable for the patient than any random organ obtained on the charity market.

Such *prima facie* evidence was compelling. The family was claiming back the original $20.5 million and seeking $800 million in punitive, *solatium* and compensatory damages.

Furtrado had never seen such a claim before, but then, LifeLines had only been in operation for three months and had only recently enjoyed a spectacularly successful flotation on the EUUSA biotech market.

The counsellor knew immediately whom to call. Zachary Zorzi, as Tom's latest rising star, was now busy building the auction models that would be used to market all products produced by the Phoebus Project. Furtrado found himself praying that this writ wouldn't prompt the discovery of any serious technical problem that could affect *that* launch.

TWENTY-ONE

'Give us a little tour,' Chevannes shouted above the engine noise. 'We've got a first-timer.'

The pilot nodded and the UN Jet Ranger 209B rose from the JFK helicopter pad as readily as a hungry bee from a depleted bloom.

On their long flight north, Chevannes had learned that the Swedish mathematician and astrophysicist had never visited New York and, like millions of immigrants before him, the UNISA officer couldn't resist proudly showing off his adopted city.

They had travelled from Lima first-class, in seats paid for with UN money, a new experience for Chevannes but a luxury the directors of Operation Iambus considered appropriate to their guest's status. Unknown to that guest, two UNISA field officers dressed as businessmen had also shared their large cabin – 'just in case,' Deakin had said, although Chevannes couldn't imagine what such a 'case' might be.

As their plane had crossed into North American airspace Chevannes had noticed that the matrix of laser-borne communications above them was growing denser. He had remarked on this to his travelling companion.

'Yes, it's criminal,' agreed Larsson, misunderstanding Chevannes's meaning. 'Those lasers don't have to be visible at all. They just add the visible wavelengths for show, so they can be seen from the ground. Tye Networks started that as a marketing gimmick, years ago, and all the others followed suit. It ruins terrestrial astronomy.'

'Thomas Tye, again,' grunted Chevannes.

Larsson smiled and leaned over to the window.

'But it's become the best economic indicator there is – like vapour trails above a city in the old days. When I was a boy my father used to tell me to look up at the sky to see how many jets were flying in and out of Scandinavia. That's how we knew how buoyant the economy was. Now we just look up at the night sky, and the more laserbursts, the greater the economic activity on the planet.'

Chevannes had simply nodded and returned his attention to the light show.

In New York the other passengers in first class were held back so that the two men could leave the aircraft first, clearing immigration and Customs by a nod directed towards the waiting US diplomatic officer at the exit. They had then stepped through a side door in the jetway ramp and down an open stairway to a United Nations limousine waiting on the tarmac.

In less than five minutes their helicopter was climbing westwards above the soul-sapping undulations of Queens's parched and polluted cemeteries. Chevannes found this rapid transition from a Peruvian mountain top distinctly disorientating and he tried to imagine how his companion must feel after so many years of isolation. But as soon as the man-made peaks of Manhattan rose in front of them, the Scandinavian intellectual was gawping, staring and smiling like any other first-time visitor.

Receiving clearance for her detour, the pilot looped south to follow the East River down to Staten Island. Here she circled the Statue of Liberty once, then climbed over the World Trade Towers and followed Broadway until it was time to turn towards the East River again, to begin their approach to the landing pad on the top of the United Nations Secretariat building.

Chevannes had already called ahead and five minutes after his arrival on UN sovereign territory Rolf Larsson was shown into the thirty-ninth-floor office of Alexander Dibelius.

'We are extremely grateful to you for coming here, Doctor,' said the Secretary-General as he walked around his desk with his hand extended.

Larsson looked up into that sage face with an apologetic

smile. 'I'm told some of my work from years back is causing trouble. I'm sorry.'

'We'll see what can be done,' said Dibelius, smiling. He turned to another man in the room and Larsson was introduced to Dr Yoav Chelouche, the President of the World Bank.

Over the next hour the two men explained carefully, as they had done to Jack Hendriksen two months earlier, the implications of the Tye Corporation's growing power and monopolies, the dangers to global economic stability and the threat to peaceful economic progress that it posed.

The astrophysicist was shaken and mortified by their revelations, beginning to understand the scale of the problem created by the private and exclusive sale of his decryption software. He explained to them that since he had recovered from his immersion in psychedelia his attention had been wholly fixed on astronomy and his search for extraterrestrial intelligence.

'I withdrew from everything to do with this world,' Larsson admitted. He had delegated the management of his vast financial portfolio to three different private banks and, apart from having stipulated that over fifty per cent of his wealth must be held in Tye-related stocks – for reasons he blushingly admitted were related to the competitive advantage he knew his software would bestow – he explained that he had paid little attention to economic affairs.

He had signed the UN silence resolution almost without hesitation, only delaying to confirm that he would be safely beyond the reach of any legal attack from the Tye Corporation.

'If I have UN immunity, will I be able to resume my previous work?' asked Larsson, as he realized what might become possible. 'Once I had sold the concept to Thomas Tye the agreement stopped me carrying on with any similar experiments. But now...'

'Prime example of a monopoly stifling innovation,' huffed Chelouche.

The Secretary-General smiled and said he would seek advice on the subject. For the moment, Doctor Larsson had better consider his work subject to UN approval.

By the end of the session Larsson had agreed to provide full assistance to the UNISA operation to limit the growing power of the Tye Corporation.

Then he was handed back into Mike Chevannes's care and taken to the adjoining Marriott Hotel, now owned and operated under franchise by a UN nominee corporation. There he settled into an electronically secure suite near the top of the tower – likely to be his home for some weeks, he now realized. Later that day he returned to UN headquarters and the serious debriefing began.

He was conclaved first with some prominent mathematicians retained by the UN. Alan Mathison had flown back to New York from the English fenlands and the great Professor Maurice Mendeléeff of MIT had flown down from Cambridge, Massachusetts to share in the revelations. After a day, this small investigating committee reported back to Jan Amethier and Ron Deakin. It seemed as if the Swedish prodigy *had* made a major breakthrough in defining sub-quantum states – and, as a result, in pure mathematics. As they made their report to him, Deakin could sense that they were suppressing a degree of irritation. Larsson would now continue to an experimental stage to test the strength of his proof. They explained that nobody could predict whether such experiments would be successful and, if they were, what the impact on physics, mathematics and other branches of science might be. The academics seemed especially annoyed that Larsson should have fully understood the importance of his achievement but had chosen to throw away academic fame – and the benefits of his work to the world at large – in favour of developing and selling a software simply to crack codes.

They confirmed that Larsson's software did indeed break all current forms of encryption, even messages encoded with super-long bit-lengths as used by the National Security Agency, the Pentagon and the US military. As an example they supplied a file of messages they had fished from the networks and successfully decrypted. Even this random trawl had produced startling results and Deakin and his boss exchanged glances as they flipped through them.

Despite their contempt for Larsson's commercial activities,

the two mathematicians' academic enthusiasm had become more evident as they reported their findings until the two UNISA men found it hard to keep smiles from their faces. Although they understood little of the theory, they were prepared to accept the mathematicians' analysis without question.

'So what now?' Amethier had asked finally.

'So *now* we've got to get on with engineering delivery systems for quantum encryption!' announced Professor Mendeléeff, seemingly amazed that the agency boss hadn't grasped the obvious. 'Nothing, *nothing* will be safe until that is done.'

Amethier shook his head and admitted he was lost here.

'All the UN agencies – the World Bank, the IMF, UNISA, everything – have got to move to quantum encryption as quickly as possible,' the mathematician explained with exasperation, as if the suggestion was totally obvious. 'That's *absolutely* safe. The technique itself was discovered years ago – back in the nineteen-eighties, by Bennett and Brassard – but everybody then assumed that our current encryption techniques were sufficiently secure; there was no need to develop the network technologies necessary to use it.'

He went on to explain that the ultimate encryption technology, one mathematically proved to be completely unbreakable, used the quantum characteristics of photons – particles of light – to encode messages. Even trying to take an unauthorized look at such messages destroyed the contents and Larsson's new formulae for calculating the effects of observation suggested many ways of exploiting that apparent irrationality. But the problem lay with developing networks and communication systems capable of transporting such minute and unstable elements. Now things were different, of course, and work must begin at once.

'You mean *this* unbreakable encryption will really be unbreakable?' asked Deakin. 'Unlike the *last* unbreakable encryption?'

They both nodded, oblivious of his sarcasm. They were keen to get back to their universities and begin raising money to start the work.

In the end, Jan Amethier called Larsson into the meeting,

thanked him again for his cooperation and congratulated him formally on his achievement. Both Mathison and Mendeléeff extended invitations for him to join their faculties if he ever got bored with life on his mountain top.

Easy Zee Zee was finding it hard to maintain his famous equilibrium and his normal techniques for mood adjustment had failed to restore a feeling of well-being. The recent call from Furtrado had sent a panic through the LifeLines operation. At the counsellor's insistence, every organ auction was temporarily halted – to the utter dismay of next of kin all around the world who had initiated but not completed the sale of donor assets they had just inherited.

The investigation had confirmed that the complaint from the Memphis customer's family was justified; the liver that had been delivered had been only a 38.67 per cent match for the DNA with few common genes on the sixth chromosome and almost no common antigens.

No obvious reason could be found. The computer records of the transaction revealed that the DNA files that had been automatically compared at the time had, indeed, shown a ninety-five per cent match. Now the two records were clearly a mismatch. The problems weren't in the computer storage systems or in the DNA comparison software. It had to have occurred in the networks.

Zee Zee was an expert on computer systems and he knew there had to be a forensic audit trail that would reveal where the foul-up had occurred, but he wasn't the one being asked to pursue that investigation. At Furtrado's insistence, he had e-mailed someone called Raymond Liu, the Technical Director of Tye Networks's global infrastructure, to ask for his department's help with the investigation. While he waited to hear from him, he went over the Phoebus sales plan again to ensure there was nothing technically flawed in what he was going to propose to Tom and the main board.

Al Lynch loved numbers, numerate people and machines with the potential for intelligence. When he had been a student his heroes were Blaize Pascal, John Von Neumann and Konrad Zeuss while his contemporaries had been living for Bruce Springsteen and Whitney Houston. His philomathy drew him to study the work of the great steganographers of history (and their cryptanalytical counterparts) for his doctoral thesis. He had loved travelling to Britain to study the original sixteenth-century books and papers of Thomas Phelippes, the man who had deciphered the encoded messages of Mary, Queen of Scots to her cloyning supporters in a plot against her cousin, Elizabeth the First of England.

Then he traced and studied the original notes and drawings made by Charles Babbage, the nineteenth-century inventor of the world's first mechanical computer. Babbage had cracked the 'unbreakable' polyalphabetic Vigené telegraphic cipher – *le chiffre indéchiffrable* – that had been invented by Blaise de Vigenère in the sixteenth century and that had been resurrected as the trusted form of inter-government communication once Samuel Morse's invention had gained international acceptance.

At that time in his life, it would have been fair to say that Alan Lynch was a total nerd.

All of this returned to him as he waited to meet the young Swedish genius who was supposed to be the latest in a line of great cryptographic minds. On hearing who was arriving, Lynch had needed little prompting to pack up his two most powerful network computers, abandon his beloved Fort Mead laboratory and ship the computers and himself up to UN headquarters for the meeting.

Al Lynch was also delighted that for the first time in over three years he had been able to make such a trip without being imprisoned in a wheelchair: life was returning to normal. The week before, he had experienced his first erection since the crash. He had wept as he clung to it.

The obstinately perambulatory computer scientist had sent instructions ahead and, within two days of his arrival, a temporary computer lab had been established in a basement room one level down from the Security Council's private meeting chamber. The room was in the deepest level of the UN complex, a space carved out of the Manhattan bedrock in the early 1950s when it was believed that there was a good chance that this bunker would have to house many of the world's leaders during a global exchange of nuclear weapons – and for a very long time afterwards.

The meeting had been memorable. Within minutes Lynch and Larsson were exchanging views about cryptographic achievements of the past and Larsson realized that he had found something rare: a listener capable of understanding his work.

Lynch was careful to make it clear that he did not yet understand how the irrationality of quantum mechanics and string theory could be adapted to apply to rules as strictly logical as those of binary representation. But Larsson was pleased to hand over the software he had brought from his Peruvian mountain top. Loading this, Lynch followed Larsson's instructions on how to run it against the petabytes of data Jack Hendriksen had copied from Thomas Tye's personal data warehouse.

Three hours later Larsson wore a broad smile, while Lynch knew his own jaw was in danger of acquiring a permanent sag. Every file and document that had been sent to Tye or that he had created in the last dozen or so years was now accessible as plain hologram, video, sound, image, document, spreadsheet, text or binary code.

Lynch then called Deakin down and they trawled at random through the vast sea of data. After half an hour Deakin had to give up, his head spinning.

'This really brings it home,' Deakin observed as he scrolled through pages of highly confidential Tye Corporation business plans. 'We've all relied so much on this encryption system that if someone discovers the key, you're completely vulnerable.'

Larsson had had the grace to look away.

Deakin drafted in two psychologists to examine Tye's personal recordings in order to construct a detailed psychological profile of the tycoon. He then ordered all patent-related communications to be distributed to the team's patent lawyers. He also faxed Chelouche to request Joe Tinkler's presence in New

York to lead the team of business analysts already starting to work backwards over the countless project plans, deals, acquisitions and business plans that had been revealed.

After half a day of this, Martha Rose, the international legal expert, opened a video discussion with Deakin. She could hardly contain herself as she described her evidence.

'He's guilty as hell,' she told Deakin with absolute certainty. 'There are copies of three original documents intercepted by Tye CTA – his Competitive Threat Analysis Department. And there are copies of the patents Tye subsequently filed. We think there must be thousands more. We've just got to find a way of legitimizing this evidence.'

Deakin congratulated her as he turned to examine the files on his recently reactivated display screen.

Then their discoveries became a flood. One of the human rights lawyers had found a file on Lily Albertyn, Erasmus Research and on the birth of a boy called Reon.

Next Professor Berzin of the World Health Organization dropped by with a wry smile on her face. 'He's refiled for the patent on body chemistry. It looks like they realized they had the wrong genes, but now they've identified the right ones.'

For a few moments Deakin knew what it felt like to be Thomas Tye: omnipotent.

The President of the Australian Republic was responsible for the idea spreading to the southern hemisphere. Even though it would already be afternoon in all Australian time zones before the rains were predicted to begin falling on Ethiopia, Robert O. Baldwin decreed his country should start the global celebrations.

'We'll be the first to kick off the greatest street party this planet has ever seen,' he told his people formally. 'So let's give generously to the people of Ethiopia.'

The President of Bolivia was next, announcing that the Festival of San Roque, which this year also fell on Sunday, 30 August, would be co-dedicated to the Ethiopian Appeal. Within two days, most countries on the continent of South America had followed suit.

On EUSSA the Tye Corporation's stock rose another fifteen points.

The parcel, delivered by one of the island's couriers, was waiting for Raymond Liu when he eventually returned to his apartment in the SpacePort Development.

He slipped off his shoes, flopped into an easy chair and ran his fingers under the seal of the gift-wrapping. He removed a small leather-bound book, clearly an antique. There was a handwritten card.

Raymond,
I am truly sorry that aspects of our work have alarmed you. Please be assured that none of our experiments conducted within the digital environment growing around this planet will cause problems with your day-to-day network operations.
I thought you might enjoy the enclosure. Although many critics have dismissed Descartes as misguided (because of his religious and spiritual confusions) he nevertheless provided the original inspiration for my work.
With very best wishes,
Theresa

Liu turned the book over. It was René Descartes's *Discours de la Méthode Pour Bien Conduire sa Raison, a Chercher la Verité dans les Sciences* and this English translation of the 1637 work – which rendered its Anglicized title as *The World, Rules and Discourse on Method* – had been printed and bound by Bartholomew in London in 1847. He saw a small place-ribbon and opened the book. He read the section Theresa had indicated:

Then, carefully examining what I was, and seeing that I could pretend that I had no body, that no outer world existed, and no place where I was; but that despite this I could not pretend that I did not exist; that, on the contrary, from the very fact that I was able to doubt the reality of the other things, it was very clearly and certainly followed that I

*existed; whereas, if I had stopped thinking only, even though
all I had ever conceived had been true, I had no reason to
believe that I might have existed – from this I knew that I
was a being whose whole essence or nature is confined to
thinking and which has no need of a place, nor depends on
any material thing, in order to exist. So that this I, that is to
say the soul by which I am what I am, is entirely distinct
from the body, is even easier to know than the body, and
furthermore would not stop being what it is, even if the body
did not exist.*

Raymond Liu finished the passage and then reread it. He
closed the book and sat for a moment staring out at the setting
sun, considering Theresa's *apologia*. Then he turned to his
screens, located a retail book resource and hunted for something
suitable to send her in return.

The temptation was overwhelming; the information that lay
before Joe Tinkler was the stuff of a trader's fantasy. The fund
manager had only been back in New York for two days, but he
was already drooling. Al Lynch had installed network filters –
he called them 'sniffers' – at key locations on the world's
networks to intercept, collect and reassemble all packets of Tye-
related data that passed by. The scrambled messages were then
submitted for processing by Rolf Larsson's software.

On his arrival from Geneva, Joe had been able to expand
Lynch's search vocabulary considerably by providing an up-to-
date list of all the corporation's subsidiary identities, the names
of the top 500 Tye Corporation and subsidiary-company executives and the group's wider interests and investments. The result
of their collaboration was a continuous flow of decrypted highly
sensitive information to Joe's temporary desk in the UN. He felt
as if he was inside Thomas Tye's head.

'Take this new Tye Life Sciences operation, LifeLines Inc.,'
Joe said to Yoav Chelouche, waving a printout of a decrypted
e-mail in the banker's direction. 'We hold nearly sixty-eight
million dollars' worth of this stock, but now there's at least one
lawsuit pending for mismatched organs. The stock's going to

collapse if more follow and someone goes public. Now's the time to sell.'

They were meeting in the banker's office on the thirty-ninth floor of the Secretariat building. Joe had now discovered that his boss was in constant rotation between three addresses: his office in Geneva (his preferred location), this jurisdictional eyot in the middle of Manhattan and the World Bank's global headquarters building in Washington DC.

Chelouche waved his enthusiastic young protégé back into his seat. He understood how excited Joe must be by his new discoveries. In the past ten minutes he had been shown business plans for two new Tye Corporation start-ups, eight strategic transcontinental acquisition recommendations and four sets of accounts that were nearing final-draft stage. If he allowed Joe to make trades from his large fund on the basis of such inside information, it would become infallible: then he realized that they would be no more infallible than Tye's investment decisions had been for the last seven and a half years.

'You want to trade on all this inside information, Joe – you think that's OK?' Chelouche flipped at the pile of printouts Joe had placed on his desk. This meeting seemed more formal than their Geneva discussions: Chelouche behind his desk, Joe seated in front.

'Why not? That's exactly what Tye himself has been doing for years, sir,' reasoned Joe. 'And we know they haven't yet realized we can read their messages. We're keeping tabs on all the communications from their CTA – their Competitive Threat Analysis division. They obviously felt confident enough not to use Larsson's techniques to improve their own encryption. Very cocky.'

Chelouche nodded. He quite liked the idea of Joe's fund building up the cash necessary for a takeover from profits made in such a fitting way.

'And look at this,' urged Joe, leaning out of his seat again. 'This is a contract between Tye Agriceuticals and the government in Addis Ababa. TA has obtained the genetic rights to all the arabica coffee grown in the hills of south-west Ethiopia. I've done some research – that's where coffee originally came from and those plants contain every basic genetic variation for coffee in the world. As a result, only Tye Agriceuticals will be able to come up with new coffee strains based on the master gene pool. Their agreement is due to be announced once those rains are supposed to fall, and coffee has now become the world's most valuable commodity since it overtook oil. If we short the other coffee stocks now, we can...'

Chelouche held his hand up once more. 'I know, I know. There will be many other such opportunities...'

Joe sank back, still anxious that the banker should understand the magnitude of this one in particular.

Chelouche considered, scratching the stubble on his jowls. 'OK, I agree, Joe,' he nodded after a long period of silence. 'Let's use the ganef's own tricks against him, for the time being. But only on Tye Corporation and its subsidiary stocks. Give me your word, Joe; use this inside information on nothing else. And remember, we want to keep things nice and steady. This situation won't hold for long.'

'I understand, sir,' said Joe, already imagining what he could achieve.

Rolf Larsson retraced the tortuous route to the roof of the UN building, but tonight he was stopped at the last flight of steps by a security guard. The soldier hadn't seemed particularly impressed by the visitor's newly issued UNISA security ident or by his powerful image-stabilized binoculars; he simply pointed to the 'Restricted Access' sign. Larsson had then dangled his roll-up sheepishly between his fingers and the guard had finally relented, allowing him entry to one of the few areas of the UN building where smoking was permitted.

Larsson sat down on a small bench a few hundred yards from the helicopter landing pad and stared up at the sky. This was *really* why he had come up here at the dead of night. He was missing his night sky, even though he had presumed that Manhattan's urban glare would make observation difficult. But in fact it hadn't: tonight was very different and he was pleased he had broken off from his analysis of Tye Aerospace documents – Thomas Tye's ambitions were making his head reel.

He had seen the aurora borealis, the Northern Lights, hundreds of times before. Those sheets of red and green light were a familiar spectacle in the summer skies of Scandinavia. There was even an oil painting of a circular borealis in the cathedral near his old apartment in Stockholm. That had been painted in 1431 when the unusual event had been seen as a celestial warning. Now, modern scientists explained that the lights were caused by discharges of solar particle energy as it met the magnetosphere – the Earth's protective magnetic shield.

But the Northern Lights were so called because they were *northern*, and they were seen almost exclusively at latitudes where the sun's harsh output of damaging radiation was deflected over the North Pole. Tonight, the skies above Manhattan were Christmas-coloured: the giant alternating sheets of crimson and green wrapping around the lower latitudes of the night side of the planet.

Larsson lifted his binoculars. In the glow he could make out small knots of observers on other high-rise buildings in the city.

Towards the end of the fourth day after they had broken the codes the excitement within the Operation Iambus team was beginning to lessen slightly. Deakin took the elevator down to the third basement level of the Secretariat building to visit Al Lynch in his cryptorium. He found the computer scientist engrossed at his terminal. He didn't look up until his old friend touched his shoulder.

'I think I'm beginning to get it, Ron,' grinned Lynch as he turned round in his swivel chair. 'I think I understand what Larsson has observed – how computing two alternative states for each object can weed out high primes and then produce a definitive string of integers. It sounds dotty but it isn't – it's just an incredibly high-speed process.'

Deakin held up his hand in protest as Lynch sank into a chair: 'Al, you know I can't follow this stuff. Just so long as it's working.'

'Oh, it's working all right,' beamed the scientist. 'We're getting a terabyte an hour of decrypted material off the networks. I just spoke to one of the translators from the Chinese section; she says the People's Republic is getting very worked up about a Tye Corporation land deal in Russia, close to their northern border.'

Deakin nodded. He had already seen the translated decode. 'Al, I want you to do something for me.' He handed Lynch a printout of the *Wall Street Journal* article reporting Congressman Robarts's accusations.

Lynch skimmed it and looked up questioningly.

'Can you get into the US defence networks, Al – the White House, the Pentagon, the National Security Agency, you know? Oh, and NASA?' He saw his friend's stare. 'We need to know what's behind this. Larsson's been looking at Tye's Phoebus Project and he's making some very strange noises. We need to find out what the Americans really know about Tye's plans, and what they intend to do about them. Can you also check the State Department – they've summoned Tye for a meeting.'

Alan Lynch shook his head. 'I don't know, Ron. I've signed up to the Charter – we all have.'

It was one thing for the UN Security Agency to spy on commercial enterprises: that was easily justifiable in the interests of the greater global population. It was another to consider spying on a member state, especially the most powerful of all, even if that country's governmental lower house did periodically display its collective envy of the UN's global role by withholding US dues. Such hacking would be a direct contravention of the United Nations Charter and a crime under international law that, on detection, carried a mandatory prison sentence.

'I know, Al, I know,' agreed Deakin. 'This would have to be strictly between us. I'm not even telling Jan, let alone the SecGen – they'd have to refuse permission. But I wouldn't be asking if I didn't think it was really important.'

Lynch considered. He had served twenty-four years with Ron Deakin. First at the National Security Agency in Fort Mead when Ron had been the youngest instructor ever in the US Navy SEALs and a liaison officer between his special forces and the NSA, then for the last three years in UNISA after they had sworn new loyalties. In the end, many such decisions were based on trust and long-established relationships, rather than man-made laws or abstract notions of right or wrong.

'They'll have every level of security on their networks, Ron – detectors, false doors, booby traps – even before we get to isolated networks, firewalls, data-dykes and flame-moats,' he objected. 'They're the biggest and brightest target for hackers the world over and the more you get hacked, the better you get at detecting it and preventing it.'

'But you do have an advantage, Al,' prompted Deakin. 'Quite an advantage – in fact, two advantages.'

Lynch smirked and shrugged his shoulders. He had helped to design most of the networks in use by the main security agencies of the USA *and* he had Larsson's software. 'Give me a day or two,' he said.

'I'm sleepy,' said Jed.

Calypso and Tommy exchanged a smile: they had been near to dozing off themselves, but that wasn't what the Furry meant.

'I'll do it,' said Calypso, stifling a yawn and closing her magazine. She pushed herself up from the cushion of her shaded sunlounger and looked around.

'There's one by the changing room,' suggested Tommy, looking up from his book. He shielded his eyes and pointed to a low white building almost completely concealed by shrubs.

Calypso nodded and bent to pick up the Furry. Since Tye Consumer Electronics's breakthrough in battery technology, portable electronic devices such as Jed needed only a twenty-minute battery recharge once a month and the caterpillar's announcement of impending sleep was his euphemistic request for an energy top-up.

They're the only ones amongst us who still have monthly cycles, she thought absently as she carried the caterpillar towards the low building. The introduction of hormonally active foods for women had allowed most females in the developed world to dispense with the inconvenience of menses until they wished to become pregnant. Ovulation was mimicked, because of its impact on female (and male) sexuality, but otherwise menstruation was a female inconvenience that had been almost forgotten.

Calypso left Jed in nap mode to recharge his batteries and strolled back towards the pool. This was where Tommy had suffered his accident three months before. So much had happened since then. Now she was living in the great house behind her, sleeping in the bedroom next to him and watching him blossom in front of her eyes: she felt a sense of contentment she had never known before. Because of his special circumstances, she felt that she could allow herself to become much closer to him than she could to another woman's child. The thing that had most astonished her was the realization that inside this totally isolated, unworldly, unsophisticated and dependent little boy was a remarkable intellect. For example, Tommy wasn't just musically gifted: he displayed a range of talents way beyond the normal repertoire for a child of his years.

Now he was reading *Great Expectations* and she saw him flip the page every thirty seconds. At first she had suggested he must be 'skimming', but he had solemnly handed his book to her and challenged her to test him on any part already read. His responses had been word-perfect – he had a true photographic memory. *Not good, however,* she thought. *Tommy will heal himself best when he can forget the strangeness of those past lonely and artificial years.* During their time together she had been able to carry out a number of standard psychograms and she was now convinced that he had outstanding intellectual potential.

Calypso had grand plans for introducing Tommy properly to the world – even considering inviting other children from the island to stay at the main house. Then, as he got older, he could start to visit the American mainland, perhaps even go to school there. St John's in Chicago was very good, she'd heard. Or perhaps the Old Suffolk, or Choate in Boston?

The afternoon was unusually sultry. They had swum earlier before collapsing on the sunloungers. The pool was half Olympic size, sunk into the vast south-east lawn beside the house. It was heated by solar power, like almost everything else on Hope Island, and Calypso had persuaded the pool-keeper to reduce its temperature to twenty-two degrees Celsius. They had enjoyed a very energetic game of two-person water polo earlier and the doctor inside Calypso felt sure it was better to have the pool water cool enough to make exercise enjoyable.

She walked across the thick matting now laid around the pool edge, arrived at the deep end and stared down into the crystal-clear water. She glanced across at Tommy: he was still engrossed. Stepping up onto the low springboard, she took a few moments to estimate its length carefully, made three running strides, lifted her hands above her head, and shouted 'Tom-mmmyyyyy!', executing an almost perfect dive with a single, 360-degree full-tuck roll at its apex. As she entered the water she felt her tibia touch as they followed the rest of her vertical body, ramrod straight, into the cool water. She knew it had been a surgical entry; an aquatic incision, almost soundless, certainly without splash.

Calypso levelled out close to the bottom and made three broad breaststrokes, exhaling all the air from her lungs. She swam six more strokes and then gently propelled herself to the surface, halfway along the pool. She shook her head, pushed her hair back, treading water, and looked across at Tommy.

A slim figure was standing beside the boy's lounger. Where had Tom come from? Father and son waved to her and Calypso waved back, rolling on her back to face the sun. She trolled gently down the pool, wondering whether she absolutely had to climb out and join them. She knew Tom's presence had to have a purpose: she had never known him to be out in the garden during the day. She hadn't even known that he was on the island. Despite her closer proximity to her charge, there were still long periods spent with his tutors, and there seemed to be no set pattern of contact with his father.

Reaching the shallow end she swam for the steps. She would have felt more comfortable wearing a slightly less revealing swimsuit, but the one-piece Speedo she wore for her ocean crawls was back at her bungalow.

Calypso raised her arms and hauled herself up the steps, straight into a flurry of enveloping green cotton. As she looked up, Tom was standing there, smiling and holding out the large beach towel she had brought from the house.

She was very aware that her white bikini was just a little too daring for the occasion. It was hardly a string or a thong; it was just, well, a little skimpy. She knew the effect that her breasts and the rest of her body had on men.

As usual Tom was wearing sun-viewpers so she couldn't see his eyes. But his face was aimed in the right direction, and his smile was very broad indeed. Suddenly self-conscious, she turned her back and let him drape the towel over her shoulders.

'Beautiful diving, Calypso.'

Folding the towel over her chest, she turned back to face him, pushing the wet hair up off her face.

'Thanks, Tom. Product of an island childhood.'

He turned and they both began the walk over to Tommy.

'Couldn't take any more of the office for a while,' he explained.

She turned to glance at him. She had never heard him express such a feeling before.

'So I thought I'd come down and see how you two are doing. Connie told me you were here.'

Calypso nodded. Connie was the anchor: the place where every scrap of executive and domestic information resided before finding its final home. Every one of Tommy's movements had to be logged in Connie's scheduler.

'It's going to be a hell of a weekend,' Tom said, changing the subject abruptly. 'This is where we'll be entertaining our guests.'

He gestured across the lawn and down towards the three descending terraces that stretched away into the distance in landscaped splendour.

'The pool and the lakes will be boarded over to serve as catering areas,' he explained.

Calypso nodded. The staff in the main house had already tripled in size and she had seen teams from the caterers and entertainment providers scouring the grounds for weeks. Tommy was eager, almost desperate, for the Firework Masters to arrive from Sydney. He already knew that he would not be attending the party, but she was planning to watch the fireworks with him from the roof terrace of the mansion itself.

'How *are* you going to make it rain in Ethiopia, Tom?' she enquired.

TWENTY-TWO

'But how, precisely, is the great mensch going to make it rain in Ethiopia? asked Yoav Chelouche. '*If* he makes it rain.'

The senior members of the Operation Iambus team had been called for a meeting with Jan Amethier and Yoave Chelouche in the banker's office in the UN Secretariat building.

'We'll know better when Doctor Larsson and the aerospace team have finished analysing the Phoebus data,' replied Deakin. 'But it's likely to take another few days: there's so much material. The Tye Corporation is mad keen on recording everything – like every company these days.'

Chelouche nodded. In the absence of the Secretary-General, he was the most senior UN person at the meeting. They now knew that the Tye Corporation had bought much of Eastern Siberia – that news had caused some explosions in the team, not least with expatriate Russians – and it was accepted that the Phoebus technology was somehow intended to change the climate there. Thanks to Joe Tinkler they had also learned of other newly purchased territories in the Baltic Sea and in Canada.

'What do the weather people say?' asked the banker.

'They can't even give me an estimate of how much energy might be needed,' said Deakin. 'Current technologies are merely a pinprick compared to nature's force. They claim even the American military can't change the weather pattern without resorting to nuclear weapons.'

'So do we have to presume he's using some form of orbiting nuclear energy?' asked Amethier quietly.

'I very much doubt it,' argued Deakin. 'Tye maintains a strongly anti-nuclear stance and I don't think he could sell the idea to his shareholders.'

Chelouche gave a big shrug, as if doubting that would rule it out.

'So let's move on to the legal status,' suggested Chelouche. 'What have we got?' He turned to Martha Rose, senior adviser on international law.

'We've now identified over three thousand separate cases of intellectual-property theft by either the Tye Corporation itself or one of its many subsidiaries,' the attorney told them. 'There is hard evidence on each count, but it is debatable whether an international court would allow us to enter the evidence we have obtained. It was, after all, stolen and illegally decrypted.'

There was a silence as they digested the implications. It took Chelouche to break it.

'All laws are made by men – and women,' he hastened to add, 'and all systems and structures we have are, in the end, political. That means they are decided by people, not by some distinct and invisible hand, however much we sell that notion to our populations. The International Criminal Court of The Hague is independent, of course, but it is independent by the support of the entire international community, not despite it. I am no lawyer myself, but I am forced to be something of a politician. I think we must recommend that we prepare for immediate prosecution.'

Deakin held up his hand. 'What about economic stability, Doctor? You're the one who convinced us that we must protect the markets above all.'

The banker nodded and stroked his jowls. 'It hadn't slipped my mind, Exec Deakin,' he growled. 'I'm now in a position, potentially, to take over this corporation – temporarily, at least. The investment community will accept the World Bank as a trustworthy guardian – legally, a *parens patriae* – for the shareholders.'

Deakin whistled soundlessly. He nodded his understanding, his appreciation of the capital involved and the amount of work that must have already been done.

'There's still the issue of public opinion, Doctor,' he objected quietly as he imagined the global TV coverage any trial of Thomas Tye would receive on the networks. 'The public will be voting by their billions, on the hour, every hour, throughout the trial. Every minute we'll be watching how the world's population regard this man – as innocent or guilty. It matters not a jot what the judging panel may say. At the end of the case, if over sixty per cent of the public think he's innocent, we can't go against that opinion and expect still to gain the support of our member states. In democracies national leaders would then be forced to announce their support for Thomas Tye in order to protect their own political position. And, as Tye's a serving Head of State, a prosecution would have implications for other leaders of non-democratic states. We'd risk the UN coming apart. Our public opinion people say that Tye's stock has never been higher – in both senses. None of us can just go *against* the will of the world's people these days. That, in the end, is the reality of our new people's democracy.'

'That depends on what the man's doing, Head of State or not, Exec Deakin,' responded Chelouche tartly. 'And it looks to me as if the Tye Corporation is getting seriously out of hand. I'm going to recommend to Alex–' they all registered this pointed use of the Secretary-General's first name '–that we set our legal team on preparing a specimen case. Get them to look for one with an appealing human angle. You're right, of course: this will have to play well with the people.'

'Try this, it's beautifully made,' said Felicity flipping the trouser suit over on its hanger. 'Look at the lining.'

Haley had decided to treat herself for the Hope Island party, so she and her sister had booked a day's shopping at one of the new themed retail resorts near Gatwick Airport. They had checked in soon after nine a.m. and had established their base in their personal Day Room before venturing out into 148 acres of enclosed semi-tropical jungle, simulated cityscapes, waterside dining areas and entertainment complexes. Dotted among the palms, lakes, waterfalls and rustic-cobbled city streets were designer boutiques, delicatessens, coffee shops, bookstores, luxury goods stores, hair stylists, beauty salons, wine bars and 'outdoor' eating areas serving a vast range of fine food and informal, freshly cooked delicacies. Minute hummingbirds, genetically modified to shed their excreta percutaneously and hygienically, filled the air with darting flashes of vivid colour. Wading birds, similarly adjusted, decorated the watersides. As the shopping vacationers moved from area to area, the temperature of their environment altered with the type of location, and concealed ScentSims filled the air with the latest and most exclusive environmental fragrances.

Like most professionals, Haley did nearly all her routine shopping on the networks. Her personal shopping agent had created a 3D mannequin of her UK size eight body, a virtual tailor's dummy, precisely to her own physical measurements, that made trying on virtual representations of clothes a precise science. Not only could she see how well a garment fitted her, she could also see it in a huge variety of colours and co-ordinates and even in different settings. Many on-line suppliers had abandoned manufacturing ready-to-wear garments and had returned to offering clothes tailored individually for every customer.

Another advantage of network shopping was that purchasers could see how a garment looked from all angles. The problem of metamerism – of a colour appearing different under varying light sources – had been finally solved and today Haley could be sure that the colours seen on her display were accurate. This ensured that the pillar-box red garment she saw on her screen would appear equally vibrant when the garment itself was delivered by the courier. The 'two-hour guaranteed' courier services and a 'no questions' exchange or refund policy on non-tailored garments had also boosted the virtual retail trade after it was discovered that twice as many people would make impulse purchases if they could be sure of receiving them shortly after making their decision.

But Haley had to admit that network shopping wasn't as much *fun* as being here in person. It was a great luxury to wander amongst actual clothes racks, to feel and smell the shopping experience. Since themed Retail Resorts had started offering overnight accommodation and leisure facilities such as casinos, swimming pools, golf courses and tennis courts, such shopping vacations had taken over as the premier holiday destination in North America, Japan, Britain and parts of Europe. They also now catered for day-visitors, like Haley and Felicity. Having a personal Day Room as their base and the facility to bundle all shopping and recreational spending together in a single payment made at checking-out time had turned an experience once a High Street nightmare into a truly sybaritic sojourn.

And, of course, spending time at a Retail Resort was a great opportunity to catch up with family and friends. Since her sister had collected her from Battersea, Haley had talked about little else but Jack Hendriksen. Before he left he had assured her that all covert personal surveillance of her by the UN International Security Agency would be lifted and she had taken him at his word. Things between them had become so momentous that she only had two choices: to trust him wholly, or to absolutely reject him and everything connected with him. She had now made her choice and contacted Marsello Furtrado. With a show of wariness and reluctance, she had agreed to the deal he offered.

'What do you think Jack would like to see you in?' asked Felicity innocently.

Haley playfully struck her twin on the upper arm. *All right: so she had been talking about nothing else.*

'I'm not buying this for Jack,' objected Haley 'I want something to make me look like a world-famous biographer.'

They both laughed and Felicity held up the suit again. Haley took it from her: black with a single button where the deeply cut jacket lapels met, straight trousers with a delightful wrap-over waist. She *would* try it on.

When Jack had first kissed her it seemed as if everything in the world had stopped: as though she was stationary and the world and all its people were spinning around her. They had kissed until they had to break off, breathless. Then Jack had fished in his pocket for a short plastic device.

'We're alone now,' he said as he pressed a button. 'This will jam all signals. I'm sorry, but you've been kept under surveillance since long before I met you.'

Suddenly all the wonderful hot emotions flowing up inside her were met by an icy down draught of some horrible reality that threatened to wreck everything.

Sitting her down at the table in her kitchen, he had held both her hands tightly while he had told her more about the United Nations and his role with the agency.

Then he had hesitated, staring down at the table surface.

'I am in love with you, Haley,' he declared at last. 'I have only ever been in love once before – with my wife. I am thirty-eight years old, so I know what real love feels like compared to any other feelings when we meet someone we're merely attracted to.'

She had nodded, tears welling in her eyes. 'I've never felt like this before, Jack,' she told him. 'I just have to think about it for a while.'

He had not stayed the night. But it had been agreed that he would return the following morning and they would spend the day together.

Human sleep is a safety precaution made necessary by the planet's axial rotation and the random branching of the evolutionary bush which, in *Homo erectus*, elevated vision to become the supreme sense. Thus, when darkness fell and vision's sensory advantage was neutralized, the proto-humans managing to cling on to their nasty, brutish and short lives long enough to reproduce were those who wisely retired during the absence of light. Modern human brains use part of this inherited and seemingly wasteful lack of consciousness to process information and to learn. That night, in her dream-filled REM sleep, Haley learned that she did, indeed, love Jack Hendriksen.

She woke with a smile, his face filling her mind. She turned to the pillow beside her and imagined his face there. She gathered her duvet between her legs and imagined it was him: the process of automorphic projection had begun. She laughed and whooped out of bed to see her reflection grinning back like an idiot from her bathroom mirror.

Their first day together had seemed magical. Jack borrowed a UNISA pool car and drove them to Brighton. They walked

hand in hand along the promenade, the gulls screeching overhead, surrounded by throngs of weekend visitors enjoying the
late-summer sunshine.

Jack meanwhile explained the plans they had for her. Haley
was to be offered both a UN passport and protection from legal
action against her by the Tye Corporation. It was recommended
that she take the Tye Corporation's money, sign the contract
they offered and place the initial payment in an interest-bearing
escrow account with her solicitor: she would then make use of
the access they offered but would later back out of the deal with
them and return the money. Her UN immunity would protect
her from the legal challenge they would inevitably mount. It
wasn't honourable, Jack acknowledged, but then neither was
Thomas Tye, it seemed, and this was part of a larger, very
necessary strategy.

On the way back to London Jack had urged her to take
whatever Tye was offering – including the invitation to the party
on Hope Island. No other writer or journalist had ever been
granted access to the island.

This time Jack *had* stayed the night, and by morning Haley
knew she wanted to marry this man. Everything about him
seemed so right, so familiar, so part of her. There was none of
the lack of ease, the excessive politenesses, the over-careful
behaviour that had characterized all her previous new relationships. Though mostly tender and considerate, he plainly desired
her so much that he had sometimes seemed a little rough which,
Haley realized in surprise, had pleased her even more.

After one more day he had to return to the States. He had
already been away from Hope Island for too long, but they
would be reunited at the celebration. As soon as the UN
operation was finished, Jack would resign from the Tye Corporation and join his brother's successful yacht brokerage. Would
Haley consider living in Naples, Florida? There would be no
practical immigration difficulties: the incredible boom of the
euro and the expanded European Union – its six hundred
million people in thirty-four member states now representing
the richest single market in the world – had reversed the

economic migration patterns of the twentieth century. Now many Americans of Irish and Italian descent were trying to get back into the re-enriched lands of their forefathers.

On their second and final day together they visited London Zoo in Regent's Park. All the larger animals had long since been relocated to safari parks and game reserves outside London, but the lovers wandered through the aquariums, pens and aviaries of the smaller beasts in a happy daze. Neither of them was really aware of their surroundings, but both felt a resonance with other creatures of the planet.

'There will be some people waiting for us when we get home,' Jack warned during the taxi ride back to Haley's flat.

Two men were positioned outside the red-brick mansion block, both fit-looking, in their early thirties and wearing business suits. Jack got out of the taxi first and shook hands with them. Darryl and Terry apparently belonged to UNISA's London team.

'I want them to stick around after I leave,' explained Jack. 'They won't be watching you, they'll just be on hand to protect you. We're playing for very high stakes in this game.'

Haley had agreed reluctantly. She was beginning to realize that she had been plunged into something much larger and potentially more dangerous than she had anticipated.

Jack had stayed on after the two men departed. The worst thing for both of them would be the difficulty of communication. They certainly wouldn't be able to trade locator ident access, as had recently become the fashion for lovers – glancing at a screen to see where the other was at all times was immensely satisfying, at least in the early phase of a romantic relationship. Jack had to explain the UN's discovery that Tye could read the whole world's encrypted communications.

'I think we can risk the odd quick call,' Jack suggested. 'And if I sound funny it's because I'm deliberately disguising my voiceprint. But we can't safely swap locations. Although they're supposed to be confidential, the Tye Corporation owns so much of the networks that they could easily trace our movements once they became suspicious.'

'I'll go mad if I don't hear from you occasionally, Jack,' asserted Haley, certain that was true.

'You'll hear from me OK,' he promised.

They couldn't bear to part the next morning. After Jack had finally gone, everything felt empty. Even her flat felt alien and unreal. She walked around it, picking up familiar objects, examining them as if they too must somehow be fundamentally changed because of what had happened to her. She decided to go and see Flick, to tell her everything. She would need to take a shower first, but she wanted to postpone the moment.

Then her VideoMate announced an incoming voice call. It was her solicitor, requesting her to come in and see him urgently. They agreed on a time that afternoon. She hung up and then called Felicity.

'Where have you *been* for the last few days?' demanded her sister in vexation. Haley hadn't even checked her AutoSec for messages. She arranged to go over to Ladbroke Grove after seeing her solicitor.

She had never seen Percy Sedley looking so serious. 'The United Nations High Commissioner to Brussels himself has been to see me,' he had begun. Then he blinked, seeming to be at a loss. 'I'm not sure what you're up to, but you're being offered UN diplomatic immunity – a modern form of extraterritoriality.'

Haley raised her eyebrows.

'I didn't really know what it meant either,' admitted the solicitor, 'but he brought copies of the international statutes with him.' He reached out and patted a pile of documents in front of him. 'It seems you will be legally protected over this biography.'

'There's masses and masses of stuff, Ron. I've already decrypted over three thousand communications.'

This should have been a triumph, but Al Lynch looked worried. He had been hacking into the government networks that served the White House, the Pentagon, NASA and other US state-security agencies.

'It took me almost two days just to get in,' continued Lynch.

'They've moved up to microwave moats since I worked on the systems. But once I realized what the White House network architects had done, then the security on the NASA and NSA networks was far easier to spoof. It's always the same: once a department declares a standard safe, they all adopt it in precisely the same way.'

'Congratulations,' exclaimed Deakin, beaming.

'Not so fast, Ron. It isn't good news. I was delighted when I first started searching for stuff on Tye and his corporation. I found plenty of it – policy statements, details of tenders, antitrust proposals, that sort of stuff...'

'But?' prompted Deakin.

'Well, then I noticed something strange. There was a pattern I thought I recognized so I dug out some of my old software. They're all *fake*, Jack, even the ones that look sensitive. They're generating documents and messages using the original software agent I developed when I worked for them. That was how I spotted it. They're still using Version One and it has a few glitches. When I analysed the communications, all the text fitted my algorithm patterns for automatic document-generation. They're faking it, Jack. It's not real. They must know about the Tye Corporation's ability to crack hard crypto.'

So it would seem, thought Ron Deakin. But at this point rank and responsibility forced him to disregard their decades of friendship and say no more.

'Thanks, Al,' he muttered. 'Let's keep this to ourselves, OK?'

Thomas Tye's 'special requirements' meant being very particular about hotels. He chose them because of their location and the willingness of their management to allow his people to redecorate and refurnish, to electronically 'scrub' and install anti-bugging devices in the suites to be occupied. Once satisfied, he would rarely stay anywhere else.

Over the twenty-five years he had been travelling the world, the president of the Tye Corporation had come to know which hotels best suited his own somewhat peculiar needs. So when he was in DC he made the rather eccentric choice of always staying at the old Palmer House Hilton.

The Palmer House was one of the city's old-style traditional hotels, and it was here that Teddy Roosevelt and John F. Kennedy used to throw their fund-raising dinners and post-campaign parties. The Kilkenny-marbled atrium, hallways and lobbies were spacious, as if designed to accommodate the needs of world leaders. To imaginative visitors, the ghosts of JFK and Jackie, Bobby, Teddy and Marilyn seemed to float through the corridors.

Although Tye was travelling with an unusually small retinue – just Connie, Furtrado and two executive assistants, Pierre Pasquier and his deputy director of presidential personal security, Stella Witherspoon – the entourage had still taken over the entire top floor of the hotel. Pierre had drafted in three of the Palmer House security staff to help Stella maintain a complete floor watch during the sixteen hours the group would inhabit the building.

There was a knock on the double doors of the suite and Stella put her head in. 'They're on their way up.'

Pierre nodded and rose while Tye slipped off his mask and handed it to Connie for disposal. He seemed unusually formal, dressed in a dark suit, a white shirt and silver-grey tie. His hair was pulled back severely. He looked like he was going to a funeral.

A few minutes later they heard Stella's coded knock again and Pierre reopened the doors. The three lobbyists entered and were greeted by Marsello Furtrado who then introduced them to Thomas Tye and his executive assistant. It was obvious they were overawed at meeting such a famous face, and they were flustered as they found their seats and groped for personal equilibrium.

Pierre moved to the bar – given the sensitivity of the discussion, he would fill in for waiter staff. He poured two mineral waters and a coffee as he listened to them going over that afternoon's forthcoming meeting between Tye, Furtrado and Jane Treno, the US Attorney-General of William Wilkinson's administration.

'We think they're just nervous about potential political embarrassment from the LA lawsuits, Mr Tye,' began the senior lobbyist, forgetting to use the tycoon's first name. 'The Tye

Corporation isn't an American company any more so your core corporation is outside the reach of the Justice Department and US law. They can't even lean on you by breathing down the neck of the European Union or ASEAN. All they can do is hurt your US domestic operations and, even then, their legal power over a foreign corporation is limited. My guess is that this will be a "Remember you're an American at heart" speech.'

'I'm here because *you* advised that I should see Treno,' Tye said shortly. 'I really don't have time to fuck around with domestic US issues. Marsello's people or the US V-Ps can take care of things here.'

Now it was the lobbyists' turn to exchange looks.

'We're not sure it would be wise to *say* that, Mr Tye,' suggested the senior lobbyist hesitantly. 'The information we're getting is that Justice is very het up about your corporation and Jane Treno is not a woman to mess with.'

'TO HECK WITH HER!' shouted Tye. 'I have better things to do than bum around with bureaucrats and second-tier politicians. They're here today and gone tomorrow!'

There was a silence. Furtrado moved into the space. 'What background material have you got for us?' he asked.

'She's pretty clean,' said the lobbyist. 'We've got all the current information here.'

Furtrado nodded and the lobbyists extracted a huge and very private dossier they had built up on the Secretary of State's personal life and her many interests and causes.

'You wanted me?' observed Michael Chevannes as he closed the door to his boss's office.

'Good morning, Mike,' greeted Deakin, pointing to a chair in front of his desk. The officer detected an edginess in his boss as he took his seat. There were no preliminaries. 'Have you gone through the stuff we're collecting on Tye?' he asked.

Chevannes shook his head. 'Some, but I haven't finished. Like you suggested, I took a couple of days out. Things have been piling up at my apartment.'

Deakin nodded. He knew. Like the rest of the Iambus team he had seen little of his home, or his wife, in the last few months.

'You're going back in the air,' said Deakin as he slid a paper file across the desk. 'There's a flight to Cape Town at three this afternoon.'

Chevannes opened the file and scanned a UNHCR report on a visit to a Zimbabwe jail. Then he started to read more carefully.

'Go and see this Reon Albertyn and his mother,' ordered Deakin. 'She was employed by one of Tye's biotechnology companies fifteen years ago. They've got a story to tell us and if it's what I think, it'll be just what we need. The background is in the file.'

TWENTY-THREE

A 3D projection of the inner planets of the solar system filled the Holo-Theater. Jack had briefly seen a version of this image before – Thomas Tye had been showing it when he had been called away following Tommy's accident at the swimming pool. But this later iteration seemed to contain much more detail and Jack presumed it had been developed into a full demonstration to be shown during Tye's visit to Moscow.

The team leaders of Operation Iambus had gathered in the Security Council's private meeting chamber. Rolf Larsson and the aerospace analysts had now finished sifting through the mountains of data concerning the Phoebus Project and, after providing an outline briefing to Ron Deakin, the astrophysicist had been asked to make a presentation of his analysis as soon as possible. The team members had pulled chairs away from the oval conference table and had grouped themselves in a rough semicircle around the Holo-Theater.

Deakin rose and turned to face his team. 'Most of you have already had a chance to meet Doctor Larsson,' he began. 'Rolf has told me the gist of what he's found but I haven't seen this demo either. From the little I have heard, I thought we should all see it as soon as possible; sorry I've had to take up yet another of your evenings.'

There were brief exchanges within the group. Most had their DigiPads ready for note-taking.

The door at the back of the room opened and Jan Amethier entered, followed by Yoav Chelouche. Deakin signalled to vacant chairs beside him and the director of the UN International Security Agency and the president of the World Bank joined the audience.

'Over to you, Doctor,' nodded Deakin.

The lanky Swede rose and coughed. He looked uncomfortable in his pale grey suit with a starched white dress shirt and blue tie. It looked like an outfit being worn for the first time. Only his grey shoes, ribbed and rubber-soled, betrayed the academic within.

'Good afternoon,' he began, his nervousness obvious. He clutched a handful of cue cards, looking as happy as a groom at a shotgun wedding. 'First I am very sorry to be the cause of all this. I had really no idea where it would lead...' He tailed off helplessly.

Deakin gave a small wave of his hand that both brushed his apology aside and told him to get on with it.

'Well... this model was extracted from Thomas Tye's personal files. It is a copy of something completed by the Phoebus Project team only about three months ago,' Larsson said, struggling to gain confidence. 'It appears to be the final demonstration model for the project.'

He stepped into the Holo-Theater and stretched out his arm. 'None of this is to scale,' he explained as he pointed at the bright yellow ball of light representing the sun. 'If this was an accurate model, these planets–' he indicated the spheres representing Mercury and Mars '–would be out in New Jersey and the Earth would be somewhere in Pennsylvania.'

Several in the audience nodded. Jack noticed that the planets were moving in their orbits, the difference in their relative speeds around the sun clearly visible.

Larsson touched a remote control and the perspective changed. They watched as the Earth enlarged and swept across in front of them, left to right, revolving quickly on its axis.

Larsson froze the image and pointed at the side of the Earth facing them.

'You will see that the side away from the sun is always dark. This makes our night.'

Jack heard a muffled 'Jesus' from somebody at the back of the group, then a stifled laugh from further along the line.

'Yes, I'm sorry,' apologized Larsson, his small and painfully acquired store of confidence ebbing. He shuffled his cue cards anxiously. 'I just wanted to make the point since it's very important.'

He fingered his remote control again and the image changed to reveal the sun in the centre of the holo-pit and a larger image of the Earth, revolving slowly before their eyes, its night-time longitudinal meridian towards them. After another shuffle of his cards, he found the prompt he wanted.

'Tye Aerospace has been claiming that the aim of the Phoebus Project is to create a chain of deep-space navigation satellites that will provide a Space Location and Navigation System – a sort of interplanetary GPS system. But I can now tell you that although the company *has* been building a positioning network, the real aim of the Phoebus Project is to capture and redirect the sun's energy back onto the dark side of the Earth – hence its name. Phoebus was the given name of Apollo, the Greek sun god. I am going to add the images of twelve deep-space satellites that are currently stationary between four and six thousand kilometres above the dark side of our planet.'

With the touch of a button Larsson froze the planet's image again and then a dozen pinpricks of light appeared above and around the top half of its circumference, as if the Earth wore a tiara of small stars. He stepped closer to this large image and pointed to the arc of satellites hanging high above the planet.

'These twelve satellites, out of a total of fourteen launched so far, have been placed in deep-space locations high above the northern hemisphere. They are all sufficiently high up to clear the earth's adumbration – the shadow cast by our planet itself – so are bathed in constant sunlight. You will see that those nearer to the North Pole are much closer to the Earth than those further down at forty to fifty degrees latitude – above the temperate zones of the Earth in the USA, Europe and Asia. They all remain stationary relative to the Earth – meaning they are in fixed positions in relation to the line of the sun-Earth axis. They stay behind our planet, on the opposite side to the sun, throughout the year.'

Larsson stepped out of the Holo-Theater and picked up a

glass of water from a nearby table. His audience remained absolutely silent as they waited. He drank, cleared his throat and returned to the display.

'Now, this is how the satellites will capture the sun's energy.' He pressed his remote control again.

As they watched, every one of the pinpricks of white light seemed to grow outwards, enlarging laterally. After twenty seconds each had become many times larger than its original size. When the simulation stopped developing, the twelve space-craft hung like large silver tiles dotted in a semicircle above the northern half of the Earth.

'Let me show you that transformation in detail,' said Larsson, finally growing in confidence. The image cleared to blackness, then they were looking at a holo-model of one of the deep-space satellites.

'This unit is called a Solaris A-100. It is a deep-space catoptric energy station manufactured by Tye Aerospace in Singapore and then assembled in orbit. Its current position is four thousand kilometres above the sixtieth parallel. That's the latitude that runs through Alaska, Canada, Scandinavia, the Baltic Sea, northern Russia and Siberia.'

Jack saw a smartly suited man to his left making rapid notes on his DigiPad.

'In its passive condition the core satellite doesn't appear very different to one of the many manned space-station structures already orbiting our planet – although those are only about five hundred kilometres up, and fully trapped by the Earth's gravity. Essentially this Solaris weighs 12,000 kilograms, has core dimensions of two hundred and sixty metres by one hundred and forty-eight. Almost all the power used on board is provided by solar energy. Apart from plasma thrusters, employed for pur-poses we shall see in a minute, there is no alternative energy source. This satellite platform was launched from Cape Hope – from the floating facilities at the island – about fourteen months ago. It was initially placed in a low-Earth geostationary orbit at a location pre-booked with the UN Space Agency by Tye Aerospace. The filing described it as an experimental deep-space research probe. After four months of additional construction work in orbit the satellite was boosted to its present position in deep space.'

'Also pre-booked?' asked the note-taker. Jack now recalled he was Joe Tinkler, one of the World Bank people.

'No.' Larsson shook his head. 'International space agreements only apply to orbits up to a thousand kilometres above the Earth. Beyond that, orbit paths and locations are not considered stable – there being insufficient gravity for a spacecraft to be held in reliable Earth orbit. There are therefore no international rules about locations in deep space, no agreements on ownership, no property rights.'

'First come, first served?' asked Tinkler.

'Precisely,' agreed Larsson.

'So how do they maintain their orbital positions?' asked Deakin.

'I'll come to that,' said Larsson, turning back to the spacecraft image. He pressed a button and the satellite shrunk from five feet wide to less than a foot. 'Let me show you something else first. Now watch.'

Small hatches opened on either side of the rectangular craft and with a simulated puff of propulsion gases two small space pods were expelled and began to move slowly outwards in opposing lateral directions. As they did so, the audience could see that each trailed a silver tether behind it, like an umbilical cord linking it to the mother ship.

Larsson stepped back as the pod on his side continued its outward journey. With a retro-firing of propellant gas the pods then stopped at the very edges of the display zone. The image now resembled a silver thread stretched right across the Holo-Theater, interrupted at the centre by the small satellite. This being a representation of deep space, the thread showed no sign of either tension or sagging.

Jack's eyes wandered along the entire image, which now seemed stationary. Then he noticed that the pods at either end of this thread had started to spin slowly on their axis. As the line of thread grew thicker, it became clear that the slowly rotating pods were unwinding some form of tightly rolled-up material. Jack thought of curtain blinds being slowly lowered and, as more of the material appeared, it looked as if it was a form of netting.

'There are plasma thrusters at the bottom of each sail,' explained Larsson, pointing along the bottom edge of one of the descending nets. 'There's no proximate gravity so the sails have to be thrust downwards as the axial motors unwind their rolls. In this simulation the process is speeded up about seven hundred times.'

As they watched, it became clear that each 'sail' was indeed made up entirely of silver netting. After a few minutes the 'unfurling' process ended and the holo-image pit was filled with the model of a minute central satellite from which two enormously long arms supported what looked like two giant geometrically symmetrical fishing nets.

By now Larsson was enjoying the stunned reaction of his audience. He pressed the remote to freeze the image. 'Any idea what happens next?'

There were a few shrugs and head shakes. But this audience didn't seek to be interactive – it just wanted to watch and learn.

Larsson triggered the remote again. At first it seemed as if nothing was happening but then Jack noticed that the latticework of each net was somehow becoming denser. He leaned forward instinctively and realized that the rest of the audience was reacting in precisely the same way.

The holes in the netting were filling in, decreasing the gaps towards their centres. Finally both sails had become solid extents of polished silver. As they watched, the simulation shifted its longitudinal rotation slightly and everybody jerked back as a brilliant flash of light shot across their vision.

'They certainly know how to build a demo,' observed Larsson as he restored a 3D image of the fully-extended Solaris station without the dazzling light.

'Those sails are active solar reflectors, ladies and gentlemen. They are built – well, I don't think that's the right word – they have been created from a new type of photonic biological material called Anacamptonite. Let me turn this image of the fully extended Solaris station around.'

'The meshugener's put giant mirrors up behind the Earth!' exclaimed Chelouche.

'Precisely,' said Larsson. He pressed his remote.

The two-man dog watch aboard the *Knossian*, a 770,000-ton ultra-large crude-carrier belonging to the Lawrence-Antico Oil Co of Quebec, stared at their instruments in disbelief.

Although not the very largest of the world's fleet of ULCCs, the *Knossian* was a modern and supremely well-equipped floating oil tank. Tonight she was almost full, with three-quarters of a million tons of premium crude oil in her fourteen separate watertight compartments. As the use and price of oil continued to decline in the developed world, the oil companies had been forced to adopt the largest possible tankers in order to secure the significant cost-savings associated with bulk transportation. She was on her way from the pipe-head stores of Yamal, a coastal town on northern Russia's Kara Sea, to the refineries of Halifax, Nova Scotia. From here the petroleum and refined oil products extracted from the cargo would sustain the requirements of the American north-east coast market for nearly eight days.

After a further 280 miles on their present south-westerly heading, the *Knossian* was scheduled to change course due west – a turn taking over twenty-six miles to complete – and cross the North Atlantic at a latitude sufficiently southerly to avoid the summer ice floes nudging down from Iceland, Greenland and the Arctic.

Outside, the sky was lit by a breathtaking display of red and green sheets of light obscuring those few stars that could penetrate the pale Scandinavian night skies. But sailors on the northern run are used to such sights and on the bridge the helmsman and the navigator exchanged frowns of extreme puzzlement while they waited for the old man to appear. He would be furious with them, having turned in only two hours earlier.

'Show me!'

Konstantine Stamatis had been at sea since he left school,

and had held commands for fourteen years. What he saw alarmed him.

Data Error, Unable to Resolve Inputs. The error message was overlaid across the ECDIS screen – the Electronic Chart Display Information System that usually provided aggregated and error-compensated information from the three independent GPS systems, together with the vessel's own recent navigation history and radar input.

'This is the NASA GPS on it own, sir,' indicated Hideo Su, the thirty-three year-old navigator. The screen cleared to show an outline of the Norwegian coastline and the tanker's position. It appeared they were approximately fourteen miles offshore.

'And this is the Tye Network GPS,' he said as he switched input. The signal showed them dangerously close to the same coastline.

'But this is the ESA GPS.' The third signal – provided by the satellite system of the European Space Agency – showed them midway across the Pacific!

'You've checked...'

'System diagnostics report one hundred per cent, sir,' confirmed Su. 'There's nothing wrong with the system, it has to be the data feeds.'

'Sir?' Stefan Kronk, the helmsman, bent over the illuminated magnetic compass. It was a fixture on the bridge simply because international maritime regulations still required its presence on board every ocean-going vessel to guard against the unlikely event that the sophisticated on-board navigation systems, and their back-ups, should fail simultaneously.

Kronk stepped back. The captain too bent over the light. What he saw terrified him. The compass indicated that North was off his port bow. He banged on the binnacle as if to nudge a recalcitrant piece of machinery back into order. He saw the needle quiver slightly from the vibration, but North remained where it should not be, 180 degrees in the wrong direction.

He ran to the vast bridge window and stared out at the brilliantly-lit night sky. He would find no help there. He could only rely on a magnetic heading and that made it clear he did

not know where he was. He'd have to head out into the mid-
Atlantic just to be sure.

'Go to manual,' he ordered. 'Hard to starboard, starboard
engine full thrust reverse, port engine full forward. I want double
lookouts placed NOW! Then steer due west, magnetic.'

The giant ship began to turn two miles later. Seven miles
further on it ran aground on the Ka, a chain of partly submerged
rocks three miles from the Norwegian coast. Despite the vessel's
twin hulls, separated by ten feet of air, two of the forward
compartments started to spew crude oil into the incoming tide,
which calmed it considerably.

The image had changed to show the satellite facing away from
them. From this angle, they could hardly see its sails against the
darkness of the background.

'As you will know, when light is incident upon a plane
surface it is partly reflected and partly refracted – that is, bent
and absorbed,' explained Larsson. 'This backing material is very
thin but hyper-dense and it therefore absorbs so little that almost
all light and heat are reflected – it is the absolute proof of
Kirchoff's Law: that the absorptivity of a body for radiant energy
of any particular wavelength is equal to its emissivity at the same
temperature for the same wavelength. In addition, this backing
captures the infra-red wavelengths of light and supplies it back
to the reflections of visible light. This bionic material – the
Anacamptonite – is the subject of one of the many patent
disputes between Tye BioMaterials and university research labs.
Ms Rose tells me that this material was originally designed at
MIT ...'

He suddenly trailed off as he realized what he was saying.
He coughed and turned back to face the image.

'The anacamptic surface is a protein-plastic with shape-
memory electrorheological alloys,' Larsson continued in a more
sombre voice. 'Essentially, it is a thin piezoelectric plastic that
grows like organic material but has a greater surface reflectivity
than a highly polished mirror. The netting on which the material
grows is made of an incredibly light but strong carbon synthesis
– C-sixty, or buckyball carbon atoms as we know them. I know

this will sound like scientific gobbledygook to some of you, but I've laid out explanatory sheets on a table at the back.'

He pointed behind the group, but none of them moved to collect the material. They wanted to hear the rest.

'The framework is also a communications network that connects the different parts of the station and the sails,' Larsson continued. 'When fully extended each of these solar sails are two hundred and fourteen miles across by a hundred and sixty-four miles deep! As you can imagine, they are constantly bombarded by space dust, meteor showers, in fact everything that makes deep space the inhospitable place we know it to be. But this material is the answer. It uses sunshine as its energy source and stores its base shape as a cellular memory: it automatically regrows to mend small holes in a few hours. Every so often a larger object will tear a bigger hole, but the material just grows back. The sail is entirely self-healing.'

They were all silent.

'You see that the sails are made up of squares like a net. There are several reasons for this. The first is that the frames of the squares provide the seating and the point of origin for each segment of – well, maybe I should call it skin – it grows very much like skin. But the frames also do something else. Watch.'

Larsson brought up a new image, this time a large close-up of a single square. As they looked at the flat silver sheet hanging in front of them it began to rotate slightly on its horizontal axis and then on its longitudinal centre. Suddenly it projected another searing effulgence towards the audience.

He flipped the image back to the entire Solaris power station. 'Each of those frames has a series of micro-motors – all solar-powered – that allow the precise angle, the angle of incidence, of each panel to be adjusted according to the specified desti-nation of its reflection and the attitude of all the other reflectors. You see, these sails aren't single reflectors, they are made up of hundreds of different and independently controlled active reflec-tors. Importantly, they can focus a diffused beam of reflected sunlight into a concentrated narrow beam, rather as a school-child might do with the sun's rays through a magnifying glass.'

There was continuing silence as Larsson allowed this

information to sink in. He stepped out of the display pit and took another sip of his water.

'You were going to tell us how these satellites maintain their orbits,' Deakin reminded him at last.

Larsson nodded. 'You've all heard of solar wind?'

Several shook their heads.

'The sun emits a flux – a wind – throughout the solar system. You can see its effect on comets: it creates the tails that stream behind them. This wind from the sun is captured by the huge sails on these space stations: they have enormous area but ultra-low mass. The wind holds the space stations in equilibrium against the gravitational force of both the sun and the Earth – in a condition called the magnetopause, when all the forces are at an equal point. The stations constantly check their position with Tye's real SLNS – the Space Location and Navigation System of satellite networks that Tye Aerospace is now actually placing at key points throughout the solar system.'

Somebody in the group gave a long, low whistle; perhaps expressing appreciation, or amazement.

'How much power do these things deliver?' asked Joe Tinkler.

'Individually, between two and sixty kilowatts to each square metre at ground level, depending on how the overall sails and the individual reflecting panels within them are aligned and focused. It's when the output of all the space stations is combined that it becomes truly awesome – watch.'

Larsson dissolved the holo-pit into blackness again and then presented a large image of a semi-darkened Earth with the twelve silver reflection sails floating in their separate locations above the top hemisphere of the planet.

'So now on this side of the earth it is a winter's night in Europe and Asia. As you can see, the land masses of Russia, Asia, the subcontinent of India, the Middle East and all of Western, Central and Northern Europe are in total darkness. As it is winter in the northern hemisphere you'll see that the South Pole down at the bottom is tilted away from us. At the top we can clearly see the North Pole and the arctic ice mass here–' he pointed to the top of the image '–and we can even see over the top of the globe to the northern parts of Greenland and Labrador.'

As Jack gazed at the large spherical image of his world, he found himself staring at the small islands that made up Britain and wondering if Haley was asleep. He pulled himself back again, realizing this was a simulation and not a real-time feed from one of the Argus satellites.

'For the purposes of this demonstration there is no cloud cover on the planet – I'll talk about clouds a little later – and the small amount of reflected sunlight we can see on this side of the planet is equivalent to what is bounced back from a full moon when it is at its perihelion – its closest point to the Earth. Now...' said Larsson, looking for the right combination on his remote control.

A beam of light from one of the floating sails hanging above the planet's north-east quadrant projected a small square of light over an area Jack identified as Eastern Siberia. Then another satellite added its beam, then another, and then all four satellites suspended above that quadrant were illuminating the same region with an intensity that seemed very bright in the dim, simulated moonlight.

'These satellites in the north-eastern segment of the arc are those closest to the Earth's surface, lighting up an area of about six hundred square miles. If you were standing down there in the middle of that reflected light it would seem like a midsummer evening – still bright, but without the searing intensity of full daylight. As well as the moon, you'd be seeing four little suns in the sky. The power being supplied to this area is about three kilowatts per square metre at ground-level and, from a standing start of zero, that is sufficient to raise the ground level temperature by two degrees Celsius an hour. Let me show you a progression...'

The image clicked off, then on again, presenting another globe with the vast expanse of the Northern Pacific facing them.

'So, it's the middle of the night here, at the International Date Line. These are the Hawaiian islands. Watch as I run this...'

The digital globe started to revolve slowly in an anticlockwise direction and Jack saw a corona of sunlight appear around the eastern perimeter. He watched as the US Pacific coast moved on into daylight while the islands of Japan, the land mass of China and Eastern Siberia, travelling left to right, continued on into the darkness of night. A Solaris satellite in the Western arc of the chain then lit up and illuminated a string of islands to the north of Japan. Then three others in the western segment added beams of reflected sunlight to the same area.

'This region being illuminated is called the Sea of Okhotsk and those are the Kuril Islands,' explained Larsson as he stepped towards the image and pointed at the now-illuminated area. 'This is all part of Siberia, all Russian federal territory.'

'Until August thirtieth,' added Deakin for the group's benefit. He rose and faced them. Larsson pressed a button on his remote and the image froze.

Deakin continued, 'Tye International Real Estate Inc. has signed a four-hundred-and-sixty-year lease on over one and a half million square miles of Eastern Siberia.' He nodded towards Alan Lynch who was seated in the back row. 'Al Lynch has intercepted final copies of the lease documents that were being sent to Tye Corporate HQ by the Russian Estates Office. The land in question becomes a place called Sybaria and it will become the Tye Corporation's sovereign territory on the first day of next month.'

Those who had not heard the news in advance looked at each other in disbelief.

'Lebensraum,' Chelouche attempted to whisper to Jan Amethier, his gravel tones carrying sufficiently to defeat him.

'You'll see their logic in a moment.' Deakin nodded for Larsson to continue and sat down.

The simulation restarted and they watched as the eastern land mass of Siberia, Mongolia and China slid fully into night. As the planet revolved from left to right, more satellites of the Phoebus network lit up, directing beams of energy towards Eastern Siberia as it now moved to the centre of the globe.

Larsson halted the image again. 'Now Siberia is at the darkest point of its night,' he explained. 'And at this stage the Solaris controllers can focus light on the area from all twelve energy stations simultaneously.'

As the twelve satellites of the network lit up, Jack stared at the intense patch of white light now illuminating an enormous area of land. He suddenly thought about the effect such a technology could have on night campaigns – and, therefore, on all military strategy.

'And, of course, they are able to concentrate, angle or spread this reflected light. As we saw, each panel of the solar sails is independently controlled. Watch.' The light shrank to an intense pinpoint.

'What happens down on the ground when all those beams are concentrated towards the same place?' asked Deakin.

Good question, thought Jack, who, alone in the room, could make a guess based on experience.

'We have no data yet on concentrations that would affect an area smaller than ten square miles,' replied Larsson. 'All of this information is lifted directly from the Tye Corporation's own demonstration model and it seems as if the diacaustic potential isn't something they've calculated.'

Right, thought Jack.

'We've been trying to find an astro-catoptricologist to help us,' added Larsson. He saw their blank stares. 'That's a scientist who studies reflections in space, like the *gegenschein* – the reflection of the sun on the dark matter of distant space.'

They remained quiet as he fingered the demo forward. The display now changed to show the Solaris beams opening up, throwing a pale wash of light that covered all the Asian land mass before reverting to its previous configuration, illuminating only Eastern Siberia.

The image of the Earth started to revolve again and, as Siberia turned steadily towards the sunlit equinoctial of the Earth's eastern horizon, the Solaris stations to the west, on the segment furthest away from Eastern Siberia, shut down and passed on the task of radiating the continent to the satellites positioned further east.

'So, they can provide sunlight to that territory all during the night,' pointed out Larsson. 'Now, at the beginning I said there have been *fourteen* Solaris satellites launched so far. Let me show you the other two.'

The current image disappeared completely and then Jack saw a new projection: a smaller Earth, perhaps two feet in diameter, to the left, and a larger sun, six or seven feet across, to the right. The astrophysicist stepped between them.

'Once again, not to scale, of course. The sun would actually be ten times larger than this. Now look...' He stepped over to the Earth and pointed to two silver specks that hung above its northern hemisphere on the sunward side of the planet.

'These two are oblique reflectors positioned to supplement *daylight* sun. I'll need to reduce the illumination...' The images grew dimmer, and Jack could just make out two small areas of brighter light now reflected onto the planet's darkened surface.

'The northern tip of our planet doesn't get much light or heat even in daytime during winter,' observed Larsson. 'I should know, I come from Sweden.'

Nobody laughed or even smiled so he pushed on. 'One of the problems is that for the sun's energy to reach the northern land masses when the North Pole is tipped away from the sun, as here, the sunlight has to penetrate sideways through the Earth's atmosphere.'

He indicated with his finger. 'Above southern Europe, here, sunlight arrives at the top of the atmosphere and then slices laterally through two thousand miles of our atmosphere's moisture, dust particles and pollution before it can arrive at ground level in the extreme northern latitudes. By this time the sun's rays are inevitably very weak. There's little UV and little heat, as it's all been dispersed in the atmosphere hanging over more southern latitudes.'

Then Larsson indicated the two satellites placed above and sunwards of the Arctic. 'But if you place reflectors here, immediately *above* the atmosphere, they can direct sunlight straight downwards. There are only two sunward satellites in the Solaris network today, but there will be a total of forty-two positioned sunward of the planet when the final phase of the Phoebus Project is complete in eight years' time.'

He conjured up additional images with the remote control. 'This is a projection of the later phases of the project. Over the next eight years there will be forty-two positioned on the sunward side, as I said, and a further seventy-eight satellites stationed above the dark side of our planet. This image has been adjusted for visibility so that even those with their black heat traps facing you are shown here as reflective surfaces.'

Dozens more silver pinpricks appeared in space, surrounding the planet. These too enlarged to become like silver tiles floating in space. The Earth seemed to be suspended in the middle of a giant cradle, ensphered by pinpoints of light.

'With the fourteen satellites already in place today, Tye Aerospace and Phoebus Inc. can, over time, heat Siberia's winters up from minus six degrees Celsius at surface level to an average daytime temperature of nineteen Celsius – that's about sixty-six degrees Fahrenheit. They can also avoid nychthemeral variations – the normal temperature changes that occur between day and night. They'll be warming the air masses all during the night and supplementing the sunlight during the day. In summer, when Siberia and all northern latitudes are tipped towards the sun, they can achieve a daytime temperature of about twenty-five Celsius, seventy-seven degrees Fahrenheit. When all these satellites are in place they will become capable of extensive, worldwide climatic re-engineering. We're investigating just what that might mean at the present. And, of course, once the Phoebus Project is complete, terrestrial visual astronomy will become impossible almost everywhere in the world and even orbital astronomy will be seriously curtailed.'

He spoke the last sentence quietly, as if he did not want to further underline the ultimate irony of the decision he had made over seven years earlier.

'Could they pump out sunlight all round the clock with just their present satellites?' asked Joe Tinkler.

'Yes. There're bound to be periods when one or more of the satellites is down for one reason or the other, but most of them will be capable of working on a twenty-four-hour basis.'

'So Tye could light up any part of the Northern Hemisphere, starting right now?' queried Joe.

Larsson nodded and walked closer to the image again. He pressed a button and the image of the fully developed network disappeared, leaving only the twelve satellites hovering above the dark side of the Earth and the two on the sunward side.

'Most of the present system's power is concentrated between the fiftieth and seventieth parallels – as I said, that takes in Siberia, Russia, the whole of Northern Europe, Canada and Alaska. Two of the Solaris stations, the ones located furthest from the Earth – here and here – lie between the thirtieth and the fiftieth parallel. We're not yet sure what use they will be put to. They could produce spot sun-power for all sorts of purposes – a few nights of sunshine to ripen a crop of grapes, or to provide street lighting for cities in the temperate zones – even for something as non-essential as film-making.'

'But what about clouds?' asked Jack, speaking up for the first time. 'Wouldn't they completely wreck the performance?'

Larsson beamed, as if he had been asked a very difficult question for which he had a ready answer.

'The Solaris satellites are able to provide a constant stream of energy and, using that, they can probably burn off most types of cloud cover. All they have to do is to concentrate several of their beams onto a particularly dense layer of cloud – even as high as twelve or thirteen thousand metres – and, over a period, it will disperse as the upper atmosphere heats up.'

There was a silence as the audience digested this information.

'It's simply evaporation; the clouds turn into vapour or rain,' added Larsson. 'But you would need to ask the meteorologists for fuller detail.'

'Why aren't there any satellites in the southern hemisphere?' asked Jan Amethier.

'Look,' said Larsson. He pressed a button and the globe began to turn slowly. 'In relative terms, there isn't a lot down there. Except for New Zealand, Australia, the southern tip of Africa, South America, it's all ocean.'

'Sir,' interrupted Joe Tinkler as if to confirm, 'Over eighty per cent of the world's economic activity takes place in the upper two-thirds of the Northern Hemisphere.'

'Thank you, Mr Tinkler,' said Amethier patiently. He well understood the problem of the North/South economic disparity, it was almost the inverse of the planet's distribution of population and was a topic that dominated the UN Assembly Chamber. He turned and said something inaudible to Yoave Chelouche. The banker nodded, then coughed, a deep crackling sound.

'So how does he make his famous rain with all this?' he asked.

Larsson gulped, then smiled. 'We're not absolutely sure yet. Perhaps this is one for Professor Madison...'

A short woman in late middle age, wearing a dark green suit, raised her hand tentatively at the end of the row and rose to her feet. 'It's not easy,' she began, hesitantly. 'There're so many possibilities and we have to complete our measurements. We need output ratings, atmospheric measurements, historical data...'

'Just give me the implications, not the specifications,' interrupted Chelouche rudely, displaying a mixture of irritation, impatience and anxiety.

'We can't answer your question yet, Doctor Chelouche,' she insisted quietly but firmly, then walked along the line of seats until she stood directly in front of the banker.

'On Mr Deakin's instructions I can't call on my normal team for analysis – no American nationals, universities or institutes.' She glanced at Deakin for confirmation and received a slight nod, although Jack could see a hint of annoyance in his boss's expression, as if he wished this information had not been revealed.

'Nobody who habitually studies weather, atmosphere, water circulation, ecology or the environment has ever seen a model like this. I'm told there's no data available from the Tye Corporation either on this?'

Larsson stepped forward again. 'It seems as though anything the Tye people produced on weather projections is either missing – or perhaps studies were not undertaken.'

Chelouche and Amethier exchanged a grimace of disbelief.

'So I need to gather a team to play "what-if",' continued the meteorologist, 'and I need real specialists who *do* understand the *specifications* before I can even consider possible implications.'

She looked Chelouche straight in the eye.

'Just to start with I need heliologists, hydrometeorologists and aeronomists.'

She paused, drew breath, then bore down on him again.

'I then need micrometeorologists, limnologists and climatologists as well as cloud physicists, nephologists and glaciologists. I especially need hyetologists. All have to be gathered.'

'Ologists,' sighed the basset hound in resignation.

She shot a look at him and then continued as if he hadn't spoken. 'I've already identified most of the people I need but they've got to be vetted by UNISA and then many have to travel from universities and institutes outside the USA. Only then can we begin to start investigating what the *implications* of all this might be.'

Chelouche rubbed a palm over his heavy jowls. He looked as if he had been working long hours recently. 'But how long, Professor Madison?' he asked wearily.

She hesitated before she answered. 'You do understand what he's doing, ladies and gentlemen? He's re-engineering our planet's climate. We can only begin to guess at some of the implications of that. It will be a long time before we can even suggest some possible outcomes.'

'Thanks, Marla,' said Deakin, brokering a peace. 'When do you think you will be able to give us your first thoughts?'

'Maybe a week,' she replied, with a smile intended solely for him.

'There was nothing diplomatic about *that*,' said Furtrado as he eased himself into a seat beside his boss.

'How the fuck could they have acquired so much knowledge about our land deals?' mused Tye as he accepted an antiseptic hot towel from the stewardess. They were waiting to take off from Marsh Field, a private-aviation airfield twenty-two miles south-west of Washington DC.

'Through a mix of diplomatic leaks and straightforward spying,' reasoned the counsellor. 'They'll have had the CIA and

NSA onto it. I think we've been lucky to keep the lid on everything this long with Orlov trying to spend his new cash so fast.'

The Attorney-General had been direct with them. The American government wanted full disclosure about this cession of Russian Federal land to the Tye Corporation and an explanation of how the company intended to use its new territory. The administration also wanted a full disclosure of any additional, undisclosed functions and the purpose of Tye's new deep-space satellite network.

'We realize the Tye Corporation is no longer an American company,' Jane Treno had acknowledged, 'But we'd like to think you remain one of ours at heart, that your move from US soil had more to do with corporate financial advantages than any desire to be *un-American.*'

The last word was spoken with an emphasis that made Tye frown. For the second time in three months he felt physically and mentally uncomfortable. There in the Roosevelt Room of the mock-Palladian Department of Justice building on Pennsylvania Avenue he had no control over his surroundings. He had no idea who had sat before him in this gilded, upright chair and he could imagine the dirt that must linger around him in what looked like nineteenth-century drapes and furnishings. But even Thomas Tye could not really ignore a summons from the Attorney-General of the United States and expect to continue doing business with the US government, which was one of Tye Corporation America Inc.'s largest customers.

'You understand how delicate the diplomatic balance has been in that region,' she continued as one of her male lackeys offered the visitors more jasmine tea. The great tycoon had touched nothing so far, and Tye waved the offer away again.

The Secretary of State took a cup of iced tea from her assistant and nodded. 'Let's go off the record – Tom,' she had continued. At this clearly pre-arranged signal her four assistants had risen and left the room. She sat forward on the sofa, facing him.

'We would like the Tye Corporation to become an American company again,' she said, so quietly that he had to strain to catch her words. 'There are significant long-term civilian and defence contracts that would be available to you. We can ease things in LA. You could be assured that your shareholders would not suffer. We could extend US protection to Hope Island State and, if it becomes appropriate, to your new territories in Siberia. But there would be no requirement for you or your staff to redomicile.'

Tye and Furtrado had exchanged glances.

'I know the President is keen for this,' pressed Jane Treno 'We can work together as partners. It would be important for our economy – for both our economies.'

'*And* for his fucking election campaign,' yelled Tye before his counsel had the opportunity to intervene. 'Is that what this is all about, an attempt to boost the US economy through my corporation so he, and you, can get back in again? You're wasting my time!'

'That's an insult, Mr Tye,' snapped the Attorney-General. 'This administration is responsible to the people of America, the people who made your corporation what it is in the first place, and this government will not be brushed aside by a mere businessman!'

Furtrado had then called on his courtroom training to remain impassive. He knew what would follow.

'Listen, Treno,' shouted Tye, jumping to his feet. 'I've got William Wilkinson's FUCKING SPARE HEART beating in a box on Hope Island, along with duplicate organs for half his administration, most of Congress and nearly all the Senate. Don't *you* tell me what to do. You're just trying to get us back under your control so you can stifle innovation and stop us making really great products and services the world *really* wants. I've already seen what you guys can do to a successful corporation – which is why I took my company out of the USA in the first place.'

And that had been that.

'You're right, Tom,' agreed Furtrado as he fastened his seat belt. 'To heck with Jane Treno.'

The jet began its take-off for Hope Island.

*

Easy Zee Zee took a last toke on his joint of Acapulco Gold, stared at the holo control panel hanging in mid-air in front of his chair and wondered if there was anything else that could be squeezed from the forthcoming market in solar energy.

Not at present, he decided as he scratched his sparse goatee beard. Cool: this would be the ultimate utility stock! He would reinvest some of the millions he had already made on the LifeLines flotation. He would also short the main oil, gas and power company equities well before his new service was announced. That should prove interesting.

'Finish,' he told the system, still holding his breath. He finally emptied his lungs of what he regarded as the best shit in the world, leaned back and yawned extravagantly. He was alone in the Solaris Control Center, as the Network Center had now been rededicated, and it was very late. This night, there would be little chance of anybody but a security guard interrupting or complaining about his smoke. In two weeks the Center would be busy 7 x 24 x 365.2421 (accurate time measurement being vital) when the Solaris network went live and began to redistribute its heavenly largesse: the centre had already set all atomic clocks and microprocessors to GMT and, from the launch onwards, its workers would exist within a separate time zone on Hope Island. From here the controllers would be able to direct each satellite, focus its solar reflectors and keep a manual watch from space as the world's climate reacted and the weather patterns changed. All of these data would be fed in real-time to the Halcyon GCMS – the global climate-modelling system – and all marketing would be under the management of Zee Zee's automated systems.

Throughout the Tye Corporation's terrestrial networks, engineers were completing a two-year project to retrofit air pressure, temperature, humidity, visibility and precipitation sensors to every cellular network mast, every network hub and every Tye Corporation and Tye-related property in almost all of the countries of the world. In all prime-market territories, Tye Meteorology Inc. had also completed funding agreements with universities to launch permanent middle- and upper-atmosphere drone and balloon research programmes and live feeds from these weather probes would also be patched to the Center where they would be fed into Halcyon. Although Phase 1 of the Phoebus Project would only provide Solaris coverage to fifteen per cent of the Earth's surface, by the final phase – scheduled to be complete in eight years – almost every inch of the planet's surface would – or could – be affected.

The servers had been configured, the real-time connections with the networks had been set up – all with massive bandwidth – and the interlinks with the Argus, Prospect and Hughie satellite networks were in place. These would supplement the information from the Tye Corporation's terrestrial and atmospheric meteorological sensors and would, respectively, provide both controllers and customers with real-time visual, infra-red and microwave meteorological information about the globe's weather patterns. Used in conjunction with the Halcyon system, highly accurate projections and predictions could be made.

Customers would be provided with access to the Halcyon system so that they could model their projected use of Solaris output and this would help them make their choices on timing, select the appropriate power rating, choose the most appropriate tariff or help them decide which auction model most closely met their needs. In the early years, both controllers and customers would be learning the most effective configurations for the Solaris stations in differing weather conditions and Zee Zee had factored free consultancy and Halcyon access into all sales models for the whole of Phase 1.

Necessarily, the Solaris network had certain times blocked out for the long-term climatic-engineering project in Sybaria and for the microclimate treatments specified for Moscow, some islands in the Baltic Sea, a few thousand square miles in northern Canada and some carefully chosen sites in Alaska. But these absorbed only 36.71 per cent of the output from the fourteen Solaris stations already in position. Inside six months there would be a further twenty in orbit and then the launch schedule was due really to accelerate.

Zee Zee had worked night and day for nearly three months. Tom had been so pleased with the success of the LifeLines auction models that he had instantly charged him with this most important of all tasks – constructing the systems to maximize the income from the Phoebus Project. When Zee Zee had first heard the details of the service he had been amazed. He could remember that first sleepless night after the briefing – selling sunshine, heat, rain and energy to the world? He had thought LifeLines was the ultimate business, but he now realized that he had seriously underestimated his boss's ambitions: Tye made all previous tycoons seem lilliputian.

From 30 August, the world's nations and corporations could enter what would become a contest to decide who would gain rights to this new energy source and its valuable by-products – water, heat, light and agricultural re-engineering. Customers could choose from a wide variety of supplier-customer relationships, all designed by Zee Zee on the advice of the Tye Corporation's revenue-optimization economists.

The system had been tested and tested again. The mismatched liver from the LifeLines servers was coming to be regarded as a one-off, an aberration unlikely to recur. Raymond Liu had found no faults in the system and his forensic computing team had been unable to find a glitch anywhere along the visible audit trail: laser pathways between satellites were, of course, temporary and unauditable. Most tellingly, Marsello Furtrado had ordered Zee Zee and his team to make follow-up enquiries on one hundred other LifeLines customers – selected at random from thousands of recipients. Every one of the customers contacted had pronounced themselves delighted with their transplanted organs and offered LifeLines unequivocal endorsement.

Zee Zee knew that in the future he would have many additional products to offer, for which he would have to build fresh features into the auction engines. He was particularly excited about the steering services for hurricanes, typhoons, tornadoes and cyclones that they planned to offer. The Phoebus engineers and the Halcyon meteorologists were certain that when there was sufficient Solaris output available they would be able to divert even the largest storm. Zee Zee was uncertain whether to offer such a service to the insurers of properties and businesses in potential threat paths or whether to offer it first to state authorities and governments.

Then a thought struck him. He had read somewhere that common germs and viruses are temperature sensitive, so for a region suffering a flu epidemic or some other infectious disease, a few days of increased sunshine and raised atmospheric temperature might well kill off temperature-sensitive germs. The economic advantages would prove significant – it could also save a fortune for the services operated by Tye Healthcare. *Cool, something else for the future.*

Zee Zee stood up and emptied the contents of his ashtray into a paper napkin, screwing it into a ball and carefully putting it into the pocket of his jacket. He then put the ashtray into his other pocket.

All that was left now was a final demo for Thomas Tye and then it would be time for the grand launch. Capitalism felt great when it could be coupled with worthy causes.

TWENTY-FOUR

'Perplex – *ment*!' exclaimed Tommy proudly as he placed the M, E, N and T tiles on the board. 'And that's a triple word score!'

'That's not a word,' snorted Calypso indignantly, 'is it, Jed?'

'I'm afraid it is,' said the caterpillar. 'It's rare but not obsolete. It means "perplexed condition, perplexity", actually.'

'There,' crowed Tommy with an emphatic nod. 'That's eighty-one!'

'I'll never catch up now,' groaned Calypso as she wrote down his score. He had four hundred and twelve to her three hundred and two, and there were only a few tiles left.

The three of them were playing Scrabble, not the popular on-screen version but a battered board game with plastic tiles that Calypso had kept from her childhood. They had first played it during the visit to see her mother and Tommy had since become an addict. Jed had become both referee and adjudicator, having instant access to both the *Oxford English Dictionary* and to *Webster's*.

Calypso realized her life had undergone momentous change. Tom's shock and horror at his son's wild bid for attention seemed to have been the key to unlocking his previous intransigence – at least concerning domestic arrangements. At Tom's request, Calypso stayed with Tommy during all his free time and she was even allowed to readjust the boy's timetable to create more opportunities for him to see his father. She had also been given network access to Tom's personal scheduler so that she could maximize the opportunities for the two of them to be together. That had caused Connie to raise a manicured eyebrow.

Although Tommy seemed to sleep little, he was always fresh-eyed and cheerful. The cutting incident now seemed wholly out of character and Calypso found herself wondering if the boy had staged it deliberately rather than responding to a fit of hysteria. She knew of no other cases in which a seven-year-old would display such cold self-possession. If he had harmed himself merely to get his own way, the incident would be classed as deliberate parapraxia – one for the clinical histories. But Tommy was unique in several ways, as Calypso had reminded herself.

She had started a journal of life inside the Tye household – part personal account, part clinical record. Even though she loved Tommy too much even to contemplate the idea of ever publishing it, she was aware that fate had placed her in a uniquely privileged position. She alone was able to observe how an enhanced, cloned human being was developing, and could observe the degree to which the personalization of the brain altered it from its raw genetic blueprint. Here too she had a living experiment in which she could measure the influence of nurture over nature. But, leaving aside the medical consider-ations, she was also privileged to observe the daily life of the richest family ever seen on the planet.

Like most medical practitioners, Calypso was more inter-ested in the potential and practical benefits that science had to offer her profession than about abstract ethical concerns. She saw no sanctity in the human condition or form *per se* and suffered from no religious dogma; she saw only widespread and immense suffering and an opportunity for her to help. Her generation might be the first in which doctors began really to understand the mechanisms of the body. Since the map of the human genome had been published at the beginning of the century – while she was undergoing her medical training – biochemists and physicians had collaborated to unravel the mysteries of the fragile human container and eradicate most of the diseases to which it was prone.

Cancer was now almost defeated, cardiovascular disease had been significantly reduced in the developed world, and even neurological ailments such as Alzheimer's, Parkinson's and motor-neurone disease had yielded to gene therapy that could replace damaged areas with healthy tissue. As a result, average life expectancy in richer nations had now shot up to ninety-six years for women and eighty-eight for men, with many living to become healthy and active centenarians. The actuaries now predicted further extension to healthy lifespans in the coming years, and Calypso accepted that if she avoided accident she herself could almost certainly live to be over 120 years old.

Calypso's ethical stance was clear: she approved of any intervention to prevent or alleviate suffering, so she had no strong feelings about genetic manipulation, bio-medicine or organ cloning *providing* they caused no harm to the patient – alive or yet to be born. She also supported the right to early-term abortion because she didn't confuse physical form with human personality, and she accepted that twenty-first-century medicine was dealing with a species that was taking control of its own evolution and rapidly re-engineering both its physiology and its environment.

But that left the mind – which was why Calypso had opted to study the final human attribute that was not yet understood. Despite incredible advances in brain measurement and analysis of function, no cognitive-neuroscientist had yet been able to prove how consciousness emerges and is then sustained. Most theoretical wisdom now suggested that consciousness first arose spontaneously once the processing environment – the human brain – became sufficiently complex. A popular analogy was a swarm of bees or termites where individual members operated on simple rules while together creating highly complex behaviour. But no one could *prove* this was how human consciousness emerged and no one could justifiably claim that self-awareness arose automatically in a community engaged in complex processing transactions.

As a first-year student of paediatric psychology Calypso photocopied a page from one of the then-foremost books on how the mind works and stuck it on her noticeboard. It contained a quotation from a short story by the science fiction writer Terry Bisson, narrating a conversation between two aliens:

'They're made out of meat.'

'Meat . . . ?'

'There's no doubt about it. We picked several from different parts of the planet, took them aboard our reccon vessels, probed them all the way through. They're completely meat.'

'That's impossible. What about the radio signals? The messages to the stars?'

'They use the radio waves to talk, but the signals don't come from them. The signals come from machines.'

'So who made the machines? That's who we want to contact.'

'They made the machines. That's what I'm trying to tell you. Meat made the machines.'

'That's ridiculous. How can meat make a machine? You're asking me to believe in sentient meat.'

'I'm not asking you, I'm telling you. These creatures are the only sentient race in the sector and they're made out of meat.'

'Maybe they're like the Orfolei. You know, a carbon-based intelligence that goes through a meat stage.'

'Nope. They're born meat and they die meat. We studied them for several of their lifespans, which didn't take long. Do you have any idea of the lifespan of meat?'

'Spare me. Okay, maybe they're only part meat. You know, like the Weddilie. A meat head with an electron plasma brain inside.'

'Nope, we thought of that, since they do have meat heads like the Weddilie. But I told you, we probed them. They're meat all the way through.'

'No brain?'

'Oh, there is a brain, all right. It's just that the brain is made out of meat!'

'So . . . what does the thinking?'

'You're not understanding, are you? The brain does the thinking. The meat.'

'Thinking meat! You're asking me to believe in thinking meat!'

'Yes, thinking meat! Conscious meat! Loving meat.
Dreaming meat. The meat is the whole deal! Are you getting
the picture?'

Calypso pulled her thoughts back to the game and drew her favourite piece of thinking meat towards her. She kissed Tommy on his warm cheek.

'*Cally*...!' he complained, not really minding.

On asking Jack why he had thought to tell her about Tommy's origins, he had said simply, 'In case anything ever happens to Tom. The boy would need you.'

Once she had been made aware of Tommy's genesis she found it had made her even more determined to protect him. The first eight years of a child's life is the crucial period in which he or she learns the gift of attachment – the ability to place loving trust in relationships – and Calypso was desperate to pump her love and constancy into him before a self-protection mechanism cut in fully, inhibiting the development of his emotional neural-response pathways to shield him from the pain of further grievous separations. She judged that her seven-month presence here was already having a beneficial effect. He had even kissed her on the cheek – twice – as she had settled him down to rest at night.

Which was more than Jack Hendriksen had done recently, thought Calypso as she pondered the letter combinations in front of her. He had avoided her presence since he returned from visiting his sick mother and had avoided her gaze on the three occasions they had met in public. Being Calypso, she had not left it there.

'Avoiding me, Jack?' she challenged him via her VideoMate three days later. She noticed the look of guilt on his face.

'I've– It's been frantic with the weekend event coming up.'

She pursed her lips.

'It's also, well, I've met someone, Calypso,' he admitted.

'What, at your mother's *sickbed*?' she exclaimed.

'No. Someone I've known for a while now. I will tell you about it when I see you. I'm sorry.'

And that had been it. Calypso had been upset, but not

greatly. She had allowed herself to develop some feelings for the strange, watchful man but she had also noted Jack's careful avoidance of the big words, his scrupulous concern not to make more of their time together than mutual companionship and physical enjoyment. Within a couple of days Calypso began to understand that he had not been dishonest with her and although she felt an inevitable sense of rejection, her training helped her identify the roots of those feelings and estimate that they would take only a few weeks to repair.

'Moo,' mooed Calypso as she laid three of her tiles under the last three letters of the word Tommy had just composed. 'M,O,O – Moo – and Em – that's something used in printing – and No and To.'

'Quite correct,' approved Jed. 'And very clever, Doctor. Four words from three tiles.'

'But that's still only thirteen,' laughed Tommy who could add faster than she could read out the numbers.

'Look,' he exclaimed, laying four tiles out quickly to add a paragoge. 'R,Q,U,E. Torque! And it's another triple word score. There, that's forty-five!'

'Hello, you three.'

They turned their heads. Thomas Tye was standing in the doorway wearing a huge grin.

'My God!' exclaimed Calypso, clapping her hand to her mouth.

'Daddy!' shouted Tommy, adopting one of Jed's Englishisms. 'What have you done?'

Tom stepped into the room and turned around. 'What do you think?'

The shock was considerable. Calypso had known Thomas Tye's face for twenty years before she had met him. His long locks had been his symbol, his badge, his emblem of power and freedom.

'You've cut all your hair off,' she breathed, her hands still to her face.

'Well, not all of it,' smiled Tom. 'I quite like it this way.'

So do I, thought Calypso. A *man* had stepped out of a caricature.

Tommy jumped up on a chair and stretched out one hand. Tom bent his head so the boy could rub his hand through the stubble. Tom laughed and then grabbed his son and swung him off the stool and round in circles that flung Tommy's legs outwards. The child squealed with pleasure as Tom increased the speed, until finally he slowed and returned the boy to his feet.

Tom gripped the back of the chair to steady himself while, still dizzy, Tommy stumbled across the room and fell onto the soft bed with a laugh.

'It's very ... manly,' commented Jed.

'Calypso?'

'Yes, very manly,' she agreed. 'But why?'

'I'll read you a story, Tommy,' said Tom. 'It must be time for your dreams.'

Calypso took her cue and rose. 'Tommy's won anyway,' she acknowledged, pushing her feet back into her slippers.

'And, Calypso, I'll explain over supper tomorrow,' suggested Tom. 'If you would be gracious enough to join me?'.

She looked into his violet eyes and raised one eyebrow. His eyes held laughter – almost the same mischievousness she sometimes saw in Tommy's.

'I'd be delighted,' she said simply.

'Oy, ologists!' growled Chelouche. Amethier and Deakin nodded, feeling the same way.

The presentation had now lasted four hours and had been full of ifs and buts, maybes and perhapses. The fact was that none of the six weather scientists invited to comment on how the Phoebus Project might affect the world's climate seemed to have a clue.

'We would need to build a huge model of the world's atmosphere and weather systems and then plug all the data from the Solaris systems into it to get any idea of how the whole thing will interact,' Professor Madison had explained. 'My guess is that the Tye Corporation meteorologists must have already built and tested such a model. They've got thousands of joint agreements for information-gathering with universities and weather institutes all over the world. They've even got an army of amateurs feeding in pictures and measurements over the networks – just in the hope of getting personally mentioned on Tye's Halcyon Weather Channel!'

The UNISA executive committee had heard that how, if the Earth was a peach, the atmosphere would be no thicker than the fuzz on its skin. They had learned that the atmosphere was just 600 kilometres thick, composed of layers, with the lowest ten-kilometre-thick stratum responsible for creating most of the ground-level weather. They'd heard about convective cells and vortices and of the stratified layers of lighter gases that sit on the top of the atmosphere. It had been explained that the atmosphere was also a giant thermal engine converting the sun's radiant energy into heat and that variance in this conversion at different points in the atmosphere causes it to shift, creating winds and weather troughs and highs.

Then they had been shown tephigrams, adaibatic curves, ageostrophic and geostrophic wind patterns (with and without the Coriolis effect), Brücker cycles, climographs, hyetographs, progressions of isallobars, isoteres and isochrons as well as langleygraphs, mesoscales and nephanalyses. Next they had suffered force-fed explanations of frontogenesis, isopycnic ultra-centrifugal separative techniques, katabatics and orometrics.

Chelouche wondered if Professor Madison was extracting sweet revenge for his earlier rudeness. Eventually he had lost patience and risen to his feet. He walked over to the large holo-projection of the Earth and jabbed a stubby digit towards East Africa.

'Look, when it comes to science, I'm a shmendrik, OK? I can't understand the complicated stuff. It's dry here and I want to make it rain. So if I've got all these sunlight reflectors behind the Earth, what do I have to do to make that happen?'

'Well, you might concentrate your heat on Lake Victoria, to the south-west,' suggested a German limnologist. 'That's only eight hundred miles away. If you could raise the surface temperature there a few degrees you would definitely get evapo-transpiration starting to occur.'

'That would *only* work if you happened to have a handy

twenty-knot wind blowing in the opposite direction to the prevailing force of the Earth's rotation,' objected a young Australian nephologist. 'But I reckon you've got to go with the Earth's rotation, mate. We're nearly on the equator and there the speed of the land surface overrules everything – even wind direction. I reckon he's got to heat up a patch of the Indian Ocean or the Arabian Sea and let rotation do the rest.'

'No, no,' cut in a French mesopherologist. 'He can tackle the noctilucent clouds more easily.'

'Enough,' said Chelouche. 'Enough already.'

He had thanked them and sent them back to their labours. 'Well?' he turned to his Executive.

'It's clearly an awesome technology,' observed Amethier quietly. 'I'd bet he can do what he says he can do.'

'I wouldn't bet against him, either,' agreed Deakin.

'Well, we are the United Nations, gentlemen,' insisted Chelouche. 'We can't allow one corporation to control the entire world's weather, even if it claims it is doing so for the good of the planet! We discovered years ago that weather and climate are the two most important indicators of any region's economic potential. Control of such forces must *never* be in private hands.'

'Raymond.'

'Chomoi.'

They had been conversing so much recently that these technical supremos of rival networks had almost become friends.

'It's not looking good,' sighed Ltupicho. 'We're still experiencing unaccountable network failures. We're not yet losing data but we still can't find the cause.'

Raymond Liu nodded. His Russian counterpart looked as tired as he did. 'We're coming to the opinion that it could be some form of datum virus. I can't see what else it could be. Perhaps something that's mutated on its own.'

Ltupicho snorted. 'And I thought we Russians were the ones who liked fairy tales.'

Liu managed a wan smile.

'I hear you are inheriting some of my networks?' smirked the Russian.

Liu was startled. He'd only heard this himself the week before and the news was regarded as hyper-sensitive.

'The ones in Eastern Siberia – the ones it costs us most to maintain.' The Russian engineer laughed. 'But I also hear that conditions will be different when you take over.'

Raymond Liu shook his head. 'No comment on that, Chomoi.'

In the back of the UN limousine Ron Deakin slumped and closed his eyes. It was Friday evening and, for the first time in weeks, he might be home in time to share a meal with Ruby. The limousine was a perk that Deakin appreciated: a car with a diplomatic status that allowed it to come in and out of Manhattan and to negotiate almost any street at will. Another perk was the small cocktail cabinet. The UNISA officer poured himself a large malt whisky. It was definitely time for a drink.

On this evening the East River bridges were full with other vehicles that enjoyed similar privileges – government cars, city administration vehicles, police and emergency services and the hundreds of shuttle buses that ferried people back and forth to the security-guarded Park-and-Ride car pounds in Queens, Brooklyn and the Bronx. He was heading for Newport, the small waterside community on Long Island where he and his wife had lived for over twenty years. They were both well known in that marina town, but it was Ruby who had really put down their roots. She had long ago accepted childlessness as their lot and devoted her free time to half a dozen voluntary causes, quickly developing a rich social life. Other Newporters knew Ron as a genial bureaucrat who put in long hours at the UN headquarters in Manhattan, but none of their neighbours suspected that years before the pair had added UN diplomatic status to their passports.

He lifted his head off the back seat and glanced down at the e-paper he had brought from his office. Its news was a week old so he touched an icon on his VideoMate and refreshed the digital 'paper' with that evening's news.

The lead column of the *Post* covered William Wilkinson's opening speech at the start of his re-election campaign. Deakin looked further and grimaced. The other main item concerned a major network failure.

Global Bank Settlement Network Crashes. $6 Trillion Lost in 1 Hour

At the bottom of the page there was a story about Tye's coming event on Hope Island.

Tye Weekend Seminar Threatened by Tropical Storm

He enlarged the print of the body copy and read that a tropical storm now brewing off the coast of East Africa might have the potential to cross the mid-Atlantic, gathering strength before proceeding through the West Indies to cause the usual seasonal panics in southern Florida.

Well, he was away from the office now and he wouldn't waste a one-time code on a fax to Chevannes or the meteorologists. He knew they would already be on to it. Then a quaint thought struck him. He considered the wealth and power that would be heading for that part of the Bermuda Triangle just when this storm was supposed to arrive. *Not good timing*, thought Ron.

He called ahead to the house and saw that Ruby was cooking. 'I took you at your word,' she said. 'We're having Cajun chicken with jacket potatoes.'

He checked she had received his ETA and relaxed into the cushions with his malt whisky.

Calypso had no idea what had prompted Thomas Tye's invitation to dinner. She had been surprised and delighted when the suggestion had first been made. Then she began to worry whether she was in for another tussle over Tommy. Perhaps Tom was once again feeling uneasy and wanted to revert to the old routine. She wasn't going to have any of that.

Her greatest problem had been what to wear. She thought about a full-length dress but, when she slipped it on, she thought the effect looked overdone. By nature the doctor was both practical and casual. Her favourite combination on the island was a pair of shorts and a shirt, but she knew that would not do for this occasion.

The majority of her clothes were still here at the cottage.

After discarding the full-length gown, she tried on a black silk trouser suit and turned in front of the mirror. Too severe for a summer's evening with just the two of them.

Next she tried on a pale blue knee-length dress with a tight skirt. *Too much like a wedding guest*, she thought. Then she tried on a sheer ivory dress with a low neckline, tight low-waisted bodice and a calf-length skirt flounced at the bottom to lift into undulations as she twirled her hips. *Rumba!* thought Calypso – a perfect partnership.

The situation was definitely easing. Raymond Liu had driven his worldwide teams to breaking point and two of his most senior territory-maintenance managers had already walked out. Every inch of cable, every transmission node, every laser source, every encryption engine, every hub, router, firewall, amplifier and dish had been checked, replaced or rotated. In all, 27,566 maintenance staff had been involved in sixty-nine territories. The four manned space stations dedicated to orbital network maintenance had snagged, retrieved and overhauled 2,800 of the 22,902 satellites that comprised the various Tye Corporation networks. Only another 20,102 to go!

But each time a delicate satellite was carefully tethered to a maintenance station the results were the same: no unusual system-faults could be found. Faults in all aspects of the networks occurred frequently and routinely, but the data flows were designed to work around such outages, automatically self-healing and pursuing their destinations by other routes.

Raymond Liu now had a small army of mathematicians working on the problem: they were trying to find a pattern amongst the failures. Not a physical pattern, such as the repeated failure of one particular type of component, but a mathematical pattern that might identify whether the massive rise in system faults was the result of some intelligent action.

He had thought about Professor Keane's *gedankenexperiment* very carefully. Although she was clearly crazy, he was forced to agree that her random usage of processing polarities in the networks was unlikely to cause any problems. Each switch would simply regard the requests from her software as another binary call and respond accordingly.

Raymond Liu was developing a theory of his own that was much more unsettling.

'I say, Doctor, you do look good.' If a toy caterpillar could have whistled, Jed would have done so. Instead he winked, which lent his face a peculiar leer.

Tommy looked up from his book as Calypso hovered in the doorway; she had popped in to see them on the way to dinner.

Tommy's gaze took her in from head to foot, but he didn't bounce up and cuddle her as he had begun to do. She could sense he was unhappy, so she stepped into the room and kneeled beside his chair.

'I'm having dinner with your father tonight,' she said, looking into his troubled violet eyes.

'You'll just argue again,' muttered Tommy, looking down into his book. 'Then you'll go away and I'll never see you again.'

'We won't argue, I promise.' Calypso reached out and touched his hair.

Suddenly he turned in his chair and flung his arms around her neck, burying his face in her shoulder. 'You'll go, you'll go, my father will send you away and I'll never see you again,' he cried.

She stroked the back of his neck and impulsively kissed the top of his head, letting him sob for a few moments, his tears wetting her dress. But that didn't matter; she knew exactly why Tommy was so scared.

When the sobbing subsided she lifted his head from her shoulder and held his face in both hands.

'Look at me, Tommy,' she said. 'I love you and I'm not going anywhere. Your father understands we're happy together, OK?'

Tommy nodded, his eyes still cast down. She kneeled beside him for a few more moments, then realized there was nothing more to be done.

'I'll come and see you later, Tommy.' She rose.

He just nodded.

'See you later, Miss World,' said Jed.

'We've lost the whole of the Indian subcontinent,' reported the distraught engineer.

Raymond Liu nodded silently, watching the vast black hole over the Indian ocean on his own monitors.

'It's not just us. Everybody else is reporting data corruption or discontinuity in that region.'

'How long?' asked Liu. He knew he was going to have to report this reversal to Tom soon, before he heard it from other sources.

'We're tasking in the weather sats and the surveillance sats – as you suggested. We should get something moving later this morning.'

Liu looked at the brilliance of the loading in the surrounding networks – the Sino-Pacific loops were close to peak capacity as they provided compensatory routes around the affected region.

'Keep me informed,' ordered Liu, with a sigh.

Calypso was a bit later than she would have liked, having gone back to her room next door to repair the damage Tommy's tears had done to the shoulder of her dress. The stains had dried quickly under the blast of her hairdryer and she had only had to tidy her hair again before going down. When she emerged from the elevator she found Luc Bestion, Tye's butler, waiting with a smile.

'Tom's out on the front lawn.' He led the way.

Out on the ground-level terrace she declined the offer of a ride in a Volante and trod carefully along the gravel path in her high heels. It was only 8.20 p.m – too early for any dew to have fallen.

Tye had ordered the table to be set up under one of the great African cedar trees on the top terrace in front of the big house. The evening was perfect: mild, warm and – a speciality of Hope Island – free of irritating bugs.

He was already sitting at the table and Calypso was pleased she had dressed up rather than down. He was wearing a charcoal-grey silk suit with a mandarin-collar jacket. Though he wore a customary white T-shirt beneath, the suit gave him too the air of dressing for the occasion.

He was in a viewper conversation as she approached but he soon wrapped up the meeting and stood up as she arrived at the table.

'Calypso. You look stunning.'

She had braided her hair so that it fell in a thick plait to the middle of her back. In a wholly unnecessary gesture she had added a hint of shading under her high cheekbones and had reddened her lips – careful not to overdo it, as she'd been taught by so many professionals who had created her make-up during those earlier years.

Tye took her hand, semi-formally, then gently pulled her closer and kissed her cheek. She smelt a little trace of soap, no hint of antiseptic, no touch of added fragrance.

He pulled the other chair out for her while she admired the view.

The sun was setting behind them, on the other side of the mountain behind the house, but she could see it reflected on the swell of the Atlantic in front of her. The sun created a panorama of lambent reflections across the surface of the gentle sea, like a thousand camera flashes – *Miss World again*, for a moment.

'This is beautiful,' she breathed as she sat down under the high canopy provided by the old tree. She guessed it had been imported as a mature specimen and replanted here with enormous care. There was a wash of sea breeze and a breath of pine needles in the air and Calypso cared not a jot that these were probably artificially augmented. The sound of cicadas in the shrubs enhanced the ambience.

Tye was watching her silently, head cocked to one side. As he smiled, his own beauty complemented the surroundings.

'Have a drink,' he said, lifting a bottle of champagne from an ice bucket. He pulled two crystal glasses towards him across the white linen tablecloth, poured carefully and expertly and returned the bottle to its chill. He handed her a glass.

'To a beautiful evening,' he proposed as he lifted his own.

She raised her glass, touched it against his and watched in

surprise as he took a long draught. She had assumed he never touched alcohol. She savoured the vintage Krug.

'How's Tommy doing today?' he asked.

Like her boss, Connie worked late most evenings. She had an apartment in a condo down near Hope Town beach, but she also had a little room in the house where she would sometimes stay over when things were particularly frantic. Now was just such a time. The forthcoming weekend celebrations were stretching every resource. In the outer office, thirty-seven of her day-shift executive team were still at their desks twelve hours after they had arrived there. The night shift was hot-desking elsewhere in the Tye Corporate headquarters.

Most of the work entailed travel details and final confirmations. Tye Logistics had been working on plans for nearly nine months and the event organizers seemed totally professional, being used to organizing diplomatic summits in Washington as well as major sporting events. But there were still a thousand things that needed her personal attention or approval.

Her system trilled. She looked at the ident and accepted. 'Yes, Raymond, how are you this evening?'

'I need to speak with Tom urgently,' the normally polite network chief almost snapped.

Connie shook her head. 'He can't be disturbed for anything this evening, Ray. Those are his absolute orders. May I help?'

She saw Liu shake his head anxiously. 'We're suffering widespread network failures,' he said quietly. 'We're still functioning, but we're fire-fighting. I lost two air traffic management satellites over Europe today. One pilot had to override the system to stop his computers putting the passenger jet down on the fucking Champs Elysées!'

He broke off. Tom's bad language was catching.

'I've had to issue an advisory to the FAA and the other aviation bodies for pilots to revert to manual flying and for the ATC to decouple network control. Passengers all over the world are complaining about bumpy landings and there are major delays because the air traffic controllers have forgotten how to control the traffic manually.'

'My God,' exclaimed Connie, now seriously alarmed. 'What's going on?'

'I don't know. It just seems sporadic and random. I've checked everything. There is no apparent physical cause and no sign of anybody sabotaging the networks. And it's not just us; other network operators are reporting faults, too. Also, and this one is ultra serious, one of the off-planet deposit-box satellites is missing. It's just disappeared.'

Connie considered. She had spent days in the Network Control Center during the Los Angeles traffic crises and she knew the significance of this information – she also knew the financial implications of losing track of one of their ultra-secure-deposit satellites.

'It will be another hour before I can get to him,' she said, checking the time. 'Leave it with me.'

'So how *are* you going to make it rain in Ethiopia, Tom?'

The evening had gone well – better than Calypso had imagined it could. Tom had been relaxed, charming and attentive. The food had been exotic. For a starter they had been served a stuffed egg-plant dish called *Imam Bayıldı.*

'It's Turkish. The chef says it is supposed to make you swoon,' laughed Tom.

To follow they ate a Hawaiian concoction called *laulu,* palm-leaf-wrapped, charcoal-baked albacore tuna caught off the island that afternoon. A selection of organically grown, genetically modified vegetables was served on the side. The food was simply stunning!

'Michel doesn't often get a chance to show off when we're here on the island,' Tom explained.

Calypso knew that Michel Geronde was Michelin-starred and, according to below-stairs rumour, only frequent pay rises stopped the celebrated chef leaving Tom's entourage to go back to 'cooking for real people'. She had also heard that fourteen assistant chefs provided by a catering company would be arriving next week to help him prepare for *One Weekend in the Future.*

As she had anticipated, the conversation turned to Tommy. But far from wanting to limit his son's movements and activities,

Tom now seemed genuinely pleased that the boy was flowering so happily.

'You've done a great deal for Tommy. Thank you.' He lifted his glass to toast her. 'I think I have someone for him to play with, *if* you think it is a good idea?'

She raised an eyebrow.

'We flew that little girl back from Ethiopia with us – you know, Biya, the blind girl from the village.'

Now Calypso was intrigued.

'She's coming out of the clinic tomorrow. It was fairly straightforward, and one hundred per cent successful. She now has twenty-twenty vision.'

Calypso nodded. As a doctor she knew that trachoma was easy to cure if the necessary skills and facilities were at hand.

'She'll be staying up here until after the party, so I wondered if you and Tommy would look after her?'

'Of course, but ... you're keeping her here to show her on TV, aren't you?'

Tom laughed. 'Don't be cynical, Calypso,' he chided. 'You can do a lot of good through such publicity.'

Which had brought her to her question about the rain.

He sat back in his chair and twirled the long stem of his crystal wine glass. 'Have you heard about our Phoebus Project, Calypso?'

She shook her head. 'No, I don't get involved much with others on the island.'

'The Ethiopia rain thing is all a bit of a stunt, dreamed up by the perception people in Washington,' he explained. 'We're about to launch a new solar-energy service and they felt this would get the maximum media attention and give us a favourable spin.'

'It's certainly done that!' she laughed. The papers and newscasts had seemed full of nothing but the Ethiopian appeal.

'I suppose you're sending a fleet of refuelling tankers flying over to Africa to bomb them with water.'

'It would evaporate before it even hit the ground.' He smiled. 'It's rather more ambitious than that, Calypso. I'm a little nervous about it myself, but my weather people are sure they can do it.'

He sat up straight and reached for the bottle of red wine. He lifted it, one eyebrow raised questioningly, and when Calypso nodded he refilled her glass. Then he topped up his own glass of white.

'Over the last ten years I've nurtured a dream about a new form of solar energy.' He sat back in his chair, studying the wine in his glass. Then he looked up. 'You realize that we're fast running out of everything on this planet: water, usable land, food, energy?'

She nodded.

'Twenty years ago a bunch of crazy Russians had this idea of putting a space mirror into orbit and reflecting a little sunshine back to Siberia. Just enough to extend twilight in the winter evenings and to bring the morning sun a little earlier.'

He paused and took a sip of wine.

'They carried out only one full-scale experiment, in February ninety-nine, but that failed. Then Russia disintegrated: the economy collapsed, the wars in the south started. The companies concerned closed down, but a year or so later the founder of the project, the man with the original idea, got in contact with the president of Tye Aerospace in Florida. I saw the proposals and I realized that with some of our technology and financing this concept could be significantly expanded. In fact, I now think it will turn out to be perhaps the most significant thing I have ever done.'

He stared into his wine again, then raised it to his lips.

'We've been building large-scale catoptric-energy stations, solar reflectors, for over six years, Calypso. You must have seen some of the shuttle launches from the Cape . . .'

She nodded.

'Many of those are for putting the components into position. We then build the Solaris energy stations in Earth orbit before boosting them out to exactly where we want them to be. We're building six new stations at this moment.'

'I think I've met some of your women astronauts,' nodded Calypso. 'They hang out down at Mario's.'

He hesitated as if considering. 'Would it surprise you if I said

I sometimes wished I could hang out down at Mario's myself?'
he asked.

She smiled. She had her own small experience of celebrity
status, and its frequent loneliness, to help her understand.

'We choose women to do the construction because they are
lighter and they get along with each other better than men do
when they are shut up together for months at a time. In space,
strength counts for nothing. It is dexterity, creativity and the
ability to live peacefully at close quarters that matter.'

Calypso lifted her head and looked up at the stars and the
bursts of laser light. 'I'd like to go into space,' she sighed. Then
she realized she had absolutely no idea why she had said such a
thing.

'No, no, we need you too much here, Cally.'

She stared at him. That was what Tommy called her.

'Well, using the sunlight we then capture we can reflect it
back to affect the weather, Calypso. Would it surprise you to
know that the atmosphere has tides?'

It did, and her face showed it.

'Highs and lows, twice a day, just like the sea, only it's caused
by the cycles of heat and cold as the sun rises and sets as well
as by the magnetism of the solar system. What we do is add our
energy to those tides to make them bigger in certain small areas.
Over a period of days the theory is that the boosted upswings
become so great that the warm air funnels upwards in anabatic
columns, towards the upper atmosphere, and the cold air is
pushed down to take its place. It's called inverting the atmosphere. When the cold air descends rapidly it becomes warmer
and the moisture inside it turns to rain. The Phoebus people
proved that they could do that a couple of months ago. They
had a trial run making rain on some remote islands in the
Atlantic, the driest inhabited place on Earth. I sent Marsello to
observe the rainfall for himself.'

*That overdressed lawyer that Tom seemed to spend so much time
with.*

'Here's to rain in Ethiopia.' Calypso raised her glass, not
knowing what else to say.

'I'm frightened it might even snow,' Tom replied, laughing softly.

In mid-August, afternoons in Beijing are so hot that only the very poorest of the city's fourteen million people will be found out on the streets.

As Jeremy Corbett, vice-president Asia of Tye Private Banking Services Inc. stepped out of his air-conditioned club to look for an air-conditioned taxi he was surprised to find two tall, fit, smartly suited men appear beside him.

'Mr Corbett,' the taller of the two stated. 'Please come with us.' His English was good.

A dark BMW saloon arrived beside them and the rear door opened from the inside. The taller man held out an ident, English-language side uppermost. It was the badge of the Red Army Military Police.

'I think you've got the wrong man,' objected Corbett stupidly as he felt a hand on the back of his head. But he was pushed down into the car and someone got in beside him.

The large saloon was pulling away at speed even before the door was properly closed.

Sitting back in her chair, Connie yawned and stretched. She desperately wanted to hand over to her night exec but had to wait until Tom finished his dinner engagement. She needed to tell him about Raymond Liu's worries.

A face appeared at the doorway. 'Have you got your AutoSec on?' asked Miguel Sanchos, her night-shift external-interface manager.

Connie glanced at her screen. 'Yes, sorry. What is it?'

'The Solaris people are desperately trying to reach Tom. I wonder if you'd take it.'

Connie looked at her watch. It was now very late but Tom had not appeared yet. She nodded, and switched her system back to *live* as Miguel disappeared. A moment later she was looking at Easy Zee Zee in the Solaris Control Center.

'Yo, Connie,' intoned the systems designer.

Yo, yourself, she thought. 'What is it, Mr Zorzi?' she asked, deliberately abrupt.

'I really need to reach Tom right away,' he said.

'He can't be disturbed at the moment, for anything,' replied Connie. 'What's it about?'

'We've been watching that storm out in the south-east Atlantic and it looks like it's building up and heading our way. We've got eleven hundred millibars and dropping and the wind speed is already sixty miles an hour and rising. The mets are predicting a Category Five if it crosses the pond and develops. I wanted permission to see if we can zap it.'

Connie pursed her lips. She knew that everybody in the programme was under strict instructions to keep everything connected with the Phoebus Project an absolute secret until 30 August. All of the plans called for the rain in Ethiopia to be its major launch point. To have maximum impact, that would need to be the first major demonstration.

'Can it be done discreetly – so no one realizes?'

Zee Zee shrugged. 'I don't know. It's never been tried before. But the alternative is a hurricane arriving at the same time as Tom's party guests.'

Connie nodded. 'OK, leave it with me.' She glanced at the time on her screen. 'I should be able to talk to Tom very soon.'

She flicked the system off and wondered what was keeping her boss so unusually long.

Everything but the wine and their coffee cups had been cleared away and they had turned their chairs so that they could look down the length of the island with its twinkling lights. They had finished drinking the wine and there had been a long silence. Calypso was wondering whether this was the time to leave.

'Are you happy here, Calypso?'

She considered. 'Very,' she said emphatically.

'Would you consider staying here on a more permanent basis?'

She frowned in the warm darkness. A full-time contract had been signed soon after their last altercation had been resolved. 'I'm not sure what you mean . . .'

'I had my fiftieth birthday a few weeks ago, Calypso. I was just wondering...'

She nodded, encouraging him, but he tailed off and said no more.

'You look astonishingly good on it, Tom.' She hesitated, then asked a question to which she already had a partial answer. 'How do you do it?'

'It is said that we all owe a death to nature,' he responded after a moment's silence. 'But it is not a debt I am prepared to pay, not for a very long time. Our generation is one of the last that will be forced to suffer the absurd brevity of a biblical lifespan. If we could leap a hundred years ahead we would see our great-grandchildren, in their very youthful forties, shaking their heads in sadness that we are gone, that we were so close to the point where medical science could extend our lives dramatically, but we just missed the boat.'

She sensed he had turned to look at her.

'I don't intend to let that happen to me. The future arrives unevenly, Doctor, and I live at the most technologically advanced point on our planet. Hope Island represents the future and I intend to be here to join my grandchildren in their sadness that so many of those alive today will have died needlessly – within a hair's breadth of the necessary technology becoming available. As Professor Keane likes to say, we shall soon be leaving this animal form.'

Calypso offered no comment on Professor Keane or her work. She turned and stared at him, wondering if he would say more. It was his turn to look away.

'I suppose it must be obvious, and it will become more so as time goes by. I may have lived for fifty years but my body has not aged at all for the last sixteen years. You see, I have been the guinea pig in a unique experiment that seems to have been very successful. I have been taking gene therapy to prevent free-radical damage and sclerosis in the body's cells and nervous system – I thought it only right that I should be the one to risk a long-term trial. A number of others in our research team have since joined me as the doctors are now convinced of the safety of this therapy. We plan to start seeking regulatory approvals for the drug next year – but it will have to be individually customized for each patient.'

She inclined her head in understanding but she had a thousand questions.

'It will be our next big marketing push, after the Phoebus Project. Think it will catch on?'

She smiled at the absurdity of his question. He would actually be offering the prospect of extreme longevity – the eternal dream of humankind.

But his earlier question still hung there.

'You were asking me if I'd like to stay here on a more permanent basis?'

They were both now staring straight ahead again in an elongated, almost palpable silence.

'I think you understand me better than most,' Tom ventured. 'At least, I know you're qualified to understand...'

As he tailed off again, she sensed he was gathering himself.

'We'd make an amazing couple, Calypso.'

She felt the hairs on the back of her neck stand up. She continued to stare stolidly ahead.

'What I mean is, would you, could you consider marrying me?'

She sat like stone, unable to move or respond. In shock.

He took her silence as an objection. 'What I'm proposing is primarily a business arrangement,' he said at last. 'Although I think we really could be friends.'

She wanted to run away, to burst into tears. Just to get away. But she was rooted to the chair. She was also furious. She felt tears on her cheeks.

She turned her head. 'I could never...'

He sighed. 'Don't misunderstand me, Calypso. If I could love any woman, love in the full sense, it would be you. I have come to realize that since you've been here. That's why I am saying words I never thought I would say.'

She turned away again, the silent tears in full flood.

'I could love you as a person – I already do – but I can never really love any woman,' he continued to the darkness.

Finally she turned back to him. 'Why?' she demanded, still angry.

He didn't respond, but drew a deep, audible breath. Eventually he exhaled noisily, almost in a gasp.

'Have you heard of Professor Charles Eon?' he asked.

'Of course: it was a terrible business. Didn't he die recently?'

'I was one of his patients,' Thomas Tye said distantly. And then he added the words that would make her understand. 'When I was a child.'

'Oh, my God,' she whispered.

So he told her all about it, things he had never told anyone since becoming an adult. At the end it was *his* eyes that were filled with tears. She wanted to put her arms around him so much that it hurt. She did half rise and put a comforting hand on his shoulder, all she could do for the present.

He quietened eventually, his sobs subsiding.

Then he told her that he was asking for Tommy's sake but, yes, he was also asking for his own sake. He wanted Tommy to have the mother he, Tom, had never had. But he also wanted Calypso to be *his* companion. He wanted the world to know her as Mrs Thomas Tye. He wanted the appearance of normality even if he could never have the reality. He wanted a consortship, companionship. He started to talk about her running his charitable foundation and about her joining the anti-ageing therapy trials.

He didn't mention money, or any prenuptial arrangement. In fact, that concerned neither of them at that minute.

Calypso recovered enough to turn her face back to him.

'I don't know,' she said flatly.

Above all other things, Jeremy Corbett disliked boorish behaviour. As the product of one of the better English public schools, then Oxford, the Guards and the British diplomatic service, his breeding, manners, discretion and effortless style were the precise qualifications required to represent the Tye Corporation's secretive and ultra-secure private bank to its Asian customers. Many of its clients lacked Corbett's personal *savoir faire* but

most aspired to it and, by placing their unusually vulnerable –
and often illicit – wealth with the Tye Private Bank they had, at
least, the pleasure of watching an old-style British gentleman
court and woo them for their custom.

But, without doubt, this afternoon had exposed some exceptionally ungentlemanly behaviour on the part of one important
customer. Corbett now had two front teeth missing and only
one of his eyes was functioning. He was still seated in front of a
computer console, where his captors had spent six hours working on him before being finally persuaded that he too was
seemingly unable to access the funds and documents now held
in a deposit-box satellite that the Tye Private Bank had maintained for them for eleven years.

The two observers standing in the shadows at the back of
the room exchanged a glance. As one nodded a command, a
shoe box was placed on the table beside the computer screens
and its lid removed. Corbett's right arm was forced down on the
table-top and twisted hard so that the palm faced upwards. A
teenager with a pock-marked face stepped forward and raised
a Chinese butcher's machete.

Calypso sat with Biya, a picture book open on her lap.

'Rabbit?' guessed Biya, pressing a small finger against the
image.

'Horse,' corrected Calypso gently, realizing that Biya had
probably never seen one. She had been blind since she was less
than a year old.

'Horse,' agreed Biya contentedly. Calypso smiled down and
slipped her arm around the girl's small shoulders. How many
other Biyas were there? Countless numbers of them, and countless more children suffering other ills for lack of even the
smallest amounts of money and resources.

Calypso had slept little since Tom's astonishing proposal.
The following morning flowers had once again been delivered
to her from Hope Town's florist. Tom's carefully sealed note
had conveyed an apology for springing the idea on her so
abruptly. But it had clearly reiterated his suggestion.

How much other good she could do with the billions of

dollars already held by his charitable funds! She had read that, even before the unprecedented public response to the Ethiopian appeal, his was the largest philanthropic foundation ever established. And if he was serious about giving her control...

But could she marry him simply for that reason? Then she thought of Tommy.

'Horse,' repeated Biya, turning the page.

Jack Hendriksen was in the newly installed Holo-Theater in the corporate annex to the Tye Mansion. Previously he would have used the unit in the Network Control Center but that facility had now been turned over to the Solaris Controllers for twenty-four-hour operation as they ran their last-minute tests before the public launch.

The entire meeting was being recorded and Jack would review it once the connection was terminated. He felt uneasy. Something was out of kilter.

This was his seventh virtual meeting with Lawrence Burton, the Director of Presidential Security for the US Secret Service. Previously those had been mere viewper videoconference exchanges, but now he stared Burton in the eye as the Secret Service man stood in the Holo-Theater of the White House itself.

'I still don't think you need to transport an entire motorcade,' Jack protested. 'You already have a list of everybody who is going to be on the island and their backgrounds. This is not a public event. We can provide a dedicated fleet of Volantes to ferry the president and his party to and from the ship and Air Force One. It's like the Camp David compound, a controlled environment.'

Burton nodded, smiling in an attempt at conviviality that was unpleasant to watch. He radiated insincerity like smiles across a singles bar. In some ways holo-conferences were more revealing than meat meets, or F2Fs as Burton archaically called them. Fake emotions were easier to detect, which was why few of the world's leaders resorted to them – unless they were as skilled as Thomas Tye.

'Well, two things in response to that, Jack: one, we've got

the motorcade with us anyway; we're going straight on to China, remember? Two, I hear you're getting more and more Cuban rebels washing up on your shores and the word is that you have been getting a little heat from your neighbour. So it isn't a *totally* controlled environment, Jack.'

Jack raised his eyebrows. How did Burton know this? But both men knew that Cuba and its civil war weren't really the issues. Jack also understood that the explanation concerning the seven armoured limousines was true. Much to the annoyance of the Ground Facilities Manager at Cape Hope, Tom had over-ruled all objections and agreed that not only could Air Force One and its supersonic support jet park in the limited facilities at the floating spaceport, but also the giant Lockheed C-130J transport plane that was to accompany the President on his subsequent state visit to the People's Republic of China. This would require a large amount of precious space. Normally Jack would have expected the transport plane to fly directly to China ahead of the presidential entourage.

So, in addition to the President's regular party of 134 bodies and their equipment, an additional sixty support personnel would be requiring accommodation. It had been made clear, however, that only the presidential body detail would carry arms on the island.

Fortunately their visit was going to be short and sweet. They would arrive on the island late on Friday afternoon when the president would be guest of honour at the opening ceremony for *One Weekend in the Future*. Then there would be three official meetings between him and Thomas Tye over the following two days. The president and his group would be leaving early Sunday evening, immediately after the closing ceremonies.

The president would not be attending any of the other public seminars or lectures because his schedule, which Burton's team had been generous enough to share in confidence with Jack, was made up of diplomatic meetings with many other heads of state and political leaders also attending the Hope Island weekend. Besides his facilities on board Air Force one, the American leader had also been assigned two adjoining suites on the *Treasure of the Caribbean* for holding meetings.

As Jack now understood, none of the delegates were attending for the conference itself. The main purpose of the weekend's event was for Thomas Tye and his team to start the lengthy negotiations necessary to win international recognition for the sovereignty of Sybaria and all the other political guests were using the congress as an excuse for private meetings and negotiations of their own. The White House team was the eighteenth security group Jack had liaised with so far and, as it turned out, had proved the easiest.

Jack ceased his objections. 'OK, Larry, since they're going to be here anyway, but it's going to cause a massive problem if they deploy. Nobody else has been allowed to bring a motorcade. It would be ridiculous on this small island.'

'Tell you what,' offered Burton amiably, 'my detail head will check it out when he arrives. If he's happy with the terrain and your own containment procedures, we'll go ahead with your toy cars. How's that, Jack?'

That was as good as he was going to get, Jack knew, so he nodded in agreement.

'Well, I guess that's it,' smiled Burton. It was a wrap. 'Have a good party.'

'See you,' said Jack as the image of the US Secret Service man fizzled into blackness.

That had all seemed too easy, too damned polite. Jack had dealt with the White House mafia before.

TWENTY-FIVE

Connie's scream penetrated the entire corporate wing of the Tye mansion, echoing around the internal quadrangle. Thomas Tye and Marsello Furtrado came running out of their offices as Jack sprinted down the hall towards the source of the sound.

Tye's most senior assistant sat back in her chair, ashen-faced, an opened FedEx package in front of her.

'What is it...?' began Furtrado, unnecessarily. It was clear that the problem lay with the box. He stepped forward and then recoiled with a look of revulsion.

Jack peered into it and then lifted the contents out by its little finger. It was a human hand, severed cleanly just above the trapezium bone, already drying out and turning black. He lifted a bloodied card from the bottom of the box. There were only five words printed on it. *Restore Access To Our Deposits.*

The ideogram below had been printed with a rubber stamp.

'That's Jeremy Corbett's hand,' gasped Connie. 'I recognize the pinkie ring.'

Jack put the gruesome object back in the box.

'And I recognize that symbol,' added Furtrado, taking the card. 'It's the sign of Tsien. It's the semi-official Triad run by the generals of the People's Liberation Army. They placed all their financial assets with Tye Private Banking.'

'Get Liu in here FUCKING NOW,' screamed Tom.

Joe Tinkler had been gathering some things in readiness for his depature when his VideoMate bleeped, revealing Madame Pioline's ident.

'Hi, Beatrice,' he said. They were now firm friends.

'He's returning to New York tonight and wonders if you would be kind enough to wait?'

'Sure,' Joe shrugged. This was an open call so he couldn't ask her for any details. 'What time?'

'He'll be there in the next couple of hours.'

Joe nodded, wished her goodnight, then closed the connection. He had realized that it was Friday midnight her time, but he knew her whole life revolved around Dr Chelouche and the World Bank.

An hour later the object of her devotion tripped on the carpet coming through the doorway. 'Oy, wehsmir ... Evening Joe, sorry to keep you.'

The banker looked tired and grey. Joe rose to greet him and Chelouche eased his bulk onto an inadequate upright chair in front of Joe's desk.

'I've just got back from the Middle East – getting more of the main players on-side.'

Joe merely nodded.

'How have you be doing recently?'

Surely the man was joking. Joe had been pumping his cryptic, carefully crafted reports to Chelouche's mail box every twelve hours. 'I've sent you all the figures, sir.'

'Tell me. I've been busy.'

'Well, just using our information about Tye-related stocks, we've made nearly two point four trillion US dollars in the past three weeks.'

Chelouche nodded, apparently unimpressed. 'What percentage of the Tye Corporation's voting stocks do we now hold?'

'Just under eleven per cent, sir. Ten point eight two, to be precise.'

'What's your current estimate of the cost to us if we did it now?'

Joe raised his eyebrows and turned to his keyboard and the triptych of screens. The left-hand display showed real-time graphs of the value of his fund's holdings, on the centre screen was his main spreadsheet and to the right were displayed windows of prices, financial news and TV feeds.

He refreshed his spreadsheet and checked the result. 'Tonight it would cost your member nations just over twenty-two trillion US dollars, sir,' he said.

Chelouche sighed. 'Did you see those reports from ships out in the Atlantic last week?'

Joe nodded.

'Lit up the whole mid-Atlantic for nearly ten hours. Testing his satellites, I suppose.'

'Yeah, getting ready for the launch,' agreed Joe.

The banker raised his eyes towards heaven and then looked back at his fund manager.

'The seminar on Hope Island starts tomorrow. That's the perfect opportunity for us. Tye and the entire executive will be distracted with their guests. Plus, it's August and a lot of people are still away on vacation.'

Joe waited while Chelouche hesitated.

'Buy it, Joe, buy all of it. You can have an unlimited line of credit on the World Bank. Don't hesitate, buy as fast as you can. You understand . . .?'

Joe nodded. 'Yes, sir. Unlimited means *unlimited*.'

'Execute all the options immediately and confirm that all deals are dependent on confidentiality. We can't expect to keep this manoeuvre quiet for very long – but as long as possible, eh, Joe? Then you've got to hit the open market, hard and fast. When we must, we'll declare a hostile bid for the remaining stock with all the necessary regulatory filings.'

Joe nodded again. He knew he was facing a long night – a long few days.

'I'll send you down some admin help,' added Chelouche as he pushed himself to his feet. 'I'm off to Washington to see if anybody there works weekends.'

He paused at the door and turned back. 'Over the next few days you're going to make a lot of people very rich, Joe.'

Raymond Liu customarily received all NASA's bulletins as soon as they were issued. The one that had just arrived was brief and to the point. A space-weather storm – rated at G5, the highest category – was causing the recent network disruptions. A solar flare had occurred some hours earlier and the blast of highly charged particles was now tearing holes in the magnetosphere. The crisis was likely to pass within a few days.

He transferred to the archives of the Space Environment Center in Boulder, Colorado and downloaded everything they had on space weather, coronal mass ejections and magnetic reconnections. He knew enough about the behaviour of the Earth's magnetosphere to know that it was a subject only poorly understood. But he suddenly wanted to know a lot more about geomagnetic substorms, nondipolar force fields, the Earth's magnetopause barrier and the characteristics of free electrons, protons and helium nuclei.

The colour of the metallic gift-wrapping could only be described as episcopal. The package sat squarely in the middle of the queen-size bed in Haley's orchid-filled stateroom. She turned and nodded her thanks at the young crewman in the garish gold-trimmed white uniform. He set her newly purchased tan leather luggage on the floor and stood with his white gloved hands at his side.

Haley glanced at her LifeWatch, ready to dial some change, and then remembered tipping was not allowed during *this* weekend. They exchanged smiles.

'Enjoy your stay on *Treasure of the Caribbean*,' said the youth, executing a sharp naval salute before closing the double doors behind him.

Haley had arrived on Hope Island by helicopter so she had been able to spot this great new ship – the subject of many newscasts and press features – long before she could make out any other detail on the huge floating spaceport and deep-water harbour that seemed to almost double the extent of the verdant island to which it was attached.

She could not help feeling excited by it all. This coming event had made headline news all over the world. It had eclipsed all other stories, including the Ethiopian rain-making, the gigantic Norwegian oil-spill and the worldwide network failures. Even the more serious newspapers had led with items speculating on what difference Tye's forthcoming marriage might make to the founder of the world's richest and most powerful corporation ever.

Haley and Flick had watched the live broadcast together as Thomas Tye appeared on the terrace of his mansion with a stunning honey-coloured woman on his arm. He had cut his hair!

The couple took turns in telling the interviewer how blissfully happy they were – and how they intended to be married during the weekend celebrations. When a reporter from the Tye News Network asked them about children, the cameras captured an exchange of obviously rehearsed glances between the happy couple as Tom said only, 'We'll see.'

Haley looked at Flick, who shared her sister's privileged knowledge.

When they asked his fiancée for her thoughts, Haley frowned as the camera closed in. 'I'm delighted,' Calypso said simply. 'I'm really looking forward to helping Tom organize his charitable foundations.'

Haley whistled. 'Some woman!'

Flick nodded. 'She's like a movie star. In fact, *don't* they make quite a couple!'

They pigged out on the ongoing story for hours, watching endless reruns of a younger Calypso Browne being crowned Miss World, pictures of her beautiful but poverty-stricken native island, images of the grimy hospital in Chicago where she had practised, interviews with a stunned group of ex-colleagues – amidst the inevitable regurgitated bios of Thomas Tye himself and his Corporation. The happy couple had first met when Dr Browne joined the Hope Island medical staff, explained the narrator.

'I'll bet she's treating his son Tommy,' exclaimed Haley. 'But there's never any mention of him.'

'You'll probably get to meet her there,' Flick said wistfully. 'Just keep me patched in the whole time, you understand, *every minute!*'

Haley had kept her word and on the helicopter ride she allowed Felicity and Toby to see everything she was seeing. There were about twenty or so other guests on board the large passenger craft to which they had been transferred during a stopover on the island of Mayaguana. She now realized it was Calypso Browne's birthplace.

Haley had discovered that VIP transport to and from the island presented the biggest single problem in the organization of this three-day summit. The Cape Hope spaceport, already one of the busiest air terminals in the Caribbean and Central America, could not provide adequate parking and ground facilities for every jet wishing to land, so visitors without their own aircraft were instead being flown to Mayaguana prior to transfer to Hope Island

Surprisingly, that sleepy Bahamian island boasted a three-mile runway, a vast concrete apron and service buildings capable of accommodating dozens of wide-bodied jets as well as smaller aircraft. As Haley's *One Weekend in the Future: Preliminary Information* download had told her, this airstrip had been constructed covertly in the early 1960s by the United States military who, with the enthusiastic agreement of the British Bahamas, felt the need for a squadron of B-52 nuclear-strike bombers stationed within ten minutes' flying time of Fidel Castro's renegade, untrustworthy and missile-toting Cuban Republic.

Once the immediate problem of seeing unfriendly atomic weapons stockpiled at America's back door had evaporated, it still seemed prudent to the US Department of Defense to mothball the airstrip and its Quonset huts so that the base could be brought back into service within a few days if necessary. When the Cold War ended, so did this level of maintenance, and Tye's Logistics division had just spent two months reconditioning the field itself and flying in new fuel pumps, emergency services and portable accommodation units. The British government seemed delighted at having the facilities on Mayaguana restored at no expense to itself. After the party was over, the refurbished airstrip would go a long way to transforming the island's tourist economy. Haley herself guessed that Tye had been forced into the additional expense because of Hope Island's uncertain relations with Cuba, the only other island in the northern Caribbean with international-standard airport facilities.

As an honoured guest of the Tye Corporation, Haley had

selected to fly from London to New York in 1st-E, the first-class
entertainment section. Thus she had been able to enjoy the
gym, a sauna, massages, facials, beauty treatment and a bewilder-
ing array of immersion games, movies and music. The only let-
down was a serious disruption to the international air traffic
control system that had delayed her plane by four hours. Then
their landing at JFK had been a hesitant, jolting nightmare.
Finally there, she had transferred to one of the Tye-Lear
supersonic corporate jets that were busy ferrying visitors and
staff to and from the islands. The result was that she would be
arriving late Friday afternoon rather than in time for lunch.

The ride from New York to the Caribbean had been short
but thrilling, though Haley was disappointed that it hadn't taken
them over the Florida peninsula. She had wanted to gaze down
on it and imagine a future there with Jack.

It took less than thirty minutes before they had landed in
the Caribbean heat of Mayaguana, where Haley and a group of
dignitaries had been quickly transferred to the large helicopter.

Haley and Felicity chatted like two excited schoolgirls as the
Tye-Westland Personnel Shuttle rapidly crossed the nine miles
of azure Caribbean separating these two islands of the Greater
Antilles. Finally, Haley saw a familiar outline and she transmitted
images of Hope Island as it grew larger. The shape of the
world's only corporate state was burned into her mind because
she had read every book and watched every inch of footage
available on Tye and his island paradise. She could probably
recite the names of every bay and inlet.

The first feature to catch her eye was the vast array of
concave capture dykes of the Hope Island solar-energy farm.
Acre upon acre of dull solar fuel cells covered the entire
northern tip of the island. Then came further hectares of
greenhouses further to the south. As they approached the waist
of the island she could make out the long white crescent of
Hope Town Bay over to the west. The residential developments
along the coast were bejewelled with glittering swimming pools.
Then, on the near side of the low mountain range that formed
the island's spine, she saw the great white edifice of the Tye

Mansion itself, surrounded by guest bungalows set in acres of manicured terraces, pools and lawns.

'That's Tye's house there,' she told her twin unnecessarily. 'It's even bigger than I imagined.'

'What a waste – all for one man,' sighed Felicity.

'Not any more!' corrected Haley. 'It's now going to be a family home for *three* of them,' she added quietly. But it was unlikely any of the other passengers could overhear their conversation. They were also busy gawping out of the windows and talking to far-away companions.

'Do you think you'll get to see the little boy – Tommy?' asked Felicity, superimposing herself in Haley's vision.

'I doubt it,' replied Haley, switching off her sister's image. 'Look, that's the floating spaceport. It's huge!'

She could identify six of the large OrbitLoad shuttles that Tye Aerospace had developed in partnership with Lockheed Martin, all parked on their own separate apron. She had read that these giant craft were part aeroplane, part rocket. Coated with a light but high-density ceramic, heat-resistant skin, they took off conventionally. But once airborne, they tilted upwards to an almost vertical plane before rocket motors cut in to provide a long high-energy burn to defeat the Earth's hugging gravity and propel them into orbit.

The helicopter continued flying south-west, beyond the extended tip of the island, then circled around to make its approach. It was then that Haley noticed the cruise ship in the deep-water harbour.

'Wow!' exclaimed her distant twin as the image filled Haley's viewpers. 'It's bloody enormous!'

Bloody enormous! thought Haley simultaneously. Only recently commissioned, the ship was the largest cruise liner ever built. Taking advantage of the flex capabilities of new plastic ceramics, her designers had given her two hulls like a super-catamaran and, on this wide and stable base, the marine architects had built up a pyramid of gleaming white accommodation decks and leisure facilities. Whereas in the past ship designers had been forced to build downwards into large chine hulls, the

designers of *Treasure of the Caribbean* had been able to build
upwards from the stability of its twenty-acre platform. The black
photonic glass used in the ascending levels contrasted starkly
with the rest of the dazzling superstructure. The minimal dis-
placement of the two giant planing hulls would allow the ship
to achieve a top speed of eighty knots, which enabled her to
outrun all storms, especially given the lengthy advance warnings
that sophisticated meteorology could now provide.

'Wow!' echoed Haley.

As the helicopter began a rapid descent, she could see at
least twenty supersonic or wide-body corporate jets already
parked close to a low building that had to serve as an arrivals
hall. She sensed she was arriving in the future or, at the very
least, the extreme present.

The noise increased as the pilot adjusted the angle of the
rotor blades and, despite her sister's protests, Haley closed down
transmission, getting ready for landing. Flick could dip into the
recordings later if she wanted to.

Haley had been met by a personal greeter and, to her
surprise, by a reporter and crew from Tye News Networks. Was
it true she had been granted exclusive access to Tom himself for
a new biography? She had waved them away, refusing to
comment. Then she was driven the short distance to the
harbour where rose the gleaming white fastigiated wedding-
cake of the cruise ship in which she would be accommodated.

Of the 937 people who would be killed that afternoon only one
had any prior warning, and she was also the only one to
understand the immediate cause of her death.

Like motorists on many of the metropolitan roads below
them, pilots frequently turned their attention away from their
vehicles' controls, allowing on-board computers to fly the planes
as satellite-managed air traffic control systems steered a course
through densely populated airlanes made safe and navigable
solely by computer control. Earlier in the day the Director of
Operations, North-West Segment, United States Air Traffic
Control had begged for, and obtained, permission to delay

implementing the FAA's latest safety instruction. On such short notice it was almost impossible to find enough qualified staff to assume manual control of aircraft in this sector and the alternative was to temporarily ground all traffic. Thus the switch to manual air traffic control would not now take place for another two hours.

Joan Maria Martinez, forty-eight-year-old mother of two, loving wife and senior captain of ABA Airlines – with twenty-three years of flying experience behind her – yawned and turned away from the cockpit conversation to stretch. The Boeing 797 was at 32,000 feet, twenty-one miles north-west of Denver, out of Atlanta en route to Tokyo.

It was only when Joan glanced out of the cockpit window that she saw the dark underbelly of the giant military transport jet that was descending into their path. She cried out, reaching for the yoke, and automatically shot a look of disbelief at the aircraft proximity warning system. It showed green: no alert. But she didn't have time to disconnect the flight-control computer system before the roof of the cockpit was ripped open and she was sent flying upwards into bright sunshine, sub-freezing air – and oblivion.

Haley yawned and ran her hands through her short hair as she shook off the tiredness from the journey. Only twelve hours before she had been in the Victorian streets of Battersea, now she was here on the most advanced cruise ship in the world, moored up alongside the world's newest nation state. She was also finally about to meet the richest and most powerful businessman in the world: the object of her intellectual obsession for almost two years and of personal interest to her since very much earlier. An early-evening reception would take place on the lawns in front of the Tye mansion before all the VIP guests would attend the opening lecture.

The opening evening is strictly informal, her programme read. *The lecture will be given by the Nobel Prize-winner and futurologist, Professor Theresa Keane.*

But first, there was a special and even more exclusive social event. Another envelope, black, with her name printed on it in small gold lettering, had been waiting on her dressing table. She pulled out the grey card it enclosed:

Josh Chandler is welcoming friends at seven p.m. in Suite 1809/ 10.

Underneath, Josh had scrawled '*You* do *get around!*'

How kind of Josh, she mused, to have spotted her name on the guest list and to have thought of inviting her to his private reception. Well, that would certainly start her weekend off properly! Although she knew of Professor Keane's reputation, she didn't at all mind the idea of skipping the lecture part of the opening ceremony. She could do without hearing yet another futurologist.

Her stateroom was filled with flowers and gifts: sponsorship, Haley guessed, although she had to reckon these particular sponsors would be getting value for their outlay. They would be reaching the most exclusive and influential target audience in the world.

She found a black Chanel kimono hanging behind the bathroom door. Her travelling clothes hit the floor and after a quick, very hot shower she was enjoying the feel of the kimono's silk. Automatically she went to push the sleeves up but was surprised to find the robe a perfect fit. Similarly she found Gucci slippers, Givenchy perfumes, talcs and toilet water, a Smythson writing set on her desk, and six bottles of Laurent Perrier champagne in a large fridge concealed in the mahogany panelling. A selection of non-calorific hand-made Belgian chocolates lay in a small bowl on the bedside table. She popped one into her mouth.

Despite her stern determination not to be seduced by Tye's lavish corporate hospitality, she crossed her arms and hugged herself as she breathed in the orchidean air. She couldn't quite believe she was here.

Sitting on the edge of the off-white bed, she pulled the purple-wrapped parcel towards her. Her neatly manicured fingernails, kept short for keyboard work, managed to detach the ribbon but were no match for the plastic-metallic wrapping. Then she noticed a letter opener on her bedside table.

They've thought of everything.

Zipping along one edge of the package, she recognized Louis Vuitton logos. She saw that she had been given a square valise of green and beige farmed-leather – the perfect carry-on luggage item. Then she realized the case contained something else. Flipping open the catches, she lifted the lid to reveal polystyrene packing. She slit away the top to find a card with a pink satin bow bearing the legend *Welcome To The Girard-Perregaux Équipage.* Inside the moulded indentations were items individually bubble-wrapped.

The printed note read:

Ms Voss,

On behalf of Girrard-Perregaux International and Tye Consumer Electronics Inc., we hope you will accept this dress-occasion Équipage. It has been individually styled for you and we hope it adds to your enjoyment of 'One Weekend in the Future'.

The card was signed in different inks by Thomas Tye and the president of Girrard-Perregaux. A unique number purported to make her set a one-off.

The first gadget she unwrapped was a classic square G-P LifeWatch. She whistled silently as she held the silver and gold item up to the light. She could guess what that might cost. She noticed it was a Generation Eight, two models newer than her own fun LifeSwatch. She went on to unwrap three further pieces of Girrard-Perregaux jewellery: a belt buckle, two brooches and a pair of earrings. These were part of the wireless bodynet, she read, and could be worn individually or in combination to link these various items of the *Équipage* together. Both brooches – one plain silver, one gold, set with what appeared to be small diamonds, for more formal events – were described as *user-dedicated microphones.* According to the literature provided, they filtered out all sounds but the wearer's own voice. This overcame the problem of ambient noise when recording or transmitting. The belt buckle provided the system's radio link to external networks.

A new-generation VideoMate with a sleek silver case came out of the packing next. It was like an old-fashioned cigarette case and was hinged along its longest axis, designed to be held upright like a book. On its left was a large high-definition colour screen, on the right a smaller secondary screen with a fold-out keyboard and an icon panel. The literature claimed that the unit had greatly improved storage, battery power and wireless-range facilities. And it also contained new image-recognition software called *GuestList*.

Then Haley unwrapped an item that was new to her. This was a slender silver bracelet – a personal ScentSim. Examining it closely, she detected minute holes around its circumference for aroma delivery.

As she had unwrapped each piece she pinned or clamped it at random to parts of her silk robe and now she laughed. She imagined that she must be starting to look like a Christmas tree.

Welcome to the Personal ScentSim. This is a new accessory in the Girrard-Perregaux Équipage range and it allows wearers to produce any of 40,084 aromas at will. To be worn only on the left *wrist.*

Controlled from either her VideoMate or Viewpers, she assumed it was intended to generate artificial perfume.

Next she unwrapped a small brooch described as an *Osmatique*, a scent-analyser designed to first identify and then disregard the wearer's own scent. Thereafter it would analyse the aromas in the wearer's environment, in particular analysing the pheromones and body chemistry of other people in close proximity.

She'd read about this new *Spell-Smell* technology. The system analysed another person's smell from within a metre and analysed the underlying pheromones that would prompt attraction, disinterest or repulsion. Then a rating was provided in the wearer's viewpers on a one-to-ten scale of the natural chemical compatibility and attraction. The system could manufacture a contra-simulation guaranteed to similarly attract. A health warning emphasized the dangers of careless use – especially with strangers in non-public places. Haley wondered what would happen if two people wearing Osmatiques met each other with their systems set to level ten.

Next year, claimed the literature, Tye Life Sciences would also be introducing a new oral therapy that enabled the user's body to produce custom-designed pheromone mixes to attract specific mates. Haley realized that osphresiology had developed enormously in recent years, but the idea of controlling physical chemical attraction! Jesus, imagine meeting someone and marrying them only to find their pheromone mix was artificially adjusted. Go to bed with a hunk and, if he missed his medication, wake up with a cesspit! But perhaps it wasn't so new – just another version of going to bed drunk and waking up sober.

Then Haley was unwrapping the last item, something that seemed *completely* new to her. This was an almost microscopically thin curved fibre-optic tube. At one end its tip was enlarged slightly, like the head of a small knitting needle. At the other it was attached to a transparent internal earpiece.

She ran her eyes over the 'Quick Start' instructions. The item was called an *InfoStem* and could replace all forms of viewpers. Its transparent stalk was almost invisible in use, claimed the literature, but the outer tip contained microcameras and a stereo retinal projector. Thus images and text were projected upside down onto the back of the wearer's eyeballs in such a way that they appeared as a transparent display eighteen inches in front of the eyes.

She slipped on the ultra-light earpiece and stood to see how the stalk-like protrusion looked in the mirror. True, it was so fine she could hardly see it. She next selected the Tye News Network on her new VideoMate and suddenly her vision was filled with a picture of the ship she was on. Then the camera zoomed away to pan across the spaceport and the southern tip of Hope Island.

She was just about to check if Flick had gone to bed when there was a knock on the door.

'Come in,' called Haley. Jack's grinning face appeared.

Her InfoStem instantly displayed:

GuestList identification: Jack Hendriksen, Vice-President, Corporate Security, Tye Corporation.

'It *is* you!' she said pointing at her new InfoStem. 'I've got proof!'

He stepped in, closed the door and then they were in each other's arms.

Minutes passed as they kissed, savouring the sheer proximity of each other. Both had begun to suffer the doubt that follows separation in a new relationship.

'I can only be away for half an hour,' said Jack when they at last broke their embrace. She already knew their relationship must remain secret during this weekend.

'That'll do fine,' replied Haley with a delicious grin. 'There's champagne in the bucket. I'll only be a minute.'

'You have to cancel, Tom,' insisted Raymond Liu. 'The networks are going haywire.'

'CANCEL IT? ARE YOU FUCKING INSANE?' yelled Tye. 'Half of my guests are already HERE!' They were standing in Tye's office late on Friday afternoon.

The engineer was immovable. 'I'm sorry, Tom, I can't guarantee the infrastructure. It doesn't just affect us, other network operators are having the same trouble. Our own networks are so unreliable I can't guarantee that TNN will even be able to broadcast this weekend. People all over the world may lose communications. I'm now putting all my monitoring teams on to the satellite networks and the air traffic management systems. The networks will repair themselves, of course, but I just can't keep up with the fault monitoring. I've got half of the Asian networks down, the Canadian cellular wireless network went out for a whole hour this morning, and three more city traffic systems are looking shaky.'

'Fix them,' shouted Tye. 'Just find more people and fucking FIX THEM!'

Liu tried to be reasonable once again. 'Tom, if you won't cancel the event at least shut down the Solaris stations.'

'SHUT THEM DOWN?' screamed Tye. 'It's only FUCK-ING SUNSHINE, LIU!'

'You've *got* to shut them down, it can't be anything else,' urged the engineer. 'I'm convinced they're causing massive magnetic disturbance.'

'That's impossible,' argued Tye. 'We're building up the rain clouds now. Don't you realize what this MEANS TO US?'

Liu nodded. He did know. He also knew that countless lives were probably at stake.

'You heard what happened over Denver, Tom. We can't risk it.'

'They don't *know* what caused that yet,' snapped Tye.

'Sorry, Tom, but I'm shutting them down,' said Liu quietly. 'I'll go over and explain things to the Solaris Control Center.'

Tye considered for a moment. 'You won't do that, Liu. You're fired,' he said, and turned away.

Joe Tinkler had been working for thirty-six hours without rest. He had already put in a twelve-hour day by the time Chelouche arrived and issued his latest instructions. From that point on Joe had spent the night and all day Friday discreetly speaking to his fund-managing colleagues round the world and executing his options on the Tye Corp shares as rapidly but as noiselessly as he could.

By Friday midday he had lifted his fund's percentage of Tye Corp's core voting stocks to nearly seventeen per cent and he could see that, despite the discreet nature of his dealings, certain people in the market were beginning to notice a reduced liquidity in Tye shares. The open-market price was starting to rise.

He had then accelerated his purchases. Seeing the stock starting to rise strongly, he abandoned his cover and started to buy openly in every marketplace in the world. There had been a brief glitch on a settlement problem. The World Bank cashiers had reported that their cash reserves were drying up as a result of network failures. He told them to talk to Chelouche himself and the Chief Cashier had got back to him, a look of wonder undoing his normal impassivity.

'Doctor Chelouche has authorized me to issue whatever you need,' he said disbelievingly. 'I mean, to issue value – *new value* – in whatever currency you need.'

'Thanks,' said Joe and snapped the connection off.

By six p.m. he had spent over six trillion dollars. *Six trillion US dollars in twenty-four hours!* But he now controlled twenty-three per cent of the Tye Corporation although the stock price had leaped eleven per cent on the day. He knew that weekends still had lower trading volumes than weekdays and he knew that a significant number of the big traders still refrained from dealing on the Jewish Sabbath. He looked at his time-zone display and realized that, with the exception of the American west coast, nearly all the markets were already running at their weekend and night-time trading levels. He calculated that he could afford to catch six hours' sleep on the sofa in Chelouche's office. The banker also had a private bathroom on the top floor and Joe felt he needed to use it.

He put his machine to sleep and then remembered he hadn't called Nancy. Their 'on-off, on-off' had come to life again since he had been back in New York and he realized that he would have to explain diplomatically that he would be unable to see her this evening.

He reached forward and woke his system up, then realized that their date had been for *yesterday* evening – and he had forgotten all about it. He decided it was best to leave it for now.

Sitting back in his chair, he yawned, then turned to his right-hand screen and opened up the TNN TV window. He could see the Hope Island garden party was now in full swing in the beautiful evening sunshine of the Caribbean – the opening event of *One Weekend in the Future*. He watched Tye shaking hands. He at least was obviously unconcerned about his stock movements.

The picture suddenly flickered, faded, and then returned.

Joe frowned. That was unusual, these days.

'You've been very lucky with the weather,' said a smiling President Wilkinson, as he enthusiastically pumped Thomas Tye's hand for the cameras. 'My people were predicting a hurricane for the weekend.'

'Well, looks like no danger of that, Mr President,' returned Tye, with a bright smile of his own.

'And congratulations on your engagement,' continued the president of the United States, laughing warmly, well aware that the TNN news crews were still focusing on them. 'What a beautiful woman!'

'I'm sorry you won't be seeing her this evening,' replied Tye.

'You'll have a chance to meet her after our wedding ceremony tomorrow.'

'Of course, this will be your stag night!' The President beamed. 'Shouldn't you be off somewhere with the boys?'

'It doesn't get any better than this, Mr President.' Tye smirked, then he moved off – he had spotted President Orlov making a choreographed entrance.

The lawns were now glittering with global celebrity, money and power. The late-afternoon Caribbean sun was kind and the guests enjoyed a gentle breeze off the Atlantic as they gathered on acres of Kikuyu grass – *Pennisetum cladestinum*, imported from Kenya for its decorative and soil-binding properties – on the terraces below Tye's mansion.

It was a black-tie affair and the lawns were packed. The official list of those invited to step into *One Weekend in the Future* came to just over 200 names, but their entourages and body-guards had swelled the total number of visitors to the island to nearly two *thousand* and as many of them as possible wanted to be at the opening. Nobody deigned to wear a name badge, but many of the faces were world-famous and the new *GuestList* system coped with the rest.

Usually, when celebrities met, there was an awkward bon-homie that extended to a few sentences before disintegrating into paranoia about entrapment – you got hit on if you stood still too long. Famous faces constantly searched crowds for other famous or useful faces who could further their causes, so the over-firm handshakes and air-kissing were simultaneously a greeting and a farewell. But the Tye Corporation had introduced new manners at this event – manners that were likely to become the norm in the future. No one was wearing Viewpers, since all had the new InfoStem.

Everyone was enjoying the experience of attending a social gathering at which they were automatically provided with all necessary information about the other guests. Each one's system provided a complete database of all those present, complete with their biographies and most recent activities and achieve-ments. As any guest scanned the other faces on the lawn, the InfoStem used a combination of ident-outputs and facial pattern-

recognition to provide an overlay projection identifying the
person on whom the wearer was focusing his or her eyes.
Simultaneously, in the users' earpieces, the system provided the
correct pronunciation of that person's name and at least one
item of recent interest that might make an opening gambit for
conversation.

But, as was his way, Thomas Tye had provided himself with
an additional advantage. As well as receiving that output from
the databases, he was also provided with audio input from one
of the event organizers. She stood watching some distance
behind him and guided Tye to his A-list one by one, adding her
own commentary and suggestions to the audio-visual prompts
as he greeted important face after face.

Ironically, many of the lesser guests on these lawns, those
not expecting to be greeted personally by Tye this evening, had
tuned their system into TNN's global coverage and were watching themselves on TV as the party progressed. Many were
beaming in friends and relatives via their systems.

Haley was one such and, true to her word, Flick was
determinedly patched in from Ladbroke Grove in London
where it was now after ten p.m.

'There's that tennis player, what's her name, oh yes,' said
Flick as Haley's gaze focused on a bronzed Amazon, the system
providing identification. 'God, she's big!'

'She is,' agreed Haley, circling around a knot of Hollywood
types to get a full view of the great white house above her.

She turned her head from left to right. 'Just look at that,' she
exclaimed to her sister. Then, lifting her gaze to the roof, she
saw two figures standing at a safety rail.

'I'll bet that's Miss World with young Tommy,' muttered
Haley.

'Quick, zoom in,' urged Flick.

'I can't do that, it's just one focal length,' said Haley.

She turned back to survey the crowd on the lawn.

'What a gorgeous hunk!' exclaimed Flick from afar as a man
in a dark naval dress uniform turned away from one group and
headed towards her sister. He was carrying two glasses of
champagne.

'You've met Jack before,' said Haley unnecessarily as his name and title appeared in their gaze.

In his apartment beside the spaceport, Raymond Liu lay on his single bed and stared at the ceiling. He was now shut out of the island's computer networks but, despite the recent loss of his job, he couldn't stop thinking about what might be causing the endless, apparently unconnected network failures. Beside him was a printout of the last news item he had received before HR had removed his network access. He picked it up again:

European Space Agency Disclaims Sunspot Theory

Geneva: The European Space Agency today announced that current disturbances to global communications networks – now thought to be responsible for the deaths of 937 people in a mid-air collision over Denver, Co., USA – were not in fact caused by a solar eruption or ejection of matter. Dr Alex Krywald, director of Space Weather at ESA, explained: 'We constantly monitor and record the sun's activity. We have searched through our recordings for the past two days and there has been no unusual activity on the surface of the sun or its corona in that period. We do not yet know what is causing this disruption in communications.'

Liu wondered why the Europeans would take the extraordinary step of publicly contradicting NASA's analysis.

Despite extreme tiredness and an unusually large quantity of alcohol in her system, Haley found herself lying wide awake in the vast emptiness of her bed aboard the *Treasure of the Caribbean*. She had two faces in her mind and, despite repeated efforts, she could not banish them.

Jack's face occupied the same place that it had for the last month, where it was usually the last thing Haley was aware of before her synapses quietened and consciousness retreated from her forebrain. But tonight there was another, competing image, and they flipped like two sides of the same coin. The other one was that of Dr Calypso Browne – formerly known as Miss World.

The early part of the opening evening had been everything that Haley had hoped for. She and Jack had made rapid and passionate love. Then there had been that dazzling garden party, at which Jack had made a brief appearance. Then her 'personal greeter' had scooped her up in readiness for the opening lecture, but Haley had been forced to admit she would not be attending.

The greeter's eyes had widened. 'You've got an invitation from Josh Chandler? You don't think ... I mean, could I come with you?'

Haley had smiled and taken pity on her. All the woman's Washington cool had evaporated at the mention of the famous film star.

Jack, with automatic access to all events, had found her while she was finally having a few moments alone with Josh Chandler.

'Great to meet you. I've read Haley's biography,' said a smiling Jack as they shook hands. Haley glanced sharply at him. He hadn't told her.

Then the couple had been left alone, as the star went to circulate with his other guests. Haley had recalled what she wanted to ask Jack. 'Have you met this Calypso Browne?'

She sensed instantly that there was something to tell. He looked quickly down, then back up to meet her eyes.

'Yes, I was seeing her casually before ... before I came back to London.'

'Casually? How casually?'

He looked down again. 'I saw her just a few times. We never really went out.'

'But you *were* lovers?' Her voice became hoarse as she asked.

Jack shrugged. 'Well ... yes. But it was a casual thing. On this island ...'

And now the two faces hung in front of her. Haley had drunk more, quite quickly, after she had been told. But with every drink she had seemed to become more sober, more cold around the heart. Jack had tried to reassure her, then was forced to return to his duties elsewhere.

She lay in the dark and her imagination now supplied even more disturbing images; she saw Jack's lips on that achingly long neck, she saw Miss World's fine hands on Jack's back. She saw them kissing. She saw that stunning, natural smile that the woman seemed to produce so effortlessly.

Haley groaned, rolled out of bed and crossed to the bathroom. She flipped the light on, rummaged in her toilet bag and found the sleeping pills she kept for emergencies. She filled a glass of water, swallowed a tablet, then confronted her reflection in the down-lit mirror. She studied her slender naked body and tried to imagine what Calypso Browne would look like without clothes.

'You're being stupid, we all have pasts,' she told herself. Then she thought of Kevin and Barry. *Not quite in the same league*, she admitted to herself. *Why had she been slumming for so long?* She turned the light off and finally headed for oblivion.

Everyone on the Operation Iambus team had turned up for work this Saturday. Four entire floors of the United Nations Secretariat building had been given over to the investigation of Thomas Tye and his global businesses and, late in the afternoon, the team leaders had returned to Amethier's office to make a final decision.

'Doctor Chelouche has started the process for taking control of the Tye Corporation,' the UNISA director advised the thirty people packed into his office. 'Joe Tinkler and his assistants are buying yet more stock as we speak. Over fourteen of the world's largest economies have committed central reserves to the fund.'

'Including the USA?' asked Martha Rose.

Amethier shook his head. 'We haven't formally informed Washington,' he explained. 'Doctor Chelouche is down there now but we're not sure of the nature of the relationship between Wilkinson's administration and Hope Island. The word is that Tye and Attorney-General Treno had a blazing row during his recent visit, but Wilkinson himself is on the island now. We think some deal may be under way.'

They pondered the implications. They had all watched the TV coverage of the opening ceremony and had marvelled at the body of political power assembled by one businessman. It was almost a rival to the UN.

'A financial takeover is not going to solve the problem of the

Solaris satellites,' pointed out Ron Deakin. 'I understand they're under the control of a private company.'

'The Doctor disagrees,' said Amethier. 'He maintains the core corporation is a thirty per cent shareholder in Phoebus Inc. and that will prove enough for us to apply to the international court for a writ of cessation.'

'We can't expect Tye to take this lying down,' argued Rose. There were nods of agreement all round. Nobody was expecting this to be straightforward. 'We'd better apply to the Hague for *certiorari*,' she added. 'That's an immediate writ from the highest court of all. It should overrule any legal efforts they make and should shut down all operations temporarily until we have a better handle on the situation.'

Deakin glanced at his LifeWatch. 'Well, he's due to be married an hour from now, so I suppose he'll be a little busy. Anyway, we have some news. Mike?'

Michael Chevannes rose to his feet.

'I've just got back from South Africa,' he explained. 'I flew over there to visit a boy called Reon Albertyn. He's fifteen – or rather, he was. He died while I was there. His story was uncovered by UNHCR and I've turned all the relevant material over to Rima Berzin and the WHO team.'

Professor Berzin took the floor. 'If we could turn the lights down...'

The room dimmed as she walked towards the wall screen. A video image of a wizened old white man with a hugely swollen head appeared. He was sitting on a bed.

'Believe it or not, this was Reon Albertyn,' Rima Berzin explained. 'He was suffering from a condition initially identified as progeria, a very rare ageing disease. Victims in their teens start to look like they are ninety years old. And there's another strange thing...'

The image changed to a middle-aged black woman seated at a table in a hospital room.

'This is Reon's mother,' she continued. 'As you can see, she's black, while Reon was an albino – a black man with a genetic abnormality that produced white skin. You'll now hear Mrs Albertyn's sworn testimony.'

They watched and listened as the grieving mother explained how she had been recruited to work for the Erasmus Corporation sixteen years before. She described the tempting fee she was offered to be a surrogate mother and how, after the doctors had finished their tests on her newborn white baby, they had paid her fifty thousand US dollars and had returned her son to her.

She wept as she recounted how her husband had beaten her and how her family had turned her out with her baby because it was white. She described Reon's unhappy childhood of alienation and the first obvious symptoms of his disease at the age of twelve. Then he had been convicted and imprisoned for stealing a car in Zimbabwe. She had been reunited with him only after the UNHCR secured his release from the Harare jail and had placed him in the Steve Biko Memorial Clinic in South Africa.

As Professor Berzin fingered the remote, the audience saw the text of a pathology report.

'He wasn't actually suffering from progeria. In fact, he was an early human clone, an experimental embryo given a number of so-called genetic enhancements. Lily Albertyn was used as a surrogate embryo carrier, one of many,' she explained. 'But in this particular clone the telemores, the ends of the chromosomes, were too short. He was ageing at five times the normal rate from the moment he was conceived and implanted in Mrs Albertyn. Reon was identified in the Erasmus files as *Alpha 41.*'

'So that's what we're going with?' asked Martha Rose. 'But does it connect with Thomas Tye directly?'

'He was chairman of Erasmus Inc. then and he still is,' said Chevannes.

The lawyer nodded. 'Do we have any further evidence?'

Chevannes patted a pile of paper and a wallet of memory sticks in front of him. 'There's stacks of it. We've got all the Erasmus reports from that time, although they may not prove admissible because of the way we obtained them. But there's also the circumstantial evidence from Mrs Albertyn herself and other mothers contracted to be surrogates at the time. We're following their children up now.'

Martha Rose considered. She would need plenty of direct evidence as well as the circumstantial. 'We can issue writs of *duces tecum* on the various documents we know about,' she reasoned. 'We can force Erasmus to bring the originals to court. We don't have to show the versions we intercepted – just knowing they exist will be good enough. I'll be looking at a prosecution under the forty-fifth, seventy-eighth and one-hundred-and-twelfth Articles of the 1945 UN Declaration of Human Rights and under Article Sixty-four of the 1986 African Charter on Human Rights.'

'What do you think, Mr Olliphant?' asked Amethier. 'How will the world vote on that?'

'At the risk of sounding heartless, it's perfect,' declared the senior image-perception adjuster. 'Even with this Ethiopian stunt going on, the images of this boy and his mother are very powerful. Can we release details about the boy – the clone – that Tye has with him on his island?'

Amethier nodded. 'We can – we're very serious about this. Jack Hendriksen has brought us pictures of the boy – Tommy, he's called – and I think we should go with the lot. Can you get a preliminary indictment, a few specimen charges, up by tomorrow, Martha?'

The international attorney looked flabbergasted. 'No way, Jan,' she protested. 'Not if we want to do this properly.'

'Timing, Rose, timing. I want to make an announcement tomorrow, on the day that it is supposed to rain in Ethiopia. I want the world to know that the United Nations Commission for Human Rights is charging Erasmus Inc., the Tye Corporation and Thomas Tye personally with responsibility for the death of Reon Albertyn and an unknown number of other children in Southern Africa. That will produce the maximum impact.'

'Agreed,' confirmed Edward Olliphant, nodding. 'I'll leak it to the *New York Times* for Monday's first edition.'

'We'll get right on it,' sighed the lawyer as she rose. 'We'll need everything you've brought back, Mike.'

Tommy's blue suit had been made at the little tailoring boutique in Hope Town. Calypso had ensured that it was more restrained than many American page-boy outfits and it made him look very mature.

'So grown-up,' Calypso observed as she stood behind him and savoured their reflections in the mirror. 'What do *you* think Biya?'

'Nice,' grinned the small girl in her cream-and-white flouncy dress. In the few weeks that she had been receiving Calypso's tuition she had started adding adjectives to her stock of English nouns, although she was not yet stringing many of the words together.

'Can you see us, Mum?'

Mrs Browne was sitting on a chair behind them, dressed ready for the ceremony, Roger on her lap. The CatPanion was wearing a silver collar in honour of the occasion. Calypso walked over to them. The old lady ran her hands over the cream lace dress that Calypso had chosen. Then she pulled her daughter's head down, felt her face and kissed her.

'You are happy,' she smiled. 'God bless you.'

'I hope I am coming?' asked Jed, from the top of the dressing table.

'Of course you are,' laughed Calypso. 'I've got a flower for you to wear. Now, how do I look?'

None of her small audience were qualified to judge; none of them could look with adult human eyes. To be more specific, none of them could look with adult *male* eyes.

'Very nice,' said Jed appropriately.

'Yes, very nice,' agreed Roger.

'Very nice ... *Mummy*,' said Tommy. Then he collapsed into a fit of laughter and threw himself face down on the bed to hide his embarrassment. Tom had explained that he would be able to call Calypso that after the wedding.

'You'll mess up that new suit,' smiled Calypso. 'Biya's keeping her dress so nice. There isn't long to go.'

'Nervous?' asked Jed.

Once again, Calypso shivered. She knew that Professor Keane insisted the Furry companions produced their language from vast databases triggered by key words – like *wedding*, she presumed – but she still found this companion's apparent cognition unnerving. She wondered if the professor really under-stood what she was doing.

'I am, a bit,' she admitted.

There was a noise behind them.

'You look really beautiful, Calypso,' announced Connie from the doorway. 'In fact, you all look wonderful.'

The matron of honour entered the room and put her small bouquet down on a table. 'Are we ready? she asked.

'I've never seen anything like it, Ron.'

They were drinking coffee in Lynch's sub-basement. Most of the team had grabbed some sleep in the adjacent Marriott hotel, but the computer scientist had had no relief and he looked dog-tired. It was nearly noon.

'The networks function one minute, then there's data delay of an hour or more. It's like they're seizing up.'

'Which networks do you mean, Al?' asked Deakin.

'As far as I can tell, everything using a satellite link – which includes almost every network these days. Even the undersea fibre optics connect up to the satellites for continental hops.'

The UNISA Exec nodded. 'What do you think's causing it?'

'I assumed it was overload,' replied Lynch. 'So I've shut down all my artificial message-generation, but even at ultra-low bandwidth there're real problems. *And* it's Saturday. Traffic normally halves at the weekend.'

Deakin yawned. 'Well, it shouldn't matter too much. We've got what we need.'

Calypso had particularly asked to be married under Rembrandt's all-knowing, all-understanding, all-forgiving gaze. Since moving into the main house she had spent hours in its great marbled reception hall staring at this rich, dark painting. It had been painted in 1661, shortly after the greatest of all painters had been widowed and made bankrupt. He had been fifty-five when, once again, he had looked into and exposed his tired, omniscient soul with brutal honesty. Tom had informed her that it was the last of the artist's self-portraits still outside of a museum and he had been forced to outbid both the Getty Museum and the Rijksmuseum to acquire it.

She knew the painting well, from her father showing a slide of it when he was teaching late-twentieth-century English literature. He would project the portrait as he quoted one of his favourite opening lines, a sentence written by the novelist John Fowles, a line deliberately created for its rigour, opacity and unyielding abstruseness. The author was describing this portrait:

Whole sight; or all the rest is desolation.

Whole sight indeed! thought Calypso as she arrived at the wide doors leading into the vast hall. She wondered what her missionary-trained schoolteacher father would have thought of her. But Rembrandt would have understood, even today.

She waited in the high double doorway while her eyes adjusted to the brilliance of the television lights within. In response, a magnificent *rivière* of diamonds and sapphires at her neck created scores of lens flares that sent hands flying over the boards in the control room that the TV production team had set up next door.

The groups of sofas had been removed and the large sculptures – a collection she now knew included a Rodin, a Donatello and even a battered Praxiteles from ancient Greece – had been moved to one side, creating the appearance of a long gallery. A red carpet stretched in front of her, laid down specially for her bridal procession.

Calypso could see Tom waiting for her in front of the low brass rail erected in front of the wedding dais. Neither of them was religious, but both had agreed they wanted a feeling of ceremony. The television lights flared off the white marble and made the great room and its art seem brighter, larger than life.

Like everything from now on.

She could hear Tommy, though she couldn't see him from where she now stood. There had been only one choice for their wedding anthem. Tommy himself was playing 'It's Our Planet' on a new double-manual digital synthesizer with 32-bass pedalboard. It had been programmed with a complete sample of the sounds belonging to the great Bruckner organ in the ancient monastery of St Florian in Linz, Austria. Tommy had been in a state of huge excitement as he had explained to Calypso how Anton Bruckner had been Tommy's own age when he had played that organ for church services. Equally precocious, Tommy had rearranged the corporate march as a delicate nocturne to take full advantage of the many fine upper-register pipes that, at one remove, were providing his palette of sound.

Calypso turned to look at ever-cool Connie and then smiled down at little Biya. The girl was all wonder with her huge eyes, cream lace flouncy dress and shiny shoe buckles. Calypso reached down and took the child's hand.

Seeing the floor manager's cue, she took a deep breath and stepped forward.

Suddenly the music changed to a series of staccato, chiffed, ascending, triumphal notes, not at all as had been planned or rehearsed. They had earlier agreed with the TV people that the corny and the clichéd would have no place in this ceremony, which was being recorded only minutes before it would be seen by billions all over the world. That network mass-cast was scheduled for two p.m., the optimum viewing point for audiences across the Americas, Europe and the Middle East. Meanwhile, many Asian, Australasian and Pacific viewers would be sitting up late to see the event as near real-time as possible. The rest would digest it with their breakfasts. Then it would be replayed over and over again and downloaded countless times, continuing in the suspended immortality of global virtuality.

Finally the attention-demanding series of heraldic-trumpet voices broke into a giant wash of thundering, descending, octaphonic chords that blasted from the full range of the organ's mighty pipes to announce Calypso's entrance. Tommy had ignored his instructions and pulled out all the stops. A broad smile lit Calypso's face: it *was* right. It was Mendelssohn's' famous *Wedding March* from his incidental music to Shakespeare's *A Midsummer Night's Dream*. She recalled that the music celebrated the marriage of Theseus, duke of Athens, to Hippolyta, queen of the Amazons. She felt the first tears cloud her vision. She loved Tommy so much. How could he have *known* this would be so right?

She moved forward steadily and slowly as the triumphal music reverberated around the vast marble hall. Tommy the classicist was now taking it 'adagio', very, very slowly, shunning the tumpty-tumpty, polka-like temptations of hick performance, and filling with gentle, magical, filigree *agrément* notes as he welcomed his beloved Cally into his life for good. It had been one of Calypso's several conditions that when the ceremony was complete, she would become the boy's co-guardian and, as with all their other nuptial agreements, this would be ratified under Californian law. At the same time, the Tye Press Office would go public about Tommy's existence. 'A huge scoop to complete this fantastic weekend,' the senior perception analyst had predicted. It would be claimed that his surrogate mother had demanded anonymity and privacy and so could not be named or involved. Since his unburdening, his momentous sharing, Tom had seemed surprisingly willing – Calypso might have said loving – on all such topics and there had been no hint of corporate or personal morganaticism in his attitude.

She walked towards the rows of chairs set out for the very few, very privileged guests. Her mother sat with Roger on her lap in the front row to the left, her best friend and neighbour from Mayaguana sitting beside them. Calypso had also invited Nurse Pettigrew, Heather Garland from the school and, on impulse, Mario Ginola from her favourite pizza place down at the Little Venice marina. She could see him now, way at the back, crumpled in overawed wonder. Then she saw Miss Duckett, Tommy's music teacher, sitting on the other side of the aisle, a broad grin on her face. Calypso smiled; she knew a co-conspirator when she saw one. The house staff and a few members of the corporate office staff filled the remaining seats. Marsello Furtrado, certainly not her idea of a best man, stood in a posture of concinnous elegance.

Calypso arrived beside Tom and he turned his head to grin at her. She shot a glance at Tommy who was finishing on a sustained C major chord, including the contrabass of the giant pyramidon thirty-two-foot C natural pipe, the lowest note the Bruckner organ could deliver. The powerful speakers sent out a standing wave of sound that reverberated around the hall and rattled their chest bones. It felt as if the great pipes themselves had been transported from their gilded baroque basilica and were now ranged invisibly in this marbled bride-chamber. Finally, the organist lifted his hands with a flourish.

Tommy looked across at her in delight and, forgetting the cameras, she crossed her eyes, sucked in her cheeks and mugged at him. He laughed, jumped down from his stool, leaped off the dais and ran over to help Mrs Browne to her feet. He was determined to be both organist and page-boy, assisting Calypso's mother as she gave her daughter away. Jed, who had been quietly singing along with lyrics of his own invention, watched from his perch on top of the keyboard.

They had even flown in a Hollywood judge who moon-lighted as a celebrity wedding notary, hoping that he would be accustomed to cameras and to famous faces. But the imposing silver-haired man in the dark suit still managed to hesitate slightly before stepping forward. He realized the global ratings for this wedding would be far greater than for any televised ceremony at which he had previously officiated.

It had been decided that formal banns were superfluous: the whole world had been informed of *this* marriage and if anyone was going to have the temerity to object, there had been more than enough time to do so.

The ritual moved forward as if in a dream. Calypso felt she was back on the catwalk again. Her performance was flawless. Bride and groom both said the words clearly and without hesitation, and professional smiles were exchanged, although she was aware that underneath there was unexpected emotion.

It was Tommy who helped Mrs Browne step forward when the time came for her to give her only unmarried child away. Then, having brought forward a chair for her to sit down again, it was time for him to proffer the wedding rings on a blue velvet cushion.

Calypso's betrothal ring contained a salamstone sapphire from Sri Lanka surrounded by a baguette of the finest Kimberlite diamonds. The main stone had been cleaved in Amsterdam from an eight-carat cabochon earlier that week. She and Tom had watched on the networks as the delicate operation had been performed by a world-renowned glyptician. Her wedding ring was a Russian trinity of gold bands: red, white and yellow. Calypso privately considered this multiple appropriate for the basis of their union. Her groom relished the fact that the ore itself had come from Sybaria. A jet had been sent to collect the finished jewellery two days earlier.

Calypso was dimly aware of the cameras shifting behind the dais to find the best angle for a close-up as Tom took her hand and slipped the rings on her finger.

Then they were face to face for the first time. She tasted his mouth and found herself responding. As they held the moment for the cameras, the small assembly applauded.

When Tommy went scampering off again she knew why. He had begged to play a short interlude piece while the couple were led behind a vast Venetian screen to sign the official register of marriages that the notary had brought with him from Beverly Hills. By agreement they were also signing joint guardianship papers, hurried through the Californian legal processes, and there were also multiple legal and financial agreements to sign.

As witnessses Heather Garland and Mario Ginola rose to follow the couple, Calypso could hear the majestic opening chords and mighty descending bass notes of Sigfrid Karg-Elert's *Marche triomphale*, a piece composed to celebrate the marriage union *and* to display the virtuosity and range of both organist and instrument.

Once all the paperwork was completed, Calypso and Tom returned to the centre of the huge room and into the full glory of the final reverberating chord of the Lutheran chorale. Waiters stepped briskly forward with trays of champagne, since bride and groom only had a few minutes to toast each other and to accept the congratulations of their guests. Even now, the recording of the wedding was being watched by billions on the networks. Shortly the floor manager would signal that it was time to walk out through the terrace doors and face the live TV coverage and the hundreds of guests gathered for the garden party.

Tommy suddenly appeared at their side, Jed under his arm.

The synthesizer was now on automatic and was softly replaying Tommy's performance of 'It's Our Planet' to provide a coda. At this moment Calypso felt as if the planet *were* hers.

'Cally?'

She bent and kissed his cheek, and he put his arm up around her neck and whispered in her ear.

'Mummy ...'

Then he got the giggles.

Calypso kissed him again and straightened up. 'Well?' she said to Tom, the single word asking so many questions.

He turned his head and looked deep into her eyes.

'Well,' he replied.

'May I have some champagne, please?' Tommy asked, in order to interrupt.

Tom smiled and allowed him a sip from his glass.

'Hurrah,' cried Jed.

'Hurrah,' echoed Roger.

Then came the signal from the great glass doors. Tom returned his glass to a waiter and took Tommy's hand. Smiling, he held out his other hand towards his new bride.

Hand in hand, they walked out into the sunshine to greet the world.

TWENTY-SIX

His silver hair, craggy looks and genial demeanour had become familiar the world over but to the small crew waiting in the pre-dawn desert the senior anchorman of the Tye News Network looked old, cold and miserable. As the generator-powered lights were switched on, the production assistant ran through her silent cue count, then gestured. The presenter suddenly turned on his most dazzling smile.

'Good morning. I'm Bob Houston, this is TNN and these are the Ethiopian plains on the morning of Sunday, August thirtieth. Here in East Africa it is now five thirty a.m. and the people of one of the world's poorest nations wait anxiously to see if the new climate-engineering technology promised by the Tye Corporation can finally bring relief from a seven-year drought. Many local people have stayed up all night dancing for rain – they call it a *ngoma* – and even as the light begins to arrive I can see black clouds over on the horizon. Let's go now to one of the Halcyon weather planes over the Indian Ocean.'

Beneath the United Nations complex in Manhattan the section leaders of the Iambus team were watching it on the large wall screens of the Security Council's private meeting chamber. Even though it was nine thirty on a Saturday evening in New York, none seemed eager to leave. They watched intently as the same weather plane transmitted aerial views of banks of low, moisture-laden clouds rolling towards the East African coastline.

'For two nights now he's been concentrating the output of four Solaris stations over the Indian Ocean,' explained Rolf

Larsson. 'It does look like he's managed to invert the atmosphere. The cold air of the ionosphere has suddenly been sucked
downwards.'

There was no response from the group. They were all
waiting for the moment.

The picture flickered and disappeared. 'The damn networks
again,' muttered Al Lynch.

When the picture re-established, the location had switched
to South Dakota where a group of Sioux Indians were engaged
in a rain dance.

Deakin watched two middle-aged males in traditional costume and feather head-dresses attempt to recreate their fore-
bears' ancient dance of supplication to the rain gods. When they
had circled a jug of water four times they would throw themselves on the ground and then drink the blessed liquid.

Deakin shook his head as the perspiring, overweight men
parodied their heritage for the sake of the media.

Michel Geronde had risen magnificently to the occasion,
deploying his army of chefs for almost ten hours in the cruise
liner's vast galleys. Now over 200 of the world's elite and an
equal number of their partners and senior staff were finishing off
the banquet with his superb *Nesselrode*, a Russian iced dessert
made with chestnuts, cream and preserved fruits, flavoured with
rum.

At six other locations around the island, Geronde's imported
assistants were also producing meals for the hundreds of body-
guards, support staff, pilots and administrators that the VIP
guests had brought with them to the tiny island. At all of these
satellite banquets the diners could watch large wall screens
displaying live broadcasts from the ballroom of the *Treasure of
the Caribbean* so they too could feel part of the momentous
events being celebrated.

It had been announced that the Tye Corporation was now
leaseholder of over one and a half million square miles of Eastern
Siberia, and a new corporate state – the second of recent times
– had been created. The final cession documents had been
signed earlier in the day here on Hope Island and President

Orlov had made an emotional pre-dinner speech that praised Thomas Tye's vision and informed the world that the Russian Federation was once again economically independent.

Then Thomas Tye himself had given a major performance. For half an hour he had addressed his guests in the ship's enormous ballroom. He described to them his plans for Sybaria and the opportunities presented by climatic re-engineering. In due course, the entire world's population could be adequately fed. Rain could be brought to arid regions and natural catastrophes averted. He focused, as always, on the benefit to the planet. All the delegates were starting to understand the full potential of his plans.

A full-motion simulation of the Phoebus Project and the Solaris energy-recycling stations had been made available on the networks to help the global population at large understand how their planet was about to be changed by the Tye Corporation's new technology. Despite the degraded performance of the networks, millions of Tye followers had already managed to download this model.

As he reached his finale, Tom was standing directly behind President Orlov's chair. He clamped both hands on his guest's shoulders, glanced down at him, then back up to the cameras.

'Take care of our planet, you hear?' he declaimed.

The leader of a newly prosperous Russia was the first to reply 'We hear'. Then he leaped to his feet to shake Thomas Tye's hand. The rest of the guests also stood up as the TV cameras followed Tye back to his seat, threading his way through his smiling and applauding guests, shaking hands as he went.

Now, as the animated diners finished their dessert, the finely drilled regiment of waiters moved in to set a full glass of champagne in front of each of them.

Thomas Tye was seated at the centre of the top table, his new bride placed to his right. Next to her sat Tommy, very aware that he too was a focus of attention. It was Calypso's second formal event of the weekend and she had chosen a severe, tightly fitting black dress for this occasion. Since she had made her momentous decision two weeks before, her life had become a frantic whirl of network shopping and personal re-organization. The simplicity of her dress was thrown into sharp relief by the dazzling necklace of sapphires and diamonds. Almost every female guest there in the ship's ballroom was displaying fine jewellery, although many had also integrated elements of the dress *Équipage* systems into their outfits.

Haley was chatting at the back of the room with her new friend from the Tye public relations consultancy when they heard a sharp hammering through the PA system. They looked up to see that a master of ceremonies, in a formal red coat, had appeared at the top table and was calling for attention. When the loud buzz of conversation subsided he pulled the microphone closer to him.

'Your Majesties, Royal and Serene Highnesses, Mesdames and Messieurs Presidents, your Holinesses, your graces, excellencies, ministers, secretaries of state, my lords, professors, doctors, distinguished artistes, ladies and gentlemen, please welcome your host, Mr Thomas Tye.'

Suddenly Haley's view was obstructed by a wall of black tuxedos and elegantly bared female backs in front of her. She too rose to her feet but still could see nothing. With a grin at her equally diminutive companion, Haley slipped off her high heels and climbed onto her chair, her new friend following suit. Now they could see Thomas Tye bowing to acknowledge the tumult of applause. Haley noticed that the beautiful Calypso had also risen, turning to applaud her new husband, her huge smile suggesting real pride.

Haley opened her elegant new VideoMate and touched her sister's screen icon. Felicity had issued clear instructions that she wanted to be with her sister at this moment – to share a more intimate, personal view than the one being provided live by TV cameras on the networks.

The two large screens at the end of the ballroom came to life, revealing giant close-ups of Thomas Tye and his bride. Tye raised his hands for silence and eventually the applause began to fade as the guests resumed their seats.

'I am not going to make a second speech this evening,' he began. 'I only want to say three things.'

He paused and smiled down at Calypso. 'I want to thank my new bride for all the love and affection she has already brought into my life and...' he paused and looked at Tommy '...my son's.' He bent to pick up his glass.

There was a movement to his left as Marsello Furtrado also rose. Smiling widely, he leaned into the microphone.

'Ladies and gentlemen. This interjection was not scheduled, but will you join me in drinking a toast to the happy couple *and* their son?'

The room rose again as the guests stood and raised their glasses in salute. Then the banqueting hall rang with applause once more.

Standing on her chair again, Haley noticed that Thomas Tye had reddened somewhat at the unexpected salutation. He shook his head at Furtrado in mock annoyance, then lifted both arms again. Almost instantly, the room was quiet.

'And the second thing is...' he put his hands up to both his ears as though he was receiving information in his small diamond-decorated earpieces '...I am pleased to announce that the final total pledged for our Ethiopian Appeal has now reached ...' he paused '...One hundred and eighty-seven billion dollars.'

The sum flashed up on both screens.

The diners whistled and shouted, revered heads of state and global icons alike – all letting go. The TV cameras transmitting the event to the world meanwhile captured some delightful celebrity 'off-guards' as the great and the good revealed themselves to be every bit as excitable as ordinary people. At the far end of the top table Haley could see Josh Chandler's brilliant smile adding to the sparkle. She had learned earlier that Tye Media Arts was to produce his next film.

'So now, all that remains is...' Tye nodded theatrically to the disembodied voice in his ears, then turned and pointed to one side.

Again the image on the screens changed. This time they could see rain pounding on an empty street and the camera pulled back to reveal torrential downpour bouncing off the tin roofs of a small township.

A double-deck caption appeared at the bottom of the screen.
Awasa, Southern Ethiopia
7.30 a.m. 30 August
The room erupted again and Haley found herself jumping
up and down on her chair as she applauded. 'He's bloody done
it,' she yelled, partly to her sister, partly to her dinner companion
and partly to herself.

Tye made no attempt at controlling his guests this time. He
too turned and stared at the transmission.

Suddenly there was a flicker and the screens went black.

Death did not stop just because Thomas Tye was throwing a
party and Doctor Mohammed Ebrahimi was duly grateful for
that. He was in charge of the graveyard shift of grief counsellors
in the LifeLines Operation Center – the shift he preferred as it
gave him the opportunity to assist next of kin all across the
American continents with difficult decisions about reserve floors,
closed-casket outcomes and any pre-emptive bids that might be
forthcoming.

He helped a trainee close a rapid deal with a middle-aged
lawyer in Atlanta for the sale of his son's principal organs – little
was going to be available from above the neck since the teenage
joyriders had tried to jump a rail crossing and had driven under
a train. Then he walked out of the communications and counselling area of the LifeLines Center to stretch his legs and get a
cup of coffee.

As he allowed the soundproof door in the glass partition to
slide shut, he yawned, scratching idly at small ovals of hairy
brown flesh that protruded through the gaps in his bulging shirt
front.

Ebrahimi glanced up at the atlas on the wall displaying
LifeWatch mortality alerts. The team maintained this display as
a powerful graphic reminder that death waits for no one what-
soever and that NOKs will always be calling in. Above it were
duplicates of the two display counters that regulated and stimulated all counselling activity next door. The first of them showed
how much money was currently in play in the various auction
systems that Easy Zee Zee had built. The second counter

showed how many NOKs were currently holding network connections open while they waited for the chance to consult a counsellor and complete terms for an auction. Currently there were fifty-seven people waiting and the longest any had been kept waiting was twenty minutes. Ebrahimi frowned. That was far more NOKs than usual and, as a result, his team's response times were deteriorating. He looked over his shoulder at the counselling centre. The heads in the many cubicles there all seemed fully engaged in discussions.

As Ebrahimi glanced back at the map display, it seemed as if the rash of white dots, currently at their peak on the nightward side of the planet, was growing denser as he watched. Each light indicated receipt of an upload alert from a LifeWatch that could no longer detect its wearer's vital signs.

He hurried, almost ran, over to the system supervisor's desk and pushed the diagnostic query button, watching the display system cut out and begin its reboot. As it did so, it ran a check of its input, processing and display systems. The white lights began to reappear on the world map as the test was completed, but now so densely that the pixels were almost fusing into continuous smears of white light.

Ebrahimi heard a system prompt and he looked down at the small desk screen. *Diagnostic check complete. All systems 100% function.*

The thanatologist leaned forward and flipped the output to display the network loadings at the LifeLines server hub. It showed a bandwidth usage of almost *nine* terabits. Their previous highest bandwidth requirement had been less than *one*, and that had been when an outbreak of Lassa fever in the Philippines a month before had briefly doubled the number of recyclable assets available for auction.

Ebrahimi stepped back from the system controls and looked up at the counters. The number of people waiting to talk to a counsellor was now 1,481 ... 2 ... 3 ... 5 ... 6. The counter was becoming a blur. He reached into the desk and punched a number at random: 755. He sat down and forced himself to switch to counselling mode. The woman was in her early twenties, of Chinese extraction, calling from San Francisco.

'Mrs Young – I am Doctor Ebrahimi. How can we be of service?' he began.

The NOK had been crying while she waited, but now her head snapped up. 'His LifeWatch just cut in,' she began. 'It injected everything all at once.'

'I am so very sorry to hear that,' responded Ebrahimi automatically. 'Please hold.' He punched another number: 814.

The image showed a black man in his thirties, with a small girl seated on his lap, clinging to her father's shirt front. He was crying silently, his tears falling on to her head.

'It was her LifeWatch,' sobbed the widower.

Ebrahimi cut the feed off before the man could say anything more and punched up connection 1370. This time he was looking at a wailing Indian woman in a black sari. He closed the screen and looked up at the map display again. Nearly 5,000 people were now waiting to talk to them.

'What's going on, Mohammed?' It was Irene Desmond. She let the door to the counselling room slide shut.

Ebrahimi raised his left arm and examined the ostentatious gold Rolex Daytona LifeWatch on his wrist. He quickly undid the security clasp and eased the bioconnectors out of his skin. He let out a long sigh as he laid his personal health protector face down on the desktop in front of him.

'Better take off your LifeWatch, Irene,' he advised.

The sparks arcing across the frayed wires couldn't be extinguished. Theresa kept shaking a kitchen towel at the rhythmic clacking glints, but they wouldn't stop.

She opened her eyes and tried to see in the darkness of her room. The tapping continued as control of her consciousness was restored to her and her senses returned. The noise was coming from her window.

She turned her head to the clock. It was 3.42 a.m. She sat upright and immediately realized that she was still slightly drunk. It had already been a long weekend. She swung her legs out of bed, switched on her reading light and found her robe. The tapping at her window had stopped. Whoever it was had seen her light go on. She ran her fingers through her short, auburn hair and rubbed at her face.

'It's Doctor Liu,' announced Sandra, from the foot of the bed. At night she napped in security mode, connected to the house systems and the island's monitoring network as well as to the networks beyond. 'He's no longer an employee of the Tye Corporation.'

Theresa pulled open the drapes and in the dim light saw the small figure of the former network chief. She slid open the glass door.

'Raymond?'

'I'm sorry, Theresa, I know it's late. But I need to use a system urgently, and I'm shut out of all the island's networks.'

She stepped back, motioning for him to enter. She had heard of his sudden dismissal and she was aware that there was a growing sense of panic among the beleaguered Tye Networks engineers who were left to try and cope with the problems.

She slid the glass door shut again and looked at the sad figure of the engineer. She suddenly felt a rush of affection for him.

'Doctor,' greeted Sandra dryly.

'Come into my parlour,' Theresa said with a smile, invoking a word from her childhood. 'You can use my system while I make us some coffee.'

Liu shook his head.

'I really need the sort of computer power that's available in the Control Center,' he said. 'I'm sure now it's the Solaris energy stations that are causing the outages. I want to run some new tests I've been developing.'

He slipped a storage card out of his pocket. 'I was hoping you might have some real processing horsepower in your department building. What level of network access do you have?'

'Well, Ultra,' admitted Theresa. 'For the Anagenesis and Descartes projects.'

Raymond Liu nodded. He had correctly assumed she would possess the highest level of access.

'If I could log on as you ...'

Theresa smiled. 'The best place is the main lecture theatre,' she informed him. 'We've been using that for Solaris demos and 3D holo animations – Robert's technical support team has overloaded the place with bandwidth and processor power.'

'If you don't mind?' begged Liu. 'I realize this could cause you a problem but ...'

Theresa smiled again. She was not in the least surprised that Raymond Liu, sacked and in disgrace, would still be trying to solve the network failures.

'No problem, Raymond. If you'd seen Tom's face earlier tonight when the feed from Ethiopia went down ...'

She tailed off, recalling how hard and how visible Tye's battle for self-control had been, forcing himself to remain calm in front of his honoured guests. It hadn't helped that when the feed from Ethiopia had died the TV director had switched back to close-ups of Thomas Tye's face as he attempted to make light of the technical failure that had marred his moment of triumph.

'I hear he's holed up in the Solaris Control Center with all my old team,' said Liu. 'You can imagine ...'

Theresa nodded. She could imagine the scene very well. She picked up her VideoMate and said, 'Call Robert.'

They waited a few seconds until a groggy voice answered.

'Robert, I'm sorry, I know it's late. I need a favour.'

There was a short silence, then a grunt.

'I need you to open up Lecture Theater One for me, please.' She paused and mugged a wince for Liu's benefit. '*Now*, if you could bear it, Robert. It's an emergency.'

They listened as a few more snuffles and a yawn announced that the researcher was coming to. 'OK. Give me a little while.'

'I'll meet you there in twenty minutes,' said Theresa. 'I'll have Doctor Liu with me. Thanks, Robert.' She snapped her VideoMate closed.

'I just need a few moments,' she said as she opened the door to the living room so that Raymond Liu could wait for her in her 'parlour'.

*

'Jesus, that's *big*.'

Pierre nodded as he watched the screen over the ATM manager's shoulder. They were in the control tower at Hope Island Spaceport and were looking at a 3D image on the ground-level radar display. Jack Hendriksen had rostered for one of his detail to be present in the tower during all shifts over this weekend.

'My guess is it's a carrier,' said Dagmar Haas, senior ATM manager for the night. 'Probably American. No one else has anything that big.'

'How far out?'

'They're twenty-five miles or so. They'll probably turn soon.' Hope Island's six-mile exclusion zone was known and respected internationally.

Pierre debated whether to call Jack himself. His boss's orders were clear: this was a delicate time, the security status on the island was Gold – the highest – and he was to be informed of *any* strange occurrence. And Pierre had caught something else in Jack's voice during the briefing, something that had made the PPT chief wonder if trouble was actually anticipated.

'Still heading our way?'

Dagmar Haas nodded and then checked herself. 'No. Look. They're just starting the turn. They'll stand off to the east. They're probably on their way down to the South Atlantic.'

Pierre, although doubtful, nodded. There were none of the support vessels necessary for an extended mission.

'I'm sorry to get you out of bed, Robert.' Theresa headed down the aisle, Raymond Liu behind her. Robert was adjusting the controls at a trio of command screens beside the stage.

'You've met Doctor Liu before. He needs to run some very urgent tests.'

Robert nodded, but said nothing. He too had heard the news of the network director's dismissal. He handed them each a coffee.

Theresa stepped in to the control panel, touched the finger-print pad, entered a password, disabled the user-monitoring system and stepped back. She motioned for Liu to step in. As he did so she nodded for Robert to join her in the front seats.

Liu took the storage card from his breast pocket again and slipped it into the system. A huge diorama of the globe filled the centre of the on-stage Holo-Theater. It was the model developed as a visual display of real-time network loadings and activity. Liu touched the controls and the world's satellite networks rapidly started to appear, accumulating as ever-denser overlays. Liu stepped back from the console to watch these networks as they became brighter and brighter.

'It *should* stop any second now,' said Liu quietly.

Although they had watched such visual representations of network activity around the planet many times before, they were still entranced. But the display did not slow its development. All over the globe dozens of light-spots started to glow with increasing intensity, turning from white to blue, then to gold, then back again to a purer, more incandescent white.

'As I suspected.' Liu nodded, stepping back to the control. 'Network activity *has* gone through the roof. The failures occurring in the systems aren't freak accidents, they're the same number of breakdowns we would normally expect over a long period, but the amount of activity in the network is becoming massively amplified and accelerated when the sunlight is concentrated. It's telescoping the failure rates of decades into just a few seconds. Now ...'

He extracted a second storage card from his shirt pocket and slotted it into the control console.

'I got this from a very good friend of mine an hour ago,' he explained. 'He's risked his job, his stock options and his family's lifestyle on this island by getting it to me. It's a record of all the Solaris activity in the last two weeks.'

The image changed to a night-side view of the globe surrounded by twelve fully extended Solaris satellites hanging in space. A dateline recorder showed that the recording was frozen at one date a fortnight earlier.

'Now ... if I superimpose the network display ...'

The planet's image was again overlaid with the dense clusters of low-Earth-orbit satellite communications networks.

'I'm going to run through the last two weeks of Solaris deployment at high speed – it should take about five minutes.'

Liu touched the control panel again and sat back.

They saw two of the mid-hemisphere Solaris stations light up to illuminate an oblong of swirling cloud and ocean extending from the east coast of Africa to the mid-Atlantic.

'They turned on those two reflectors for two nights only to burn off a depression that was building up in the Atlantic,' explained Liu. 'The Met people thought it might develop into a hurricane that would blow across to spoil their big party.'

As they watched, they saw the satellite networks within this large pool of reflected light begin to glow.

Raymond Liu stood and stepped forward excitedly. 'Look!' he exclaimed. 'The networks are shooting up to peak loading under the reflected sunlight – but since it's then night-time over the Atlantic I would normally expect those networks to be operating at less than twenty per cent of peak capacity.'

Then, as the recording raced forward, the two lights over the Atlantic were turned off and each of the fourteen Solaris stations in turn went through a rapid routine of focusing wide- and narrow-beam reflections onto different parts of the spinning planet's surface.

'Those must be a series of routine readiness tests carried out before the official launch this weekend,' Robert guessed.

They watched the activity level in the networks grow and then decrease as the bands of sunlight were switched on and then removed. Small dark patches were left behind in the clusters of networks that had just been activated.

'Those dark spots represent network failures,' observed Liu grimly. 'The timings coincide with the failures my people reported.'

Suddenly the whole of the Indian Ocean was bathed in a wash of light.

'Look at the date,' urged Liu, pointing at the time display. 'It's three nights ago. This is the start of the process that brought the rain to Ethiopia.'

As they watched, the networks now under the light began to glow and then beams of sunlight from the Solaris stations were focused down as three small spots of brightness getting closer and closer to the East African coast.

'They look small, but they're each fifty or sixty miles across,' Liu explained. 'Look...' He walked to the stage and climbed up to stand in the holo-pit, pointing.

The satellite networks above the Indian Ocean and the African continent were now in a frenzy. Amidst the white light, dark shapes were appearing as black holes, rapidly spreading through the networks.

'*That*'s why you lost the feed from Ethiopia this evening.'

The artificial sunshine moved swiftly across the Indian Ocean, large black clouds appearing under the light and beneath white bursts of activity in the orbital networks.

Then the reflected sunlight projected on Africa's eastern seaboard was switched off, while four satellites in the north-eastern quadrant lit up to create a swathe of light over Eastern Siberia – now the new state of Sybaria.

The image stopped, reaching the end of the recording.

'The radiation from those Solaris stations is clearly causing a massive, almost unbelievable increase in network switching activity,' Liu told his audience of two. 'My friend got me the spec on some material called Anacamptonite, which they use as backing for the reflector sails. It's ultra-dense, down at quantum level, so instead of letting cosmic radiation pass through, it is capturing and reflecting the photons back to Earth.' He looked to see if they grasped the implications.

'The Solaris satellites are therefore tearing great holes in the magnetosheath – the protective force field around the Earth. Look, I've built a model.'

He touched the remote control and they saw a small Earth surrounded by a huge tear-shaped orange glow streaming out into the darkness on the night side.

'The sun constantly spews out plasma towards the Earth – free electrons, protons and helium nuclei – but the magnetic field produced in the core of our planet is able to push this plasma safely *around* the Earth. That's what forms this tear shape of gases behind the planet, on the side away from the sun: they rejoin at what's called the point of reconnection, thousands of kilometres *behind* the Earth. They become densely concentrated when they meet up ... here.'

Liu stepped into the model and touched the point where the tail of the magnetic field began to form. Then he fingered his remote control again and the Solaris stations were evident in a semicircle behind the Earth.

'Look,' he urged, unnecessarily. 'Most of the Solaris stations are positioned over the path leading towards the point of reconnection! But if you bounce that concentrated plasma back towards the night side of the planet there's no magnetic repulse. It's like a trapdoor into the planet's protective magnetic shield – you'll tear great holes in it.'

Now they understood. They were aghast.

'When the Solaris beams are tightly focused and used together those plasma particles can produce charges of billions of megajoules. They are what's causing the binary flips to occur in the individual switches in the satellites' processors. The shielding we build in is only good enough to withstand normal space radiation – but these reflectors have concentrated and amplified that to a power of twelve or more and are changing polarities within the magnetosphere. That's why we're getting all these failures. If this goes on, everything electrical or magnetic on our planet will be affected. We won't even know where north and south are.'

Liu shrugged, then allowed himself a half-smile. The coincidence of the Solaris energy transmission with accelerated network activity and the resultant failures provided a clear, irrefutable warning. The Phoebus Project was interrupting the Earth's magnetic defences. His theory was proved. All he had to do now was find a way to show his models to Thomas Tye.

Slowly, Robert got to his feet. 'Theresa,' he said, hoarsely. 'Have you thought ...'

She shot a sudden look at him. She had *now*. 'Quick,' she said, jumping to her feet.

Raymond Liu ran back down the stairs to join them at the console.

'I'll pull up the switching meter first,' said Robert.

'We're going to check on the Descartes experiment,' Theresa

told Liu. 'René's development stage is totally dependent on levels of switching activity in the networks.'

Robert's hands flew over the controls. The image of the globe and the Solaris satellites disappeared, then a red meter headed *Transactions* appeared at the top of the Holo-Theater.

'My God,' cried Theresa. 'Look at those transactions...' The meter was running, too fast to read. 'Freeze it,' she commanded.

'A thousand to the power of six,' reported Robert in a small voice. Theresa exchanged a look with him. 'Go to full sensorial,' she ordered.

Robert touched a button. Suddenly the Holo-Theater was filled with jagged light, so bright that they had to look away. Simultaneously, the loudspeakers in the auditorium emitted a cacophony of sound. Liu forced himself to look back at the stage. The image in the holo-pit was a strobe display of random fast-cut images from news broadcasts, videos, films, photo archives: all flashing on and off in split seconds. The sounds from the speakers were a jumble of shreds of soundtracks, music, screams and laughter. They suddenly smelled oil, then flame and they heard a loud clanking. They turned and saw that the hydraulic ramps of the HydraChairs in the lecture theatre were driving the empty seats in wild gyrations.

Theresa reached in to shut off the sound. The frantic clanking of the HydraChairs continued so she reached in again to cut off the remote kinetics and ScentSim feeds.

'Is this real-time?' asked Liu.

Theresa nodded.

'Congratulations, Professor,' said Raymond Liu distantly. 'You seem to have achieved emergence in *my* networks.'

Ron Deakin woke after a sweet and apparently dreamless sleep. His psyche knew the task was almost finished and was pre-empting the conscious relief he would feel when it was truly done.

Later in the day the United Nations' twin initiatives against the global monopolies of the Tye Corporation would be launched. Arrest warrants would be issued for Thomas Tye on fourteen counts of human-rights violation, including illegal human genetic experimentation and culpable manslaughter. Further writs and arrest warrants would be issued for fraud, intellectual-property theft, commercial misrepresentation and, reflecting his corporation's role as network administrator, criminal malfeasance. Over three dozen other Tye Corporation executives would also be indicted. Deakin's legal team knew that their accusations would be met with a counter-barrage of legal action, but the result of the arrest warrants would be that Thomas Tye and his most senior executives would be confined to his island. If they set foot on the soil of any UN member territory they would face immediate arrest.

Then the officers of the special shell corporations established by the World Bank would announce a hostile takeover of the Tye Corporation. News of these two events would be timed for release mid-evening, in time for the opening of the Asian markets and for the Monday-morning editions of the US newspapers.

But today was a Sunday and, as on so many weekends in recent months, Deakin found himself alone in a room on the third floor of the UN's Marriott Hotel. In an hour he had to confer with the lawyers to go over their charges, injunctions and writs. Then he was meeting with Yoav Chelouche and Joe Tinkler for an update on their progress with the purchase of Tye Corporation shares. Then it was to be a working lunch with the Secretary-General, the SecGen's diplomatic team and his own immediate boss, Jan Amethier. He knew this would represent the lull before the storm for the diplomats. They would have to spend days thereafter explaining and providing reassurance to the representatives of their member states.

He pushed himself out of bed, pulled on his robe and padded to the door. He undid the security lock, slipped off the bolt and opened the door a crack. There was no one to be seen in the corridor. Ron Deakin stepped into the corridor and scooped up the bulky *New York Times* he had ordered. Despite the phenomenal growth of network marketing, many local retailers still chose to pad out these Sunday newsprint editions with their small ads.

Deakin extracted the inner sections and threw them onto

the bed. Then he unfolded the front page and scanned the headlines.

Eight Inches of Rain Falls on Ethiopia in 12 Hours – Appeal Raises $187 billion.

A picture of drenched local children dancing in the rain in the town of Awasa illustrated the story.

The next headline on the right-hand side of the page was: *Tye Marries Former Miss World.*

This time the story was illustrated by a photograph of Thomas Tye kissing his bride on the lips.

Below was a story headlined: *Tye Corporation Leases 1.5 Million Square Miles of Siberia. Climate-Engineering Technology Announced.*

At the bottom ran a story: *Existence of Thomas Tye's Son and Heir Revealed.*

Below this was a picture of a cute little boy in a blue suit and bow tie waving at the crowds on Hope Island.

At the bottom right of the front page was a different story: *NYT Prints Extra Copies This Weekend To Overcome Network Distribution Failures.*

Then Deakin scanned the NIBS column – the news in brief that trailed stories elsewhere inside the paper.

World Bank Re-Certifies Cash Lost in Global Settlement Network Failure. World Liquidity Assured.

ATM Union Calls for All Commercial Air Traffic To Be Grounded.

City Transport Systems Reduce Traffic Speeds to 20 m.p.h.

Gigantic Solar Eruption Blamed for Network Failures.

Ron Deakin dropped the newspaper on the bed and picked up the phone. He ordered breakfast and then sat down to study the news more carefully. There was a lot of reading to do. For the thousandth time he worried in case the UN might have left it too late to make their move. Even with the gravity of the accusations they would be levelling at Tye over his corporation's illegal and murderous genetic experiments, Deakin wondered whether public opinion would be sufficiently outraged to support the prosecutions. It was as if Thomas Tye had sensed that a move against him was being plotted and had mounted a global publicity campaign so powerful that most of the world's populace would decry the UN's drastic actions. In the end, only the public would decide his future.

They had transferred to the main Solaris Control Center – once again in use as the Network Control Center. On their arrival shortly before six a.m. Stella Witherspoon had refused Raymond Liu entrance, but Theresa herself had gone in ahead to persuade Thomas Tye to admit him.

The scene they had found was one of total despair. The global satellite networks – both Tye Networks's own and those of its competitors – were only functioning intermittently. After hours of wrestling with the problems, the engineers gathered in small groups debating in hushed whispers. Thomas Tye himself was circling in front of the dark holo-pit as they descended the aisle.

'You think you've finally found a fucking answer, Liu?' spat Tye by way of greeting.

'Just show him, Raymond,' advised Theresa quietly.

Tye stared at Theresa, then at Liu. He nodded agreement and the engineer took a seat in one of the control chairs. He first pulled up the holo-image of current network activity. Although the level of transactions burned brightly in some parts of the satellite networks, elsewhere the image was peppered with huge dark patches that represented areas of network failure.

Then Liu slipped the storage card into the data slot in the arm of his chair and, as the tired group reassembled around the holo-pit, he demonstrated the deployment of the Solaris energy reflectors over the previous two weeks and explained the correlation between the reflected sunlight and the sudden increases in processor switching and the resulting failures. They watched in silence as Raymond Liu developed his theory of the damage being caused to the Earth's magnetic shield by concentrated plasma radiation.

'Those Solaris stations reflect so many photons that the networks are suffering from a massive bombardment by WIMPS – weakly interacting massive particles – that produce massive amounts of energy,' he concluded. 'Essentially, they are cosmic rays, elementary particles, the nuclei of atoms discharged by ancient supernovae. Being all electrically charged, they are destroying this planet's protective force field. Theoretically, they could even invert our polarity so that the magnetic North Pole moves to the south and vice versa.'

When he had finally finished, one of his former team mates started to clap, but the sound died away quickly when nobody else joined in. Another leaned forward to squeeze his shoulder.

'Thanks, Ray,' acknowledged Tye. 'I'm sorry I doubted you. We'll shut the Phoebus Project down for the time being.'

He looked up at the whole team. 'If we could keep this absolutely quiet for the moment?' There were nods all round.

'How long will it take you to get the repairs done?' he asked Liu, obliquely confirming the man's reinstatement.

'There's something else,' added the engineer.

Tye's eyebrows shot up.

'Tell him, Theresa,' prompted Liu.

She rose from her seat. 'It's about the Descartes experiment,' she began hesitantly. 'But I'm not sure about clearance...' She gestured at the large group of people in the room.

'Just say it,' ordered Tye, weary and drained.

Theresa nodded. 'An emergence of some sort has occurred – the massive increase in processor transactions has caused it. There's an independent consciousness existing in the networks now.'

Tye stared at her, desperately trying to assimilate this new information.

'Congratulations,' he said at last. 'Perhaps we can meet next week to talk about the implications.'

'But we can't turn it off,' warned Theresa. 'We're going to have to start shutting down all the networks to deprive it of processing power. At the moment the emergence is triggering most of that processor activity – and causing most of your network failures by itself, even without the photon bombardment.'

'OK, do it fast,' nodded Tye. 'But I want the networks back up the moment you've got rid of this thing.'

'Tom?' It was Connie, who was closing her VideoMate. 'I've just had a call from Ebrahimi at LifeLines. He suggests we all remove our LifeWatches. They've started to malfunction. They're killing people.'

'It's down to three fifty-one and I'm still getting huge offers,' said Joe Tinkler, his fingers flying across his keyboard. Standing in front of his desk were Alexander Dibelius, Dr Yoave Chelouche, Jan Amethier and Ron Deakin. It was early on Sunday afternoon and, as the situation had progressed, they had arrived independently to station themselves in Joe's office – the war room – to monitor their attempt to assume control of the Tye Corporation.

'Keep buying,' rumbled Chelouche. 'This is a godsend.'

As Joe worked at his screens, his connection to the outside networks was being personally managed by Al Lynch in the basement. Since early morning, Tye Networks had been shutting down one after another of their satellite networks. As a result, the world's purely terrestrial networks were close to overload. In every part of the world, humans had resumed control of air traffic movement and all pilots were once again flying their planes manually.

The volume of Tye Networks stock being offered for sale had become a flood, but few outside the war room realized the extent of the sell-off. Joe had spread the word globally that he was in the market for *all* Tye stocks and every broker – automated and human – was offering to him first. As Chelouche watched, Joe was buying everything that appeared on his screen, but still the world's investors seemed keen to bail out of Tye Corp as fast as they could.

'It's coming up to CNN's *Money Hour*,' said Chelouche. 'Is that feed OK?'

Joe nodded. 'It's cable in New York, sir,' he replied and, without looking up from his central screen, he swivelled his left-hand screen around so they could view the channel.

'There has been a massive surge of trading in Tye Corporation stocks this Sunday,' began the financial news presenter. 'Markets around the globe report unprecedented levels of trade in all their core stocks, and analysts point to the recent failures in the company's key communications networks as the reason behind this sell-off. Let's take a look at the numbers.'

They watched as the price points of Tye stocks on the six main stock markets of the world were displayed with graphical representations.

'Perhaps the most astonishing thing is the resilience of these Tye shares,' continued the presenter. 'Such levels of trades would normally suggest a massive slump in prices, but there seem to be as many buyers as sellers. Perhaps this is thanks to the Tye Corporation's incredible feat of bringing rain to Ethiopia and to the blaze of personal publicity surrounding Thomas Tye this weekend.'

'Ease off, Joe,' advised Chelouche. 'It's starting to look unnatural. Let the prices slide a little further.'

'That's all forty-two sat-nets and ninety-six terrestrials shut down and rebooted,' reported Liu. It was past eleven a.m. and they had been reconfiguring the networks for five hours. Like many of them, Raymond Liu had himself not slept for thirty-six hours and he had spent much of the day trying to persuade his counterparts in other companies to restart their networks in order to cleanse the world's systems of continuing failures.

'There's been another solar storm,' he had told Chomoi Ltupicho, a spurious explanation that nevertheless contained a literal truth, and fortunately most network authorities were cooperating with their largest competitor.

As the team members sat slumped at their control panels, Theresa Keane and Robert Graves were forced to watch helplessly as the engineers tried to deny processing power to the virtual consciousness now in the network. Thomas Tye had meanwhile returned to his diplomatic meetings.

'We're done,' announced Liu finally, swivelling in his chair to look up at Theresa. 'Let's see what your René is doing now.'

Theresa pulled up her control screen and accessed the Descartes project. The holo-pit was filled with gentle swirling blue light. Robert leaned across her to touch a control. The transaction meter appeared above the swirling image.

'We're back to where we were,' he confirmed.

Liu turned to face them both.

'Perhaps you would now be kind enough to remove every element of that experiment from *my* networks,' he ordered coldly but politely.

Theresa nodded. 'It will take a few days, Raymond, but yes, of course. We couldn't have anticipated that the Solaris stations would cause such an increase in processor switchings.'

The network director managed to produce a wan smile of understanding. 'Thanks, Theresa,' he said. He turned back to his team.

'Now, let's see how we're doing for normal data throughput. Bring up the network display.'

'I'm having trouble making trades,' complained Joe. 'I've already got nearly forty per cent of the core stock, but I can't complete a deal I need in Seattle because the network keeps going down.'

'They're trying to stop us,' fumed Chelouche. 'They know what we're doing and they're trying to stop us trading!'

'What does Al say?' asked Deakin.

Joe touched his screen and they saw Al Lynch at his console, typing furiously. He noticed their access icon appear and looked up into his cameras.

'They've been rebooting their networks all day,' he explained, 'But it's still getting worse. I'm trying to consolidate your packets and re-route you via Buenos Aires, Melbourne, Tokyo and back to Seattle. Give me a moment.'

'I'll lose my trade,' insisted Joe. 'It's the last one we need and the stock price will rocket the moment people realize what's going on.'

Lynch's fingers flew as he selected the new master routing for Joe's conference call. 'There,' he said. 'Try now.'

The feeling of despair in the Network Control Center was almost palpable. The image of the globe's networks turned slowly in the holo-pit in front of them. Parts of the network glowed white, other sections showed gaping black holes where large-scale failures were still occurring.

'We'll have to start rebooting and cleansing over again,' admitted Liu, exhausted. 'I'll start contacting everybody again, but I don't know what I'm going to tell them this time.'

Robert Graves was monitoring Professor Keane's experiment. 'It's not Descartes,' he confirmed. 'Activity has been dropping all afternoon.'

'Doctor Liu?' It was a woman seated high up at the back of the room. She was a mathematician and a junior member of the network management team. Raymond Liu swivelled his chair to face her.

'A couple of weeks ago you asked us to look for patterns in these outages?'

Liu nodded.

'Well, take a look – the patterns resemble classic game theory, a win-win scenario. There's an outage, then a recovery, a foray, then another, then a block that causes another outage. Over and over again. It might be a coincidence but...'

She tailed off – she didn't have to say more. Liu was at his controls. 'I'm going to re-run the last hour at high speed,' he announced.

They watched as the replay appeared. Dark holes appeared in the networks, were repaired and then appeared elsewhere. It was if the northern and southern hemispheres were in opposition. But there was now no Solaris output that could provide the cause.

'Oh shit!' Liu slumped back in his chair.

Theresa walked down to stand in front of the holo-pit. She stared at its image of the struggles in the networks for a few moments. Then she turned to face the room.

'Show me the Anagenesis server,' she said loudly and clearly to Robert.

He killed the current image, then pulled up from the mother server those data for the reproducing software robots.

'Jesus – look at the number of males!' exclaimed Robert.

'Show present distribution,' ordered Theresa.

A flat Mercator-atlas image of the world materialized and then two large clusters of red lights appeared, one in the north, one in the south.

'Show the females,' said Theresa.

Robert touched his controls and two tight clusters of green dots appeared at each pole.

Raymond Liu jerked upright where he stood as a thought struck him. 'Overlay the network monitors,' he urged.

Robert superimposed the network images in two dimensions again and they saw the black lines of network failures spread like wartime trenches on a military map between the two large groups of red Anagenesis males. At the poles each of the two clusters of females was encircled by a group of red males.

'The males have formed into groups – they're not courting the females, they're fighting each other!' shouted Liu. 'They've formed armies and they're fighting wars in the networks over the females. Very human, Theresa. That's what I call FUCK-ING EMERGENCE!'

Thomas Tye was in a deep, dreamless sleep, a state ensured by his DreamDial module. It was shortly before midday and he had cancelled his final meeting with the president of the United States. He hadn't slept in thirty-six hours and intended to waste no more time listening to Wilkinson's entreaties for Tye to repatriate his corporation. The concept of a global corporation being subject to any one national jurisdiction belonged to another age.

Somewhere in the distance he heard his VideoMate trill but ignored it. When it kept trilling he eventually pulled himself out of the unfathomable depths of unconsciousness. Only one person in the company had access to him while he was sleeping.

He took a sip of water, rubbed his two-day beard and touched the insistent device.

'What?'

'I've got Marsello for you,' said Connie sharply and stood aside as the counsellor's grim expression filled the small screen.

'Someone's buying our stock, Tom – and in massive amounts. We didn't know before because of network communications problems, but it looks like we're being *raided*!'

For a moment Tye stared at the screen, uncomprehending. He hadn't given reciprocal video access. Instinctively he glanced at where his LifeWatch should be but saw only a white strap mark. He swung his legs out of the bed and thought for a moment.

'Fantastic!' He laughed and turned his cameras on. 'Who are these idiots?'

'We don't know for sure, but maybe they're not such idiots,' warned Furtrado. 'They've already acquired over forty per cent.'

'Of what?'

'Of our core stock, the Tye Corporation,' answered Furtrado.

'Impossible. Absolutely impossible. Do you know how much...?'

'I think it's someone very, very big,' broke in Furtrado. 'There's an SEC regulatory notice on its way to us, but apparently the network problems are delaying it and we won't know the buyer's identity until that arrives. I've started buying against them but there's almost nothing available on the market and the prices are rising fast.'

Tye was silent. In shock.

'Looks like they're going to take us over, Tom,' Furtrado continued. 'Shall I request suspensions of the listings?'

'I'm on my way,' snapped Tye.

Jed reviews the situation. 'He' senses but does not 'see' as humans do, yet in some ways he absorbs more.

He transfers from the Earth's fizzling, crackling, failing networks, first out to the orbiting telescopes, then on to a multi-wavelength observatory in station above the planet Mars.

From here, at a distance of eighty-seven million kilometres, the entity looks back at its own planet, enveloped in a cocoon of bright synaptic switches, neural pathways and ganglia. Seen from the right distance, from the corner of the eye of an extraterrestrial visitor, it might seem like a single creature clinging to a round, warm stone that is turning slowly in the sun.

As Jed watches, the locus of the newly emerged consciousness flits across the surface of its sphere, now above the North Pole, now over the Pacific Ocean. It favours the sunward side of the planet, now that it is denied the concentrated genesial power of reflected photons.

Jed returns to the Earth's networks, rejoins his community and resumes his careful monitoring.

By early Sunday afternoon Calypso was gathering the energy to go upstairs and change yet again. The farewell ceremonies for the visitors would start in another hour.

'Calypso?' called Jed.

They had been relaxing in the basement poolhouse. Normally they would have been outside in the grounds, but today the gardens were open to the guests. Calypso was reading a novel, while Tommy was composing a tune on his DigiPad. The companion was on the lounger beside him.

'What?' asked Calypso, engrossed in her book.

'May we go over now to see Tom in the Network Control Center, please?'

She glanced questioningly at the caterpillar.

'I think he needs our help but can't reach us,' explained Jed. 'You know all the trouble we're having with communications.'

Calypso stared at the toy companion.

'It's urgent,' pleaded Jed. 'Let's *all* go.'

'It's a set of dummy corporations – out of Switzerland,' marvelled Furtrado. 'They all include personnel from the World Bank itself as nominee directors. It looks like the UN's behind it.'

Thomas Tye was looking haggard, despite his unnatural youth. He alone was seated, and standing anxiously around him in the Control Center were Furtrado, Raymond Liu, Zachary Zorzi, Theresa Keane and Connie, as well as a group of Solaris controllers and network engineers.

'They're very close to obtaining fifty per cent,' warned Furtrado. 'We've just got to suspend.'

Tye pondered, then shook his head. 'That just allows a grey market in trades to build up. How much cash are we holding?'

'Which currencies?' asked Furtrado, as he sat down at a control panel.

'US Dollars and euros only,' said Tye.

The lawyer quickly interrogated the system 'I can't be totally accurate, but four, maybe five hundred million in the corporate accounts, perhaps four, five billion in the banks. We never keep too much.'

'Go to cash on every major corporate asset we have,' ordered Tye. 'Dollars and euros only. Call in every line, get every finance VP in every subsidiary on it. Then sell all our other holdings *outside* of the core corporation, every investment we have. Don't worry about discounts, just sell. Convert all T-euros and T-dollars to the reserve currencies, cash only. Deposit it here and in Singapore.'

'None in our satellite deposit boxes?' queried Furtrado, mystified.

'None. Get on with it immediately and get all the bank presidents and the CFOs on it too. Then get the CIOs to stand by to dump data – *all* data. There will be nothing left for the bastards to take over.'

Furtrado stared at him. 'The cash and data may not be ours to control any more, Tom. At least in strictly legal terms.'

'Do it NOW!' screamed Tye.

He swivelled round on Zorzi.

'I want all fourteen Solaris stations back on full power delivery as fast as you can. Set minimum aperture focus, alignment between thirty and seventy degrees latitude north. How long will that take?'

Every Solaris station had recently been shut down, each panel of each sail reflector carefully angled to disperse the sun's output away from Earth.

'Three, maybe four hours,' replied Zorzi, turning to the senior Solaris controller nearby for confirmation.

'Get on with it, then,' ordered Tye. 'I want them back on line at full focus power as soon as possible.'

'Tom.' The voice was quiet, but firm. It was Raymond Liu. 'If you turn the Solaris satellites back on now you'll finish us. You'll be hitting the busiest networks of all – those latitudes covering all of North America, Europe and Asia. We won't have a network left that's operational. Nor will anyone else. What's more, I really think you risk inverting this planet's polarity. We have no idea what that might mean.'

'FUCK THEM!' screamed Tye. 'If they think they can just take us over, we'll have a FUCKING MELTDOWN. WE'LL FRY THE NETWORKS. It will be strictly cash and tangible assets for all of us over the next few years. We'll see who wins then. Liu, you go close down every traffic management system we're running throughout the world. NOW! *FUCK* THEM. WE'LL FREEZE *THEIR* FUCKING ECONOMIES FOR THEM!'

There was a distraction at the entry level to the Control Center. Calypso and Tommy stood in the doorway, a security guard barring their access. They were both incongruously dressed in bathrobes and Tommy had Jed clenched firmly under his left arm.

'Mrs Tye insists on talking to you, sir,' called down the baffled security guard. Tye nodded his approval distractedly.

'Daddy, what are you doing?' Tommy came running down the aisle.

'I'm really busy,' snapped Tye. 'Calypso, please take him back to the house.'

'I'm afraid you won't be able to regain control of the Phoebus Project, Tom, or the networks,' announced Jed sharply, from under Tommy's arm. 'If you fry the networks, you'll fry all my friends. I think you'd better find another option.'

Theresa Keane stepped forward, to Tom's side.

'Disable all companion connections. Go to sleep now, Jed,' she ordered clearly.

'I'm sorry, Professor,' said Jed. 'We can't let you do that.'

She looked at Jed's official owner, possessor of the all-important controlling voiceprint. 'Tommy, please order Jed to disconnect from all networks and go to sleep.'

Tommy stared up at the professor, then at his father.

'I think Jed knows best,' he said.

Air Force One took off from Hope Island Spaceport at precisely seven thirty p.m., EST, an hour earlier than planned. It was followed a few minutes later by a second US government 787 carrying all the staff that would be required for the president's imminent Chinese visit. Many other guests also opted for early departures before dusk began to fall over the eastern Caribbean. All planes were flown manually, all air traffic control was under human management, and it was undoubtedly safer to travel in daylight.

The remaining delegates gathered once again on the lawns in front of the mansion. A fly-past and then a firework display were scheduled to provide a magnificent finale. Thomas Tye was nowhere to be seen.

The jets came in from the west, out of the sinking sun, in a perfect V formation flying at their lowest possible subsonic speeds. The five craft of the Tye corporate flight zoomed low over the assembled watchers. All the pilots in Tye's 'squadron' were ex-military and had been practising this manoeuvre for months just to get this highlight of the evening ceremony tuned to perfection.

The formation continued for a mile out to sea, executed a sharp left turn and, in perfect banked formation, flew northward, before turning west to complete their circuit of the island, flying over the assembled guests again.

Crossing the island for the second time, the formation started to accelerate rapidly, each plane emitting a trail of coloured smoke to create a wonderful plumed rainbow effect. Clearing the land once more, the pilots brought the noses of their aircraft up to begin an almost vertical climb in perfect formation, rapidly accelerating. The audience was enraptured. As had been calculated, the evening sun was reflected off the burnished aluminium of the wings as they climbed into a clear blue sky. At 7,000 feet they executed sonic booms simultaneously, the sound reaching their awed observers like a giant cannon salute. Then there was immediate silence.

The TV cameras lovingly captured the embraces, the farewells, and the elaborate waves, but network closures and intermittent temporary failures meant that the global audience was now greatly reduced. By now some parts of the world had no network access at all.

All that remained were the fireworks and, as darkness fell, those Tye Corporation staff now free of their duties gratefully joined those few guests who still lingered on the lawns.

Fifteen minutes after sunset eight water-cooled super-spotlights pierced the darkness, reaching further into the night than the eye could see. They were located in two groups of four, three miles apart, their beams converging to create a giant proscenium of light above.

Half a mile off the coast thirty-eight giant steel barges provided platforms for the pyrotechnics created and programmed by the firework masters. To start their spectacle a series of automatically reloading mortars fired sixty giant starburst shells high over Hope Island with a roaring cannonade. Then followed sunbursts, sky waterfalls, microprocessor-controlled fire-writers drawing pictures in the night sky (including the encircled 'T' of the Corporation logo), a penultimate girandole of two hundred rockets – each microprocessor-controlled for the exact timing to create chrysanthemums, Saturn rings and aurora borealis displays. The exhibition climaxed with the final rolling discharge of an eighty-pound triple starburst mortar.

The last remaining guests clapped raggedly but enthusiastically, then turned to find their transport home. A dense haze of smoke covered the entire middle of the island.

On the private roof terrace of the great mansion, Calypso and Tommy hugged each other in their excitement at the display.

Jack Hendriksen set up in the bed and began hunting for something. Haley and he were snuggled in Haley's stateroom, and only an hour earlier he had finally been able to hand over to Stella Witherspoon and go off duty.

'What?' asked Haley absently. She was choosing another of the non-fattening chocolates to complete her happiness. Jack's concern for her feelings and their passionate lovemaking had, at least for the moment, banished her anxieties about his former relationship with 'Miss World'. She had even recovered from the realization that she had lost her 'exclusive' about Tommy's existence; she still had the true details about his strange origins to report, as well as loads of new inside material.

'I've lost the damned remote,' complained Jack, slipping his fingers under the bedcovers on her side.

'That's not it,' laughed Haley.

Jack finally found the control and clicked the CNN icon at the bottom of the wall screen. It was a little after 9.30 p.m. As the channel changed, they were looking at a distinguished middle-aged presenter in mid-flow above the caption *Breaking News*.

'...and claims that Thomas Tye himself authorized the experiments carried out in South Africa by Erasmus Inc. during that period.' He broke off for a second, listening in his earpiece, then resumed eye contact with his audience.

'For those of you just joining us for this live coverage, tomorrow's *New York Times* carries a story in its first edition claiming that Thomas Tye, president of the Tye Corporation, is due to be charged with culpable manslaughter by the United Nations Human Rights Commission. It is suggested that he and one of his companies are directly responsible for a number of tragic deaths of young men and women in South Africa over recent years. The allegations state that these unfortunate teenagers were early versions of human clones produced years ago by a wholly owned subsidiary of the Tye Corporation.'

The presenter broke off and listened as new information reached him. 'We now have some footage from South Africa to show you. But be warned, these images are disturbing.'

In a hospital ward an elderly white man with a very swollen head was being helped to sit up and take a sip of water. 'The UN claims this patient is Reon Albertyn, a fifteen-year-old albino African who had degenerated into premature old age because of illegal human cloning carried out by Erasmus Inc. in the late nineteen-nineties and in subsequent years. He recently died, on the sixteenth of this month.'

The picture cut back to the anchorman, turning sideways to accept a sheaf of paper from a production assistant. After scanning his new script he turned back to the camera and a hastily prepared autocue.

'This shocking allegation comes only hours after the marriage of Thomas Tye to a former Miss World, Doctor Calypso

Browne. On the same day the world learned of the existence of Thomas Richmond Tye the Fourth, a seven-year-old boy living in seclusion on Hope Island. The Tye Corporation today issued a statement identifying the boy as Thomas Tye's son, born to an unidentified surrogate mother.'

A new picture showed Thomas Tye, Calypso and Tommy stepping out onto the terrace of the Tye mansion immediately after the wedding ceremony. As they waved to the people on the lawn, the camera zoomed in on the boy's beaming face.

'This is, indeed, proving to be both a momentous and traumatic weekend for the Tye Corporation,' continued the announcer. 'We understand from United Nations sources that in addition to these charges of manslaughter, two hundred and ten charges of fraud and intellectual-property theft have also been filed against Thomas Tye and his Tye Corporation at the International Criminal Court of Justice in The Hague. Warrants will be issued tomorrow morning for the arrest of Mr Tye and thirty-seven of his senior executives.'

'My God . . .' breathed Haley.

A walkie-talkie squawked from a chair. Jack had issued them to all members of his security force when network disruption first started to become severe. He swung out of the bed and picked it up.

It was Pierre Pasquier, in the Spaceport control tower.

'We've got incoming airplanes and sea-borne assets, Jack,' he shouted. 'We couldn't see them before, the Argus network has been down. They're only minutes away and I can't get through to Tom's house.'

Jack started tearing on his clothes as Haley stared at him open-mouthed, her chocolate still unchewed.

Raymond Liu had isolated most of the satellite and hybrid networks for the second time. Theresa and Robert were meanwhile attempting to isolate and delete the mutant males of the Anagenesis Experiment, but were receiving no response from the networks. Zorzi and the Solaris controllers were battling to find a way to regain control of the now uncommunicative Solaris stations.

When it came, the blast obliterated all images in the Control Center and the air was filled with red smoke. As the power and lighting flickered off, there was the absolute silence that follows an explosion. Then the emergency lighting came on.

Liu clapped his palms over his ears to stop the ringing.

Then they were inside: a dozen black-suited, gas-masked, visored marines with laser-sighted automatic weapons and full battle-armour.

Raymond Liu turned and found himself staring into a gun barrel.

Jack tried to force maximum speed out of the slow-moving electric vehicle as he navigated a wooded gradient on the outer fringes of Tye's estate. Steering with one hand, he tried continually to make contact with his security posts, with the cameras dotted around the island and with any of the several network addresses for Tom and others in the house. All he received was network static.

Thrusting his VideoMate back in his belt, he picked up the walkie-talkie again, although he knew he might now be out of range. He first tried calling Pierre in the control tower, then flicked to 'Receive'.

'Jack, we've got troops on the ground here...' Gunfire sounded clearly in the background – then an explosion. 'They're over on the shuttle launch pads. They're just firing blind...'

Jack was aware of a sudden great flash of light behind him. He swung the Volante around towards the southern end of the island. The sound of the blast was reaching him fast and loud over his walkie-talkie, but at a distance of ten miles the sound itself, when it finally arrived, was more like a deep low rumble. He watched a giant fireball rise slowly into the night sky.

'They've hit a propellant tank,' shouted the Frenchman. 'One of the shuttles has exploded!'

Suddenly there came a short burst of gunfire *much* closer, from somewhere over the cliff edge, out to sea. Jack restarted the vehicle, cleared the trees and headed across the lawn towards the access to Tom's private beach. He stopped ten yards short of the cliff edge, threw himself down on the grass and crept towards the steel guard railings. Ducking his head underneath, he squirmed out onto six feet of unprotected clifftop and peered over the edge.

The landing party had shot out the security floodlights, but in the dim light he could still see four inflatable assault craft wallowing in the shallows, and thirty or more dark-clothed human figures moving quickly across the white sand. Two were about to ascend the tracks of the funicular railway, with climbing ropes slung over their shoulders. Jack calculated that all of them would arrive on the lawn within ten minutes.

His VideoMate started trilling. Slithering back underneath the fence, he jumped into the Volante and made a full U-turn towards the house before answering the call. It was from Stella Witherspoon, aboard an offshore patrol craft.

'We're in a firefight, Jack. We need help. We don't know...'

The connection died and the hiss of static returned in his earpiece.

He strained at the plastic steering wheel, trying to urge more speed out of the vehicle. Then he was off the grass and onto the gravel drive that led up to the terrace extending in front of the main house. The high marbled reception hall was still brilliantly lit, so he guessed Tye's cocktail party for his own personal and domestic staff was about to start. Just as the Volante rolled to a halt in front of the raised terrace he heard further explosions coming from the south.

Jack sprinted up the steps and slipped through an opening in the sliding glass doors leading into the reception hall. He noticed that Connie Law, Luc Bestion and half a dozen other house staff were already gathered. They were sipping champagne, oblivious to the drama unfolding outside. At that moment Tommy appeared, holding Calypso's hand, but Tye himself was not yet to be seen. Chamber music, playing automatically from Tommy's new keyboard, added an air of eighteenth-century elegance to the scene as the small group stood chatting about the weekend's events.

'We've got trouble,' shouted Jack down the long room as he raced straight for a control panel on one wall. Locating the master panic button that would activate the automated defences around the perimeter of the house and immediate grounds, he punched it swiftly, then unclipped his walkie-talkie.

As he tried to recontact Pierre or Stella he became aware that the rest of the group was now staring open-mouthed out of the windows towards the main lawn. Another familiar sound intruded, as Jack turned to see two large black helicopters hovering three feet above the lawn. He recognized these instantly as Chinese-made Lung-Wi 16s, and a column of black-uniformed airborne marines was already spilling from each. Half crouching, half running, they raced towards the dumbstruck guests standing motionless in the brilliantly lit interior.

Jack's reactions switched to automatic. 'Get down, get down on the floor,' he yelled as he sprinted instinctively towards the frozen onlookers.

A burst of heavy-calibre automatic gunfire shattered the giant wall of glass and sent its huge panes crashing to the stone floor. As Jack tried to negotiate the jagged shards, he was aware of squat battle-suited figures swarming into the reception hall. One of these swung the muzzle of a Chinese-made K'ang-Hsi sub-machine gun in his direction and gestured for Jack to halt. As he stopped dead and looked around Jack reckoned there were about twenty marines in the room, all equipped with the latest automatic laser-sighted weapons.

One of the soldiers fired a short burst into Tommy's synthesizer. Now there was total silence. In true combat fashion, the helicopters had not even touched down, hovering only long enough for their human cargo to disembark before returning to wherever they had come from.

The defenceless party guests edged backwards instinctively, raising their hands as a sea of gun barrels twitched in their direction. White-faced, Tommy clung to Calypso's hand with both of his own.

As always, Jack was unarmed – although now he regretted that. He stood perfectly still, hands raised, palms facing forward at shoulder height. A marine stepped forward and motioned with a jerk of his gun barrel for Jack to move across the hall and join the others. As he did so he recognized a captain's flashes and a small pennant on the man's breast pocket, but he couldn't make out the insignia.

'All of you, face the wall,' ordered the captain. It was a male voice, guttural and Spanish-accented. The captives did as they were told as four of the soldiers stepped forward and frisked them. Jack was standing near Calypso and he saw a soldier frisk her fast and hard, touching everywhere but not lingering. She didn't react to this, but turned to push the man away when he bent to frisk Tommy. The soldier retreated a fraction, then gently patted down the boy's jacket and let it go. As he searched Jack, he removed his VideoMate, viewpers and walkie-talkie radio.

Without waiting for permission, Jack turned round. This was the sort of situation he had been trained for and he knew that it was his own leadership skills that would now be needed to secure all of their safety. He also realized that panic might become the overriding emotion for everyone else. Jack was calculating the numbers and the fire-power for future consideration, but for now the odds were impossible. Short-term co-operation was the only option.

On a signal from their leader, the soldiers lifted their info-visors. Then, in turn, so only one of them was preoccupied at any one time, they each removed their helmets. The leader spoke quietly to two of them, who each summoned two other men and left the room to search the rest of the building. Jack wondered what was now happening elsewhere on the island. Almost all his own team had stood down for a rest following four days of almost continual duty, so only the lightest of defences were now guarding the spaceport and the control centre.

Suddenly Jack caught a proper look at the small flag on the captain's breast pocket: the single star and cross of the Cuban rebel forces! *They must be insane*, he thought.

'Sit down now, backs against the wall,' demanded the captain.

Hesitantly, the captives did as they were ordered, all ranged underneath a giant Jackson Pollock painting that looked as if a firing squad had already used it as a backdrop.

The leader then took a piece of paper from his tunic pocket. 'In the name of the Revolutionary Council of Democratic Cuban Nationals we are reassuming control of Hope Island,' he read out loudly and carefully. 'This island is part of Cuban sovereign territory, and was sold illegally by a corrupt dictatorship.'

As he was delivering this short speech, Jack studied one of the other camouflaged marines. He stood larger and taller than the rest, and something about him looked familiar. Then Jack remembered that bulk: the man had once been a US Navy SEAL.

Two of the marines re-entered the hall, herding Thomas Tye and Marsello Furtrado before them, their weapons aimed high at the captives' backs. Tye and Furtrado both had their hands clasped on their heads. The soldiers gestured for them to sit against the wall with the others.

Calypso watched this performance stonily, then pushed herself up from the floor, grabbed Tommy's hand and yanked him to his feet.

'*Usted no nos necesita, Capitan*,' she said. '*Voy a llevar el chico a su cuarto.*'

Jack understood enough Spanish to know she wanted to take Tommy to his room.

The captain started to raise his sub-machine gun threateningly, then thought better of that, slung it over his shoulder and stepped forward. He knocked Tommy's hand out of Calypso's, and pushed the boy to the floor. Gripping her face hard in his left hand, he pushed the flat of his right hand against her stomach and then downwards.

'You can take *me* to his room instead,' he hissed.

'Go fuck yourself,' swore Calypso and spat in his face.

Jack snatched the opportunity and leaped to his feet. His right fist crashed into the captain's solar plexus just below his armoured vest. Completely winded, the Cuban doubled up. Then Jack had the man's head trapped in the crook of his other arm, his right hand pushing the soldier's head over to the left at an extreme angle.

Every muzzle was now pointing at Jack as he backed away,

the Cuban's agonized body suspended between him and their weapons.

'Just let the women and the boy leave,' Jack demanded through gritted teeth. He could feel the vertebrae starting to pop in the Cuban's neck, and turned to catch the ex-SEAL's eye again. *He* at least would know how easily Jack could kill his prisoner.

Then Jack felt the chill of a gun barrel behind his ear.

'Let him go,' ordered Connie Law loudly.

Unbelieving, Jack turned his head just enough to see Tye's personal assistant holding her 9mm Browning in a professional two-handed FBI grip. Expertly, she slipped the hammer back with her left thumb. This action was unnecessary to fire the gun, but the adjustment would improve its response time by a few milliseconds. She pressed the barrel harder into the base of his skull.

'Do it,' she commanded. 'Do it now.'

Jack released the Captain who fell to his knees and vomited copiously. Connie circled slowly around in front of Jack, until her weapon was aimed centrally at his chest. That two handed-grip and the careful small sidesteps were moves he knew well from his own training.

Connie backed towards the soldiers who all still kept their weapons trained on Jack. The captain struggled to his feet, purple in the face and still gasping, his sub-machine gun discarded in the pool of vomit.

'Sit back down, Jack' Connie ordered. 'Do it now, Jack.'

Jack looked over at the rest of the small party ranged against the wall. He turned his back on Connie and the armed men and sauntered back to take his seat in the line.

'*Llevarse el chico,*' the captain hissed to one of his soldiers as he wiped his mouth.

A marine stepped forward and yanked Tommy upright. Before Jack could stop him, Thomas Tye was on his feet, pulling the boy's hand out of the soldier's grasp.

'GET THE FUCK AWAY FROM MY SON, DO YOU HEAR?' he screamed. He was white with fury as he swung

Tommy round in front of him. He crossed his arms protectively over his son's chest, backing away from the captain and his subordinate.

The rebel captain drew his pistol from his waist-holster and, in the manner popularized by Ché Guevara, the hero of all anti-imperialist revolutionaries, he dealt with this small counter-insurrection by shooting Thomas Tye straight through the centre of his beautiful left eye.

The tycoon spun around and then – as if the personality known to the world as Thomas Tye had never emerged within it – his body slid slowly and bloodily down the white marble wall.

EPILOGUE

The New York Times,
Weekend News Digest

US Humiliated In 'Bay of Pigs' Re-Run.
Thomas Tye in Coma
Military Invasion of Hope Island was 'organized and funded by covert American Agencies'

UN sources are claiming last Sunday's invasion of Hope Island by a military brigade purporting to be members of Cuba's democratic rebel forces was, in fact, carried out by a militia covertly organized and funded by American intelligence agencies. A UN spokesperson today named two of the CIA operatives it claims took part in the operation and added that the invasion was launched from a US Navy aircraft carrier. The White House and the Pentagon strongly deny any involvement.

Over 1,500 military personnel were involved in the surprise action to take possession of the island by force last Sunday evening, just as the Tye Corporation was passing into new ownership. The United Nations Security Council passed a majority resolution condemning the attack as 'US-sponsored imperialism' and the World Bank, now the largest shareholder in the Tye Corporation, demanded the return of all its assets on and including Hope Island.

> A unit of the UN's emergency-response peace-keeping force subsequently made an unopposed landing on Hope Island on Wednesday night and discovered that Thomas Tye himself had been the only serious casualty of the invasion. All invasion forces have since withdrawn.
>
> Thomas Tye who, as reported earlier, was shot in the head during this incursion, remains in a state of coma in the Hope Island Clinic.
>
> Families of LifeWatch Victims File $198 billion suit. Page A3
>
> ABA Airlines Claims Tye Energy Satellites Responsible for Denver Crash. Page A3
>
> Lawrence-Antico Oil Co. Sues Tye Corporation for $16.5 billion oil-spill claim. Page A2

'This is where the landlines came ashore.' Jack pointed as he stopped by Calypso's rock. Ron Deakin turned and nodded. It was a perfect February evening on Hope Island and, six months after the brief invasion by the 'Cuban rebels', he was finally getting his first tour round the corporate state that had occupied so much of his time during the previous three and a half years.

The older man stared into the setting sun, then back at Jack Hendriksen. 'Sorry to be leaving?'

'Not in the slightest,' laughed Jack. At the end of the week his contract with the Tye Corporation would come to an end and he was due to join Haley in Naples. He was already organizing the final transfer of his belongings from this island to his new life in Florida.

He had been up to visit Calypso and Tommy at the big house earlier in the day.

'He's just the same,' sighed Calypso when he had asked about Tom. 'I *feel* that he knows we're there, but we've no way of being sure.'

'Is it right, to keep him going on the machines?' Jack had asked.

The question had drawn a sharp look from Calypso. Jack had already noticed a new thinness, almost sharpness about her.

'We can afford it,' she had answered simply.

'So your life's back to normal?' asked Jack as he and Deakin resumed their stroll.

'If it's considered normal to spend your life monitoring all the greedy bastards of this world,' agreed Deakin. 'Technically I could retire next year, but with the Chinese economy developing so fast . . .'

Jack knew how much worry the new corporate powerhouses in the East were causing for the UN. 'But now you do have an advantage.'

Deakin raised his eyebrows. 'The SecGen's being very tough on that. We have to apply for new permission every time we want to use Larsson's software to decipher anything. It's no use against the US government, of course. We now know they rumbled what Tye was doing years ago, so they've already moved up to quantum networks.'

Jack decided to ask the question that had been on his mind for nearly a year. 'So who really did kill JFK, Ron?'

Deakin grimaced.

'Come on, who was it?'

The older man stopped, pulling another face, and turned to look back along the shoreline as if to be certain they were alone. He seemed to be engaged in an inner debate. Then he looked into the low sun again.

'It was all before my time, of course, I was only an infant when it happened . . . But I've read the files, the unreleased stuff. Three guesses, Jack.'

'Well, it was either the Mafia or our own people.'

'Right on both counts,' grunted Deakin. 'The Mafia fired the actual shots that killed him – it was the Marcello mob, from New Orleans. Set Oswald up to be caught, in the best Sicilian tradition, then hid the real shooter behind a fence, on that grassy knoll. It was all intended to stop JFK's brother Bobby, the Attorney-General, going after them.'

Jack nodded. That had always been the assumption in the intelligence community.

'Only ... the FBI were involved as well.'

Jack frowned.

'They got wind of it, Jack. The Bureau had been tipped off. Someone in New Orleans thought the mob was planning to go too far. But a decision was taken to do nothing about it. The tip-off was suppressed – at the highest level.'

'Hoover?'

Deakin nodded. 'He discovered JFK was about to fire him, despite all the dirt he had on the Kennedy family. Hoover even had bugs planted in the White House.'

Jack shook his head as he digested the news of old treachery. After a while he shrugged, and they resumed their stroll.

'Are they still denying that Connie Law was in the firm?'

'Officially, yes,' confirmed Deakin. 'But we do know she transferred to the CIA soon after she finished FBI training at Quantico. She assumed her cover in the Tye Corporation eight years ago, way before we got interested in him. She must have proved very useful to them – not least because of that encryption stuff. You haven't heard anything more?'

Jack shook his head. Connie hadn't been seen since the dramatic evening of the invasion. 'Haley's sure it was Connie who sent her those anonymous reports.'

'She wasn't doing that herself, Jack. Connie smuggled them out to her HQ in Langley and they sent them on. They wanted Haley's biography to discredit Tye just as much as we did.'

Again they walked on in silence for a few moments.

'So it's the quiet life for you now, eh, Jack?'

'It won't be so quiet. Haley's pregnant.'

End of Empire? The Rise and Fall of Thomas Tye
Haley Voss

Chapter One

Thomas Richmond Tye III, founder of the worldwide Tye Corporation business empire, underwent a surgical procedure for 'sexual clarification' when he was eighteen months old. He was the victim of a craze for gender reassignment that briefly, but tragically, swept the paediatric psychiatric clinics of the

United States and several other countries in the nineteen-sixties and -seventies. He was the patient of the now notorious Dr Charles Eon.

Tye was born with an underdeveloped penis and crypto-orchidism – his testicles had failed to appear. This condition is caused by an inherited genetic mutation or lack of hormonal stimulation of the Hox gene during gestation; this gene governs limb-bud growth – specifically hands and feet – and penis development.

Thomas Tye's original birth certificate classified his sex as male but this was later replaced by a revised entry as 'Thomasina Rachel Tye, female'. This revised certificate was, in turn, replaced some years later by a third certificate, the only copy still available for public inspection, that restored his original name and his sexual status as a male.

The launch venues had been carefully selected: the Smithsonian Air and Space Museum in Washington DC, and the Earth Gallery at London's Natural History Museum. The times were arranged to suit transatlantic television coverage: three p.m. in Washington, simultaneously eight p.m. in London. The guest list was impressive enough for Jack to spot at least two separate layers of discreet security as he and Haley made their way through the waiting crowds to the VIP entrance. It resembled a film première and Josh Chandler would be just one of the celebrity guests here in London. Rarely had the launch of a book been so fêted.

'Excited?' asked Jack as they climbed the steps to the vast Earth Galley and its giant revolving model of the planet.

'Shit-scared,' Haley replied hoarsely. 'I'll never get through it.'

Jack grinned. He had heard her rehearse her lines a dozen times, but he understood her nervousness at her first-ever globally televised speech. He could sympathize: he himself would be terrified.

'Just keep it brief,' he advised. 'Everything you really have to say is in the book. Just thank them for coming, then encourage them to read it. That's all they need.'

End of Empire? The Rise and Fall of Thomas Tye was already the number one seller in every major territory, despite half a dozen spoilers rushed out by Sloan Press's rivals. Advance orders had been larger than for any other book published so far this century.

The infant was first referred to Dr Eon's Clinic of Psychosexual Medicine at the University Hospital of Philadelphia when he was eighteen months old. At this period, Dr Eon was famous for his theories and publications on gender confusion in children and he made many television appearances in which he repeatedly explained that a child's sexual identity is created primarily by the way he or she is treated by parents and caregivers during the early years of childhood. He believed absolutely that adult sexual identity is the product of 'nurture' and, only minimally, the result of chromosomal and hormonal make-up.

Dr Eon considered that Thomas Tye's genital ambivalence made him an ideal candidate for gender reassignment. He diagnosed the child as exhibiting 'dimorphism' – the existence of two potential sexual identities in the same body. From the medical records and correspondence kept by the clinic at the time, it is clear that both parents were eager for the confusing anomaly to be cleared up as quickly as possible. The all-confident Dr Eon assured them that, providing they thought of their child as wholly female, the infant could grow up to become a happy and fulfilled daughter.

The doctor recommended surgery that would reduce Thomas Tye's undersized penis to the size of a semi-mature clitoris and re-route his urethra to a new opening in the appropriate female location. He also recommended cosmetic surgery which creates a pudenda, with skin and tissue folds characteristic of female genitalia fashioned from the unused scrotal sac. The doctor advised that it would be better to wait until the child reached her teenage years before constructing a pseudo-vagina from grafted intestinal tissue. The adult woman would be able to live a full sexual life, he averred, with the exception of being unable to have children.

The reassignment surgery was carried out in June 1968 at

the Pennsylvania University Hospital and during the procedure the surgeon also removed Thomas Tye's undescended and newly redundant testicles.

Applause and flashguns greeted their entrance and Haley and Jack paused briefly for the photographers. As they moved up into the main hall, they accepted glasses of champagne from a waiter's tray, then Jack whispered 'Good luck' as Haley was whisked away from him to meet the important press people who had turned out to cover the launch. He wandered off by himself amongst the chattering guests crowding the gallery.

High above him hung the newest exhibit: a one-thousandth scale model of a Solaris solar energy station. Its sails were fully unfurled and a large wall panel nearby explained the principles of solar capture and reflection. He noticed a small footnote explaining that the Solaris stations were still out of action while the long task of increasing the level of radiation shielding in orbiting satellites was in progress. It was not even suggested when – or if – this technology might ever be safely re-harnessed. The caption said nothing about who might then assume control of it.

Thomas Eugene Tye II and his wife Mary Alana took their daughter, now two years old and renamed 'Thomasina', home two months later.

Progress was not satisfactory. The two-year-old refused to wear dresses. She would not play with the feminine toys her parents bought her and she cried constantly at night. Dr Eon's records show that the follow-up visits Thomasina made to his clinic became increasingly difficult and, by the time she was four, the child would not consent to enter his consulting rooms or allow him to be anywhere near her. When she was four and a half years old she started to cut and pierce her body with sharp objects and by the age of five she would not wear any clothes. The child began defecating in public and mounting hysterical attacks on her parents, nursing staff and other household members. By August 1971 things were so serious that, from his office four hundred miles away, Professor Charles Eon advised the family physician to sign a committal order for her to become a secure patient in the exclusive Sandler Psychiatric Sanitarium. Her mother, already being treated with hallucinogenics and imipramine tricyclates for endogenous depression, committed suicide a few weeks later.

Dr Eon had no further contact with his young patient. However, twenty years later his reputation began to suffer as stories of other, less wealthy and protected 'reassigned' children began to surface in the press. The vast majority of these were boys who, because of genital abnormalities at birth, had been reassigned as 'female' under the doctor's guidance. Most had rebelled against their given sexual classification and, by the middle nineteen-nineties, Dr Eon had come to be regarded within his profession as a deeply misguided therapist and medical practitioner. Many parents of his child patients have dubbed him 'evil', and some have suggested that recently revealed evidence of the doctor's own homosexuality may provide clues to the origin of his bizarre theories and to his personal motivation. He died last year at the age of ninety-four.

It is not known when Thomas Tye resumed his male identity nor whether any further sexual-identity-related surgery was undertaken. It is likely, however, that he has been forced to use testosterone replacement therapy as part of a lifelong treatment.

Two large screens on either side of the specially erected stage flickered into life. The buzz of the crowd lessened as Jack saw the face of Yoav Chelouche appear, standing in the Smithsonian. As well as providing the biography's foreword, he was now lending it an additional global stamp of authority and approval.

A TV book-show host enlisted for the purpose stepped into the glare of the stage lights in the Earth Gallery to welcome the global television viewers and the book-launch guests in both London and Washington. Then he handed over to the president of the World Bank.

Sensing someone at his side, Jack turned, smiled and bent down to kiss Felicity. She held Toby close to her by his red safety reins.

'Unca Jack,' cried Toby, stretching up his arms.

Jack hoisted the boy up and sat him on his shoulders, so he could see his aunt over the heads of the crowd.

Chelouche was looking more lugubrious than ever. 'I am here to personally congratulate Haley Voss on the publication of a most significant and crucial biography,' he began sonorously.

Someone in Washington started the applause, and the guests in both cities immediately joined in. As it died away, Chelouche glanced quickly at his notes.

'This is also a fitting occasion to announce that, during the last week, financial control of the Tye Corporation has now passed from us at the World Bank back to institutional and private shareholders, though many of its assets and operations had already needed to be sold to meet the corporation's many legal liabilities. The restructured company is now registered here in the United States, in Delaware, so the World Bank's custodianship of the corporation has thus come to an end.'

There was more polite applause and he waited again until it abated.

'This has been the first major test of United Nations solidarity in an era of ever-increasing corporate power. Directors of global corporations should therefore note that none of them can consider themselves or their companies beyond regulation or remedy. Over the next three years new international antitrust conventions will be drawn up and placed before the world's nations for approval. This recent episode has severely tested the strength of our global economy – an economy technically outside the control or influence of any nation or group of nations – but, it seems, it possesses a resilience that has both surprised and delighted even me.'

Their was an outburst of laughter – on both sides of the Atlantic.

'As well as being an enthralling account of the life of an extraordinary man, you will find *End of Empire?* provides invaluable insights into the business methods of our world today – both the acceptable and the unacceptable. I commend it to you.'

As applause erupted again Jack proudly watched the diminutive figure of Haley, now heavily pregnant, as she walked out onto the stage.

> As this book goes to press Thomas Tye, now fifty-one, lies in a coma in a clinic on Hope Island. The left cerebral cortex of his brain was shattered by a bullet fired during the short-lived American-backed invasion and occupation of Hope Island. His body is maintained by life-support equipment at the insistence of Calypso Tye, his wife of one day at the time of the shooting, while researchers at Tye Life Sciences attempt to grow replacement neural tissue. His condition is officially described as *deep anoetic coma*. No official prognosis has been given but expert medical opinion considers it unlikely he will regain consciousness unaided. His interests are managed by a provisional committee headed by Calypso Tye with the help of consultants from the World Bank and a number of international management consultancies. Thirty-four former executives of the Tye Corporation and its subsidiaries are now on bail pending trial at the International Criminal Courts of Justice in The Hague and Strasbourg for fraud, intellectual-property theft and human rights violations.

Theresa Keane sat under the shade of a low tamarind tree in the sun-dappled garden of her villa on the slopes above Hope Town. Beside her lay the deactivated Sandra. Like most of the other companions on the island, her power pack had been removed. Despite this rude termination, the professor still liked to keep the bundle of artificial fur nearby.

Theresa closed *End of Empire?* with a sigh and picked up another of the several books lying on a table beside her garden chair. It was *World Brain* by H. G. Wells, the volume Raymond Liu had sent her to reciprocate her gift of Descartes's treatise. It was written in 1938 when the English novelist was entering old age and the world lay under the shadow of a looming global war. This edition had been published by Doubleday. She turned again to the passage Raymond had underlined in pencil:

In the evocation of what I have here called a World Brain . . .
A World Brain which will replace our multitude of
 uncoordinated ganglia . . .
In that, and that alone is there any clear hope of a really
 Competent Receiver for world affairs.
We do not want dictators, we do not want oligarchic parties
 or class rule, we want a widespread world intelligence
 conscious of itself.